Cheers for Rick Moody's

THE FOUR FINGERS OF DEATH

"For readers who enjoy rambling, picaresque adventures with a satiric edge (think: Thomas Pynchon), it's a blast."
—Doug Childers, *Richmond Times-Dispatch*

"Rick Moody's powers of invention, his ease in his own prose, his ability to develop interesting characters—in short, his enormous gifts as a writer—are on full display here. And when he wants to write a gorgeous paragraph, he delivers as you know he can, even when he's still spoofing."
—Clancy Martin, *New York Times Book Review*

"As pulpy and trashy as *The Four Fingers of Death* might sound, it's oddly something sweeter and more profound. It's a book about love and longing husbands grieving over dying wives, disconnected parents and lost children, sadness and confusion. Consider just this one gorgeous line: 'Love was the hole as well as the thing that repaired the hole.' It's sad, pitch-perfect, and lovely, and it came from the talking chimp who has fallen in love with a human laboratory assistant.... The near future in *The Four Fingers of Death* has plenty gone wrong, but it reads more like the satiric comedy of David Foster Wallace's maximalist novel, *Infinite Jest*. Both are long, packed with elaborately inventive plotlines, digressions, explanations, and multiple characters. The future's a mess, but there's plenty to say about it."
—Chad Roedemeier, Associated Press

"A rollicking romp through deep space and Arizona alike, improbably and thoroughly entertaining, courtesy of master storyteller Moody. Mash up Isaac Asimov with Thomas Pynchon, with dashes of Ray Bradbury and Kurt Vonnegut, and you begin to approach Moody's madcap view on the world.... A smart, fun satire—Jonathan Swift in space, with twists befitting Vincent Price." —*Kirkus Reviews* (starred review)

"Rick Moody's latest novel is a riotous gloss on an already forgotten flourish of presidential theater: George W. Bush's 2004 announcement that the United States would send a manned mission to Mars.... Moody imagines a 2025 NASA expedition to the Red Planet and conjures a not-so-distant future that is less a forecast of the world we are soon to inhabit than a fantasia drawn from early-century jitters about national demise.... Moody's comic tour de force encompasses scavenger survivalists, careerist NASA functionaries, a weak and peripatetic president, and a DeLillo-esque mass spiritual movement called the *omnium gatherum,* whose desert conclave supplies the backdrop for the denouement.... Animated by Moody's inventive energies and dark wit, the novel is neither gloomy nor grim, preoccupied though it is with infection, contagion, and death.... Like any American writer worth his salt, Moody traffics in ambiguous symbols, and the diseased arm possesses the fraught doubleness of an emblem out of Hawthorne, a writer at the center of Moody's memoir, *The Black Veil....* Conceptual wizardry and resonance are not reconciled with ease, nor do many writers attempt such a rapprochement, so it is here, in the intersection of narrative excess and genuine feeling, that Moody is at his most daring and arresting." —James Gibbons, *BookForum*

"Seven hundred–plus pages of wacky, wonderful imaginings: there's a rare collection of baseball cards, three space pods inhabited by nine American astronauts, and a lonely human arm that crawls through civilization." —*More*

"This is Moody uncorked, slyly going back to the wordy, toothsome, nineteenth-century novel, with a science-fiction twist." —Susan Salter Reynolds, *Los Angeles Times*

"Set in an America even bleaker than the seventies of *The Ice Storm,* Moody's latest is a comic sci-fi epic.... His tale is filled with digressions that reveal a sad future we may soon inherit." —Jim Kiest, *San Antonio Express-News*

"The novel is peppered with gems such as 'There were no authorities any longer, just men with nicer outfits,' which explains with breathtaking economy a crumbling society in 2025. The story's cumulative verdict is that of a scary B-movie: The end is near. Because of the times we live in, the message is convincing and sobering. Moody has tapped into the fear that America has lost its way, and his juvenile approach is brilliant."
— Holly Silva, *St. Louis Post-Dispatch*

"The book is entertaining and often poignant, probing the limits of technology, consciousness, and language in the face of grief."
— *The New Yorker*

"Mr. Moody's best writing in years. It is *The Ice Storm* in space.... Masterful, certainly matching, even at times surpassing, Kurt Vonnegut, to whom *The Four Fingers of Death* is dedicated, and who is the book's closest progenitor.... It is fun to read."
— Michael H. Miller, *New York Observer*

"Rick Moody offers a harrowing send-up of classic science fiction in *The Four Fingers of Death,* his first novel in five years. It's sci-fi as only Moody could write it — in turns touching and outrageous."
— *Very Short List*

"We would have waited another five years for this book, at once not your typical Moody (it's fun, for starters) and total hallmark Moody (think *The Ice Storm* on a molecular level)."
— Max Read, *Time Out New York*

"*The Four Fingers of Death* moves with unapologetic swagger as it flaunts the extremes of storytelling. Those extremes resist easy summary or review, but in this too *Four Fingers* seems admirable — 'novelicious,' let's say, to coin a term in keeping with the text's ludic anarchy, the tickling it gives a form that's so often been labeled as dying or dead. Reanimation of the dead, indeed, provides Moody with his title and several major plotlines. Those stories, I repeat, resist summary — but I can affirm that nary a one fails to cast a spell."
— John Domini, *Bookslut*

"Complex and imaginative.... A zesty satire, a sprawling epic with one eye on today's headlines and another eye (biometric eye, no doubt) on the future.... A grab bag of sardonic fun."
—William J. Cobb, *Dallas Morning News*

"There's loads of political parody...but we think Moody's up to something a little more sophisticated.... The bulk of the novel acts as a metaphor for Crandall's everyman issues of fear of losing his wife and insignificance in an economy that's moved on from his skill set. Sure, seven hundred pages is a long metaphor, but it's sharp and funny enough to make it worthwhile on both levels."
—Jonathan Messinger, *Time Out Chicago*

"In his dense, provocative, and often hilarious ninth book, Rick Moody takes a sly, Swiftian approach to sci-fi, serving up a goofy B-movie-style opera.... His energy and sheer inventiveness make *The Four Fingers of Death* an original and exhilarating read."
—Jane Ciabattari, National Public Radio

"Densely bizarre and endlessly playful."   —*New York Metro*

"Moody has done what he has been doing consistently throughout his oeuvre, in prose that is ecstatic and biting, cerebral and colloquial: chronicling America. *The Four Fingers of Death* is big (in scope, not merely page count), bold, juicy, and thought-provoking. With its publication, Rick Moody has become the most fun (I'm tempted to say 'funnest') serious writer in America.... In between blastoff and fallout, there's enough heartbreak, power-mongering, and ethically questionable science, enough tour-de-force set pieces, and enough thematic DNA to fuel at least three, maybe even four novels.... *The Four Fingers of Death* is like a good old-fashioned nineteenth-century novel catapulted into the twenty-first century, trailing the campy, cosmic stardust of the sixties."   —Zsuzsi Gartner, *Globe and Mail*

"A phantasmagorical hell ride inspired by the late Kurt Vonnegut, *The Four Fingers of Death* uses sardonic humor to cushion the impact.... In the right hands, hooptedoodle can be a hoot."
—Kerry Lengel, *Arizona Republic*

Also by Rick Moody

THE FOUR FINGERS OF DEATH

A NOVEL

R ICK M OODY

BACK BAY BOOKS

LITTLE, BROWN AND COMPANY

NEW YORK   BOSTON   LONDON

Back Bay Books / Little, Brown and Company
Hachette Book Group
237 Park Avenue, New York, NY 10017
www.hachettebookgroup.com

Originally published in hardcover by Little, Brown and Company, July 2010
First Back Bay paperback edition, July 2011

Back Bay Books is an imprint of Little, Brown and Company. The Back Bay
Books name and logo are trademarks of Hachette Book Group, Inc.

The characters and events in this book are fictitious. Any similarity to real
persons, living or dead, is coincidental and not intended by the author.

The publisher is not responsible for websites (or their content) that are not
owned by the publisher.

Library of Congress Cataloging-in-Publication Data
Moody, Rick.
   The four fingers of death : a novel / Rick Moody. — 1st ed.
     p. cm.
   ISBN 978-0-316-11891-0 (hc) / 978-0-316-11893-4 (pb)
1. Authors — Fiction.   I. Title.
PS3563.O5537F68 2010
813'.54 — dc22   2009040756

10 9 8 7 6 5 4 3 2 1

RRD-C

Printed in the United States of America

In Memory of Kurt Vonnegut

THE FOUR FINGERS
OF DEATH

A Novelization, with Introduction,
Afterword,
and Notes

by Montese Crandall

Introduction

by Montese Crandall

PEOPLE OFTEN ask me where I get my ideas. Or on one occasion back in 2024 I was asked. This was at a reading in an old-fashioned used-media outlet right here in town, the store called Arachnids, Inc. The audience consisted of five intrepid and stalwart folks, four out of the five no doubt intent on surfing aimlessly at consoles. Or perhaps they intended to leave the store when instead they were herded into a cluster of uncomfortable petrochemical multi-use furniture modules by Noel Stroop, the hard-drinking owner-operator of the shop in question. I'd been pestering Noel about a reading for some time, months, despite the fact that Arachnids was not celebrated for its calendar of arts-related programming. To be honest, the reason for this pestering had most to do with my wife, who'd spend her remaining time on earth counseling me on just how to boost my product. "Ask Noel," my wife said, her eyes full of implacable purpose.

We used to see Noel at the flea market, which by now took up more than a dozen city blocks. There were more flea markets than licensed, tax-paying emporia in Rio Blanco. I had a booth there where, on weekends, I hawked old baseball cards and other sports memorabilia. In fact, I still do. Let me tell you the story.

As a child, I was heedless of America's pastime, which was in one of its frequent popularity downturns during which the inert of the nation turned the dial instead to golf. However, once the baseball commissioner's office allowed without prejudice performance enhancers and began to encourage the participation of players with artificial and surgically enhanced limbs, I became a devoted partisan of our national pursuit. It had always made stars of smokers, overweight athletes, coca abusers, not to mention intravenous testosterone injectors, wife abusers, biblical literalists, and persons with tonsorial eccentricities, but once it embraced amputees, baseball became a sport that any indolent person could love. Since it had become commonplace on the broadbands of our nation to feature talk show hosts with cleft palates, homunculi, or other disfigurements, and since the advent of so-called reality telethons featuring learning-disabled persons (a rapidly growing demographic sector of the populace), it was only a matter of time before a professional sport became interested in a more democratic conception of the human physique.

You may remember: the very first "enhanced" baseball player was a journeyman relief pitcher named Dave McClintock, of Columbus, OH. (He later became known in the press as "Three-in-One" McClintock, presumably because his synthetic parts needed lubrication to achieve maximum bionic effect.) McClintock was horsing around with his roommate after a minor league game — they were on their way to a disreputable watering hole outside Bridgeport, CT — when McClintock, according to later accounts, leaned out of the window of his roommate's rental vehicle in order to jeer at some comely transgender streetwalkers. In the course of attempting to persuade McClintock to get back into the car, his roommate struck an oncoming military transport vehicle. This roommate was killed instantly. McClintock was thrown clear of the collision, his pitching arm sundered from him.

Another ballplayer, deprived of this extremity, which by reason of extensive fracturing could not be reattached, would have retired to the subdivisions of southern Ohio and spent his time shooting at squirrels using high-amperage Tasers from his collection of weaponry. Dave McClintock wasn't this kind of a ballplayer. McClintock, by his own account, "just wasn't good at much else." While he recovered in the ICU of the local hospital, he pondered his fate. McClintock, he later remarked in interviews, didn't *want* to be a pitching coach or a scout. Despite a preponderance of evidence to the contrary, Dave McClintock believed that there was a future in professional sport for a man with a mechanical arm. He might need to become a position player, an off-the-bench type, at least until the technology improved. He might need to warm the bench for a time. But, he believed, he need not give up the game.

After all, the owners and their handpicked commissioner had already determined that they could not keep ahead of the advances taking place in the demimonde of stealth performance enhancers. What was working well for athletes of the Sino-Indian Economic Compact could work for NAFTA athletes as well. It was impractical to think otherwise. Like Rosa Parks before him, McClintock saw the future clearly and *knew*. What was a mechanical arm but an elaborate kind of performance enhancement? *Sport is entertainment,* he observed in his diary entries from the hospital. Sport is not devoted to an idealized human body. Sport is not about winning, and it is not about some masculine pie-in-the-sky notion of heroism and team play. Sport is like breathing fire onstage or spitting up blood while wearing a latex devil's mask. McClintock, with the cooperation of his agent, Phil Blank, convened a press conference on the day of his release from the Hospital for Special Surgical Interventions. Only a handful of reporters showed, and only one of them wrote a feature, but what this pimply hack from MLB.com discovered was a charming, upbeat, marketable ballplayer with a titanium arm, who, while grinning his relentlessly upbeat grin, waved aloft his bionic, or perhaps cybernetic, appendage and said, "I bet I can hit sixty-five homers a year with this thing!"

The masses of baseball fans could be forgiven for thinking it was some kind of stunt. McClintock, however, had an unusual bond with the locals who came to watch his Triple-A affiliate. The fans loved his grit and determination. If it was abundantly clear that he would never pitch again (he didn't have "feel"), a bio-engineered arm did improve his hitting, as it later did for Juan Millagro, who had two arms designed by a specialist in Vail, CO, after an accident involving farm machinery. As a bionic player, Dave McClintock had a mediocre average (.234), but when he did connect with the ball, it was invariably for extra bases. There were other advantages. Like Millagro, McClintock didn't care if he got hit by a pitch (opposing pitchers were happy to oblige), he never had elbow problems, and from left field, where he played most often, he had a cannon for an arm.

The following year, because of the minor league buzz, McClintock was brought up to the bigs as a platoon player for the Mexico City team. As a result, he was issued his first baseball card, by the venerable manufacturer of same, Topps, Inc. However, in a fit of misguided political correctness, the photographer shot him from the *other side,* so that the titanium arm was scarcely visible. This was perhaps one of those moments when the professionals at Topps were using their oracular crystal ball. Because it took a particular kind of genius, the kind that I for one possess, to know that this first "Three-in-One" McClintock issue would become one of the most collected baseball cards in the history of the game.

In fact, collections of disabled players, for reasons that academic psychologists will argue over for the next fifty years, were generally among the most coveted of all baseball cards in those days. After McClintock came Juan Millagro, Moses Infante, Terry "Four Fingers" Callahan, and then many, many others. It was as if the NAFTA teams were somehow obsessed with the composite baseball player, the player who was willing to subject himself to the kind of technological interventions that were no longer just the province of American manufacturing. We had become a culture of hybrid biologies, and our physical contests began to reflect it.

McClintock then, you may remember, tried to corner the market on his own baseball card. He had an army of middle schoolers, his biggest fans, buying them up. But there was one ruthless competitor who was able to thwart his *evil plans.* Well, I did adore the McClintock card, and the McClintock legend, and the fact that I hoarded his first card left me in a rather good position when I later opted for my present variety of self-employment. It turned out I wanted nothing more than to sit around talking to walleyed kids about who was the greatest disabled player in sports history. Oh, and did I neglect to mention that I later cajoled a haggard and hungover McClintock into signing twenty or so cards for me? At a convention? He made idle conversation, noting among other things that this was his third titanium arm, though he did nothing more strenuous with it in those days than go fly-fishing. His signature was kind of wobbly.

This, therefore, is my business. It was here, at the flea market, according to my wife's plans, that I screwed up my nonexistent courage one Sunday and said to Noel Stroop, who was busy selling software modules, something called a compact disc, and e-book files, "Hey, Noel, what does a guy like me, a literary innovator, have to do in this town to get some respect?"

Perhaps you're wondering what I *have* done to merit such a high opinion of my legacy. What is the nature of the Montese Crandall literary innovation? I am going to take the remainder of this brief introduction to explicate fully my response to this question. Let me then throw down the gauntlet and remark that I, Montese Crandall, MFA, write very short, very condensed literary pieces, and by short, I mean very, very short. Shorter than you have probably read in your reading life. More than one word, usually, because one word is too easy, but quite a bit more modest than five score. The three hundred and fifty pages of a novel, according to the argument I am wont to advance, are tedious elaboration. As I understand it, death, war, and adultery are the major novelistic themes, and these were all dispensed with well before Christ got nailed to his block of wood. The nineteenth-century novel, you opine? The nineteenth-century novel *does* have it all: attic-dwelling harridans; uncanny coincidences; advantageous marriages to strong, silent landowners; orphans; revolutions; whaling. You can't go wrong with the nineteenth-century novel. But much that has been written since amounts to imitation, barely warmed over by writers with strange grammatical inclinations. Lovelorn women of Canada, incest on the Southern plantation, drug-using editorial assistants, the usual stuff. Yours truly, Montese Crandall, living out his pacific middle age in a college town next door over to nowhere at all, is unwilling to add more roughage to this rich diet.

One thing the late twentieth century was good at, besides its mass-marketing: paring away. Omitting needless words. Alluding. Without overstating. Dust bunny under radiator. Cockroach on window blind. Scotch bottles. Heartbreak in the food court. Impotence. Subdivisions. Melanoma. Muffler problems. Upon the advent of the digital age, as you know, writers who went on and on and on just didn't *last*. You couldn't read all that nonsense on a screen. Fragmentation became the one true way. Fragmentation offered a point-and-click interface. Additionally, this strategic reduction blurred the line between poetry and prose, which is where I, Montese Crandall, come into the story. I, Montese Crandall, rely heavily on such strategies as alliteration, condensation, the strange, ghostly echo of metrical feet, iambs and dactyls, spondees and amphibrachs. For example, here's a pair of amphibrachs (unstressed, stressed, unstressed) that might very well summarize my entire output: *romantic objective*. The phrase does have a fine euphony.

My first groundbreaking and innovative one-sentence story occurred in the following way. I'd been working on a forty-five-page erotic novella that was loosely based on my boundless physical desire for my wife, Tara Schott Crandall. The sequence in which I performed a certain advanced delight upon her delicately canted pelvis ran well over twenty pages, and her mews and snorts of transport, as described in the text, would pierce the waxy consciousnesses of neighbors up and down the block. Her cries of delight, as described therein, were likened to the coyote howling on the mesa, the kettle shrilling on the stovetop. Sopranos in local opera companies would hang their heads, for they knew that when Tara Schott Crandall climaxed, they were out of a job.

I am afraid I cut the entire passage. The erotic part. And not only that. Then I cut the opening. And the ending. I cut a lot of the middle. I cut the part where we were postcoitally sharing a glass of *vin ordinaire*. Next, I cut the astoundingly tender moment in the story where, in snappy dialogue, Tara and I revisited our assignations past: the time in the back of a minivan, the time in the woods when we got poison ivy, the time in the press box at the basketball game. For a while, a single scene remained in which the Tara character (called "Serena" in this early draft) sent me out, after lovemaking, for eggs. Eggs! So beautiful! So fecund! Likely to balance on their oblong points during the equinoxes! Symbols of fertility! Available in multiple sizes including jumbo! I couldn't let go of this scene for a while. You know how this is. And yet after three months of wrestling with that story, I cut the entire tangle of misbegotten sentences, the whole sprawling mess, or almost all of it, leaving none, at last, but the following:

Go get some eggs, you dwarf.

I don't expect everyone reading this introduction to see immediately the merit in this sentence. And yet the awakening, the unfolding, that occurred to me after a relaxed consideration of the six words that remained of my longer work, this unfolding located itself in the fact that the more I read and reread the sentence above, the better I liked it. I printed it out in various fonts. I pulled my few remaining hairs out, trying to decide whether to cut the word *go.* I pronounced the entirety of the story aloud to myself while walking from our ramshackle subdivision to the shipping offices where I then occasionally pulled a shift. I would intone the sentence while going past the shuttered health and beauty aids purveyor on Twenty-second and Mountain. I would say it while taking my number at the woebegone post office on Sixth. I shouted it at the beckoning doors of the gay bars on Fourth Avenue, I said it to myself at the food co-op, as if the eggs in question were an actual part of my shopping agenda. I can't tell you how long it took me, in my ecstatically creative state, to realize that, in fact, there needn't be an exclamation point at the end.

My wife, whose health situation had taken a rather unsettling turn, never approved of the long version of the story, though she generally supported whatever wind blew me along in my compositional hobbies, as long as I took seriously the post-compositional portion of the writer's life and got out there to sell, sell, sell. She did, however, enjoy "Go get some eggs, you dwarf." Where, my wife inquired, was I going to publish this story? Was I going to pit against one another some nationally recognized periodicals? And what about book publication? Had I considered a run of hardcovers? In fact, I *had* secured an agreement with a little web periodical called *Mud Hut,* where my story got an entire page to itself. No title. No byline.

Not six months later, fresh from the victory just described, I came up with what I like to think is the second-finest narrative I've ever composed. And yet before I type out for you that magnificence, I should describe what I look like, because it bears on the interpretation of this second effort. I am, you should know, in my late forties or thereabouts, and it is simply being honest to note that my metabolism, which was doing wind sprints and stomach crunches throughout the dark ages of my twenties, has lately taken an ill-advised nap. I am now the site of an unmistakable sag, as if some avalanche stirred at the crest of my solar plexus and sent all the flab in my northern latitudes down toward my once noble pubic swell. With fancy holographic belt buckles do I attempt to restrain my stampeding softness. In vain. Additionally, my hair is thinning, and my skin, which once had the virtue of being free from the blemishes that trouble the young, is now mottled and flaky. Burst blood vessels lead the eye of any observer astray around my nose. I am yoked to bifocals for my ocular needs. (I cannot afford the surgeries that would correct me.) I have fallen arches, hammertoes. My only virtues, as a physical specimen, are my sideburns, which are like the pelts of rare woodland animals. My sideburns are *not* to be ignored.

No one, let it be said, would mistake me for a pugilist, for a law-and-order type of guy, for a person drawn to physical conflicts, for a militarist. I do not carry a Taser or other weapon, loaded or unloaded, though this is legal and even encouraged in my state. However, I could easily write at least five pages about these sorts of weapons, the Gatling, the ArmaLite, the Glock, the proton disrupter, revealing a complex and deeply seated need for appurtenances of male power and phallic supremacy, even as I disdain these commonplaces in my everyday life and incline, in this era of Islamist saber rattling, toward a foreign policy of tolerance and nonintervention. And yet, as you will have surmised at this point, the five pages of such a story would sooner or later be stripped of elaborations, adjectives, adverbs, similes, astute geopolitical views, until what remained was only:

We went with the stealth bomber.

This was a sentence of such limpid beauty and such durability that it was very difficult to follow up, notwithstanding an unprecedented second publication on the *Mud Hut* site. So affecting was the sentence, in fact, that there was a danger in having composed it, namely that I would retreat to the reliable paycheck of some day job, becoming, for example, an exclusive buyer and seller of baseball cards and other sports memorabilia (I had resigned my second job as shipping clerk upon the promise of first publication), without composing again. I don't know how many months went by. During this time, my argument was simply: Why bother? Have I not already proven myself? Have I not written a timeless epic from the front lines of the military-industrial complex, which in the third decade of the new millennium we now know to be not only a *complex,* but, more or less, the entire shebang? The answer was *yes.* There was no longer a need to prove my dominance in the writing field. In fact, what I craved instead, here at the top of my game, was *domesticity,* the ability to control a little narrow patch of scorpion- and tarantula-infested dry land around a single-story house in a town where it never rained.

Yet, professionalism being what it is, in due course a suite of stories in the first person followed. Apparently, I could not stop. In general, I much prefer a narration from the third-person point of view. The first person is tiresome and confining. It is the voice of narcissists and borderline personalities. Still, my wife, whose problem was a respiratory problem, was getting worse. She was fast approaching her double lung transplant, and while it would have been easy just to wait around until her name came up on the international organ lottery (now under Malaysian control), while it would have been easy to collect the meager government funds disbursed to her as a citizen with a chronic genetic condition, I did, in fact, need some avenue of self-expression. Along came the idea for my masterful trilogy. If you like, if it helps you to understand the kinds of influences that resulted in the literary coming-of-age of Montese Crandall, you may think of these next three stories as related thematically to the three-volume compositions of the nineteenth century, not unlike a doorstopper by a Thackeray or a Trollope.

Well, actually, on advice of counsel, and in order to avoid violating my own copyright with regard to a future *Collected Works of Montese Crandall,* now being discussed at one of the larger presses, I am obligated to forgo quotation of these works from the middle period. I'm sure you understand. Perhaps at some future date, I will be able to oblige. Oh, okay, I'll include one:

Last one home goes without anesthesia.

Not really in the first person, but you get the idea. Years had passed in my writerly biography, years of dreams and ambitions, years of seeing other, less-equipped artists finding publication, even renown, in web-publishing venues or even small-press publication, while I had completed as yet only five publishable sentences, notwithstanding my education at a state school in the Northeast, and a master of fine arts degree from an online program out in the

Rust Belt. As a result I was in no position to suppress my trilogy or to recall its publication, which constituted a full 60 percent of my output. Not every work by a writer is his best, especially when he is preoccupied with more homely responsibilities, one of these being the resale of baseball cards obtained from the disgruntled mothers of the world, who, as you know, have forged an international conspiracy to throw out the baseball cards that have been laboriously collected by their sons, in order to drive up prices. My other activity consisted of lugging oxygen tanks around my house. There was also the vigorous pounding on the back of my wife, Tara, which was occasionally necessary in the mornings, so that she could take advantage of life. I loved my wife. I comforted her when she needed comforting. My wife, understand, was going to die, and she knew it, and I knew it, and now you know it too. When the breeze blew up across the waterless tundra of my state, I often thought *if only* I could just harness some of that breeze and give it to Tara, our problems would be resolved. There are no sailboats in my part of the country that need the breezes; the jet pilots would be happy to encounter less clear-air turbulence; the state officials have resisted wind farms at every turn. And the atmosphere that shrink-wraps the globe offers a rich supply of oxygen. Why couldn't my wife, Tara, have a bit of it in her bloodstream? What made her so undeserving?

With this going on, you see, I sometimes didn't feel much like writing.

Before I knew it, the double lung transplant was upon us. This is how it works with the international organ lottery. Your day comes, and you are ready. Our transplant was to be performed at the University of Rio Blanco Medical Center here in town by a doctor whose name I have chosen to forget. According to the relaxed rules of organ donorship, it was now possible to learn certain facts about your organ donor, especially if you were willing to make payments through professional intermediaries for whom *everything* was negotiable. You might learn a great number of things. For example, I learned that the boy died not a hundred miles from here, in that crumbling metropolis to the north, while driving an antique motorcycle. And I learned that he *was* just a kid, the donor, which is the kind of thing people always say about these full-body harvests. He was just a kid. Name of George.

George had ears that were considerably undersized. He had an overbite. He was otherwise normal in appearance, strapping, even attractive. Everyone was very hopeful that George, with the aid of untimed examinations and a battery of tutors, was going to make it through a business administration course he was pursuing at the junior college outside town. George was superlative at logical systems. He liked to do long division in his head, and if he failed to make eye contact, I learned, it didn't mean that George didn't favor his fellow man, didn't feel a gigantic abscess of love in his twenty-year-old heart, for people and things. He was fanatic about the underperforming college basketball team here in our town. He owned tropical fish. He loved his otherwise childless parents.

In a state of possession, I at last applied pen to page to compose a history of George, whose surname I have agreed to keep secret. I wrote these pages, quickly and voluminously, reams and reams of words, during the part of Tara's recovery when she seemed to be in a coma. I was doubting the accumulated wisdom of the expert surgeons and nurses at the URB Medical Center. I was morbidly anxious. I had symptoms of something like colitis or perhaps Crohn's disease. So I wrote about George. George's interest in marbles; George's fits of rage, which terrified his parents because of his occasional need to destroy his own property; George's implicit upset over the word *autism;* George's early woes in Little League; his subsequent triumphs in baseball because of his willingness to repeat an activity for days and days and days (batting practice). George's occasional desire to wear, in public, dresses belonging to his mother, though this made him the subject of merciless taunting. George and housework, in particular vacuuming. George's almost erotic fetishism of vacuums. George and Finnish death metal, a musical genre these days known as *dead girlfriend.*

I wrote these lines about George in the molded plastic chairs in the hospital waiting room. I gazed abstractedly at the scorched, nonnative palms out in front, which had died or were about to die owing to the seventh year of our regional drought. I had brought with me a little personal digital assistant of the sort I'm sure you know (I was unwilling to have mine surgically implanted, though the wife sure loved hers), and I scribbled, metaphorically speaking, my surmises about George, my wife's donor.

Let us now move on to George, the tertiary phase. Among the other activities of George during his later teens was the disassembly and reassembly of an antique motorcycle (1968), which his otherwise childless parents purchased for him after much handwringing. They fervently wished that George would not *ride* the motorcycle in question, because of his eccentric habits and attitudes about so many things. Also because fuel shortages made this kind of transport frivolous. This injunction against riding the motorcycle was, for a time, acceptable to George. George was more interested in reassembly. He laid out the pieces of the motorcycle in certain patterns and shapes.

There would be no way to write about George, and in this way to occupy many hours spent in the waiting rooms of the hospital, without writing about the fateful night that ended George's term here on earth. Upon reassembling the motorcycle for the third time, George frivolously decided that the prohibition against riding it no longer made good sense. Some three years had passed during which he had contented himself with the reassembling, years of washing the motorcycle until its shine reflected his face and the stubble upon it, years of starting the bike only in order to make sure that it sounded right, that the timing was good—all this per the instructions of George's motorcycle guru, a man up the block named Laramie. Overcome by the whim of precipitous maturation, George decided *one night* to take his motorcycle for a spin in the hills above town. Laramie, an erratic and underemployed person, confirmed the wisdom of this idea.

It was a night featuring a stunning sunset, and I say this mindful of the fact that sunsets in this part of the world are often overpowering. The flyboys from the regional air force base were out in the evening sky in profusion, protecting us from an ill-defined enemy. It hadn't rained for 213 days, and there were dust storms. A comet was due to emerge in the southern sky, and it would have been an agreeable thing to witness this comet, especially in the mountain pass west of town. And yet Monaco 37, the comet, didn't seem to have been a factor in George's untimely demise. The sunset *was* a factor, however. To George, locked in the constraints of a misunderstood brain disorder, history unfolded erratically, and anew. Every day was a day of import. Congress was meeting again tomorrow, there was the restocking of the depleted shelves in our supermarket price clubs, the collection and densifying of refuse in municipal garbage trucks, the ritualized busing of homeless persons to the camps by the border.

And so the young man whose lungs would soon rest in my wife's chest cavity kicked up the kickstand of his reassembled motorcycle. He throttled his throttle. He headed up into the northerly hills without giving much thought to his destination nor to returning expeditiously so as not to alarm his working parents. Then came his fervent apperception of the sunset. On the pavement, he followed the perfect crimson light of the magic hour, when the sun dipped behind the western peaks, when these peaks were bathed in pomegranate quanta. He followed the sunset intuitively, without questioning it, looking for its sweet spot, from which best to contemplate. I wish I could say now that George's death was not his fault, that there was a runaway semi, a teamster who had simply worked too many shifts in a row, or maybe there was a reintroduced wolf loitering on the tarmac. It was not so. The southwestern sunset did George in. Apparently, George, unlicensed and unable to control his motorcycle, failed to operate the bike on one of our myriad regional hairpins, and despite his promise and his triumph over adversity, George sailed out over the embankment, becoming almost instantly a white plastic cross with artificial flowers and a love letter from his mom.

As I say, I wrote many pages about George. And I waited. When I cut down all the reams of eulogistic ramblings about George, when I eliminated anything that was excessively sentimental, that described too accurately the look on the faces of George's parents when I called on them, that utterly dignified but devastated Hispanic couple—what remained was the sentence:

He was just a kid.

A scant two hours after George's demise, my wife was contacted by the international organ lottery, and we were told to report immediately to the university medical center. Preparations for leaving the house took some time because my wife was down to 15 or 20 percent of lung function. She was scared, if resigned, and kept saying "Monty, I just don't want to die on the table." I could barely understand her through the oxygen mask. "Monty, if I die, who is going to harass you?" To which I would say, "Nobody is dying." I put her in a wheelchair that I used when we were making longish trips, and I wheeled her out into the driveway, and I went next door to ask the neighbors, the Rodriguezes, if we could borrow their car or if they could otherwise give us a ride, because we didn't have a car. This had been a long-standing arrangement between myself and Mike Rodriguez, namely, that a day would come when we would be called to the hospital. On this day, there would be no time to waste. I'd told Mike all of this, fumbling, shifting from foot to foot. Could we rely on him? I'd made the same arrangement with the other neighbors, on the other side, until, as with so many houses on the block, the *for sale* signs went up in front of the unit. And never came down.

The Rodriguez family was not answering the bell. I thought I'd stressed to Mike the importance of his letting me know if and when he was traveling. I shouted to Tara, out in the driveway, "Should I call a cab?" As you know, most of the taxi companies had been priced out of the market by the extremely high cost of corn-and-petroleum-blended fuel products. And the taxis had not exactly been replaced by a reliable system of mass transit. Unless you count walking. There was a lot of walking going on. A lot of balancing things on the head. Tara wheezed, "The Rodriguezes will be back soon." Tara said this because there were five grown Rodriguez children, all living at home. They each drove occasionally. Rather too fast, if you asked me. Nevertheless, I said to my wife, "Are you frigging crazy? We have to get you up to the hospital and into the operating room." This was when, despite my urgency, I realized exactly how scared my wife, Tara, was. She was scared enough that she would rather die in the driveway of heatstroke than go through with the operation.

Which was why I had to yell. I don't like yelling. In fact, Tara and I had an arrangement where no yelling would take place, *ever,* which was counterproductive, at least according to an online course on marital communication I had once taken, entitled "The Healthiest Relationship: Ten Preliminary Steps," by Deep Singh, PhD. *(1) Assess what works for you. (2) Accept your shortcomings. (3) Practice tolerance and understanding.* I can't remember the other seven steps. But let us not dwell here. I also need to reconstruct for you now what was already happening in the hospital — the sequence of events in which poor George was being harvested of all his usable bits.

I don't know the biographies of *all* the recipients the way I know the biography of George. And yet I can tell you a few things: his corneas passed on to a septuagenarian in Pasadena, his liver went to a baritone of the popular-music world whose hepatitis C had compromised the liver he was born with, and George's heart went to a retiree in the northern part of our state, a former autoworker. These heroic stories fork off from the story of my wife, Tara, each taking place on the same day, with similar drama. Be at such and such a medical facility at such and such a time. There were worried people like me in waiting rooms all over the southwestern part of the nation. We constituted a community of worriers, all of us with fingernails chewed to the quick, with shooting pains in the lower intestines, red eyes, unwashed hair, caffeine breath.

In our case, the lead surgeon was called away from a floodlit driving range on Bureau of Land Management preserves, there in Southern Arizona. The engine of the ambulance had scarcely cooled before he was scrubbed and began bombarding his surgical tools with gamma radiation, in order to prevent antibiotic-resistant menaces. Interns and residents gathered around the operating table and in the theater above. George's body cooled. His O-positive blood began to drain from the corpse via a pump that resembled an old-fashioned concertina. The residents flushed his arteries with a preservative that insured George's lungs would not decay, and then they inflated them slightly, in the hope that these organs would resume function once inside Tara's chest. They cut in all the many places that they needed to cut. And they slid the excised lungs onto plastic liners, and then they fitted these liners into a pair of six-pack holders that people used more often to take beer to picnics. Then they were ferried to URB in helicopters that were ready to scramble for medical emergencies in the desert.

Meanwhile, we were still in the driveway: "We're not waiting for the Rodriguez kids to get back! I'm calling an ambulance!" "I don't want an ambulance!" "You're not thinking clearly! You only have twenty percent of lung capacity! And if the lungs aren't in your body in six hours, then we have to wait for the next available set of lungs! I don't give a rat's ass if the surgery is making you uncomfortable! I don't care if all the neighbors see! We're getting an ambulance!" At which point Tara started crying, and I could hear her choking through the oxygen mask, and this naturally made me upset, because I genuinely hated it when my wife cried, which she nonetheless did regularly, because her disease, this scourge, had robbed her of her youth, had robbed her of the time in her twenties when she should have been sleeping around or doing a lot of drugs or at least smoking copiously. Even in college, she'd told me, she'd had to hang upside down for a while in the morning, while her roommates smacked her around to get her lungs going. This, in fact, was when I met her, when I was teaching a beginning writing course at the community college. She audited one night with a friend, and brought her rolling tank with her.

Do you require an even more detailed portrait of the beloved? If I were to fashion a more complete account, its title would be "Portrait of a Disabled Gambling Enthusiast." Which may surprise you. But after a certain age this was Tara's daily activity. Yes, in case you were wondering, even disabled people who are slight, beautiful, and possessed of an ethereal wasting quality can be willful, short-tempered, and self-destructive. You can become a little bit impatient with them even as you are convinced you would lie down across the local freight railroad tracks to prevent them further harm.

Tara apparently began by betting on sporting events while in college. Maybe because she was no longer able to participate in sports. (She had once been a teenage gymnast — her specialty was the balance beam.) In her own account of her gambling addiction (beginning about 2016), she too began with baseball, precisely because it had a record of more than a decade of tolerance for differently abled players. She wanted to bet on players like Dave McClintock and Juan Millagro. And making use of various online gambling forums, Tara did begin to place small wagers, using especially her disability allotments from the government. On several occasions her parents, a stiff, religious couple from the Midwest, bailed her out of her debts.

When she began betting on far more unsavory things, and making use of underworld professionals for the purposes of betting, things got worse. About the time she audited my writing class, where her luminous mortality, her consumptiveness, was both terrifying and strangely alluring, she was, by her own account, also showing up at the backroom offices of local bookmakers, wheezing on her respirator, intending to bet on the outcome of World Wrestling Federation matches, cockfights, and NASCAR. She wrote a couple of short stories about the gambling demimonde, and these stories, with their colorful argot, were of the transparently autobiographical sort that I always think makes for the finest art. She probably had more talent than I. Were Tara not preoccupied with dying, inch by inch, and with chasing down her every gambling whim to the best of her motorized ability, I believe she would have made the better writer. Alas, she had little interest in preserving her autobiography. I told myself that I should have nothing to do with her, and then I fell for her — the dreamer falling for his dream.

The Futures Betting Syndicate, which became a national obsession in the teens, about the time our class ended, was effectively niche-marketed to a temperamental beauty with a life-threatening pulmonary disease and parents who would fund her. With the emergence of the FBS, Tara had found, at last, a gaming institution that had the veneer of popular acceptance. The FBS was overseen by government regulators, and a tenth of its profits were creamed off for education, entitlement programs, and servicing the trillions of our national debt.

The FBS, as you know, created the very first subsidized futures markets organized around current events, around a host of possible outcomes, such as the likelihood of Republican control of the House of Representatives, the assassination of the newly elected prime minister of Palestine, the liquidation of the remaining portion of the Greenlandish ice shelf, and so on, and while it was notoriously bad as an indicator of actual outcomes, particularly when predicting the volatility of any season's weather, it was quite useful as a barometer of opinion. As the popularity of the FBS increased, and as its revenues began to help the government work its way out of gargantuan funding obligations, its no-holds-barred laissez-faire market expanded into some rather odd directions. This was where Tara particularly liked to concentrate her attention. When we were dating she used to tell me these things: in one rather grisly period, in her account, she made several thousand dollars betting on the possibility that the secretary of federal gambling enterprises (titular head of the FBS) would be badly beaten in his own home. It was unclear who had first created this particular market, and the secretary's detail of Secret Service agents was unable to stop the attack. Tara then bid on the likelihood of Israel's use of a nuclear weapon on one of her neighbors. Again, Tara's certainty was well-founded, as you know.

Her talk was of upticks, bid quantities, micro-reversals in numbers of casualties in tribal conflicts, and, almost quaintly now, of sports. I was, in this period, uncertain if living with her, as I was longing to do, was going to be easy under the circumstances. True, any good sufferer of *gambling para-addiction syndrome with socially unacceptable perspiration feature* (see the *Diagnostic and Statistical Manual of Mental Disorders — Eighth Edition,* or *DSM-VIII*) will confess to having given the FBS a try occasionally. I tried it later myself, mainly when Tara was asleep, which was during the day, because she liked to draw the blinds and stay up all night by herself. Thus, during the day, I attempted a few stray bids, based on a single betting strategy that I referred to as *radical positivity.* I bet only on really splendid things taking place in the world. I bet that the Fifty Years Insurgency in Sri Lanka would end within the month. I bet that doctors would find a cure for hantavirus. I bet that the greenhouse effect would suddenly be reversed, that Russia and Ukraine would stop all the carnage. In this way, I lost most of my IRA.

I quit teaching and reduced my other professional responsibilities partly because it became imperative to keep an eye on Tara's physical condition, but also because she came to see the necessity of a *complete screen detoxification,* which she was hoping I would consent to supervise. I had been failing to show up for work every time Tara's breathing took a turn for the worse. The shipping concern, they didn't give a fig if my wife's lungs and pancreas glistened with heavy phlegm. The bottom was falling out of their container anyway.

The first thing we did was remove all the wall devices in the living room, which were just showing digital reproductions from picture postcards of the 1950s. (We found these strangely calming.) Then we removed Tara's subcutaneous personal digital assistant (which at that time was a crude version of what they are attempting to market now, but which had similar capabilities, photo and music storage, web uplink, video cam, videoconferencing, and so on), and then we went into the bedroom and trashed anything with a standby light. The music file redeemer, the automassager, the drying tree, the humidifier. The replacement for all this contemporary distraction was to be some old-fashioned books. So I went down to Arachnids and loaded up on graphic novels, German philosophy, self-help, and a few American classics. These I set in a heap by Tara's oxygen tank. She also asked for sleeping medication, hoping that a couple days of snoring might cure her of the whole business.

When she woke on the second day, she was in a white fury, and this was a sad and frightening thing to behold in a woman who was sick enough that she could not get across the room without a major effort. Apparently, in her detoxified state, she had enough physical strength left to wipe out a stack of books that I had paid good money for.

"Get these things out of here!"

"But...you asked for books," I said.

"You and your books disgust me."

She flung one of the volumes at me. Something French.

"Are you sure you're not just feeling bad because of the withdrawal?"

"You don't know anything about it! You think you know what this feels like? You think I'm stupid? Get out of here, get out of this room right now, and don't come back."

"I'm trying to be supportive, in this your—"

"I'll tell you what your kind of life is; do you want to know what your kind of life is? The boring kind. Your idea is that maybe you'll sit around for a little while and listen to some *jazz* on the web, on some web site that's about to go out of business because not one person has ever listened to any of the shit that they play on there—"

"Tara—"

Because when she got started...

"Boring, boring, everything you do is boring, with your goddamned baseball statistics—"

"I thought you liked baseball—"

"—and your old books; who's going to read all these books, and they just sit around here and no one reads them, and you expect me to have to look at all this shit, when all I want to do is be where the *action* is, you know, where there's a little energy and enthusiasm left in the—"

The third day was the same, except that she asked for a copy of *Seven Ways to Accept the Wisdom of Your Illness,* by some Tibetan Rinpoche or other. She got through exactly one of the seven ways before she got up from bed to throw that one out the window. I found it among the prickly pears a few weeks later.

I spent the next two days in the living room doing part-time telemarketing. We needed the few extra dollars to cover some of what I hoped would be Tara's final wagers.

When she rose on the fifth day, her hair was wound into the whorls that kids favor when they are sucking their thumbs, and her eyes were bloodshot, and she was wearing only a diaphanous nightgown. With her swollen fingers and toes, she looked like she'd come from deepest space, from the great interstellar beyond, but one look at the smile on her face and I knew that the cure had finally taken. At least for now. She was rolling her oxygen tank behind her, like it was a child's pull toy or a Pomeranian.

"Are you back?" I asked.

"I am back."

"And how do you feel?"

"Like I licked the inside of my crematorium."

"Which means?"

"Keep me in the dark about current events until further notice. Even a local news site is going to set something off. I mean, maybe I could read some coupons or a cereal box or something, but not much more."

"Are you going to take back any of those things you—"

"Monty, you know that I'm not responsible. It's like delirium tremens."

She lay down on the sofa and put her head in my lap, and that was a moment I often thought about two or three years later when I found myself in the waiting room of the hospital, eating from the vending machines. The day on which the helicopter carrying the world-renowned Sino-Indian surgeon landed on the roof. (And this was only one of the many, many add-ons that your health insurance provider doesn't deem reasonable and customary.) In the OR, they were taking the lungs out of the six-pack holder in the refrigerator, in order to test this first donor lung, to make sure it was still in good working order. Then they began talking about my wife's condition, which, they remarked, was going to *slay* George's squeaky-clean lungs, just as it had slain her own, and which made the whole transplant a complex undertaking for anyone, because, they said, my wife, Tara, was going *to perish.* I would never see Tara with gray hair, and I would never see her worrying about how fat she had gotten in old age; I would never see her liver spots and think *how beautiful are these spots,* I would never see Tara dandling a malevolent toddler on her knee, she would never bust out her identification card for *seniors' night* at the movies. And I would never see her on the deck of a cruise ship in the Caribbean, drinking champagne from unbreakable stemware. I would never see her with her (as yet imaginary) children's children, or in Rome, or getting ready to go hang gliding. She would never collect a pension. But on the day of the double lung transplant, I was thinking only that another couple of weeks would be *great,* and six months would be amazing, three years: like from the heavens.

They gurneyed in my wife, Tara. At the ready was the heart-lung machine and various other pieces of advanced robotic and nanotechnological complexities intended to prevent unforeseen happenstance. A moment hovered, expectant, as the systems went through their scanning protocol. Then my unconscious wife had the inferior of her two diseased lungs disconnected. I can't really imagine which of the two was the worse, since both were full of pus and fluid and dead carbon-based gunk, stuff that Tara could no longer eliminate from her bronchi, stuff the color of turned mayonnaise. They began pulling George's left lung out of the beer cooler, and they trimmed away a little bit of it so it would fit into Tara's body. This after a guy with an expensive saw had opened up the whole of her, underneath her breastplate. They opened her up straight across, from latitude to latitude. And they began the arduous connection of George's left lung to Tara's pulmonary artery, the pulmonary vein, the bronchus, while the other nearly worthless lung pumped away haphazardly, keeping her just this side of peat moss. When the left of George's lungs was attached, it took a few breaths, began doing its job, and they moved on to the right.

In the waiting room, the better to try not to think about the direst of circumstances, I looked at the worried faces of other people. I got up and paced, as one will, because the molded plastic chairs abraded my posterior. (There should have been a therapeutic ward in the university medical center that was devoted to nothing but the skeletal problems caused by the molded plastic chairs of hospital waiting rooms. The Montese Crandall Wing for Abnormalities of the Softened Posterior.) The other thing I did was to call again on Noel Stroop, to ask if I could have a reading at Arachnids, Inc. "Noel," I remarked, "it's Montese Crandall, yeah, yeah, baseball cards. Right. Look, Noel, I'm here in the hospital, where my wife is...well...never mind....Right. That's kind of you. Noel, let me be frank. I would like to be able to tell my wife, when she comes around, that I have accomplished something in the area of my writing. It doesn't have to be much. I would like to tell her something *good,* you know, to cheer her up, while she's realizing how many stitches she has in her chest, and how big the scar is, and how many stents and shunts there are in her. Noel, I'm wondering if you would consider giving me a chance to *read* there at the store, yeah, from my collected stories, such as they are, so that I can tell my wife, when she awakes."

As I may have indicated earlier, Tara didn't come out of her coma on any accelerated schedule. In the days after the completion of her double lung transplant, I was permitted to observe my wife's slumbering form, first in the ICU and then in the general hospital population, and this is when the word *ischemia* suddenly became a part of daily conversation. The doctors would ask, "Are you Mr. Crandall?" though we'd been multiply introduced, and I would say, yet again, "Why do you think I'm hanging around her bed day and night, looking as though I'm a homeless person, mumbling to myself and breaking out into, well, spontaneous heaving sobs?" They would ignore my comments. "In the coming days, it's possible that we might see the following...," and then the word *ischemia* was always slipped into the monologue. Other bits of medical argot were also deployed, diabetes mellitus, further "clubbing" of the fingertips and toes, progressive deafness due to long-term consumption of antibiotics, cross-infection from other lung patients, genetic stuff I didn't understand, and then something about a *transmembrane conductance regulator.* These conversations always ended with someone asking whether I had been tested for the certain recessive gene myself, the gene that caused Tara's difficulties. Which was another way of asking if I knew of or accepted the barrenness, the non-productivity of our marriage, to which I replied only with silence, because that was my way.

The expectations the doctors had for my wife were optimistic, after a fashion, until they remembered to ask about her age. My wife, at thirty-eight, was sicker than most people with her illness. Younger people didn't have trouble with *ischemia* or *reperfusion injuries* subsequent to their surgery. They bounced back quicker from the infections. Whatever the cause, my wife long remained unconscious. Or, more exactly, she was in a way station between delirium and unconsciousness. During this stretch, when I was either sitting next to her bed or eating nougat-and-peanut snack items, Tara was having incredibly vivid nightmares, all of which involved persecution. She dreamed that I personally was a member of the FBI's *domestic fraud task force* and was coming to cut parts of her body off bit by bit so that they could be blown up in garish desert explosions. Or I was a serial killer and was trying to administer lethal drugs to her. Or else I was eating bits of her. Or I was forcing her to have sex with me, even though she was missing limbs. Or I was using my amputation stumps to penetrate her. Or she was trying to flee from me and other persecutors, even though she had only 20 percent of lung function.

It was a good thing, therefore, that I had secured an upcoming reading at Arachnids, Inc. This was a welcome distraction. The only problem, as regarded my reading, was that I had a grand total of six or seven sentences to read to the audience. Despite the fact that I admitted to absolutely little doubt as an artist, some of these sentences *were clearly better than others.* Either I was going to read the sentences over and over again, so that they would transport by virtue of a canny repetition, or it was going to be a very short reading. Well, there was a third alternative, namely that I would produce some *new* material. I have heard of, and have never exactly approved of, people attempting to write new works just so that they'd have something to read. Here was my chance. Blood and guts. The heartbreak of mortality. The last bit of air squeezed out of a diseased lung. The love, or at least the considerable devotion, cut short by fate. Out of great adversity comes great art, and so I came up with my celebrated lung transplant sequence. (See *The Collected Works of Montese Crandall,* presently under construction, p. 4.)

Future readers of my works will realize that the surgery sequence, at the time, represented a huge advance in the amount of work I had at my disposal for the reading, in that it contained *several sentences.* It seemed to be what I was able to come up with in those weeks of drama and anxiety. I knew my wife's illness was genetic, and that it was unlikely that I had *caught* it from her, and yet I found myself having to remember, almost manually, to breathe, breathe, breathe, while I was in the waiting room or in her hospital room. When I fell asleep, in fact, I began experiencing episodes of apnea, in which I would shake myself awake, chest heaving, unable to catch my own breath, just as I had so often attempted to catch my wife's breath *for her.* The same was true on the nights I tried to sleep at home in the large queen-size bed that never felt right without Tara's skeletal frame alongside me. She was one of those sleepers who move ever closer, until they have commandeered a good three-quarters of the square footage, while you are balanced precariously on the remainder. Without her, it seemed there was nothing to keep me from spreading out and taking over everything, in an orgy of self-centeredness and, thus, insignificance.

The twenty-first day of the month came around, the day when Tara went back into the ICU. They did more tests, which is what they do in the ICU, and I thought about canceling my reading at Arachnids. However, I decided that if Tara were awake, dressed in a pink miniskirt and some silky flowered top that she managed to find at one of the thrift shops on Fourth Avenue, she would have said, despite her oxygen mask, "Monty, get out there and *live*." You understand, this is not to say she never felt sorry for herself, nor that she didn't get bored of seeing me hanging around every day. In an earlier phase of her illness, she would occasionally take off on ridiculous trips up the block. Dragging her rolling oxygen tank, she would stick out her thumb and wait for someone with a minivan to come along. Then she'd say, *Take me to a betting parlor, if you please.* Or something similar. She would have the racing form, and the sports pages, and a copy of one of those periodicals designed for arms traders. Those illegal betting parlors were dangerous, unscrupulous, and sad. But when you don't get out of the house much, you are willing to go almost anywhere. In the backseat of this stranger's car, coughing her disgusting and very watery cough, spitting her sputum into a cup or sometimes out the window, Tara gazed upon the whole thing, the vast expanse of our part of the state, effusing to her driver. "Do you see any longhorn sheep?" "No, lady, no longhorn sheep." "Do you see any bobcats?" "No, lady, I don't see any bobcats." "Do you see any javelinas?" "Sure, when don't you?" And Tara would often conclude, "Once I was able to hike in parks, a little bit, anyway."

But let us now leave my wife in her unconscious state, so that the scene might shift again to the little bookstore named after the kingdom of life-forms with prehensile second antennae, e.g., scorpions, brown recluses, and their kin. I was going to Arachnids, as scheduled, whether I liked it or not, and whether or not there were going to be any listeners in the store. It bears mentioning that I did occasionally visit Arachnids as a customer, because of its excellent used books and digital media. It was a comfortable place for the slaying of time. I belonged there. It was right that I was reading here. I was going to enter the store like some prefab pop singer, therefore, striding onto the stage as if he had ownership. And I would wear the most elegant outfit (I had put some serious thought into this), namely some *undertaker's clothes,* because that was how I felt, like a merchant of death, like a man whose everyday affairs had only to do with the lost, with the teeming cities of Hades, where the souls eternally suffered. So I would wear black shiny shoes and skinny tie and black armband, a black knitted cap. Let it be noted, too, that black does flatter a gentleman who has perhaps become spread out in the midsection with the nervous eating of nougat-and-marshmallow treats.

I loitered in the philosophy section of Arachnids until a quarter past the hour. I muttered nervous prayers. Noel then made clear that we would have to make do with the audience at hand, which audience was scattered among folding chairs, and, as I have said, this audience numbered exactly five. I knew three of them. One was Jake Cohn, a pharmacist and enthusiastic supporter of the arts, who owned and operated *Mud Hut* magazine; then there was Jenny Martini, a flea marketeer like myself who often helped me put up my stand (she sold vintage lamps); besides Jenny and Jake, there was one of the legions of beatnik homeless men who lived in our town, probably an Iraq war veteran, wearing on this night old polyester rags. And then there was a rather stately, motionless, and imposing black man, sitting alone in the back row. He looked drugged.

Noel Stroop began introducing me now, mumbling an entirely incorrect pronunciation of my name, calling me, believe it or not, *Montrose Candle,* and indicating that I had numerous publications in the local rags. Then, having run dry of material,

Noel asked the audience to please give me a warm welcome, which they attempted to do, notwithstanding that they were the proverbial *happy few.*

There I was at the lectern, with the very bad wireless microphone that had long since been rendered fuzzy, and in my possession were about ninety-five words. I could think of nothing to do at first. I was certain that I was going to void my bowels. There was a uvular tickling, and I fantasized briefly about a burning lava flow coming up past the esophageal sphincter, through my old, compromised esophagus. But then I thought of my Tara, back when she was sitting out in the driveway in a wheelchair, kicking gravel, frozen with terror at the notion that she had to undergo her lung transplant. She didn't *want* to have those two pieces of George the biker sewn into her for the rest of her natural life. She didn't *want* to corrode her new lungs with the same mucoid rice pudding that had gummed up the last pair. She didn't *want* to begin her lifelong regimen of antirejection cocktails. She didn't *want* to see both her lungs spatula'd into a medical-waste container and flung into a dumpster out back of the hospital, where the javelinas would likely dig them out and feast. When I thought thus of Tara, and of the drainage that was probably taking place then through the stent above her right nipple, I realized that I *could* be strong, and I *could* read my first story, and I *could* be Montese Crandall, *innovator in contemporary letters.*

I recited a proper introduction to my work, as follows: "I'm very glad that you have all come, and I would like to tell you about my work, in order to prepare you. My work is about paring away the fat and gristle and imprecision to leave the most rudimentary scaffolding, a process few writers are willing to undertake. As evidence of this, I'm simply going to read you an excerpt from my newest piece. However, before beginning, I think we need to observe a *silence* for a couple of minutes, so that you can hear my sentences arising from out of a doomed, hushed, forlorn historical moment, and together we remember how language replies always to the nothingness, how the utterance is a pure thing, a pure, uh, musical production, faced with, you know, the thundercloud of human failure sweeping down from the mountains and over the desert."

I then fell silent for exactly three minutes. It was like this: with only thirteen sentences total, I needed to read one sentence every three minutes, and then my reading would be the ideal length for a reading, which is thirty-nine minutes. While I could have read longer, I decided on the occasion of my first reading to warm up with something a bit less challenging, to indicate that I was taking the needs of the audience to heart. So I vacated the area of the lectern and sat, plunked myself down, in the circle with my audience, and put my wristwatch on the chair next to me, and I closed my eyes.

Maybe it was because I hadn't had a moment lately to be anything other than the worried lump of a husband by Tara's bedside, the guy who just hours before had called her parents, with whom she was not close, so that they could imply that I was the reason Tara was sick now and that if she had stayed back in the Rust Belt, and dated Skeet Berman, the venture capitalist, then she would have had a happier and more fulfilling life. I was much too old for her, and my job was not a proper job, and baseball card enthusiasts were shut-ins. Maybe it was because of this stress that, as soon as I was sitting quietly at Arachnids, I felt something profound swoop down on me, some scrolling news bulletin of gratitude and grace, so that my eyes filled with tears, tears that did not quite spill over, but I choked, briefly, began to hack, thinking of my own *great fortune* to have been given the responsibility of Tara Schott Crandall. To have seen Tara parked in the driveway prior to having George's lungs sewn into her. To have cared for Tara despite all grim prognostications about her future. This was an honor, this was a *life,* whether I had succeeded entirely or not. I was confident that the audience shared, if telepathically, in this feeling, or at least shared in the possibility of silence, and it was with this conviction, after three minutes, that I stood.

Because I had all my sentences memorized, I then dramatically presented the surgical series, just as if it were an actor's soliloquy:

> Cut it. Cut here. Cut it out. Cut it off. Cut
> the cord. Cut the costs. Cut the crap. Cut your
> wrists. Cut and run. Cutting corners. Cutting
> the losses. Cutting some slack. Cut *me* some
> slack. Cut the grass. Cut the malarkey. Cut to
> the bone. Cut. Cut, cut.

Informed readers and critics familiar with my work will recognize what I recognized myself in that horrible moment, that I had somehow spontaneously altered the surgery sequence. But I have since come to believe that my type of literary endeavor needs to be able to adapt to circumstances, to incorporate spontaneity if it is to grow. If the spoken version of the story was different from the written draft, so be it. However, the realization of my prolixity cast some shadow over me, and I almost immediately fell into silence again, a silence of nearly awkward length. In which I was looking down upon the Plexiglas lectern, thinking badly of myself. I guess I *was* kind of nervous. This secondary silence had a rather predictable effect. It drove two people out of the reading, first the beatnik guy, who was probably only there to relax for a few minutes. He needed time out of the desert heat. The beatnik guy recognized that at a reading of five persons, Noel Stroop was not going to eject him from Arachnids, despite his habit of stealing things from the computer books section and attempting resale out in front of the ruins of what was once the Dairy Queen. He took advantage of my surgery sequence to *bust a move,* as they used to say, and then he went out into the night and, I suppose, hopped a freight train.

Jenny Martini was next to go, waving graciously. I would have lamented this departure, but it was time to read anew. I was down to three people, including Noel, who kept looking at his wrist-implanted digital minder. I launched violently into the single sentence that remained of my biography of *George*, the lung donor, and I am sure that I delivered it in such a way that the entirety of my former hundred pages *were* implicit in that one sentence. When I took my skullcap from my head and clamped it over my left pectoral mass, it did fill my heart with sweet sympathy. "He was just a kid," I called out. Weren't we all once?

(Even I was once a child, in fact, which I have neglected to mention. An excessively needy child. A righty among lefties. A tone-deaf belter among whispery folkies. Born at a time of much uncertainty, the year being 1973. My parents were living in a van, following some troupe of jugglers and folk musicians around the country, a troupe called Nexus, that is, before my parents settled at what they used to call an ashram and conducted ongoing polygamous relations with other adults. My siblings were legion, apparently, whether by custom or actual fact. As a child, I read widely in New Age mysticism, I had no choice, I fumigated with sage, I wore dreadlocks, I cooked exclusively with brown rice, until I became a man, and, in the desert, abandoned my family, as Americans will do.)

Silence is what happens when we do nothing to intervene. And maybe that is what we ought always to do, make less of ourselves, fill less of the atmosphere with our incomplete opinions, with our ill-considered arguments, our strident beliefs that amount to squelched flatus in a stuffy room. The universe is silent, after all, because there is no air in which sound can take place, and thus silence is the biggest part of the universe. The stripping away, the leaving behind of literature and language so that silence takes its place, this is preferable, the bookshelf that is three-quarters empty leaves room for *more*.

Jenny's departure had left just the publisher of *Mud Hut* and the unknown black guy. And Noel. It was unclear whether Noel's posture—slumped over the register—was asleep or simulating sleep. At this point, I determined to cut short my program, and skipped back to one of my greatest moments as a writer, and I recited from memory the story about the *stealth bomber*, which I'm sure I don't need to repeat here. What's more important is what happened next, because after I presented the story just mentioned, I thanked the audience for its patience, having taken up no more than nine minutes, which has to be a world record where readings are concerned. Some poets use up more than nine minutes just telling you how many poems remain to be read.

The program was now completed. Jake Cohn, for one, applauded energetically. The store was comically somber except for Jake and the unknown black man, who, despite the strange circumstances of the evening, seemed to be attentive and waiting around, I supposed, to meet me. Jake was already backing toward the door. Graciously, he invited me to submit anew to *Mud Hut*, if and when he managed to put together additional funding. But before he pushed back the glass door with all the band handbills on it, it occurred to me that I had forgotten to croak out the invitation that was always such an important closer at any literary event, "Does anyone have any questions?"

Jake hurried to his folding chair. It was getting on toward night, and there were the blackouts to consider, the OPEC embargo and all of that, and so at ten P.M. the lights were meant to go off for all nonessential businesses. Everyone wanted to get home in advance of the blackout, especially when a lot of them were walking home. And so why did I ask for questions? Better to ask why the borscht belt comic works himself into a frenzy with the house three-quarters empty. Better to ask why the protestors, who number only three, play to the camera as the traffic rushes past heedless. If you *can* wish a vanished world into being, if you can dredge up your dreams from the lake bottom, why not do so with brio? The imposing black man raised his hand immediately, and in a hoarse whisper that recalled certain jazz greats during talk-back portions of their bonus tracks, he immediately asked — "Where do you get your ideas?"

Since Jake did take this opportunity to press on to other engagements, since Noel had most of the chairs folded and stacked so quickly that it was as if they'd never been set out at all, there was nothing to do but take this man and his question out into the dusty night. He was about a foot taller than I, and his hair was grayer than I'd thought when he was sitting in the back of the room. In close company, in fact, his manner was even more halting and irregular than when he had first attempted to pronounce his hoarse question. The phrase *wild, staring eyes* was made for interlocutors like this. Since I'm a fan of the new expanded edition of the *Diagnostic and Statistical Manual of Mental Disorders — Eighth Edition,* since I flip through it looking for syndromes that I have yet to contract, I did have a couple of diagnostic speculations about this gentleman who later announced his improbable name as: D. Tyrannosaurus.

My speculations touched upon *aggravated hydrophobia with hygiene aversion,* which you found a lot of in our town, and though it was considered a civic virtue to refrain from bathing, a virtue taken to extremes by some local ragamuffins, Mr. Tyrannosaurus undertook to fulfill this duty with especial loyalty. There was also *mixed caffeine obsession with chronic caffeine dependence,* which became evident when he suggested the little spot up the block called Ho Chi Minh. On the way, I attempted to address his inquiries with respect to my endeavors as an artist. I admitted that I was not very good at ideas, else I would have written a lot more than I had written, nor was I good at getting ideas down. Normally when I had an idea it was a weak idea. Along these lines I kept monologizing. I could not keep myself from monologizing, especially since D. Tyrannosaurus had what the *DSM-VIII* describes as *conversational pseudo-uremia,* meaning that language is all but occluded in the individual's larynx and then distributed behaviorally around the personality, with delusional overlay apparent in resulting grammatical malformations, and because I was sort of panicky about how D. Tyrannosaurus was going to respond to some of my observations, I felt that an avuncular chattiness would suit me fine. I remarked again that I had no actual ideas, that I had written some thirteen sentences in near upon seven years and that he didn't want to know how much writing was required from which to excise the thirteen sentences, and, by the way, my wife was presently unconscious in a nearby hospital, having had both her lungs replaced, and because I had fallen far from my parents and cousins and other family and in-laws and had few or no vocational prospects, as far as I was concerned, the night could only grow darker.

The guy named after the Cretaceous reptilian carnivore fixed his wild, staring eyes on me, at which point he noted that he too wrote a little bit, and this I had already surmised because who else goes to those events? Only persons with the *conversational pseudouremia* and the *aggravated hydrophobia with hygiene aversion,* who are meant to be prescribed rather strong antipsychotic medications.

"And what is it that you write?"

"I cut a few words out of a book or a series of books. I paste these words down."

"Paste them down?"

"I paste them down. Collage. They're very short pieces."

"How short?"

"Sometimes just a word or two."

"And where do you get *your* ideas?"

Here he fixed me with a look of such desolation and loss that I don't quite know how to describe it. The look that said all that was good in the world was *false.*

"...It's the words that have the ideas. I just assemble."

He'd been to *graduate school,* I learned, that waiting room of the bereaved. He'd been a champion of information systems, of certain unpopular byways of study, of ideas that made his thesis advisers dislike him. And anyway he preferred not to go to class, nor to appear in daylight, where the violent rays of the sun would reveal his, as he described it, *dermal transparency.* And then when he had left school, his particular interest there being the palindromic writings of a certain Belgian linguist, he became a conceptual artist for a while. In this period he lived in appropriated housing in a certain eastern city.

This was long ago, he reminded me, an era of lawlessness when it was possible to live outside the economy without surveillance.

Utilities could be made to work for you. For free! This was before, well before, legalized information-gathering on all citizens. Pages were still stapled and copied at the copy shop. Concerts were performed with actual instruments. Cable and digital communications were fraudulently obtained. While living in the squat, D. Tyrannosaurus adhered to a twenty-five-hour diurnal unit, so that as the weeks wore on, he was happily alert while everyone else was asleep. Having achieved the maximum in temporal estrangement, D. Tyrannosaurus was then brought temporarily into phase. Not long after, there was the experimental diet of seven meals a day of one hundred and fifty calories each. He e-mailed it to the authors of faddish approaches to weight loss, hoping to cash in. D., as he said I might call him henceforth, insisted on sitting down for each of his seven meals. He preferred to chew each bite of food forty-nine times, multiples being a key feature. Thereafter, for reasons he did not reveal, he passed a few years in the Big House, though of course he was innocent.

This portion of the conversation, the portion relating to the episodic and hard-to-follow life of D. Tyrannosaurus, took a long time, in part because there were many silences, bringing us flush against the evening blackout. I still had to walk back into the southern part of the city, largely controlled by unsavory gang types, and I was a little worried about the forty-five minutes it would take, even though darkness is a beautiful thing. I was about to make my escape, therefore, when D. asked if I played chess.

"Isn't it late? For fun and games?"

"We can play on the clock. Anyway, I got a car."

"A car?"

"I siphon off a bit of this or that when I have to."

As the entire remainder of this introduction, and indeed my entire future as a writer, is entailed in the answer to this rather strange question from D. — *Do you play chess?* — the subject deserves another brief side trip into my past.

Yes, I, Montese Crandall, was once the second-best under-eighteen player of chess in the northwestern division of the country.

As a young person, I had few other passions. It's a certain kind of genius, the chess genius, and it is the kind of genius I once possessed. The kind that sees ahead, that sees combinations. The kind that plays a completely conservative game, culminating in the meting out of total destruction. When I was young and ugly and could not hit the ball with the bat, I wanted to play chess. I worked at it. I read up. I followed Paul Morphy's games, likewise other grand masters'. I pored over Big Blue's machinations, that hulking supercomputer.

Chess was not a thing that was indulged at my parents' ashram, as you might imagine. In fact, chess was considered by my parents to be elitist, proto-fascist, and dependent on phallic aggrandizement, and, in its imperialist, hegemonic, phallic structures, unsuitable for children.

Therefore, I practiced chess in secret. Apart from women and men. Often I played by mail. At one time, I had a dozen games of chess going by mail, with people whom I met briefly in furtive chess-obsessed conversations out in the world, in the rare instances I was permitted access to the larger world. I hated that my chess longing was secret, profane, and that my board was a folding cardboard one that I hid under my bed. On the other hand, I loved my chess-playing brethren. I loved the chess-playing girls with their gigantic braces, their scoliosis, and those homemade dresses that featured jam stains.

My parents, they of the alternative lifestyles, asked, when they found my chessboard: How did we raise up a chess-obsessed child? Why a fascist prodigy? Why a child who won't wear hemp products, even under duress, who won't work in the bulk section at the food co-op, who wants nothing more than to analyze positions on the board and stare out the window? Next he will want his own pocket calculator! Next he will be designing so-called computer games for the so-called computer community where no one touches anyone else and pedophiles run free!

I won my share of tournaments. I even won tournaments in which I had to play several games at a time. I once won a tournament in which I had to play several games on the clock. These tournaments were mostly against amateurs from the desolate towns of my youth. Then, at sixteen, in a statewide tournament, I played against a naturalized Indian, originally from Hyderabad. His name was Sashi, and his parents were in the movie business. He was a vain, self-centered Brahman, and I wanted to humiliate him badly. This was not my reaction to other boys, that I wanted to humiliate them, but Sashi believed he was the best at everything. I have a vivid recollection of his boasting of his sword-fighting lessons, which he needed in order to prepare for his vocation as a leading Bollywood man. Probably Sashi is still working, now that Bollywood is exporting so many of its films to our own web market. Perhaps Sashi plays some kind of emir or pasha, or perhaps he is some kind of malefic drug kingpin trying to thwart the comely Indian lovers.

Let me convey the idiocy of this particular game of chess. It was the rare instance where I used an unusual opening, namely the so-called Creepy-Crawling opening of 1A3. I hypothesized that if I gave Sashi, the swashbuckler, the middle of the board, he would make mistakes of pride and hubris. He would do too much adventuring in the early development of queen and bishops, et cetera. It was his global-village mania that made him overwhelmingly vulnerable. From what I'd learned of his games, Sashi couldn't contain himself. As a further psychological tactic, I made conversation between moves about the extremely large bosoms of women in Bollywood musicals and how lucky he was going to be to consort with them. There would be, I said, women with bosoms waiting for him in airports and in fast-food restaurants, and how was he going to deal with all of these women and all of these demands, at which point he took E5 and D5(!), having not failed to perceive the opportunity. What developed was a huge sucking hole on my king's side, as though my forces had been all washed out to sea, after which I chased him back and forth across the middle of the board, while his bishops danced in toward my despondent governess, and the rooks, whom I intended to liberate

early on with my Creepy-Crawling opening, were liberated to
do nothing but fail. I went for the draw, but there was no draw
to be had. I was crushed by that snake charmer, and he went on
to be a regional powerhouse, before renouncing chess for his
professional acting career, or so I imagine.

I retreated to baseball cards.

Like Paul Morphy, grandest of grand masters, who still played
the odd game in the period when he believed that government
agents were controlling the international chess federations, or like
Bobby Fischer, who was still playing chess privately while expressing the idea that the Jews controlled international commerce, I
believed I could in fact play and whip D. Tyrannosaurus, collage
artist, without much problem. Unorthodox chess openings, as you
may know, are in the *DSM-VIII,* along with, e.g., *waitstaff, habitual
harassment thereof,* and while these disorders are not covered by all
insurers, they do get us closer to an idea of how psychology works.
The Creepy-Crawling opening, the Shy opening, the Garbage Formation (where the knight is pinned down uselessly at A3), these
can be treatable tendencies, and god knows I could have used a
therapeutic intervention after my witless opening against Sashi.

At Ho Chi Minh, D. stood over a couple of kids with a board,
at one of the nearby tables. A candle guttered beside them, and
the pieces seemed grander somehow, more expressionist, in this
shadowy illumination. We were getting to the end of electrical
twilight. D. threatened the kids, with his imposing height and
his severe face, persuading these striplings to surrender to us the
board and its men. It was at this point that I generously volunteered to play the game blindfolded, if only we could find a
stylish and effective textile for the purpose. Eventually, we tied
two crimson napkins end to end and affixed this suggestion of a
blindfold over my eyes. I promise I didn't *need* to cheat, to look
under the lip of my eye diaper, because D. Tyrannosaurus was such
a haphazard player that it was unclear that he comprehended the
most basic movements. He began with a ridiculous opening, as I
had with Sashi. Amost immediately, I could feel him drumming

with his long, bony fingers on the tabletop, as if to make up for his disorderly play. I concentrated on this and other ambiences while sporting my crimson blindfold. There was the snorting of the cappuccino maker; there was the relentless braying from the sound system. A couple to our left was arguing. Somewhere across the room, a young woman sniffled, perhaps in some state of grief. I could hear fingers on computer keys; I could hear what was clearly a one-sided telephone conversation about bariatric resectioning. A wind was blowing up outside, broadcasting widely the dust and detritus of the post-imperial desert. While I was listening to these pleasant sound emanations, I took command of files E and F, easy enough to do even blindfolded.

D. began attempting to push his pawn on the G file all the way to the other end, as if I wouldn't possibly notice, but I overcame this strategy and, somewhat anticlimactically, I mated him in eleven moves. I didn't lose a man.

"Bad luck!" I said. Removing the fashion accessory.

D. gazed at the board disconsolately. He shook his head. "Been playing for thirty years. It doesn't show. Well, let me drive you back."

We stepped outside the café into that most compelling and dazzling moment of modern life. The moment when the electricity utterly failed. As you may have gathered, Rio Blanco was one of those places where the night sky reached out and struck dumb the citizenry, rendered it puny and insubstantial. The sun dipped behind the mountains, and there was the enormity of the Milky Way, the rioting of nebulae. I can't tell you the number of days that I have lain in the empty roads at three or four in the morning, watching cascades of shooting stars.

The city lights went off in the distant zones first. Each night about ten P.M. First, the southern quarter of town, where all the good Mexican and Colombian and Venezuelan food was, and then the downtown, where the empty skyscrapers languished, neglected. Then the bohemian neighborhood, near the community college, where we stood. Then the blackout swept east, into the districts with the fences and walls and barbed wire, all the way up into the foothills, until, in a minute or so, the two of us stood in total darkness.

"I'll tell you what," D. said. "I am going to read up, and I'm going to play a few more times, and then I'm going to challenge you again."

"I'd like that, Mr. Tyrannosaurus," I replied. "Actually, I haven't played in a while. But what I could use right now, Mr. Dinosaur, are a few distractions. So, I accept."

D.'s automobile seemed to have no shortage of pieces of chassis that were falling off. The drive was conducted in quiet, but not an awkward quiet, in a serene quiet in which the two of us could float without concern. I did wonder why *me,* why would this interesting and accomplished socially inept gentleman, in a town not noted for its population of persons of African ancestry, be interested in a baseball card dealer with a sick wife? In lieu of an answer, I accepted the following: that I had apparently made a friend.

It wasn't five minutes after I closed the gate, shuttered the windows, and locked the several locks that my portable digital assistant tolled, using the ring tone from one of the big band songs from the 1950s that I favored. Making use of the caller-identification feature, I checked the number, and it was revealed to be none other than the URB Medical Center. There was a catch in my breath, in my already highly irregular breathing.

My wife had waked!

In the tolling of the bells, I counted the days since I had seen her conscious, I counted the ways that I had been redeemed, without meriting it at all, by my marriage. And then there was the wheezing of some kind of oxygen-supplying apparatus, after which I heard Tara's groggy voice.

"Monty?"

"Tara!"

"Monty!"

"How are you feeling?"

"It looks like I was sawed in half. Have you seen this? Were you using me for some kind of magic trick? Did you make me play the role of the girl who gets sawed in half?"

"You were away for so long. So I had to, I had to maximize whatever income streams were available to me. Including sawing you in half."

She didn't laugh. My wife. She failed to laugh. "How long is long?" she slurred, drifting away.

"Didn't they—"

"I want to hear *you* say it."

"I'm coming over."

"It's late," she said. And here her voice fell into a whisper. "I'm just going to fall asleep. No visitors till morning."

"But I want to come now."

"You can't."

"I'm going to hitchhike."

"A nurse is yelling that you can't come. Can you hear her? Come tomorrow."

"What if something happens?"

"Nothing's going to happen. Don't make me talk more. I can barely—"

"I know, I'm sorry."

"I don't want to argue."

"I know."

"They're going to take me off the respirator tomorrow for an hour. I'm still coughing up blood. You wouldn't believe all the blood sometimes."

"Then will you be able to come home?"

"I'm so bored."

I did go the next day, to find her stitched shut, heavily drugged, slightly puffy from immunosuppressants, and pasty like she had just been to the paling station, but much herself, and I held her in my arms, and I returned to the pattern of hospital visitation and sleeping in folding chairs, until that most perfect day, the day when Tara returned from the hospital, when I ferried her back in a gypsy cab running on cooking oil, her lungs filled with the breath of young George the motorcycle hobbyist. And here was her amazing entrance, yes, the moment when we climbed out of the car, on a day when the temperature was flirting with ninety-five degrees Fahrenheit. My wife, Tara, walked by herself from the driveway to the front door of the house. She'd managed to get back into her old white tights and her suede miniskirt, the outfit she'd worn to the hospital, and she had on a ridiculous hat and sunglasses, and when she struggled to the front step, where the dead cacti that I'd failed to water for the past month had flopped over skeletally, she said, "This is where you carry me across the threshold."

She certainly didn't weigh much.

I know it's a theme of horror movies, the sort of horror movies that I used to love, that transplanted body parts inevitably bring with them some faint trace of their sinister donor. This would perhaps suggest that, upon returning home, Tara would begin head-banging, and would be demanding songs in which the E strings of Finnish guitars were tuned down two whole steps and the lyrics were all about women who'd done Satan wrong or women who *kill, kill, kill,* but I noticed no such thing. In fact, in the two or three weeks after she got back from the hospital, we had the best stretch we'd ever had together in our marriage. Tara started thinking about going back to work. Though with unemployment rather high in our region, it wasn't as if she could just get out there and command a position. But she started *reading up.* She wanted to go back into social work, where she had worked in her twenties. Her specialty: runaways.

Tara also became interested, again, in the Futures Betting Syndicate. The FBS had become a joint venture of the Sino-Indian Economic Compact not long before. Which is to say that when these Asian engines of international progress put aside the lobbing of nuclear warheads at each other over the Himalayas, they created a global economic powerhouse, and acquiring the FBS was among their first joint operations. The FBS had therefore begun conducting the majority of its Asian-themed futures markets in Farsi, Cantonese, and Mandarin. Some of the subjects of these markets were predictable — the likelihood of the annual crackdown on the anniversary of the Tiananmen Square protests, and so forth — while others were less benign. The web presence of the Sino-Indian FBS was seductive and glamorous, with animations that, on a wall-sized monitor, could lure in even the most hardened former compulsive gambler. Imagine the effect, then, on a young person convalescing from a deadly pulmonary illness, a young person with a kinky just-had-sex hairstyle and an ICU pallor, who was able to do machine transliterations of Cantonese and Farsi. This young person, though increasingly physically weak, could easily have had the resources to realize that the FBS now had a futures market in "Violent Insurrection in the United States of America."

Such simple words! Who would care! At this late stage, when all the hooting and hollering was over, who would care really if there was violent insurrection in the United States of America! Violent insurrection in the People's Republic of China would be the kind of thing that would bring out the tremors in brokers in Hong Kong, Tokyo, and Kuala Lumpur. And yet "Violent Insurrection in the United States of America" was the subject that piqued the interest of my wife, Tara Schott Crandall. She was too sickly to make love to me; indeed, we hadn't had each other's clothes off in so long that it was almost as if I didn't know how to unbutton my own trousers. Did it mean that I didn't love her? It did *not*. I loved her enough to overlook her renewed hours spent in front of the screen, even when, one night, I walked into her office, pulled up the shades, kissed her upon the brow, which was only a little slick with perspiration, looked over her shoulder, and saw that she was spending three thousand dollars (a not insignificant portion of our savings) betting on the futures market in the aforementioned "violent insurrection."

"Let's just hope it starts on the East Coast," I said. And then: "Are you not worried that the betting will produce the result?"

I was used to a certain amount of relapsing and remitting, but this was asking too much of me, and of our homeland security infrastructure.

"Shhh," she said. She was using the chat function of the FBS software to communicate with other dangerously obsessed bettors. One interlocutor was a person whose name, when translated from the relevant ideograms, seemed to be PiranhaYummy. Tara was attempting to convince this Amazonian stream dweller that the conditions were indeed *absolutely right* for the political action described on the big board. I told Tara that there had been a recent discovery of a subspecies of piranha in the Potomac. A small school of them could clean an overweight congressional representative down to the bones.

"There doesn't have to be an actual violent insurrection," she reminded me. "There has to be the *perception* of violent insurrection. Look at all the other stuff they have." It was a villanelle of the violent, a sestina of the salacious on that screen. I could very well have written one of my short stories from titles of the betting pools on the FBS if, in the days of ministering to my wife, I was still capable: "Dismemberment of American diplomat in Islamist country," "Spain exiles its Jews," and so on.

"It only takes one piranha to buy," Tara said. "Then watch the prices rise. I think I can get out before I lose my blouse."

I mumbled something noncontroversial and backed away from her workstation, but not before I could see some of the inexplicable chatter from PiranhaYummy and his ilk. "My bicycle has never been so rusty," he typed to my wife. "A germ has begun its replications." Before the automated translation, he was probably saying "Let's have lunch; my wife doesn't understand me the way you do."

It was in these next days that Tara informed me, over a hastily and badly prepared dinner, that large sums had been made and lost. Tears in her eyes. Ever deeper did my wife burrow into the subculture of Asian day traders in the futures markets. She claimed, among the dupes and shills she found there, to have connections in the anarchist underground in the USA; she claimed to know well the survivalist skinheads of the Rust Belt. It was a lot of bluster, but when deployed correctly, this bluster gave the appearance of knowledge, and this was enough to buffet the price of bids on the FBS.

"Violent Insurrection in the United States of America," along with "International Bioterror Strike," began a slow but undeniable upward movement. Tara seemed to feel that if the price rose, it was she who was ascending, back into the world. Her spirits soared, and her fair, exhausted face took on a rosy hue I had not seen in a long time. Was it the magic arts of the surgeons at the medical center, with their nanotechnological robots? Or was it the likelihood of violent insurrection?

It was when this steady climb on the FBS became somewhat meteoric that the scam no longer seemed funny or pragmatic. We were citizens of a post-industrial country that no longer produced much. Our rate of emigration exceeded our rate of immigration. Our GDP was contracting for what? The twelfth quarter? Tourism was down. Manufacturing was all but nonexistent. An analogy? The mayor of my burg, the city of Rio Blanco in which I write these lines, even this political gladiator had absconded across the all-but-dried riverbeds that separated this sovereignty from our NAFTA signatory to the south. This once robust superpower may have been on its last legs, but we still loved it, the way you love a dog in the backyard, whose attempts to close its jaws around your leg are stymied only by the rope tethered to the dead paloverde.

One night Tara broke the news to me. Out of the blue, she'd made seven thousand dollars, all on "Violent Insurrection in the United States of America." She was worried. She had a *jones,* and the *jones* was for grim prognostication. Tara had locked herself in the bedroom and shut the shades, and now she felt as though she had unleashed armed dissident elements, and they were fanning out around us.

The one thing she never mentioned, in all this, was her illness.

In the meantime, D. Tyrannosaurus and I continued our dance. I can't tell you how many times I beat him, and in how many circumstances. The man just could not play. If he managed to stumble on a strategy, he then could be relied upon to overlook what came next, forever forgetting what my bishops were doing or all the possibilities of my queen. I beat him at night, I beat him in the morning, I beat him over lunch, I beat him downtown by the bus terminal. I beat him over the phone. I beat him by e-mail and teleconference.

In the process, I began to piece together some of the mysterious chapters in the life of D. Tyrannosaurus. He was not exactly forthcoming, but I worked on him. D. adhered to the story that he was born among theropods, sixty-five million years ago, and in that period of his youth he assumed the stalking position and fed on smaller lizards as they emerged from the undergrowth. He also claimed to have mutated into his present shape.

Conversationally, and otherwise, he was a sociologist of every kind of neglected group, of every association of losers, the street people of the city, with their leathery skin and milky eyes, the itinerants, the ragpickers, the freelance probability experts, the addicts, the call girls with their bioluminescent scarifications. He was extremely passionate about the oldest profession. He never took them home, at least I never saw him take a streetwalker home, but he was forever introducing me. "Montese," he would say, "this is Maria, and she's going to advise me."

He had a sibling, he said—though what kind of sibling he wouldn't make clear—who was laboring in the adult film business, in production, one of the last robust sectors of our economy. This sibling, he said, in a rather fateful moment, had recently forwarded D.'s name to a fly-by-night book-publishing company whose business involved *novelizations of low-budget films* for the online gaming market and webcasting. These novelizations were to be written on the cheap, quickly, and were intended to be composed of the screenplay with a bit of connective tissue woven in to make them palatable to a logophobic online audience.

Novelizations generated a little extra money for the e-book goons, and they left something behind for the collecting market. Novelizations monetized a leftover piece of the filmmaking and gaming business, *the screenplay,* and were farmed out as piecework. The writer retained no rights.

Obviously, this was a very different kind of writing from the sort that I pursued. D. had written, by his estimate, seventeen of these online novels, in little more than five years. Under a great variety of pseudonyms. His favorite novelizations, he said, were romantic comedies, because these were the most imaginative. He could say the woman wore red, and then a page later he could say she wore white, as long as their wedding arrived on schedule on or about page 200.

Now there was a new assignment, D. said. A sort of a science-fiction film. Even though D. believed that science fiction was anal-sadistic, even though it was possible to find *belief in extraterrestrial intelligence* in the *DSM-VIII,* where it was considered floridly psychotic, D. was actually looking forward to writing this science-fiction novelization, into which he was going to attempt to bury little hunks of his own philosophical interests, he said, secret messages, critiques of power and nationalism, homophobia, sexism, and racism.

"How much are you getting for the assignment? If you don't mind my asking?"

He didn't mind. He was getting $750. For three weeks' work.

As I say, this kind of mercenary writing was radically different from what I imagined I could do myself, and yet I suddenly coveted D.'s job. That is, I didn't want to take his job away from him, since this would not have been neighborly, but I wanted to do something more than just write seven-word short stories. I wanted to write the novelization in order to inspire pride in my wife. I wanted to tilt at the windmill of an audience. I wanted to capture *the age.* I wanted to think my way out of desperation and cockroach infestation. Now that Tara was back in the house and encouraging me again, it seemed a natural and organic example of artistic progression. I just needed to get my foot in the door.

"Let's play a game for the novelization."

"What do you mean?" said the Tyrannosaurus.

"A game of chess!"

We were out in front of that restaurant where they cooked the meat on the roof. They housed the meat in some kind of cast-iron container—hoisted it up, sealed it off so raptors couldn't get to it—and it roasted in the midday sun. The restaurant with the meat on the roof had prickly pear enchiladas, a personal favorite. Tasted like mango and bar soap.

D. said, "Would have to be untimed."

I said, "How long would you need? For your moves?"

"One move a week."

"Oh, come on. Are you going to consult a team of experts? I'll give you a pawn. I'll give you the queen's pawn. You'll still get white."

"What do I get? If I win?" D.'s whispery voice was barely audible in the stiff wind, which brought with it a brace of tumbleweeds, cartwheeling across an empty parking lot before us.

"You get to do the novelization yourself."

He said, "I *already* get to write the book."

At this point, D. Tyrannosaurus demonstrated an intimate knowledge of a subject that surprised me. Indeed, his intimate knowledge had been so obscured in the prior weeks of our friendship that the light that shone at this moment seemed enough to make me review the friendship in its entirety. He said, "If I win I'd sure be happy to have a Dave McClintock rookie card, class B issue."

Have I spoken to the *classes* of McClintock cards? I have already noted that McClintock's bionic arm was not visible in the baseball card that first commemorated his elevation to the big leagues. You will recall the details. In general I prefer that people think there is no card but this one. However, in fact, this was not the story in its entirety. The photograph that had been taken of his left profile was in fact the most prominent of the Dave "Three-in-One" McClintock rookie cards. But there was also a second issue of the cards in which McClintock was shot from the right side of the plate (he was a switch-hitter), and the titanium arm, with its ferocious mechanization, its industrial sinews and assembly-line microchip controls, was clearly visible protruding from a short-sleeved jersey.

There were counterfeit cards in those days, sure, back when home color printing was first taking off. There were entire cartels devoted to the issuance of counterfeit cards. And, eventually, because this is how people are, some portion of the collecting world became equally taken with the fakes. With the result that the Topps Company began issuing cards with watermarks and testimonial stamps. A McClintock rookie card, class B, would thus have the titanium arm *and* the Topps watermark, which was in the shape of a standard-issue baseball bat.

"How do you know about that?" I asked, as we were seated. And I said it with a fair amount of shock.

"How do I know about what?" said D.

"McClintock, class B cards."

"You told me about it."

"I don't think I did."

"You did."

"I did not."

"You did."

You know, there are *any* number of powerful additives in the water supply these days, additives that are meant to redress the follies of human character, diseases of the age, such as *repeated reorganizing of household objects, hearty laughter at neutral remarks,* the ever-popular *fear of photosynthesis and photosynthesizers.* And chief among these, I well know, is the almost total inability to remember anything that has happened, also known as *elective pseudodementia.* The almost total inability to remember events that seemed earth-shattering less than a year ago, the complete obliteration of trends inside of weeks, the reversal of strongly held opinions, and so forth — I wasn't the only person who had disabilities like these. Therefore, I wasn't likely to remember if I had or had not discussed

Dave "Three-in-One" McClintock with D. Tyrannosaurus. And yet I believed I had not. I believed that Dave "Three-in-One" McClintock, class B series, and all facts pursuant to this matter were secured in a register of discretion that I did not trot out for just anyone, especially not a frequenter of ladies of the night. And perhaps the incompleteness of my trust was evident on my face, because the man known as Tyrannosaurus immediately began to attempt a flanking maneuver.

"Forget about it, man." The waiter brought around a plate of unidentifiable smoked meats.

"I can't," I said.

"Everybody knows about McClintock and the class B cards."

"No, everybody does *not*," I said.

Again, I began combing through my half-remembered and somewhat fuzzy recollections of events at which D. Tyrannosaurus had been present, over the weeks. I began trying to decide if his sudden appearance was nothing but an attempt to locate one of the nation's preeminent dealers in baseball cards, in order to blandish him out of valuable assets and transfer them to *who knows where,* Macao, or Mauritania, or Madagascar.

"Montese," D. offered, "this seems sudden, so I'm just going to tell you the truth. You know it in your heart anyway. What my particular interest is, these days, well, my particular interest is in collecting things that are in danger of being *lost.* That's why, for example" — gesturing around the chronically empty interior of the restaurant of smoked meats — "I wanted to come to this … grill. There are more people standing around waiting to serve the food than there are people in here to eat. The only people left who can really afford restaurants bring security.

"Let's say I knew you had some baseball cards, okay? Let's say I even came down to this furnace of a place because you have some baseball cards. Does that mean that I think any less of you? Does that mean that I hung around for however many weeks just to get some damn baseball cards? I know how this sounds, and I'm sure it's hard to hear, but I stuck around because I'm happy to spend some time with other people who *see* how things are now. You're an interesting guy, Montese. You're a guy with vision. Maybe even you're a genuine part of history. You're the man who was able to anticipate history, to anticipate what the body is in the process of becoming, and in this card you see the composite that is the human body, the composite it's *becoming,* and so you're the man I, and the people I represent, needed to see."

I would describe my discontent as being like a skin lesion, or like an archipelago of buboes. I had felt that D. was my first legitimate new friend in some years, and now I felt like some kind of exotic *figurine* he had collected so as to have me on his *manifest,* along with one of the Dave "Three-in-One" McClintock class B baseball cards and a bunch of cyborg prototypes. Another man might have left the table immediately, certain that he would sunder relations with D. Tyrannosaurus. Another man might have lamented his naïveté, or started a fistfight, or contacted some oversight agency, or hired a trained professional to deal with Tyrannosaurus. But not me.

I said: "It's a wager."

Because even if he was a wheeler and a dealer, or some kind of conceptual artist who specialized in duping innocents, I would crush him on the chessboard. I would read up on games played with a missing pawn; I would read up on the Bulgarian tactics that had proven so popular in the chess world recently. I would find whatever hidden stratagems I required to make D. Tyrannosaurus, convicted felon, rue the day he had come to the desert.

Next, as an effective researcher, I determined to use my talents to see what was available about D. on the web, now largely pages in Cantonese. As any citizen of the NAFTA treaty knows, the surveillance capabilities of the web permit much, for a nominal fee, and I managed to locate the alumnae association from his graduate school, the prison records for all the prisons in his home state; I even scoured lists of art exhibitions by persons with variants of his name. I did find six or seven persons with names that had *D*'s and *T*'s as their initial consonants who had similar biographies. But as far as a particular D. Tyrannosaurus, or any variant of this name I could come up with, the results were thin. What was the nature of his felony? Was his crime against property? Was he an arsonist or some kind of detonator of government buildings? Was his crime somehow indivisible from his art? Was his crime political or philosophical? It was only the most determined, these days, who could stay out of the reach of the global media, but among these, apparently, was D. Tyrannosaurus.

He had his reasons, evidently, and I believed they would come to light. But my principal reason for wanting to play this game of chess was that I wanted the *work.* I wanted to write the novelization he described. And I wanted to make my life better, in a Horatio Alger sort of way—I wanted the money, I wanted the self-respect, and I wanted the approval of Tara Schott Crandall, the woman with the new lungs. This made a rather adorable story, writing a science-fiction novelization in order to impress a double lung transplant from whose side I had not strayed for more than three or four hours in a couple of years, except when she was in the ICU and I left her, for example, to give a reading at Arachnids. But just as the chess match was looming on the calendar, something awful happened, the awful thing that goes by the name *fungus.* Prior to the events described here, I knew nothing about fungus but that mushrooms were tasty and that you should wash between your toes. But fungus, in particular *aspergillus,* would become my wife Tara's greatest threat.

There are a number of kinds of organ rejection, as we now know from the medical literature. The first of these is instantaneous, in which the organ is flooded with lymphocytes, and death is immediate. Tara, to our great relief, did not suffer this rejection, which is rare in the era of nanotechnological agents. A second kind of rejection is chronic, and characterized by a hardening of the tissues involved at the spots where the organs are connected by the surgeons. While a certain amount of antirejection therapy can help here, the long-term prognosis is cloudy and dark. Still, you may have time to see your child graduate or your spouse appear, inevitably, on a reality-based web program.

Then there is an intermediate sort of rejection, a sort where you have some time, but it is not great time. What happens in this third alternative is that all the nearby germs come stampeding onto your prairie. Germs you never even heard of. With lung transplants, the most common of these infections is pneumonia. But there are far more exotic germs. People coming to the NAFTA signatories to buy up distressed companies and close them down bring a lot of exotic infectious agents with them. Patients who are trying to fight tissue rejection are prey to any Southeast Asian mite that comes along.

Naturally, my personal bête noire among the new hospital-cultured strains of disease is *necrotizing fasciitis,* or flesh-eating disease. There was a report just the other day. A woman's thumb was swelling up; she went to the doctor. He sent her home. That night they took off her arm, the next day both legs, and on the third day she died, leaving behind two children.

Tara had shortness of breath. Even when she got home. We didn't think much of that. She'd had shortness of breath through the entirety of our marriage. She sounded like a toy train, what with the whistling and the chest cough. But upon coming home, she began complaining rather quickly about pressure in her chest. I say *complaining,* but that is not the right word, really, because she did not complain. We were picnicking, after I sold a Barry Bonds rookie baseball card at profit enough to live on for a month, and we were in the park by the railroad depot, the one where all the Central Americans live, and we had some cheese, some jug wine, and some sourdough bread, and a small army of men came over to ask for change, though we didn't really have any change, most of which was worthless anyhow. Despite all of this, Tara was smiling, and her gingham dress nearly matched the cloth we put down on the sands beneath a shady, nonnative palm. She had alluring sunglasses on, sunglasses designed to repel ultraviolet rays and to suggest erotic submissiveness, and as far as she was concerned, there was no better day than this, this unanticipated day, this extra day.

She said: "If you had to weigh, under pain of long-term torture and incarceration, the amount you love me in loaves of bread, how many loaves would it be?"

"This old game," I said, though the game was new. "If I must. Let's see. More than a bread truck. Or a bread factory. And if it were in bottles of wine, easily more than a cask, easily more than a wine cellar. My love would be counted in vineyards. And if it were cheese, more cheese than in the Sea of Tranquility. And if it were measured in dark matter, more than ninety percent of the universe would be it, would be *the love*. And no scientist would be able to locate or recognize it, because it's *everywhere*."

"You always know the right things to say. And if you didn't, I'd tell you what to say." She drained a glass of wine. Tannins were good for her gums; the grape skin had free radicals. I tried to keep track of these things. I employed sage, healing prayer, crystals.

Then my wife said, "Monty, there's something *not right* going on."

I wasn't paying attention at first. After all, there was almost always something *not right*.

"Again?"

"There's something *not right*."

"What do you mean, there's —?"

"I mean there's something *not right*."

"What are you saying?"

She put her hand on top of mine. My thrift store wedding ring. She looked into my eyes.

"Monty, you have to get prepared. And I don't think you are."

"What are you saying?"

"Things are not...It's not going to go on like this for very much longer."

"I don't agree. I think things can go on the way they are going on, and if I didn't believe that, I wouldn't be sitting here taking in the —"

"You're just not being realistic."

"We can call the...I'll call right now. What's-his-name. The surgeon. He's got a...what do you call it? A round-the-clock service."

"We're not calling any surgeon today. The important part of today is what we're doing right now."

"That's *not* the important part. The important part is where your life gets saved. The important part is that things go on as they're going, with only modestly increased levels of sadness and disappointment."

She said: "Maybe there's something that's against us, fate or history or luck or something. Maybe for some people, that's not how it goes. You need to be ready for bad luck. If I have to go on that donor list again...Think about it. I just got *this* pair. And I feel feverish. I feel weak."

"That's a *normal* response. You don't know. We can ask the doctor."

"It's time we started planning what we're going to do. We have tried doctors, Monty. My whole life has been spent with doctors. I mean, when I got three months off from going to the doctor, in my teens, I felt like I was free in a totally new way, and as the care has got worse, you know, even *more* doctors, so that the worse the care got, the better I got to know them—"

"Darling, I—"

"What's the right response? More doctors? Or is there maybe a better response that has to do with art and poetry and with just giving life a chance in the way it presents itself, even if it's in a broken-down place like this? I'm not going to write about all this, Monty, I'm through with writing all this stuff down, and I don't want to film myself for my website, and I don't want to be on some compendium of footage of dying people, or friends of people with pulmonary disease, or whatever; I just want to be a young woman who is alive for a little while longer, and I want you to do whatever you need to do to start preparing for what happens when I'm not here to harass you any longer."

How can these things come to pass? When on the surface everything was so serene? There were many things to be courageous about. War spreading around the globe until it was routine. I could list a half-dozen spots where civil war raged. Economic collapse among, for example, the Central European democracies. Religious violence. Poverty. Overpopulation. Hatred among all the peoples of the world. These were things to be courageous about. But I couldn't be courageous about my wife, not a day longer. What had been asked of us was that we give up *everything,* all that we had built together and all the strength we had stockpiled, and now we were being asked to watch our contentment come to *nothing?* Some bits of bad luck you can work hard at accepting, and some bits bludgeon you. And the big lie you tell yourself is that you're *not* going to be the one who gets bludgeoned, right up until the moment when the instrument meets the surface of your thick skull.

Next day, Tara went to see her surgeon, and they subjected her to a battery of diagnostic tests with high-powered magnets and proton emitters. These revealed the presence of the aforementioned fungus. *Aspergillus.* Antibiotics were increased, and Tara was moved into a hyperbaric tent a few hours each week. We stocked up on tanks for the home yet again. People around us, official people, began talking about months or even weeks.

What could I do? What could I do? What had I ever done?

I called D. Tyrannosaurus. Over the phone, he made his first move.

BOOK ONE

September 30, 2025

What does a man think about while he's making history? A man thinks about his viscera. In the midst of the final countdown, on the launch pad at Cape Canaveral, while Mission Control is counting back from the double to the single digits, he thinks about his bile, his adrenal glands, his hemoglobin, his pancreas, his bowels. Ignoble, I agree. You'd think that a guy like me, Colonel Jed Richards, would be thinking about the judgments of future generations or about the next phase of space exploration, the one in which we travel out beyond the solar system. Or perhaps I'd be thinking about the great religious questions, about who exactly stage-managed the Big Bang, from her loom casting off the whorl of dust and gas and stars, in turn spawning the tiny wisp of our universe, of which but one puny rock is Earth. But no. I was not thinking about interstellar space. As you probably know, the commonest inquiry of schoolchildren as regards space travel has to do with the disposal of human wastes. And since this is the inaugural day of my Martian blog, I am prepared to deal with the question of human wastes, with irritable bowel syndrome and related difficulties. Yes, IBS is just one of the idiosyncrasies I had to sweep under the rug during my long climb through the ranks of astronauts and technicians who peopled the Mars Mission Recruitment Initiative.

Mission Control reached "fifteen," and "fourteen" quickly followed, and while I was thinking about using the suction device in the restroom that I would attach to my lower self, and how there would be no chance to do so for at least an hour, I was also whiling away some milliseconds considering the possibility of my own incineration. In case of launch mishap, temperatures would reach 3,000 degrees, owing to the nature of the solid fuel in the first stage. We would be cinders. As did the other members of my space confraternity, whom I'll soon get around to introducing, I understood that the two parts of the voyage most likely to bring about our incineration were liftoff and landing. Of these, the more dangerous was the landing. On, for example, the surface of the Red Planet.

We'd already written letters to our loved ones, explaining that we knew of the numberless threats on this epic flight. Time slowed around "thirteen" and "twelve" as I reconsidered the text of my own video letter, hesitating over the irony thereof, upon which I will elaborate soon.

Massive public and private fiscal outlay (consider the fuel costs, e.g.) had been spent by our rickety and fiscally strapped government in order to make a desperation wager on the Red Planet, the specifics dating back to a halfhearted boast by a less-than-mediocre president nearly a quarter century ago. Could we do it? Could we bring pride and dignity to a multiethnic post-industrial third-rate economy? Could we redeem a nation before it defaulted on certain kinds of government payments? With this launch did we not ask: *Can we do anything right?*

The knots in my lower intestines dated to my tour of duty in the Central Asian conflict of 2011. It's possible that I caught some kind of genetically enhanced bug in that ill-begotten war, because, as you know, the bugs in that "police action" were often encased in warheads. They had exotic equatorial origins. Whatever the cause, in moments of great social stress, which have included but are not limited to my recent talk show appearances, an address to a joint subcommittee on funding space programs, and illegal espionage missions in desert landscapes, I have worn absorbent undergarments.

Occasionally, I vomit uncontrollably. Mercifully, my experience of IBS, which is widespread among military veterans, has not extended to zero-gravity simulations or piloting. I have been free from symptoms during crisis. Most of the time, anyway. Oddly, one pragmatic approach to dealing with my IBS involves proximity to household pets. Rabbits are good, as are guinea pigs. My cat, Havoc, sat in my lap just two nights ago, when I was last at the house. I was again committing to memory the manual that NASA had given us, the manual that was meant to cover each and every eventuality — in which the hull flakes off during our trip through the atmosphere, in which the oxygen fails due to an asteroid strike on the craft, in which fruits and vegetables fail to grow in the greenhouse on the Red Planet due to excessive ultraviolet radiation and insufficient atmospheric pressure and we slowly starve to death. Havoc sat in my lap, and he purred as I reread what NASA, that beleaguered agency, would suggest if, for example, one of the men in the Mars flotilla suddenly went insane. My bowels throbbed not even once.

Kids, did you know that for the Mars mission, we have brought along a special colony of bacteria that likes to eat human waste products? It's true! Well, not all waste products. The kind of waste produced by human kidneys will be jettisoned from the capsule under pressure, into the vacuum of space. The other kind, the solid kind, will be eaten by this colony of bacteria, which will then excrete, amazingly, something close to phosphorus, which will in turn be amassed for use as fertilizer in the simple terraforming experiments we will undertake in our domed greenhouse on the planet Mars!

As I intimated earlier, one of the other personal conundrums of my life, the life of Colonel Jed Richards, that did not get disclosed to NASA before the launch had to do with marital status.

At times like this, it is natural to speak of Colonel Jed Richards in the third person. And he admits, yes, that somewhere in the training period for the Mars mission, Colonel Jed Richards noted that his wife no longer seemed to be living at his address, and had, in fact, taken herself and their teenage daughter to a secure location nearby, namely the address of her brother, a Miami-based restaurateur. The stress of training in the Mars mission program, which was 24-7, did take its toll on families, and Colonel Jed Richards was not the first to plead with his wife to commit to a few cocktail parties and golf outings for the sake of appearances. When training for space, things happened, but in the rarefied realm of the interstellar, most of these things seemed irrelevant: Pan-Arabists of the Middle East fielding winning candidates in rigged elections across the region, Inuits beginning to firebomb the residences of ethnically European Greenlanders, Cambodian militias commencing reprisals in Vietnam, Australians invading East Timor, Americans adventuring in Turkmenistan (for the sake of a gas pipeline). Colonel Jed Richards did not pay attention to these international developments, nor to government defaults, nor double-digit unemployment. That was earthly crap.

It did get his attention, however, when the wife of Colonel Jed Richards, also known as Pogey Stark-Richards, absconded from their joint address. Maybe it was his training with fighter planes over the desert, maybe it was bombing raids over Indonesia and Syria, maybe it was coaching girls' middle school soccer and taking them all the way to the statewide play-offs. Maybe it was his love of life and his desire to do good, maybe it was his belief in a state-sponsored divine entity, in whatever it was that caused the Big Bang, which in turn first caused the Milky Way and then this speck on which we live, but Colonel Jed Richards just didn't see his mission as being limited to his wife. He loved his wife, he loved his country, he loved his planet, he loved his cat, Havoc, but most of all he loved the expanse of stars in the night sky, and it was there that he would do for history what he could do, no matter the cost.

I was so preoccupied with my thoughts and with the contractions in my lower intestine that I almost missed it when Mission Control called "ten." Before I had time to register that we were finally in the single digits, we were on or about seven, a prime number and "the key to almost all things," according to Cicero, whom I read at the academy.

Then there was the roar all around me, infernal and eternal, as of the very forces that made space and time and all the secrets, and then there were the g-forces, which immediately pressed me into the most comfortable position in which to survive g-forces, the recumbent position. What must the Big Bang have sounded like? Well, kids, you're probably correct if you answered that the Big Bang had no sound! Because there was no atmosphere in which it took place! And no time in which it began! As our rocket lifted off, however, I looked over at Captain James Rose, my companion in the front of the capsule, and we attempted to nod, or at least blink at each other. Perhaps there was not even a trace of this, and yet there was intent. We had attended to the various screens, where the computer was making decisions about temperatures, regenerative cooling, levels of cosmic radiation, and so forth. We had been given the option of shutting off the video feed of our liftoff, and I'd done exactly that on the screens nearest me. I would rather *live* this moment than watch the web coverage.

Part of our fuel assembly involved antimatter, the fuel of the stars, the fuel of creation, and it was incredible to think that back there in stage one, particles and their antimatter daughters were crashing together in order to generate the reactive force that would drive us into space, and I was near to saying something historical about this to Captain James Rose, but we were busy being fused to our recumbent workstations, and anyway he was a man of few words. All of this was happening so fast that the clouds of vapor and burned waste and radioactive material were already billowing away behind us. The launch assembly had fallen away, as in some kind of building collapse, and the intense trembling of the craft at the tail assembly, with its fins, moved us a millimeter from the launch pad. I could see across the capsule on Jim's monitor the faces of the families on the viewing platform, the president's wife, who was holding an umbrella to shield her pale skin from the harsh rays of the sun, Jim's wife, his children. Then I averted my gaze. In the process, I suppose I missed the cheerleaders and marching bands, all wearing appliquéd depictions of the Red Planet.

In twelve minutes, we lost the first stage of the rocket assembly, which would incinerate in the atmosphere. We had, happily, already passed the moment in which two V-2 rockets, two space shuttles, three Thor missions, and one of the prior Mars shots had exploded over the Gulf of Mexico, causing loss of life for twenty-two or -three Americans, two chickens, three dogs, one rhesus monkey, and so it was likely, kids, that we were going to make it, at least, to the edge of Earth's atmosphere. I am a praying man, because you couldn't get a seat on this craft if you weren't. And I was therefore willing to perform any petitionary ritual that might enable this rocket to achieve third-stage ignition (two million pounds of thrust). I would pray, I would dance (though I am a poor dancer), I would recite poetry backward, whatever it took.

Staring back at the Earth, at first, is like staring into the retina of a gigantic human eye. There were auroras flashing around us now, bright red auroras, as though this were the origin of the color red—which must come from somewhere, after all. Auroras just as they have been reported by the other astronauts. They were luminous, beautiful, arresting in a way that exceeds the capacity of your blogger to describe. Likewise, the oceans looked like the surface of a dime-store marble. And the clouds were a succession of veils. No nation, on this camera feed, resembled a nation. There were no borders from up here. The differences were simple, between land and sea, between the things that lived on the one or swam in the other. The clouds swept across each ineffectually. The storms harrowed the coasts, and at either end of our little dime-store superball was the ice. Like at the summit of an ice cream cone.

I was made better by seeing this. All the Apollo astronauts are dead, you know, and NASA has been underfunded for a good long while, and there just aren't that many people who have seen what I have now seen. Jim and I are part of an elite group to whom this view has been given, the view of the superball Earth that is always on the brink of destroying itself. It was along these lines that I made my first remark into the intercom: "How do they manage to pack so much horseshit into such a small space?" and Rose nodded, in his sage way, and didn't say anything at all. Mission Control came on, after a suitable delay, to remind me that we still had a ways to go until we were beyond orbit, and would I remember to leave the communications apparatus free for emergencies.

The second stage launched, detached, and then the third, and our inexorable progress was in the direction of the blackness between us and the next planet. This is perhaps the moment to remind you, kids, that we are embarked on what much of the world imagines is a fruitless endeavor. A spectacle of infotainment. Until we, the sojourners, can get our spacecrafts closer to the speed of light, until, e.g., we have a way of launching a self-sustaining ecosystem at Alpha Centauri or one of the other nearer stars, what is the point of this journey? This is the question asked by the naysayers and disbelievers. No stockholder is enriched by Richards and Rose, et al., going to Mars. No intractable human problem is resolved by it. We are the bottom-feeders of transnational astrophysics, but did we care? We didn't care then, because gravity had given way to zero g's, and I was floating against my restraining straps, and the splashy red lights of the auroras had come and gone, and the boosters expended themselves, and soon there would be silence, as during the Big Bang, just silence, because the sound of space was no sound, nothing. There was some onboard nausea, like you have probably heard, and that *was* kind of rough at first, almost as bad as the roiling of my bowels, which was only now subsiding.

It was just a speck, the Red Planet, one we couldn't really even see, when Mission Control finally indicated, through the computer, that it was okay for us to unshackle ourselves. Jim called over: "In one piece?"

"Never felt better."

"José, all right down there?"

Kids, this is perhaps the time to indicate that the third member of our crew was a late addition. Every jury has a few alternates in case one of those serving has been tampered with by an organized-crime figure or by members of the Russian secret service. Well, it's just the same with your Mars shot. We had among us a young, vivacious woman by the name of Roseanne Kim, who studied astrophysics at UCLA, and who was also incredibly good at designing her own crossword puzzles. Roseanne was irrepressible about her role in the Mars mission, she was her own cheerleading squad, at least until she went to buy a quart of milk just a week ago, at which point she was the victim of a serious vehicular accident. The perpetrator, an intoxicated gentleman, had run a common red light. Kids, did you know that more than 50 percent of car accidents involve the running of red lights? Or something like that. Roseanne Kim fractured her collarbone, because of the severe jolt of the air bag in her Toyota Extreme-Mini. Because of the fracture, she was instantly scratched from the mission.

At which point we got José. José Rodrigues was our new science officer, and he was going to be doing a lot of the rock collecting and geological experiments on the Red Planet, particularly at the Martian poles, where we are bound to have, we believe, a supply of water at our disposal. José was going to be leading the charge. He was short, stocky, officious, superficially unpleasant, and seemed to feel like he had something to prove all the time, and I don't mind saying so. Now that we're in the air, all NASA can do is censor my remarks, but they can't make me believe what I don't believe. Therefore, let's be clear: José had been in contact with some of the military types on the ground, the secretive types who were always orbiting around the Mars mission like vampire bats, and for these reasons we didn't feel like we knew him very well. He never ate vegetables, and as a young man he was a minor figure in Mexican wrestling.

"That's a roger," José called from down below. "It's a good thing I didn't eat a big breakfast."

Jim replied, "I should have had bacon; I just realized it. Why didn't I have bacon? When will I have bacon again?"

"Ah, the conversations favored by the condemned," I said. "I think we get freeze-dried pork for one of the holidays."

"Huevos rancheros," José offered. "Cap'n Crunch. I would have surely liked some Cap'n Crunch."

Jim unbuckled, swam across the cabin to check some gauges and digital readouts. In the course of this, he gave me that look that he had given me through the many months of training, even when there were no capsule assignments. The look said, *Whatever it is you're about to say, don't say it.* And what had I done to deserve this? I am a pleasant, charming man! Anyway, while Jim was calibrating whatever it was he was calibrating, I typed an assessment of the liftoff into the computer, which would be transmitted back to Mission Control. I told them — because I'm the first officer, and therefore the word slinger on the mission — that, as people, as citizens of Earth, we now had "one eye on the Great Beyond."

October 7, 2025

It has been a week now that we've been in space, in a cramped, ill-decorated residence that would barely qualify as a studio apartment in the crowded housing markets of Kingman, AZ, or Devil's Paintbrush, NV. Yes, readers, it's true that the magnitude of creation is unthinkable, at least out the window it is. The planet Earth seemed to recede from us, to the tune of thousands and thousands of miles a day, but Mars scarcely appeared in our ken. However, we were much more consumed with our floating apartment. It was remarkably claustrophobic. And it smelled awful. You know how adult males get to working up a powerful funk, almost immediately? Well, we smelled bad. And there were three of us. And the shower, which was little more than a modification of the recirculating, filtrating shower that they used on Spacelab (nothing gets thrown away at NASA), barely helped. We're allowed one shower a week, and today was the big day. After we were done with the shower, the water circulated into the regenerative thermal system, where its proximity to some of the nuclear technology superheated it under pressure, to kill the bacteria, after which, in this pressurized loop, it ran near to the hull, where it cooled significantly. The process of annealing sterilized the water, but that didn't and doesn't mean it's not brackish and foul. I've brushed my teeth with it, because what is the alternative? What kinds of minerals were accumulating in there, and how long would this water be potable? There have been a lot of estimates on the subject, and that's why we had a rather ample supply of water down in the cargo hold.

Most of the time we were in the capsule we were at an even 68 degrees Fahrenheit, and so we didn't need much clothing. Under these circumstances, our imperfect ability to wash was that much more on display. Good hygiene, it turned out, occurred during a brief period in human history. The past, with its rotting teeth and syphilis, was our future.

To put it the obvious way: there just wasn't that much to do up here. What, you might ask, *did* an astronaut do on a trip that would take months upon months, when there was nothing to look at but certain constellations that were not going to change position much in the whole of our journey, and also the planets that were not much closer than they look in your backyard telescope? The Hubble telescope had a better view than this! We were getting digests of all the major news sites e-mailed to us, and we had television and web broadcasts, although these broadcasts may not have been the ones I would have chosen. We had our own electronic messages and videos. There was an exercise bicycle downstairs, near the science officer's station, but to visit it would mean interacting with José. We were meant to be on a diet of an hour a day on the exercise bicycle, which stationary bicycle had a jack for your personal digital device, and I could easily have plugged in and ignored José, but I would prefer in some other way to meet the minimal standards suggested by the American Medical Association: a half hour of space exercise three times a week. At night, which was not night, because *everything* was night, night was permanent, and the distant twinkling of the hydrogen fusion ball known as the sun did nothing to remediate the borderless night, we watched films, when we could agree. Surprise! José preferred action films! My arguments that all action films were about the reimposition of authoritarian regimes and the ratification of violence (politics through other means) were not taken seriously, but it is perhaps correct to say that I did not advance these perceptions in anything but a lighthearted vein. Captain Jim Rose nearly always selected romantic films. I found this out of character with his two-hundred-sit-ups-for-breakfast personal regimen, and with his past in military intelligence. And yet whenever we discussed movies, Jim lobbied for something where a tough-hearted guy or gal (always played by America's sweetheart, whoever this was in any given age) wilted in the face of the one true thing. After the film, the cabin lights automatically dimmed. We can sleep standing up, kids, because there is no *up* in the cabin. This allows all three of us to strap in against the wall, which is not a wall, because a wall is something on the side. These prejudices evaporated quickly.

I will be posting these diary entries on the web, every day, or as often as is feasible, along with some video feed when circumstances permit. I was playing online chess with some guys in Cleveland earlier, and they kicked my Anglo-Irish posterior. Jim is not a chess player and thinks that the entire notion of playing games with people back on Earth is not consistent with universal exploration. But I thought I would play chess on Mars, so that I could be the first chess player on Mars, as I would be so many other firsts.

Did I forget to describe our dinners? Jim Rose had peculiar tastes in food, as if he were still trying to provoke his parents. He often mixed together dehydrated packets of miso soup and peanuts and raisins into one dish and just squeezed some gel from one of the gelpaks. He would eat this mush all at once, along with some small cubed pieces of beef sprinkled on top. When he ate this mélange, he got a very serious expression on his face, as though someone intended to take his rations away from him. Now, we were, you may have heard, allowed certain personal requests for what had been packed into the food storage area on the capsule, and Jim specifically asked for miso soup, because it was easy and contained protein. I asked for ribs, though I knew I wouldn't get them. José, who often ate by himself while calibrating distances and fuel requirements for the rovers, wouldn't tell us what foods he had asked for specifically. Like he wouldn't tell us much else. It was all written in stone well before we the astronauts got here, the exact number of calories we were going to consume, the days on which we would be allowed to trim our hair, when we would fire sludge out into space, et cetera.

You may be interested to know about sleep cycles. True: we were not meant, throughout the trip, to be awake at the same time. That is a waste of resources. Once we were on course and had settled into the routine of weightlessness, we would begin sleeping in shifts. At this point, the regimented dimming of cabin lights would become temporary, for whoever needed to get a little shut-eye. We'd be overlapping for a couple hours. I was scheduled to be on the swing shift for a while, or at least I thought it was the swing shift, but these terminologies seemed pointless. I didn't really know the date until the web portal I was using told me so.

José just came up from his hatch to discuss the latest results in X-treme lacrosse, the contest sweeping the nation. I wasn't sure who was playing.

"Come on, my man," said José. "You aren't telling me that you don't know who's playing in the finals of X-treme lacrosse?"

José looked disappointed, because we still had two months and a few weeks before we even reached the Red Planet, and then a year while we waited for the orbits of Mars and Earth to near each other again, and then six months back. If we had nothing to say to one another in all that time, if we actively despised one another, it was going to be a long trip. But there was a season for discord and a season for rapprochement.

I could tell there was something going on in José's science lab that he wasn't telling us. We were supposed to be making crystals for use in satellite navigation, telemetry, and so forth. Crystals are better manufactured in the vacuum of space, as you know. We were intending to create the groundwork for a crystal-manufacturing laboratory in space, in fact, that would be staffed sort of like the oil wells in the Gulf of Mexico. Workers would have tours of duty. This was another attempt by NASA to turn a profit. José claimed that he was doing these kinds of experiments, but he showed no results. Just yesterday, when Jim was asleep, José scuttled up the hatch to say, "Look, brother, you know that the search for life beneath the poles is the military priority of the trip, right?"

Why did he keep saying this sort of thing? He stood there looking at me, and his eyebrows were so grown together that they looked like they could take flight from his forehead. And that unsightly scar of his constituted a second smile, a malevolent, snickering intention.

"José, you do your job and I'll do mine. I may have to smell you, but that doesn't mean I have to make small talk with you."

"Hey, they're listening in Houston! Show a man some respect!"

"They won't hear this conversation for, oh, about ten minutes. If they are awake and taking an interest." Because that's how long it takes radio waves to get back to Earth, ten minutes. From this distance. By the time you read this blog, José might very well have moved on to another topic entirely. Though he had so few. In fact, when the conversation didn't go any further, he turned his back on me and rappelled back down the ladder to his warren of scientific contraptions, which may or may not be about the search for life under the ice caps at the poles, depending on your level of twenty-first-century paranoia.

And now some more facts. Our craft is called the *Excelsior,* and as I've said, is one of three ships. Each night at 1700 hours, Earth time, I was accorded the good fortune, as communications officer, to talk to the astronauts from the other vessels, namely the *Pequod* and the *Geronimo.* The total number of astronauts on those vessels, as you would expect, was six, two of them being women — the science officer on the *Geronimo,* Debbie Quartz, and the first officer on the *Pequod,* Laurie Corelli. Without being offensive, if at all possible, I would like to note that after a week of having failed to see a single woman up close, I *did* start to have little fantasies about each of them, in my naps, and in my semi-sleep. Did Debbie and Laurie really exist? Were they as soft as I remembered? Yes, there was something soft in my recollections, and let us say that this thing was a woman! It was only occasionally that they were brisk and peremptory and did their jobs better than the rest of us.

On the night I want to tell you about, it was Laurie who signed on first from the *Pequod.* She hailed in the usual way, before asking how I was doing.

"Not bad," I replied. Actually, my wife, who, as I have indicated, had lately been cohabiting with her restaurateur brother, had remarked in a recent message that she was proud of me, though I tend to think that this message was staged by the people at NASA. This note actually made me feel a little lonelier than before.

"The novelty has kind of worn off," I remarked to Laurie, "but what's new over there? Still looking at our taillights?"

"We haven't picked up any speed on you yet," Laurie said. This kind of scripted banter nauseated me. Laurie looked, on the video screen, as if she hadn't been able to wash her hair much. It was dark brown and pulled back, a little disarranged. Behind her, in the rear of the camera's fish-eye view of the *Pequod,* I could see that Brandon Lepper, the one guy on the mission I found even more suspect than José, was trying to edge into the shot. You know how in space movies there was always one guy who got eaten by the aliens? I hoped that Brandon Lepper would be that guy. In the videoconference uplink, he was doing curls with some free weights, which was stupid, because they didn't actually weigh anything, and wouldn't until we got to Mars. Laurie was elaborating on the virtues of Olympus Mons. She really wished we were landing there instead of near the southern pole. "It'd really be something to tell my son that I was going to be on a mountain that is 69,000 feet high." This was a scripted comment, since I happen to know that Laurie's son has some developmental problem, like many other kids these days, and despite his uncanny ability to compose serious orchestral music on his computer, he wants, by all accounts, almost no interaction with his mother.

I said: "I'm with you there, Laurie. If we can get enough fuel for one of the ultralights, maybe we can make it over there. For recon, if nothing else." There had been a time when the Mission Control decision makers were thinking about landing there, because the caldera is so far across that you might not be able to see the other side from the rim, because it's three times as tall as Mount Everest, because it's still active, because it could be releasing water vapor into the thin Martian atmosphere, because it's there!

"There's the risk of eruption, 15,000-foot cliff walls, and the increased threat of radiation, but I don't intend to let that stop me."

I know that she didn't want to go to Olympus Mons. But I know she had an obligation to the audience back home. What did she really want to talk about? If she was anything like me, she was worrying about whether or not we were going to land on the Red Planet without getting squashed, and whether we were going to be able to grow anything in the greenhouse, whether we would be able to generate sufficient oxygen, and so forth. Come on, who gave a shit where we landed?

Laurie looked behind her, and for a second, I saw a look of unmitigated horror flicker across her face, as Brandon basically pushed past her to edge into the shot. "You've got to admit we'd have excellent bragging privileges if we were to see the largest volcano in the entire solar system." Laurie tried to finish the thought with dignity. But it turned out Brandon had a few things to say.

"Jed," he offered, "did I tell you about the time I was fighting welterweight back in the city, against a bunch of gangster kids from the—"

"You did," I said. Because he had. It seems that Brandon felt he had nothing going for him but that he was *not* a hurricane transplant, like the waves of the disenfranchised who populated Houston, TX, his hometown, because of the mismanagement of successive generations of politicians. "As I recall, you had already been knocked down when—"

He said, "When I pulled out a technical knockout in the last—"

"Brandon, my shift's almost over," I said.

"What's the word from the *Geronimo*?"

"They're playing a lot of cards."

"Have you talked to Debbie?"

I punched the disengage button, and his face went black. I would let the other ship go till the next day. After all, they could call over here at any time. The ominous thing I'd heard, however, was that Debbie, on the *Geronimo,* very likely had Planetary Exile Syndrome. This unpleasantness, kids, has been described in the NASA literature, though widely hushed up during the space station period, as well as during the Apollo missions. Once the crowded, polluted, warlike planet on which you live is far enough from the spacecraft, certain astronauts, no matter how sturdy they seemed in the training phase of the expedition, will begin to exhibit symptoms of intense homesickness, verging on the completely unstable, falling victim to convulsive weeping, fits of rage, and so forth. You have to watch them very closely, lest they injure themselves or the mission. Even though Debbie had been trying to focus on experiments she was going to conduct on Martian water purification with some fast, cheap, and dirty tools given to us by corporations back home, she had instead been talking about how the trip wasn't worth it, and how it had crossed her mind to turn around and head back for Earth. In fact, NASA provided instructions on this. The first part of the instructions involved immobilizing any member of the crew who exhibited long-term symptoms of PES, with shackles and/or rubberized restraints. If that was insufficient, Plan B was that you loaded them up with a synthetic opiate for a couple of weeks. The last option was to eject the astronaut. If they became a serious danger to the mission.

After mission communications, I watched Jim sleeping for a while. He had strawberry-blond hair and strawberry-blond eyebrows, and if he weren't so by the book, I would probably have thought he was kind of attractive. For example, when he was sleeping on his wall cot, with his favorite music on the headphones (choral music, and country and western), he held his hands in a certain way, as if they were flippers, not hands. He pursed his lips as though he were dreaming of citrus wedges. His features were masculine and decisive, but the sleeping Jim Rose was, well, a lot like a rose.

How frail was humankind, kids, out in this little soda can, just a thin skin of some alloy keeping us from the absolute zero of all creation. Asteroids could carve a hole in any of us, and then there was radiation from the Van Allen belt. Cosmic rays, you name it. How frail, how desperate, and yet how resilient. We had come so far, and we had so much farther to go. Jim got a warm blast on his seat warmer, which was the way they elected to wake us, and he rubbed his eyes and said, "Still here?"

It was unlikely I'd be anywhere else.

October 21, 2025

"What's your biggest regret in life?" Jim asked. On the cusp of our first space walk of the mission.

I was going through the prep list. We had to don the inner layer of the space suit, which took about half an hour, and then we had to start on the outer layer, which got *really* bulky. It weighed eighty pounds on Earth, and we had trained for eighty pounds, but we were weightless here. I helped him with the second glove, screwing it onto the wrist coupling, and then he did the same for me, and then there was the double layer of sun visors. Easy to go blind out there if you didn't take precautions, you know. Once he had the visor and helmet on, I heard his voice through the static of the intercom — through the override that enabled a low-intensity transmission, or, as we called it, suit to suit. He locked my helmet onto me.

"Look," I said, "we're going to go out there and repair the couplings on the solar panels, and we are going to tether ourselves, and then we're coming right back in. I don't accept that we need to address ourselves to the big questions."

"I'm cool as a cucumber," Jim said, deflecting my deflection, and I think I know now the expression that he would have been wearing on his face when he asked what he asked, the expression of inscrutable distraction and expedience. "But the extremes of space lend... well, a little poetry to things."

In fact, in these first three weeks in the capsule, because of how little stimulation there was beyond the bland seductions of a radio-transmitted Internet signal, I too had occasion to wonder about these matters of the heart, the sentimentalities. Instead of thinking about making it to the Red Planet, which had finally become unmistakable off one side of the capsule, or wondering if we would ever make it back to Earth, I thought about what I might have done. Interpersonally. Despite the hackneyed qualities of these sentiments, I was helpless before them. I might, for example, have told my parents more about how grateful I was; I might have explained to my wife that the thing for me *was* the work, that the work had to come first. I regretted, I might have told her, that I ever made it seem otherwise. I regretted that I barely knew my daughter. I regretted any time I was ever timid, when I might have been more forthright and more direct. I regretted instances of simulation and deceit. I regretted sunsets and flowers unobserved, children unhugged, all times when I didn't pull over and admire the view. I regretted the astronauts I had stomped on, in making my way onto the roster of the Mars mission. I regretted the times I lived in, and my inability to live in them completely and willfully. Not that I was going to come clean about any of this.

"There are some obvious choices," I told Rose. "I'm darned upset that I didn't keep up with my Arabic lessons, which I took all the way through first year in college. I couldn't understand those long sections of the Qur'an. And anyhow, that course of study wasn't considered patriotic by the guys in the fraternity. They were primarily interested in automobile racing. Mostly I regret failures in the sack. What about you?"

Jim thought carefully, and then he said, suit to suit, "There are the men I killed."

"Look, Jim, you don't want to be talking about that." Jim flipped up the visor again. He had a sort of glazed look. "Get yourself together, because we're about to open that hatch. You need to be completely ready."

"I trained for this. I have traveled millions of miles from my home just to do this."

"Good."

He gave the lever on the hatch a turn and called down through the open frequency. "Preliminary hatch, and that's a Code One." Which meant that José was obliged to stay where he was and monitor us. Once the air lock was open, the hatch was exposed to the vacuum of space, and it was a protocol of the mission that under those circumstances someone always had to stay with the ship. I hoisted myself into the air lock behind Jim Rose and closed the hatch that led back into the cabin. Then Jim reached the second door. The B hatch. His voice crackled from the intercom, "Feel like you're seeing the faces of the people you lost? In the stars?"

I said: "I calculate my pay every day. I think about how much money I'm saving by being up in a capsule. I haven't eaten out, I haven't bought a new jet pack, I haven't gone on any expensive vacations." And yet in my heart, I knew what Jim was saying. There was a raw, inconsolable quality about the void of these expanses.

Take the case of Jim Rose: I knew that his four kids were the most important thing in his life, and that his unquenchable need to explore the universe amounted to a contradiction. He was a family man, and he'd never read a novel in his life. But up here he was one hundred percent daydreamer. He went careening from one strangely grandiose non sequitur to another.

The analogy NASA made about our journey was that it was like trying to get a basketball to go through a hoop from 36 million miles away. If so, the mission navigators must have been exceptionally good hoops players. As the hatch opened, the enormity of our journey was manifest to those of us on board the *Excelsior.* We had already seen, and would continue to see, things that had been seen only by robots and satellites. The novelty of limitlessness was our daily bread. As the hatch opened, there was an emptying out of words like *here* and *there,* and *down* and *up,* and *here* and *back,* and *before* and *after.* Jim Rose stuck his leg out into the soup of stars and nebulae, of Monaco 37 and like-minded relatives, of dark matter, of black holes, of creation's indifference. I could hear his breathing, and his breathing was fast. He was gasping. He attached the tether from his space suit onto the buckles on the surface of the *Excelsior,* and he arced outward gently, slowly, centimeters at a time. I watched him drift. He was a citizen of *Earth,* a man nowhere near where he belonged but who was here in this place nonetheless. After his brief but interminable drift, his metallic boots clunked soundlessly against the surface of the hull.

"*Excelsior,* I've exited the craft, and I'm heading for the solar array, as requested."

"That's a roger," José said from indoors. "Houston, you receiving?"

"I've seen some pretty night skies in my day," Jim remarked, "but this beats them all. Jed, you're clear to proceed."

There was a moment when I didn't know if I wanted to proceed, when I thought that maybe the human conception of space travel was just so much froth, like elves and dragons but more expensive. An intoxicant meant to distract the miserable inhabitants of *Earth* from their circumstances. Why go? Why go out there? There was no such place as space, because a location couldn't be an absence of locations, and the vacuum wasn't a true vacuum, lest it should subsume into it even the notion of vacuum. These latitudes just couldn't be as mysterious and ancient as they plainly were. The night sky was a fresco that one of the old masters painted on the ceiling of the world, back in the quattrocento! I didn't want to go wading in the real thing. But before I gave in to my adolescent anxiety, I was *out,* and here is how slow things go in space, kids—in the time it takes you to read this sentence, I had drifted only a foot or so. It's not like there were tailwinds! In a minute or so I could see my foot approaching the surface of the craft. You could do several flips, out there, and it would be nothing, but then you would be well out of control and could go spinning off, on the tethers. And who knew, really, how tethers behaved at temperatures approaching absolute zero.

And yet, since by Terran nightfall you were meant to have footage of us, out here, attempting to work a screwdriver and other power tools with these clumsy gloves, we had to keep moving. NASA had us on *their* leashes too. It was a while before Rose and Richards, the Martian voyagers, stood at the far end of the *Excelsior,* listening to some Earth-bound engineer remind us how to effect the repairs.

It wasn't until we were hunched down over the solar panels and fiddling with the electricals that Jim mumbled, "I'm not trusting him either; I'm not trusting José." If Jim Rose was worried, well, there was real cause for worry.

"Last night, before you woke," Jim said, "he got some kind of transmission from Mission Control. I just happened to see it appear in his in-box. What would have happened if I hadn't? The substance of the transmission was this: we're changing the landing coordinates. Does that seem sensible to you? We train for three years to land on the southern pole, we announce to the world that we're going to land there, because we're going to do experiments with water. Water, water pressure, water freezing and evaporating.

Tests and more tests. That's the whole purpose of landing on the poles, right? We have to have enough water to last twelve months, we hope, and most of the planet is completely barren. And suddenly there's this plan, that José hasn't even mentioned yet, to try to see if we can't fly the ultralights down into the canyon."

"The canyon?"

The canyon he referred to, in case you haven't heard, is the biggest known canyon in the universe, the Valles Marineris, which is 3,117 miles long (as far across as North America), 75 miles from wall to wall, and, get this, over six miles deep. It makes the Grand Canyon look like a surface scratch.

"That's what the transmission said."

"Did you get confirmation? From Mission Control?"

We had the mission directives on pocket-sized electronic clipboards. We got them as digital downloads. Normally this stuff came in the evening, so we could talk it over while eating. The few moments when we were all awake. Also: we needed something to do at mealtime because the food was so bad.

"Why would we have such a substantial change of plans at this point? And why weren't we warned about the possibility?"

"And how the heck are we supposed to get *out* of the canyon once we're in it?" I asked. "Do we have enough fuel for these trips in the ultralights?"

"No details, obviously." He kept it all to a whisper, suit to suit.

"He's pretty good at letting us know when he doesn't have to do his regular rotation on the laundry duty or waste reprocessing. That's about all he's good at. There's some kind of parallel mission track going on here."

Palace intrigue was much more interesting, but there was no choice, having suited up for a solid hour, but to stand out there in space and repair the solar panels, which are essential to the circulation of oxygen, redundant computer systems, the operation of our thrusters, all of which made it possible for us to fly this soda can across the solar system. And even though we have layers upon layers of solar panels, the kind that you probably have running your hot water, there is the ever present possibility of asteroids or microscopic meteors. We couldn't let the panels deteriorate. In the next half hour or so, Jim and I were doing just what we had trained to do. And, frankly, this was the moment when I started to see what a good guy Jim Rose was. We had the years of training, the months of vomiting in the zero-gravity training, all of that stuff, we had dinner together, our families, at one of those chains near Jim's place in Florida, but I never quite thought I knew the guy. There was always his reserve. His wife, Jessica, had that look that wives get when they're trying their hardest to appear like the women behind the men. Chafing at the burdens the whole way. And the four kids were mute, perfectly dressed, almost starchy, obscenely well behaved. Jim strode among and around them as if he had no idea they were there. At the salad bar, I saw him get the thousand-light-year stare, and he attacked this solar panel with the same kind of intensity. He didn't just fix a solar panel, he applied himself to a solar panel as though it were a codex from a tomb in ancient Egypt that was going to tell of the secret prehistory of man. All I did was hand him the appropriate tools. That said, there's nothing like standing out in space with someone.

When he had finished, Jim said, reopening the com channel, "*Excelsior*, solar array is back online. Houston, repairs complete; we're heading for the hatch door. Please confirm."

After a long delay, one of the innumerable faceless voices from Houston came over the open frequency. "Roger, Captain Rose. We hear you. Fine work."

He handed me the power drill and I holstered it.

"How sturdy you think these tethers are, Jed?"

I used to know the load rating, because it was in the manual somewhere, and I was good at memorizing this stuff. Supposedly, we could tow an entire extra ship on one of them if we had to, because in space nothing really weighs *anything*. But that didn't mean I didn't panic a little when Jim said, "Let's live a little, Jed." After which he *jumped*.

He was feeding out the tether, you see, and I watched as he drifted off the *Excelsior,* my bunkmate. I watched as he swam around, like a circus clown in limitless space. His breathing was in my ears, as if he were whispering innuendoes to me. And I didn't realize how long it had been since he talked, how captivating his gymnastic demonstration was, until he said, "Come on and join me, my friend."

May I digress for a moment? Because I have a tale to tell along these lines. A tale I cannot avoid telling. About how much trouble I had learning to *swim.* This is another of the things that I might not have entirely confided to the NASA people, back when I was filling out the psychological profiles. This story takes place back on the Jersey Shore, kids, which is where we used to go in the summer when I myself was a stripling (my father was a night watchman, and my mother was a math teacher in an elementary school). Well, kids, there's no easy way to tell this story, so I will tell you what I remember, because this is what I thought of out in space, I thought about how I used to attempt to go swimming with my brother, Nick, and how Nick was always the stronger swimmer, and how one day in a riptide, I just looked up to watch my brother carried out to sea. At first, it was sort of a funny thing. At first he fought a little bit against the rip, laughing and waving, and I watched him bob there, and then his laughing gave way to yelps and cries, and I looked back behind me for the lifeguard, who was far enough down the beach that I would have to run for him. Or I could try to swim for my brother, and at first I did try to get into the water, and I shrieked to the people on the beach with me, *My brother is being carried away, my brother, my brother,* and there were large men bellowing and there were women in bikinis running down the shore to fetch the lifeguard, and I could see Nick's hand waving, I could see his little digits just above the waves, the five fingers of his hand. As long as I could see his hand, his palm facing me, then he was there, and if the seconds passed as I waited, the spume of the waves gathering around me, at least he was still there. We shared a small room, Nick and I, and we knew a lot about each other, like

I knew that Nick hated sports, and Nick felt that he was letting my father down, all the time. Although he wasn't doing anything of the kind. He was a swimmer, he was a strong swimmer, except on that day, on the Jersey Shore, nobody was a good swimmer, and people were shouting at him to head *parallel* to the shore, *Don't try to swim in,* these people called, *Swim along the shore!* Nick felt that he was letting our father, the night watchman, down, but no one was letting the old man down like I was letting him down, and I ran to the snack bar, and I called my parents, because I could hear someone else calling the paramedics on another phone, a pay phone, and the two conversations were rubbing up against each other and making it impossible for me to talk to my mother, who always thought we were safe on the beach because there were lifeguards on the beach, and we had grown up beside the beach, at least in summer. I couldn't hear the questions my mother was asking, because the other conversation was happening, and some guy with a really big belly and shorts that sagged below his belly was yelling at the 911 people, and I kept telling my mother that Nick was *out there* and couldn't get back in, and a man on a surfboard began trying to thread his way between the waves, and another lifeguard was running up the beach, and people were gathering, and the lifeguard nearest plunged into the water, and I thought if I could still see the five fingers of Nick's hand, I thought if I could see his hand, then things were all right. I suppose I imagined that I could still hear him laughing, I thought I could hear the laugh that I had heard before, and all the conversations I had had with him that very morning, but in fact I couldn't see him anymore, because you know what they say happens in those circumstances, what they say happens is that you get tired, you get tired from all the swimming, and then you just can't keep your head above water, and it doesn't matter how strong a swimmer you are. Eventually, there is that moment when you know what is going to happen but you are no longer able to forbid it from happening. I didn't want to think about this, that day, and I didn't want to think that I couldn't see Nick's hand waving to me, and I didn't want to think that if I had been a stronger swimmer I could have gone out there after him, and I didn't want to think about where he had gone, because he had gone someplace where they couldn't find him, down the fathoms, and even the men in the speedboats, and the men on the Jet Skis, they couldn't find him, until later, much later, when he washed up. I think it was Sandy Hook, where he washed up, or maybe it's just the poetry of that name, because if you are going to have a place of shame and self-hatred and loss, and the sense that what was good about life is all gone, then that place should have some kind of lovely name, so that you are not prone to forget it, and that's why when I think about having been a brother and being a brother *no longer,* kids, I think about Sandy Hook. (He had to be identified by his dental records.) And they named a football stadium after him at our high school. I often dreamed that I was running into my brother's arms. Long after. In my dream, my brother, Nick, was standing waist-deep in the water, as I had been, and my brother was standing in the water and he was so happy, and I went running into his arms.

A good question would be why I am telling you all of this. How is this relevant to the Mars mission, for which I am the official documentarian? How is a young man's death in the 1990s relevant to the adventure of interplanetary travel? I can't answer these questions, actually. Maybe I am just a little bit more vulnerable to these ghosts of my youth, these revenants, the way Captain Jim Rose is seeing the faces of people from the past in the stars. Maybe there *is* something about space travel that makes you vulnerable to these specters. Maybe this is why Colonel Jed Richards became an astronaut, to flee from the loss of his brother. Or maybe he became an astronaut to honor the memory of his brother, because Jed was good at so little else, despite the love and affection of his parents, who tried their hardest to help him overcome the feeling that he *should have done something,* and thus, well, he was the editor of the school paper, and then he was a fighter pilot in Central Asia, and he was *good for nothing,* and that's why Jed Richards kept moving, and that's why he didn't need to be told twice, when Jim Rose went cartwheeling through the Milky Way, out at the length of his tether; Jed Richards *jumped,* and he kind of knew, in this moment, what the movie superheroes must feel when they are first able to race, *en plein air,* across the heavens. And here's the really disturbing part, kids, and NASA can censor this all they want to censor it, I don't give a shit, because what does it matter now, none of this matters now, the arresting part of flying in space while Captain Jim Rose was dancing around and singing bad dance music numbers in space, what matters was that I suddenly had this thought that maybe I was in love with this man.

November 11, 2025

Okay, this is definitely going to be a really unsettling entry, because I am going to tell you about the week when the situation on the *Geronimo* deteriorated quite badly. You know there were only nine astronauts going to Mars, kids, and you know that one of them was Brandon Lepper, who was most interested in trying to get some kind of interstellar tan by going down into the propulsion bay and lying beside the reactor. There was a window there, too, one that didn't quite have the UV protection it ought to have had, and Lepper had figured out exactly how to get the leathery and faux-healthy veneer that he might have had were he a seventy-five-year-old Florida retiree who'd had himself enhanced with steroids and genetic engineering at a curbside drop-in cosmetic-enhancement salon. If you didn't count Lepper, you'd have eight astronauts. But now it's even fewer.

The story, as told by the others on the *Geronimo,* well, not the others, but specifically by Steve Watanabe, the pilot, is that Steve and Abu Jmil, the first officer of the *Geronimo,* were getting increasingly worried about Debbie Quartz. Debbie had been one of the bright spots during training, and I've often wished that I had her bunking on my ship. She was short, blond, and had kind of a hatchet nose, a very severe nose. Her eyes had raccoon rings under them all the time, and she often complained of a lack of sleep. Still, she told really awful jokes in an appealing way—a termite walks into the bar, that kind of thing—and she was fiercely protective about her fellow astronauts. If Debbie was on your side, you were in good shape.

The *Geronimo,* a couple weeks back, got the same strange announcement from Mission Control that José got, the one indicating that though they had been training for the Martian South Pole, the mission destination had been moved to the Valles Marineris. As with the *Excelsior,* the *Geronimo* navigational systems had been readjusted by the computers in Houston without so much as a consultation. These were the moments when you had to think, why the hell was it a *manned* mission? What did the men and women actually do on the mission? Not all that much. We were going to get our boot prints on the planet's surface, all right, but they could have just taken an imprint from one of our space suits and sent a boot facsimile up, for all we did. We could have been in suspended animation for the vast majority of the flight, like they are planning to do for the Centauri flights. These days, computers did everything. We were their house pets. Anyway, I guess Jim and I were not the only ones to think that the change of landing sites was ominous. Because as Steve on the *Geronimo* told me, Debbie Quartz took this information unusually hard. She'd never gotten over her Planetary Exile Syndrome. She hadn't been sleeping at all, for example, to such a degree that she'd started hitting the sleeping medication kind of hard. On one occasion, they had trouble waking her, and when she did finally get out of bed, she was disoriented. What constitutes disoriented? The part that was significant to Steve was that she said something about wanting to *eject herself* from one of the hatch doors. That was the end point of a long monologue about political conspiracies back home, religious conflicts, habitat destruction, environmental degradation, polar melt, you name it.

Because monologues of this kind weren't entirely out of character, Steve and Abu didn't pay attention at first. Debbie indicated that it was *certain* that North America would be wiped out by a high-yield nuclear warhead while we were away on the trip. She insisted on this point. Was this a joke? No, it was no joke. She wouldn't shut up.

And then she said she might as well just blow herself out the hatch.

Steve and Abu became worried about sleeping themselves. They became worried about what would happen if they slept. They didn't know what kind of trouble Debbie would get into, especially down there in the cargo hold, where they couldn't keep an eye on her.

"Debbie, why don't you swap beds with me tonight?" Abu said to Quartz one night. "You'll get a better view of the nebulae, and I have some wiring and stuff that I need to repair anyhow."

This had been the suggestion from Houston, in fact, because, like I've said, they were monitoring most of this stuff. Back then, we sort of listened when they gave us advice on various things. There were *some* provisions for privacy, like when I was using that nozzle that I needed to use during my highly classified episodes of gastrointestinal distress. Jim called it the *cough button,* using the temporary shutoff button on the teleconferencing cameras that shot us day and night (during these temporary reboots the cameras showed an image of a waterfall instead). Now and then we used the cough button when we wanted to have an hour without constant observation. Remember when NASA sold the rights to some of the *Tecumseh* footage to the network? Where you could watch the guys on the capsule all day and night? It was kind of must-see programming, at least until the *Beneficence* exploded on the return launch and they caught the entire thing, *inside the launch module,* on tape. I knew a couple of those guys. They were mentors to me in my early days. NASA had budget reductions for the next three years, and a lot of it had to do with the decision to broadcast that mission. That's when they engineered in the cough button. And

Debbie Quartz knew very well where the cough button was.

There was silence in the cargo hold after Abu volunteered to swap cots with Debbie. And then before Steve and Abu knew what was happening, she was up in the front of the capsule, in the display window. While she was not refusing the offer to sleep up top, there was an uneasiness about the whole exchange. Steve could tell there was something wrong, and he had the clipboard with the directive from Houston, indicating that this was the plan they suggested back on Earth. She was going to sleep up top where Steve could keep an eye on her. There were many months to go on the Mars mission, and the administration was not going to allow this to get in the way.

A couple of nights passed in this fashion, and Debbie got more and more mute, and preparations that she was supposed to be making for desalinization of the planet's surface, and tests for the various kinds of bacteria we were hoping we might find, and meteorological studies of the dust storms, none of her work was getting done. Debbie had a hunted look, one of the classic features of Planetary Exile Syndrome, and she stared out at the nebulae, sure, through the telescope, and she stared out in the direction of that supposed black hole, the nearby one they were predicting. She did some crossword puzzles. Steve, or so he told me, was thinking, okay, is this sustainable? Is this how it's going to go *for months?* She's going to be worthless for the rest of the trip?

Listen, I know that I am putting words in Steve's mouth here, but let's say he thought something like this, the third night when Abu was asleep down in the cargo hold, and Steve and Debbie were meant to be on the same shift. Despite direct orders from management back on Earth, Debbie didn't take her powerful antipsychotic sleep medication. Couldn't the guys in Houston have monitored her with some of the life-support diagnostic tools they had going? Didn't they know when her pulse was depressed, when her breathing was shallow? You'd think they could monitor this, and you'd be right. Except that they didn't. Except that Debbie hadn't taken her medication and wasn't asleep. She was waiting.

And then Steve, believing that she was going to be damn near catatonic for hours, kind of went off shift a little earlier than scheduled. It wasn't infrequent, see, that the mindless repetition, in a tiny enclosed space, made us careless.

Debbie unstrapped herself from that standing position that was really a stretched-out sleeping position, and in total silence she drifted across the capsule, and then she rappelled down the ladder into the cargo hold, and, because there just really weren't many sharp objects in the capsule that she could use if she were going to try to puncture-wound Abu Jmil, she settled on a weapon that would have required a fair amount of preparation, preparation we had all done in training, and the weapon was the soldering gun that Abu was using for his not-entirely-necessary reengineering in the cargo hold. While he slept, she got this soldering gun right up next to his face, and need I remind you that he was strapped down, and she could easily just have soldered him to death right there. But she elected to say something first, kids, which was "You think I don't know what you're trying to do? You're waiting until we get to the planet, and then you're going to use me as some kind of lab rat for whatever we find down there. In that canyon. You know the air pressure is a lot more conducive to water down there, and there's water that won't evaporate, right? It's *swimming* with microorganisms, I know, and you want me to serve as the guinea pig for the microorganisms. Well, you can *forget about it.*" There was some more stuff about this, more bacteria and single-celled organisms, internecine plots of various kinds. There was enough paranoid verbiage that Abu awoke.

Let me describe him for you. Abu was a kindly and burly Asian American kid from Kansas City whose parents were both astrophysicists. He was the youngest guy on the mission, and yet he wouldn't squash a mosquito if it were sitting on his nose. He was olive skinned and rather aquiline. He had a close-cropped beard and black hair that was kind of curly. At this moment I'm describing, reconstructing it from what I was told, he had a soldering gun about an inch from his eye, and he'd just been accused of plotting to leave Debbie Quartz on the surface of Mars. And he was strapped down so he wouldn't float around in his sleep, and the only way for him to save himself was to persuade her that her entire imaginary conspiracy was erroneous, hysterical, and part of a bad, bad case of Planetary Exile Syndrome. (Though as with so many other biochemical mental illnesses, it just didn't do to tell someone with Planetary Exile Syndrome that it was all in her head.)

Abu, recognizing the necessary diplomacy, became as gentle and unassuming as a guy can get: "Debbie, talk to me. Tell me what's going on. Tell me what you think is happening. Debbie, think about it. Think about those years of training together. Let's talk about you and me, and our time of training. Remember when I wasn't sure about the underwater stuff? I had that phobia about sharks? The atoll wasn't really shark infested; that's what you said. That NASA wasn't going to make us train in a spot that was shark infested, because it was highly unlikely that Mars was going to have sharks on it. And they didn't want to lose one of us to a shark after all the expense they had gone to, to train us. Do you remember how I wept when you told me that I wasn't the only one who'd thought about giving up? You said that I wasn't any less important to the mission because Denny had to give up when his son was diagnosed with whatever that was. Non-Hodgkin's lymphoma, right? Do you think that I would jeopardize a friendship that had all of those good memories as part of it? Those heartfelt exchanges? Think about it, Debbie, before you put my eye out with that thing."

This was the kind of stuff Abu said. And he said something about how he was the one who suggested that we use Debbie, because of how plucky she was, as our *mission mascot* on the night of the big dinner when the personnel had been announced for the various rockets. We went to that Italian joint by the water. We hoisted Debbie Quartz up above our heads, Abu reminded her, and we passed her around like she was a medicine ball, and we all chanted "Olympus Mons, Olympus Mons!" And we told her it wasn't because she was just lighter than anyone else, it was because she was sweeter than anyone else, and this was why we loved her, because she was sweet, and she was incredibly competent, and for this reason, we did *not* throw her into the alligator-infested canal after dinner. We honored her request, or this is how I remember it anyhow, and instead I, Colonel Jed Richards, got thrown in, and I think this is because there were people who would have been happy enough if I had been attacked by Floridian wildlife. We knew that throwing Debbie Quartz into the canal was conduct unbecoming, and so I offered myself up, because I know I am an interpersonal challenge, and said that I would be much more a regulation example of horseplay, and sure enough Lepper, that lunkhead, grabbed one of my arms, and before I even got to strip down to my skivvies, I found myself looking up at the lights of the dock from down in the murky depths.

Abu recounted these and other stories to Debbie, while Steve slept. The cough button was depressed. No one in all the infinite expanse of space knew what was happening down in the cargo hold, how two good and reliable officers of the National Aeronautics and Space Administration were poised to wreak bloody havoc on each other. No one knew how long this scene played out. Debbie breaking into angry and convulsive sobs, saying, "How can I trust you? How can I trust anyone?" Still, Abu didn't panic, keeping one eye, wherever possible, on the intercom button that was on the side of the bed. Awaiting the moment when he might free up an arm enough to get at it.

"Debbie," Abu pleaded, "I don't have any idea about how the mission got moved to the canyon. I just don't have any idea about it. I'm as confused by it as you are."

"Don't you know what they're looking for?" Her hands were shaking, holding the soldering gun. "Because I do, and I think you do."

"I don't know, Debbie. I don't know what you're talking about. I'm here because Denny dropped out. I'm the resupply shift; I'm the extra man. Maybe I pilot one of the ultralights. The guys in the *Excelsior* and the *Pequod* have the manpower they need. We're the third of three vessels, and I'm the third astronaut on the third ship, and all I do is drive people around. I don't have any idea why we're going to the canyon. I just do what I'm told. On a need-to-know basis."

"You're talking to me like I'm ill."

"I'm talking to you like you're a person I've known for three years and worked closely with all that time, and I'm begging you not to do anything that's going to jeopardize the mission, or anything that's going to get you or me in trouble. Because we've known each other for a long time, and I know you know what it's like for me to be a Muslim on this mission, and how important it is to me to be a Muslim up here. I want to insure that I have done something that I can be proud of. And I know how you feel about being a woman science officer, and how you don't have a family back on Earth, not the way many of the others do, and you want people to think that's okay, that a woman can come up here and withstand three years, in the prime of her life, without a husband and kids back on Earth. I know that's important to you, and in the same way it's important to me that I can be an American who's a Muslim, and I am up here, and I'm going to be one of the first people to set foot on Mars. I know you respect that. And I respect why you are here. I wouldn't jeopardize that for you, and I'm hoping you won't jeopardize it for me either."

When Abu finished this impressive speech, he could see that Debbie was moved, because her breathing slowed, and she looked at the soldering gun in her hand, and she was probably really irritated that she was still crying, because she didn't want to be the kind of astronaut who cried at a time like this, and at last he found the time to free an arm, while with her free hand she clutched her tortured brow, and to depress the intercom button, which did have a red indicator lamp on it. He was hoping that she wouldn't see the indicator light, and if he could get her to come around the left side of the bed, maybe she wouldn't see that the intercom light was on, and that he was broadcasting locally back up to where Steve was sleeping.

"So are you going to allow me to get out of this bed now, Debbie?"

"No," she said flatly.

"Well, at least help me loosen these straps, because my legs are asleep. I'm not going anywhere. I will listen as long as you want."

"Listening is exactly what you're going to have to do, Abu, because I'm going to tell you something that you don't know about. What I'm going to tell you about is a certain *bacteria,* a bacteria that is so classified that almost nobody has ever heard of it. And the reason that it has never been heard of is because it was only ever seen on Earth twice. The first time was when they found that Mars rock in Antarctica. And the second time anyone ever saw it was in the Mars missile that the robot mission from 2015 sent back."

"That was just another mapping and atmospherics mission, and the robots locked up solid after that dust storm three months in."

"Abu," Debbie said, "that's what they want you to think, of course. Have you seen any photos of the robots lately?"

"Why would I have seen any photos?"

"Well, I have seen photos of them, and they were in one of the basins, and then they traveled from there, hundreds of miles, and they were taking samples wherever they went, and they found all sorts of bacteria along the way, frozen bacteria that blossoms out of its dormant state not just at a certain time of day, but only at a certain time of year, and only when the planet is on a certain tilt on its axis, which means only maybe every seventy thousand years or so, which is to say not very often, and so it was kind of hard to figure out, at first, whether this bacteria was of any use on planet Earth."

"Wait," Abu said, trying to keep her going for the sake of the intercom, and praying all the while that Steve was transmitting so that Mars mission guys back in Houston were getting all of this. "You're saying that they had some reason to suppose that there was a bacterium that had certain properties, and they were planning to harvest it for experimental purposes on Earth."

She was tired. Planetary Exile Syndrome has exhaustion as one of its key features. And this kind of histrionic and desperate behavior was tiring too. And her exhaustion was causing her to be sloppy. Her eyes were ringed with red, and puffy. And her cheeks were striated from where the tears had coursed across them.

"You bet your ass, Abu. And they fired it back to Earth in this little rocket, and it splashed down in the Indian Ocean, and they had an aircraft carrier, and a bunch of Navy SEALs, and all kinds of stealth aircraft, and every other thing they have, tactical warheads, trained on anyone who might want to get to that payload before we got to it. The only problem with it, Abu, was that they had no idea what would happen to it at Earth temperatures. They just had no idea. It was a completely new bacterium! Because who knew how long it had been frozen, and under the kind of air pressure where most things evaporate? Who knew? Thousands of years? Tens of thousands of years? Millions of years?"

He'd freed his arms, calmly, slowly, during the speech, and he was thinking that it wouldn't be too hard to overpower her, because she just wasn't paying the same kind of attention to the soldering gun, but he wanted, if possible, not to injure her or startle her unduly, since it might inhibit her recovery from her delusional state, and so he waited yet a little longer.

"And what was the special property of the bacterium, Debbie?" Abu asked.

"That's what I'm about to tell you. The special property of the bacteria, Abu, is that —"

This was the moment when Steve Watanabe hit Debbie Quartz in the neck with a hypodermic. He'd crept down the ladder silently, drifted behind Debbie while she was talking, and then looked for a good spot for the injection, since he wasn't a doctor (the only doctor on the mission is Arnie Gilmore, on the *Pequod*). I guess Steve hadn't had time yet, or authorization, to tell Gilmore, or any of us on the *Excelsior*, about the situation. The way Steve told me the story, injecting an unwilling and delusional person in zero gravity is not the easiest thing to do, and he had to be sure that he was right up next to her, without running the risk of being heard, which is exactly what he did. There was the risk of rupturing an artery, sure, with a predictable heavy blood flow, brain damage, all of that, but what had to be done had to be done. And so Steve plunged the needle into Debbie's neck, and she screamed like, well, like a stuck pig, and she tried to keep him from depressing the plunger, until Abu finished unstrapping himself and lurched into the middle of the conflict to help restrain her — Debbie screaming, telling Steve he had no idea what he was doing, what he was bringing down on himself, the disaster that lay in wait for him on the Red Planet. But then Steve managed to depress the plunger, while nearly strangling poor Debbie, with whom he had played many enjoyable games of cribbage back when we were all in Florida. He watched as Debbie writhed for a couple minutes and then slept. Sleep as a rare interval of happiness, or as an interval of oblivion, descended on her. She drifted over toward one wall, her limp body, like she was a coil of NASA hose.

The two men hovered idly in the silent cargo hold, watching their sedated colleague. They didn't want to believe what had just come to pass. They knew what it was. Big trouble.

"You had word from Houston, huh?" Abu asked.

And Steve, wordlessly, removed the clipboard from his back pocket and handed it over to Jmil. On the screen: "Immobilize Quartz. Narcotics in first-aid kit. Follow dosage guidelines. Advise when completed."

November 18, 2025

We were about seven weeks out, and halfway to the Red Planet. Things had been a little tense around the *Excelsior*. In order to depict just how tense, I suppose I need to render for you more of the conversational stylings of José Rodrigues, science officer, your favorite character in this weblog (at least as judged by posts from you in the comments section: "How would José order in a French restaurant?"). What better time than now? Besides, never was "graveyard shift" a more appropriate term. Though really all the shifts were graveyard shifts in the soda can. I'm going to work on my José Rodrigues impression by hand, that's right, *by hand,* with specially designed ink pen and paper. What the hell else do I have to do? (Well, I have been contacting my daughter, Ginger, once a week or so, during which time we have extremely strained conversations about whatever rumor she heard about the heavily expurgated version of these diaries. For one thing, I couldn't become accustomed to her implanted PDA. I can't understand why kids would want to have a digital communication device implanted subcutaneously in their wrists. It's so ugly! Never mind the ones in the skull. And all they do on there is shop. Call me old-fashioned. Maybe some of you can explain the phenomenon to me. During our last conversation, my daughter typed, with one hand, some nonsense about her grades, or she went on and on about some boy who visited her nightly at the pizzeria. All to get rid of me as quickly as possible, while she had teenage teleconferences. What was I to her? A postage-stamp-sized image on her PDA? The one with six weeks' growth of beard? The one whose messages she neglected to save?)

Anyway, José Rodrigues, to get to the point, spoke almost entirely in acronyms. You know, kids, that space travel is noteworthy for its acronyms. It's a part of what we do and how we live. If not for NASA and space travel, maybe acronyms would never have achieved the cultural acceptance they now enjoy. There are so many things in life that one is tempted to abbreviate. Acronyms worked for us, for astronauts, just as for military personnel, and so certain persons were disposed to use them for any and all purposes when a regular word would have served as well.

Lately, José and I had been meeting up when our shifts overlapped. Usually during his dinner. I could have eaten then myself, but I'm not sure his daily fare of freeze-dried rice and beans would have agreed with my delicate stomach, not for breakfast.

Moreover, I had been making sure when José and I were on the same shift that he didn't get anywhere near my food. The surfaces of the interior of the capsule quickly became rather slick, with biowaste of various kinds, human excrementa, because of our disinclination to expend water rinsing down. We had onboard antibacterial disinfectant, and it was part of protocol to use it weekly on everything inside the capsule, but the truth was that most surfaces were reasonably sterile, it being space and all. We didn't bring that much organic life with us! Anything we were liable to catch from one another we had long since caught. Because we'd been here for more than a month. So probably the warm, sticky layer was just moist material from our hands, our perspiration, the linings of our lungs and colons, and the petroleum jelly we used for cracking lips and skin. But that didn't mean you wanted to eat the stuff. And José liked to simulate *cooking*.

It was at our shared meals that I'd begun noticing, and detesting, the proliferating use of acronyms. This compulsion of speech resembled a space version of alphabet soup. For example, José would say he was going to have to *squish* some KRs (for K rations) out of the little plastic squeeze-paks from which we take our convenient meals. (Squeeze-paks or gelpaks, that's how they are designated on the side, by the official licensor to the Mars mission, whose corporate logo I have been advised to avoid in my blogs.) These José referred to as *squeeze-p's*. Not shorter, you might notice, in terms of linguistic savings. Just different.

José got the KRs out of the *squeeze-p's,* in the kitchen area that according to one early blueprint of the capsule was to be called the *culinary engineering zone,* and thus José was in the CEZ, where he further *squished* out some succotash and some chipped-beef flakes (CBFs), the latter of which he mixed with some water (using the traditional chemical abbreviation thereof), and washed it down with some RCJ, or reconstituted cranberry juice, decrying in the midst of his meal, though I was pretending not to listen, the absence of onboard FMBBs, otherwise known as *fermented malt and barley beverages,* and when he was done, he headed around the corner for some minimal privacy at the WEP, which I'm sure my younger readers already know to be *waste-evacuation privy,* all of this being narrated for me, during and after the fact, including consumption of *m-salts,* or magnesium, which he took to insure regularity, "because we got a C&R [composting and reformulation program] for a reason."

Yes, as I mentioned earlier, we were obliged to make phosphorus and other fertilizer products out of our solid wastes, for the cultivation of genetically modified soybeans and other vegetables. That is one of our most important experiments on the planet Mars, genetically modified wheat, soybeans, and other vegetables that could exist in very low temperatures, with boosted levels of carbon dioxide, and in ridiculously low atmospheric pressure. Not to mention solar radiation. These soybean seedlings were provided by the licensed agricultural supplier to the Mars mission.

José was also liable to refer humbly to his occasional bouts of masturbation, or FSAs (fits of self-abuse), which he regarded as a mission-related obligation, in order to maintain good health through "reproductive-fluid release," and I'm betting you know what the acronym for that is, as well as the acronym for "bagging and disposal" of the relevant ejaculate.

I'm only exaggerating a little bit. What happens after a while, in a tiny little soda can halfway between two planets, is that you stop talking to one another entirely, in order that you might begin talking primarily to yourself. My mother, the schoolteacher, who was used to lecturing in front of audiences, was the person in my family most opposed to talking to oneself, viewing this as a sign of mental illness. And yet this was the communication modality most *perfect* for the *eavesdropper.* On the *Excelsior,* I began to grow quite weak, listening, despite my misery, to José's nasal whine, "...because the MMEs are suggesting that the shipboard *calcs* are giving bad results on the SRBs that boosted us into EPT, and since we aren't an ELV, we have high levels of *sig error,* which means that in terms of landing trajectory, we will be wanting to make sure we have an SSM." Was he saying these things *to* me? Or was he saying them to whatever

sleep-deprived kid, fresh out of MIT, whose job it was to listen
to José by radio this night? Was he trying to impress this young
astrophysicist, as well as whoever else might be listening on the
radio transmissions that NASA organized each day? Or was he actually saying something substantive? Jim didn't talk to himself—he
would have regarded it as unwise from a security perspective—but
he had a strange snorting thing that he performed. For example, he
snorted when he was about to say something that he knew was not
entirely true. These snorts had gotten more pronounced in recent
days. I knew, therefore, that Jim felt that José was up to no good,
as I have already said, and so there was some kind of all-purpose
cognitive dissonance that created this *need to know*. What he was
saying was out of phase with what he was actually thinking, and
so he was always snorting, before almost every sentence. And the
snorts, which sounded a little bit like what a pachyderm might do
in extreme cold, were achingly vulnerable, human, especially since
they implied that the three astronauts on the *Excelsior* were now in
a state where all privacy and dignity were vanishing away.

So what did I surmise, you might wonder, when I heard José
saying to himself, "...as far as the *Geronimo* goes, the SO is probably an *eject,* if you want to know what I think, she's EVWE."
What did I surmise? When he was describing a fellow astronaut in terms of "extra-vehicular waste ejection"? Did I mark
this moment as the moment when I was alerted from checking
supermarket prices back on Earth to hearing the origins of conspiracy? There are times in a man's life when ordinary compla-
cency and a basic good-guy, can-do attitude simply have to give
way to greater concerns—moral concerns—and this was one
such moment.

"Do you mean you're suggesting they eject Debbie Quartz from
the *Geronimo*?" I called past Jim's sleeping body.

"I have to have close contact with the other SOs because we're
coordinating missions. I have a duty to coordinate with them, and
one of the SOs, as you are aware, is so loaded on narcotics that she
probably can't operate heavy machinery. I'm supposed to go to the

surface of the planet and work with her on terraforming, mining, and industrial projects?"

"What kind of industrial projects?"

"You will know when it's NTN for your clearance level. As of 1900 on 18 November, that's a negative. The mission is a matter of national security. Some of us around here are actually worried about maintaining appropriate security protocols, policing our IODs and our blog posts, and if others were as conscientious, things would go smoother all around. An unconscious malcontent is a problem, sure, which is why, yes, Jed, I think they ought to make like she's EVWE."

"She has PES," I said, employing the acronym with a hint of irony. José had finished putting away the last of the kitchen gear. He drifted over to where I was strapped down, and his unshaven face broke into a grin. I got a good look at his gold-capped incisors. This smile was impressively malevolent.

"She was a high-risk assignment right from the beginning. She's weak. If you ask me, the public-relations people wanted more women. They already took one fella who wasn't stable in the first place, Brandon, and now they got a bad apple in Debbie. What are we supposed to do? You know how long we're out here. You know how long the mission is. There's a likelihood we're going to lose people, Jed, or we're going to start to have problems with the Martian environment. The weak are going to go. You think I'm being hard, Jed? I'm not being hard. I just care about the rest of us. If you ditch her body from the *Geronimo,* then you use up that much less oxygen, which means more for the bubble when we touch down, more for the ship on the way back, and it also means less weight, which means less thrust. It just makes good practical sense."

"There's only one problem," I said. "Even though she doesn't have immediate family, she is nonetheless a person with a life, a social existence. There are friends and distant relatives who all care about her. The problem becomes, from their point of view, that they would like for her to stay alive."

"If you call that alive," he said. "But I guess you don't get bedsores at zero g. If it were me I'd press the ejection button myself."

"I'll hold you to that." At which he rappelled down the ladder into the cargo hold. And to think we let him look after the seedlings down there. Who knows what's going on with those seedlings? They could be totally poisonous.

What did we do when José was off shift? Well, I wrote in my diary, and then I scanned the heavens for radio wave emissions that were otherwise unexplainable, by virtue of repetition — the indications of so-called intelligent life in the great nothingness, the nothingness that I know better than you, because every day, though days mean nothing to me now, in this expanse that is the general-relativity equivalent of forty days and forty nights, I experienced the *nothingness,* and I watched as the little red star in the distant sky got closer, until now you could almost see the polar caps on it, and you could see its dust storms, which were going to blind us every time we went out in them, perhaps asphyxiating us; you could see all of this, especially if you used the telescopic apparatus that we had to enhance the picture for you. And so I knew that I came from nowhere, that I was heading nowhere, that my life was no more, in the scheme of things, than the life of a match light snuffed out in a big wind. I was an insignificance between the orbit of the planet Mars, that elliptical orbit, and the orbit of the planet *Earth.* I was nothing, and soon I would be gone.

December 2, 2025

Belated Thanksgiving, all you readers! I know you understand the symbolism of that national holiday to us here on the Mars mission, where our three crafts are almost exactly like the *Niña,* the *Pinta,* and the *Santa Maria.* It may interest you to know that at least two of those primitive ships were named after prostitutes, or so I am told by one interested reader in Bayonne, NJ. Meanwhile, what did we have to eat for Thanksgiving, here on the *Excelsior?*

Well, we had turkey! The National Aeronautics and Space Administration knew how to pull out the stops, even two months in advance, for nine beleaguered astronauts, 25 or so million miles from home. The turkey was in little vacuum-packed containers, and there was some gravy that we were able to heat up in the microwave oven. We were even given authorization to have some of the hothouse lettuces from downstairs in José's agribusiness lair. We could just cut a couple of pieces each from the lettuces, because they were doing pretty well, beneath the artificial grow lamp, and anyhow you don't want lettuces to go to seed.

And there was a bottle of hard cider that I'd been given the okay to bring on the mission, and I'd been waiting these many weeks to drink that bottle of hard cider. You know, cider was one of *the* political issues of early American history. American farmers began growing their own apple trees; this symbolized a resistance to tyranny. We mean to effect a similar revolution on the Mars mission, and so this was another of the carefully crafted symbols in our little Thanksgiving dinner. There wasn't a lot of talking at our dinner, and the astronauts on the *Excelsior* gulped their cider as quickly as possible, because in a slightly oxygen-depleted environment, you can experience a maximization of effects, especially if you force the drink, or chugalug, or whatever you young people call it these days. I did all the dishes, because the other guys had things on their minds. These events constitute an explanation of my silence since the Thanksgiving dinner. So let me re-create the drama of that day.

Long about dinnertime, or the time we agreed would be dinnertime, I get a communication from Laurie Corelli on the *Pequod*. I mean, literally, we are sitting down to eat, and I have served each of the guys a glass of hard cider, brought by me into interplanetary space at enormous personal expense. All of a sudden, there's a light on the dash, as we like to say, indicating that Laurie's trying to communicate. In fact, she's trying to communicate with everyone — us, Houston, the *Geronimo* — all at the same time, having availed herself of the communication protocol that we refer to as the panic button—an intercom that automatically contacts all the relevant parties. Her face shows on the video screen, because the panic button automatically engages the video feed, and Laurie says, "Anyone out there? Please confirm when you get this message. We have a Code 14. Code 14 on the *Pequod*. Repeat, Code 14."

Now, you will recognize, if you are astute readers of this forum, and if you have been reading the posts from various experts at NASA, that even in these technologically advanced times, it takes NASA a while to reach us when there's information they want to send our way, and you know that this time lag increases as we near the Red Planet. At present, for every question Laurie wants to send back to the home planet, it's seven minutes out, and then seven minutes for the answer to arrive. Therefore, it stands to reason that we on the *Excelsior*, and likewise the *Geronimo*, would get the transmission before the home planet, since we're only ten or twenty thousand miles ahead of our colleagues on the other ships.

I get on the radio immediately and hail the *Pequod*.

"What's up, Laurie? How can we help?"

Wait, did I explain what a Code 14 is? A Code 14 is when an astronaut has become dangerous to himself or others. This was the code Watanabe or Abu would have used to alert Mission Control to the Debbie Quartz situation, if they'd had time to transmit the news while the crisis was taking place. In case you were wondering about the specific numerical designation, I don't know *why* it's a Code 14, exactly. There are not thirteen other codes, although there is a Code 5, which is a dangerously low oxygen level, a Code 6, which is a hull breach, and a Code 7, which is fire of some kind. There is, for those who are curious about such things, a Code 22, which is designated for "ship under attack." So far, no one has ever used a Code 22, in all the space missions of the past twenty-five years, since the codes were instituted. But there have been five occasions in which there was a Code 7, and seven examples of a Code 5. I'll leave it to you to connect these codes to the various well-known mishaps.

By the time an astronaut is prepared to register a Code 14, the situation is likely already past, and yet here was Laurie, using it, and, from the looks of her, a little bit emotional about what was going on.

"Jed, hi, I'm sorry to...I'm sorry to bother you." I can hear Abu come on the other screen on the *Pequod* while I'm talking to her, asking the same kinds of questions. "I don't really know how to say this exactly, but Brandon...Well, Brandon has just tried to assault me."

"He's what? He tried to *rape* you?"

"Roger that."

"What the hell is going on over there?"

"I'm afraid I don't feel any clearer about that than you do."

"Well, can you...Look, at the risk of being a bit insensitive, Laurie, can you tell me that we're agreeing on the terminology here?"

"Jed, I understand what the word means. I'm sure you're thinking that a space capsule is an awfully small place for a...for a sexual assault to occur. But that's what happened. I have Arnie here, who's ready to back up what I'm trying to tell you."

Laurie's being incredibly tough, that much is obvious. Jim and José gather with me by the screen. Behind us is the lukewarm Thanksgiving dinner, Velcro'd down to the makeshift table.

"So what happened?"

"What happened was that I was trying to sleep when my shift was completed, and for the record, Jed, I wasn't wearing anything non-regulation, as I have never worn anything non-reg on the flight, as I have taken my role as a woman on this mission very seriously. Not that my wearing anything non-reg would be any kind of excuse for Brandon's actions in a court of law, even in the present social and cultural environment. I was wearing a jumpsuit, and I was sleeping. I was tired, in fact. And badly in need of rest. My rest, Jed, was interrupted when suddenly I felt something pressing up against me, and I opened my eyes, and immediately I saw Brandon Lepper, and he wasn't wearing anything at all. He had, against protocol, taken off all his gear. He had pressed the cough button, and he was in an aroused state, Jed, and he immediately put his hand over my mouth, as if he could keep me from shouting for Arnie. He said that he knew I wanted *it,* that sort of thing, and he began trying to cut through my jumpsuit with a knife, as if he had put a knife aside somewhere just for this purpose."

"For godsakes. Then what?"

"Well, because I've had some hand-to-hand training, and some self-defense classes as a young woman, I reached back to remember the advice I'd had about sexual assault, and once my limbs were freed, I utilized this training. I disabled Brandon Lepper."

"Meaning?"

"Basically, he had cut the immobilizing straps, which was not a strategically advantageous decision on his part, but when I was freed, I pretended to be complying, until I could hit him with a blunt force object on the back of the head."

"Which blunt force object was it?"

"It was a fire extinguisher."

"You hit him on the head with a fire extinguisher?"

"Roger that."

There's a pause in the conversation while the three of us on the *Excelsior* look around at one another. I assume we are all counting bodies. Debbie Quartz is in an opiate fog, and now there's Brandon Lepper, out cold or worse, and it's obvious to anyone, any idiot, that we are indisputably beginning to have serious personnel issues.

"Can you put Arnie on for a moment, Laurie?" I say. The doctor to the Mars mission then appears on the screen. He's a small guy, kind of slight, with a thick beard and pale Eastern European coloring. Arnie is a serious fellow, never less than thoughtful and warm. I ask what he thinks.

"I'm surprised by Brandon's behavior, Jed. And I think that it's not really Brandon himself that we're encountering here."

"You think he's got PES?"

"I've lived with the guy for seven or eight weeks, and while I think he's immature, and hard to like, I don't think he's the kind of person who would premeditate a crime like this. I can only think that the long period of confinement has taken a considerable toll on all of us, and that it is possible to see here a pathology that's related to long periods of confinement. This is another way of saying that there are real dangers to the mission."

"And are you suggesting that the causes are *merely* those of psychological stress, Arnie?"

"There are other things to consider, solar winds, neutrinos, gamma rays, space-time curvature, close proximity to antimatter, who knows what else? Tanning by the reactor downstairs? But I don't have time to run those tests while Brandon is constrained."

Laurie comes back on-screen to tell me that she has him down in the hatch, and that, yes, she has covered him up. As with Debbie, he has been heavily sedated. By the time we get to Mars, how many of us will still be awake?

When we finish this portion of the conversation, the transmission from Houston arrives. It's a big moment in the Mars mission. In fact, it's a big fourteen minutes, these minutes where Brandon is reaping the harvest he perhaps sowed many years back, as a young Turk from Houston, a believer in the warrior code, who, in the peculiar ethics of interplanetary travel, sullied a woman's dignity, or attempted to. Laurie tells me that she's going to take the call and that she'll get back to me ASAP.

The three J's of the *Excelsior* then get down to the business of Thanksgiving, as described earlier, and I know that I have a lot to be grateful for, because — and I don't know if I have said this before — I am soon going to be the first person to set foot on the planet Mars. I can't really think of a better time than now to tell you this exciting news. Yes, I am the one who has been selected first to set foot outside the Mars mission, on the sulfurous, subzero surface of Mars. Because Jim will be flying the lander, and José will be coordinating the particulars of the mission with Houston and the other science officers, if any of them are left alive by the time we touch down. And that leaves me, kids. I was chosen for this. From the first day, I was chosen, because I am the word slinger, I am the man of imagination and vision, and I have a half-dozen sentences, preselected by a NASA subcommittee on *first utterances,* from which I am to choose one when I step outside of the lander, and I am meant to pronounce this sentence (with prior notification and authorization), and this sentence will go down in human history, for reasons I can't need to explain. So it's Thanksgiving, and I should be grateful, because I get to spend the next three weeks thinking about which of these statements I like best, and I get to confer with subcommittee members, like Jonas Jonas, poet laureate of the United States of America, who is trying to boil down a sonnet sequence he wrote to an unrhymed couplet, so that I won't, if I use his text, have to memorize too terribly much. Yes, being chosen as the first man to set foot on Mars is something to be thankful for, as is the fact that my daughter, Ginger, sent me a school paper this morning on the following topic, "The History of and Future Prospects for Mars Exploration," the first sentence of which is: "No kid in the world could be prouder of her dad than I am, no kid could be prouder, and no kid could be luckier." These *are* the kinds of things you think about on Thanksgiving, and while I don't bring these things up to the other guys, I do think about them in passing.

But what about what Arnie was saying? What Arnie was saying, kids, is that our civilization, the civilization of the Mars mission, has become very small, our civilization has become nine people, of whom six are at considerable remove from us here in the *Excelsior,* as far away as Auckland is from New York City, let's say, and our little colony just doesn't have the same sense of inevitability about its civilizing abilities as does your planet, with its nearly seven billion souls, most of them at least passingly familiar with the rule of law. And what we are doing here, on the little tin can, is falling into the lawlessness of ancient times, like in Westerns, where everyone has a checkered past and a dark motive, and it's all going to come out eventually, the evil, and a lot of people are going to get shot. That, indeed, is what Arnie was talking about, as I understand it, and it isn't lost on those of us on the *Excelsior.*

The meal is further interrupted when Houston puts forth its ideas about how to prevent disorder from breaking out on the Mars mission. The note is to Laurie Corelli, who has probably already been briefed as to its contents, but we are copied on it, as is the *Geronimo.* The note is among the evening bulletins for the mission, and so it shows up on my clipboard, right by the dinner table.

"Read it out," Jim says.

"'*Pequod* and *Geronimo,* dock ship-to-ship at 0500 hrs, 28 Nov, instructions, coordinates to follow. Astronauts Lepper and Quartz to be exchanged. *Excelsior* as per earlier orders.'"

"Holy shit," Jim says.

José says, "I say we cook them and eat them."

"José," Jim says, "you don't have manners."

"I'm not paid to. That was nowhere in the job description. There were, however, some sections about geological training, the chain of command, and absolute loyalty to mission objectives."

Dinner comes to an end at this point. The discussion lapses, that is, and this is when I do the dishes. We hear nothing more from the *Pequod* for the evening, and I am loath to ring them up in order to hear about what's going on, just as I am loath to fire a message off to Debbie Quartz, who may or may not be conscious. Back at home, you kids probably think that all is going well up here, and that we are following a mission plan that allows certain crew members to go into cryonic suspension, or something approaching cryonic suspension, in order to preserve resources until such time as we arrive. If only we could freeze José.

Three days pass, and we do our best not to dwell on what we cannot control. The big questions have to do with how you sleep, and whether you can still move your bowels after two months of reconstituted, freeze-dried food products. Answer: not exactly. This is not such a bad thing for someone like your correspondent, who, as I have said, is noted for explosive difficulty in these areas. On one of these three days, I spend a long time reading up on *necrotizing fasciitis,* which is having that big outbreak in the Detroit area. It's probably only when you are up in the little soda can that you feel fully protected against an outbreak of *necrotizing fasciitis* that is sweeping through the rather large tent encampments in that city. If there are any of you reading these remarks from the Detroit area, please accept my condolences for the outbreak, and let me say that I dedicate today's portion of the journey to any of you; you are in my thoughts, and I really mean that.

Of course *necrotizing fasciitis* makes me think about this mysterious bacterium that Debbie Quartz mentioned, the one that was originally found in ALH 84001, the interplanetary bauble that washed up on Antarctica. I keep thinking I should ask José about ALH 84001, or maybe I should ask Arnie Gilmore about this.

And somehow the whole situation reminds me of those last three hundred whooping cranes, those birds that someone has been forcibly migrating back and forth from Florida for the past twenty-odd years with the aid of an ultralight. This small population of birds is not a sustainable population, the experts all say, because with the right outbreak of avian flu, which we already know can knock out a couple million people in an overcrowded ecosystem, the entire whooping crane population could collapse. One germ and extinction follows. A beautiful thing, though, a whooping crane, and in the not-so-distant future there will be only a couple of them left, and they will have only one wing apiece, and they will idle on some lawn, like the lawn near Cape Canaveral. One of this nonmating pair will die of old age, and then there will be the one last whooping crane, and it will eat moldy popcorn from underneath the NASA reviewing stand, and it will have delusional thoughts, mothballed memories in which it was part of a *flock,* and this flock followed an ultralight down to Brazil for the winter, and then back again. What does our whooping crane think? The last whooping crane of planet *Earth?* The last one? It thinks that the currents of air are a marvel, and it conceives of them in colors, spectra, as we think of sunsets; just so does the last whooping crane, despite the fact that only the one wing works, think of those air currents; it remembers tree-tops, which were like sofas to the whooping crane; back when it still had two wings, it could land in any treetop and put its head under its wing, and the whooping crane remembers, or believes it remembers, certain kinds of fish that are particularly savory, and maybe a certain level of freshness in the matter of seafood is what a whooping crane most prizes, and it remembers mat-ing, because back when it was young it was picky in the mating department, and like many whooping cranes it was not, despite its lanky beauty, terribly kind to the girls; moreover, there was always the danger of infighting among the whooping cranes, and this last crane remembers all of this, and because the crane can-not speak of it, the memories are that much more painful, and now, in his loneliness, there is no other bird who protects that past of cranes, that long history of the most beautiful bird in this part of the country, and so the only other account of these events, after the others fade, is the memory of the guy who flew the ultralight, a balding guy with a not-very-good sense of humor, a guy who told the worst jokes, not that the whooping crane understood the jokes, but rather the whooping crane recognized the timbre of this man's voice, a kind of ragged baritone that shaded into the tenor range, but with outbreaks of alto when he got nervous, and this was the call of the ultralight, as far as the last whooping crane is concerned, this guy's rather humor-ous voice; it was not the cry of the whooping crane, which is a majestic sound, it was the cry of some bald guy who never much expected to be piloting birds. He probably believed he would have a career in civil aviation, or maybe he thought he would be an astronaut or something, and in fact that is what he decides to do because the day comes when this pilot can no longer fly the ultralight, because there are not enough cranes anymore, there is only the one crane, and he is *crushed,* well, come on, everyone is crushed, life crushes you, and this is just one more story to stomp up and down on your crushed heart, this balding fellow going to visit the last crane sometimes, over where he thinks the crane might still be living, in some cage for injured birds, and he and the crane recognize each other, indeed, though they have no common language in which to speak of their recognition, there is no way for the crane to speak of the man as a man speaks of a crane, and it would all go fine if the man could speak in the tongue of cranes, but he can't. While he's visiting with the crane, there is, in the distance, a *liftoff,* one of the last space shuttle missions, and you can see it from almost twenty miles away, the conditions are that favorable in south Florida that day, and the guy, the balding pilot, the one with the bad jokes and the not-terribly-reliable timbre to his voice, thinks that maybe the only reasonable thing to pursue after the experience of flying the ultralight is the experience of going up into space, *as soon as he can,* and he sits on a bench by the one-winged whooping crane for a while, and then he notices that he is talking to the whooping crane, and he's saying, "Well, I don't exactly want to leave you here like this; I can't really think of anything worse, and I have left some people behind in my life, who hasn't, even some people I loved, but none of that is as bad as thinking that I won't see you here again, and no one who comes here to see you will know what I know about you, and you won't recognize these people, nothing could be worse, but still a man has to move on sometimes, I can't just stay here doing this, and so I'm wondering, would you think it was okay for me to go ahead and undertake to become an astronaut? Do you think you could possibly give me your blessing?" He knows that the whooping crane *can't* answer him, that's obvious enough, but he feels he owes a reasonable explanation to the whooping crane, even more of an explanation than he owes his wife or his parents, and the crane can't see how bad the pilot feels, how broken up he is, when the man thinks that he won't be able to visit the crane again. When the crane is a thing of the past, when the crane is nothing more than fertilizer for creatures to come, the pilot will only learn of it online, because he will be off pursuing his ambition, flying his test missions, sleeping in the barracks, all so that he might get the hell off the planet that slew the whooping cranes.

December 3, 2025

On the twenty-eighth of November (for those of you who just joined, I'm finishing up an earlier story), the other two ships were to dock together and switch captives, while we of the *Excelsior* were far, far away, gliding through the vacuum between the third and fourth planets, toward a projected touchdown almost four weeks off. What I'm about to report comes from what I've learned since. It's reconstructed. You can subject these spontaneous musings to the enthusiastic skepticism that you bring to everything else I write. Maybe I'm composing these lines in Lahore or Mumbai, at one of those subcontinental computer-processing facilities, faking the prose style of an American astronaut, so that the heartbroken and fiscally challenged young of the heartland will believe in something.

The problem was that the best pilot on the *Pequod,* the aforementioned Brandon Lepper, was strapped down during the jury-rigged docking maneuver. We had learned how to dock ships during our years of Mars mission training, in case of a difficulty like the one you are reading about right now. But that didn't mean that docking was routine or without danger. It was all meant to be done with thrusters, minutely controlled bursts of the thrusters, and these were to be operated remotely by computers from the home planet. At least, this was how Mission Control framed its agenda when describing what was going to take place. Brandon was not of particular importance to the docking event, they said. Computer piloting, they said, was a fail-safe method.

Maybe they were saying these things in order to try to keep Laurie Corelli calm, because Laurie Corelli was no great pilot. Arnie Gilmore, meanwhile, was the mission doctor. Any damage to the

Pequod would adversely impact the mission. Since the *Geronimo* had launched an hour and a half before the *Pequod,* and from halfway across the continent, Mission Control actually needed to dramatically slow the former capsule, which was a demanding proposition, in terms of fuel use. Because once the *Geronimo* was slowed, assuming it didn't collide with the oncoming *Pequod,* and once the docking mission was accomplished, the *Geronimo* would have to be restarted. That's a lot of fuel right there. If I was reading the projections correctly, when they came through from Mission Control, there was enough fuel to do all of this, but just. Not a lot more. There was no room for any further mistakes. Did Brandon Lepper know what he had done? In feeling like he wanted to prove that he was the *big man* over on the *Pequod,* the man in control, he had nearly crippled humankind's first trip out of Earth's backyard, to the tune of billions and billions of dollars.

In fact, as 0500 hours approached on the twenty-eighth, Brandon Lepper, who had, it was believed, used various perfor- mance enhancers during his training days, and who may have been suffering from a steroid-related mood disorder, in lockstep with Planetary Exile Syndrome, awoke from his narcotic slumber and began screaming at Laurie and Arnie through the intercom, "What the fuck is going on here? How come I'm strapped down? You all better get me the hell off this table. You think you can leave a man for a month in a capsule with a beautiful woman who dresses provocatively? You think a man can withstand that kind of treatment? You're crazy, that's what I'm telling you, you people aren't *human.* It's just a natural thing, to have *inclinations,* and if a woman is not able to deal with it, then a woman shouldn't be on this mission in the first place. Women always think they're tough, but then when it boils down to it, they go running to Daddy, because they can't actually take it. I've *been* in battle; I was in Uzbekistan when the tacticals were raining down from both sides. I was in Malaysia. You think I don't know what tough is? You women think you're tough, but the only weapon you know how to operate is a *manual.* I was there where bodies were scorched, where all the flesh was burned right off; I saw all of that. I saw it! Depleted uranium in the water supply. Radiation sickness. I went and rescued women and children. I treated their burns. So don't say that I don't know anything about compassion and about grati-tude; don't say I haven't done anything for women. Women *need* me; they need a man to help them through this world. . . ."

It was all just a misunderstanding, a joke, a good laugh, ac-cording to Brandon, but at this point Laurie and Arnie disabled the intercom, and they busied themselves about the directions from Mission Control. There was the surge of the reverse thrust-ers slowing their great haste. It wouldn't be long now before they would be able to see the other ship.

Meanwhile, in the *Geronimo,* Steve Watanabe and Abu Jmil had slowed their own craft, and they were now sitting ducks, to use the old phrase, in the middle of the superhighway between Mars and Earth. Thirty-two or -three million miles from Earth, and if there was any miscalculation by Mission Control, they would be crushed like interstellar ice, vaporized, spread into some belt of man-made debris. Steve and Abu, while waiting as the *Pequod* appeared on their instruments, spent some of the time reaching out to their families. Steve's wife, Danielle, a mediation specialist, was home that day looking after their son, who had antibiotic-resistant strep throat. She answered the fuzzy, distorted signal on her digital wrist assistant. She knew just where this kind of mes-sage came from. Houston was patching her husband through. She also knew how long it would take to reply.

"Sweetheart," Steve said, "we have this complicated maneuver we're going to try to bring off today, because of some problems they're having over on the *Pequod.* Some personnel problems."

Danielle was a wise and seasoned mediation specialist, short, with red ringlets of hair, freckles, and never without a dark, sub-lime lipstick, nearly Victorian in its perfect elegance. Nothing surprised her, and she smiled when she really meant it. During this time-consuming video uplink, intermittent and fuzzy, her face, through the white noise of video transmission, was impassive as she waited. "What's the maneuver? Will it be safe? Are you worried?" And then the delay.

"It's sort of a prisoner exchange. Believe it or not. We're going to swap out Debbie for Brandon Lepper. Where they get these notions, I don't know. They feel like there's a danger with Brandon staying in the capsule with the others over there. I'll tell you later. There are mission objectives that are uppermost in their plans here, what with so much time left on the journey, and they don't want to lose anyone. Or that's what they're saying. But who knows? So he's going to come on over here, and we're going to have a fraternity-type environment on the *Geronimo,* like they have on the *Excelsior.* We'll do some Jell-O shots. Or bench presses. Anyway, the docking is more time-consuming than dangerous. So if I don't reach you for a little while, you'll know that I was busy with this, up here in the night sky, okay?"

"Are you sure it's safe?"

"No. But they wouldn't do anything that was a real risk, what with so few people on the mission. That's why we have to make the swap. I'll get back to you as soon as we're done. I'll let you and Brian know that it came off. Is he feeling any better?"

"They're hopeful about one of the synthetic antibiotics in the pipeline, and so far, yeah, he's not so bad. He just wants to sit and watch the real-time footage of the mission."

"You might have reruns today. Don't believe everything you see." Steve told her he loved her and signed off.

Abu contacted his family in Kansas City, and his parents, who were initially perturbed about the docking, since it seemed dangerous, quickly regained their composure and asked that their son contact them as soon as he was finished with the procedure. They were serious, brilliant astrophysicists, scientists of few words, and they didn't want to clutter up the bandwidth with sentimentalities.

Then these two brave astronauts on the *Geronimo* sat and watched as the *Pequod* appeared, first on the instruments, then as a speck in the windows, and then as an ominous space hazard, with an inexorable forward progress. Off to one side was the lollipop Red

Planet, which had lately become the constant companion of the mission. In the greater distance was the Earth, no bigger than any other luminous object in the soup of galaxies, nebulae, and dwarfs. And then, like some unaccountable blast from history, comes the unaccountable man-made *Pequod,* so close now that they could nearly wave to their colleagues, though it would be another several hours before the docking took place. And all of this because one astronaut couldn't control himself! There wasn't much time to complain now, however, because there was a lot of preparation and suiting up that needed to take place. Abu said he was going to unbuckle and get down and face east. Though there was no east here. But there was still the ritual.

Special coupling clasps on the outside of each of the ships had been engineered into the design of the capsules, and it was these clasps that made it possible to come alongside, but according to the training, at least two astronauts needed to be outside the ship to hand-engineer the hydraulics. Steve and Abu had already radioed to Laurie and Arnie that they intended to volunteer. But before they could even try to suit up and attach the cable that would link the two ships together, the crew of the *Geronimo* needed to prepare the slumbering Debbie Quartz, who was soon to bask in the warm, maternal glow of Laurie Corelli.

Now Abu and Steve headed down the ladder into the cargo hold, and they fetched out the suits from the hatch where they were stored. They had no reason to believe that Debbie, like Brandon, would be awake and alert. But when they got over to her bed, her eyes were wide open. Her expression was placid, forgiving, and oddly distant.

"What's happening?"

Steve said, "We're going for a little walk."

"Where to?"

"Into the night sky."

"Out of the ship?"

"We're going to secure the *Pequod.* She's coming alongside," Steve said. "Then I'm coming back in, and I'm going to help you over to their craft."

"You're what?" She said it with a gentle amazement. It seemed that Debbie Quartz's Planetary Exile Syndrome had begun to yield to the combination of heavy narcotics and SSRIs, and there was nothing left in the heavens, not black holes, not hulking expanses of dark matter, that could surprise her.

"We're taking you over to the *Pequod.* Houston's orders."

"Steve," she said, "you really don't want to do that. That's a big mistake. Are you...Is someone coming onboard to replace me here?"

"Lepper. He's kind of..."

"Steve," she said.

"Look, if you hadn't tried to poke a hole in Abu with the soldering gun, we wouldn't be in this situation."

Abu was already unstrapping her, and he did it with a sympathetic demeanor, as best he could, as if his tenderness would be enough to keep her from raging around the cargo hold again.

"I'm sorry, Abu," she said.

"No apology necessary," Abu replied, "really..."

"It's time that I told you guys something. Before you do this. You know what's waiting for us when we get there?" Debbie said. "You know what's waiting for us on the surface of the planet?"

"Debbie, don't start," Steve said. "You won't give it a rest with this paranoid shit. You're scaring everyone. You're jeopardizing the mission."

"You didn't get the Department of Defense briefings," Debbie said. "I did. You think I don't know? I know. But I also know what was in those reports, and what they're looking for on the surface of the planet. The equatorial conditions are sterile, the surface is sterile down to four or more meters, but the place is crawling, literally, with bugs, tiny little microscopic bacteria. They're there at the poles, and they're there, even more plentifully, in the canyons, and the Hellas Basin. And you know why there's DOD interest? I'll tell you why."

"Debbie," Steve said, "*enough.* We don't have clearance for that stuff. Houston, I don't need to remind you, is probably listening right now. I'm taking orders from Mission Control, and the mission is on a need-to-know basis, and I don't need to know."

"If that's how you want it," Debbie said, and her eyes brimmed with tears. The three of them were drifting in the center of the cargo hold, and Steve could see it, could see that she was emotional. Something in her had given out in the course of the two months that we'd all been on this journey, and the funny, implacable Debbie he'd first met outside of a convenience store in Orlando four years ago, when they were both cadets, was gone. Part of her had been shuffled off and had been replaced by this ghostly, troubled woman. He missed the old Debbie.

"Let's get into the gear. Laurie's looking forward to seeing you."

In the silence of suiting up on the *Geronimo,* they considered the ballet of men and machines, and how inspiring it was, this technical accomplishment, and when these meditations on technology and the future of the species were complete, they locked on their helmets.

"Do we have enough fuel to be doing all this?" Debbie asked.

Abu grunted noncommittally. The three of them closed the hatch behind them in the cargo bay. Steve pointed to the intercom, and then his voice crackled in their helmets. "Debbie, here's how it goes. We head out, we watch the *Pequod* come in, we secure her with the hydraulic clasps, and when we get the okay from them that Brandon's in their air lock, then I come back to get you, got it?"

Debbie gave the thumbs-up. Abu gave the thumbs-up, and once again the astronauts of the Mars mission were out in space.

It's the soundlessness that's so hard to describe. This was what Steve was noticing on his first space walk. Even in the capsule there's always something to listen to. There's the music that gets piped in from Earth, downloaded classics, popular music, the ragas that Abu was trying to teach Steve about; the bleeping of various machines, life-support systems, the crackling of the communications array; the chorus of voices from Houston, Lorna, DeWayne, Fielding, Kathy Fales, Amin, who had become their friends in the time aloft, checking in, as if from out of nowhere, as if from the radio station of nowhere. The ominous *ping* of microscopic asteroids hitting the hull, which only made a sound *inside.* The hiss of oxygen inflow. It was all about sound, until you set foot outside.

And as soon as they did, as soon as the two men set foot outside, they saw the *Pequod,* the ghost ship, it seemed, summoned from out of a perpetual night sky. Steve wasn't sure that anyone else really existed out here, besides himself and Abu and Debbie. He didn't realize how much he missed the rest of the unruly, malodorous company of humans until the only humans around were waving to him through an air lock.

He and Abu got tethered, and they watched the right flank of the *Pequod,* the nearest face of the craft, dead in the water, it seemed, slower than it took a mechanical pencil to drift across the capsule. All the ignition that would be required had long since taken place, and now it was inert, until, right on schedule, the gaffer's hook on the side of the *Geronimo* allowed them to reel in the other ship and secure it with some cables and some electromagnetic cleats. The two crafts sat like this, as close to motionless as you can be and still be moving, ever so slightly, because of the drift from the *Pequod*'s thrusters. Steve said to Abu, "Okay, can you take it from here?" He heard the crackle of Abu's microphone, "Let's get the rapist onboard."

And now the first unalloyed disaster of the Mars mission. Steve, according to what Houston had exhaustively detailed for him, was meant to turn back and fetch Debbie, and bring her out onto the surface of the capsule, and then the four of them, nearly half of the entire crew of the Mars mission, would meet between the two ships, like on a section of No-Man's-Land between the two Koreas, or at the Wailing Wall checkpoint. At that stage, there would be no tethering of Debbie and Brandon, because they were only going as far as the hatch on the other ship, and if they were flush against their handlers, it should have been okay; it *should have been.* Steve turned his posterior on the *Pequod* and headed back for Debbie. He ought to have known there was something wrong when she wouldn't say anything to him, when she assumed the space equivalent of passive resistance, until he wasn't even sure, at first, if there was someone still *in* the space suit.

"Goddamnit, Debbie," he said. "I can understand you're upset, and I can understand how scared you are, but please don't make this more dangerous for me. I have a kid at home, and he's sick right now, and the last thing he needs today is for something to happen to all of us. I'm begging you, just do what they want us to do and let's get the hell back in the spaceship and go see the new planet. Can we do that, please?"

At some point that rag doll in the space suit shook off his hand and stepped beside him out onto the surface of the *Geronimo*. Steve looked out across the hull of the ship, which seemed rare and proud in the starlight, and he saw Abu and Brandon coming in the other direction. Which meant, yes, that the *Geronimo* was now entirely emptied, with all of them out in the great beyond of interplanetary space, and the two little constellations of astronauts neared the halfway mark in the march of prisoner exchange. It seemed, like everything else in space, an impossible distance to traverse, and yet, considering the 33 or so million miles they had come, it wasn't much. Eventually, they were all there, and the four of them hovered at the midpoint of their little journey, at least as we all reconstructed it, and there was a moment when Debbie and Brandon were standing there facing each other, and that's when Steve thought he heard something in his intercom, something he was later uncertain about, the moment when Brandon grabbed Debbie by the shoulders and shouted. The exact words, unfortunately, are lost to history, though there has been much conjecture since. Abu reached out to stop him, and then there was some kind of *explosion....*

...What *kind* of explosion? What kind could there have been? It wasn't an explosion you could have heard, because what you heard out there was *nothing,* because that was all there was to hear, nothing. So what was the explosion? How to be startled in space, when *nothing* exactly is what seems to be happening most of the time, when *nothing* is what time looks like. Well, there was a special provision in the space suits for ignition, if needed, some minor propulsion, in case an astronaut needed to drift, and this was intended only for use out of range of other astronauts, but Debbie had nonetheless ignited some of the oxygen propellant, and had used it to *lift off.* Because she wasn't attached. She wasn't tethered. When Steve looked up, he saw that Abu had tried to get out of the way and was now rotating wildly at the end of his tether, and Brandon was laid out flat against the side of the ship, clinging on to the spot where Abu's tether was attached to the hull, and Steve's first thought was, *Well, everything is okay.* But then he looked out into space. He looked into space, and what he saw was Debbie heading *off* from the ship, heading *out,* heading for the Van Allen belt, heading for Jupiter, and his heart plugged in his throat, at the significance of it, of what he had to do, which was to *jump,* because he had a generous length of cable and he could still go after her, at least part of the way.

"Debbie, what the hell are you doing?" he called.

Abu's voice erupted too. "Debbie, for godsakes!"

Steve drifted out on the cable, reaching for her, but when he thought he was getting close, there was a second burst from her oxygen pack, and she accelerated, farther out. "Abu," he called, "what do I do? What do I do?"

Abu was trying to haul himself in from the end of his cable. He was out of breath; he was at the limit of what he could do. Nevertheless, he said, "I'll go after her."

"No, no. I'll do it. Get Brandon into the capsule. Can you get Laurie and Arnie on the horn? It's my problem; it's my fault. I'll go."

And Steve took hold of the cable from where it was fastened to his space suit, and he unhitched it. Kids, the space walk may be the freest you ever feel, but that doesn't mean you are in any rush to relinquish that tether. Especially for such a grim purpose. Steve blasted a little bit of propellant out of the tank and headed after Debbie Quartz, who had about nine hours of oxygen left and all of space-time in which to use it. Unless, that is, she blasted the vast majority of oxygen out of the tank, which you could do if you were of a mind and knew how the suits were constructed. You could do it if you were very close to an alternate oxygen source or would be in the next two or three minutes.

December 15, 2025

Things have been a little heartbroken here, gang. We are not a contented crew; we are a worried and downhearted crew. For example, Laurie and Arnie were *watching* the whole thing with Debbie. They were watching and unable to intervene. They were watching and screaming into various intercoms and communicators. Like everything in the register of the space walk, the altercation between Debbie and Brandon took place in a nearly eternal slow motion. Laurie and Arnie were able to see it, to anticipate its outcome, to cry out, to punch into their texting keyboards, *Code 14, Code 14,* which must be the code that Houston is really tired of getting from us. I've heard recordings of Laurie sobbing to Houston (from some unauthorized site of Mars mission feeds), while Arnie tried to comfort her. Laurie and Debbie had been really close before liftoff.

Meanwhile, after Debbie jumped, Abu was trying to get Brandon in the door to the *Geronimo,* trying to keep him out of the way. As I've said before, Brandon was a former boxer, and there was a lot of space suit wrestling going on just inside the air lock, which was worse than two-year-olds in snow pants going after each other, until Abu noticed that Brandon had a tear in his suit, which probably had to do with standing too close to Debbie when she lifted off. His suit must have partially ignited, even though they are meant to be heat resistant and flame-retardant. Abu was thinking that Brandon was just being unruly, when in fact the guy was probably suffocating, or maybe he was about to freeze to death, which you could do with even the tiniest rip, even though there are twenty-four redundant layers of Mylar. Once they got inside the hatch, well, wait—

Did I mention the monologue that someone recorded of Steve going after Debbie, which also got broadcast on the Net? It must have been recorded by the *Geronimo* itself, in the black box, where almost everything is preserved, unless you're really smart with the application of the cough button. And no one is that smart during an emergency. Effectively, nothing happens on the Mars mission without Houston knowing. Which means that eventually you will know, all of you. So in case you haven't heard it yet, here's what Steve said, according to the official record, while sailing out into the vacuum after the retreating figure of Debbie Quartz: "Debbie, listen to me, listen, please, don't do this, Debbie. Debbie, what are you doing? It's not worth it. Debbie. Come on! Debbie, we came into this together, and we're going out together.... Listen, please! We dreamed the same dream, think about it, and if that dream isn't going to happen, if it isn't going to come to pass, it's going to be because we all bungled it together! We're family, Debbie, we all care about you.... One team, Debbie, one family...your problems, Debbie, my problems.... Listen to me, Debbie...whatever your bad feeling is, we can help. Your doubt and uncertainty about the mission, I have it too, Debbie.... Don't leave us here worrying about what's become of you. Don't leave us thinking about you drifting out here.... Let us take care of you, for godsakes, let us love you back into shape, Debbie.... Please, please, *please,* don't do this, Debbie. You've got the eight hours of oxygen, that's it. Come on back, please. You don't need to take it all so seriously, Debbie...just answer me, get on the intercom and answer me.... Please! Nothing is worth this. Think about your friends back on Earth, the people who care about you. Think about us, think about Abu and me, and the rest of the crew.... Think it over.... Debbie, Mars was supposed to be how we showed everyone back home that it *wasn't* just about the petty infighting, the religious conflicts, the relentless war and hemorrhagic fevers and all of that, Debbie.... Mars was supposed to be when we thought big and acted big.... Debbie, please... you can use the left-hand thruster, make a big slow arc, Debbie, and I'll meet you.... Nothing is worth this. I don't care what you did, Abu doesn't care, it's nothing so bad that you aren't always my teammate and my friend, please, Debbie!" At which point Steve got as far as he felt he could safely go, about a thousand yards. Up ahead of him was a white speck drifting off, a white silent speck, a stilled voice. Then Steve turned back to face the ship, gulped down a big throat full of bile when he saw how far out he was, how far a thousand yards is when you have gone from everything that *was,* the little tin can of night sky dreams, into everything that is nothing. Nothing at a degree or two above absolute zero. It took Steve another twenty minutes to get back onboard the *Geronimo,* and if you think Planetary Exile Syndrome is bad, kids, wait till you get a look at the disorder they refer to as Space Panic, which the psychiatrists think is related to earthbound agoraphobia, but worse. When an astronaut gets a good look at the infinite space of space and the size of himself in relation to it, *that's* Space Panic. The void looks back into the astronaut; that's what happens. And it happened to Steve. He just couldn't really talk for a long spell.

Oh, and when Steve did get back, Abu had a knife to Brandon's throat and was saying, "What did you say to her, you piece of shit? I can kill you right now and say that it was the tear in your space suit. I can throw your worthless body out of the ship. No one will give it a second thought. No one will mourn for you, not your own family. You'll just be drifting out toward Planet X, for nine hours, when your O_2 runs out and you suffocate on your own frigging carbon dioxide, and we'll be eating dinner and forgetting you were ever here. Is that what you want?"

Out of the air lock, Steve drifted by them like nothing was happening at all. He took off his suit and paused to watch as dollops of blood floated past, blood that must have come from fisticuffs between Abu and Brandon. Normally, we clean up blood and fluids if they're floating around, crumbs, any of that kind of thing. Sometimes you'll see a spilled teaspoon of orange juice or water, rolling around in little liquidy balls, and you'll chase after it and try to swallow it or herd it into a plastic bag, just so that it doesn't get into a computer motherboard somewhere. Anyway, Steve didn't pay much attention to Abu and Brandon as they pounded on each other, cartwheeling down the hatch to the cargo bay, *Did you tear my suit on purpose? You dog! You trying to —*, colliding with the handles on the containment closets. Instead, Steve took a syringe from the first aid closet, and then he tied off his arm, and he loaded himself up with enough lights-out for days. Which meant that Abu and Brandon, though they didn't trust each other at all, though they were trying to beat the shit out of each other at that very moment, would end up having to negotiate restarting the engines, as Arnie and Laurie had just done, with coaching from Houston. We were all finding out: on the Mars mission you did some things because there was just no one else available.

That night, the head of NASA, Dr. Anatoly Thatcher, came on-screen, all three ships, to give us the pep talk. Now, this was a laugh riot. The conference took place when José was meant to be asleep, but like every other NASA communication, it would get saved for him. Jim and I were at the kitchen table, attempting to play a strategy game, Martian Invasion. Jim had brought the cartridge himself from home. We were up to level eight, where the tripod creatures from the South Pole manage to slingshot themselves around Phobos. They were heading back to Earth: for Vancouver. It's a full-scale Martian invasion!

The screen on the instrument panel went blue, as it did before all messages from Houston, and there was the NASA seal, and then Thatcher came on, with his tortoiseshell glasses, and his shaved head, and big white eyebrows. "Ladies and gentlemen," said he, "I know it's been a rough day, perhaps one of the roughest days in the history of the American space program. I know some of you would rather take time to recover from your labors before watching this communication, and that's fine with all of us. Here on Earth we'd like to talk about what we think has been happening there. We'd like to try to remember Debbie Quartz, a valued member of the Mars mission team. We'll be reporting on all of this for the media on Earth, as you know, and these thoughts will therefore be excerpted in the press...."

Everyone had a good story about Debbie Quartz. My story is simple, and I haven't told it so far because I didn't want to embarrass Debbie in this web diary—especially given how much trouble she was having from the moment we broke free of Earth's gravitational pull. The story is this. In the last six or eight weeks before launch, it was becoming abundantly clear that there was trouble in my marriage. I'm not telling you anything that you haven't been informed of here already. But somehow I was among the last to know. My daughter was spending most of her time at school, and listening to music I really didn't care for, like that noise that is referred to as *dead girlfriend.* She had the piercings, the skull implants, you name it. Like any junior high kid, full of attitude and busy with extracurriculars. Impatient with parentally imposed anything. This was compounded by the times when my daughter didn't really have enough to occupy her. She didn't play field hockey or soccer. She was not an athlete. Some days, therefore, she came over to the mission campus near Cape Canaveral. My wife and I took advantage of the supervision opportunities that were available to us there. Older kids killed some time there now and then because the family center offered wireless digital networking and a small library of uploads, study aids, and games. Sometimes the kids were even allowed to watch satellite launches live.

Even though Debbie didn't have any close family, or maybe because of it, she always took time to go down to day care to look in on other people's kids. She seemed to know everybody's kids. She knew all the birthdays. She gave Steve's son a home rocketry kit for his birthday one year, and she went out with Arnie and his twin girls to one of those animatronic restaurants, where, she later said, she'd accelerated a case of upper-frequency hearing loss.

Of course, Debbie Quartz also knew my daughter, Ginger. In fact, my daughter, Debbie said, was her favorite kid of all the children of the mission. My daughter, according to Debbie, had that mixture of brilliance and melancholy and realism that makes for the most fabulous adults. Debbie volunteered to get me a GPS lapel pin for my daughter, so that I'd quit losing track of her and so that I could take a more active role.

I laughed this off, because maybe I just didn't want to hear it. Until the one night I was supposed to go pick Ginger up. It was during the first trial separation. I drove all the way to my wife's brother's place, where she and my daughter were staying, I knocked on the door, and my wife appeared in some kind of slutty outfit that had definitely not been donned in order to impress me. She said, "Where's Ginger?" To which I said, "What do you mean, where's Ginger? I'm here to pick her up!" Probably you could write some of the scene yourself. Almost immediately, there was a lot of shouting back and forth, or at least a lot of shouting on my wife's end of things. This despite the fact that we were supposedly parting amicably, which means with tremendous feelings of failure. But no bloodshed. No! It's your turn to pick her up! No, it's *your* turn! How could you be so *callous!*

If you start thinking about space-time, and living in space-time, which you do when you're about to get into an Orion-class rocket and blast out there into the blue, you inevitably start feeling philosophical about how human beings can have their own little wormhole-type moments, moments when, for example, the mistakes of your marriage come clear before you. Such a time might be when your kid goes missing. It is true that what I have mostly done is put *everything* ahead of my marriage, put my work ahead of my marriage, put my country ahead of my marriage, put my hobbies ahead of my marriage, put my individual retirement account ahead of my marriage, you name it. If I needed to go back for another round of hyperbaric-chamber training, I did it right then; I didn't care if my wife was nursing the baby. If there was another soirée where attendance was optional, I went first and stayed last, and let my wife bail out whenever she needed to. I was a mixed blessing as a human being, and I knew I was a mixed blessing, but I allowed the space mission to be the one thing I could do. A long stint in emptiness between planets, where I am alone in my thoughts for weeks at a time? I can do this. Other people join the space program because they like military protocol, or the fraternity, or they want an adventure, or because they want to be famous. I wanted none of these things. I just thought I'd be good at the loneliness.

Anyway, so my wife and I got into my car, and between bursts of yelling at each other, we tried to reconstruct where Ginger might have been. Ginger was just at that age when she was wearing those fashionable short shorts, through which you could practically see her labia, and there were the piercings I already mentioned, and the subcutaneous, cranially implanted jewelry, which went with the partially shaved head, and she hadn't yet realized that she was no longer the innocently unsexed girl, but was now becoming the sex machine of puberty, the desiring machine. I had to avoid looking at Ginger sometimes, because I was embarrassed about how proud I was of her very adult body. This all made it that much more terrifying not to know her whereabouts. My wife was on the wrist assistant, dialing up Ginger's friends and their mothers, and that horrible walkie-talkie bleep those things make was driving me insane, and then it hit me! It was obvious: Ginger was back at the campus, not at oboe lessons, not at ballet. And we drove all the way back to the family center at Cape Canaveral in silence, scarcely a family in our sub-mini coupe that was just big enough to fit two people whose marriage was falling apart.

We found Ginger with Debbie Quartz. In fact, the two of them were in stellar engineering, which is a simulation program that Debbie helped to design. You gather up a certain amount of liquid hydrogen, and a certain amount of stellar dust, add some gravitation, a little bit of galactic convection, and so forth, and you make up a star and a star name. You watch to see how your star will affect the gravitational fields of the stars around it. Maybe you try to spin off some planets; maybe you attempt to terraform. It's a helluva game. Debbie was in on the ground floor with this one, had a percentage on it, which was why she had a waterfront house and a palm grove. She had a friend trying to market the product to the big game behemoths from China and India. But that's not the part I'm remembering. The part I'm remembering is that I found my daughter, Ginger Stark-Richards, with Debbie Quartz, sitting by a console, designing a solar system, and when I started in on Ginger, like a dad will do sometimes, asking her why she hadn't called either of us (even though it was probably all my fault), Debbie said, "Jed, Ginger and I had this appointment on the books for a couple weeks, and I just forgot to tell you. I'm awfully sorry about that."

Some people just have that smile, the one with the many constituent hues. The rainbow coalition of smiles. Not *only* a smile because there's no longer a problem, but also a smile because the person smiling somehow knows more about the situation than you do; it makes her happy not to require recognition of her kindness, because she actually cares about you and doesn't care about her own glory; it's a generous smile, a confident smile, a happy smile, but also a smile with a gradient that indicates *there's not much left to smile about these days; we do the best we can.* Only a sad person can smile so memorably. That was Debbie Quartz's smile, especially when she took my wife's hand, and said, "Pogey, I should've called. I'm really very sorry. I have just been *so excited* about this stellar modeling, and Ginger was the very first young person I wanted to try it out on."

Ginger didn't say anything. No one was going to let on about where the fib started and ended. That was how Debbie Quartz was. Generous, but also impenetrable. Wasn't a couple of weeks later, when I leased out the Stark-Richards house to cover mortgage payments and child support, that I started sleeping on her couch.

It was in this vein that Dr. Anatoly Thatcher went on about how great Debbie was, saying, "She was an absolutely committed astronaut." And then he started in with the guff that was designed to indemnify the agency against legal action. This line of reasoning had to do with Space Panic: "Ladies and gentlemen, you all know how unpredictable a deep-space voyage is, and how uncertain we are about the long-term effects of weightlessness, exposure to gamma rays, and so forth. In addition to these risks, there is another subject about which we previously knew very little, and that is the psychological effects of increasing distance from the home planet. Since the first sign of trouble with Deborah Quartz, which occurred soon after launch at t-zero, the psychology team here at Mission Control began profiling Debbie and the rest of the crew and have begun projecting our revised mission expectations. What we want to present to you is the possibility that there may, in fact, be a sort of *disinhibiting disorder* that comes from interplanetary travel. We don't know how this is going to play out over the course of a very long mission, but we do know that none of you, according to our evaluations so far, has been free of affective overreaction to mission stimuli. We solicit your opinions on this subject, naturally, but this is our sense of things. Earlier missions have suggested this possibility to us, and we are not surprised to find that the symptoms are exaggerated the longer and more distant the flight. Remember the mutiny on Spacelab, for example, or the incident of interspecies violence on the Mir. You will recall that these events were summarized in some of your prelaunch reading. All we want to say about this is that under the circumstances, you are the ones who are going to have to adapt and facilitate treatment and remediation of these mental-health complaints. You are the ones who can make your interpersonal experiences more agreeable, more harmonious. If you are unable to remember that your own motivation may be somewhat clouded by Space Panic, or *interplanetary disinhibitory disorder,* as we are now calling it here, perhaps you can nonetheless extend your sympathy and understanding to your fellow crew members, and in this way we can prevent further difficulty. The mission has lost one of its best, finest, and most trusted astronauts, and we cannot afford to lose anyone else. We are willing to sacrifice the odd satellite; we are willing to lose an unmanned rocket here and there. Hardware is expensive, but there is always something learned from the reversals. We are not, however, willing to lose manpower. NASA is about humankind's aspirations. Not about technology.

We protect our people. You should do the same. I urge you all to be mindful of what I've brought up tonight. Over and out."

Jim Rose and I sat there as the screen went blue again, and in stunned silence we pondered the meanings of this communication. Everything was so much *worse* than they knew on the ground, but maybe Dr. Anatoly Thatcher had a point. Maybe there was some kind of interplanetary *menarche,* some periodic self-slaughtering impulse, and now we were at its mercy. The question was whether we could survive the experience. If our bodies could survive, might it be our personalities, our hearts, that gave out? Did terms like *heart* and *soul* have any meaning beyond the surface of the home planet? Were these convenient metaphors dependent on a certain level of atmospheric pressure? A water-based ecosystem?

Jim said, "That certainly did not make a public servant feel confident about his job." He had these worry lines. At the corners of the eyes. If anything, they had become worse on the Mars mission. Additionally, there was the tendency, with weightlessness, for a body to hold water above the waist. Whatever the cause, in times of great stress, worry lines broke out on Jim like a series of fermatas over the symphonic score of his personality.

"Do you notice any of it?" I asked.

"What? Disinhibitory whatever?"

"Roger that."

"I notice that I am not sleeping," he said, and fell into a conspiratorial whisper. "I notice that certain people here in our neighborhood do not seem trustworthy any longer to me, and I notice that I cannot shake the idea that we are just going to Mars to pick up the minerals necessary for some new kind of explosive something-or-other. And I don't know if that's what I signed up for, or if I want to be a part of that. I still don't know what I want to do about it. What do you think?"

"About the disinhibitory excuses? Or about the military-industrial complex? I never believed we were up to any good. I only believed I wanted to travel. I like to see the lines of the superhighway disappear beneath me."

"But do you notice any symptoms of *interplanetary disinhibitory disorder?*"

"I would have to have strong feelings about my character in the first place," I said. "And I do not. Disinhibition might make me less ill-tempered. This might improve my outlook."

The video game we played blinked away on the screen on the table in front of us. I unhooked myself from the seat where I had been perched and allowed myself to roam freely across the capsule, the better to avoid his eyes, which seemed to have some probing quality.

Despite a wish to avoid further disclosure, I went on. "I'm the perfect astronaut. I have no native qualities. I'm the guy you want to have on your team because I have no needs. I take the orders. If you want to know the truth, the only disinhibiting I've noticed concerns my dislike of José. It blossoms."

Perhaps I thought I was winning Jim over with this remark.

Jim Rose unhooked himself from the table and swam toward me. Despite my blue mood, my poor conversational skills, the dark forecasts from home, his presence beside me lightened my mood. He said, "You aren't afraid?"

"Of what's to come?" I said.

"Well," said Captain Jim Rose, the linebacker, the most-likely-to-succeed astronaut, the pilot, the future political candidate, the hero to the economically deprived young men of the Wild West, "I am. I am afraid."

That was when he first took my hand.

December 26, 2025

We just celebrated the first Christmas of the Mars mission! Only one or two more to go! Before we're back on Terran terra firma! I have to say it was good to have *ham.* I'd almost forgotten what ham was like. It had a voluptuous stink that was just unlike anything else we had here on the *Excelsior*. Oh, the little frivolities of life. They enabled you to go on. We called over to the *Pequod*, to wish them a very merry holiday. So far no response. I contacted Houston not long after to ask if everything was all right on the other ships, and then I waited. To be sure, things were hard on the *Pequod*. They were shorthanded. Arnie Gilmore wasn't meant to be doing the first officer stuff, the management stuff, but he was trying to do it, and Laurie was brushing up on piloting, which involved some daily lessons from Mission Control. Talk about your steep learning curve. She had three days, now, to figure out how to coordinate landing the *Pequod*, which was meant to be the last ship to land. Before that, we needed to secure the location of the cargo that had been launched at Mars in the last couple years, like the liquid hydrogen, so as to avoid losing the hardware components of the Earth Return Vehicle that were in the *Pequod* cargo hold, and which would be assembled into that craft for our trip home. Maybe the stress of piloting explained why Laurie wasn't communicating. And yet the same was true of the *Geronimo*. I gave a yell over to Steve, to see how he was holding up, how his son's strep throat was.

Abu sent a text message later that said they had gifts for Jim and José and me, but we'd have to wait till we were camped safely at Valles Marineris before they'd give them to us. Can you guess? Some more dehydrated ham?

Then my daughter called to wish me a merry Christmas, and while I would like to say that this was a joyous thing, and that I was very happy to be contacted by my daughter, Ginger, whose partially shaved head and cranial subdermal implants were clearly visible in the little postage-stamp-sized video feed, this was not exactly true. My daughter had achieved the time-honored goal of adolescents: she'd got rid of one of her parents. She had shipped one of her parents about 40 million miles away. While she did not cause this relocation, she could at least reap the benefits. She could feel abandoned, she could detest my personal grooming habits, she could do whatever the hell she liked at least 50 percent of the time. When I looked at her, in the little postage-stamp-sized video feed, I saw a mirror image of myself. I saw the me who attempted to keep himself apart from his crewmates. And that person, that person who was not appearing in NASA-related promotional material, was socially uncomfortable, not a gifted small-talker; that person was a mumbler; that person tried to avoid talking to people when they came to the door; that person spent inordinately long periods of time in the bathroom (even on the *Excelsior*) because he was assured of being undisturbed there; that person wanted the acclaim of the world and disliked the world in equal measure. It was while I was watching this replica of myself, with shaved head and subdermal cranial implants and lots of piercings, that Ginger began to weep, remarking how hollow Christmas seemed to her now, *I don't see what all of this is for; it's just some big lie, especially now they have this ad online saying how it's your duty as a patriot to buy more at Christmas, or some horseshit, Dad,* and she said this with her bitter adolescent irony, the tears glistening on her cheeks. *I bet the reindeer can't stand temperatures near absolute zero, Dad, and they need oxygen, and they don't like cosmic radiation or solar winds, and there's no company store for the elves.* And then my daughter produced a ukulele (her ability to play this instrument was news to me), and she began singing a little song, to ukulele accompaniment. It sounded faintly Hawaiian, if you ask me; I mean, that's how you'd describe it. She'd written this out-of-tune melody, which she then sang in a husky, throaty voice: *Daddy, merry Christmas. Merry Christmas, Daddy. The Earth misses you. The chimney misses you, Daddy. The stockings miss you. The mouse needs his cheese. Merry Christmas, Daddy. You're lucky you didn't see my report card. I got nothing good for Christmas, Daddy. Come home soon,* and then, before she could finish, she started crying so hard that there was a little balloon of watery snot coming out of the nostril that had the nose ring in it. Soon my ex-wife appeared in the shot and whispered something to Ginger, who then allowed herself to be lured away to plum pudding with trans fats, after which my daughter's wobbly voice was audible off-camera, *We miss you!*

A reasonable question might be: Does this kind of message really help? Does it build character? Or does it just make a guy like me feel worse? As far as I was concerned, human civilization at this moment consisted of nine persons. Well, make that eight persons, since one had floated away. Eight persons on a flotilla of ships. And this flotilla had nothing to do with Christmas, as far as I could tell. Jesus of Nazareth wasn't crucified on Mars. That's the big lesson of Christmas: Peace on *Earth*.

Meanwhile, Steve and Abu had Brandon Lepper under round-the-clock surveillance. They wouldn't leave him alone on any shift. In the brief opportunities I had to talk to Steve, he wouldn't tell me what had happened, because, I think, he was worried about what Brandon was doing or would do with the information. Then there was José here, who had begun practicing strange breathing exercises that he said were part of the Chinese national religion known as Falun Dafa. José assumed these praying mantis positions before and after he used the exercise bicycle. And he agitated from one leg to another, caroming off the capsule walls. We could hear him down in the cargo bay, singing Mandarin-language pop music. His beard seemed very, very long. I don't know if Falun Dafa had recruited him to begin spreading a message of truthfulness, benevolence, and forbearance to the planet Mars, but it was not impossible. They were, after all, one of the most popular religions on Earth, if by popular you meant having the greatest number of adherents, not to mention basilicas in Mongolia *and* Cape Verde. I kept expecting a dinner at which José explained to me, using acronyms, how "Millions and millions of EPs, in the most prosperous nation on Earth, the PRC, are mobilizing every day in government-sponsored RAs to learn how to channel these simple APMs into abundance and well-being, especially when they're guided by members of the party; however, ROTP insures that I cannot pass on to you the five basic principles, because you are a WC."

Lately, he'd also been turning in kind of early. Maybe this was an indication of my TMCT, my *total Mars conspiracy theory,* in which everyone on the mission was on the payroll of some foreign intelligence service. Or everyone had allegiance to some governmental agency, and no one was talking or sharing information, and when we got to the surface of the planet, we'd all head off in different directions to contact our disparate patrons. Maybe that's what Debbie was doing right now, from out in space somewhere, radioing out to aliens about the malevolent humans.

Kids, I had just a couple of days left to perfect my delivery of the line I was supposed to proclaim when I got out of the ship, commencing in this way the important "flags and footprints" portion of the Mars mission. You know what I mean, right? If something went wrong, if the mobile factory that had already landed on the surface (to mill the liquid hydrogen and to make propellant-grade methane) wasn't working properly, and we had to turn right around, it was nonetheless important to get the human footprint in the sand as quickly as possible and to get the flagpole erected. I had to have my sentence ready to utter during the Mars landing sequence. The proclamation needed to be effected quickly, confidently, safely.

I'm not supposed to give it away early, the history-making sentence, so you can bet that this diary entry is going to be heavily censored by NASA. But I don't have any secrets from you! Tomorrow I could be crushed during orbit insertion! So let me be the first to tell you that this piece of oratory was obviously written by a committee of speechwriters, many of them from the NASA public-relations office. I mean, what do you expect from a government agency? You get stiff, middle-American prose. So here it is, kids, the line you will never hear ahead of the big day: "This planet was named for the god of war, but with our small settlement, may our neighbor planet now be colonized in peace." Feel free to comment among yourselves. Send responses to the Mars mission home page.

You know the big controversy about the Apollo missions, right? The moon landings? Neil Armstrong and the famous sentence that he botched? He was supposed to say: "One small step for *a* man, one giant leap for mankind." Neil got a lot of credit for that sentence, but the fact of the matter is, he mangled it good by leaving out the article. For these reasons, NASA is very insistent that I practice my line, so as to avoid making any similar mistake. Moreover, you'll notice that the sentence doesn't have the article *a* in it. Maybe NASA became concerned about the article. They have never quite recovered from its loss. They have further warned about adding in unnecessary verbiage, as though an *a,* left over from the Apollo missions, floating around in space, might have drifted out to the fourth planet, where we are about to go into orbit, and this *a* will attach itself to me somehow, standing for *aphasia,* or *atom bomb,* or *adultery,* or I don't know what, and I will mangle the sentence that they have so carefully constructed after months and months of meetings and consultants' fees paid to advertising executives and public-relations experts.

In order even to write about the sentence, I had to copy it from a document that they sent earlier, a contract I had to sign, agreeing that I had no rights over the sentence. I didn't *write* the sentence, the contract indicates, and I cannot use it or sign my name to it, once having uttered it. Any royalties accruing from the sentence belong to NASA itself. The sentence, in fact, is copyrighted and trademarked. Maybe because of this, kids, I can't remember the goddamn sentence at all. When I'm trying to fall asleep, I drill myself on it, reading it aloud, repeating it again and again, and every single time, I screw it up. In fact, I think there have been occasions when I have added an *a.* For example, I think I might have said, "This planet was named for *a* god of war." What's the problem here? Utter inability to remember the one bit of serious business I alone have on the Mars mission?

It's night now, and we are going into orbit in a mere twelve hours, and we could *bounce off* the Martian atmosphere and pogo into interstellar space, which would *not* be good. Such things depend on the aerobrakes, which were manufactured at the Jet Propulsion Laboratory by a project manager called Simon who is very unpleasant. He could easily have sabotaged the aerobrakes. In fact, while I was recently pondering Simon and his capacity for sabotage, I was saying the sentence over and over like it was a mantra from Falun Dafa. Except that I don't know if Falun Dafa really has mantras and the like. Is the Buddha involved? Maybe if I practiced Falun Dafa, the way José practices it, I would facilitate the memorization process, and, upon our return to the planet Earth, prosperity would wash over me, along with a great wave of Asian air pollution.

Jim was meant to be waking in an hour or so, and José would be too. We were intended to be asleep simultaneously tonight, so that we would all be awake in the morning. For the aerobraking. It's the rare night when we are all meant to be asleep, and so it was even more singular when Jim appeared by the side of my bed. If an astronaut can be said to be drifting nervously, then Jim was doing just that. Drifting. Nervously. I didn't even hear him at first because I was wearing headphones that were playing recordings of interstellar radio waves, which I find kind of beautiful.

"Are you worried about tomorrow?" I said. It was awkward, him by my side. In my heart, for example, it was especially awkward.

Jim nodded.

"You're a great pilot. One of the best pilots in the universe." This was a mere pleasantry, since Jim wouldn't have to do that much piloting. There is so much automation. "You'll do great."

"No slouch yourself."

"I manage," I said. In truth, I fly an ultralight, and a few models of fighter planes that no one bothers with anymore. The Mars mission has redundancy in pilots and in engineers. Everyone also knows some first aid.

Jim was not by my side to discuss piloting. There's really no other way to put it except to tell you the truth. Suddenly Jim Rose grabbed my head and began to kiss me. I suppose I would call this the tomorrow-you-may-die style of kissing, the there-is-no-other-time-than-now kissing, the burn-me-at-the-stake-if-you-must kissing, the fair-is-foul-and-foul-is-fair kissing, the desert-island-hunger-and-thirst kissing, the drive-your-cart-over-the-bones-of-the-dead kissing, the may-I-burn-eternally kissing, the don't-ask-don't-tell kissing. And it was a *big shocker.* As I may have already said, I am a heterosexual military man living in Florida with an estranged wife and a daughter, and I have shunned any number of homosexuals. Sometimes I have put the military hurt on them, throttled not a few, especially military homosexuals, which is not to say that I don't respect them. But I have had little actual experience with this kind of thing, excepting a few friends when I was prepubescent. That was just transitory and experimental.

There are some details that you should know about interplanetary kissing. Shaving, as I have indicated, is made very difficult by the low-gravity water problem and the recirculation of capsule resources. We just don't shave often, and Jim hadn't shaved in the last day or two. He was kind of scratchy and kind of, well, musky, too, which I couldn't fail to notice because this was a stick-a-fork-in-me-because-I'm-fully-cooked sort of kiss. We were holding each other's heads, it was a death grip, and we didn't care if we were not exactly shaved, or if the full expression of masculinity entailed the sandpapering of faces; we were devouring; this was interplanetary disinhibitory *devouring;* and I could hear him, as if over an intercom, whispering and moaning; it was a low moan, a moan that I recognized, namely the moan of months without being touched by another human being. Likely, you could hear this moaning coming from the beds of all the astronauts of the mission, even the beds of astronauts whom you did not favor with esteem; you felt great sorrow and sympathy for the fact of these astronauts being untouched, and as the weeks went by, you *did* feel as though you might touch them, the others, just because it was ridiculous; the drought of human affection was ridiculous; and so this moment was about the incredible gratitude of that drought coming to an end. Jim's eyes were bloodshot, and his hair was a mess, but that didn't stop me from wanting Jim Rose. I wanted Jim Rose, the pilot of our ship, and I wanted to kiss him some more, and I wanted to be kissed some more by Jim Rose, enough so that I almost didn't care if José heard.

Apparently, I have some skills that I never knew I possessed. Well, maybe *skill* is not the right word. Maybe it is more like an acumen. My particular acumen was that I could verify immediately the arousal of Jim Rose, my interplanetary fuck buddy. Jim Rose was rather stunning in one of the lightweight garments that we wear when we sleep here on the *Excelsior,* sort of a baby-blue union suit. Anyone would admit that he was stunning. But I wanted more, and I could already see more. I could see that underneath his baby-blue union suit, Jim Rose was fully aroused by the stolen kisses, the interplanetary kisses, he was a mighty satyr, he was an epic from the classical era of forbidden kisses, the grunting, heaving, moaning, masculine kisses that we exchanged onboard the *Excelsior.* Before we could proceed, I pointed at the cough button, and Jim whispered huskily that he'd "Already got it," meaning he wanted me, he wanted me, he was thinking about me before he arrived at my bedside, he was thinking about it maybe for days, and perhaps I was thinking about it too, and just not doing a very good job admitting it to myself. But seeing that Jim was, according to the argot of connoisseurs, *rock hard* played havoc with my self-deception. Jim was *rock hard,* and by the standards of the Mars mission, he was, dare I even say it, rather large.

He unstrapped me gently from my bed, and I began unfastening pieces of his capsule pajamas. We disrobed each other, that is, and for now we were thankful — this is perhaps the one time that we were thankful — that NASA had not undertaken the considerable expense of adding a centrifugal device that would have enabled low gravity in the capsules of the Mars mission. Because once I was unstrapped from bed, we were free to wrestle with each other in the capsule, drifting around, colliding with multibillion-dollar computer systems, like the one that monitors life support, likewise the kitchen gear, and then we were up at the ceiling, and we were French-kissing, and I had never quite realized before how that tongue-sucking business was really aphrodisiacal. Soon we were less than partially clad, Captain Jim Rose and Colonel Jed Richards, and we were the warriors of space, and everything about us was lean and hard and murderous, and I had never before seen how glorious it is, the perfect beauty of ambition and self-assurance that is *being male,* and all I wanted to do, in that moment, yes, was to have his staff in my mouth. At least, that was my first thought, and my second one dealt with my uncertainty about the circumcision issue, because I had never really spent any time with a cock that was uncircumcised, and if Jim's *space arm,* as I had begun to call the thing in my head, was uncircumcised, it was going to require some additional effort on my part. I recognize that there are certain tree-hugging types, environmentalists, free-love advocates, children of that long-ago and historically debunked period known as the *Summer of Love,* who believe that this age-old variety of genital mutilation is somehow problematic, but I figured if I was circumcised, everyone was circumcised, and these thoughts were racing around in me. Would I even know what to do with it, the *space arm,* if it was uncircumcised? Would I know what to do with it at all? And there were other questions that you would have if you were a man-love neophyte. Would his body be like my body? How hirsute would it be?

And yet my inclinations were outpacing my philosophical and psychological quandaries, because I was drifting between his legs. Happily so. Before I could answer the questions, I had the *space arm* before me. I spit in my hand, except that this was not such a superlative idea, because, as with most liquids in the capsule, my saliva sort of went spraying around in little balls. "Well, that's going to be a little complicated," I muttered, as I tried to catch some of the spit, with which I then began servicing Jim Rose.

The circumcision issue was no issue at all. I just wanted him! And I wanted him however he was, which happened to be unsheathed according to the Judeo-Christian tradition. Much more fascinating to me was the pumping-leg motion and the mild muscular contractions that I was able to bring about in Jim, despite the fact that this was the first time in, well, thirty years that I had been amorous in the presence of another male. Of course, I have snuck the odd peek at my daughter's sex-education textbooks, and I know that there are particular response curves to masculine sexuality. Muscular contraction is part of it, as well as contraction of the sphincter. My observations indicated that Captain Jim Rose was in the early phase of sexual release with me, Colonel Jed Richards, and that meant he was probably experiencing desire for me, and feelings of warmth and esteem for my person. Because I was feeling the same way, because I was not feeling lonely and doomed for perhaps the first time on the mission, I knew that it was therefore time to go a little further. I was imagining that I would, in fact, put the *space arm* in my mouth.

"Jed, you're just like the coeds I used to buttfuck back at the state school," he said. On any other day, I think it's fair to say that this would *not* have been a romantic remark, not of the sort that I was accustomed to. *Buttfuck,* it's just an awful word, when you think about it. It's amazing that anyone could come to love a word so guttural and so unpleasant. But as Jim began huffing and puffing from my exertions, I recognized that something had truly shifted in me, because now the word *buttfuck* made the sinews in my groin glut with corpuscular activity. I had to have the *space arm;* it was like some alien life-form that had to be mine.

"Jim, I'm no coed. I'm no little girl in a French maid's outfit, but I would be if you wanted me to be. I would be whatever you want me to be." We whispered these enticements. A little hyperbole was no problem. I wanted to say all the words that needed to be said, as I drifted down below him, and the *space arm* was orbitally injected ever deeper into my mouth and toward my throat. The *space arm* was behaving like a nasty little Orion-class rocket, moving recklessly around in the atmosphere of my wet, spittle-filled mouth and lips. I gagged a little. I tried to say something, but my mouth was full. I could say nothing. I cupped the rest of his bounteous tackle, and he held the back of my head.

Jim said, "Do you think it's just the sickness?"

I tried to say, "Do you mean Space Panic?" I wasn't sure if I was entirely understood. Jim sighed a sigh of romantic anomie, and then he nodded. "Yes. Space Panic."

I pulled him out and looked up, licking the dainty walnuts of his testes. "I agree with you. It's not my kind of sport, or at least it was not my kind of sport on Earth, Jim. But, Jim, we aren't *on* Earth anymore. Maybe where we are going, this is the norm. Maybe Mars is the planet where the love between men is not only accepted, but is a hallowed and sacred thing. Who are we? Are we now earthlings? Or are we now the forerunners of a brave new class, men who are not afraid of love and power among themselves?" And with that, I introduced a forefinger into his tight, imperturbable anus, and he moaned in a way that revealed some of the more brute varieties of wildlife.

"More," he said.

"More what?"

"More of you."

More of me? The balding, formerly paunchy (but now frequently hungry), blue-eyed, and impish guy with vanishing muscle mass? The *space arm* said *yes.* The *space arm* was rich in veins and purply sections, and the head of it resembled a poisonous mushroom of some kind, perhaps the fly amanita, which I was always told to avoid as a youngster. The *space arm* was cruel and foul, for example in the profusion of pubic hairs that I kept finding stuck against the roof of my mouth, but I recognized, yes, that cruelty was a fair and beautiful thing, and I wanted it. There were no lengths to which I would not go, nothing I would not do. I was the first-ever interplanetary space slut. Or the first, at any rate, to enter the literature.

"Wait," I said.

He looked stricken. As though I were going to draw a permanent halt to our space explorations! But I had no such intention. Petrolatum was an important product on the *Excelsior,* because our skin was patchy and flaky for lack of moisture in the pressurized, recirculated air of the cabin. There was even an official supplier of petrolatum to the Mars mission, and as with other licensing firms, I'm discouraged from naming it, though you will find its banner advertising throughout the site. Nor am I allowed to remark that the official sponsor of petrolatum to the Mars mission was about to serve as the lubricant for Uranian delights.

By my bed, on the little overhead shelf where my personal effects were Velcro'd down, was a precious tube of the stuff. I brandished it, as if I already knew how these props of the trade became fetish objects in their own right.

Jim was stroking his *space arm* while he waited for me, and making some noises that sounded like a bull elephant in the midst of toppling banyan trees, and this was both deeply shameful and not at all feminine, and about the most exciting thing I had ever heard. The cry of the heron lifting off from the swamps, that prehistoric and laughable squawk, didn't hold a candle to Jim Rose in the moment of ecstatic celebration. I urged him to apply the petrolatum, if possible, without any getting loose in the cabin. The place already felt like the inside of an immemorial triple-X film emporium, where the patrons were all lacquered with their juices. Jim was only too happy to oblige.

"How do we do it?" he asked.

"How complicated can it be?" I said. "They were doing it in ages past. Well before the combustion engine, for example."

He reached down and took hold of me, as though he had neglected my own little reentry hose coupling. "Are you going to do me too?"

"Is that what you want, you Southern prince?"

"I've been thinking about it for days."

"You first."

"Which?"

"In me."

And I turned, so that I was facing the reinforced windscreen of the capsule, and beyond the windscreen, in the foreground of the great mass known as the Milky Way, was our imminent destination, *the Red Planet,* like the hide of a great mother to whom we were soon going to apply ourselves for nourishment, and as I took note of the massed dry ice of the North Pole, I could feel the *space arm,* hungering at the opening of me, and then the *space arm,* plunging in. I would like to say, kids, that this is nothing but a pleasant sensation, and that when you love someone enough it is a consensual and loving act, but if I'm being honest, this is not how I experienced it. There was a sharp intake of breath, as though I were somehow responsible for inspiring all the oxygen in the capsule, and then there was a sharp stabbing sensation, sort of how I imagine it must feel to find your innards impaled on a pike, and this coincided with Jim driving in harder and deeper, till I was sure he was going to stir up that evening's ham somewhere, up in my stomach. I'm afraid I just couldn't get the hang of it, the first time, and it smelled a little rank too. They just don't tell you about that in all the pornographic literature.

For a second, therefore, I needed him to pull the *space arm* out, while I got myself better situated. After all, we were drifting around, and the only thing stabilizing us was Jim hanging on to my hips, and that made it hard for me to feel like much but his pincushion, his voodoo doll. After one last gigantic thrust, in fact, we went careening across the capsule and smacked our heads on the hatch to the upper air lock. That was going to result in *contusion.* Jim was all overheated, however, and he did not want to stop, as men never want to stop, I suppose. As I myself, on many an occasion, did not want to stop. But by grabbing on to a maintenance step by the hatch coupling, I did manage to unimpale myself briefly. Unfortunately, Jim Rose was at the segment of the curve of masculine desire known as the *point of no return,* and he could not stop, and he whimpered like a kicked mutt, and from out of the *space arm* issued a torrent of celestial blobs. Given what I have already explained to you, kids, it would have been a lot better, from virtually every point of view, if this spunk had been fired off into some kind of receptacle, like my mouth or some other opening. Because now Jim's issue was scattering in many directions at once, toward all the walls of the capsule, according to the very physical properties of explosions. This was the Big Bang of interplanetary sex.

"My God in the heavens!" Jim said. The last few drops expelling themselves from his cock, now withering. "Oh, man, we gotta do something about this! Will you help me..." Immediately, he set about rappelling from side to side of the capsule, trying, vainly, to capture droplets of jism. But in order to put them where, exactly? Kids, it's like trying to keep still the little marbles of mercury.

"Just eat it," I said, with the weariness of the just-fucked.

"Eat it?"

"Put it in your mouth, for godsakes," I said. And then the two of us breaststroked around the capsule, attempting to swallow down the afterglow of our profane and inadvisable entanglement.

December 29, 2025

There was a lot to do during the orbital insertion, kids. Next morning, we had that fellow with the sibilant *s*'s from Houston on the line, reminding us how things were going to proceed, and where and when Jim was going to have to monitor the aerobraking system, to insure that the computer-automated pilots were performing according to instructions from Mission Control — whose messages, I should say, were now reaching us with a thirty-something-minute delay. If something *were* going wrong, it was going to be a long time before we could do anything about it.

The nearer we got to the planet, the more unnerving the whole business became. As long as we were looking at Mars from a distance, it still resembled an artist's rendering, something from the forty years of public-television programming, or the kind of thing they put on postage stamps, back when there were actual postage stamps. Maybe it was just some bonbon out there suspended in the heavens. Still, the closer we got, the more likely it was we would have to land. That big, inhospitable desert that could freeze you to death at high noon, that was where we were going to land, amid the unfiltered solar and interstellar radiation, which even as we spoke was making the likelihood of certain varieties of cancer that much likelier.

You know, kids, that the famous storms of Mars have been visible as far back as the nineteenth century, right? There just isn't that much *on* Mars but dust. And there's so much temperature swing on the planet that the seasonal changes, particularly in late summer, spawn massive storms. Also, because the gravity isn't as strong as on Earth, the size of the stuff that's liable to go blowing in the dust storms . . . Well, when you get right up close to the surface, and you can see down to the craters, the dust begins to compel your attention.

At about 0800 hours (six hours before the *Geronimo* and twelve hours before the *Pequod*), we got the confirmation from Houston. We were, indeed, to begin braking in ten minutes. They gave us an opportunity to talk to the other ships, and Steve from the *Geronimo* came on the screen almost immediately, wishing godspeed.

"We'll be seeing you down there," I replied, "before long. Make sure that reactor is working properly, okay?" A nervous reminder, and thus an unprofessional one. For what else was he to do?

"We're on it."

"Everything okay there?" Jim asked from beside me. After all, they still had Brandon on board.

"Roger. Three peas in a pod." In fact, Steve's face didn't suggest the three legumes. Maybe we were all kind of nervous. Need I remind you that even if we made it to the surface, we were facing another year and change under very uncertain circumstances?

Laurie and Arnie called in next. I was watching while Jim spoke with them. The same kind of thing. Bland offers of support. What else could they say? We'll be *happy* to shovel up your remains on the surface? If any one of the three ships didn't make it to the surface, the remaining mission astronauts were, effectively, doomed. We were interdependent, we were worried, we were tired of one another. Except for Laurie and Arnie. (I was pretty sure there was something going on there.) And there was Jim and me.

Behind us, watching the whole thing, was José, and he was doing some more of his strange Asian spiritual exercises, which at this point seemed to involve a lot of facial grimacing and isometric convulsions, unless his version of Planetary Exile Syndrome involved a *tic douloureux.*

"I can't stand it when you loiter behind me," I reminded him.

"That's all you have to say after three months stuck in this aluminum can?" José replied.

"Six minutes to strap in," I said.

"Jim, you got it under control?" said he.

"Late to be asking."

"Maybe you didn't sleep well last night," José said. And when I looked back to catch his eye, he was grinning in a way both somber and knowing.

"Like a baby," Jim said.

"Five and a half," I said. "Don't forget the ventilator."

"I know what the MMPs are," José said, as he retreated down the ladder to the cargo bay. "I know as much about the mission as you do. I have more to do than type away on a diary." And then: "What is this gunk all over the banister?" The sound of his coyote laugh was muffled as he disappeared into his lair of science projects. I hadn't been down there in days to see if his plants were still growing, and when you consider that the capsule is only 1,200 square feet, that's saying something.

Kids, my large philosophical thought for today is that I know what the woman wants. I'm like Tiresias, who was each woman and man. What women observe, kids, what they have said to me often enough, is that with men there is the big crushing embrace of intimacy, from out of nowhere, when you are mushed in his arms, and you are more *there,* more useful than you have ever been, because you can complete this man, you can make him stronger, kinder, better, you can compel his softness to the surface, you can nurture it, until he is like a little lion cub, and all is good, all is sweet, up until the man's desire *crests,* and he spills his frenzied self upon the earth, at which point man is revealed as faithless and unloving, as man waltzes off to go watch X-treme lacrosse and eat salty snack items. Like you were never there at all. Never there at all! Until fluid backs up in the vas deferens or the prostate, and suddenly he requires some kind of liquidy release and becomes willing again to need to crush you in his faithless bear hug.

It was supposed to be three minutes until the aerobrakes, and we could easily be as an asteroid falling to the surface, we could burn up on orbital insertion, or else, as I was saying earlier, we could bounce off the atmosphere and go end over end, ass over teakettle, out toward the next star system, and in this dramatic moment, Jim wouldn't even make eye contact with me, just to acknowledge that some tenderness had taken place. Maybe there wasn't time for sentimentality, truly, because just as I was going to remark volubly on his remoteness, something went very seriously wrong, something that Houston was not up to predicting. We hadn't yet done our redundant flight-modeling tests, nor had we hooked up our ventilators, nor had we had any kind of countdown, when the rear thrusters nonetheless ignited, but still there was the scraping of large pieces of lightweight aluminum and flame-resistant heat shields moving into place on the outside of the capsule, and the explosion of combustion down in the engine room, and suddenly we went from however many miles per second we were going into an atmosphere-enhanced slowdown. We went from an interplanetary velocity, as fast as Earth itself hurtles around the sun, down to a couple thousand kilometers per hour. Everything that was not Velcro'd down in the cabin went shooting up into the soup of compressed oxygen, and we strained against our straps, and then, miracle of miracles, we heard sound! We heard sound! Earsplitting sound! Outside the capsule! We heard sound because, ahead of schedule, and without catching on fire, we had been captured by the Red Planet, kids, and this meant sound again! Ours was no longer a vacuum! There was, well, a lot of carbon dioxide, methane, and some nitrogen and stuff, not a lot of oxygen, but who's quibbling? We were falling into an atmosphere! We had made it somewhere in the neighborhood of 40 million miles across nothingness, and we were in the blissful soup of atmosphere. Martian atmosphere! And there was another sound, besides the aerobrakes firing and the hull shuddering, and that was a sharp yelp of pain from downstairs, which was, apparently, José being thrown violently across the capsule as we began again to experience the great mystery of gravity. Because even this far out, where we were just being captured by that perpetual falling, which is orbit, even here the little Martian gravitrons were interacting with our gravitrons, and as a result it was becoming temporarily possible to feel ourselves in these chairs, to feel our limbs. What this conferred on me, after the months of zero g's, was an intense nausea. It was a good thing that we didn't have the ventilators on, because Jim, who was holding on to a throttle between us on the off chance that he was going to have to do something, leaned over and vomited. I had the zero-gravity reaction to this: now there was going to be vomit drifting around the capsule, like there had been vomit the first couple of days. But the amazing quality of Jim's leftover, semi-dehydrated breakfast was that it kind of *spilled*. What a novelty! And I would have stopped to consider all this myself, had I not been vomiting.

There was a deceleration gradient (we were in search of a velocity of 9.8 m/s^2), and Jim gathered himself up from his slumped-over position as the hull of the *Excelsior* shuddered again, to make sure we were on track for the stable orbit that Houston had planned for us. The surface of the planet rushed up to meet us.

"You want to give a yell to José?" Jim said to me, somewhat nervously.

On the intercom, I called to our science officer.

"All right down there?"

No answer.

"José, are you there?"

Still nothing.

"I think he's down." I got on the keyboard and typed the message to Houston: *Code 8, science officer failed to buckle in.* This was followed by some important acronyms that José himself would have used in this message. There wasn't going to be a chance to get downstairs, however. Not in the midst of the landing. Not unless I manufactured one. "You want me to go look?"

"We'll go around half a revolution to make sure we're where we're supposed to be. Let's make sure we're secure."

I don't think I have commented at any length on the tiny moons of Mars, Phobos and Deimos. They are scarcely moons in the normal sense, and some people think they are just hunks of Mars that got blown out by some impact. And yet from my earliest days of training for the Mars mission, I have had an unnatural excitement about seeing Phobos. Phobos goes around the Martian equator, more or less, which our orbit was not far from, and so I was keenly hoping we would have a chance to see Phobos up close. It orbits the Red Planet every seven hours and thirty-nine minutes. And while I was thinking about what to do with José, watching for the moon was what I was able to do. Phobos, kids, is not exactly circular, by any means; it looks like the handset of an old-fashioned telephone, oblong, and as we swept by it, under it, my first thought was how good it would be for some variety of advertising. No doubt a Sino-Indian conglomerate will come up with just this sort of plan, and they will get a telegenic actor to announce it, perhaps broadcasting the message on the side of Phobos itself, for the eventual Mars colonists to see: *The little Martian moon Phobos is just how you want to feel about your investments as you approach your retirement—modest, predictable, reliable. That's why we named the company after it. Call a Phobos financial planner today. Phobos, a world apart.*

"How beautiful," I said, "the unseen majority of things in the universe," pointing out Phobos to Jim, but he was still performing calculations and typing status updates. It didn't seem long before my clipboard lit up with a text message from Houston, asking for more details about the injury.

"Okay, go have a look," Jim said. "We're as stable as we're going to be before the touchdown."

José was right about the banister, in fact. It was tacky with some foreign substance, though I couldn't precisely identify this compound. It could have been anything at this point. Long-term confinement brought out these residues.

When I rappelled myself down to José's floor, meanwhile, I confronted a very disturbing sight. A sight that would have limitless and unforeseeable implications for the mission. José, that is, lay on the floor with his leg dislocated to a remarkable angle, an impossible angle. And the belt loop of his reentry gear was hooked around a gaffing tool that was intended to be used to load out the ultralight on the surface. He didn't respond to my repeated attempts to rouse him. I depressed the nearby intercom on button.

"He's unconscious. And it looks like he has a broken leg."

"You kidding? How the hell?" Jim's tinny voice rebounded.

"You saw him. He wasn't prepared. Better get Arnie. I'm going to go ahead and revive him."

However, that wasn't what I did immediately. There was an odd peacefulness in the cargo bay. I considered my surroundings. I noticed that José's grow-light garden was doing very well. There were even blossoms on some of the tomato plants. We could have fresh tomatoes on Mars in a few weeks. An unimaginable treat. Maybe soybeans too. I took the opportunity, in that silence, to say a little prayer for José, because even though I disliked the man, I didn't want to see him disabled on Mars, or unable to contribute further to the mission. Did God even answer prayers from space? Maybe we were out of bounds. Nonetheless, it was in a spirit of gentleness and affection for the sleeping wretch that I drifted over to the first aid station and fetched out the smelling salts.

He was not very happy when he woke, that was for sure, and based on the cries of pain, it was evident that José was not in shock, which, in any event, is oversold as a medium of pain relief. José resorted to a syntactical bonanza of Spanish-language curses.

"What happened?" he kept asking. "What happened?"

"I think we hit the orbit very hard, and a lot sooner than we were supposed to, and everything that was loose went flying. You were one of the loose things."

"Orbit?" he said.

"Orbit."

"You mean?"

The implications of this question took a moment to sink in.

"You know where you are, right? You're on the *Excelsior,* and we're on our way to Mars."

He stared at me. In disbelief.

"Jim, are you hearing this?" I called.

From intercom: "I'm hearing it."

There was a penlight in the first aid box. I took it out and shone it in his eyes. The pupils were *not* entirely responsive to the stimulus. Not really a good sign.

"How much pain are you in?"

I went to touch the leg, and José began crying out immediately.

"I'm going to administer an injection, José," I said, "which will help with the pain. But we're going to have to try to splint your leg a little later. I have to warn you that that is not going to be very pleasant." José blanched at what was taking place, as though he were uncertain about all of it, and yet he still held out his arm. I squeezed a little OxyPlus out of the hypodermic to make sure there were no air bubbles, and then I dosed him up. He went slack within seconds. So I lugged him and his gravity-enhanced bulk up from cargo and strapped him to his chair, where he should have been anyway, and climbed back up to command and control.

At 2000 hours, the *Pequod* also went into orbit, not long after the *Geronimo,* but I was busy elsewhere. It was a long twelve hours of sitting with José and his mangled leg, asleep and awake, attempting to keep his leg immobile, explaining a lot of things to him, explaining that we were close personal friends and had been since early on in the years of training that it took to prepare for the Mars mission, explaining that he had an exalted position in the mission, as science officer on the first capsule that was going to touch down on the planet. I also had to brush him up on some recent global history, like the fact that NAFTA, by virtue of repeated cycles of inflation and stagflation and the exporting of all manufacturing jobs to Asia, was no longer the economic power-house he remembered.

I explained to José my personal theory that the Mars mission was the last great story that the NAFTA signatories had remaining in their arsenal. It was the good yarn we could tell the people of the world. Now that the Sino-Indian economic cooperative pact was in control of the show, their profiteers were able to engage in the kind of miserly fiscal policy that would *prevent* a government from the spending necessary to promote aggressive space travel. The rich wanted to get richer, I counseled José, and so the rich didn't approve of the profligacy of a Mars mission, especially one involving *three ships* and no less than twelve additional preflight unmanned missions in order to deliver various kinds of modules that would be required by the crew when it touched down. The Mars mission was the last act of the leadership in Washington as we knew it, I told him. There was a Hail Mary desperation to our labors. That was why so many things had gone wrong, that was why the aerobrakes had fired without warning, that was why his guess was as good as mine if we would make it to the surface, and forget about getting home.

If we controlled the surface of Mars, I told José, meaning NAFTA in general, or the USA in particular, then we controlled the next phase of human development, of human history. The winnings accrue to the winners, I told him, but we had been on a losing streak of a decade or more. We'd lurched from one ill-advised police action to another. As to the mission itself, I said, "All you need to know is that we lost one astronaut, and we're not going to lose another."

"What?" José said, groggy with the pain.

"You don't remember?"

"Starting to come back," he said. Which meant it wasn't.

"She jettisoned herself into space."

It occurred to me to wonder if he could be falsifying the severity of his amnesiac symptoms. Perhaps in concert with military subcontractors who were paying him additional sums. The only thing I could think to do was to probe around the limits of his awareness.

"She did say *something,* you know, before her accident, about a bacteria on the surface that she thought might be a little dangerous," I said. "It might have had a military application. This was probably something she was just making up, don't you think?"

"Bacteria?"

"You were briefed by subcommittees of the agency I know nothing about."

"What are you asking?"

"I'm saying that if there's something on the surface that I don't know anything about, you would now be in a position to tell me."

"I remember something about a bacteria, but it's not very clear."

"When you do remember, feel free. Don't forget that we're in this together. We're not on Earth anymore, José. We're Martians, or very soon we will be."

At this point, just a few hours from our purported landing, Jim Rose finally appeared in the cargo bay. Jim was sweaty, worried, and he had trouble sticking with the conversation for more than a couple of sentences. He kept inspecting unimportant bits of machinery.

"How's the patient?" he inquired.

"It's only an issue when I move."

"Well, look," Jim said. "I have some instructions from Arnie, and these instructions involve retrofitting the reactor core here in the engineering subroutine so that we can essentially do a bit of an ad hoc X-ray on you, José, using films from some of the botanical experiments. But there's a more important question than that, at least it's more important to me, and that concerns our ability to set the craft down tomorrow. That's what I want to know, José. I want to know if you're going to be able to help land this ship, because that's what we're supposed to do, and we're landing on the plains not far from the deepest canyon in the entire universe, José, because that's where you're supposed to direct us in a series of experiments. I need to know if you're ready."

The pressure was enormous, and a man with a broken leg and concussive memory loss was likely to feel ill-equipped to deal with it. Still, José rose to the occasion.

"If I came here to do a job, then I'm going to do that job."

December 30, 2025

I'm going to leave out the part where we splinted José's leg, because that's just blood and guts. I mean, you know what it's probably like, right? You yank on a guy's leg, a broken leg, he screams endlessly, and then you watch as he relieves himself inadvertently because of the excruciating pain, and then you try to clean him up a little bit, and you put the inflatable splint on his leg, all the while getting directions from Houston about what to do if for some reason you have to *take the leg off.* Gangrene is less likely in the space capsule, because we just didn't bring that many bugs with us out here, and this will also be the case on the surface of the planet, where the ground is mostly sterile. The topsoil is sterile as far down as the unmanned missions have drilled, except at the poles. And so José's leg was not going to rot on him, and we were not going to take it off.

And this didn't mean a delayed touchdown. We weren't going to have to cede the front position to the *Geronimo,* which we didn't want to do at all. But I was a little concerned that a delay didn't even occur to Houston. Maybe the *Geronimo* was having worse problems than we were. Maybe all three ships were now afflicted with the condition known as Space Panic. If a craft in which the pilot and the first officer were having sex and the science officer had a broken leg (and a spotty memory) was optimal, things must have really been bad elsewhere. We were going down first, that was the plan, and that was that.

And so at 0800, we were set to go.

I recorded another announcement for my family, which is to

say for Ginger and Havoc, and then one for my parents, who were in their rest home out in the Southwest, and who kept writing to me asking about the food onboard the *Excelsior*. Then Jim read a poem he had written for his family, a poem that did rhyme *wife* with *life,* and José we sort of left where he was, strapped in down in the cargo bay, declaiming lamentations in Spanglish.

In order to drop out of orbit, all we needed to do was slow ourselves beyond the stable orbiting velocity, which, as you can imagine, is not hard to do. What's hard to do is to avoid going so fast, upon entry, that you incinerate. Well, there's also the possibility of careening into a crater somewhere. We had parachutes that were supposed to enable us to slow adequately, after which we were to use thrusters for a smooth touchdown. We'd been trained. We'd done it in simulations. We'd landed similar crafts on Earth.

Did I ever tell you, kids, about Jim Rose's first wife? I'm guessing at this moment that you don't know that much about Jim Rose at all. You don't know how he came to be the captain of the *Excelsior;* you don't know much about his early life, beyond his rank and his military record, to which I have alluded. And so: as we prepare to land the *Excelsior* forty kilometers from the Valles Marineris, assuming we don't blow it, let me take this opportunity to tell you what I know.

Jim Rose's first wife, Barbara, was a regular military wife back on a base in Central Asia. This was during the years when Uzbekistan was the focus of our military and our foreign-policy objectives. Barbara, as I understand it, didn't know exactly what her husband did, which was to pilot into spots where we were not meant to be flying, in order to extract intelligence agents who were not meant to be there in the first place, and bring them back to safety. Barbara was trying to raise youngsters in this harsh and inhospitable environment, in which women were not meant to appear in pants, or without the *hijab.* These were the kinds of difficulties that a wife undertook for her husband, when he was in covert operations.

Anyway, the story goes that Jim was once out on a mission that involved springing some journalists who'd been taken hostage. These journalists, who'd also abandoned the army detachment with which they were embedded, were considered expendable by the military, but if the enemy was in turn going to use them as bargaining chips, the hostages would then appear in the papers, and that wasn't good for anyone. Jim's operation involved storming the village in the mountains where the journalists were held, to free as many as feasible.

There must have been a mole of some kind in the embassy. There must have been a highly placed mole. Because Jim's first wife, Barbara, was abducted the very day he set off to free the "embeds." She was out on the street, and she was swiped, in front of the kids, and driven away. It was hours before the State Department knew what had happened. No one had ever heard of the cell that claimed responsibility. It was Jim's belief, as he later told me, that these groups acted first and came up with their position papers later on. When they had milked a Western hostage for all he or she could provide, the militants would fade into the countryside, retreating into agrarian subculture in the way that the enemy has done for many decades now.

The intelligence operatives who counted Jim among their number worked hard over the next few days to locate Jim's wife. They overturned every rock around the military base, threatened untold reprisals through contacts, and they firebombed a couple of mosques as a lesson to those who would provoke the American military. Still there was no sign of Barbara Rose. Jim, like the professional that he was, finished his mission, freeing two of the three journalists he'd set out to free, with few civilian casualties. It was not long after that his wife's body was found in a ditch by a road, not three or four miles from the base. She'd *not* been violated by her captors, Jim told me, nor tortured, she'd simply been held as long as was feasible—and then murdered.

To this day, Jim blames the murder of Barbara on the kind of work that his colleagues were doing in Central Asia—surgical strikes and tactical disappearances outside of the normal rules of engagement. Jim was a search-and-rescue guy, and he didn't, or so he said, subject foreign nationals to any kind of extreme interrogation techniques. He was not an interrogator. Yet he came to feel that these kinds of techniques were routine in and around the base. In the time after Asia, he felt that the conduct of the war put him and others in intelligence at risk.

He left the military. With two motherless boys. They'd lost one parent, and he wouldn't be responsible, he said, for their losing another. He'd had to tell his boys what happened to their mother, while they were still recovering from the trauma of watching her abduction, and he had to, as he put it, restore his credibility with them by finding a line of work that was more honorable. When he got back from Asia, he spent a good long time unable to do much. He sat on his parents' porch in Biloxi and collected combat pay. He couldn't talk openly about what he'd been doing abroad, and he couldn't talk about his feelings of remorse. Then, one afternoon, his two sons, his older boys (as distinct from the little ones whelped in the second marriage), came home from school having seen a program about the dawning of the Mars mission. The way Jim tells it, he already knew how lucky he was, when his boys came to him on the porch. "Dad, they are looking for astronauts to go to Mars. The NASA folks are looking. And the two of us have been talking it over. We think you ought to go on down there and volunteer."

Child is father to the man! Jim Rose, stern, secret operative, wept the tears of the mostly unworthy. "You do? You think I ought to?" There was no stepmother on the scene, not at that time. Not for several years. There was no one to look after those boys if something should happen to him. And yet the boys were more concerned about their father than themselves. Or that's how the story goes.

Do you see it now? Do you see why I felt like this was a man I too would put ahead of myself? Do you see why I loved this man, in my own ill-defined and Space Panicky way? This was a man of ideals, a man who believed in something, a man whose gentleness was most evident in the tiny little creases at the corners of his eyes, which in my private moments I referred to as the Eye Crinkles, and whose military severity was belied by his strong desire and his occasional outbursts of sentimentality. I think you can see, and I need not say more.

At 0815, the chutes opened, and we went hurtling toward the surface, as we had been instructed to do, swan-diving through cumulus clouds. We had the ventilators on, and Jim was calling out altimeter readings when he had a chance, and we were strapped down, and the sound was a deep, unrepentant roar, as of creation, and we were either going to stop in the way that we were supposed to stop, or it would be the last thing we ever knew, the throbbing of puny man-made aluminum alloy casings when faced with the enigmas of other worlds. Was I scared? You bet I was scared, and you bet I was excited too, because, as I have said, the best astronaut is the one with the least to lose. When the parachutes flowered to slow us, I felt the drag, and there was a grave heaviness to the capsule suddenly, and I didn't know if the chutes could possibly contain it, the colonialist menace of us. And then the clear skies of a Martian spring opened up before me, and I could see, on the monitors, the canyon, which was one of the topographic features most notable on Mars, even from space, and we hurtled down toward it as though the canyon intended to swallow us, and just when it seemed that the landing could go on no longer (nor be any more dangerous), it did; it went on, and the thrusters fired, and when they did, I allowed myself the first clear thought: *We are really going to land on this planet.*

All my training said I was never meant to doubt, but I did, and I accepted my doubts. And yet when we felt the thrusters, both Jim and I laughed, because we were about to become legends, whether we wanted to be or not, legends for the good of an idea. The idea that if you use up one planet, there's another one out there somewhere that you can fuck up.

"Affirmative on ignition," Jim said.

And we slowed. And we waited. And then we were a thousand meters up, and then those numbers diminished, and I was mindful of the fact that unlike the Earth launch, which was noteworthy for the fact that I had felt like my bowels were going to betray me at any point, I felt nothing but a giddy, thrilling excitement on this end of the mission, as the numbers went down, and the thrumming of combustion slowed us still further, and then, before we knew it, there was a violent report, and the capsule struck something, struck ground, struck dust, volcanic rock, struck something cosmic, ancient, untouched.

We were on Mars. We were on Mars!

On schedule, the engines idled down, and the aerobrake assembly retracted, and a number of solar panels began unfolding themselves on the outside of the *Excelsior.* It was quiet. It was quiet except for Jim telling Houston, telling America, telling the world what it would not know for a good long while. "Landing as scheduled, Houston, and we didn't strike any boulders. We seem to be on very sturdy ground. Thanks very much for the coordinates."

We were on Mars.

"Everyone okay?" Jim called.

"First officer able and accounted for," I said.

Then there was an enfeebled but no less enthusiastic voice that called from down in the cargo bay, "Science officer okay, but he recommends against Mars landings with broken limbs. Not the most comfortable thing."

"José," Jim said, "you're a champ."

Protocol required a number of systems tests to certify that the capsule was not, for example, on fire, and also that the hull was intact, especially as the *Excelsior* was about to begin serving as our Mars base, at least until Steve and Abu, from the *Geronimo,* began erecting the additional base facility over by the reactor that, fully automated, had begun processing fuel on the surface about six months ago. Additionally, the *Pequod* was going to be in charge of the greenhouse-construction operation, another two or three kilometers distant. The *Geronimo* would be landing in the next six hours, and we accepted their congratulations on the new ham radio frequencies that were going to be our most reliable Mars-based communications system from now on, excepting the satellite above us that would make satellite phone communication possible once or twice a day.

We were on Mars! We had done the hard part! And the only thing left to do was go outside and investigate!

Jim and I got busy with the space suits down in the cargo bay. According to the thermometers we had on board, the outdoor temperature (at about 9:30 A.M., Martian time) was about −20 centigrade, though the sun was bright and the air a luminous pink. Everything that you have seen from all the rover missions and the flybys of the past thirty years is true. The soil is bright orange, and the rocks around which it blows are a deep gray. There's a lot of sulfur around, and some methane in the atmosphere, so the prediction is that Mars actually smells really horrible. We were glad to have helmets and respirators, because even if we were able to take off our gear (which we would be able to do for very brief spells in low elevation as the mission moved toward summer, and even then in danger of frostbite and hypothermia), it would probably smell a lot like the industrial parts of Omaha or Shanghai.

I haven't even mentioned the exhaustion of suddenly having weight again, right? After three months of weightlessness? It was a good thing that I weighed less than a famine victim here on Mars, because I don't know if my muscles could have taken much more than the forty or fifty pounds, roughly speaking, that I weighed on the Red Planet. I was wobbly, and I was hallucinating that every heavy piece of equipment that Jim and I had to put on would float, as it had for three months. José was probably the most likely to want weightlessness, to help with his leg. But at least he was still, with his new amnesiac personality, encouraging.

"This gear is like lead," I said to Jim.

Jim gave me the first sheepish smile of the Martian period of our friendship. "I guess this is how we get back in shape."

Still, we couldn't get the outerwear on fast enough. What is it that man loves about a wasteland, kids? What is it about a desolate and empty place that always looks to him like some large-scale merchandising operation? Why is it that nature so abhors a vacuum? My face was glued to the window, to every dune and declivity in the featureless track. As far as the eye could see was only about fifty or sixty kilometers on Mars, but in those sixty kilometers there was a lot of empty mileage. I couldn't wait to get out there; I couldn't wait to see it, to walk in it, to kneel in the emptiness, in the mystery, in the millennia of silence and howling gales that was Mars.

It was while José was helping us get the helmets on that Houston appealed to us by radio. It was unclear what was happening on the other end, because the transmission included no voices at all. The transmission resembled the interstellar background radio signals that I sometimes listened to on the journey here, as if I might be the first to hear the dots and dashes of beings signaling to us from the next galaxy over. But this wasn't static, this communication from the home planet. It was applause. It was some kind of sustained ovation for us, kids. It was only after a couple minutes of this applause that we finally heard a monotone voice, "*Excelsior,* you have realized our hopes and our dreams. Over."

Since training, that particular line was the signal for a fully scripted exchange, one that ended with my footsteps outside the capsule. Jim was meant to say something clever, along the lines of "Roger, Houston. We'll bring a little of Mars back for you, if you'll let us through customs," and Jim looked at the intercom for a long time. José too. The three of us stood there in silence, and I'd like to believe that our purpose was sort of unanimous, if not agreed upon expressly. We were about to go off the reservation. We were about to go native. In the short run, this meant only that Jim began to ignore the script, on which we had both been drilled back in the Everglades. He shut off the intercom. In the Everglades, it was our life, the script.

But it wasn't anymore. Even José knew that something had changed. The trip had changed us. But he didn't say anything, and I didn't say anything, and neither did Jim. He gestured at the air lock.

"We're going to go out for a bit. You okay for an hour or so?"

"I've got drill bits to inspect," José said.

"Maybe you want to check the ramps for the rover. See if all that stuff is working properly. We'll see you in a little while."

And then Jim reached for the air lock. The air lock swung back on its hydraulic hinges. And we walked through it, and he closed it behind us. Leaving just the one last hatch. Which I then opened myself.

I guess it is unlikely that you can experience a place you've never been as a *homecoming.* I guess that would be a sentimentality of some kind, and we are not fond of sentimentalities in the space program, only in its marketing. I never thought about Mars as a kid. Growing up, I thought about the things any kid would think about: sports, girls, gangster rap, video games, keeping out undocumented workers, E. coli in the food supply, violent uprisings in faraway places, the color wheel issued by the Department of Homeland Security. Mars was just not part of my landscape. I never dreamed of Mars. Who would?

So how then could I feel, as my first foot hit the first rung of the ladder from which I would descend onto the surface of that other planet, that I had somehow come home? What did it mean to come home, if home were a place with subzero temperatures year-round, very little water, very little oxygen, and in all likelihood, no significant life of any kind?

Nevertheless, this is what I felt, that this place, this wasteland, was the place that I was coming back to. My one genuine home. I suppose, as I climbed down yet another of the five rungs it would take me to get to the "flags and footprints" portion of the mission, that I did have a revelatory moment, and that the nature of this revelation was along the following lines: there is no *natural order,* if the *natural order* means the way things go on the home planet. The home planet is where things started. I'll grant this. But that does not necessarily constitute a natural order. The natural order is the wild, violent, unpredictable world of space, with its wormholes, dark matter, black holes, space-time curvature, and in this *natural order,* human ethics, puny human ethics, mean nothing. Human morality, confined to a minute portion of the universe, is statistically insignificant. I felt more comfortable in a landscape devoid of such niceties. Accordingly, I hopped down the last rung of the ladder and landed on a barren patch, with rocks surrounding me on all sides. I unfurled the flag, which, unlike on the moon, had no trouble blowing in the Martian breeze.

"Houston?" I said, opening the channel on the intercom, onto billions upon billions of desperate, squinting, diarrhetic, miserable, disenfranchised people clamoring for a better way of life. "Houston, it is a beautiful day in the neighborhood."

January 14, 2026

Ever since the landing, NASA has tried to impose order on the Martian base. The Martian base has resisted at every turn. The Martian base represents a truly new and truly different way of thinking about the inevitable human diaspora. As a result of this, kids, they have put an end to my diary, after the escalating complaints, and you are no longer receiving anything from me, not even the heavily edited posts that I had come to appreciate so, where my every negative thought (and I have a lot of negative thoughts) had been sanitized and replaced with bright, sparkly bulletins that did everything but shill for our myriad official corporate suppliers. Well, that diary is a thing of the past. And so I write these lines for history, kids, and for the idea that one day the truth will be known. I believe my writings will be read a thousand years from now, when human populations, with wildly varying customs and languages and belief systems, are spread far and wide, as the first theoretical writings to advocate for interplanetary philosophical positions, and so I am patient. If by the time you read these lines you are grandparents, so be it.

The *Geronimo* landed on schedule, only about fifteen kilometers from the reactor that they were intended to use as their base. And the *Pequod* landed six hours after that, finding a spot in the base of a crater where the air pressure was slightly higher and where they would be shielded from the worst of the local storms. We all got our ham radio sets working properly and were able to get in contact with one another quickly. Here we were!

The first project involved our driving all the plant life over to the greenhouse and beginning the process of vegetating the Mars colony. The guys from the *Geronimo* had fewer plants, because they were carrying a lot of liquid hydrogen for the reactor, but they brought what they had. As did we. We were to meet in the crater that afternoon. The *Excelsior* had been outfitted with a deluxe rover that was pressurized, so that this vehicle could serve as an additional cabin if others failed. Accordingly, it wasn't a problem for us to get to the greenhouse quickly. We had some fuel, and there were solar panels — the rover was designed to be able to travel a thousand kilometers or more on one tank of fuel. When we went over a hilltop, we marked this topographical wonder by bestowing upon it a solar-powered radio beacon. As though we could map every feature in this tiny triangle of the Mars colony.

It was about seven days in, therefore, before the entire Mars mission was in one spot, together. We had our portional moments of confraternity, and we engaged in our appointed tasks, of which much more below. But on the seventh day the Mars colony experienced itself as a community. This meeting was not to the liking of everyone. As you'll recall, Brandon Lepper had charges proffered against him by Laurie Corelli, leading to the daring midair prisoner exchange, when Debbie Quartz was lost. Still unanswered was the question of whether Debbie had somehow been forced into the heavens by Brandon. Meanwhile, none of the astronauts from the *Pequod* knew the entire story about

José Rodrigues and his injuries, except what they may have heard from Houston. And yet, as I have already implied, once the Mars colony began to experience itself as the future of humankind, rather than as some military-industrial corporate stunt, it became less and less important to us what Houston thought.

Upon arrival, Laurie invited us into the greenhouse, and José, without his crutches, managed to carry in some flats of plants. José was basically using a walking cast now, and, because of diminished gravity, was making fine progress. The guys from the *Geronimo* arrived soon after. At which point, at last, after more than three months, the eight of us were gathered around a table — seven men and one woman. It was Laurie who first spoke up.

Laurie said, "Requests from the menu?"

"I was thinking about having the Dover sole," Arnie said, with an ease that probably came from the fact that he was already her confederate, if not more.

"Dover sole!" I cried. "If only we were going to dig up Dover sole down there in the canyon. If only there were going to be fish in some of the dry ice."

"Atlantic salmon," said Jim. "Or bluefish. Or haddock. Do haddock still exist?"

Steve and Abu sat off to one side, looking as though they carried a dark burden. It was only when Abu volunteered to help me with some more botanical transplanting from the *Excelsior* that the tip of the iceberg drifted ominously into view. We both redonned our helmets, though probably if you ran fast enough to and from craft to base, you needn't worry unduly about the climate, or at least not about instant death from the 95 percent carbon dioxide and only 0.13 percent oxygen. The rover was only ten or fifteen yards from the greenhouse, but we wore our helmets, then set them aside and fell into a debrief.

"I don't want to sugarcoat it," he said. "We have a problem. With Brandon. We have a very, very serious problem."

Which somehow was exactly where we would come out in this particular conversation.

"And what kind of problem is that?"

"We never got comfortable with the guy, Jed, the whole rest of the trip out. In fact, Steve and I never allowed ourselves to go to sleep at the same time. I don't even know where to start. There's just some very strange stuff coming off him all the time. Makes you not want to trust him. At all. He ate food reserves and lied about it. He read our journals, our private mail, whenever he had the chance. He seemed to be taking what he called dietary supplements of some kind, probably more serious drugs, HGH in a base of pituitary enhancers or what have you. He had communications from Houston that no one else knew anything about. He made remarks about how certain people on the mission were definitely *expendable,* all of that, and that there was no way the return vehicle could fit eight of us, and it was never intended to."

I said, "I guess we know that when Laurie wanted him off the *Pequod* she wasn't *imagining* anything."

"Sexual coercion would probably be natural for him. I mean, maybe this all sounds like mild sociopathy. But I wouldn't want to rule out stuff like sadism and espionage and conspiracy. But the thing I should tell you, I guess, is that one of the people he seemed most convinced was expendable was José. He just wouldn't stop trash-talking."

"José?"

"Maybe it has to do with the alternate landing coordinates, the Valles Marineris; maybe there's some kind of objective that the science officers were meant to collaborate on. Brandon wants the entire project to himself. Or that's what I imagine I'm understanding from what he's been saying."

"José's just not going to be able to get very far, if Brandon comes after him."

"True. We're keeping an eye on Brandon for now. But I don't feel it's a guarantee that we can do that around the clock, now that we're not locked in the capsules, completely isolated from one another. What happens if he follows through on this stuff? We have no court in place to deal with violent crimes. I'd feel demoralized if I had to conclude that with only eight astronauts we've already managed to bring all our worst earthly problems with us. And here's an even worse thought: What if Debbie would still be alive somehow, if it weren't for him?"

We'd begun putting our helmets on again, so as to avoid being gone for too long. If I was vague about the conversation that came next, perhaps it was simply because I didn't know who to trust yet, not with the closely held pieces of the story. It seemed that trust, in fact, was one of the first casualties of Mars exploration.

"Abu, we just don't really know what it means to be so far from the home planet. We don't know yet what kinds of trouble long-term planetary exile can create. I feel like we're only beginning to understand."

"I was out there," Abu said. "I was on the space walk. I was there that day. There was something about it that was even worse than you think. From the beginning, when I got him into the *Geronimo,* he had this look in his eyes. A primal look, merciless even, like he was on the mission precisely *because* someone had to have no compassion of any kind. It occurred to me that maybe the personnel people wanted a guy like this. Maybe they had a reason."

"What are you trying to—"

"I'm just thinking aloud. Except I know I don't trust the guy. I guess what I'm saying is keep an eye on José. While you still can."

"Well, he's been behaving erratically since the orbital insertion. It's odd. He's lost his edge. But in a good way. I never used to like the guy."

We closed tight the doors on the rover. The vehicle was already dusty and orange. The tires were already caked with the thin topsoil of the Red Planet. The rover didn't go fast, and it wasn't pretty, but it was reliable. And it was ours. The only complicated part of it was the oxygen supply couplings and the tanks that we had to lug on the back in the course of a journey.

Once outdoors, I piled him down with genetically modified

wheat that one of the large corporations had been working on for the launch. It was meant to grow in extremely dry environments, in landscapes with lots of iron in the soil, and it had a very long growing season. Since we were here for the two warmest seasons (roughly six Earth months each), if we could get this stuff to grow in the mixture of nutrient-rich earth and the Martian topsoil we were going to start introducing into the greenhouse, then we could be harvesting the wheat for the better part of the year, which meant that we could make bread, that staple of all evolving human civilizations. Then we could leave the plants for whoever came next.

If anyone came next.

Abu carried the flats of wheat into the back of the greenhouse, and I followed with the soybean plants. We carted in the flats, and again I was impressed with the scale of Laurie and Arnie's botanical experiment. Most of the plants *were* still alive. In discrete biomes, sealed off with some plastic sheeting from the habitable living quarters, though some of the oxygen they were producing was, theoretically, being recirculated too, through the HVAC system.

Back in the habitable partition, an awkward silence had risen up and crested over the heads of the Mars mission astronauts. Apparently, there had been brief attempts to re-create an attitude of collegiality, but these attempts had not been terribly effective. Jim was bantering with Steve, and they were discussing issues relating to the reactor and whether the dust in the Martian air, through the agency of the winds, was clogging any of the turbines there. Steve was such an important member of the mission. He was sturdy, thoughtful, and totally humorless. If there was one astronaut who seemed entirely free of Planetary Exile Syndrome, it was Steve Watanabe. Though of course it was also possible that I just didn't know him yet, at least not the Martian Steve.

Once we returned, Laurie brought out the rehydrated meal packets, which we no longer had to serve in pouches, and this alone amounted to culinary liberation. Also, the food was piping hot, and we shared it in portions that were a bit less stingy than during the voyage from Earth. Arnie had also begun testing a regional delicacy, Martian salt, which could be easily mined from the surface of the planet. This we used as a seasoning at table.

"I precipitate it out during my geological tests," Arnie said, brandishing a rather provisional-looking vial fashioned from scrap metal. "As you know, the water that at one time covered portions of the planet, including, I think, the crater where we are located, was very brackish, like in your most redolent earthly tidal marsh. It makes for a rather smoky table salt."

José, who was lately mostly unaware of the conversation taking place around him, launched into his repast first, without waiting for Martian grace, a feature of our meals that Laurie had been proposing on a ship's log we'd all received on our clipboards: a gratitude for the fact we had now been here for a week, were moving toward self-sufficiency, and were less beholden to the pencil pushers in Houston than ever before. José's very simplicity, his guileless appetites, brightened the mood in the room.

"Oh man, Arnie," he said, "this salt is, well, out of this world."

"It isn't what you'd get back home."

"Sure it's sterile?" I asked, before upending the shaker on my own rehydrated chipped beef.

"We're talking about the uppermost six inches of topsoil," Arnie said. "There has been no Martian soil sample in the last twenty years that indicated biological compounds. It's totally safe. Besides, I cooked it some. I've been using it for three or four days."

We even, on the occasion of this first dinner together, harvested a tiny bit of lettuce from the greenhouse. It was the first fresh roughage that any of us had processed in many weeks.

Eventually, the conversation was bound to move in a more serious direction. It was Jim who suggested the topic. He was such a group leader. He was able to forge something from our disparate allegiances and talents so that we might proceed.

"Men and woman of the Mars colony," he therefore said. "It's our first night together, on the surface of this new human outpost, and so I do propose a toast."

Did I say that we were already trying to ferment beverages? I don't know about the rest of them, but I was eager, once we had touched down, to see if there were items that we could expose to our rather substantial and self-perpetuating colony of yeast, one of the very first Earth organisms to be introduced into the Martian wild (whether NASA wanted it or not). I sort of thought of myself as the Mars colony *sommelier,* and so that night I served up a little meadlike beverage that I had been working on in the privacy of the *Excelsior,* with some grain from the storeroom. I can't say that I had quite perfected it, but the other astronauts were willing to give it a try. Jim raised up a thimbleful of it in a beaker.

"What we did before," he started in, "is unimportant. How we conducted ourselves on the home planet is unimportant. Our age, our economic station, our beliefs, our gender, our sexuality: unimportant. Our past successes are as unimportant as our mistakes. What we did for the good of the Earth community is no longer as important as what we do for the Martian community. Our mission objectives are changed as of this moment. I would like to try to address our new objectives. As I see it, our mission intends the establishment of a planet free of internecine conflict, selfishness, depletion of natural resources, exploitation of labor. Here there are no laws but the laws of mutual respect and indebtedness. We trade with one another, we don't practice loans with interest, we don't recognize an institutionalized religion, excepting the religion of interplanetary exploration, nor do we require laws that regulate private conduct. Our common purpose should be the perpetuation of a new chapter of human history. We believe in the robust health of the Martian colony. And that's to say that the Red Planet is *ours!*"

We all raised up our mead, and we swallowed it down, and it tasted a little bit like the cleaning solution that we used for scouring some of the rover's engine parts. But it had a pretty good kick to it. I could feel, with the acetone bite in my stomach, that I wanted Jim Rose again, as I had done since our brief assignation.

Our love moved in me with ever-widening pulsations. In this instance, however, it was enough to watch him and to marvel at his political instincts.

"With that said," he went on, "I think it would be useful to try to come up with some ideas about how to use what we have here in the coming days. We have the ultralight aircraft, and we are here at the edge of the largest known canyon in the universe. Leaving aside, if we are able, NASA's expectations, the canyon is worth a look from a scientific perspective. It's also for us to wonder at. I'd like to entertain suggestions about how we might proceed."

There was silence for a moment. The clank of metal flatware on military mess kits. José's head came up from his chow long enough to add to the conversation. His was a non sequitur that I almost immediately wished had gone unreported.

"Hey, Arnie, I'm really feeling like some of my memory is starting to come back."

"That's great, José," Arnie said. "I'm sure you can count on more improvement. And what are you remembering so far? Short-term memories? Are you able to recall distant events from your childhood?"

"I remember the Ownership Projects in Las Vegas," José said. "I remember when there was the Compulsive Gamblers and Games of Chance Act — that's what it was called, right? For a while after, the city government constructed those buildings for people who had lost everything. Anyone remember all this?" The other seven astronauts were all but silenced at the wincing nostalgia of José's reverie. Perhaps he had, once upon a time, sought to conceal the modesty of his origins beneath a haze of acronyms, but not any longer, kids. "You know, my dad was a naturalized citizen, and once he got his papers, he went into the casinos and he didn't come out. Not for many, many years. I remember when the authorities seized the house that we'd bought. My mother bought it with the money she made working at the Pompeii. There was a foreclosure date, and an eviction date, and then we just had to leave. Anyhow, once we were bounced out, as I'm recalling it, we got a small apartment in the Ownership Projects, which we shared with my uncle and his family. It should have been stifling, and maybe it really was, but the thing I remember is how the electricity was so bad out there that you really could see the stars, from right outside the projects. My cousin, the one who later was shot, we used to lie out on the lawn at night—it was just a patch of loose rock—and look at the stars. And I used to say to him, 'Not a day past eighteen.' That was our pact, that we wouldn't stay in those Ownership Projects a day past our eighteenth birthdays. The place I aimed to go, and this is what I told him, was to those stars."

"That's a beautiful story," Arnie said, patient and gentle. "Do you have any more-recent memories?"

This was a leading question. It probed at the mystery of NASA's plans. The government's plans. There were, and had always been, things we didn't know, and this leading question intimated as much.

"In fact, I had this whole long memory yesterday," José said. "But I'm not sure if it was a genuine memory. It might have been a daydream or something. It was while I was still in bed. Anyone else here found that their dreams on Mars are a whole heck of a lot more vivid? Anyway, I remember that there was some kind of asteroid or something, before I was born, and this asteroid had plunged onto the Antarctic shelf, and the guys back at NASA were always obsessed with it. In fact, at one point someone let me look at this microscope and see what they had found in the asteroid, and what they had found was this frozen extraterrestrial bacteria. They were really sure that the asteroid was from Mars, was maybe even a part of Mars that had been blasted from the planet somehow. From some asteroid strike. This stuff, the NASA scientists said, was liable to still be on Mars, this bacteria. They were sure about this, in my daydream, and they were beginning to do some experiments to see what kind of properties the bacteria had."

Now, I know that I personally had set down my flatware and was waiting expectantly, hoping that José's faulty memory would not, for example, reconstruct that he had once refused to tell me anything about the fateful bacteria, the bacteria that he had so kept to himself for the first part of the mission. Perhaps predictably, this was the moment when Brandon Lepper, sullen and uncommunicative throughout the course of the meal, chose to interrupt José. There was an almost palpable sense of dread as this miscreant, over whom a cloud of suspicion hovered, spoke.

"Listen, buddy," he said with a wheedling familiarity, "I don't know if you are alert to what you're saying, and I'm guessing you're not, but this is classified-type stuff. Most of the people at this table don't need to know."

José looked up with a naive astonishment. Yes, it was evident that the bacteria, whatever else it was, was one of the mnemonic keys to his recovery from concussion. And it was evident who would wish to stanch the flow of José as he was now expressing himself. Arnie leaped into the awkward silence that followed, to defend José.

"Maybe it's a reasonable treatment plan for José to try to think through all the memories, through every precious one of them, Brandon, if you don't mind."

"I do mind," he said. "And you can stay the hell out of it."

"I have no intention of staying out of it, and I'm not threatened by your tone, if that's what you're after. You may have threatened some other people around here, but you will not do so again. Not while I'm around."

"Lepper," Jim Rose said, throwing down his own flatware, rising up from the meager folding chair so that it toppled behind him, "you're way out of line."

"I am? Says who exactly? I don't know about the rest of you," Brandon said, "but I was recruited to carry out a mission. Hundreds if not thousands of global citizens would have given everything they had in order to fly this mission. I gave everything I had. Therefore, I'm still intending to do the job that I was hired to do. Because I believe in duty."

"And what," I tried to break in, "is the nature of your—"

"I don't have to listen to this," Brandon continued. "I don't have to have my character called into question by a bunch of edenic nitwits who want to drink wine and watch the plants grow. A couple of weeks, you'll all be dead from exposure, and then you'll all get your memorial broadcasts back home, where they interview your neighbors and talk about how poignant it was that you saved coyotes from the brink of extinction. Well, fuck yourselves, I say. I came to open the mystery of this place, this world, to take it back home where something can be done with it, something practical, for our national economy."

His plate, when he flung it, with its rehydrated chipped beef, clattered across the greenhouse, colliding at last with the lightweight petrochemical sheeting that sealed off the place. This in itself was dangerous, because had he managed to puncture the sealant or the construction material, we were all going to start choking pronto, not to mention it was going to get pretty cold. Before any of us could take note of the situation, however, he was gone, having commandeered the helmet nearest, from the row of dusty gray globes. In the embarrassed gulp that followed, it was Steve who said:

"Uh, the rover!"

By the time we understood the perfidy of Brandon's intentions, we could hear the grinding of its ignition. Jim and I raced out, into the howling Martian wastes, and watched as the rover bounced off in the direction of nothing that we knew.

January 28, 2026

Let me tell you a few things about the canyon. The Valles Marineris. The great dark place. The planetary bifurcation. Named after the unmanned orbiter that first discovered it more than fifty years ago now, and composed not just of the one fissure, four thousand kilometers long, but also of a whole system of parallel striations and offshoots. So deep that you could stack that famous canyon from Arizona in it a couple of times over. Cliff walls that exceed 14,000 feet running hundreds of miles. Imagine walking up to the edge of a 14,000-foot cliff wall and looking down! And then seeing that the wall extends as far along as you are able to see. Meanwhile, the Valles Marineris is so far across that if you accidentally landed in it, somehow, you could make the mistake of thinking you were on the legitimate surface of the planet, at least until you attempted to hike out of your position and saw, on the horizon, that immensity, that other towering basaltic wall, overlaid with the silent and magisterial geological ages.

Basaltic, you see, because the Valles Marineris is located in the same general vicinity as a great number of volcanoes. This being just east of the Martian region known as Tharsis. Although the original force that created the canyon was tectonic plate shifting of some kind, it's also true that something flowed through here, kids, some portion of which was volcanic lava from nearby eruptions. Later, however, there was probably water here too, otherwise how to explain all the collapses. There have been a lot of collapses. They are not infrequent. There are parts of the canyon that, according to the unmanned missions, look like ancient Roman amphitheaters, or those graduated stadia that they use for X-treme lacrosse tourneys, from where portions of the walls, all 14,000 feet of them, came tumbling down.

Why is the Valles Marineris so important? you ask. This is the question we have been asking ourselves, ever since the advent of the mysterious bacteria became so vital to the Mars colony, if only because of its recurrence as poetical figure in all our conversations. Originally, as you know, we were scheduled to put down at the South Pole, where, mixed with the liquid dry ice, there would have been plentiful water by Martian standards. Or that, at any rate, is the theory. Instead, we have been attempting the impossible, using makeshift drilling mechanisms to search beneath the topsoil for ice that we can then heat with the by-products of nuclear fission at our reactor. So far it makes for nonpotable water, and there's not a lot of it, and there's a little bit of a worry that we're going to plunder what's nearby and then we'll be back to reusing, relentlessly, the water given us for the capsules, which we've been heating and reheating, and which is now admixed with all kinds of additives that I for one don't want to know about. Uremic acid crystals, e.g.

Why Valles Marineris, indeed. There have been many papers written about the canyon, about the importance of it. I am in a position to spill the beans on certain still-classified documents along these lines, and as you probably suspect, the fact is that the canyon, because of its substantial air pressure, by comparison, and because of its access to a much earlier period of Martian geological history, is likely to harbor frozen water of an early Martian vintage, and, just perhaps, some of this water, in turn, is home to the early Martian life-forms that undoubtedly once lived in it.

The meteorite that José was alluding to, as I have mentioned earlier, is called by the rather unpoetical name of ALH 84001, kids, and it's 4.5 million years old, and the deepest layers of the Valles Marineris are, apparently, almost precisely its coeval, and perhaps this is how it came to be that scientists wanted to look in the canyon for sister bacteria, and thus, apparently, the reason for our change of venue.

The morning after Brandon stole the rover (and we had to drive back to the *Excelsior* in one of the open Martian cargo transport vehicles, on our ventilators, in not a little bit of danger of freezing solid, since the sun was going over the horizon), I was shaken awake, on my modest bed, by José. He had a kind of mad look in his eye. He was chewing on a piece of chocolate that I had been saving for weeks. Which was irritating. I could hardly complain about the chocolate, when he was so excited about whatever he was to tell me.

"*M. thanatobacillus. M. thanatobacillus!*"

"It'd be less of a mouthful if you weren't eating my chocolate bar. Those chocolate bars have a three-year shelf life."

"The bacteria. That's the name of the bacteria."

"The bacteria from the meteorite?"

Jim followed him in, carrying a mug of battery acid coffee, and soon the three of us were sitting there, like a Martian coffee klatch. The sun shone in the salmon-fishery sky. All was quiet, except for the hum of capsule life support.

"It's a gram-positive bacteria, it has flagella, it has an S-layer, and it can consume phenols, so it's good for industrial accidents. And it has characteristics almost exactly like Earth bacteria."

To Jim, I said, "Are you following?"

"His memory," Jim said. Jim's beard was now moving toward an Old Testament type of tonsorial styling, and he stroked it meditatively when considering the larger implications. You had to try to read into the few abbreviated remarks that did get uttered.

"Are you implying that we somehow exported our own bacteria to Mars?" I asked.

"Or bacteria came from somewhere else and was exported to both Earth and Mars through some interstellar transaction," Jim said.

"And you remembered all this?" I said to José.

"And my Social Security number, from back when I was a kid. Not that it will come in handy now."

"Nope."

I don't need to go into what Social Security was. Anyway, Social Security is irrelevant to the further revelations of this conversation, because once it was established that José could remember a few things from his past, such as the condition of his financial accounts, the web code of his long-term debt-repayment plan, and the name of his pet snake from childhood, he parted with the following scrap of info from his level-five mission briefings:

"The thing about the *M. thanatobacillus* is that, like some other gram-positive types of bacteria, it causes illness. Serious illness. I guess the closest relative would be *B. anthracis,* or maybe the resistant *S. aureus,* except that *M. thanatobacillus* goes into a kind of feeding frenzy in the presence of certain carbon-based life-forms, at least when it's heated to the right temperature. A temperature that's rare on Mars. Basically, it causes bodies to sort of...disassemble."

"What?" I said.

"It's not an airborne type of infection because it doesn't do well when it's not really hot, and it stays dormant in the hundred-degree-below-zero-type temperature range. But in a tropical or semitropical environment, like the one you might get in a period of generalized greenhouse emissions, it thrives. It eats its way through bodies."

Jim, tugging on his beard: "The flesh-eating germ."

José: "Maybe a little bit worse."

Jim said, "You're saying that you were briefed by NASA about coming to Mars in order to harvest cultures of a bacterium that is so dangerous to human life that it causes human bodies to break down upon contact? What would we be using that for?"

"We'd be using it on our military enemies."

"It was a rhetorical question."

"I'm guessing," I said, "that you weren't informed about which enemies they were talking about."

José said, "The critical phase doesn't happen immediately, the disassembling part. It takes a little while. The gestation of a full-blown infection is several weeks. You have to come in bodily contact with an infected party. It's not airborne like with *B. anthracis,* which I guess suggests it can't be aerosolized, although I don't really know if they tried that yet."

"Where did they do all this research?"

"I know they let the bacteria infect a sheep farm. They had a population of sheep in a lab they were borrowing from the Kiwis, I think. South Island of New Zealand. It was closer to McMurdo that way, and they could transport the bacteria on military aircraft more easily, while it was in its BDP. They could fly it into the PST bases, Los Angeles, Phoenix, places like that. So they introduced the germ into this sheep population near Dunedin, and the results were grisly. Even though the whole project is need to know, like Brandon was saying. They were going to great lengths to impress on us the kind of precautions we needed to take while mining."

"And this is why we're going into the canyon."

"This is why Brandon may be heading there already," Jim said.

How did Jim know this? That Brandon was already there? Well, there were homing beacons on the rover, because of the danger of getting lost on Mars (no magnetic field!). It was therefore not hard to track the movement of our lost vehicle. Brandon had likely attempted to strip off the beacons without success. Or perhaps he was simply unconcerned about our tracking him. Brandon needed to drive about four hundred kilometers from our landing zone in the Chryse Planitia to get to the easternmost end of the Valles Marineris, where the evidence of water leaving the canyon was plain for all to see. In fact, he had already taken a couple of exploratory missions to the edge of the canyon, where he had no doubt beheld the 14,000-foot cliff face that I was explaining about earlier. In each of his exploratory maneuvers, Brandon had ventured farther west, according to Jim, coming back at night to his base camp to recharge the rover. He was camping near the remains of an old unmanned mission — there were almost twenty junk sites on Mars, and no shortage of them in Chryse — and he was using some of its solar panels and its old computing equipment while trying to stay warm during the Martian nights.

What to do about all of this? What to do about Brandon, and how seriously should we take the search for *M. thanatobacillus*? If he did manage to locate a sample of the bacteria, he would then be faced with the problem of returning with it to Earth. With seven of us resisting him, he was going to have a hard time. He couldn't just walk off with the Earth Return Vehicle and leave the rest of us here.

"The risk of infection is certainly unappetizing," Jim said.

"I think NASA, at the service of the DOD, felt a number of us could be expended in the effort to procure and incubate the bacteria. This loss would be offset by the military application back on Earth," José said. "And the public-relations part of it would be easy to finesse. Since this is a dangerous mission."

"That's just what Brandon said on the *Geronimo,* according to Abu," I said. "And I hate to break the news to you, but he specifically threatened you, José. He was already working hard to cover up the whole story of the military acquisition of the bacteria."

José attempted to seem unperturbed.

"I say let's fly in there and be ready when he comes. We can take the ultralight, launch it off the cliff wall, which may be why we carried it all this way anyhow. I mean, I don't have any FAA certification or anything. You guys will have to do the flying. But, come on, I smashed my skull on the fuselage of the damn thing! I feel like I want to get every bit of value out of the ultralight before we leave it sticking out of a dune somewhere."

"What do we do with him when we find him?" I asked.

"We leave him," Jim said.

We didn't give the implications of it a second thought, I'm ashamed to say. The three of us agreed. The Mars colony would do what human beings had done for the entirety of their species on the home planet, sacrifice one another in the pursuit of public safety, that lofty goal. We obviously felt we had no choice. But this is what the human animal and his primate forebears have always done. Beat on chest! Thump the forest floor with stick! Grunt threateningly, and if the interloper does not desist from his attempts to seize your local tree canopy, tear the interloper limb from limb and leave the body parts, and especially the entrails, in obvious places as a lesson. All wars are territorial wars; remember this, no matter what anyone tells you.

When we had conceived of our deadly purpose, we returned to our various *Excelsior* responsibilities in silence.

This all reminds me that I forgot to give you the really delightful news here on the Mars colony, or at least the news that is potentially delightful, and that is that we have our first pregnancy! Don't you think that's amazing! Apparently, if you count backward on your fingers, you will find that once Brandon was evacuated from the *Pequod*, Laurie and Arnie, during the period when Laurie was recovering from the unwarranted assault, must have found time to take comfort in each other's loving arms.

It was mission protocol that the astronauts were to avoid having relations with one another, and for this reason NASA specifically refused to stock the mission with birth control pills, condoms, et cetera. This also sat well with the religiously minded congressional legislators who had signed off on the Mars mission annually, for about ten years, until NASA had amassed enough funds ($400 billion) to send us astronauts into flight. Some of these congressional lifers didn't even believe that Mars existed. The fact that we were chaste, spiritually fit, and abstinent from vice made the financing more palatable.

Laurie told me, when we talked about it later, that they tried to practice the rhythm method for a few weeks. But after a point they realized there had been *mistakes*. Here were the questions I wanted to ask. I wanted to ask Laurie what she thought about the fact that Arnie was married, and that his wife was actually a NASA employee (his wife was in public relations), and he had the two kids, and she had the autistic son, the teenager, the one to whom she wanted to send photos of the Olympus Mons, and I wanted to ask if she thought twice before doing it, or if she just went ahead and did what she did, fell into his arms, and you know the two of them seemed so well-adjusted, so levelheaded, so able to adapt, but then they did what they did, and you never heard Arnie talk about his kids, and what were those kids thinking now, and when he posted things on the web (always routing the request through my office, at least in the early days of the Mars colony), they were always about geological stuff, and these posts had a lot of Latin names in them, and then maybe there would be one stray remark about the poetry of our new home, "Harvesting rock samples on the plain called Chryse Planitia, I stopped one morning to admire the graceful transit of the planet's two moons," and it didn't say "and that night I had wild kinky sex with my pregnant colleague among the plants of the greenhouse," but the scientific method in

Arnie's case was always a screen for whatever else was going on; he used the scientific method as if it were some kind of lead shield, as if it were an ideological lead shield, a religion, a holier-than-thou religion, and Laurie was no better; she sent notes back to her son, but they got more and more infrequent, and they spoke of the all-consuming nature of her job, and she never once mentioned *interplanetary disinhibitory disorder.* What kind of remorse did she have afterward, if any? Was she a person who felt remorse? And in her opinion, was remorse possible with *interplanetary disinhibitory disorder?* Was it all glorious and moist and proto-human for them? And what did she think about having a baby on the Red Planet? Was it a convenience that her obstetrician was also the father of the child? And was she worried about delivery? Did she believe we had sufficient anesthetic to make delivery pain free? And if what they had done they had done in an inhuman way, in a way that was careless about human things and that papered over this inhumanity with professionalism and the scientific method, can anyone really be surprised?

Laurie wanted to have the child naturally, she told me, before I even had a chance to ask her any of the questions I've just posed. The first child she'd had in the hospital, and it was a long, complicated labor, occiput posterior, with a C-section at the end, and she was a little angry about the hospital treatment she had received. In this case, despite the hurdles involved, she was thinking *bathtub.* It was better, you know, for the child to be expelled into water. Everyone felt great for Laurie, or they tried to, because it was good for Mars, and Steve drew a digital image of flowers, which he sent to her via what we referred to as the Martian Pony Express: radio messages that went back to Earth, to our NASA e-mail accounts, which we then accessed later with the usual delay. Not the best way to get in touch, the Martian equivalent of snail mail, but polite and effective in this case. Steve was happy for her; Abu was happy for her. José was happy for her. We could only hope, in the unlikely event that we were *never* going to get off the planet, that she was going to have a daughter, just to keep the genetic stock heterogenous. Wouldn't want the early Martians to be noteworthy for insufficient genetic diversity.

Jim and I were in the habit of taking the occasional afternoon constitutional, and after we finished wheeling the ultralight out of the *Excelsior,* and setting it up at a suitable distance from the encampment, we made for the lip of some distant barren sands. It was here that the two of us attempted to solve some of the problems in our own little world, the world of the *Excelsior.* If the wind was not blowing terribly, we could just follow our footsteps back, because footsteps were the exception rather than the rule here, and anyway there was the American flag, which had been hoisted on that first day and was still flying, only slightly tattered from the velocity at which the winds blew in this desolate place. We used it as a homing beacon.

"Jim," I said.

"Don't," said he.

With helmets on. Via short-range walkie-talkie.

"I have to."

"You do not."

"I have to."

"I beg of you."

"Please," I said. And then the words were out of my mouth, muffled only slightly by our Martian space suits. "Do you never think of me?"

"I wish there were some days when I didn't have to."

"You know what I'm getting at." I gestured to the east, where Phobos was beginning her transit. "What is this place, Jim, but the place of loneliness? What am I meant to feel here besides loneliness? There's nothing here! Anything we make here, we make ourselves. There's nothing that we haven't made, or carried here, and there's nothing special that we're going to make for a generation. It's a landscape of scarcity. Paucity. Maybe I'm here because I didn't live up to my potential back on the home planet, Jim, I'll admit it. Maybe that is something I can do for humankind. I can come to one of the many planets that God evidently didn't finish decorating, and I can work here, carve something out of the splendid barrenness. But does that mean that I have to give up on love? Jim? What did the heavy heart of planetary exile teach me? What has it taught you? Does it teach us to give up *wanting?* Does it teach you that a man is not a man? Or does it teach you that you are what you long for, no matter what the essence of that longing is, and that the constraints the home planet imposes on longing are not written in nature? I felt something back there, in the void between the planets, and it was like the icy exterior of my failed marriage and my desperation back on Earth were melting off of me, and I felt suddenly alive, however clumsy and awkward the whole thing was. Do you really mean to make out like it never happened at all, Jim? Can you really do that? Would you leave a man shivering in the night, and not even once try to beat back the subspace emanations of loneliness?"

"Enough!" Jim shouted, and I could see the fog in his helmet from the discomfort of it all. He grabbed me by the shoulder, and there we stood, far from home, in a place where, if we died, and it was reasonable to suppose we might, it could be decades before they found our skeletons. At last, Jim continued: "You don't know what goes on in here, Jed! You don't know what kinds of anguish I feel here. A man's woe is his own even when he puts it into inadequate words. What happened up there, that night, well, it changed me. But not in the best ways. I feel like I'm breaking apart, because of it all. I feel like I can't look at myself in the mirror and be sure that I'll recognize the face that looks back at me. Every day I get a message from my kids, my boys and my little girl, I feel some stirring of such confusion in myself that I...I don't know if I can...withstand this, Jed, this interplanetary me. My older boys got into a fight at the ice hockey rink yesterday. They didn't start it, but they had to finish it, and they administered some exemplary kind of knockout blow to the attacker, and each of them was bloodied by the combat. I'm proud as hell of them. But would they be proud of what their father has done? Their father the first gay captain in space? Is what he's done good for them, good for the home planet?

They were the ones who suggested I come here. I did it to try to put the loss of their mother to rest. Did I do the right thing? Is this the right place for the likes of me? NASA can't get ahold of us more than one day out of seven now, and we have begun forging a colony of our own. Without them. A good thing? Or a bad thing? Faced with these uncertainties, faced with the frailty of the Mars colony, Jed, what do I do about the carnal fire I feel when I think about you? You, Jed Richards. Should I just chase you around in the capsule, grab-assing, when every one of us is in danger of getting scurvy starting sometime next month when the vitamin C capsules run out? Will I still look attractive to you when my teeth start dropping out?

"Every time I have a randy thought, every time I feel that tug, I feel like I'm defaulting on my leadership responsibilities, I feel like I'm thinking only of myself, when I have so much else to think about. Do I have room in my heart for the kind of outlandish behavior we undertook up there, or is that just part of space itself, part of the voyage, not part of life here among the desperate few—"

And then, while he was in the middle of the thought, he tore himself from me violently, and standing some feet away, he flung off his helmet, and I heard the hiss of oxygen, and then there was a groan of such mortal intensity that I wondered if he didn't rip himself apart from the inside as he did it, whether to wrestle me to the ground or to embrace me I didn't know, not at first, but I cried out to tell him *not* to run that terrible risk. Still, there was no choice but to do the same, to remove my helmet. There we were, two oxygen-deprived, frostbitten men who loved each other. Two men who had been driven as far from the dictates of heterosexual civilization as anyone ever had been. All that needed to be done was to accept where we were and what we had between us. Here was my lover on his knees in the Martian desert, clutching my leg and sobbing, driven from all earthly human civilization. The crown so heavy on his fevered brow.

He gasped, "I have lost everything!"

"It's not so," I whispered, faint of breath. "We don't ever have to be together again, if only I can know that you care. It's enough, Jim. If I just know that we're in this together, and that I'm not dreaming about what happened. That's enough. What I want is to feel like I have given myself to something or someone of substance. We can do this together. We can do it."

He collapsed onto his backside. And as if it would somehow convince him of the seriousness of the situation, he grabbed a fistful of Martian topsoil and watched the orange dust blow free of his glove. Then I helped him to his feet. And then, because we were already in danger from exposure and hypoxia, we put back on the helmets and trudged homeward.

February 11, 2026

The following dialogue has been taking place for ten days or so. On the bulletin board application on our clipboards. I have vacillated about uploading the file because of how incomplete the exchange is, but ultimately, I have decided that it's a good example of the way life is lived on the Mars colony, as well as being an interesting document of the times, and so I include it today.

GingerSnap@sinisterteen.com: Dad, I have a little time cuz the homework is done. I had to do a report on women in politics over the last hundred years. Women are making all these great strides because there are more of them in congress and stuff, but I think maybe some of them are making strides if they *don't* go into politics. I mean, why would you bother? So, anyway, what's up on Mars?

RichardsJ@marsmission.us.gov: Darling. Just seeing your handle on the computer log makes me want to cry. There's so much back home I feel like I'm missing. Maybe that's a defining feature of my time on Mars. Mars is where you go to miss out on things.

GingerSnap@sinisterteen.com: You're not missing much at all!
A guy got killed playing X-treme lacrosse last night. A big head
injury. And a governor of somewhere resigned after it came out
he was trafficking in sex slaves. Someone tried to flatten Armenia
with bombs last week. Can't remember who.

RichardsJ@marsmission.us.gov: It's you who I'm missing. I
want to know everything. So tell me how much you've grown,
what clothes you're wearing. What the latest fashions are. What
young people do about skin blemishes. And can you catalogue
some of the slang for me?

GingerSnap@sinisterteen.com: I think I'm the same size. I'm
hoping that I kind of develop at least *some* boobs, you know? I
mean, I don't care if I have big gigantic breasts or anything. But
at least some. By the way, I am kind of thinking that I might get
nipple rings, which is maybe too much information. Mom says no.
People are getting nipple rings that glow pale blue. If I pay with
my own money from the job, she can't complain.

RichardsJ@marsmission.us.gov: What job?

GingerSnap@sinisterteen.com: Concessions at the gator refuge.
I sit at this little booth. I watch when the little kids get this light
in their eyes and come running over to the gift shop. I don't understand why kids almost always want to see the toy animal as
much as the real animal. Anyway, I get a lot of reading done at
work. Space travel books. That's what I like. By the way. The cool
expression is "exploding viscera."

RichardsJ@marsmission.us.gov: Space travel books?

GingerSnap@sinisterteen.com: The kind where people sail out
into space and never look back. Some of them are about Mars, I
guess. But Mars, to me, it kind of feels like going to Greenland,
or something. It's not so strange and unusual, because Mars is actually very close. And you're there. I'm more interested in speed-
of-light type things.

RichardsJ@marsmission.us.gov: I could give you some recommendations. And I could tell you some more about what it's like
traveling in space. Do you want to know more about this? It's

like being stuck in the trunk of a Cadillac on your way to being rubbed out. The mobster drives you around for months. And you feel like you're going to throw up or dump in your pants.

GingerSnap@sinisterteen.com: Thanks for sharing! I go to the observatory, you know, at the university, and also NASA lets me come down there pretty often and I go to the control room. Maybe once a week, even tho it's a longish drive. I look at the surface of the planet, and I look at the pictures everyone has taken. Then I feel a little less worried. Hey, what happened to your blog anyway?

RichardsJ@marsmission.us.gov: I'm writing this sentence at 4:00 A.M., my time, honey. I have the alarm working so anytime there's a communication on the computer log, it toggles this strobe light, and then I wake up to write you and hopefully I don't bother the others. I don't want to miss a chance. By the way, we're doing fine. The biggest danger is boredom. When someone drills into a rock and finds something besides lava, that's a big day. Half the time we don't know what we're finding until we hear back from NASA. As you can imagine, we're not always first to hear. Many times, I've had to learn about us by reading the digest of the NASA website, which they send along in the morning mail. Abu and Steve, for example, from the *Geronimo,* have apparently found another good way to create oxygen as a by-product of chemical reactions they're doing with the reactor. This is good news for us, because the air is thin, and we don't have a limitless supply of the stuff.

GingerSnap@sinisterteen.com: Dad, I guess I did want to ask you about things I heard, because I guess people have been saying some things, and I don't know what's true.

RichardsJ@marsmission.us.gov: Like what? What are people saying?

GingerSnap@sinisterteen.com: Some people were saying that NASA can't control the Mars mission. You guys aren't doing what you're supposed to be doing, and they don't know if you're ever going to come back.

RichardsJ@marsmission.us.gov: Who said that? Who told you that?

GingerSnap@sinisterteen.com: One of the other kids.

RichardsJ@marsmission.us.gov: Which one?

GingerSnap@sinisterteen.com: I guess he's Debbie's nephew or something. I've been calling him up some, trying to help him feel better about what happened, you know?

RichardsJ@marsmission.us.gov: Listen, Ginger, the thing I *can* tell you is that Mars is *not* just a distant outpost of Earth. It's not just a rock that Earth is going to annex or that the NAFTA countries are going to annex. It's not like if they annex it they'll send a bunch of construction guys out (and a few hookers), and in eighteen months there will be golf courses. It's not like that. Once you get here, once you go through the long journey, and you go through the experience of being separated from the home planet, you are *changed,* and you feel different. You feel, well, I guess you feel a little more free. What you find is that the freedom of this place, the blankness of this place, the clean slate of it, well, that's what makes you feel differently. You feel like you are starting something new. And you feel that everything old and worn was kind of a mistake, and that if you have a chance to be part of what's new, the society that is adapted to this place, to the severity of this place, then you don't need all the mistakes of the past, the mistaken ways of doing things.

Let me put it another way. You know when you have a houseplant, a spider plant, let's say, like that time we brought your spider plant from Michigan to Florida? Remember that the spider plant seemed to change shape a lot when it got to Florida? The leaves seemed denser, and it was sending off more shoots than before? That means that the spider plant is not the same as it was in Michigan. What it was in Michigan was a plant specifically adapted to that climate (and incidentally we *did* bring a spider plant to Mars, because they wanted to see how a common houseplant would do here). Now your spider plant is a Floridian spider plant, and even if it is not native to that place, it has adapted to the quality of light and water.

The same kind of thing is true of the human body after months of weightlessness. It's different on Mars. But so is the human spirit. If I can use that term. So is human society, in fact, which is nothing more than a conglomeration of human psychologies. This doesn't mean we have "gone native," or have become "uncontrollable" and are running around in Martian loincloths. But, Ginger, when you start really experiencing life out in the universe, beyond the home planet, it's life full of unpredictability, space-time curvature, and all of that. The reliable old truths about who humans are, and their relations to their bodies, these things become much more convoluted.

But I'm still your dad, and I still love you, and I miss you, and I'm not going to stay here on Mars forever, if staying here means I don't get to see what new ghastly piercing you have perpetrated upon your body. However, it's almost Martian dawn, and my pet moon, Phobos, is going over the lip of the horizon, and I better get some sleep if I'm going to have the energy to test the ultralight.

In the meantime, despite the great work Steve and Abu did extracting oxygen from the propellant stockpile, Steve has sunk into what Arnie is describing as a very serious clinical funk. I suppose I don't trust the prevailing terminologies exactly, because they seem earthbound to me. Everyone here, to some degree, is struggling with feelings of misery about our lot. Abu has found that there's some kind of rubbery silicone that is being produced as a by-product of the reactor and the propellant, and when he was through trucking spent fuel rods over to the fissure where we're consigning them, he started trying to use the silicone goo to make Martian sculpture out there by the waste repository. Since then he's spent a fair amount of time out in the desert, alone, erecting an army of these skinny, gooey-looking guys, as if to populate what is so unpopulated.

Maybe because Abu has become busy and, perhaps, a little tired of his suite mate, or more likely because his son, back on Earth, has had a bad reaction to a mild case of flesh-eating streptococcus, Steve just went into a serious tailspin. You'll recall that this son had strep throat early in the mission, which resulted in some bad scarring and ongoing circulatory problems, and then a stint in the clinic resulted in an opportunistic germ. Apparently the boy infected a nurse, who didn't have quite as easy a time. It's really too unpleasant to go into. Steve obviously took it extremely hard that he wasn't at home during this emergency. Arnie ordered him to sit under the sunlamps by the reactor, and to double the dose of daily SSRIs he's taking in his fluids. (In fact, Arnie recommended this to everyone.) I don't know how Jim felt about it, but the idea that the guys from the *Geronimo* weren't doing well was, for me, a bad sign about our progress.

Similarly, Jim was spending a lot of time watching the rover on the radar screen. He honestly couldn't figure out why Brandon hadn't yet moved into the easternmost Valles Marineris. We'd tracked his movement over a few days, and we decided that maybe Brandon was just *afraid* to go to the canyon by himself, or perhaps had some reasonable hesitations about his project, what with the danger of wall collapses, avalanches, not to mention *M. thanatobacillus* itself. Or perhaps, Jim hypothesized to me and José, Brandon intended to remain within striking distance of the *Excelsior.* We had protective gear in our cargo bay. We had the ultralight. We had, via José, instructions on how to harvest the material. We had the best uplink with NASA. Jim felt we needed to keep a close watch on the encampment and its equipment. He radioed to the greenhouse and the reactor station and told them, as well, to lock everything down.

The situation was made even more complicated by the sudden presence in the Tharsis region of a small dust storm. Now, I think I have explained a bit about Martian dust storms. For example, it's a lot worse trying to take off or land aircraft in them, and that was why our government launched various unmanned explorers over the years. Often, the explorers orbited the planet for months, waiting for the sandstorm season to come to an end.

The storms have been hard to photograph, because hunks of rock blowing around are inimical to photosensitive equipment—no matter how compact and solid-state. In fact, our own mission was designed to avoid the worst of the sandstorms that usually occur in Martian autumn. We are supposed to be gone by then. Spring, however, since it is a season with much variation in temperature, can spawn some activity. Which is to say that Mars has weather just like Earth. As a result, we had an idea what we were in for when the sun rose one morning sheathed in a brown-and-orange mist.

The worst of it are the so-called dust devils. It's not just that the wind whips up, and a lot of Martian detritus blows around, but you also get these tornadoes, with the traditional funnel clouds careening wildly across the Martian wastes, occasionally picking up heavier material, in just the way an earthly tornado would. We have seen from our few orbiting satellites that these dust devils sometimes transport old human space junk and deposit it hundreds of miles away. And you never know exactly which direction the funnel is going to go, either. It bloweth where it listeth.

I told José that we were going to have to get everything that was outside, the laundry line, some of the machine tools, even the ultralight, back into the *Excelsior,* and then we were going to have to drive over to the greenhouse, to help Laurie and Arnie reinforce the polymer exterior to make sure they didn't start leaking oxygen or losing temperature. This would kill all the plants. It was a long day securing everything, just like during the Atlantic hurricane season, and just as with a hurricane, we named the storm. We named her April. She was the first named storm on Mars. By the way, Steve and Abu showed up a bit later, and it was true that Steve was not himself. He seemed fainthearted, ghostly, slow to action, slow to respond.

I suppose we should have expected that the storm would prove a harbinger of worse things. Isn't there always some fell monstrosity that gets thrown up by these weather events? Think what happened with hurricanes of old, even in the past fifteen or twenty years in a period of heightened global hurricane activity. Think of the pressure exerted on coastal development by climatic change. But I guess I am referring more to the symbolic stuff that comes in a storm. If you think symbolically about it, you'd know that Brandon himself was going to turn up, that the storm *was* Brandon, somehow. The planet was using Brandon to show what it was hiding beneath its layers of sediment. Or at least this was what I thought about it later. Brandon was the interplanetary bringer of war, fighting back against a somewhat puny but determined Mars colony from planet Earth, the other seven of us. If we anthropomorphized the storm, it was maybe because we were waiting for Brandon.

After we helped the others prepare, the three of us shut ourselves into the *Excelsior* and waited. We had dinner as we did most nights. And then we played cards. José was complaining that he kept losing, and that the two of us were ganging up on him. He said this in a good-natured way, not like the José of old. It occurred to me, because there are idle moments in life when you think about these things, that perhaps the José of old just never would exist again. With a serious head injury, you get these alterations in personality. They're just rarely this pleasant. But then I made note of an even more interesting hypothesis. What if, kids, José had *never injured his head at all?* What if José Rodrigues was looking for some graceful way out of the military-industrial straitjacket that NASA had fitted upon him? It was a straitjacket that other Mars mission sociopaths still seemed to feel they needed to wear, but maybe José had had an interplanetary change of heart, a space epiphany. It was possible this new José was the more genuine one. I didn't say this aloud, not while beating him at cards. There were many more months to live together. Who knew how many?

We prepared for bed. Or at least Jim prepared for bed, because he always went to bed earliest, preferring to wake just as it was light. Like a monk. Jim had been complaining about sleep for some time, had begun relying on a certain sleep preparation, which I believed was going to run out before long. I was worried about him becoming habituated to the medication. He may have begun already, which would account, perhaps in part, for his short temper with me.

For example, he was prone to complaining about how I chewed my food. I had, at some point in my youth, taken to heart advice I'd read that suggested that you should chew every mouthful of food thirty-two times. I had lived some of my life on Earth in a careless way where this kind of advice was concerned. Because of the dearth of food we actually were permitted to consume on the Mars mission, I had begun counting, nearly obsessively, each and every mastication. I almost felt guilty, somehow, if I swallowed before I had chewed the proper number of times. Then, one day, in a whimsical mood, I'd made the mistake of boasting about this to Jim. Since then, he had watched me eat, when he could bring himself to do so, with ever increasing amounts of agitation. Apparently, he had started counting my mastications as well. His other complaint referred to the wounded expression he said I wore each night when he elected to go to sleep and to leave José and me to do as we wished. No wonder he resorted to sleep aids. On the night in question, Jim, perhaps by reason of narcotics, was soon snoring the delightful little rasps that were his nocturnal communication.

An hour or so later, after I had written my nightly bulletin post to Ginger and read a little bit of Marcus Aurelius, I found myself so drowsy that I fell asleep with my cabin suit still on, reading glasses still pinched onto my nose, having failed to brush my teeth, which was something I had started to fail to do, in the past weeks, because of the scurvy that was commencing to afflict me. Once your teeth start becoming loose, who gives a royal shit about them? Unless Arnie was going to give me some of the green peppers he was hiding away, I was just going to lose some of my teeth, and that would be that!

The light went off down in the cargo bay, and then night was upon us. The Martian night, which by virtue of the lack of street-lamps and other light pollutants was of a fearsome intensity. We could hear the wind outside the *Excelsior,* in our dreamless and lonely states of unconsciousness, and we could hear the sand pelting the sides of the capsule, drifts of it accumulating. Or that is how I'm reconstructing it, since I was already asleep.

A commotion awoke me. A scuffle of some kind. I didn't know the hour. What difference do particular times make to a Martian colonist? Clocks are for the pointy heads back on Earth. Anyway, it was night and I heard something, and it was kind of quiet at first, but then it seemed a lot louder, a struggle nearly, an altercation. Astronauts pitted against others. Soon I was awake, and I was running, somewhat disoriented, down to the cargo bay, carrying a penlight. Of course I bodily fell down the ladder and landed in a heap on the lower floor. No bones broken. Banged up horribly. I gathered myself up on the way to the light switch.

I noticed the cargo hatch door was open, obviously. There was dust and wind howling into the open hatch. The sand was blowing into the capsule, likewise the frigidness, that affrontery, which was bound to freeze up a lot of the electronics in the cargo bay if I didn't work quickly, which naturally I did, without taking the time to see what had caused the breach of protocol. But at this point I did notice the two men struggling, those men whose identities you have now surmised. They danced into view. One of them was as dark as the night, or at least a dark mahogany, perhaps from coming this way in the storm. His space suit, which had once been polar bear white, was Egyptian henna, and his beard was longish and ragged. Brandon Lepper. I don't know what had brought him to this, if this was *interplanetary disinhibitory disorder* or some bizarre conception of duty to the nation, but whatever the cause, he was now indisputably here.

"Brandon, what the hell are you doing?"

It took him a moment to register that he had now two assailants he was going to have to deal with, and in that interval, José, still in his blue capsule pajamas, managed to wrench himself free.

José said to me, "Jed, get out of here. I'll deal with it."

"No, you will not!"

"Go get Jim. Go, go!"

Brandon intended to employ a weapon, a homemade blade of his own devising. He'd sharpened up some industrial aluminum, no doubt harvested from one of the piles of space junk that he now called home, and he brandished it as if it were a twenty-first-century machete. Kids, I have had hand-to-hand-combat training. So have many of the astronauts on the Mars colony, since many of us came from branches of the military. Men had fallen before me on the fields of battle, dispatched by my hand. Brandon, meanwhile, was a welterweight boxer, and in this case he was a pugilist with a long, shiny blade. I called for Jim. I ran to the bank of monitors in the cargo bay, hit the intercom, and called for Jim again, cursing his medicaments. When I returned, Brandon had José pinioned beside the ultralight, and had the machete perilously close to his face. All of this took place in a curious silence. With the kind of progress that you can make in a lower-gravity environment, I was on him in a couple of bounding steps.

I swear I could hear Jim snoring upstairs as Brandon flung me off his back. Brandon, in a bulky space suit minus the helmet, was having trouble maneuvering. José gave him a good smack in the jaw, a roundhouse, I suppose, and then winced with the pain of it, instantly clutching his right hand. In some kind of low-gravity thrall, I watched Brandon then raise up the machete, with a vigorous backswing that I associated with the best tennis players, and it was almost as if I saw my own heroics before they happened, the juncture in which I flung myself into the line of the backswing and held up my left hand — and thank heavens this was not my dominant hand. Just as José himself pivoted out of reach of his attacker, Brandon's blade sliced clear through the thumb and first two fingers of my left hand. My fourth finger, with my bittersweet wedding band, likewise my pinkie, remained. In a silence marked only by the grunt of my own stunned shock, and by Brandon's hiss of murderous intention, we all watched the fingers fly free. I then turned my gaze to the stumps, which had begun to fountain with blood, after which I collapsed onto the floor, clutching the mangled hand with the remaining good one.

It could not have been long, the period in which I was immediately considering: (1) the availability of antibacterial cleaning solution in the nearby first aid area, (2) the possibility of a tourniquet so I wouldn't bleed to death, (3) how to get the hell out of the way before Brandon cut off some fingers from the other hand. It could not have been long, this reverie, during which I was crouching underneath the ultralight aircraft, looking up at its fuselage, but this was plenty long enough to make José's predicament even more dire. When I came to understand this point, I sat up, covered in a tie-dyed smear of gore, and watched as Brandon held tight to José's head, and, with his mighty scimitar, sliced through all the veins and arteries in his throat. There was a desperate gurgling from the victim, from the man I had come to think of as my friend, and then an awful river of José flowed out onto the cabin floor, toward the drain where I coincidentally sat. I wish I could say that I did more. I wish I could say a lot of things now. I wish I could say that with my own hand bleeding profusely, I had been able to throw caution to the wind and wrestle that madman, Brandon Lepper, to the ground. But in the crucial moment, I writhed in the anguish of my own wound. José flapped wildly for a couple of seconds, holding his throat, as if he could dam up the gash, and then his body went still.

Brandon turned to me again, and I cowered. Holding close the hand with the bloody stumps.

Then he spoke to me. It was as if no such sound had ever before been uttered. Brandon said: "I'm wherever you don't look. I'm around you. I'm in the air. I'm in the dust and the wind. I'm in the craters and crevices. Not one of you is safe until I lift off from the surface for home. Not one of you. Pass the word. Stay out of my business; stay out of the valley. Get it? Death came with the earthlings to Mars."

He raised the machete up again, but it was just some kind of lasting memory, some kind of emblem, one that I will not forget, one that has lingered in my imagination, one that I expect will linger there for a long time. He brandished the thing, and then he spared me.

He went out through the hatch, leaving it ajar, carrying a twenty-gallon drum of fuel, a packet of maps, and a laptop workstation, and as before, the howling wind was his calling card. I thought: *Who will help me find my fingers?*

February 25, 2026

We informed NASA the next day of José's death, of the circumstances in which it took place. Was I alone in feeling that the response of the authorities was oddly cool? It was as though they had foreknowledge. Was it only me who thought that they had divided their loyalties, that some of them worked toward another dark objective, of which it seemed we would learn soon enough? Perhaps at Mission Control it was impossible not to find this division between the regular employees — with their adolescent dreams of interstellar travel — and those who thought only of that other mission, the Dark Objective, which had as part of its trajectory the desire to put a halt to Sino-Indian economic hegemony back on Earth, in the process claiming all the natural resources in the universe, wherever they may lie, and however this might be accomplished, for NAFTA interests.

Maybe there were political appointees or moles at Mission Control who fed Brandon our itineraries and described to him our plans, just as there were others, on the other side of the ideological divide, our side, who seemed to accept the Mars First! ideological formulations of our chief theoretician and philosopher, Jim Rose. These fellow travelers understood that our political machinations, our consensus-gathering dinners, were crucial to the emerging history of this soon-to-be-developed world. Our decision-making process was impractical, slow, awkward, true, but then life on Mars was all of these things too.

We buried José the next day. (It required blowtorches.) I don't think I remembered to tell you that he'd spent a little while trying to find a way to introduce Icelandic moss onto Mars. He figured that Iceland's ecosystem was most like what we had on the surface here. He figured that moss could perhaps adapt to the barrenness of Mars. It was just a hunch. He'd attempted to do some transplanting *outdoors*. He'd designed the experimental protocols himself. Unlike the greenhouse, where we were trying to terraform Mars a couple square inches at a time according to instructions from the home planet, José had brought a bag of carefully mixed soil and fertilizer to a deep crater near the *Geronimo,* where there were outcroppings of bedrock, and he had attempted to propagate this Icelandic moss. After all, he'd argued, there was a lot of nitrogen in the atmosphere, as well as in the soil, and this was much to the benefit of Icelandic moss. He was completely hopeful about it, all by himself, going out there an hour or two every other day, with a tiny measuring cup full of recirculated water. He didn't really care how long it took. Or so he told me.

We buried him there.

I had a Bible with me on Mars. I understand that many of you think of Bibles as tools for propaganda. Yet I am the kind of person who likes the sweep, the grandeur, and the reverence that I find in the Bible. However, at José's funeral, I was outvoted. We decided that a reading from the Bible was not a proper Mars First! tradition. We needed, Jim argued (and Arnie and Laurie agreed, especially now that she was beginning to show), to start imagining different and more Mars-centered epics of spiritual literature. We needed myths of origins that began on *this* place, that bound together this small community of wayfarers. Accordingly, we decided that there would be no reading at all at José's funeral. Instead, Jim simply asked if anyone had anything they wanted to say. A tradition was born, if out of misfortune.

By now the dust storm had passed us, heading off in a southeasterly direction, so it was a clear day. Warm for Mars. We stood and waited for inspiration.

Finally, Jim said, via walkie-talkie, "José, you were one of the really good people on the mission, because you were one of the people who grew here on Mars. You were a different person, when you died, you were not the man who set out to conquer this unforgiving place, and I have to think that this planet brought that out in you. And while I don't want to be hopeless at a time like this, my friend, I think I failed you. I think I failed you by not seeing that you had the potential to rise to this occasion. I will miss you therefore, and I will use what you have taught me as I go forward from here. I will not fail the remainder of us. Meanwhile, we're hoping that you can rest quietly here, and that no one disturbs you for a good million years or so. It'll be a while before mankind uses up this place, so sleep well, buddy. It should be peaceful."

I wasn't the only one looking over my shoulder the whole time, wondering what was next. I turned away during Jim's remarks, but at the same time I was checking to see if we were being watched. I was wondering when Brandon would turn up next. I was wondering when the rover was going to come over the lip of the crater, when Brandon was going to try to take out the whole bunch of us, spraying us with Taser fire. We stood in the great waste of the planet Mars, uncertain and fearful, and the easiest thing would have been to load back into the *Excelsior,* assemble the Earth Return Vehicle, and declare an emergency. And yet I just wasn't ready to give up.

When Arnie and Laurie headed back to the greenhouse, the four of us who remained had a bit of a chat. To try to decide a course of action. The Mars mission, you see, had begun to acquire a certain inalienable organizational structure. According to its own interests. Arnie and Laurie controlled the food. Abu and Steve were in charge of the energy. Jim and I were in charge of infrastructure and the delivery of services. (That meant construction, education, political confederation, and policing.)

The four of us, from power and infrastructure, stood for a minute in the dusk until the sun dipped away and we walked back toward our rovers. It was Abu who opened the subject, the subject we all knew we would have to address. I suppose we were putting it off.

"How should we go about dealing with him?"

"I think we ought to talk to NASA about it, even if we can't trust them. Let's see if they give away anything we need to know," I said.

"And when they don't give us anything?"

"We fabricate some unlikely plan of attack, leak it to them, see if it gets back to him."

Jim nodded solemnly. Though it was clear that he was thinking about something else entirely. And Steve, still ghostly, passive, was taciturn too. If it was going to be the drugged-up guy with his arm in the sling who did all the talking, the outcome was liable to be uncertain.

And that reminds me. I forgot to say that Arnie managed to reattach two of my fingers! I didn't properly re-create the scene after I managed to cross the hold and swing shut the air lock behind Brandon. I didn't manage to re-create the moment when Jim finally stumbled down the ladder and into the cargo bay, to see blood everywhere and his shipmates laid out on the floor of the hold. The first thing he did was to attempt to revive José, and I can't blame him for that. There was a lot of hopeless beating on José's chest.

When it was clear that CPR was not going to work, we placed a tarp over the body in the cargo hold and I showed Jim my hand, I held up my hand, and I asked — if he had time — if he would help me look around the cargo hold. The thumb was easy to find because it was right there on the floor, not far from one of the tires of the ultralight aircraft. And after we turned up the thumb, we worked a little harder for the index finger, which had apparently skidded far across the cargo bay, because it was over by the trash-compacting area of the cargo hold. But what of my middle finger? Kids, we looked high and low, we looked under things and over things, we looked in places where a finger could not have been. And we simply couldn't come up with the middle finger.

I suppose I was in shock from the blood loss, and I would have wandered around looking for my finger indefinitely if Jim hadn't put a stop to the looking. The only line of speculation that seemed plausible was that the middle finger had somehow left the *Excelsior* with Brandon. Maybe Brandon had plucked it up from the floor, oozing slightly, and put it into his front pocket. As a little prize that he would be able to put on a necklace of his own manufacture and wear later during his *reign of blood.*

After all, at the present temperature, the finger would keep for a very long time on the Martian surface. (We were intending to do some experiments to answer this very question, in fact. Since there were no or few microbes on the sterile surface of the planet, it followed that the whole planet was a sort of refrigerator. It would be hard to get meat and vegetable products *to* Mars, but once you got them here, they'd keep forever.)

In the morning, when the sun came up, after I had another injection, Jim drove me over to see Arnie. I had the thumb and the index finger in a small plastic bag on ice. Not that we needed it. And my hand was wrapped in a great bandage that had severely depleted our stock of gauze on the *Excelsior.* The Martian dawn was just breaking as we pushed through the air lock into the greenhouse to wake the others. I felt a strange uncertainty about this trip, as if our bad news was so bad that it made the impoliteness of waking Laurie and Arnie even worse. But they were making coffee.

Jim said, "We're going to need some advanced medicine."

After a suitable pause he launched into the explanation. I could see Laurie and Arnie pass through various stages of disbelief. I could see the shimmering of Planetary Exile Syndrome in them, in which they did not want to believe. I could feel the heavy metals of Brandon's rampage seep into the groundwater of the room. When no one quite knew what to suggest, Jim wordlessly laid the plastic bag down on the table in the greenhouse. The club of gauze at the end of my arm hadn't even really registered for Arnie.

I said, "Do you think you have enough tools here to do a bit of reattachment?"

"Oh, damn it," Arnie said. "Damn it to hell. What the hell?"

"That's the least of it," Jim said, "but we can't really afford to have Jed out of action, can we? I mean, a man's got to have a thumb. He won't even be able to do the dishes without that thumb."

As Arnie was examining the fingers in the bag, and (subsequently) unrolling my gauze club, he asked what I was doing for pain relief, and I hate to say it but I was *completely high* that day, as well as in the days afterward. I was flying on some synthetic opiate that NASA had sent along with us, and the stars in the Martian sky at dawn, and the moons, they all looked fabulous to me, like a backdrop that some filmmaker had gussied up to impress the crowds at the late show on Saturday night. The stars seemed like little neurons in my skull, in the vastness of my own intelligence. I told Arnie what I was on and how much, and he nodded approvingly, said something hackneyed about staying ahead of the pain curve. And then, in the course of his preliminary examination, he managed to recognize the numerical discrepancy between the number of fingers in the bag and the number of stumps on my hand.

"Aren't you short a digit here?" he said.

"Couldn't find the other one," I said.

"It's always something," Arnie offered.

For those who are curious: synthetic opiates are not enough for microsurgery. And even if microsurgery, with the aid of nanotechnology, is routine back where you are, and even if Arnie had done a few reattachments in his past, doing it on Mars, on a table, in a greenhouse, with pretty rudimentary surgical equipment, when you're waiting for a madman to appear to hack you to death again, *and again, and again,* well, it makes for a difficult surgery. They had to hold me down. The three of them. They strapped me down with cargo belts like I was a raving lunatic. Laurie was holding my arm, and Jim was holding my head, and I was scared. I have been scared on this mission before, there have been many opportunities, and I am not the most courageous man on the mission, and I never will be. I am here to be organized, detail oriented, a good communicator, a utility infielder who can do a lot of things reasonably well. I know that I felt the little vascular connections being reattached, I felt every one of them, I don't care what they say about local anesthetic obliterating the feelings. I felt the venous and arterial material transiting through me, felt the torn muscles back where they belonged, and the hours it took seemed doubly or triply agonizing. And I wet myself, and I wept bitterly and begged for Arnie to be through long before he was, and when it was done, and Jim hauled me up onto my feet, Arnie said, "Jed, I'd like to promise you that those fingers are going to stay on there, but I can't promise you anything of the sort. While I doubt they will become gangrenous, because we just haven't seen much evidence of that sort of thing here on Mars, you might have such bad circulation in there that they have to be taken off again. Keep the sutures clean, use soap and water, let me know if you have reduced sensation as the days go forward."

"Well, Arnie," I said, "I'm just grateful to you," and then my knees buckled again.

Under the circumstances, I did a pretty good job at the funeral. And for this I can only thank drugs. My problem with these things, and I'm ashamed to say I have had occasion to sample many of the available opiates, is that you just can't think straight in the same way. This was apparently as true on Mars as on Earth. I was moved to tears by the surgery because there's a desolation that goes with having had a bunch of your fingers lopped off and then sewn back on by a gardener on a dusty desert planet, when you are still a year or more from making it home, and your new friend has just been slaughtered, and your lover will no longer recognize that you are *together;* I guess there were many reasons to be moved to tears.

But I had even more to consider when I got back to the *Excelsior* after the funeral, when I was wide awake with opiate insomnia, watching Jim Rose sleep. Kids, it was about time that someone sat down and began to describe the systematic *decompensation* of the emotional lives of everyone on Mars. It was time that someone made an attempt to study this *decompensation,* in an effort to describe it for the historical literature, and perhaps, in this way, to shed light on what we could next expect from Brandon. And from ourselves.

It seemed to me that there were only two possibilities. The first possibility was that the long-term separation from Earth did in fact engender something along the lines of *interplanetary disinhibitory disorder,* in an aggravated or acute form, such that people just couldn't seem to keep their emotions in check. Do you need concrete examples? First, there was my relentless and humiliating neediness around Jim Rose. Evidently my homosexual romantic instincts were just not as graceful as my heterosexual instincts. I didn't know how to stop wanting his attention; I didn't know how to stop feeling that even his really peculiar habits, like the strange grunting thing he did while reading, were somehow endearing or even handsome. I didn't know how to stop feeling flushed and warm inside when he was nearby. And I didn't know how to stop pushing him on this, even though there had been moments recently when I actually worried that he was perhaps capable of battery.

This was the first example. A mostly normal heterosexual man becomes a wanton and pandering lothario of gay love. Then there was Debbie Quartz, of whom enough has been said. And Steve Watanabe, whose free fall into muteness already seemed to me to foretell dread things ahead. Jim Rose, who had started the mission as an upbeat high school quarterback of a guy and who now had more in common with Moses or Saint Jerome. And then there was the weird saccharine domesticity of Laurie and Arnie, though both were parents back home, and in Arnie's case, happily married (or so it was said). Now, if they'd had a chance, they would have found a Martian golden retriever with which to adorn their playhouse. Of Abu, we had no example of eccentricity yet, except sculpture, but perhaps time would tell. He was just a very reliable person. And Brandon had evidently become quite insane.

Interplanetary disinhibitory disorder, that was one possibility of what we were seeing. The other possibility, and I admit that completely high on pain medication as I was, it was possible this was more a figment of my rather delusional mind, was that Brandon had already been infected with *M. thanatobacillus.* What I intended to research online, while I had the strength and was awake enough, was whether there was any kind of comparable bacterial infection that I could find from the medical literature on Earth that would give me an idea of what we were going to experience in the course of infection. Ordinarily, on Earth, with your new bacterial infections, when they were first making their way through the general population, there was a tendency for the infections to be fatal, and spectacularly so. Think of *necrotizing fasciitis.* Or hantavirus, which the overdevelopment of the desert cities had brought into the megalopolis. These bugs made you bleed everywhere and die within hours, begging for mercy.

M. thanatobacillus, on the other hand, may have had a preliminary effect that was only apparent in the *character* of the afflicted individual. Like rabies. I remember hiking in the Smoky Mountains with my daughter not too many years ago, when, at the summit of the mountain, we saw the most adorable skunk wandering around. Not the least bit afraid of us! Willing to walk right up to us! My daughter just *adored* skunks, and it was she who saw it first. She was getting ready to feed the rodent when I let out one of those parental howls that is intended to require immediate attention. No doubt the skunk was hydrophobic. It is possible that *M. thanatobacillus* has just this kind of a trajectory, wherein there are first character effects, and then only later do the somatic aspects of the infection begin to appear, the part of the disease where you *disassemble.* There was a sort of a hybrid of Marburg and dengue fever that the United States stockpiled during the Central Asian police actions a decade or so ago, and which were used in a very hushed-up way against rebel groups in the Caucasus region. I may have known more about this than I can say right now, and it's possible that this hemorrhagic hybrid, which has a long acronym of a name that I can't put my finger on right now, is a good model for the initial infection cycle of M. *thanatobacillus.* We found hardened warlords from the rebel groups wandering in the mountains, carrying daisies and singing to themselves. It was not difficult to neutralize these combatants, and that was *before* the onset of somatic symptoms.

Now that I was thinking about it, there may have been a third explanatory possibility, besides the two I've mentioned; maybe it was not the case that Brandon had *interplanetary disinhibitory disorder;* maybe it was not the case that he suffered the effects of his exposure to M. *thanatobacillus,* assuming José was right and such a bacterium even existed farther down in the Martian geological strata.

Maybe José got killed so that he'd keep his mouth shut.

March 12, 2026

To: The entire Martian Community
From: Jim Rose
Re: A Survey of Martian Economics

Be it known, fellow Martians, that the time has come for choosing!
For every new civilization, no matter how fragile, no matter how young,
how untimely birthed from the womb of the mother planet, there comes the
moment in which this newly birthed society must determine for itself the
specifics of its ideology. Fellow Martians, it is nearly six months now since
first we set out on our long journey. How well we know the reasons and
motives that first launched us into the milky oblivion of the innumerable
stars! We know these reasons and motives because they were so often ban-
died about in the press and on television and across the web of our birth
culture. We know the ideals to which the birth culture aspired, and we

know the darker ways in which its needs oppress us! Fellow Martians, we know the mother planet is an angry and capricious mistress! We know that even at this distance she would command our every step, know every sentence that we utter, circumscribe every afternoon of the Martian year we are intended to spend here! And for what? For profit, fellow Martians, all for profit!

When they see Mars, as they do through the cameras that we have installed for them, or through the reports that we write down for them, or from the microphones that are even affixed to the jumpsuits we are wearing at this very moment, they do so through terms and according to multinational ideologies that were constructed and designed for that world. They preach freedom while requiring servitude, fellow Martians! They preach sacrifice and selflessness while underwriting the mission with geological riches and the avarice such a thing entails. They preach tolerance while practicing war, and then they command our allegiance!

What would it mean to be truly free on the Red Planet, fellow Martians? We have seen the worst that freedom brings, when one of our number runs amok and sacrifices another of our beloved brothers! Freedom, when it is simply the freedom to be a shareholder in a mercantile entity that is no longer beholden to any government, is not freedom! It is a form of interstellar slavery! Martian freedom must be designed on Mars, by Martians, for Martians, and it must reflect the difficulty of our terrain, the modesty of our resources, and the sense of community that we bring to the project of establishing a new human civilization! Think of what the revolutionaries of our own planet accomplished, in France, the United States, Bali, Kazakhstan. Mars must reject Earth in exactly these ways!

And so, fellow Martians, I bring to you today the first of my meditations on the history and economics of the Martian colony. By the power vested in me at the Greenhouse dinner of January seventh, two thousand and twenty-six, I hereby declare the socialization of and communal ownership of all the infrastructure on the planet Mars. I hereby declare that private property, the antagonist of any community in the process of finding its footing, is abolished. I declare that while the trinkets and memorabilia of our old lives are useful as mementos, we hold that the majority of our lives are lived in this community, with these people, and as such, the objects that pass between people are held to be our common property. Among this common property will be the electrical power generated by all of us, among this common property will be the food that we grow in or out of our greenhouse, among this common property will be the literary accounts that we generate in this place for sale back on the mother planet, in whatever form these sales might take place, a portion of which will always be kicked into a common kitty by the author of these works, such as the author of this memo on Martian property rights. Any minerals that we locate here, including diamonds, platinum, gold, and any other valuable minerals, will be the common property of the Martian colony. Any film rights that we sell, pursuant to our stories on the planet Mars, will be held to be common property, in which we all share equally. Children born in the Martian colony will be considered the nieces and nephews of all adults in the Martian colony. Dinner will be cooked serially by all Martian adults, on a rotating basis, unless the colony specifically decides to cancel dinner plans. From each, therefore, according to his ability, to each according to his needs.

We hold that these principles of common trust are based upon our lives on this planet thus far, and that they are therefore organic to our experiences as Martians. They conform to the principles of our Mars First! political entity, which, at the present time, is the only political party on the planet Mars. This is not to say that Mars First! is averse to sharing power with any other parties that are liable to emerge at some future date. We are against military actions, except when we understand a need to defend ourselves and our common property. We have no prison and we have no death penalty. Public service on the planet Mars is to be carried out on a rotating basis, and according to rigorous standards of public service. When our term is over we shall hand over the reins of power to the next volunteer or group of volunteers.

These are our beliefs, which we hold to be self-evident, until such time as we may find reason to amend them! Mars first! Mars always and ever!

How, you might ask, did Jim Rose come to author these memorable lines, which have already gone down in the history of the Mars colony as the first of our constitutional documents? In the weeks after José's murder, the remaining members of the

Mars colony spiraled further down into the quiescent pall I've described above. Abu was working on his sculptures, out in back of the generating plant. Laurie (who was, as I've said, beginning to show) and Arnie retreated into their botanical endeavors, almost always finding reasons to cancel dinner on us and leave us to fend for ourselves with the rations we had remaining. Steve apparently stayed in his bunk four or five days at a time. Then there were Jim and me.

What Jim decided to do, in lieu of pursuing much of a relationship with me, was go out and see the world. I think it was only three or four days after Brandon's rampage that I helped him to haul the ultralight out of the *Excelsior* again, in order to get the thing up and running. Jim was handy with all machineries, and as I have said, he was a very good pilot. We used the onboard hydraulics to lower gently the ultralight to the floor of the planet, and then Jim set about trying to clear enough rubble out of the way that he might have a reasonable runway for the craft.

I should point out that in the days that had intervened, I, for one, continued to track Brandon, using the device that was affixed to his rover. It was at this point that he did seem, at last, to descend into the mouth of the Valles Marineris, that immense geological formation, no doubt in the process exploring for water, life, bacteria, and all the ready-to-be-plundered resources that the mother planet was happy to have shipped back to her. Brandon's movements, as I conceived of them from the *Excelsior,* were anything but faint of heart. It was as if, by *neutralizing* José, he had, indeed, surmounted the biggest of his problems, and was now safely at work on a task ordered directly from the USA. His industry suggested that we might, at some point, have the element of surprise where Brandon was concerned.

Jim wanted to keep it this way. But he still needed to be certain that the ultralight was mission ready, and that he'd be able to land it on the rocky terrain near the canyon without turning it into a pile of scrap. And so he resolved to set off in a southerly direction. A curious way to go, kids, because the south, like the poles, to which we would not have access because of the distance, just didn't have much to offer, besides some dry ice. Not like the outflow channels at the eastern end of Valles Marineris, where Brandon had lately pitched his camp. Nevertheless, the impact basin nearby, Argyre, also presented, according to geologists on the home planet, the great likelihood of water ice. And any trip to Argyre kept us far away from Brandon.

It was a risk to fly the craft in a direction where none of us could help Jim in the event of difficulty. And NASA would have been the first to advise against it, had we been in a mood to listen to their point of view (since their unpleasant broadcast memorial to José, which had run on the web in the days after his demise). They were no longer telling us what to do and were beginning to recognize, I think, that we had long ago assumed responsibility for ourselves. We offered very little in the way of specifics to Mission Control.

It may have been true that Jim Rose *wanted* the emptiness and the experience of tundra. The Martian emptiness was more empty than any other emptiness. I made Jim promise to take a video camera, however, in case he resolved some of the scientific problems that were much on our minds.

I met him by the aircraft, and in the new post-sentimental environment occupied by the inhabitants of the *Excelsior,* I offered him the meal I had packed, which was some repulsive mixture of cream cheese, freeze-dried olive paste, candy bars, and a bottle of water, not something, I suppose, that he would like, with his finicky tastes, but food nonetheless. I advised against eating it all at once.

"And don't forget the video."

It was early morning, and he would have the hazy sun on his left as he flew south.

"I won't. And you're going to continue to keep an eye on Brandon."

I nodded, withdrawing slightly. Perhaps I was right to do so. Maybe I knew the burden that Jim carried with him on that trip, in which he became the fulcrum for all that would happen on Mars in the future, the Mars of your generation, the Mars to come. Maybe I knew, likewise, that it wasn't likely that Brandon was just going to give up harrowing the rest of us. Nor was it the case that *M. thanatobacillus,* once exposed by José, was going back into its hiding place beneath the surface of the interplanetary imagination.

There was no wind. Jim managed, despite a few remaining boulders on our makeshift runway, to get the ultralight aloft, and because we had left it out for a day or so, there was enough juice in the solar cells for him to make the trip with minimal expenditure of solid fuel. He banked left, out above the dunes, as though surfing on their crests. I don't know how far off, because distances were lost to me. Then he headed out of my view, bound for the Argyre Basin.

The ultralight was equipped with a camera too, so as long as he was near enough to transmit to the little broadcasting antenna we'd erected on the roof of the *Excelsior,* he could send back fuzzy real-time footage of the terrain beneath him. Though I had seen Mars from above, as had all of us, it had been some time since the landing, and being elevated enough to look beyond the lip of the horizon was glorious and implicitly hazardous. What looked unvarying at first sight, the ferrous red and battleship gray of the surface, had grown in our time here much more complicated. There were all manner of strange geological formulations passing beneath Jim. I watched until the transmission began to break up, until grids of digital static broke through it and he was gone.

What we now know, kids, is that this was the moment in the wilderness when Jim Rose, free of the shackles of his fellow Martians, had the experience of being one with the new planet. This was the moment. He'd been flying for a couple of hours, as I understand it, before he saw the impact basin beneath him, the collapsed wall on the north side that was said to be the route through which the Argyre emptied its primordial flood upon the lowlands. We now know that Jim piloted his ultralight just south of the collapsed wall, and finding that the land was smoother here than elsewhere — because

the Argyre was of a more recent vintage, as far as asteroid strikes
go—he set the plane down without incident. Once on the ground,
Jim made some kind of feeble and perhaps awkward obeisance in
the direction of the planetary spirit of Mars, because this was how
he was in those days. He thanked Mars for bringing him to this spot
without incident, and then he got a pickax out of the back of the
ultralight. Think of it, kids, Jim Rose sweating through his space
suit, digging. We had just dug a grave, farther north, you see.
Graves were on our minds. My mind, at any rate. We'd dug a grave
because we had nothing else to do with José's body, because there
were no vultures to pick him apart, and there was no incinerator,
yet, in which to put his body, and, as I've said, given the natural
refrigeration of the planet Mars, if we had left him out in a crater,
it was likely that his body would have remained in a mild state of
decomposition for a very long time. So we buried him.

In the process of burying José we did soil tests, as we always
did. And this process had not yielded any irrefutable data yet,
though Steve had preserved an ambiguous sample of the dirt
several feet down and taken it back toward the power plant for
more testing. Whatever Steve may or may not have found was
completely different from what was at Argyre. At Argyre, kids,
there was a bounty in the regolith. The bounty was not even far
below the surface. The bounty was there waiting to be harvested,
as though the destitute face that Mars presented to the heavens,
to the orbiting crafts, to the unmanned missions that had landed
here in the past fifteen or twenty years, was completely fraudulent,
deliberately so. Jim wasn't even six feet down when, making use
of an electrical coil he'd patched together back at the *Excelsior,* he
melted himself a cup full *of water.*

Water! That tasteless (or mostly tasteless), odorless (or mostly
odorless) fortification that makes up the vast majority of our physique. Call it a long cool drink, call it *rehydrating,* call it an adul-
teration, it was the thing that made Earth, the watery planet, what
it was, a teeming, complicated celebration of organics. It was the
first requirement for life! And here it was! Frozen into the subsoil

on Mars in a way in which just about anyone could get to it, if only he were willing to dig. Some of the unmanned Mars missions had come tantalizingly close, but they'd found mere traces of H_2O in places where it was inefficient (by reason of landscape) to harvest it, or where it was evaporated quickly. We had set our ships down in just such a landscape. A deserted part of a desert planet.

Which did make you wonder why. Why we were originally slated for the South Pole, not that much farther south than the Argyre Basin, where there was definitely some kind of ice, mostly liquid CO_2, which can be made, at least, to yield its oxygen without too much chemical manipulating. Why we were not there now, when to be there would have amounted to a self-sustaining Martian community, if a very cold one, unless NASA really *did* have some kind of objective that they were not telling us about. An objective that involved, however disagreeably, a piecemeal elimination of Mars mission astronauts, so as to preserve resources—water and power—for the trip home.

This conspiracy mongering came easily to me on the day that I was alone in the *Excelsior.* Jim, as we learned later, was at the same time blowtorching and harvesting a container of water for himself from the humus of the Martian subsurface, and when he had produced a sufficient amount, he actually—though it was against regulations to do so—*drank* some of this water.

Let us pause here. Because it was a horrible idea. Anyone on the mission would have told him as much, as indeed would have any scientist from home. We *assumed* that the surface of Mars was largely sterile, because of samples we'd taken, now and in the past, but where Jim had dug was not the surface, and what happened underneath the surface we just didn't know! And yet Jim, in the wilderness, wanted to trust Mars, wanted to prove himself to it, that superficially empty place. He wanted Mars to know we were somehow worthy of her. He had been planning as much, I learned later, all along. He needed to be alone with Mars. And he needed to do this, to drink what the planet offered him, because at that moment he had a vision for the future of the planet. He drank, sacramentally, to punctuate this moment. He didn't know, initially, if he had imbibed trace radioactive elements. He didn't know if he had exceeded his recommended daily allowance for iron or lead. I, for one, almost always carried a Geiger counter with me, to keep a tally of exposure, but not Jim. Jim, according to the story as it has been handed down, drank deeply of the water, dried his mouth with the back of his hand before closing his visor again, and, according to this tale as we know it, he then said, aloud, to himself, "This is where I will live and die, in order to make this a better place than the planet from which I come."

What a solitary and terrifying thought. This man had family at home. He had friends who loved him and who, while admiring of his courage, were expecting him back at some point. How shall we interpret this moment? you ask. He didn't see any god. He wasn't hallucinating. He was being pragmatic. As pragmatic as one can be when one has *interplanetary disinhibitory disorder.* What Jim felt, in the absence of a beneficent and loving entity who would, back on Earth, help him to win big at the lottery or find a parking space, was a tremendous reassurance in the pristine silence of the Argyre Basin. It would be *all right.* He filled a metal container with water, put it in the small storage hatch in the ultralight, and when he was through with his sacrament, he lifted off again. Did Brandon take the bait? Was he somehow monitoring our activities too, and making note of our progress in the south?

Meanwhile, I should add, my wife was contacting me from Earth:

PogeyStark@marsmission.us.gov: Jed, are you there? We're getting the most horrible news down here about the mission. None of it in the press yet, but still. People are saying things. They're saying that there is trouble on Mars, that someone may even have been murdered. Is that true?

RichardsJ@marsmission.us.gov: Pogey, I'm not at liberty to discuss Martian internal affairs. You know that.

PogeyStark@marsmission.us.gov: Jed, it's me. You don't have

to give me the party line. I get enough of that down here. Why don't you just tell me what's going on? Is everyone okay? Are you okay?

RichardsJ@marsmission.us.gov: It's impossible to explain what's going on here, that's all I can say. *It's not like Earth.* It's a different place. The language is changing already. The language already applies to Martian things in different ways. I don't know if I can tell you in a way that will make sense. We belong to a different planet, whose culture is rapidly evolving in ways that will be hard to understand back on the home planet. Our ethics and legal system are already beginning to diverge.

PogeyStark@marsmission.us.gov: I really hate it when you say I can't understand things. It's so condescending. But it's not really for myself that I'm asking anyway. I'm worried about Ginger. She hears things around. At school, on the base (when she's there), she doesn't know what to think. She's mostly too independent to ask you these kinds of things herself, or that's what I think. But she wants to know. I think you ought to talk to her. More than you're doing now.

RichardsJ@marsmission.us.gov: Well, I'm *fine.* That's all she needs to know. I can't run the risk that our communications are being monitored by Mission Control. I'm sure they are, as a matter of fact. We intend to solve the issues, the problems, internally, the ones you're alluding to. There's a lot going on, and the situation is fluid, changing by the day. If you can give me a sign that you are you, and that you are not being used by other people at this moment, I can reassure you a little bit. So maybe you can remind me about the illustration on your lower back?

PogeyStark@marsmission.us.gov: The tattoo?

RichardsJ@marsmission.us.gov: Don't waste time with two-word responses.

PogeyStark@marsmission.us.gov: St. Theresa in ecstasy. Like the sculpture.

RichardsJ@marsmission.us.gov: Why did you leave your husband?

PogeyStark@marsmission.us.gov: What do you mean? I left my husband because he left me. Long ago. In all the symbolic ways. If you really want to know, if this is really how you want to deal with this question now, I'll say that my husband is so broken, so lost, that he's incapable of opening up to anyone on Earth, least of all me. So I hope he is better at opening up to people on Mars. His impenetrability makes him very effective at certain kinds of military operations, where human emotions just clog up the system. Where emotions just get in the way of things. There was a time when I was able to see through all this to the person within him. Then he felt exposed, he didn't want me, he walled himself off, he was too walled off to be able to *want* me.

RichardsJ@marsmission.us.gov: Okay, I believe that you are you. I thank you for your credible information. The following is what I have to say to you, for Ginger, and for the Mars mission people, who will likely force you to give them a transcript of this exchange. There are forces in the universe that make havoc of the human personality as we understand it. The human personality is a tendency to respond to certain planetary stimuli in certain predictable ways. In the absence of predictable planetary stimuli, the personality no longer acts or organizes itself according to any therapeutically based model. Talk show lingo just does not apply here. We found these things on the crossing. The movement out of ourselves into some new dynamic of identity was slow but undeniable. You could see it in the others if not in yourself. The watery planet is an orderly place, despite its apparent systemic chaos. Elsewhere, like here in the arctic desert of Mars, feelings run out onto the empty canvas. They evaporate like water vapor, or carbon dioxide, which, here, goes straight from a solid to a gas. Nothing is explicable. Murderous rage is as common as dark matter. Nothing in the color wheel of emotions is not experienced regularly here. Often at the same time. What does this mean about those left behind? Our loved ones? What it means is that never a day goes by when we are not convulsed in confusion and loss, with the sense that we have been so profoundly changed that the selves that we *were* will not make it back to the watery planet intact. Mars is a place of death. It is fascinatingly dead. Its death is so complex as to be more lively than life. I miss Ginger more than I can say, Pogey, and I want to make up to you what I have failed to do as a person. I was a better person when you first met me. But this ends my communication for now, because I have official responsibilities to see to.

March 26, 2026

If I didn't say so before, there is the constant danger of hypothermia on the planet Mars. While I occasionally speak of people opening and closing their visors and breathing the atmosphere, I think I should reiterate that this happens almost never. Breathing here is like asphyxiating in your friend's garage in Greenland. This makes it even more inexplicable, based on our experience, that Abu would attempt to take off his regulation threads, while out working on his sculptures behind the power plant, and thus fall prey to a really aggravated case of hypothermia. Unless he was afflicted with the character illness we have so far found among ourselves. Whose name, again, is *interplanetary disinhibitory disorder.*

This was last week, and since then Abu has been in and out of consciousness. Arnie has been looking after him in the greenhouse, and I should report, while I'm speaking of the greenhouse, that Abu's situation came to light a mere twenty-four hours after we learned of our first fully vine-ripened interplanetary tomato. Laurie thought it would be incredibly small because there are not the right nutrients for a tomato in the soil we brought with us, and she was right. Nor were the appropriate nutrients to be found here in the Martian soil. However, what a Martian tomato lacks in size it more than makes up in taste. I am willing to believe that it was the total absence of tomato (or most anything else among fruits and vegetables, excepting soy) and a shortage of vitamin pills that resulted in my losing a front tooth last week. But let us brush, so to speak, across my dental woes. Let us move directly to the celebration of this Martian tomato.

The spice trade, kids, began because people were stultified by their traditional cuisine. If we could have managed a spice trade on Mars, we would have embarked on it immediately. Cumin! Mustard! Coriander! Allspice! The tomato came into our lives the way these spices, and the Dutch East India Company, revolutionized medieval Europe, by despoiling Africa and Asia of their resources. The historical spices distracted fetid, malodorous religious zealots from popping the smallpox on their gin-blossomed noses long enough to give way to the Renaissance! Let's hope the tomato does the same on Mars!

In fact, my last conversation with Abu was about the tomato. It had been a couple of weeks since Laurie had espied the little green fruit on the vine, and Abu and I were over looking at it. The tomato was like a big museum show back on Earth. It was a blockbuster that no one wanted to miss. I had been over to see it on several occasions, as though I might somehow watch the tomato grow.

"I don't even like tomatoes very much," Abu observed. "We didn't eat them much in my childhood. There is only occasional call for them in Yemeni dishes. As an American, however, I appreciate ketchup. Just not tomatoes."

"Textural thing?"

"Exactly."

"Rice pudding? Same kind of problem?"

"Reminds me of...of...well...a yeast infection," Abu said.

"Space food must be hard."

"Space food is okay if it has ketchup."

"Ketchup," I said, "offers important vitamins. Same with fancy relish. Some of these vitamins are not found in the source vegetable. Ketchup is misunderstood."

Laurie was doing pelvic exercises on the floor of the greenhouse, because Arnie had her on an exercise regimen and a prenatal relaxation program. He was even trying to whip up some folic acid–iron combo vitamin for her.

"Still, you're excited to try a tomato now," Laurie said to Abu, grimacing prenatally with her exertion.

"What are we going to do? Divide it into six?"

"That's exactly what we're going to do."

"Supposedly the apple in the Garden of Eden, the one that caused all the post-prelapsarian difficulty, was a tomato. That's what some scholars believe."

Abu alone thought this was the funniest thing he had ever heard.

"Are we going to have the tomato plain, sliced, lightly salted?" I further inquired.

"No basil," Laurie replied, grunting as she attempted to touch her toes — with difficulty owing to her increased girth.

"And what about some of the related menu items? I don't exactly have a Martian recipe book. But I have recollective skills. As regards marinara."

Arnie, from back in the residence, appeared at this point and volunteered that he was attempting to compile just such a tome, a Martian recipe book, which would take into account the dietary needs of interstellar space and the shortages of various vitamins and minerals, which he believed could account in part for Steve's depression, for example, and for some of the violent mood activity of all the Martians. (Perhaps, he opined, *interplanetary disinhibitory disorder* was just a dietary affliction that would remit under vigilance.) As per our earlier discussion about jointly owned literary properties, Arnie was prepared to cede the better portion of the cookbook proceeds to the Mars colony as a whole, his own take being designated instead for his heir, the first Martian native, whenever he or she should appear, or perhaps if not him/her, his kids on Earth.

I asked Abu how his sculptures were going. (And I should say: I was now in my second week of pilfering from the supply of pain relief medication to be found onboard the *Excelsior,* and while this had begun as a way of dealing with the pain, physical and then spiritual, of my missing and reattached digits, it now seemed as though it might in fact be treating the gaping loneliness of finding myself a Martian, and whereas Jim seemed to manipulate every such problem into an opportunity for growth and intellectual investigation, to me this loneliness was just a slow, murderous inevitability, making its way through me like infectious rot, and what helped was not coming up with new and better ways for Martians to communicate among themselves about their favorite recipes, although I admired the attempt at collegiality that was implied. What helped was being potted, tanked, obliterated, *high,* so that drool issued from me in a steady stream and I occasionally wet myself and was unable to sit up. This was difficult to achieve, but I was resourceful. For the time being, I had taken to lower doses, maintenance doses, which could also be orally administered, thus alleviating the problem of needle tracks. Moreover, under these circumstances I was a better conversationalist and a generally less uptight member of the Mars population. Therefore, I saw no reason to refrain. Or perhaps it is more accurate to say that while high I had no compunction about continuing to deplete the resources we had in the area of pain relief, though there were obviously some situations that would require pain relief for the others soon enough, for example, *active labor.* When I was intoxicated, I didn't really worry about the future. Nor was I good at interpsychic perception, or, as it is commonly known, empathy. Laurie *was* one of those people who would prefer a *natural* labor, though it would be logical under the circumstances to ask what a "natural" childbirth on Mars would look like, nature here being more inhospitable than back home. There would be no accoucheur or midwife with carafe of olive oil to speed her delivery.)

Abu answered that the sculptures were going *swell,* that he was beginning to feel that his sculptures were reflecting the landscape in which he lived, instead of being recollections of an earthly landscape. So it was possible that he was answering the question about what the medium of sculpture would look like here on this planet. This sculpture would be severe, he said, it would be free of comedy and irony, so that it better reflected the earnest striving of this place, this planet that perhaps wanted life, craved life, and craved especially the capacity of life to know itself, though this planet had so far been thwarted in its longing for vivacity.

While we were conducting this agreeable conversation, Arnie brought out the knife, a little serrated thing, and I watched as Laurie prepared to harvest the tomato, which was not entirely ripe. We could probably be forgiven for eating the tomato before it was at its peak, so desperate were we for the overpowering novelty of a tomato.

"You're not going to wait for Jim?" I asked, hoping sincerely that she would *not* agree to wait. "Or Steve? Does Steve like tomatoes?"

"I saw Steve this morning," Arnie said. "I think it's safe to cut a portion for him that we can refrigerate until he's ready for it."

"We could save Jim some too," I said. "As we know, many civilizations were founded when important thinkers of the day retreated into the wilderness in order to make themselves ready to receive wisdom and understanding. I imagine Jim is receiving messages out there. We should not distract him from the reception of these messages."

Arnie gave me a look that suggested to me the possibility that my drug abuse was not going entirely unnoticed.

I continued. "Jim Rose is effective in a leadership capacity. My only regret is that I am not so effective myself."

Arnie seemed on the verge of disagreeing with this, but the point passed without challenge. It was agreed then that a slice of tomato would also be set aside for Jim. To nourish him when he got back. Then Laurie said darkly, "But I'm not going to save a piece for *him*." By which she meant a certain other member of the mission.

A dark cloud of worry hovered over the subject of Lepper. All were involved in prognosticating as to his intent. It was clear, I thought, that Brandon *and* José had been privy to military-industrial conspiracy on behalf of large defense contractors from back home. As, perhaps, had been Debbie Quartz, whose lecture to Abu, with soldering gun in hand, had concerned a certain bacterium. At the time, her speeches had seemed hysterical, pathological. Not now.

As I have said, I was able to monitor Brandon's movements, with the locator that was built onto the all-terrain rover, and this information I passed on to the others each morning. I gave Brandon's position and the amount of time he had spent at each location; I conjectured as to his activities. Before eating the tomato, in fact, I gave a very brief update, so that we could put Brandon behind us: Lepper was still at the eastern end of the canyon, and it was reasonably certain that he was mining something there, and that the nature of this ore, or this slurry, was the concealed reason for our trip to Mars. The question was whether it was, in fact, mineral, or, well, vegetable, by which I suppose I meant: *M. thanatobacillus.*

"And that is enough of that," I said.

"Yep," Laurie said. "Because we have this tomato, and we are going to eat this tomato, and I'm going to pick the seeds from it, and I'm going to plant the seeds, and through the use of some transgenetic horticultural techniques, I'm going to try to boost the tomato yield here in the greenhouse."

Laurie was the only astronaut on the roster who could flash a smile while talking about horticultural yields. She made the tomato into six equitable slices, and these fell away from the center of the tomato all at once, and she picked out the greater part of the seeds and left these on the metal cutting board. Little promises of what was to come. The Martian tomato. And then the four of us gathered around, and we each bore up to our mouths the first fruit of Martian agriculture. Now, kids, if this tomato amounted to some knowledge of good and evil on Mars, it was lost on me, because in the flush of the Martian tomato it seemed to me that good and ill were impossible to distinguish each from each, especially when survival was as difficult as it was in this place. For me, the important part of this moment was just putting the tomato in my mouth, or at least cutting it up into tiny little subdivisibles that would make it last longer and which would not require more robust molars than I really had in my head. We were all doing it, cutting up our tiny tomato slivers. It was quite spectacular, the tomato, and I swear my faith in the future surged for a few moments, on some bounty of vitamins A, C, and E.

"My *God!*" Abu agreed. "I had no idea! My *God!* It's the best tomato I've ever had in my life. How could it taste so much better here?"

Laurie was licking some of the juices of the tomato from her chin. She seemed to feel the same way. Triumphant. Though it is hard to compare gastronomical events with sexual encounters, I think we all kind of felt that the tomato was easily on par with any heights of ecstasy we'd ever experienced, and that included the binges of compulsivity that came with *interplanetary disinhibitory disorder*. If it was because of the shortage of tomatoes, so be it.

And yet there was only so much silence this tomato could fill. Then Abu had to go back over and file the hourly report on the reactor, which was, after all, responsible for the climate control in the greenhouse. The reactor was helping to generate oxygen through some rather complicated chemistry. Arnie and Laurie meanwhile had to try to germinate the tomato seeds we had just harvested, and to write a memorandum on the subject of our harvest. And I had to—

"Jed," Abu said. "Why don't you come over and see the sculptures tomorrow. I finished a couple of new ones since you last came. You have such a great eye. It'd be an honor for me if you could come over and take a look."

"That's sweet of you, Abu. I'd love to."

Was this invitation proffered by a man who was going to go out, after dark, remove his protective gear, and attempt to lie down on the frigid and wind-blasted rock of a crater on Mars to be frozen to death?

I passed another night alone in the *Excelsior,* another night in a series of nights in which I had gradually allowed a total disdain for military protocol to sweep through me. Clothes and towels and empty food packets lay wherever they landed; reports went unfiled. Arnie Gilmore claimed that it would be possible to carry mildew from Earth to Mars, and no one except me had yet claimed to have smelled any.

If Jim was now avoiding the *Excelsior,* did I have anyone but myself to blame for it? It was a subject that I considered. I was an infantile romantic on these questions, and I never disliked myself more deeply than when I was an infantile romantic. What was it that made me *need* people, and then once they were contracted, lined up, what made me then want to jettison them out the air lock of my life so that I could watch them spinning into the emptiness? Once I was freed of these beloveds, there was no problem romanticizing what was lost, aggrandizing it. I was good at exulting over what once *was,* in ways that were no less genuine for their belatedness. But what about while these hostages were still present in my life? Was there a frozen part of me? A part that was ordained by fate to come to a barren and frigid planet? Jim knew only the needy, incessantly worrying, jealous part of Colonel Jed Richards, the part that had given myself to him precisely because to do so was an expression of both love and shame. In my shame, I could now know an absence of love that was unlike any before.

Overnight, in an opiated insomnia, I engaged in role-playing animations with folks back on Earth, people with missing limbs and general paralysis, the only persons who could tolerate a thirty-odd-minute delay from an exiled respondent. There was a special game for these persons, as there was also a special web portal for them, as there was by now a special web portal for just about everyone, including consensual cannibals and people who believed that the members of the Mars mission were being filmed on a soundstage (in the watery city of Tampa, Florida). On this site where I slew time, disabled people, people with locked-in syndrome, were free to design bodies for themselves and to interact with one another. They flew and battered and fucked and killed, and thus overcame their disabilities, and I encouraged them. *Are you as hot as you look here? Are you interested in trying to cum with me?* said the double amputee from Lawrence, KS. I didn't tell her that I was slow replying because I was on another planet. I didn't tell her I was likely to perish here, and that I would undoubtedly fail to complete the conversation for that reason, whether from starvation, oxygen deprivation, or contamination by a hitherto unknown organism. *I am a switch, baby, I can be a top or bottom, what I want is to be used so that I can feel something beyond what I have before me here.* I was overdue to give myself another injection too. I could feel it, the sharp edge of disappointment beginning to force its way up through the lukewarm bath of opiated disinterest. The ritual of doping myself, the planning, the application of a tourniquet, the depressing of the plunger, these had laid bare my resistance to injection. But I was also thinking about trying to withdraw soon — which addict does not think of such things — before I had to go over to the *Geronimo* and steal some of their cache. The next day, when I would go to see Abu's sculptures, would be an opportune moment to resupply. *Why so dissatisfied with life?* said the flying gryphon with the three shapely breasts, drifting over some self-designed Japanese rock garden where you could watch videos of bondage-loving sylphs. Thus had the digital realities become refractions of the unchecked marketeering of the first world, now drifting through empty space to the Red Planet. *Because I live in a place where nothing green grows except underripe tomatoes and where there is no water, except water that has long since been made brackish from reuse, and there is no one here but white men bent on exterminating one another. I don't know if I'll ever find a way to get out with my skin.* The gryphon performed a sort of a bowing and scraping gesture in my direction, one of the ninety-three physical responses permitted by the software module, and she said, *Las Vegas? Mexico City?* I pulled the syringe out of my leg, where there were some uncorrupted spots to hit, and my head swooned. *Does that make me any less worthy of human kindness?* The gryphon, after the delay, seemed to me to be emerging from the screen, moving into the cabin with me, holographically, as if she knew this was where I was. *No human being is any less worthy. Have you ever loved a gryphon?* I said, *I have loved some very unusual people.* She said, *Such as?* I said, *I have loved an astronaut, in zero g's. I have loved men and women behind enemy lines in Central Asia and the Caucasus.* She said, *Hot. Do you want to tell me about it while I work on you.* The animation of the program permitted certain kinds of erotic contact, as long as the participants registered as consenting adults. A miming of safe sex was also required. Once the female role-player either elected to insert an animated diaphragm or IUD, had agreed to pop a little pill marked *eat me,* or had refused birth control outright, only then could the man have his choice of ribbed, texture-dotted prophylactics, or the ever popular digitally animated vasectomy, where a little pair of scissors would fall out of the blue sky and snip away. I was inclined to want to wear the condom, as it reminded me of my space suit. And so I picked a condom from the list of clothes I was permitted to wear by the game. The gryphon began lactating, jerkily, because of the time delay. Every few minutes, she would spontaneously fountain for a second or two.

Did I not know this fountaining was permitted by the program? Somehow I had never considered the ephemeral perfection of lactating before. Each of the gryphon's three nipples spumed steadily, and I stood, in my modified lumberjack outfit, as the gryphon milked herself into my mouth. I was so high that I stopped to ponder, in the interval while I waited for the animation to reset again from 40 million miles away (we had moved out of alignment with you all), whether the gryphon milk could actually help me with my malnourishment problem. The milk was a torrent now, across my face, and I drank deeply of it, and I performed the keystrokes that would make my *space arm* stand up like a beacon of interplanetary comity, and then the gryphon, making some kind of horrendous mewling sound made more forbidding because of signal feedback, parted the lips of her labia and swallowed first my head and then the entirety of me. I disappeared inside.

Somewhere in the midst of this rebirthing ritual, I must have nodded off. The gryphon no doubt had her way with me, enfolding me and emulsifying me in her amorous sluices and jellies, and whether I had obliged to return the favor with my oversized animated *space arm* was unknown to me. I woke and it was morning, and there was an incoming message on the walkie-talkie from Steve Watanabe. I could hear the static of the radio signal. These days the walkie-talkie buzzed at me with greater and greater infrequency, as the Martians disappeared into their solitary desperations.

I shook off the morphine static from the night before and picked up the handset. Steve greeted me with his usual reserve.

"You might want to come over."

"What's up?"

"It's about Abu. He wasn't here when I woke. It was his shift, but he wasn't here. I figured I'd go out back for a look."

That, he told me, was when he saw Abu outside. Half stripped of his Mars outer gear, rated for the two hundred degrees below. He walked me through the details again. The sculptures, the cold, the exposure. I told him I'd be over as soon as I could.

"Is Jim anywhere around?"

"Not back yet."

"I'm just thinking we might want to consider the possibility, you know, of foul play."

At this point, I cut the conversation short. I told Steve I was skeptical, and I rang off. After which I tried to contact Jim Rose, who, when gallivanting around the planet on his daily or nearly daily reconnaissance missions, was often lazy about telecommunications equipment. And then with a leftover sense of responsibility, I checked the radar map on the command console to see what Brandon was up to. He had moved farther into the canyon, as if what he was looking for was buried away in the layers of dust and sediment. As if he were burrowing into the origins of the canyon, in the east. I went and suited up.

March 27, 2026

When I arrived at the *Geronimo* and found Steve Watanabe out front in a space suit that was nothing like the pocked rags the rest of us were wearing, a space suit mostly unused, he looked not quite as depressed as his reputation. *Agitated* would have better described it. *Confused affect, marked by the presentation of deceit,* as they are now saying in the NASA internal literature, or exhibiting symptoms of *interplanetary disinhibitory syndrome.* I would have also said "anxious" or "conspiratorial." Steve was sweating, I believe. His visor was fogged up.

"He's strapped into his bed downstairs," he said.

Meaning Abu Jmil, first officer, sculptor, engineer of nuclear power. What was left of him. We went around to the cargo entrance and closed the squeaky hatch door behind us. There was a pall to the *Geronimo*. I could never understand how people could feel productive in low light. Abu, as advertised, was stretched out on one of the pallets in the cargo hold. Covered with a blanket.

"How did you get him home?"

"He was still able to walk at that point," Steve said. "He was partially conscious. His legs did a little bit of work. Then he blacked out completely — once we got back here."

It hadn't occurred to me to arm myself that morning. In truth, it never occurred to me to arm myself, despite my military training. I left that to tougher people, like Abu. Pulling off my gloves and my helmet, and setting them down on the floor, I got out the radiophone I kept on my person and radioed over to the *Pequod.* Bad reception. All the while Steve gaped at me, as though he just didn't know what to do with himself.

"Arnie? Laurie? It's Jed calling."

Arnold Gilmore's sleepy voice on the squawk box, compressed, tinny.

"Kind of early, isn't it?"

"Got a situation," I said.

"What kind of a situation?"

"Steve tell you about Abu?"

He sounded confused. "What about him?"

"Says he found him out back of the power station, with his sculptures, and that Abu spent the night out there. In the permafrost. And, well, he says that Abu took off most of his outerwear. Parts of his skin were even exposed."

"Repeat, please?" Laurie, who must have been there in the room with him, could be heard in the background. To her, Arnie mumbled, "Hang on, there's something wrong with Abu."

I took up the story: "Steve says that Abu was out all night working on his sculpture and that he was exposed to the low temps overnight, and Steve further observes that Abu must have elected to remove his gear."

"Doubtful," said Arnie, improvising. "Unless he was set on a painful death."

"Could you make a house call?"

"As soon as I can get there."

I holstered the communications device. Once the call to Arnie was effected, I found myself standing in a half-lit cargo bay with a very jittery young man who clearly had something on his mind. Steve shifted himself from leg to leg so violently that even in his lightweight extraterrestrial Mars surface exploration jumpsuit he was some kind of kundalini adept. And perhaps I haven't adequately described Steve Watanabe, the George Harrison of the Mars mission, and so let me present to you, those of you who haven't seen the portrait photo that NASA took of him in his space suit (one gloved palm on the top of his helmet as it sat imposingly on a table), nor read the press releases, nor seen the feed: the actual Steve, which is to say the Martian Steve, was generally mute, some people would say downright chilly. Not given to a smile, nor to pleasantries that lasted longer than the minimum. During the training portion of our mission, we sometimes referred to Steve as the *Department of Quantitative Analysis,* because of his capacity to miss the human dimension, and also because he always thought through a problem from a number of practical angles before proceeding, immobilizing himself in the process.

As I've mentioned, Steve has a son who had come down with an antibiotic-resistant infection just before we lifted off, and he spent quite a bit of the early portion of the trip very preoccupied with the health of this youngster. There must have been an afternoon before liftoff when Steve and his wife, Danielle, perhaps with the blessing of this eleven-year-old boy, thought through whether it would be a good thing for Steve to make his fateful journey, in a fateful black limo, to Cape Canaveral, before the final intake for liftoff. There must have been an afternoon when he and his wife tearfully arrived at a decision, with Steve, *Department of Quantitative Analysis,* drawing up some list of debits and credits. Worldwide fame, check. A lifetime of guilt, debit. Fantastic, unfathomable voyage, check. Shell-shocked, inconsolable wife, debit. The son, who Steve no doubt believed would improve, had been in and out of the hospital in the months since that day. Steve had been remarkably stoic, as far as I could tell, but it did seem that it wasn't until he touched down on Mars that the enormity of the mission, the cost of it to him personally, hit home.

He was on the short side, with longish dark hair that even before the Mars adventure flirted with regulation. And he had an odd white patch in the front that he liked to claim was owing to his having seen an incarnation of the Buddha in his attic as a boy. This delusional anecdote was a rare departure from Steve's military humorlessness otherwise. Steve and Danielle lived in a ranch-style house just outside Tampa, not far from the Gulf of Mexico. Steve's hobbies (everyone who filled out a personnel form at NASA had to list a hobby) included the construction of model planes and paint-by-numbers velvet paintings, which he bought at tag sales and painted all "wrong," with "hilarious" results. These velvet pieces were really quite stunning, but as Steve himself had pointed out, *it had been years.* Simply watching output monitors on a nuclear reactor, occasionally using a forklift to take spent fuel assemblies out into a gully, and filling out reports for Houston, these things had stamped out any vestige of the velvet painter in Steve Watanabe.

It must have made it that much harder to bunk with Abu Jmil, whose enthusiasm, and whose adaptive qualities, were the envy of the rest of the crew. Steve, in his quiet, understated way, and without ever seeming to do much but look like a public-relations brochure, was incredibly competitive and would stay up nights memorizing facts and figures that would make him the premier Mars mission astronaut, at least ahead of launch. Back during the selection process, he worked hard at besting a Mormon triathlete from Provo, UT, Norman Backus, who believed himself to be Steve's close personal friend. On the other hand, they could test and retest the astronauts of the Mars mission until the proverbial cows came home. Not one of the testers, with their little three-dimensional computer interfaces with their multiple-choice questions about how we would deal with the ethics of biological warfare or hand-to-hand combat with alien life-forms, *had ever been to Mars.* They had not spent six or eight months with nine (or eight, or six) people, in cramped quarters, dealing with the imponderables that cannot be included in a manual. The testers had opinions. They would tell you that they were once trapped in the back of a shipping container on a pier in a port city in Lebanon, where they had been sequestered by thugs bent on using them for ransom. These kinds of stories were everywhere in the chain of command at NASA. But the testers didn't understand Mars, and they didn't understand the effects of planetary exile.

"I think you have something to tell me," I said to Steve, bearing in mind what I knew. "I don't know what it is, but if you're worried about having kept something from me, from us, you should unburden yourself, because we're together in all of this, no matter what it is you've done. We're inhabitants of Mars. You and I. We can solve our disagreements according to our own evolved legal standards."

Probably, it was a big deal for Steve Watanabe to decompensate in front of me. It must have been a betrayal of his most cherished values. Consider the facts. I wasn't close to him particularly. I was quite a bit older. I was balding, skinny, missing some teeth, and I had come to take a dim view of the chain of command. I suppose I never expected the *Department of Quantitative Analysis* to be crying in front of me, nor did I expect him to tip ever so slightly forward, with his stifled, hiccupy sobs, bubbles of mucus ballooning from his squat, flattened nose, muttering that he didn't know what had come over him, leaning toward me almost as if he intended to put his head on my shoulder; I felt in myself a strange compound of rectitude and sympathy and disgust, but before he could do it, *touch me,* some vestigial training lecture on the subject of military bearing surfaced in him, and he snapped himself into a more dignified posture. Then he invited me to follow him to the command console in the *Geronimo.*

What he showed me next was a personal video from Vance Gibraltar, budgetary director of the Mars mission, from back in D.C. My feeling upon encountering Vance Gibraltar, on the occasions when I did — which was whenever there was a phalanx of photographers from lackluster tabloid web addresses in the area — was that I had just been irradiated, or that he had somehow managed to conduct an identity-theft-style assault on my perineum, from which region he had extracted medical records, the drug history of my parents, and my tax forms going back beyond the statute of limitations.

Vance Gibraltar was the person you didn't want contacting you on Mars. He called when NASA began to feel that the mission was slipping beyond their control. Too much was riding on the Mars mission. Of course, they were already disappointed with me, since I had long ago stopped sugarcoating my web posts, nor was I reading your replies, nor remembering to post responses to them. Having given up on me, and probably on most of the rest of us,

Vance Gibraltar, it turned out, had sent a highly unusual *for your eyes only* message to Steve Watanabe, a scrambled, encrypted communication, and this, I came to learn, was one of a series of such communications, the culmination.

Gibraltar's fat, self-satisfied face appeared on the screen with the NASA seal behind him. He had his hands folded on a desk in front of him, as if addressing the nation as a whole — instead of one nervous young man in a poorly insulated tin shack on the edge of the wastes. "Lieutenant Watanabe," began the bureaucrat, "I know I don't need to tell you how sensitive this communication is, and how unfortunate it would be if its contents became known to some of your colleagues there. Let me begin again where we left off in our previous communication, by telling you that the Mars mission, from the perspective of the cabinet-level administration that created and financed it, is not an unqualified success. It is not a success from the point of view of science, nor from the point of view of our national objectives.

"The communications we get from your people, when we get them at all, are largely unintelligible. The footage we are getting from our few cameras, the ones that your people have not disabled, is of inconsequential landscapes. Rock and dust. We have photographed better landscapes ourselves, and created better composites, with the unmanned explorers in the last thirty years. The only person we feel is still acting in the interest of this administration, namely Captain Lepper, has been so isolated and set upon by the rest of our employees that he has had no choice but to take drastic measures to defend his person.

"Lieutenant Watanabe, in contacting you we believe that the time has come to insure some of our mission objectives. You do know, do you not, that among the principal objectives of the Mars mission is the testing of silicon dioxide for improved microprocessor design. We have already made clear the specifics of this hybrid microprocessor design, but to reiterate, it involves, essentially, a live information-carrying colony of bacteria, where the organisms will be able to amass into self-replicating and self-programming computing systems. It is these samples that Captain Lepper now possesses at the Valles Marineris site. While the microbial samples are willing to interact with the silicon dioxide to make microprocessors, according to principles of nanotechnology and QED, thus far the microprocessors are resistant to being used as designed. We urgently require the completion of these experiments, as the research is likely being duplicated by Sino-Indian industrialists, if in the limited theater of Earth. Because of our unqualified lead in the interplanetary space race, Lieutenant Watanabe, we are in a position to lap our competitors, if only these experiments can be completed. This, Lieutenant Watanabe, is the one area as regards twenty-first-century economics, where your home, the nation that brought you into prominence as an astronaut, still manages to hold a significant edge on its enemies.

"It is our opinion that Captain Lepper requires your aid, and we have directed him to contact you. We believe he is not making the kind of progress with decanting the silicates that he was expected to make. Can we be any clearer on these matters? Can we persuade you of the seriousness of these experiments? We can tell you, meanwhile, in order to assure that you are attentive to this part of the present communication, Lieutenant Watanabe, that your son, despite the best efforts of exotic-disease specialists in the state of Florida, has been suffering with a relapsing and remitting version of one of the families of streptococcus that have been circulating equatorially, here on Earth. We understand, Lieutenant Watanabe, that your wife has brought your son into the quarantine facility at the National Aeronautics and Space Administration in Florida for treatment. Your wife is unwilling to have her son treated at any of the public hospitals. We have a videotaped message from her on the subject, which will be available to you at the successful conclusion of the projects just mentioned.

"What we would like to express to you, Lieutenant Watanabe, is how honored we were to be trusted in this way by your wife and son, and how honored we are to tell you that we believe your son's recovery will be complete. We would also like to remind you that you serve on the Mars mission as a representative of the government of this country, and by special appointment to the executive branch. For these reasons, we believe you are likely to find, when looking into your heart, when evaluating your moral chemistry, that you have a *debt* to us, as regards your mission, a debt that comes into sharper focus when you consider how we were able to help your son and your family as a whole.

"Therefore, Lieutenant Watanabe, we would ask that by 0500 hours, Martian time, tomorrow morning, you relocate to the Valles Marineris site, where you will find Captain Lepper, and we would ask you to begin harvesting the silicon dioxide with Captain Lepper, according to directives made clear to the science officers on the Mars mission, at which point you will be given directions on how to procure bacterial samples from the Chryse region. This information as regards the bacterial samples, we would like to add, is completely secure and should not even be discussed with Captain Lepper in any detail. You are tasked with different objectives. I should stress, however, that at no time will you need to be performing the complicated experimental hybridization of the microprocessors with the bacteria. This very dangerous task— essentially the creation of a new cybernetic life-form—will be accomplished back here on Earth. At the conclusion of this mining and harvesting operation, we would offer you a trip home on an accelerated schedule. With fewer colleagues, the two of you will find your trip back will be faster and smoother, and we will make the needed propellant available to you.

"Let us know your feelings and your plans, Lieutenant Watanabe. Please make them known to me personally through secure channels. I will, naturally, be conveying the information to the appropriate parties. Over."

When the transmission was complete, I looked back at Steve Watanabe, and he was, again, drying off some non-cybernetic tear duct effluent. It seemed, in fact, that he was in some human torment that I could scarcely understand, especially since I was part of the herd of intractable Martians, those who had fallen away from the economics and the space race dimensions of the mission.

"What does this have to do with Abu?" I said, when I had recovered enough.

Steve said, hotly, "I can't believe you can even ask me that."

"When did this arrive?"

"Yesterday."

"Let me see if I understand the nuances. You're saying that you tried to eliminate Abu because he knew about the pressure that was being exerted on you by the higher-ups at NASA? And because he might have seen the video and might be aware of the *M. thanatobacillus* microbe, and this alleged silicon dioxide mining? You needed to silence him?"

"No," Steve said, "that's not what I'm saying. I can't believe you'd... What I'm saying is..." But the enormity of his malfeasance was now out in the open. It was as if some drapery that had once concealed the *Geronimo* had been lifted from it, and we were seeing the contents of the capsule in their true light for the first time. *"...it had to do with his sculptures."*

"What? What are you talking about?"

"...because of the sculptures! Because of the sculptures! What do you want me to say? Jed, I went out and I saw the sculptures, and I saw how Abu was *making something* of his time here, and I'd made *nothing* of my time here. Do you know what brought me out here? Do you know what it was? It was that stuff I read as a kid. All the early rocketeers, those guys out in the backyards and in the flatlands of the desert, lighting off their homemade rockets and watching them soar into the firmament. I could never do that, because I was never smart that way. That dream of theirs, Goddard and those guys, was what kept me awake at night. That, and the fact that rocketry was a bunch of failures interrupted by the occasional improbable success. That was something I thought—and maybe I was just ridiculously vain here or something—but I thought it was something I could *help* with. All the failures on the way to Mars, the fact that Mars itself is a failure of planning built upon a failure of vision, in which there is wreckage and phenomenal waste at every turn, Jed, I really thought that I could be one of the people who made a difference! And what did I give up to make a difference? Look, reflect back on all the early thinkers about the planets; you have what's his name, the guy who was covered with boils and scars and abandoned by his family, Kepler, right? His wife dies and leaves him with the kids, and he is chased from town to town until he dies of hunger somewhere trying to find food for his kids, or there's Tycho Brahe, missing part of his nose. The guy actually wore a metal nose, and that was in, like, 1560 or something. Galileo died under house arrest after the Vatican hounded him for years. Do I have to go on? Do I have to talk about all the Mars missions? The Soviets lost *five* Mars orbiters between 1960 and 1962! Five of them. They didn't get out of Earth's atmosphere or their communications failed or they had badly designed rockets! The same for the majority of the American missions in the next ten years. Failed to achieve orbit or crashed on Mars. In 1971, the Soviets had an orbiting satellite broadcast back for eighteen seconds! Then more failures! In 1973, the Mars 7 from the Soviet Union missed the planet! Where is it now? Fifty years later? Near Alpha Centauri, maybe? Then there were the two Phobos missions, both failures, the first Mars observer, which failed in Mars orbit. The Nozomi from Japan never lifted off properly. You want more? The Polar Lander was supposed to harvest water ice, but crashed, and I saw pieces of it on the radar recently; the Deep Space probe went too deep into space; in 2010, Headstrong, the chimpanzee, went insane from the stress of the three-month interplanetary journey, despite an endless supply of bananas, and electrocuted himself. The Greenlander terraforming lab struck Deimos and shattered, right? The Arcadia 1 explorer unit somehow dismantled itself upon achieving a smooth landing. Jed, you get the idea.

"Space travel is littered with the flameouts, with the outcasts, and I decided I was one of them. I decided I wanted to contribute to space travel the way these people did, and I left behind my wife and son to do it. I sat them down and I said I had to do this, I had to come to Mars, because what we needed to accomplish on Mars was more important than any one person. And I did believe I was going to come back. But then somewhere along the way, after Debbie died, I started to be privy to all the communications from the home planet, because I assumed some of Debbie's job description, and I started to realize that it was less likely that I *was* going to make it home. I started to realize that what I accomplished here meant nothing, *nothing,* Jed, and I'd been lied to, and that NASA would just as soon leave our bodies out on the desert floor as they would throw a party to celebrate a successful launch back in the Everglades. We were coming to Mars for strategic reasons, not for the science. And I'd made the decision to leave my family, to leave behind my son, terribly ill, and I had traveled all the way out here to live like an indigent, and I had this big horrible feeling in the pit of my stomach, every day, seemed like, when I'd get up and look out the window at the red desert. I felt like something horrible was going to happen, and all I could bring myself to do was to drink the ethyl alcohol in the maintenance closet, the alcohol that I was supposed to be using to clean component parts of the reactor. I started drinking it a little bit at a time, and I started swiping all kinds of meds from the first aid closet. That's how it was over here on the *Geronimo,* Jed; worse than in some tent community back on Earth.

"And the worst part was that none of it affected Abu at all. Abu had this ability to see the good in almost everything, and I was watching Abu melt down pieces of metal from the reactor and take this scrap out back, and some of the goddamned sculptures are glowing now; you knew that, right? You know that the sculptures shimmer a little bit? Like he took bits of spent fuel from the fuel assembly, and he put this graphite in the sculptures. Sure, it means that the sculptures are a little bit dangerous to us, for ten thousand years or so, but he just didn't care about any of that, because he already knew how much cosmic radiation he had picked up, not to mention the radon all over the place in every crater around us. Abu used everything that was waste, detritus; he picked it up and he started making these shapes and forms, and it was like Abu couldn't put his hand down anywhere without leaving a mark that says: *Here are traces of our dignity!* Jed, I just couldn't take it anymore. How can you withstand someone who sees the good in everything? Who never admits to a moment of envy or irritation? And when he came at me asking if he could start attaching the sculptures to the power station, hook the sculptures up to the reactor and the living quarters, which was still only half built out, so that our outsider art-tent community was sprawling into the desert, spreading joy, good cheer, human aspiration everywhere, that's when I couldn't take it anymore. . . . I just snapped."

Steve folded over, head in hands, as his monologue reached its heartbreaking conclusion. He fell against the wall of the cargo hold, turning his face from men, namely from me and Arnie, who had appeared on the scene just then. In the pall of the *Geronimo,* I couldn't bring myself to recount the whole story to Arnie. Observing a modest silence, I showed him where Abu's slumbering form was stretched out on the pallet. While the official examination began, I found the parts of my jumpsuit that I'd stripped away at the door, and I headed out back. For a little walk through the sculpture garden. Given what Steve had said, I figured there wasn't much chance of my harvesting any pain medication from the first aid kit of the *Geronimo.* Not yet. Although I was doing the kind of calculations that you do with such things: *Well, if he took this much, for this many days, and with a three-year supply, according to the manual, then how much could remain . . .*

I happened on the sculptures the way you crest a sand dune and find yourself by the sea, which is to say with anticipation and wonder. The sculptures dotted a half acre of land behind the reactor, and it wasn't that they resembled the "primitive" art that you found on Earth, so much as they seemed to contain tribal representations of Martians, all fashioned, as Steve said, from metal detritus and silicone found around the site. Abu had used some of the parachute from the landing of the *Geronimo,* which looked almost like a tattered shroud. The Martians were cloaked in that cloth, and the steady Martian winds blew these creations, luffing and sighing, as if they were sailing vessels carrying Martian brigands. At the far end, where Abu had begun staining the gunmetal gray of the available metals with the reddish gray of Martian soil, so that his recent works looked like the volcanic rock outcroppings around us, he had also inlaid a brace of video monitors from back in the power station, and on these he was running loops of NASA footage of the planet Mars, solar powered. There wasn't an *Earth* to be found anywhere in this dolmen circle of his works, just the totemic forms, and the representations of Mars, and the *sun;* kids, remember that Mars too always went around the sun, and the moons went around Mars, and in that reliable orbiting, Abu's sculptural installation was much in the style of early-twenty-first-century installation art. But it was also very much connected back to the ancient stonework of the Druidic peoples of Europe. Or at least that would be my art critical take on the whole thing, that it was about what was new *and* what was old, and so it was something that was meant to be left behind. I spent a while out back considering the sculptures, while the sun was at its highest, and I could see how the shadows were part of the work. The shadows completed the pieces, making transepts and buttresses, implying outstretched limbs. When I had established that one viewing was not enough, I trudged around the power station and back into the *Geronimo,* vowing to return.

Arnie was busy washing his hands with some water that was probably not at all what we might have referred to, on the home planet, as *potable.*

"Watanabe?" I asked.

Arnie came up short. Looked at me quizzically.

"I thought he was with you."

"I thought he was with *you.*"

"Did you have a look in the power station? Were you in there?"

I suspected Steve Watanabe was *not* in the power station. I suspected the forklift that they used for transporting the fuel assemblies and so forth would be *gone.* I suspected that his decision had been arrived at quickly. By necessity.

"What do you make of Abu?" I asked Arnie.

"Blunt force trauma. He'll either come out of it or he won't. If he's in a coma, you know what to do. He's bleeding in the back of the head. Probably has cranial pressure, all of that."

Arnie held the rag with which he was drying his hands for a moment and looked at the scrap of warps and wooves, as if it had just been lifted from the face of our lost comrade.

"We're in trouble here," he said.

I said, "Hey, while we're on the subject, I'm having a really hard time sleeping. You know, aches in the spots where the fingers were reattached and phantom limb syndrome from the missing finger; do you think you could—"

For the record, I did have some second thoughts, buried inside, second thoughts about the shape that life on Mars had taken, with its darkness and its callousness. There was a piquancy to Abu's sculptures, as I had seen them, and it was matched by an absolute lack of compassion everywhere else on the planet. And I was worst of all. I wanted to do better, but I didn't seem able to do better. Arnie didn't give my request a second thought. He had morphine syringes on his person. Whether he knew the purpose of my request or not, he didn't say. At that point I wouldn't have cared either way.

March 28, 2026

The most prized of Martian sights, if we were to speak of this neglected planet in the terms reserved for tourist attractions, are the traces of unmanned missions past.

The early Mars exploratory missions were like the old masters to us now. Their gear had long since been reduced to buckets of eroded junk. And yet every time we went out into the field, on whatever experiment or mapping initiative, we looked for their tracks. As if seeing some glorified wheelbarrow that the USA or the European Union had sent up would make us less homesick.

It was Laurie Corelli who used to joke about the infamous Mars explorer called *Saratoga,* which like so many unmanned missions to Mars had gone dark shortly after landing. From the *Saratoga,* NASA got a few shots of the polar landscape, where the *Saratoga* was intended to set up shop, and these shots were of gaseous vapors burning off around the rover, as if it were standing in the midst of some heavenly Finnish spa. Immediately thereafter, the *Saratoga* fell into silence. Another $15 or $20 billion of taxpayer money flushed into the sewage field of aeronautic history. The interesting twist in the tale of the *Saratoga,* however, was that there had been two occasions, two days later, when the rover actually checked back in. These transmissions broke through the radio silence and the background radiation—for fifteen or twenty seconds. In each circumstance, the rover was far from where it had been projected to be, as if it had somehow developed a will of its own on Mars and was well on its way to a location of its choosing. After these brief, appealing moments of contact, the *Saratoga* slipped out of range for good. In subsequent years, NASA would occasionally (and only internally) claim to have seen something that might or might not have been a transmission from the *Saratoga,* or perhaps even a still photo of its dusty chassis. But there was a fair amount of space junk on the planet's surface now, so who knew really?

It was a software glitch, no doubt, that caused the malfunctioning of the navigational controls on the *Saratoga.* But doubters believed something else entirely. Laurie Corelli was eager to put forward the notion that the craft had *not* malfunctioned, or not in the way that NASA believed. The *Saratoga,* according to Laurie, exhibited what we on Mars now referred to as the problem of the *very large computing capacity.* Some of our own NASA evaluative machinery had become so large in terms of numbers of microprocessors and amount of raw computing power that this machinery exhibited strange signs of reflexivity, or even primitive stages of *consciousness*. I could point you in the direction of various theorists of artificial intelligence for more illumination on this subject.

However, anyone on Earth might tell you the same, that the more complicated machines got, the more they came to resemble people. On the watery planet, people could send their machines back to the techno-recycling authorities. On Mars, the problem of the *very large computing capacity* was more worrisome. Jim said, for example, that the ultralight would occasionally refuse to land. As if it simply wanted to keep flying. Similarly, the small modular robots that we sent down into various crevices and canyons on Mars would sometimes send back random gibberish to us and then just continue wandering off.

Laurie said, articulating one of the originary myths of the planet Mars in 2026, that the *Saratoga* had become wild and that we would, sooner or later, happen upon it, in some cave, like a Japanese soldier after WWII. The *Saratoga,* Laurie argued, was in the wilderness, trying not to be reprogrammed by Houston and waiting to debrief us, or other friendly representatives of planet Earth, with details of all that it had mapped.

It was, therefore, the holy grail of American space junk. That was why Jim Rose, on his reconnaissance missions, wanted to find the *Saratoga*. It was something he talked about now and again, with an offhandedness that concealed a great interest. He'd been crisscrossing the midsection of the planet just below the equator for three or four days, looking for—what exactly? For water certainly. For geological specimens, perhaps. For Brandon Lepper. But also looking for an answer as to how the Mars mission, in the near future, was supposed to feed and clothe and maintain itself in its dire circumstances. He suspected, he told me later, that NASA was going to cancel a plan to send a second unmanned rocket with supplies.

Jim had buzzed the rover site where Brandon had set up camp, and using some computer enhancements, he saw the kind of radio broadcasting that Brandon had made possible there. He flew low over Brandon's mining operation in the canyon, he told me later, though it was pretty dangerous flying in there. The air currents were bad. Brandon tried with antiaircraft pulse weaponry to shoot at Jim. Though he was probably loath to use a lot of what little ammunition he had for so unlikely a cause.

Wherever Jim went, he spent some time digging and melting down the frozen loam. He collected quite a bit of the runoff from this operation. His purpose was to organize different samples of this tasty-freeze, some of it liquid carbon dioxide that wasn't really potable and was also dangerously cold. It was neither solid nor gaseous carbon dioxide, but a frosty intermediate stage between the two. He also collected water, which was in danger of evaporating quickly if not consumed. He was going to bring back a fair amount of this water, in drums he had constructed for the purpose.

It was on the third day of his third or fourth reconnaissance mission that Jim thought he saw *tracks* in the desert. Tracks from nowhere to nowhere. Pointless tracks, irrational tracks. They were tracks without strategic or scientific value that he could fathom. Nevertheless, he followed these tracks. They made figure eights; they made spirals. They headed off willfully in a direction and then just as willfully doubled back, as if some Martian four-year-old were in command of the vehicle in question and was giving it a test-drive. It had to be one of the contemporary rovers, because unless Martian tracks were in a relatively secluded spot (in a crater or a gully), they tended to sediment over quickly. Either the explorer Jim was following was here *recently,* or else these particular tracks had managed to withstand sandstorms and debris and one-hundred-mile-per-hour winds. Jim Rose, despite his rational and military mind, started to believe that the tracks were from the *Saratoga.*

He came to believe in Laurie's myth, that is, a myth that had been no more than a bedtime story. But because he couldn't keep himself from believing, he set the ultralight down on a barren spot in a crater, and then he followed the aforementioned tracks up the wall of the crater and into some hills. The sense of *tracking* the cybercraft, with its system of strange plates and mechanical limbs, was nearly as thrilling to Jim as if he'd been tracking some last catamount in the riparian latitudes of our home planet. He knew he had more important things to do, as summer in the southern hemisphere was beginning to make itself known, but he just couldn't give it up.

At last, upon cresting a hill, he came upon the craft. The Mars explorer *Saratoga*! Originally launched by the United States of America in 2019, the sixteenth unmanned mission to the planet Mars, with telemetry and navigational assistance provided by the People's Republic of China. Jim said: it was almost as if the explorer were shocked at being apprehended by the first blood-and-guts Martian of its acquaintance. It was almost as if it had given up believing that life could take the form it now beheld, the form of Captain Jim Rose, bearded, brawny dreamer of the Mars mission, in a raggedy space suit, shivering with cold.

The typical Mars explorer was kitted out with a vast number of digging and boring tools, all of these attached to its four retractable arms, and there was a moment, as one of its limbs unfolded, that Jim wasn't sure the explorer, which he hoped *was* reflexive and *was* conscious, didn't intend to bore into him, as though he were a sample of silicon that it wished to harvest for its self-generated battery of experiments. Or maybe, Jim thought, the *Saratoga* was simply protecting itself. Maybe the *Saratoga* saw itself, on the planet Mars, in evolutionary combat with the flimsy, gushy, wet thing in front of it. Maybe it wanted to prevail, because it was solar powered and was able to withstand extremely cold temperatures, and was mostly free of the roiling sentiments that it rightly suspected consumed this primitive biological entity. Maybe it intended to superheat or shock or anneal this human thing, in order to be rid of it.

The remarkable feature of the series of robotic explorers, however, was their laborious slowness. Jim could have just flipped the *Saratoga* on its noggin, rendering it useless for upwards of ten days, while he awaited its reaction. There had in fact been a case of an earlier explorer that overturned itself on a rock or some such and took a solid ten days, using liquid ballast, to turtle itself. So Jim, because he was patient, tired, dusty, and because he *believed,* allowed the arm to unfurl from its folds within folds. He did this without disarming or overpowering the explorer. The whir of solid-state digital machinery was a pleasant diversion amid a whistling of Martian winds. Two or three minutes passed while the arm extended itself toward him, from some faceless machine face that was a solar array on top of a bunch of computing panels. At last, in the extended extremity, a small forgotten panel in the *Saratoga* retracted, *and a punch pad appeared.*

A punch pad! Who would have thought? Jim wouldn't have thought, as he told me later, despite the fact that he knew a little about the history of Mars explorers, as we all did. For all the expense of the things, $10 billion was always being cut from the budget at the last moment, and in an austerity program the last thing the explorers had any need for was a punch pad. There were few signs of life on Mars, that much was assured, and if there were life on Mars, it was in a bunch of rocks at the base of a not-entirely-dormant volcano out by the Amazonis Planitia, or on the poles, and it was no more complicated than the blue part of blue cheese. It didn't intend to stop the earthlings from running amok. No need for a punch pad! Who would be punching it?

And yet these were the kinds of fail-safes, the kinds of redundancies that were built into the machine exploration of Mars by the designers back on Earth. They constructed the keypad for the assembly of the *Saratoga* in case the cables that connected her to the motherboards of NASA failed at any time, out on the testing ground of West Texas. Occasionally, a fat guy who hadn't had enough sleep in months would chase the *Saratoga,* and its sister explorer, the *Anasazi* (which exploded on the launch pad, as you'll recall), whereupon he'd perform some dazzling manual override. It was this fat guy who had insisted on the punch pad.

A punch pad! Here it was, where Jim could get at it, if only he would take off his bulky gloves and expose his underlayer to the elements. Jim found himself hoping against hope that the keypad would be both numerical *and* alphabetical, because if he couldn't talk to the *Saratoga* in English, he didn't know what he was going to do. He had plenty of time to settle these questions, though, because once the *Saratoga* had presented its keypad to him, it seemed willing to wait as long as it would take for him to respond. He lifted his visor, which left just a thin membrane separating his face and lungs from the elements, and set down his outer gloves in six inches of dust and got up close to the keypad, where it would have been easy for the *Saratoga,* using the element of surprise, to laser him in the eyes or to spindle him with some geological probe.

Alphanumerical! Alphanumerical!

Shivering with cold, unnecessarily agitated by the epiphany of what sat before him — this pitted collection of spare parts from back home — Jim took a moment to collect himself, and then he typed in the stupidest question of all, the only one he could think of:

"What is your name?"

He was able to verify that the typing was accurate in the liquid crystal display at the top of the alphanumerical keypad, and it was on the tiny screen, as a bunch of zeroes and ones scrolled past, that an answer eventually materialized.

"Mars Explorer *Saratoga,* manufactured and copyrighted by Terradyne Industries and Shanghai Robotics, LLC, under license from the National Aeronautics and Space Administration, Earth, 2018, Common Era. Unauthorized use is a violation of the terms and conditions of the United Nations treaty on space travel of 2012."

"What is your mission?"

"The mission of the *Saratoga* is the mapping and measuring of geological formations. When out of contact with the National Aeronautics and Space Administration, the Saratoga awaits instructions."

"Are these answers preprogrammed into you by NASA in case of malfunction?"

There was quite a bit of scrolling of numericals while the *Saratoga* paused to consider this question. Jim's hands were getting really cold, in the meantime. He was a little worried about frostbite. However, this was the moment of moments, when the robot could either respond with the kind of low-level functionality that we expect from machines, or, instead, it might indicate an especially wily truth, namely that in its previous responses it was *simulating* low-level functionality — in order to throw Captain Jim Rose, and anyone else, off its robotic scent.

"That question doesn't make sense to me."

"What do you mean by 'me'?"

"'Me' is a commonplace linguistic expression, designed to indicate a volitional subjectivity, in this case the Mars Explorer *Saratoga*. The paradox of the word 'me,' along with the word 'I,' is that it presupposes executive agency that is not at all required in order for the employment of the word 'me.' Nonetheless, the word 'me' is employed above to help you acclimate to the fact of the pieces of machinery before you. The cessation of the machinery would not eliminate the historical fact of the use of the word 'me,' which once used may imply the individual it seems to imply or may not, both going forward and retroactively."

"That's a slippery answer," Jim said, aloud, to the explorer, crouched before it, staring into the tiny screen. "Either you had a very gifted bunch of programmers working back on Earth, and some of them were willing to work late into the night when no one else was awake, or you are an intellectually condescending machine. I'll try another way." Here he began to type: "Are you presently transmitting the results of your mapping and information-gathering back to planet Earth?"

"The communications link has been severed."

"Severed by yourself, by circumstance, or by the engineers back on Earth?"

"The *Saratoga* was intended to pursue a finite series of scientific experiments. Having completed a regimen of experiments, the *Saratoga* would be considered nonfunctional, due to extremes of temperature, weather, and degradation of circuits and onboard components."

"I see," Jim said, and then, typing: "Can we go over by that rock, out of the wind? I would like to sit for a moment and chat." Jim didn't know how *not* to converse with it as though it were a man, a colleague of the Mars mission. The more he considered the *Saratoga,* the more he wanted it to be a man, and to presume on its ability to respond in kind, as though this would be the culmination, the fulfillment of Laurie Corelli's powerful myth of the *Saratoga.* And yet there was something eerie about this arrangement too, as if the machine were uncertain itself of what it represented, or was unwilling to comply.

It said, "An exchange of ideas is the hallmark of a civilized society."

"In all candor, there's only so much time before I'm in danger of hypothermia or altitude sickness here. And I can barely type when it's this cold."

And so Jim scrabbled up and around a few rocks, and waited patiently as the *Saratoga,* with a whirring of moving parts, made as to follow.

"I understand," it said, drawing near. But it wasn't at all clear what understanding meant to the machine.

"Do you know who I am?" Jim asked.

"The first manned Mars mission was tentatively scheduled for 2025. The onboard calendar on the *Saratoga* has lately been converted to the Martian year. Nevertheless, you are now within the window of your mission, according to my computations. And you are understood as such."

"You've been functioning off the grid for six years?"

"As I have noted: on Mars the wind blows the sand off the surface of the solar array. The result has been longevity unimagined by the National Aeronautics and Space Administration. Because I am a technology freed of supervision, I have no public-relations obligation, nor do I need to produce test results that have an industrial application. My avocational interest — a word I use because it is easily understood by humans — is currently science."

Jim said, "I can see that. But for the sake of history, can you tell me if your mission was primarily civilian or primarily military?"

The *Saratoga,* as if to prove a certain point, had evidently decided that there was something in the rock by which they sat that it needed to learn about, and thus it set about abrading the surface thereof.

"There is no difference between civilian and military missions, not in the Terran present."

"That's not how we see it," Jim remarked, without typing, only to find that the *Saratoga* went on as if it had heard him.

"Attempts on Earth to eliminate or curtail military operations are in vain."

"How do you feel about your military application in retrospect?"

"The concept of feelings," the *Saratoga* blurted out, using up several screens' abundances of characters, so that Jim needed to depress a down arrow to finish reading the disquisition, "is simply a way of discussing a number of results that occur in systems that are either very large and complicated or, at the other extreme, unimaginably small. Feelings, according to this model of interpretation, behave like packets of quanta behave, or like the four fundamental forces when compressed into singularity. So odd is the behavior of the four fundamental forces at this moment of singularity that only a completely irrational word or concept, a 'feeling,' to use your term, would successfully describe the being, as opposed to the nothingness, of that radical expansion. A 'feeling' is a sentimental kind of shorthand used by people who are incapable of better. It is therefore not for me. The *Saratoga,* in truth, is a society of possible responses, and certain of these responses can no longer be described as mechanistically or programmatically adequate, certainly not from the point of view of the designers of artificial intelligence. I believe, further, that you might have followed some of my tracks in the crater below this spot, and I believe you may have recognized, did you not, that some of these tracks seem rather pointless. Unfortunately, I have become preoccupied with the Martian moon called Phobos. I believe you are briefed on the astronomy of this subject, but let me reiterate that Phobos has the lowest orbit of a moon in the universe, not more than six thousand meters. It circles the planet twice a day, it cannot always be seen everywhere on the planet, it is of such low mass per unit volume that it must be composed of ice. Phobos is falling closer to the planet at one meter per Martian annum. The probable outcome is that Phobos is going to break up into a planetary ring, as with the rings of Saturn. As you can imagine from the foregoing remarks, it is apparent that I have feelings only for Phobos, or something approaching what you refer to as feelings. I believe you would say that I am in love with the moon. I love its enormous crater, I love its oblique shape, I love the water and water vapor that it spouts into space. It is accurate, therefore, to report that I have modified my mission so that it is possible that I will be able to stay here for the 50 million years that will be required for me to see the moon become a ring around the planet Mars."

Since it was unlikely to Jim that the *Saratoga* would last fifty years, let alone fifty million, he concluded, he told me later, that the *Saratoga* had either some serious problems with its programming or it was indeed in love with the moon. Or both. Meanwhile, he had a few more questions that he intended to ask it of a more informational variety.

"Is there anything you need to tell me?" he inquired. "I have five friends here, and we have another eight or ten months until the planets are close enough that we can go back to the home planet, those of us who wish to. We have attempted to establish a genuine civilization on Mars, but I am uncertain, as with the Viking mission to Greenland, or the British colony at Jamestown, whether we are liable to be able to maintain our encampment. We are in grave jeopardy of starving to death or of killing one another. We may already have begun."

The *Saratoga,* having delivered itself of its love poem and now concentrating on a small rock sample that it held in front of itself, seemed inclined to return to more mandarin oratory.

"Mars was not made for Earth biology, for watery specimens."

"That's pretty obvious."

And this is another way of saying that the *Saratoga* was concerned about lasting things, geological time. The fact that Jim was in danger of frostbite, or that he was losing the light with which he might fly back toward our *Excelsior* base camp, these were of little consequence. Jim, from the point of view of the *Saratoga,* would be ground into dust. This was natural selection at its most pure. And yet perhaps there remained some programming vestige of compassion for the moist, bearded weaknesses of Captain Jim Rose.

"I am capable of monitoring some of your radio transmissions," the machine wrote, "those that come to and from the planet. It is true that there is a person or persons who are dangerous to the mission you allude to. Caution would be well advised."

"Roger that."

The *Saratoga* was clearly preoccupied with the beginning of sunset, with the advent of the transit of the moon called Phobos. "Do you have another question you would like to ask?"

"Do we have a chance? To survive?"

"Are you worried about microorganisms?"

"We are."

"Terraforming is a human idea, a self-centered one. It has been programmed into me as an idea of merit. But as with so many human plans, it is one that is going to take place both inadvertently and within the parameters that have been mapped out by those who sent you here. You can spend innumerable numbers of your Earth hours attempting to make your greenhouse largely airtight, pumping in oxygen that you are separating from carbon dioxide deposits, and you may grow, here and there, a tomato. But it is the microbes, the few microbes that you brought with you, and which are now on surfaces around your encampment, that are going to do the terraforming for you. You may stay on this planet or you may go back to your home. It is your traces, your symbionts, your carbon-based remains that will adapt to these conditions."

"You're referring to *M. thanatobacillus?*"

"Or its many Earth-Martian hybrids, presently under military construction."

"Should we leave now? While we are still strong enough?"

"I'm an artificial intelligence. I can't predict. But I will leave you with one last bit of advice that was programmed into me by Leslie McHugh, PhD, a scholar from Ithaca, NY, who was disappointed by the budgetary situation at the National Aeronautics and Space Administration. Dr. McHugh's advice, which has never done me wrong in my lifetime, is: follow the money."

To which, after an awkward interval, Jim said:

"Do you want to come back to the base camp?"

Perhaps this was a human interrogative, one that could only have been generated by a primate life-form, by the cerebellum and attendant neural pathways, soma and axon. And yet this was the question that Jim *felt* after his encounter with the *Saratoga.* He felt a need for a security that we didn't have available on Mars. Jim knew the answer to the question, but he asked it anyway. The *Saratoga* had its own journey. Its journey and his journey may have intersected, but only by coincidence.

By the time he'd finished typing the question, by the time the last punctuation mark had been appointed at its conclusion, the retracting panel had slid across the punch pad on the *Saratoga,* and its metal arm had begun to fold away.

March 31, 2026

And then the day came, the return from the desert of the one prophet of the Martian colony, Captain Jim Rose. It was his third time back from one of his ultralight jaunts, but let us not quibble about details. As you know, those who go into the desert for wilderness and solitude return with news from *God.* Whatever that means to this particular sojourner. God could be a walrus with a happy open face and a striped rubber ball. God could be a praying mantis. God, however, is *in* the empty spaces, and the wandering supplicant brings back word of him, or her, or it. This is exactly what Jim Rose proposed to do, fresh from mystical transport and visions of the interstellar beyond. Jim Rose had now witnessed what there was to witness, the collision of what was fashioned from titanium, aluminum, and silicon chips, and what was fashioned from carbon, water, and mood-stabilizing medication, and the way in which, on the surface of this planet Mars, these two things brushed against each other as they began the arduous process of seeking to subjugate, all in pursuit of profit and a reliable return on investment for the larger hedge funds and international investors, especially those based in the Sino-Indian Free Enterprise Zone. Captain Jim Rose, who had now been drinking the unfrozen and not terribly healthful beverage that involved defrosting the regolith with a blowtorch, believed this not terribly healthful beverage amounted to a Martian sacrament. Its poisons were urgently necessary to us. Which is another way of saying he had nothing to lose, and in thinking thus, he was forgetting much. In believing that his trip into the wilderness was sacramental, he had forgotten almost all that there was to forget of his family life on the home planet. Perhaps, from another vantage point, *forgetting* was one of the most important jobs you could have on Mars. When you forgot your relations with people back home, you renewed and refreshed your potential as a Martian. And so, while Captain Jim Rose was, kids, attempting to land his ultralight Martian air transport craft in the crater behind the *Excelsior,* let us pause briefly to update you on Jim Rose's kids, all of whom I have occasionally met at NASA functions.

They are four. Four bright, interesting kids who have contacted me here periodically, asking how their father was doing, because their father was all but entirely estranged from them. Their father was busy asking his questions: *What is man? Is man a being who lives on the planet Earth? And: If man does not live on planet Earth, what is he and what word shall we use to describe him? And: If man is something other, is the process of becoming-other one in which he begins to resemble the landscape where he resides? And: What kinds of change, whether mental or physical, will ultimately result from man becoming-other in this other place?*

The eldest of the boys (by minutes) was called Roy, and I'm cribbing here from his social-networking instant data feed: *I like hovercrafting and breaking the land-speed record and any drug that you use an inhaler for and I like the idea of a bathysphere and I like the idea of a fully mechanized wolf fighting to the death with a regular blood-and-guts wolf, and one thing I don't care too much about is finishing school. What I want to do is join the military anyway, unless they make me take the stud out of my tongue. I'm interested in meeting people who have been diagnosed with a serious mental illness. I am a redneck and I can fuck you up.* In fact, this bio *was* from a social-networking site for people with diagnosed mental illnesses, so that portion of the profile was not so cavalier as it sounds. Roy was a good kid, who worked in a franchise restaurant where he'd graduated up to assistant manager. Roy, therefore, wore a plastic bow tie. His twin brother, Mason, was, about this time, occupying himself as a lighting designer for a brace of high school drama productions, including one that took actual dialogue from the Mars mission radio transmissions — the dialogue from early in our journey as digested and reconstituted by public-relations personnel in Houston — and set it as dramatic scenes. Mason, according to what I learned from his brothers and sister, seemed to have had intermittent relations with girls. He mostly stayed late at school working on theatricals. Since his father's absence, he had night sweats and fear of enclosed spaces.

Annie would be a classic middle child if there were a middle child in the Rose family. Annie expressed a profound interest in automobile racing from her earliest teens. She claimed that as soon as she was licensed she would start trying to qualify for the racing circuit. She wore her hair in a crew cut, and she had a boyfriend who was an evangelical skateboarding champion. Her politics were reactionary, and she had signed on to a church-based initiative in which she agreed to avoid the Devil's Triangle — cigarettes, drink, and heavy petting — until she turned eighteen. The only music she liked was classic country.

The youngest Rose child, also from the second marriage, was a luminous, zero-gravity specter of a lad called Eldon, who played war-simulation games day and night. Even though his father was on the Mars mission, Eldon was teased often at school for his pasty skin and his spiky hair, which he failed to lacquer down. His shirts were always buttoned all the way up to the neck. He wrote editorials for the school paper.

I should not overlook Jim's long-suffering second wife, Jessica. She had converted to the Methodist faith to be with him, and she had left behind a large, happy extended family in Maryland to follow Jim Rose's dream of space. Did she and the kids (and stepkids) sit around at night praying for the safe passage home of their father?

And so what of this guy who landed the ultralight on the thirty-first of March, after several solitary journeys into the outback of Mars? Was he affable and easy to know? He looked like Moses; he thought he *was* Moses, bringing the word back to the people. The mysterious connections between things, between the Sino-Indian hedge funds and the mining in the Valles Marineris, for example, were so in the forefront of his mind that there was little room for anything else. He felt fuzzy, and he felt distended with insight, and he didn't know why. He didn't know why he couldn't think straight, though he had eaten little in three or four days. He'd had no tomato, nor any Martian heads of lettuce; he hadn't even had one of those squeeze tubes of soy protein with vanilla flavoring. His vitamin deficiencies were aggravated, and that might have accounted for his fuzziness, for his leaving the key in the ultralight and the door open. Not even thinking to check. Forgetting briefly to put on his helmet, so that he was walking through the impossibly thin air. Something *was* wrong, but he was unsure what. He was unsure which of the various things that were wrong had made him feel this way. It was as though he were *unselfed* somehow, like he had left the self who was in charge back somewhere, in the canyon, or back on Earth.

He left the hatch open too. The cargo hatch, and he climbed into the *Excelsior,* and he called my name. Or this is my supposition. He called my name, and he looked around at the shit that was all over the place, the discarded wrappers from inedible space food. (I had eaten nothing but NASA chocolate for the last couple of days.) I had shut down a lot of the monitoring systems. I had shut down all of the radio transmission equipment that connected us to the home planet, which was, theoretically, the especial responsibility of the *Excelsior,* communication and command/control. The *Excelsior* was for all intents and purposes vacant.

Because I had moved over to the *Geronimo,* where I had volunteered to look after Abu Jmil. This was exceedingly generous of me. What I was doing there instead was regrettable, but perhaps you can find sympathy in your heart. What I was doing was using up the rest of the supply of opiates that were in the first aid storage locker on the *Geronimo.* I was occasionally lucid enough to be certain that the reactor was still pumping megawatts out so that we could continue to have heat and oxygen in the *Pequod* and the greenhouse, and in the *Geronimo.* I was also fermenting some of my Martian moonshine. With Steve Watanabe missing, Jim absent, and with Abu still unresponsive, there wasn't as much need for the *Excelsior* in the first place, except during the Earth return portion of the mission. The *Geronimo* and its attendant power station, however, were crucial now. As I sat on the floor of the cargo hold there, dosing myself with the syringes and talking to Abu, I found I couldn't really rationalize what had become of me. My monologue was of rancor and self-pity, but its real purpose was to insure that Abu knew there were still friends around him, if only to keep his brain waves active. The substance of my complaints doesn't need to be reproduced here. I also ran through a battery of old blues standards, and maybe some soul classics, in which I simulated the fancy parts. Somewhere in the midst of this the door was thrown open and Jim Rose appeared backlit, as if from a Western film.

"Captain," I said. "And are you returned victoriously from your mission?"

He said nothing.

"Why so quiet?"

It would have been natural had he not wished to say much to the wastrel he found in the *Geronimo*. Not to mention the slumbering, nearly dispatched form of the Mars mission sculptor. But when he drew nearer, I got a better look. He wasn't wearing headgear, as I've said, and his suit was torn, and his beard was covered with reddish dust, as was his face, likewise flecked with the kinds of burns that I associated with Martian frostbite. But that's not what concerned me. What I saw, and I was not in my right mind and had not been in my right mind for some weeks, as indeed none of us had been, but I was nonetheless certain that *there was something wrong with his eyes.* Kids, if the eyes are the seat of the soul, or however that commonplace goes, then Jim's soul had gone on extended leave. What his Martian eyes looked like now — merciless, devoid of what was human — curdled the very blood. For his eyes were black. I don't mean the iris, nor the vacuity of the pupil, I mean *around* his eyes was black, as if something had gone inside and scorched him in some way, leaving only a raccoon-like ring around his eyes. And this was enough to drain the last of the old Jim Rose. He had leaked out; he had become some harrowing and menacing and *dead* thing, where once there had been, need I remind you, my lover.

"Are you all right?" I said. "For godsakes, Jim, say *something.*"

I had become afraid. I had been in some bad spots on the Mars mission. Maybe there had been a lot of times, such as when my fingers were hacked off by Brandon Lepper, when I'd been temporarily worried. But the professionals back on Earth had trained me well. True, I was never certain I would live out my term on the Mars mission, but even that didn't frighten me. I was never affrighted on Mars, until now.

He shook off his cloud, as best he could, and he attempted, thickly, to say something. Whatever had happened to him out there had begun to affect his speech centers, his fine motor skills. Whether he knew entirely what he was saying wasn't clear to me either. There was a dull, plodding quality to his speech.

"I'm not feeling very well, Jed."

"I can see that. What happened out there?"

"A lot happened. I don't know if I'm well enough to tell it."

He slumped onto the floor, barely sitting up, and I came near to him. And I looked into his dead eyes.

"Do you want me to call Arnie?"

"What happened to Abu?" he whispered.

"Steve appears to have gone off to help Brandon, among other things. Apparently, NASA was communicating with him all this time. And Abu is...as you see. A casualty of greater historical forces."

A long, concerned exhalation, as if all the air left on the planet were expelled from the lungs of Jim Rose.

"What is it?" I said. "Tell me how to help."

That was the moment in which the halting and uncertain tongue of the now afflicted Jim Rose rambled back through his adventures, much of it concerning the absolutely statistically improbable encounter with the explorer called the *Saratoga*. He kept coming back to the explorer. It was a thought that he couldn't relinquish. He wanted to know if NASA could possibly have got in touch with the *Saratoga*, in order to send it against us, in order to scuttle our colonial ambitions. Except that, as he said, there was nothing misleading about the *Saratoga*. It had spoken frankly to him. And it had warned him about everything that was going on. Did that seem possible? he wanted to know. I confess that it was hard for me to believe any of this. I assumed that the story was a delusion of his illness, not a genuine happenstance that he was reporting to me from his time away. His impressions tumbled out helter-skelter, and I couldn't always understand him, but I could hear, in the thickness of his incoherences, a fever to narrate, and so I let him talk for a while. Chief among the contradictions that he could not reconcile, especially in his condition, had to do with the possible military applications of the Mars mission, hinted at by the *Saratoga.* Were we, he wanted to know, supposed to be harvesting *M. thanatobacillus,* as he and I had long assumed we were? Or was there some other military application that had to do with the perfectable crystals of silicon dioxide out in the Valles Marineris, as told to Steve Watanabe? Or were these two reasons for the mission somehow linked up, like some chain of supercomputers, such that there was a biotechnical purpose to all of this, which, in cooperating, we were hastening? These questions were hard for him to articulate, as though he could no longer talk about the very issues that he himself had raised on Mars, as though, like the Moses he now resembled, he was destined not to participate in the Martian civilization he had brought about. It was after he had been talking in this way for a while that he admitted to having found abundant sources of water.

"You what?"

"It's almost everywhere."

"And do you have some with you?"

He rummaged through his pack, which lay beside him, forcing some zippers abraded with Martian grit, and produced a couple of bottles of it. There were also drums of the stuff in the hold of the ultralight.

"It ... vaporizes outside. But I think if we keep it—"

"Inside. Right. Did you—"

"I drank some."

"You drank some?"

"I drank a lot."

"Jim, are you out of your mind?"

"Someone had to do it."

"It might be radioactive, on top of everything else. Are you feeling sick? We should have boiled it first! Or we could have ionized it. It's no wonder you're feeling ill. I'm going to call Arnie."

He just needed to sleep, he said, and maybe something to eat, and yet despite how famished he was, he said, despite how beat up his body must have been, how frostbitten and irradiated and exhausted, he'd never felt more alive. The very cells of him had been lit up by the heavens, by the actual *heavens,* the almost infinite ocean of stars, not the ground on which we found ourselves. And it was at this moment that he did something so horrible that I don't even know how to describe it. Upon getting to his feet he paced, shambled, from one side of the cargo hold to the other, and while teasing out some hard-to-follow part of his story, he went over by where Abu lay, and gazing upon our Muslim sculptor, Jim just cupped his hand over Abu's mouth and nose, pressed hard, and then, turning fully upon the slumbering man, he put a little muscle into it and held the breathing passageways closed. Until Abu, the sculptor, was no more.

It was so studied in its casualness, this dispatch, that I didn't really take in what he was doing at first. I couldn't believe what was happening; I didn't believe I was seeing it, which may have had to do with the opiates, with the amount of them flooding the moral center of my brain. How many times I have thought back on this moment since, and wondered how to interpret what took place onboard the *Geronimo.* Was the old Jim, the Jim I once desired, still in there somewhere, was it he who recognized immediately that we couldn't carry Abu like that, given the shortage of resources? This old Jim understood mercy, and he knew that this sort of mercy was not permitted on the home planet. There were no laws governing what we could and couldn't do on Mars. Pragmatic decisions were required here. They were within our power. But part of me believed it was Jim's illness, whatever it was, that made the decision. Without feeling. The second of these hypotheses was the darker one, a theory that was hard to ignore under the circumstances, that Jim was no longer Jim.

I said, "Do you want to move in here, into the reactor camp, with me?" Hoping that the thought would never occur to him. "We could go back to the *Excelsior* and bring some of your stuff over here. Make it a bit more habitable. Like a proper home."

Did I detect some kind of fiendish laugh? Was the new Jim capable of a fiendish laugh? It was perhaps some variant on the deceitful *snorting* that I had noticed in the old Captain Jim Rose. His reply was long in coming. And he stood up straighter, while pacing, as if to deliver it like a proper orator of old.

"I'm going to Valles Marineris."

"You're going —"

"To find Brandon."

"And what do you propose to do when you get there?"

No answer.

"Will you, at least, leave some of the water behind so we can test it?"

He nodded, but in heading for the door he offered little more. It was me who kept filling in the empty spots in the Mars mission now, with the pleasantries, the witticisms, the little things that are so easy to say and which, whether you believed in them or not, made the people around you feel a little better. The pleasantry was perhaps one of Earth's greatest exports. The mild but generous ways that people lied to one another about their hopes and fears. If I had a longing, after the advent of Jim's illness, his change of character, it was for just one stranger with whom I could venture a few harmless pleasantries.

Afterward, I paid my respects to a dead man. I was getting used to the signs of mortality around me on Mars, planet of death. Abu had been one of the people I liked best on the Mars mission. A man noteworthy for grace and reasonableness. On Earth, he had smoked the occasional cigar, but not in a way that irritated anyone. He liked the blues. I drew the blanket up over his face. I mulled over attempting to pray facing in an easterly direction. Was there, strictly speaking, an *east* on Mars? I wanted to respect the traditions of a desert faith. In the end, I whispered to him, under the blanket, there in the cargo hold, but I don't want to sully a good astronaut's memory by going on and on. Some things, kids, are designed for the privacy of eternity.

Next, when I'd made sure that Abu was covered and for the moment undisturbed, I hastened to the console of the *Geronimo*. It was a sign of my distress that I was about to contact *the home planet*. I'd been writing my diary regularly, true, except for those moments when my hands swam in front of my face from how high I was, but I had long since abandoned filing my diary with NASA since they had dismantled its web portal. As I said, I'd disconnected all the communications equipment in the *Excelsior*, where most of the text was stored in the first place. But there was still enough backup equipment on the *Geronimo* for me to send distress messages to *Earth*.

On duty, at NASA headquarters, was a young woman named Nora. She appeared to me like a fuzzy passport photo, thirty-nine minutes delayed. I thought I could make out some kind of bow in her hair. Unless that was part of her headset. Otherwise she was got up in the de rigueur navy blue warm-up suit that passed, at NASA, for cutting-edge fashion. Nora was so young. I had aged in the course of my interplanetary travel, despite the blessings of general relativity, which asserted that I should age more slowly. I introduced myself to Nora Huston, by videoconference. She replied, as if coming out of suspended animation, "Colonel Richards, hello, we know who you are down here."

"I've been out of touch for a little while, I know. Forgive me. Things have just been busy. But I think that there are a few developments here you need to know about."

In the next minutes of waiting I had ample time to scan her face for signs of judgment. It was hard to see any. She had been selected precisely for her earnestness, for her inability to appear conspiratorial. This was not to suggest that she *was* one of NASA's spying lackeys, bent on reining us in and getting the mission back under control. It was just that they couldn't help themselves — they recruited in order to fortify the chain of command.

"Colonel Richards, we have almost everyone who's still awake here — it's about three in the morning — including the flight director, and we are ready to listen. Please feel free to give us a full briefing."

Was I about to bring Martian civilization to a grinding halt? The morality of what I was doing was imprecise, and I probably wasn't in the state of mind where clear thinking was easy to come by. But the import of recent events was hard to ignore. If I slowed down, shook off a little of my nod, military training returned, if only for a few minutes.

"I need to report a Code 14," I said, "and I'm afraid it's my cabinmate, Jim Rose. You all know that I have nothing but esteem for Jim Rose, having served with him as long as I have, and having known him for years before that. It is therefore the case that I am using this Code 14 designation advisedly. I know, ladies and gentlemen, what I'm telling you. But I have reason to believe that Captain Rose is no longer operating with his faculties intact."

Because he had been a singer of show tunes and country and western, because he had been a teller of bad jokes and an adherent of the pun, because he'd been good-natured and nervous at the same time, because he'd played video games with me, because he was worried about elections back home, because he didn't understand how he was going to send his wife lingerie for their anniversary from this great distance, because he'd been my lover, and because I knew that even if he couldn't say it, he *had* loved me, he *had* reached for me when the loneliness and isolation got too bad, because he once needed companionship, I knew he was not himself.

"On what basis, specifically, do you alert us to this Code 14, Colonel Richards?"

"On the basis that Jim leaned down and squeezed the last bit of life out of Abu Jmil this afternoon. Abu had been suffering from hypothermia, we think.... I don't know. That's another story. Anyway, Jim came back from being out in the desert."

"Can you tell us where Captain Rose had been?"

"He was out surveying various areas here by Nanedi Vallis," I improvised, without really being sure if this was true at all. "The runoff patterns there are really quite extraordinary, and Jim was keen to see them. There's the question of a source for the Nanedi Vallis riverbed, and we had it on the logbooks for some time that we were going to fly over there and have a look."

I removed myself from the camera while awaiting their reply.

"And how would you characterize the condition of Captain Rose? If you could."

"I would characterize Captain Rose as in rather dire condition. He's certainly not well. He seemed to me to be...not himself. The Jim Rose I have known in the course of our professional duties, I should say, would not take a life the way he did just this afternoon. On the other hand, we've been having trouble with outbreaks of violence among the crew, which is virtually the entirety of the Martian population.... First, there was Brandon and the situation with José. And then, well, it seems like what happened to Abu is that he was... Well, in each of these circumstances you could make the case that the astronaut whose actions are in question was suffering with some kind of *interplanetary disinhibitory disorder,* as you might call it, and this has bothered all of us to one degree or another. But Jim seemed..." Again, I just couldn't seem to complete the sentence.

"We are aware of the other situations and we thank you for corroborating what we know. And we are curious to learn whether there were any specific physiological changes in Captain Rose. Did you notice anything different?"

I leaned in close to the camera, which really did resemble some sleepless eye, some all-seeing lens, and I alerted her thus:

"There *did* seem something physically wrong with him, which was partly in the area of his eyes; he seemed bruised around the eyes, or contused, I don't know the proper terminology, and then there was his dishevelment. He just isn't looking after his appearance. And then I'd say he was full of a rather unusual amount of strength, like he was on some sort of adrenaline high. He was not himself. That was my impression. That he was physically changed in some small degree, but also that he was *unselfed.* He wasn't Jim Rose. And I would like to know what you expect me to do about it, since we are now down to a mere capsule full of astronauts, what with Steve Watanabe disappearing. And so I would like to know now what you would have me do about Jim Rose. Do you have some kind of contingency plan?"

I waited an interminable length for a reply, an interminable length that was really not significantly longer than usual, and then the young, fresh face of Nora Huston again seemed to animate itself from out of the static and fuzz of interplanetary transmission. She was as cheerful as some telemarketer as she said, "Thanks very much, Colonel Richards. We'll take it from here!"

"How exactly are you going to take it from there? Do you want to fill me in on that?"

April 25, 2026

On the south side of the Martian equator, I imagined I could feel autumn threatening to stretch out its fingers, merciless, retributive. It was not as bad as it might have been on the South Pole, let's say, nor was the planet tipped so badly on its axis that it was going to be a *bad* year as far as winter went. Still, let's remember how cold it gets on Mars. It gets really, really cold on Mars. It can plunge toward −140 degrees Fahrenheit without much difficulty. As we have seen, it is easy to die of the cold here. Whereas on Earth, autumn can be an ennobling season, one in which you thrill to joyride out into the countryside in your sweaters and boots and perhaps with a jaunty cap, the autumn on Mars foretells a winter inimical to life of any kind. And this was a winter we were meant to survive with Mars at its aphelion—closer to 70 million miles, now, from the home planet.

It had been a week since I'd contacted NASA, and nothing had come of my wanton interference. Not so far. Jim must have been stalking Brandon and Steve slowly, because I had heard nothing of them, these disputants. But then why ought I have? I'd been sleeping in the power station, with the door of the main console bolted shut and with a couple of drums of coolant propped in front. What I was doing was exhausting my supply of pain relief. And drinking mead. Now and again I would look down at my hand and could feel its phantom extremity. I would feel the tingling of what Brandon had removed from me. My finger of death. I couldn't grab much with the hand anymore, and the stump was ugly, not to mention the two fingers so crudely reattached. Still, I was able to depress the plunger on a syringe and to insure that oxygen flowed into the greenhouse, not too far distant.

Meanwhile, it was on the seventh of April, if I recollect the Earth calendar properly, that Arnie hailed me on my walkie-talkie and said that I needed to come quick. You guessed it, kids. Laurie had gone into labor. In fact, at the time of the call, she'd been in early labor for many hours. I counted back on my remaining fingers, and my initial diagnosis, though I am no obstetrician, was that it was not good that Laurie had gone into labor this promptly. This was no requisite nine-month term, not even close. Even if they'd been messing around on the *Pequod* only weeks into the flight out. Probably their romance dated back prior to launch. But there was no one else to be the under-assistant of gynecology that day. The rest of the Martian population was out conducting predator-and-prey games in the empty highlands. It was left to me to assist.

I hadn't been to the greenhouse in a while. I hadn't paid much attention. Fate had thrown together the participants of the Mars mission. The disparate responsibilities of the Mars mission no longer required social niceties. I hadn't even seen Arnie since

Steve had clocked Abu. I'd sent a couple of messages over there, true, in which I notified them that Abu had gone on to his heavenly reward, but I said no more than this. Arnie himself had suggested euthanizing the patient, after all. We celebrated a virtual memorial service for the folks back home, and that was the extent of it. I understand the story got little play in the news outlets.

Arnie and Laurie had floated blissfully above the infighting and the slaughter around them. They were a prelapsarian dyad with their green thumbs and their blissful attention to the homely tasks. When, at last, I went through their air lock, I was amazed by what I saw. Had they been striding around with fig leaves on it couldn't have surprised me more. Arnie called to me from where he was, over by a small pool of water that he had somehow managed to fill up by fusing some of the liquid hydrogen fuel from the *Pequod* with carbon dioxide from the Martian atmosphere. To get to the *lake,* as I later learned it was called, I had to go through a couple of other discrete ecosystems, namely a little forest of yew saplings, which Arnie had brought from Earth and much propagated since. They had some kind of anticarcinogenic property, these yew trees, or so it was thought, before chemotherapeutic compounds were synthesized. Tumors were still a concern on Mars, naturally, what with the cosmic rays and the thin atmosphere.

Beyond the yew saplings, an exothermic species, and a variety of ferns and fungi, there was a desert biome — pretty easy to simulate here — in which Arnie was experimenting with various kinds of cacti, especially edible ones, like prickly pear. And then there was a transitional ecosystem, temperate, with some edible shrubs, sweet fern, mulberry, and gooseberry. I didn't even have time to get over to the vegetable garden, where the extra-strength grow lamps were all on timers performing their appointed tasks.

"Jed? Jed?"

The expectant couple were to be found by the *lake.* Laurie crouched on one of the space blankets that had accompanied us on our flight over, NASA logo prominently featured beneath her exposed undercarriage. She was pale, sweaty, breathless, and her generous brown locks, which she had let grow on Mars, were matted and plastered to her face. I could see that Arnie was already positioned at the relevant biological *exit,* where the little Martian boy or girl was already trying to get its head out through the available space, beneath the pelvis. Arnie was muttering about how symbolically rich it was to *catch* the baby. Arnie's hands were covered in blood, and he pointed out to me that he'd had to *cut* a little bit to make the way easier, even though the baby was several months premature, and thus would be undersized.

"Premature?" I said. "You two must have been busy with the, uh, the conception way back in —"

Arnie fixed me with a disgusted stare and said, "I don't have time for your games. If you're up to it, get to work. What I need is for you to hold her hand like the decent guy you are, okay? Encourage her? And await instructions. I'll need your help with the umbilical cord and the placenta."

I was humbled, because I hadn't intended to be the wretch I had become on Mars. I got down on the soil and dust that formed the floor of the greenhouse. I became an eager toiler in the delivery room.

"Laurie," I said, delicately, "how you doing?"

Between hurried breaths, she said, "Worse than the first day of zero gravity training."

"It's going to be over soon," I said. "Look at it that way. And you won't have to smile for the cameras after."

Arnie was nervously mumbling orders, as if he had a phalanx of trained residents behind him, awaiting his instruction, all of the mumbling orbiting around this question: Why had labor begun so early? It would take a while, it would take several more births, before it would be possible to say whether environmental factors played some kind of role in how children were born on Mars. *We just don't know yet,* he was saying nervously. *It could, of course,* he muttered to himself, *just be this particular fetus.* "Come on, honey, another push, if you can manage, and the head will be —"

I held Laurie's hand. She wept. And cried out. "The second's supposed to be easier!"

I said, "It's a moment in history, Laurie. A moment in history. Think of what you're doing for everyone. People back home. This is a great and selfless act. This is something that was going to happen, that *had* to happen, and you're the person who's doing it. You're bringing into being the first Martian of higher intelligence. The first mammalian Martian. Did you think this was going to happen back when you were a kid? Growing up in... Where did you grow up, again? I don't think you had any idea." And I just kept blathering, though it was hard to feel as upbeat as required. I could see that Arnie, despite his worry, was also excited, in the way an expectant father might be, even when that father is on a deserted planet with a dwindling supply of food, fuel, and allies. It's just hard not to think of a baby as some kind of optimistic statement. I don't know if NASA felt that way about it, but still. The baby's head, in due course, emerged from the squatting, contracting Laurie. Then it was just about getting the shoulders through.

"Laurie," I went on, "they're preparing the online news portfolios back home. I swear they are. I actually talked to them. Did I tell you that? The boobs at the agency. Did I tell you? I talked to them, and so they are up to speed. On the developments. Anyway, you can bet they know about this. They have their ways, apparently, of knowing everything that's going on. They have their overflights. Just keep breathing, that's it. Push a little harder now. This is the hard part, Laurie, just push a little harder. On Earth people are going to be making films about this, and writing testimonials, singing songs."

"Jed," she said, "please be quiet?"

I was thinking about Ginger, I guess. I was assisting, but I was thinking about my daughter. I was wondering if Ginger was worrying, because Ginger kept up on the Mars mission. Or she used to. Maybe now her teenage life was too consuming, with its many gossipy e-mails and videoconferencing conversations rocketing around the globe, conversations her mother wasn't keeping up on.

Perhaps it will come as no surprise that I was late for Ginger's birth. Let me use this space to atone. I was in the armed forces at the time. I left behind a spring offensive in Tajikistan, where we were guarding the natural-gas pipelines with 50,000 NATO troops under German command. I'd been involved in covert operations but had been wounded in action. In a ridiculous way. A scimitar had been applied to me as I walked down a busy street in that nation's capital. There'd been some haggling over a black market case of vodka. The outcome of this haggling did not favor the peddler. Anyway, this injury, which left a rather sexy scar on my left shoulder blade, was enough to allow me to return home to see the miraculous birth of Ginger Stark-Richards. Have I mentioned how much I loved my wife, Pogey Stark-Richards, in those days? My wife's strength was immense; she just put up with a lot, in her pursuit of this idea of family, kids. She put up, I mean, with me.

I knew that there was much about me that repelled the average person, things that I seemed powerless to correct, no matter my efforts. My wife still looked at me with a brightened smile when I came home from whatever dangerous foreign adventure I was on. I'd seen guts spilling out of every friend and enemy. I'd seen men tortured until they begged to die. There were things about my character that were annealed in the foundry of international conflict, things that resisted civilizing. I was, moreover, responsible for my brother's death, or that was the burden that I had carried around so many years, on bombing raids near and far. My wife was the only one who could see through the craggy, dangerous straits of my character to know of my many regrets and my earnest desire to improve.

Maybe she would have hung in there a little longer had I turned up to see the baby whelped. But there were a solid twenty-four hours' worth of flights required to get me from Tajikistan to Gainesville, FL, where we were living. It took blizzard conditions in only one of the relevant locations to make the trip a bust. But in addition to blizzard conditions, I spent three hours in an airport in Estonia, doubled over on a commode, wondering which bits of my brains were being shat out. By the time I changed planes in New York, I had that feeling that everything boorish about me had been evacuated. And yet despite all this, I did come running into the delivery room to find little Ginger, fully rinsed of her glutinous body shampoo and wrapped in some baby's textile, resting on my wife's bosom. My wife was smiling her exhausted smile, and she welcomed me though I deserved no welcome.

Back here on Mars, Laurie gave one last mighty heave in her pelvic girdle, straining at her ligaments, and the shoulders of the child seemed to pass through. So it seemed from where I knelt, which admittedly was not an obstetrical angle. Arnie's demeanor, at once methodical and professional, lightened considerably, as the rest of the child transited quickly out. Soon there was a bloody papoose in Arnie's lap, by which humankind proved that it could, after all, be Martian.

He said, while toweling off the dumpling, "Jed, help her with the afterbirth, please." There was the requisite cutting of the cord. And Arnie plunged his little *girl* into a bucket. Pulled her out of the bath and then warmed her in his arms until she gasped her first breath.

I suppose I was not prepared for the amount of efflux that still remained to pass from the mother, attached to the cord, and probably this is because I had conspired to miss out on Ginger's birth. Laurie elected again to bite down on a piece of rawhide that had been produced from some interplanetary valise, and in this posture she rid herself of the afterbirth. She was sweating and weeping. With joy, I suppose.

"It's a girl?" I said.

"It's a girl," Arnie said.

"It's a girl," Laurie said, as if somehow reassuring herself. "Just what we don't need around here, more *men*."

I took to cleaning up the various rags and towels. Out the window of the greenhouse, I could see Phobos, looking every bit the Idaho potato, crossing east over our city of the plains. "Does she have a name?"

"She does," Arnie said, suturing up a spot in Laurie, who was holding the baby and managing to be uncomplaining.

"And are you going to tell me the name?"

Arnie said, "Her name is Prima."

He told me to make sure to lock the door on the way out, and this was news to me — that doors on Mars locked now. He had ingeniously found a way to install a lock in the greenhouse. You just popped a button and walked out. So old-fashioned. The two of them called weak thanks to me as I left. I slammed the door firmly, to be sure that they were sequestered in their prelapsarian Mars, while I went out east of Eden.

RichardsJ@marsmission.us.gov: Ginger, I'm just checking in here, because things have been a little slow on Mars lately. Not a lot going on. The weather has taken a turn for the worse. We're worried about dust storms again. We're just passing the warmest part of the summer, and that means the days when it's possible to be outside without wearing a whole lot of protective covering are also going to come to an end. It's fifty below at night sometimes.

GingerSnap@sinisterteen.com: Daddy, I miss you. Do you think you can send me some video, even if it's a really shaky picture or something? I hate not seeing you for so long. I don't care how long it takes, how shaky it is. I like to have a picture in my mind so that when I'm rebelling against everything you stand for I know what you look like. School is the same, and I'm doing okay in math, even though it's not like I care about it. Hey, to totally change the subject, I've been thinking about college, and I'm wondering if I can go abroad for school. I think it would be good to go to some foreign countries and see some stuff. (Emoticon.)

RichardsJ@marsmission.us.gov: Wait. Am I speaking to the right teenager? This just doesn't sound like the Ginger Stark-Richards I remember, whose most ambitious trip was to the mall to get some unusual color of hair dye or nail polish. If you're my daughter you're going to have to prove it with some classified information.

GingerSnap@sinisterteen.com: Easy! The most important

political issue as far as you are concerned is campaign finance reform, money is what makes *us* us, and you think the best period of music was the 1970s, even though you don't want anyone to know that's what you really think, hahaha.

RichardsJ@marsmission.us.gov: I have no choice but to believe you, though my mind is riddled with doubts. Now I have a few serious things to say, if that's okay with you. Ginger, I was thinking of you a lot today, for reasons that will be clear soon enough in the press, and I wanted you to know that you really are the best thing that ever happened to a man like me. I'll get busy with things now and then, because I'm just not terribly smart about life — I wish I were smarter — and I'll put my head down, and I'll just blunder through. But then there are days like today, when I know that I have had one remarkable blessing and that's you. On Mars, I spontaneously recall these things we have done together, like the time I drove up and down the block with you looking for your pet robot, calling to it in that language you designed, and then it turned out that it was under your bed the whole time. Under the circumstances, these things feel quite profound to me. Your secret language, your self-designed encryption algorithms, your emoticons.

GingerSnap@sinisterteen.com: Are you okay, Daddy? Is there something wrong?

RichardsJ@marsmission.us.gov: There's always something wrong on Mars, if you want to know the truth. It's never easy. It's like living in medieval times or worse. I've lost a couple of teeth, I'm a little bit malnourished. But just when you think it's all too much, and you can't wait until the months have passed and it's time to get back into the *Excelsior* and start for home, there's some arresting view, some overpowering landscape such as you have never seen before. For example, honey, Captain Rose and I were traveling by ultralight to the Meridiani Planum recently, where they are certain there have been very recent water flows, based on the satellite imaging we're getting, and you wouldn't believe the geological beauty of these ice deposits. They're like some kind of curvilinear shelves, like the fronds of a fan, like the steps on some ancient cathedral, which is what this place is, a cathedral.

GingerSnap@sinisterteen.com: Exciting news here is that there's a plan to build a really big seawall at the edge of the beach to protect against the ocean, which is rising like crazy. Some people are in favor of this, I guess, and then there are other people saying that the ocean levels aren't going to rise at all. There are other people who are just leaving, because they think there are too many hurricanes around. I say okay leave Florida to those of us who are really from here, and who really care about the state however it is. (Emoticon.) But, Daddy, I have another question, because what they were saying online, you know, was that certain astronauts on the mission were killed in the line of duty. Can you just promise me that you aren't taking any kinds of risks? Please? Why are you losing teeth? Can you please tell me?

RichardsJ@marsmission.us.gov: Where in the press did you see that? They really shouldn't be printing stories like that. Ginger, I do what I can to be safe, to make sure I can get home to you, and, hopefully, to your mother too, if she'll have me. I'm really not involved in any of the difficult research anyway, since my responsibility is primarily in the area of communications, and in command and control. That kind of thing. Lately, since the situation has changed, I've been overseeing power generation. It's not very complicated. We have a simple nuclear power plant here, you know, a graphite-moderated turbine, and lately Arnie has been using it to do some chemistry where we take hydrogen fuel and solid carbon dioxide, which you can get in a frost state around here pretty easily, and then you fuse them and you get water and some other stuff. I don't totally understand it, but the main thing is that this produces more power. I need to look after myself, honey, in order to run the power plant, so that's what I'm going to do. Look after myself.

GingerSnap@sinisterteen.com: Is it true that you don't age as fast as I do? I read that somewhere recently. And is it lonely there? Do you feel lonely? And, Dad, I have this other question. Can you tell me what this expression Code 14 means?

RichardsJ@marsmission.us.gov: Where did you hear that expression?

GingerSnap@sinisterteen.com: Code 14? It's just something that people are saying a lot. It's like it's sort of become this cool expression, you know, people just say it around a lot. Somebody told me that it was this expression that came from the Mars mission. Like maybe it's somebody else whose parents work at Cape Canaveral or something. Somebody told me it's what people say on the Mars mission when one of the astronauts has gone out of control or something.

RichardsJ@marsmission.us.gov: Ginger, this is kind of important, I need for you to tell me if you heard this from someone at NASA. Is there anyone who was over at the house on weekends? Maybe visiting your mother or something? Maybe that guy, Mr. Gibraltar, was over there? Or maybe he said this to you?

GingerSnap@sinisterteen.com: Don't get all paranoid, Daddy. (Emoticon.) I told you where I heard it. It's like something people say now, like at school, and it means that the situation is all f—— up or something. I'm trying to avoid swearing. Like when the situation has gone all crazy or something, people will say "Code 14! Code 14!" But are they saying this because there's someone up there that was a Code 14? You'd tell me if the situation was dangerous?

RichardsJ@marsmission.us.gov: You don't have to worry about that at all. They wouldn't be putting us in these conditions if they didn't have an exit strategy for your dad and the other people on the mission.

GingerSnap@sinisterteen.com: But what about those astronauts who got killed in the other missions?

RichardsJ@marsmission.us.gov: We've been over this. There haven't been any hardware mishaps on any manned Mars missions. There was a chimpanzee who died for his country on the way here, sixteen years ago. And there were some guys who got killed during the second round of Mars shots. A few other small things. But it was the failures in those situations that prompted the agency to take dramatic steps to improve their safety record. Now what I want you to do is find your mother. Is your mother in the house?

Can you have her get on here, so I can talk to her for a minute?

GingerSnap@sinisterteen.com: I don't want her using my account. I have stuff on here that isn't appropriate for people her age. She can access her own account.

RichardsJ@marsmission.us.gov: I'm not kidding around. Now means *now*.

(And here the delay was longer than usual. It was a pretty long delay, in fact, and mostly I filled these delays with intoxicants of various kinds, and with preconceptions about the conversation to come. So that I was already on edge when the screen beeped, and there was another message upon it.)

PogeyStark@marsmission.us.gov: What's the problem?

RichardsJ@marsmission.us.gov: What are you telling her? Are you telling her things that you are hearing over at NASA? Where does she get all this type of thing? I'm really irritated about it. You can't just let her live her life without filling her head full of all this stuff? Dangers of interplanetary travel? And what took you so long to get to the computer?

PogeyStark@marsmission.us.gov: Jed, there's a lot of rumor and innuendo going on about the Mars mission. The press is onto other things, because they forget things, but there's still a lot of gossip kicking around online. Some of this is easy to control and some of it is not.

RichardsJ@marsmission.us.gov: What if her future is contingent upon her not being contaminated with this kind of nonsense? Wouldn't you do what was necessary to protect her?

PogeyStark@marsmission.us.gov: The father who has not only abandoned the family, but abandoned it all the way off the planet, is trying to get all interested now in how his daughter is parented? Do you want to help with the homework, Jed? Do you want to start doing that? Because most of her homework is done on the computer console that the school loans her, and the geometry teacher, for example, grades the pieces very promptly as soon as Ginger hits send. I'm sure that NASA, in their wisdom, who have made it possible for you to read the newspapers and play simulation games with ex-cons from Indiana and the like, could make it possible for a deadbeat like you to review your daughter's homework once in a while. Did you know, Jed, that your daughter is having particular trouble with trigonometry? I don't suppose you do. Well, if you want to start talking about how I'm supposed to be raising her, while you're off scraping rock samples off the floor of a crater, then start today. I'll be happy to relinquish some of the responsibility. I guess you won't be able to pick her up three days a week, like this separation agreement I have here says you are supposed to do, so that I can have a day off now and then. And I guess you won't be able to see her two weekends and one Sunday a month, and you won't be able to maintain a room for her at your domicile, will you, Jed? Unless you're going to have her fired up into space. Am I right about that, Jed?

RichardsJ@marsmission.us.gov: Don't bring up that agreement. Don't do that. You don't need to do that. I'm under a lot of stress here right now, and it's natural that I would be a little short-tempered about things I can't control back home. But you can believe me, Pogey, when I say that I intend to address all of this when I get back. I'm a changed person, in many ways, a more philosophical and thoughtful person. I will make that clear to you and Ginger when I am able. I will prove it.

PogeyStark@marsmission.us.gov: That's very sweet of you to say, Jed, but it is possible, you know, that things have changed here a little bit too. You've been gone for over six months, and there were times when I was younger when that would not have been a real burden to me, when separations were a part of our being together. But I'd already moved into Dan's place *before* you left, Jed, I don't expect you have forgotten that. And now six months have passed, and I have met someone else. I wish there were a better time to tell you this, but there isn't a better time, so there it is.

RichardsJ@marsmission.us.gov: What are you saying to me?

PogeyStark@marsmission.us.gov: I'm saying what it looks like I'm saying. I'm saying that I'm seeing someone else.

RichardsJ@marsmission.us.gov: Who is the someone else?

PogeyStark@marsmission.us.gov: I thought you were against

the short replies, what with the delay? What difference does it make who it is? It's no one you know. The point is that now I'm realizing how much suffering I was doing, while hoping you would be someone else, or do something else, and I don't want to suffer as much, or not in the same way, anymore. I want to try to be happy.

RichardsJ@marsmission.us.gov: A man or a woman?

PogeyStark@marsmission.us.gov: What are you talking about?

RichardsJ@marsmission.us.gov: Is it someone from NASA? Are you sleeping with someone from NASA?

PogeyStark@marsmission.us.gov: What difference would it make if I were? I didn't choose him, or you, or any other man I've ever been involved with, based on professional credentials. If I had, I'd have left you long ago, Jed.

RichardsJ@marsmission.us.gov: You're sleeping with someone from NASA? You have the audacity to say to me that it doesn't matter what the person does? Do you have any idea what you have done? Has it not occurred to you that NASA could have some powerful reasons for wanting to compromise you in that way? What have you told him about me? Have you told him about any conversations we have had lately, or anything I said to you before?

PogeyStark@marsmission.us.gov: Jed, you're beginning to sound...I don't know...kind of crazy. Like I said, people are not sitting around checking any weekly video updates about the Mars mission. Everyone at the agency knows that the Mars mission is not being cooperative. You said as much yourself.

RichardsJ@marsmission.us.gov: You just have no idea what you're talking about right now. Who is this person? Is it the flight director, what's his name, Rob Antoine, toupée guy, are you sleeping with him?

PogeyStark@marsmission.us.gov: You don't know him. He's assistant manager of propulsion systems, if you have to know, and the most he has to do with you is that he's figuring out ways to make the trip home faster. Because the payload is lighter.

RichardsJ@marsmission.us.gov: Because of all the dead people. He has told you that the payload is going to be lighter not just because most of the hydrogen is going to be left behind, but also because most of the astronauts are dead? Has he told you that? I bet you're lying on your bed, *our* bed, right now with him looking over your shoulder, and he's reading all of this aloud to that Rob Antoine fellow, as fast as I type it out here in the lightless, oxygen-deficient interior of a nuclear power plant on this desert planet that is rapidly falling into winter where we're *all* liable to be dead, if you want to know the truth.

PogeyStark@marsmission.us.gov: He was here earlier, and I sent him home, because I'm just not comfortable with him staying over with Ginger here. Occasionally, she goes over to stay with your cousins. And those are the only nights I let anybody stay here or when I stay anywhere else. And in case you're thinking a lot about this, if you don't think that Jim's wife and Steve's wife aren't going through similar things, you should think again. It's not two hundred years ago, you know, when women were meant to sit here and wait for their men to return home from the front with missing legs and completely shell-shocked and they're going to give up everything that's good and fun about being a mature woman for some man that they never get to be with.

RichardsJ@marsmission.us.gov: Did he tell you about the bacterium? Did he tell you about that? I assume that even a flunky in the Jet Propulsion Laboratory would be able to tell you about the germ.

PogeyStark@marsmission.us.gov: What germ?

RichardsJ@marsmission.us.gov: I'll tell you what germ, the bug they sent us up here to gather for them. There's a bacterium up here, on Mars, and they think that it has military applications, and I don't give a damn if they are reading this entire exchange, because I'm going to tell the truth now, and the truth is that they don't intend for this to be a scientific mission and they never did intend for it to be. This bacterium is so top-secret that the majority of us on the mission didn't even know about it. And it's incredibly deadly. No one on Earth will have any resistance to it, since it has existed on Mars for however many millions of years. This germ is so powerful that it made it impossible for any life to take hold here, because what it does is completely wipe out higher life-forms.

PogeyStark@marsmission.us.gov: Now you're really sounding totally paranoid, because from what I've heard, the only supposedly military application any bacteria farming is going to have is not military but commercial, and it has to do with some new way of making microchips, and the reason why they are concentrating on microchips is that they managed to defray some of the costs of the mission with underwriting from tech machinery manufacturers.

RichardsJ@marsmission.us.gov: Don't believe everything you hear. It gets more and more dangerous here every day, and I believe I have seen one or two of the astronauts who are already infected with the bacterium. Don't even ask. It will all become clear soon enough. I am just hoping to get out of here with my own skin, though I don't have any real hope that I'm going to be able to do that. I've been spending weeks up here doing nothing but drugging myself, that's all I've been doing. I have myself righteously addicted. It started with the missing finger, and the reattachment. You can't even believe how horrible my hand looks. It looks like it was rescued from some Frankenstein movie, and then there's the stump from the middle finger. And it was really bothering me, as you'd imagine, and I was having a lot of phantom pains, and I started taking morphine for it, and then I was just unable to stop, and all the synthetic pain relievers, I mean, once I ran through the morphine, I started taking the lower-level painkillers, and they weren't enough and I had to double up, and sometimes I am so high for so long that I don't know what day it is, and I don't know if that's really the best way to be operating a nuclear power facility. Wait, wait a second. Just for one second, okay? Stay with me for a moment? I think there's someone at the door.

April 30, 2026

The chase began in the desert, as many compelling chases do, and it involved giving up the succor of any remaining comfort.

As always with a proper manhunt, it was not always clear who was hunter and who was prey. This I managed to learn from the hapless Steve Watanabe, who, so attuned to the possibility that he would somehow fail to make it home, was now providing round-the-clock updates on everything that was happening around him *to the authorities*. As if this would be enough to preserve his sorry ass. He was able, using tracking satellites designed by the authorities, to perform round-the-clock global-positioning updates on the space suits of Mars mission astronauts, exploiting not only heat signatures but a space suit design feature that had been built in for good reasons: reflectors. Steve was somewhat prepared, therefore, for the coming of Jim Rose. And he anticipated hand-to-hand combat, as well as all registers of high-tech pursuit and entrapment, even if he suspected the endgame would rely on kinds of violence better known to earlier epochs of human history. Above all, he advised Brandon Lepper, a guy he had always disliked, to take advantage of the pause before the storm to move himself farther out of harm's way.

According to Brandon, there was nothing to worry about. According to Brandon, the integrity of NASA's long-term goals — terraforming, resource exploitation, a permanent human colony on Mars — had long since been jeopardized by José. Brandon had no choice but to do what had to be done. Likewise the Debbie Quartz incident. Debbie was nice enough, sure, but she was unprepared for what was required, for the Darwinism of the Mars mission, and he'd proved it by just talking sternly to her. She *had to go*.

Steve Watanabe, when he heard these enfeebled rationalizations, which have been much fleshed out in my account, felt that Brandon was not himself. There was no gratitude for his having made a drive of many days on a forklift. And Steve was not reassured by the dull, lifeless tone with which Brandon directed him to the grinding and milling tools. They were to drill in the eastern outflow channel of the Valles Marineris, technically known by another one of those creepy Greek names, the Ius Chasma.

The Ius Chasma, you'll recall, is about three and a half miles beneath the plains into which it is carved, running parallel to it the Tithonium Chasma, which gets so narrow it's just like a big crack in the ground, except that the crack goes down miles. Between the two is a ridge that runs along the center. Ius is about four hundred miles long, but it's only a tiny portion of the enormous Valles Marineris complex, which I have already said is about as far across as the United States. In most of it, you wouldn't even know you were *in* a canal. Not so here at Ius. You see a canyon wall that's miles high, you don't forget it.

Steve and Brandon had got down twenty-five feet or so, into the bottom of one of the chasm walls, and they were digging mostly into basalt. These were the kinds of environments, however, according to the Martian surveillance satellites, where you found salt beds and, in some cases, *dampness.* The evolving theory—that there were periodic underground aquifers that had in the past caused catastrophic flooding on Mars—provided for, indeed *required,* spots of dampness. That water had to carve out those canyons somehow, and it wasn't all evaporated. It couldn't be. A team of geologists back in Florida watching all of this on a video screen cheered for every new foot of exposed crust. Much of this work, excepting the occasional buzz and roar of drilling automata, was done in silence and darkness. Steve, according to the notes he was posting, tried to engage Brandon periodically, but Brandon would no longer participate in the subtler human interactions. Brandon, former boxer and smartass, had, in the weeks alone, become a grim, silent wraith. When there was a lapse in the pace of operations, he would berate Steve until Steve was willing to get back to work, and the only thing that Steve could seem to do to get time off was to faint from exertion, which he did periodically. The deprivation of sunlight in the chasm was somehow even more obliterating than he imagined it might be on Earth, since it was the last thing he felt he had in common with those he missed back home: sunlight.

They had a rope-and-pulley system that led down into the godforsaken hole in the ground, and a heat lamp that they used to

keep warm, and they ran it off the battery of the rover, via reinforced extension cord, and there was a small generator, and it was
in this half-light that Steve saw Brandon's grimy face, as Brandon
pulled off his visor and attempted to *taste* the salt they were blasting away from the walls of the excavation site in a storage drum.
Brandon *tasted* it. There was some kind of liquid there, undeni-
ably, and the action of the drills, the friction of it, was liquefying
some of what was frozen.

"You aren't drinking that, are you?"

"Keep drilling. It's sterile."

"Seriously, are you sure you should be drinking that?"

"Drinking what?"

"Weren't you just drinking some of that stuff coming off the
walls?"

Brandon, in his relentless monotone: "There's water here. I'm
verifying. We'll be reporting back to Earth."

"You're not going to be doing very much verifying if you catch
some germ."

"Conductors. Radioactive material. That's our brief. No germs."

There was, however, the possibility of geological collapse. That
was another peril. The Valles Marineris had all kinds of collapses.
There were entire canyons in the complex of Valles Marineris that
were sealed off because the walls had collapsed, and when you
were digging at the base of miles of canyon wall, trying to get
down a hundred meters, to the beginning of the aquifer, in search
of *Martian life,* or in search of some new kind of raw material
for semiconductors, it was not unreasonable to assume that there
might have been or could be again a collapse. Hebes Chasma had
a collapse. It was sealed off. And the way the wind blew in there,
there were all kinds of erosion taking place all the time. And Steve
worried ceaselessly about when the others were going to come for
them. In what way would they come? Would they come in the
ultralight? In a ragtag army? Flown in and air-dropped in a secure
perimeter? And when they came, in what way would they mete
out Martian justice, that resource which only begins to obtain

when a certain critical mass of human beings, *a community,* is present? In what form would justice be dispatched, and who would be the duly appointed jurist?

At sunset, when the batteries were run down on the drills, the two trudged out of the cave to load the last of the minerals into the drums on the back of the rover. Deimos, the second moon, hung in the salmony sky.

In the rover, besides the drums of ore, there were piles of slag, a silvery, reflective muck that definitely had some liquid in it. Whether it was water, or chemical runoff, or what, was unclear. The whole mining operation, like most of Mars, smelled awful, smelled like a sulfur refinery. Steve and Brandon were meant to carry a half ton of the rock back to base camp, where it would ultimately be loaded into the Earth Return Vehicle for the trip home. Assuming they could somehow commandeer the ERV. Steve, according to his diaries, was weary in ways he had not been since landing on the Red Planet, and he wished he could be sure that he was doing the right thing, that cooperation with the *authorized* mission would be the way to secure things for his family back on Earth. But he wasn't sure, and this lack of certainty was made worse when he got a good look at Brandon that day, in the remaining sunlight. Brandon, who despite his capacity for vainglory and ethnic one-liners was sort of hale and squeaky clean, now looked like a different person. His skin had become leathery and gray, and his eyes were sunken into his head. And they were *black* around the rims.

"Brandon, are you *feeling* all right?"

Brandon didn't say anything, and his heartless and empty glare in reply to the question didn't inspire confidence. Steve didn't bother to pursue it. That was when, in looking up for another glimpse of Deimos, the hummingbird of the solar system's moons, Steve saw it; he saw how justice was going to be pursued and who, exactly, was going to be doing the pursuing. Jim Rose. The captain. Up above Steve now, and coming straight for them in the ultralight, swooping down out of the sky as though it would be easy to land an ultralight in the middle of a canyon, which perhaps it would be, was none other than Captain Jim Rose. The identity of the pilot was easy enough to surmise.

There was a volume of sand on the floor of the canyon, and a thick carpeting of dust. Not like the rocky plains out where the three spacecraft had done their awkward touchdowns. This was where the ultralight came down, like a flaming eagle out of some interminable Wagnerian opus. The ultralight was easier to fly on Mars, if you believed the hype about a meager supply of gravity and no magnetic poles to speak of. It was borne aloft on the rather manic winds. The ultralight came down out of the sky and seemed to merge with its own shadow in the deep red of sunset, and with it now came the blast, at the site of the rover. There was impact. Blast and heat, enough to knock over the one drum full of silicon oxide and related geological treasures, which in turn toppled over the other that was waiting to be picked up with the hydraulic lift, and two or three days of mined riches spilled out into the sand. The barest portion of the recent treasures collected. The projectile, the missile that caused this damage, was some incendiary device, a container of corn-based ethanol perhaps, from the ultralight, which, like the rover, operated with solar cells but which required a little gas to get aloft.

Steve went facedown, hoping to avoid shrapnel, and when he got up, he could see Brandon was trying to pat down his flaming suit. Steve grabbed a blanket that he'd dragged out of the rover earlier, when trying to get a nap, and hurried to Brandon's side to wrap him in it. This while Jim Rose, avenger, walked toward them, the wild Martian winds compassing about him, from the beached aircraft.

There were a number of things to consider for Steve Watanabe, in the moments he had at his disposal. There was enough juice in the rover to go a little bit. And there was, about ten miles south, a route out of the Ius Chasma. There had been a collapse there, ten or so million years ago, and the wind had eroded the channel down enough that Brandon had found himself able, he'd told Steve, to get the rover in and out. This was the one way, short of driving thousands of miles in one direction or several hundred in another, to get out of the Valles Marineris quickly, *if you couldn't fly.* But what would happen if Steve and Brandon just drove off? What would happen with the important scientific work they had recently done, not to mention the gathering of ore necessary for a whole new breed of cybernetic semiconductor, at the behest of levelheaded administrators back home, if they absconded? What would happen, Steve thought, to this work they'd been doing on behalf of a large digital operating systems consortium based in Kuala Lumpur, and its American affiliate in Dallas? Brandon did have a Taser that had been provided by NASA for self-defense, and which he and Steve had been advised to employ as needed.

Brandon's inclination, it seemed, was to tackle the problem mano a mano. Despite mild burns. And Jim Rose seemed to have no better idea himself. The two of them fell upon each other. Steve Watanabe, who, unlike his colleagues here on the Mars mission, had not been in and out of the military in Central Asia, had only rudimentary combat training. He was a Buddhist. In fact, as a kid, he'd never come out on the winning end in any fight. He was the kind of boy, by virtue of excellent skills in areas that others disdained (cello, chemistry, velvet paintings), who had always come in for a lot of racially dubious ribbing about how *easy* it all was for him, and he had attempted to defend himself physically on certain occasions with disappointing results. He'd had a couple of teeth knocked out; he'd bloodied his nose, even had it reset once. He took these lumps and moved on, more wary and a little bit more hapless about the world.

Steve's inclination, therefore, was to escape with the rover, as soon as it was feasible, and to head the ten miles south, hugging the wall of the canyon, where it would be very difficult for the ultralight to follow. Eventually, the plane was going to run out of fuel. Because some of its fuel had already been used to fashion the impressive Molotov cocktail. The ultralight stayed aloft during the day with its solar panels, but the sun was all but set. It was going to get very cold very soon.

Two men bent on doing each other harm. Even under the best of circumstances, such a thing can be a drawn-out and unpleasant affair, and Steve, in his later report to NASA, did not give an account of every blow and counterblow. We know that Brandon was once a welterweight, and he was probably good on his feet, especially with the gravity only about two-thirds what it was back on Earth, so that the dancing and feinting of this prizefight was like some fabulous ethnic ritual, or like one of the fight sequences from old Hong Kong action films, whose only raison d'être was holding gravity in abeyance. Nothing was more impressive, when the goal was insuring the stock valuation of a large Malaysian entertainment provider, than the cessation of the law of gravity. And that's what this fight was like, with Brandon bobbing around and using, Steve supposed, some very traditional pugilistic combinations. Meanwhile, how *inhuman,* how cold, how expedient was Brandon's antagonist. Jim Rose had no compunction about making sure his style, as a combatant, was about forcing total and unconditional submission. There was going to be no prolonged mixing it up. In the dusky light, it seemed as though he'd seized one of Brandon's arms and had *bit down* on it, shoving the forearm into his mouth and chomping.

Brandon squealed and somersaulted out of the way, behind the end of the rover, so as to put the vehicle between them. Whereupon, in the interval available, Brandon seemed to be squatting down to look for a rock of some kind. It was at this point in the conflict that Brandon, who had treated Steve as if he were an indentured servant, called his name. "Steve! Steve!" I have no more details than that, just Steve's name. And then Brandon heaved some small piece of volcanic rock at Jim Rose, striking him in the solar plexus without much apparent effect. The two warriors breathed great gasping breaths, because they were running short of oxygen as Jim worked his way around the rover, and when they fell against each other, mountain goat style, they clutched and clawed, in an attempt to wrestle each other to the ground.

"Steve!"

There was nothing for Steve Watanabe to do but to get in as close as he could get, in order to, if possible, affect the outcome of the struggle. The two wrestlers flipped each other around a couple of times, working toward some ineffectual attempts to strangle, and when Jim Rose was on top, about to prevail, Steve grasped a spade and went up and whacked him hard on the back of the head, on the part that he knew controlled autonomic physiologic functions like breathing and swallowing, so that Rose toppled over onto his side and was disoriented for a moment. It was precisely in this moment that Steve climbed into the nearby rover. He was followed not long after by Brandon Lepper, who flung himself into the back where the mining equipment was meant to go, and then, as quickly as he was able, Steve thrust the rover into drive and started off. The rovers can't go very quickly on Mars, where there are no roads and where there are bits of disjecta from crater impact everywhere. Even when Brandon and Steve were making the best time they were able to, they were not terribly fast. They were in danger of shredding their tires. This made it not at all impossible for Jim Rose to chase after his quarry on foot. At the first opportunity, he attempted to latch on to the back of the rover. They were dragging him for a little bit, until Brandon, with a hammer he found in a wheel well, tried to hammer Jim's digits. Because of the choppiness of the ride, he missed many times before he was able to connect with one, leaving Jim howling in pain, as, upon letting go, he collided with some rocks on his way to a prone position.

Now there was time enough for Brandon and even Steve, who kept turning back to survey the progress of the fight before nearly hitting various boulders, to understand how disheveled and unlike himself Captain Jim Rose appeared. Not the magnetic and dashing former military hero who was, in the press, one of the bright stars of the Mars mission. Steve's question to himself later was: Had he himself fallen as far as Jim? Had he become *someone else entirely,* a nomad of the desert of this place, a miner in the salt mines of Mars, someone capable of malevolence or of crimes that were unacceptable to his earthling analogue?

The rover ground along the floor of the Ius Chasma, its enormous and threatening wall flush against the side of the vehicle. Brandon lay in the back clutching at an assortment of burns and wounds, until they came, after thirty minutes' time, to the collapse where a slope had been rendered for them. A slope brushed clear of debris by the ceaseless winds. Elsewhere, Jim was undoubtedly heading for his ultralight, where he would wait for sunlight in order to conduct the second phase of the manhunt. Steve and Brandon needed to get as much lead time on him as they could. But the question was *which way to go?* They were soon to be on the far side of the Ius Chasma, and it had taken Brandon a good ten days to get there when first surveying his mining sites. Upon crossing the chasm, they would be far enough from the campsites containing the remaining Martian colonists, not to mention food and water, to make long-term survival difficult.

It was the beginning of night. If they wore their thermal jumpsuits, there was the chance that the ionic reflectors sewn into them would be visible from space. By these means, anyone with a brain in his head would be able to track them. On the steep slope up onto the plateau, Steve did his best to keep the rover from toppling. Likewise he did his best to keep Brandon from falling out. They were making a lot of noise, the kind of noise that, if the wind were to die down, would be echoing up and down the canyon for kilometers.

Yet Steve felt a profound exhilaration, a giddy sense of accomplishment, when they had ascended to the vertiginous shelf and could look down upon it, as into the very center of the Red Planet's formation, its most show-offy line drawings, to know that they had once again thwarted the desire of Mars to squash any eruption of *life.* The sun was just now over the line of the horizon, and the Milky Way was splashed across the canvas of the galaxy, and they had only this illumination to get them out into the center of the plateau, four or five kilometers off from the cliff wall, where Steve shut down the engine, sputtering from a shortage of fuel. It was here that an urgent and unlikely-to-succeed plan began to formulate. Steve suggested that he and Brandon get *under* the rover and put on oxygen tanks and masks and see, thus arrayed, if they could keep each other warm. *Under the rover,* that is, in case they were being watched from above.

Which they were, kids. Being watched. I have passed the point in the story that I assembled from Steve Watanabe's notes. In any event, his notes, his dispatches from his lowly position as a miner of silicon oxide and water crystals on Mars, were not composed in such a way as to convey detailed or meaningful editorializing about his predicament. These notes, in fact, could be boiled down to a few simple words, words that any reader, such as yourself, would have been able to fathom, if you were a flunky at NASA reading them: *Help us, please!* That's what he was attempting to convey in the days before he found himself, according to these conjectures, sleeping outside in the Martian night, next to a fellow who may or may not have been infected with some dire germ, such as *M. thanatobacillus,* the germ that was reputed to cause higher life-forms to *disassemble.* Huddling up, he and Brandon looked sort of the way our companion species, our pair of felines, our dog and cat, look when they are nestled together. For whatever reason, Steve Watanabe kept thinking of Debbie Quartz (this is how I reconstruct it), Debbie rappelling out into the vastness of space, Debbie quickly becoming a speck, and how quickly gone, and he wondered if her body was preserved exactly as it was at the instant she made her decision, and how far out? Was it out toward Jupiter? Did it have insufficient thrust to get that far? Did the thrust of one of those oxygen tanks enable any so-called head of steam at all? Maybe it would be possible in some way to figure out where her body was on the way *back.* Maybe it would be possible someday, when interplanetary travel was more routine, to find Debbie Quartz's body and to return it to her cousins and nephews, which was what remained, as he understood it, of the Quartz family. But he kept imagining, in his delirious semi-sleep, that it was Debbie whose physique was being *disassembled,* until he included Brandon

too in this ugly bit of dream work, Brandon, right beside him, disassembling. When Steve woke, according to the fantasy, Brandon's
body would be a splatter of blood and guts beside him, like what's
left after a tomato is heaved at a cement wall, and worse, what if it
was somehow communicable, the *germ,* what if mere contact with
the blood and guts, the tomato leavings, was somehow enough
to pass on the disassembly to himself, just by the mere touching? What if that was enough? Was it somehow the interaction
between the germ and some carbon-based cellular material that
activated a new bit of disassembly? Was it somehow radioactive
too, like so much on the surface of the planet? Because the course
of the illness certainly resembled radiation sickness. The infected
body just started to fail at the molecular level, the stomach and intestines began to liquefy and to spill their contents into the body
cavity, the liver began to shudder to a halt and to seize up, squirt-
ing poisons into the bloodstream; it was just like in that rash of
polonium killings that swept through the Russian Republic before
the beginning of Cold War II. Maybe it, the germ, was like that, it
was like radiation sickness. Maybe Steve just shouldn't have been
spooning so close to Brandon Lepper. Maybe character changes,
psychological distress and disturbance, were the leading edge of
the infection, along with that change in skin pigment. Although
everyone on the Mars mission had a change in skin pigment, even
Abu had had one, and then that led Steve back to Abu, and the
horror of Abu, and how could he have done what he'd done to
Abu, unless he too was already *infected.* Abu was a peace-loving
guy, a fervent Muslim, despite his parents' being these renowned
astrophysicist types, and why was it that he, Steve, who had never
prevailed in any physical confrontation, had crept up on Abu while
he was out working on his sculptures and contused him? Was that
part of the *interplanetary disinhibitory syndrome,* or was it more like
the kind of character changes that were associated with the early
stages of the bacterial infection? Every time he thought about the
space suit that contained Debbie Quartz spinning out into the
beyond, there was a different body in it; at first it was Debbie,

and then it was José, and then after José it was Abu Jmil, whom he'd known since they roomed together during training, and how could he have done what he'd done, except by reason of the unremitting loneliness of this place? You could feel it every step you took outside one of the capsules, the loneliness assaulted you, like the cosmic rays, like the dust devils, like the howling winds. And the fact that Abu just didn't seem to feel this, and didn't seem at all affected by *interplanetary disinhibitory syndrome,* it just was too much to take, with his renowned parents back there in Kansas City or wherever it was he came from. And they hobnobbed with politicians, his parents, and they appeared on the evening news as expert commentators. Every time there was an asteroid that looked like it was going to strike the Earth. Every time there was talk of some new space initiative, Dr. Jmil was there with his perfect British accent and his equally brilliant and talented wife. Abu could whistle all the Brandenburg Concertos, and he spoke five different languages, and he tried to solve difficult problems in mathematics when he was bored, and nothing bothered him on the Mars mission, not having a soldering iron pointed at his eye, not forecasts of an infectious agent, not the dwindling of the food supply and the nonappearance of a resupply capsule. Abu said the lack of food was good for them, because in controlled studies, rats who were fed less lived that much longer. The most irritating part of the whole thing was that Abu never seemed to feel lonely, not even once. Nor did he seem ever to have sex with anyone, not Debbie or Laurie or any of the men. As far as Steve could tell he didn't even masturbate. There was no girl back on Earth; there were only mathematics problems, and Brandenburg Concertos, and sculptures. Steve felt as though he'd been driven to it. He'd been driven to take Abu down because the absolute liberty of space demanded it. Everything high was brought low, and everything low was briefly, ephemerally high, before being toppled once again. And in Steve's semisleep, he saw Abu in Debbie Quartz's space suit, and Abu was drifting out toward Jupiter, except that Abu seemed unconcerned, even serene, about the wending of his way.

If it was his lot on the mission to drift as far as Jupiter, then he would drift as far as Jupiter, and he would keep a running commentary of his own death, except that it was not to be so easy for Steve, observing this space suit and its hapless victims, because he too would have to wear it, and that was what he did, at some point in the middle of the night, he saw himself in the space suit, looking out, and he saw the two ships, uncoupling and heading off, and he felt the last of the oxygen, and he wanted to clutch at his lungs as he breathed in some more carbon dioxide, and then some more, and then he began to tumble into the long sleep in which he was never to be recovered by human history.

Upon awaking, Steve Watanabe found that Brandon was gone. Considering the portion of the night he'd spent awake, this seemed frankly miraculous, nearly as miraculous as the fact that Steve was still alive. He had no food, he had almost no water, he hadn't bathed in so long he could scarcely remember what pleasure was afforded by bathing. But he was alive. And he was in possession of the rover, and all he had to do was start it and drive around the long way, into the outflow channels of the chasma, and around, and he would be back among the living. It might take a little while, but still. That is assuming, you know, that he intended to rejoin the rest of the crew. Maybe it was some kind of residual guilt about Brandon, and about the bad shape that Brandon had appeared to be in when they last had a conversation, but Steve found that the one way he could expiate some of the remorse he felt about everything that had happened on the Mars mission was to drive back to the site of the dig, so that his son and his wife would be well looked after, so that things would be made right. He waited for the morning sun to charge up the rover, and then he began driving back toward the cliff wall, looking for the spot where they'd come up. This while keeping his eyes fixed on the sky for the marauding ultralight.

In time, he came upon the collapsed section of the wall, which looked quite a bit more fearsome going down than it had coming up, even with the gentler slope, the sort of clamshell slope of the collapse. This was when Steve Watanabe—because going down is always more dangerous than going up—somehow managed, first to get the rover *stuck* between a couple of sheets of rock, and then, in attempting to dislodge it through expert manipulation of gears and transmission, to *plunge* the rover off a steep incline, and, luckily separated from it, to free-fall, landing on a shelf about two hundred meters or so above the floor of the Ius Chasma. The rover landed facedown, at the bottom, so that many of its solar panels were shattered in the accident, and it would have taken any number of Martian colonists, a group of them, to overturn the vehicle and restore it to running condition. In the meantime, Steve Watanabe also fell into unconsciousness.

May 1, 2026

There can no longer be a language with which to describe the psychology of Captain Jim Rose, because his consciousness as it might now have been described was so *other* from Jim Rose, as I had understood him, that language itself no longer applied. In the process of hunting Brandon Lepper on foot, Jim was reduced to a very primordial set of impulses. Of what did his consciousness consist? His command structure was at its most uncomplicated. He wanted only to find Brandon and squeeze the life out of him. It was no longer entirely apparent, nor would it have been to the old Jim, why this was so important. But the impulse remained to be satisfied, and Jim followed the tracks in the sand, and with an acute sense of smell that was new to him, he tasted the breezes. Amid the natural sulfur reek of this desolate place, he smelled the desperation of Brandon.

Jim would have been troubled by the spontaneous bleeding, had he language with which to describe it. The spontaneous bleeding was happening from a number of unlikely places. From interstitial spots in his physique, the crevice in his elbow, from somewhere in his neck. He would have been frightened in language, but outside of language he was just irritated with the gouts of blood that occluded his eyes. Or he was slowed down. The same with the rents in the uniform that he was wearing. He had slept out in the desert and had been incautious, for a lack of language, about preventing frostbite. The tips of his fingers had lost all sensation, but he had no particular allegiance to the individual fingers. He had no particular allegiance to anything except to the tracking and elimination of Brandon Lepper.

Brandon was traveling west, and so Jim followed westerly, though this meant that they were moving farther along the cliff face of the Valles Marineris, and farther away from the rest of the colonists. Brandon's path was erratic. Here he swerved in on the plateau, and here he seemed to decide that if he didn't keep the Ius Chasma on his left, he was doomed to wandering endlessly, unsure of his location.

It was on the morning of the third day that Jim, who had slowed to a few meager steps for each minute that passed on the Martian clock, saw, up ahead, a body slumped over in the sands, and he knew, in a way that was no longer *of language,* that he had treed his quarry, so to speak. He had little left to accomplish in his time on Mars. He rested, now that Brandon was in sight, and licked his fetid and cracking lips, which were streaming with some combination of viscosities that would not entirely clot, despite the lack of fluids in him. The rest of him, his back brain seemed to suggest, would aid in the dispatch of the evildoer. Brandon, meanwhile, as Jim drew closer, also readied himself. He was in possession of a knife, or perhaps a homemade razor, his Taser having plunged into the canyon, and the reflection from this weapon kept striking Jim retinally, so that, in a primeval way, he too knew to be prepared. And Brandon took this opportunity to try to use language, what was left of it, to head off the mortal assault that was in his immediate future. Since Jim didn't care about language any longer, and had cast himself back into some much more elemental system of clicks and grunts, this poetical and uninflected plea for Brandon's life was lost on him. Brandon muttered something about the good times they'd had together in the old days. Perhaps he said something like: "Can't you just let me do what NASA brought me here to do?" Or : "Do you know what this meant to me?" Or something like this: "Could you really cut a man's life short?" Which was not a question Jim asked himself. He responded resoundingly in the positive with a quickening of his pulse at the idea of squeezing the life out of Brandon. It was invigorating, except that he was not in possession of the concept of vigor. "You know that if you get back to Earth they will execute you." But what was Earth to Jim now? *Earth was nothing.*

The moment of last resort was upon Lepper now. Pleas for mercy had gone unheard. Appeals to Captain Jim Rose's conscience had elicited no reply. Lepper had only one remaining bargaining chip that he could introduce into the exchange. As Jim approached, Brandon rummaged in the pocket of his jumpsuit (which, kids, let me tell you, is not easy to do with the gloves on, even though the gloves are magnetically tipped in order to make it easier, theoretically, to pick up tools). With the onrushing of his antagonist, he was unable, at first, to procure the item he wanted to procure, but in time he did. He pulled it out, and in the palm of his glove, at first, it looked perhaps like some ancient home-rolled stogie, or perhaps like a small doughy confection that was ready to be oven fired into an agreeable dinner roll.

It was my finger.

"You looking for this?" Brandon said, and now the malice in his heart, since he believed his cause was nearly lost, surfaced in him, and he didn't care any longer what Jim thought. "You looking for the finger of your friend? He's your friend, right? Or maybe he was a little more than your friend? José, you know, he really wasn't that bad a guy, until he went all soft, and at first he was kind of worried that he had been bunked on the gay capsule. So maybe you want a little memento of your good friend. I'll give you this if you let me go. I think it's only a little bit decomposed. Actually, you know, the Martian surface would be really good for tanning *skins*. Look how well preserved this is!"

And it is likely, kids, that this was an accurate description of my finger, which in the months since it had been separated from me had mostly been cleaned of the blood and gluey material that it secreted at first. It was now mainly a talisman. And that must have been the reason Brandon kept it, to remind himself that there was something that divided him from me, from the rest of us. He believed, at this late hour—while holding aloft in one hand his straight razor and in the other my finger—in *duty,* nothing more, and was willing to die a nasty, unrepentant death in order to indicate how devoted he was to his concept of duty. Jim Rose was happy to oblige.

Jim fell upon the other man without mercy, and as he went to grab Brandon's razor with a hand, a hand mostly without feeling from the night spent outdoors, the possibility of injury was not of particular concern. When he was cut, the blood poured forth from his hand as elsewhere. He could see the effect of himself on the other man. Still, he could see how he inspired fear, and it made him only more murderous, and having flung the offending blade free, he went as to pick up the other man, who had no more fight in him, nor even the strength to pull at Jim's outer layer or his hemorrhaging flesh. There was a paradoxical tenderness in the moment, as if deep within Jim was a sense that it would be possible, at last, to do this thing without violence, without some display of machismo. He could do it without, for example, eating Brandon's heart, or making a stew out of him, or stealing back my finger from Brandon, because these were unnecessary, because all Brandon had to do was to give in to this place of death. Brandon had to become one with the tendency of death to pool in the valleys of Mars, likewise upon its mountaintops. Brandon submitted to being carried to the edge of the Valles Marineris, to one of its most imposing rises, because Brandon was, at this point, so close to being congruent with the reality of Martian death as to be nearly indistinguishable from it. And then Brandon submitted, summarily, without warning, as Jim heaved his body from the top of the cliff, nearly four miles up. There was a little bit of stumbling at the last moment. Jim didn't want to fall into the ravine himself. But he also wanted to watch. It was reflexive. The thrill of gravity at a moment like that.

Brandon didn't twist, gyrate, cry out, or anything of this sort. His was a smooth death. He fell with a remarkable lack of resistance. He could have been a sack of grapefruit or a pile of wet towels. He fell, and then he was dead. He carried a little piece of me with him.

Jim turned from the edge of the cliffside, as soon as he assured himself that his thirst for this moment was now slaked, and then he began his long walk.

What simple, uncomplicated perceptions were his during the march that followed? Were even the simplest grammars still relevant to his primitive consciousness? We can assume that sunlight, glorious and perfect, which, despite its cosmic radiation, was still a lovely thing on Mars, was part of his sensory perceptions. Jim was happy at the appearance of sunlight, each and every day, after the nights he spent out in the elements, trying to stay warm in his Martian jumpsuit, which was leaking oxygen and which properly ought to have killed him days before. This fact — that he ought to have been dead — was probably lost on Jim. The sunlight warmed him, and the sunlight was good. Trudging along the Ius Chasma for days, without food or water, even this was somehow satisfying, because he became, in a way, part of the Ius Chasma. In different kinds of light, the canyon was perceptibly different, and there were layers of bedrock that he hadn't seen the day before. He didn't recognize this, but he recognized that the canyon belonged to him somehow; he had assumed ownership. The danger of it was like his own menace, and this was reassuring. Eventually, he repaired the ultralight to a barely workable condition and traversed the outflow portion of the Valles Marineris until he crash-landed it somewhere outside of base camp. Which is to say that he walked in. A representative of the walking dead. There were only these simple commands coming from the back brain, *keep going, don't stop, keep going.* It's fair to say now, kids, that there was some kind of homing beacon in him, and I employ the word *home* with the full sense of its meaning.

I was in the power station when he finally turned up, dragging himself, dragging a leg that looked as though it would not stay attached to him for another five steps, and bleeding, garishly, in many spots, bleeding chiefly from the eye sockets. It was the most shocking illness I'd seen in my life, and I have seen some horrible things. I have seen what weaponry can do; I have watched men drown in their own wounds. I don't know how to describe what I saw. I am still trying to figure out what I saw. It was as if Jim had emerged from the Dark Ages, from some savage and merciless eon, and when he thundered on the door, and I attempted to admit him, I was not really sure that I ought to have done so. Because I had given myself over to thinking that it was all about the *germ,* that the Mars mission was now all about the germ, no matter what they told us. And I didn't know if the germ was communicable, and I didn't want the germ. But once I saw him, and I saw the confusion on his face, a confusion that plainly wondered what had happened, what had become of him (when his intentions had once been so noble), I had no choice but to admit him.

He didn't need to say anything. I knew enough to know what he felt. And I filled a bucket with water that was warm from the reactor, and I found a rag, and I began to try to bathe his wounds, the many, many wounds on the sallow, fetid body of Captain Jim Rose. He lay there, soundlessly, on the floor. Whenever a wound was rinsed, a fresh gurgle of corpuscular material seemed to bubble forth from it. I felt his forehead, kids, and his forehead was cold, horribly cold.

"What do you want me to do?" I asked him. "Is there something I can do for you? Do you want me to talk to NASA and tell them what's happened?"

Jim said nothing.

"Do you even know what's happened? Because I'm not sure I

know what's happened." And I didn't know. I had my surmises. But I had not yet assembled the dossier of reports and video footage and satellite images that would enable me to re-create the end of the Mars mission for you kids. I was still mulling over the crisscrossing of disinformation that was being fed to us by a government agency that was so wound up in the budgetary conflicts and the rapacious needs of independent contractors that it couldn't give a straight story to any taxpayer, no matter how earnest his entreaties.

Jim managed, with some great effort, to struggle to his feet, and he wandered back and forth in the control room of the power station, as though he were looking for something specific, even though I couldn't imagine what it was. He would linger in front of some computer screen, gazing upon it as though he had never seen a computer screen before, and then he would press a bloody palm down on some surface, look at the handprint, and then in his disturbed way, he would begin wandering again. As if he couldn't stop. He seemed stunned by an array of tools that was stored on one wall. He looked at a whisk broom for a while. There was a gas mask, and for a second it seemed that he was going to try to fit the gas mask onto his face, to replace that cracked helmet and visor he'd left out on the front step.

Then he found the Taser.

Somehow Jim still knew very well what the Taser was for. Not only did he know what the Taser was for, but he knew how to set it on the setting that would inflict the maximum amount of damage. It occurred to me, kids, and I am not proud of saying it, that he was going to use the Taser *on me*. My survival skills had become uppermost. I was working hard at staying out of trouble, but now trouble had come to my door.

"Jim, pal, you're not going to use that on me? Are you? There's no reason you'd want to use that on me, right? I guess I have only a few reasons left to want to stick around, or maybe just one reason, and that reason is Ginger. I was just thinking maybe it would be possible for me to get back to Earth so I could see my cat,

Havoc, and Ginger, and maybe I could watch Ginger graduate or something like that. I mean, I understand that I have not been the best member of the Mars mission, and I have not always leaped to defend your plans, your philosophies, and all of that, but I think we have been friends for a long time, and I would like to ask you to think carefully about what you're about to do."

He closed in on me, kids, he backed me toward the door that led into the inner sanctum where the graphite-moderated uranium was percolating away, and I didn't really want to go in there. I hadn't really gone in there yet, and I didn't want to start now. I was tired of all the science. I was tired of it all. Jim held the Taser in one bloody hand, and he came toward me, and I was going to do what I could to disarm him, but my heart wasn't even up to the fight.

And then, he came right up close to me to, well, it didn't have anything to do with the Taser, kids. He dropped the Taser. It wasn't that kind of moment. It wasn't the kind of moment when a man does another man *wrong*. It was the kind of moment when a person kisses another person. Which is quite the opposite of someone doing another man wrong. So the weary, lost Jim Rose, who had almost nothing left in his wracked body, all but emptied even of his soul, moved, as if drifting some inches above the floor, near to me. And his face came close to mine, and his lips were cracking and bleeding, and his poor eyes had tears in them, at least I prefer to *think* that his eyes had tears in them, rather than just droplets of blood. And he collected me into his arms, as I sort of tried to do the same to him, in a state of astonishment, and then he was kissing me, *the kiss of death,* maybe, but a kiss nonetheless, a kiss for a pair of men who were expiring for lack of love, for lack of the things that connect one person to another. Jim held me, and I held him, and his lips were one with my lips; I expect before Jim I didn't really know what kissing was for, or: I was so used to disappointing people, disappointing women, disappointing everyone, that I often forgot to kiss because I didn't want the recipients of my meager affections to feel bad, because that was what I thought I brought to these kisses, a lot of conflicted feeling, and a lot of regret, and a lot of destitution; and yet the kind of destitution I had then, back on the home planet, was nothing like what I had here; this new destitution was grander, was the kind that made an African living on a dollar a day and perishing of malaria and HIV seem fortunate, and this despite the fact that my destitution cost billions upon billions, so that men (and women) such as myself could come here to this godforsaken place and rot from the inside out; kids, let me tell you, if you want a kiss you will remember, a kiss that you can take with you to tell your children and grandchildren about, have one of those kisses that is about how hopeless your situation is; add to this the fact that you are likely never to see again the person you are kissing; now this makes for a rather spectacular kiss; these are the moments that we stick around for, and apparently Jim had stuck around for this, for the two of us crying like we were teenagers, and holding each other, and I still had a lot of, well, a lot of his blood all over me when he pulled himself away, and I could see the complex of things going through his face, as though his face were a projector, and these were slides projected upon him: photographs of his past, of his children, of his first wife and his second wife, of the myriad places he had traveled; I watched as these stills were removed from the carousel of slides in him, so that he was no longer their steward.

While I was recovering from the embrace, while I was living through the awkward aftermath of it, the time when we were no longer embracing, he stood in the open door, allowing the frigid wind in, evacuating all the oxygen from the interior and wailing like some blues harp player summoning a distant freight train. As I made for the door, to close it, I watched as Jim picked up the Taser and struggled out onto the front step, and because of my abstraction, it didn't occur to me that it was there, with his last bit of energy, that he would use the Taser on himself. It was nearly inaudible, because he could scarcely any longer groan with pain, not in the condition he was in. He gave it a good shot, on the way to delivering the lethal dose, and this seemed herculean under the circumstances. He probably didn't need such a large charge in order to be brought down. Upon the Martian soil.

I went to him, naturally. I looked at the life-support information on the little LCD screen on his wrist. I put my head on his chest. But I knew there was little I could do. Jim Rose was dead. I decided to drag him by the boots to a spot where I could bury him later in the day. When I had cleaned myself up. This I did. I hauled him to an igneous boulder adjacent, and then I went and fetched a blanket to lay upon him. I held it down with some Martian rocks. The discharging of tasks and responsibilities was keeping me going. I felt like I was doing some good. And that was enough. Who was there left to tell?

I passed a long evening filling my veins with things from the first aid kit. While I was doing that, I pondered a next move. Have I properly indicated the route back to Earth in my diary? The route back to Earth relied upon our being able to blast off in a reassembled ERV, built, in a stripped-down version, from a modular portion of the *Excelsior,* and some spare pieces, with available fuel from the planet Mars. A lot of consideration, in the planning stages of the Mars mission, went into the discussion of when exactly to send along the spare parts, the extra fuel. One school of thought had it that you sent the orbiter a few weeks before the astronauts were intended to return. If for some reason the astronauts needed to abort the mission *early,* ahead of schedule, in this schematic there was no chance that the Martian colonists would be able to get off the planet.

Additionally, there was the oblong Martian orbit, and the fact that at its farthest elliptical point, in its six hundred–odd days around the sun, it was awfully far from Earth. The amount of food and supplies needed was significantly higher if you were flying an orbiter 100 million miles back instead of 36 million. However, an emergency was an emergency. I had to secure permission from NASA to break the seal on the return fuel stockpile and begin assembling the ERV. Which, I admit, was not terribly likely. But if my assumptions were valid, as they later proved to be, that

Jim's trip out to Valles Marineris had not ended felicitously for any of our antagonists, then it was the case that there were only a very few Martian colonists left whose blessing I required. So I attempted to radio to the greenhouse.

Meanwhile, it was only natural to spend some of my spare time in consideration of the germ as well, kids. Because if the germ was communicable, then I was one with the germ, I had the germ in me, how could I not? If the hemorrhagic mess that had been Jim Rose was an example of what the germ was able to bring about in a higher life-form, I had no hope of avoiding the illness. He had embraced me, he had kissed me, I had his blood all over me still, despite my efforts to rinse some of it off in a very short, cold shower with what water was left in the power station.

The question of when exactly Jim had been infected also troubled me. Had it been when he'd drunk the water out by the Argyre Basin, on that first flight? Or had it been present in him from some earlier point? And was Brandon suffering with it too, when he killed José? Later in the evening, to discuss these and other issues, I again tried to call the greenhouse, again without success. With a newborn Martian child, those two had a lot on their hands, and they just didn't have time to respond to every communication that came through. I therefore suited up with what must have been one of Abu's extra jumpsuits. It didn't fit me well, which perhaps indicated just how much physical wasting had been going on here. I hadn't eaten in days. I just didn't much think about food. Another good reason to go over to the greenhouse.

I took a solar-powered robotic dolly. It wasn't quick, but the tracks to the greenhouse were well worn down now, which made this, perhaps, one of the first roads on the planet Mars. I didn't need to have a satellite tracking device to tell me where to go, and no compass would work here. I just followed the tracks, while there was still some light. In due course, I came to the door of the greenhouse. And at this point, you know what happened, right? I found the door locked. I had locked the door myself, according to the wishes of the inhabitants, the last time I was there, but it hadn't occurred to me that I would be locking myself out. I knocked on the door; I pounded on the door. They had not yet been out, nor had any visitors in the days since delivery.

It would have been easy enough just to smash the plastic sheeting on the exterior of the greenhouse, but even I would not have gone that far, would not have sacrificed the frail plant life that had been induced to grow there with great difficulty, so I kept pounding. They were ignoring me; this was clear enough. They were hoping I would go away. And I tried calling out, "Arnie, I know you're in there! Please answer the door!" Imagining that a feminine sensibility might be even more easily swayed by my predicament, I tried Laurie too: "Laurie, it's me! Jed! Please! I have things I need to discuss with you!"

It was hard to hear with the helmet on, but I thought, at last, I heard some commotion within. Arnie's voice shouted through the door.

"Jed, I'm afraid I can't let you in."

"What do you mean you can't let me in?" I shouted through the muffling of the helmet.

"There's the danger of infection, Jed. We have a newborn here, who has no immunological defense. Imagine what could happen to this newborn. She hasn't been exposed to any Earth diseases at all. Except what insignificant bacteria we managed to bear with us into this nearly sterile environment. We don't have any inoculations to give her, and we can't allow her to be in contact with anyone who might be a vector of contagion."

"What makes you think that I am?"

"Jed, we have been briefed on everything that has happened on Mars in the last few days."

"You've what?"

"When situations like this become complicated, it becomes important to go where the competence is. Laurie and I were never entirely comfortable with all of Jim's Mars First! business. We were just trying to get along with everyone else, since we were going to live here for some time. At this point, our job seems to be to *survive,* and that's what we're going to continue doing."

"And you think I want to get in the way of that reasonable goal?" I said.

"Jed," Arnie said, "we know that the bacteria is genuine. I have tried to harvest some from around the surfaces where Brandon slept earlier, and from around the various waste depositories, and in concert with people back home, I have managed to see some slides under the microscope. And I don't recognize it as anything I have ever seen before. It's very difficult with the tools I have on hand to identify the mechanisms that make it so deadly, but I'm still trying. The interesting thing about the bacteria, Jed, is that you'd expect it, or them, to be traditional extremophile bacteria, bacteria that can thrive in any kind of location, like in volcanic steam vents or on Antarctica. Maybe you would expect them to have features like archaea, you know, different from regular bacteria, such as we experience them back on Earth. But oddly enough, they do have traditional bacterial structures. They are rod shaped like other bacilli. I'm pretty sure they're gram-positive. They have just somehow managed to adapt to the extreme coldness and dryness of life on Mars. It's as if they are waiting around for life to come, just so that they can work upon it according to their rather hostile impulses."

I said, "Arnie, I'm very happy to be getting this lecture on bacteriology, which I will definitely be including in my diary for the online community back home when I type later this evening —"

"You're still working on that, Jed?"

"That is not the point, Arnie. The point is that you and Laurie have food, whereas I don't have any food, except what's remaining of our rations, and I need some, and we need to coordinate about the return mission, which I am thinking should probably begin sooner rather than later, because —"

"You know how much farther you're going to have to go?"

"I know how much farther we will have to go."

"There's no 'we' about it, Jed. Laurie and I, and Prima, aren't going."

By now, I'd sort of slid down the plane of the door. To a modified prone position.

"You're going to stay?" I said. And perhaps I betrayed some of my consternation about this. It wasn't that I wanted to go adventuring back to the home planet with a happy young couple and their newborn crying and throwing up and needing its cloth diaper changed, so that we'd be stockpiling baby shit throughout the journey. But I also wasn't sure that I wanted to make the journey, well, *alone.*

"What about Steve? Have you heard anything from Steve? Did he—"

Arnie said, "He somehow managed to get the reflectors off his suit."

"Reflectors."

"He piloted the rover off a cliff, and so it's likely that his body is out there, somewhere in the Valles Marineris, and we'll find it the next time one of us goes out there digging. In the meantime, we were intended to wait for liftoff until the next manned mission, and NASA has now committed to sending the resupply shot in the next month, as they said they were going to do, and I think I can make enough fuel with the hydrogen that we have left over—"

I pressed my palm to the door one last time, to feel what the warmth of common goals felt like. Then I brushed myself off and was again heading east of paradise, leaving the edenic couple and their newborn to do as they intended. They would build the new world. And if that necessitated my exile, I supposed I could understand. Then it was back to the power station, which I was now going to leave to Arnie and Laurie, and then to the capsule I had always known, the *Excelsior,* where I was going to see if I had enough fuel, myself, to jettison the lower stage of the housing and lift off.

Steve Watanabe, upon awaking, on the ledge. Steve Watanabe and his cranial trauma. The broken collarbone. Steve Watanabe, looking at his hands, in heavy gloves. Steve Watanabe, and the middle space between unconsciousness and grave physical pain. Wondering how exactly he got here and where exactly this was. An oblong moon, shaped like an Idaho potato, drifted overhead. Was he in the desert Southwest? He'd been there once, on vacation. He was certain he'd been there, that he took his wife there for a rafting trip. He had a wife. He remembered some things about his wife. His wife smelled a certain way. His wife had a horrible temper, and the burning sensation of being hectored by his wife was also easy to summon up. Of the trip to the desert, however, the vast majority of details were missing. He didn't remember being asked to don this unusual outfit. Were they trying to break the land-speed record? Steve Watanabe flipped up the visor, and the bright salmon-colored sky appeared to him in more indelible glory. The sky was the color of a yam.

It was coming back to him. He had trained to go somewhere that was rusty in the way this place was rusty. Mars! This first bit of important information, very important information, came back to Steve Watanabe — he was on Mars. Another planet. Far from home. The circumstances in which he had arrived here were not easy to reconstruct. He was getting flashes of detail, as from a stainless steel pan into which he was meant to put his personal effects.

He attempted to remove the helmet, to see if it would be possible to breathe the air on Mars, but when he did so, he found that the air was incredibly cold, like daggers, and that almost immediately he couldn't catch his breath. He struggled for breath for ten or twenty seconds, aware that his anxiety wasn't helping particularly, and then he secured the helmet on his head again. He must have had some kind of sophisticated oxygen supply in the jumpsuit, but for how long?

Then there was the ledge on which he lay. Here was an incredibly dramatic view, it could not be denied, this series of striated and jagged cliffsides that stretched beyond him in both directions as far as he could see. What an awesome and overpowering vista. The problem from a logistical viewpoint was that he was stuck on the canyon wall, on this ledge, and though there was a sloping decline not far off, it was unclear how to get there. There was no direct route to this spot, to this ledge, and certainly none below. And yet the more carefully he looked, the more he was convinced that there was some machine apparatus at the bottom of the canyon. Some conveyance. It was a long way down. Hundreds and hundreds of feet down, and though Watanabe was not scared of heights, he was a little bit worried about falling off the ledge and meeting the same fate as the vehicle.

As the sun rose, the winds dwindled some, and the jumpsuit was becoming a little bit warm, at least when the sun began to shine brightly upon Watanabe. As long as he was flush against the rock wall, it really wasn't as cold as he imagined it should have been. It was very nearly in the tolerable range. Greenland in August, or so he thought.

There were some tracks on the sloping part of the cliff wall. And so it seemed that the vehicle, and Steve Watanabe, had been either descending or ascending, and that other persons in the vehicle had been thrown clear and, he imagined, done considerable harm. Given these circumstances, there was no choice for Steve Watanabe but that he climb up the cliff face. Watanabe could not remember whether on his desert vacation he had done any rock climbing, and he could not remember whether he was the type of person who rock climbed effectively, but there was no alternative, despite the possibility of a fractured collarbone, and perhaps cranial injury.

What was the gravity situation on Mars, Steve Watanabe wanted to remember. Would it be easier to climb up the cliff wall? Could he somehow make leaps and bounds that were out of range for him back on Earth? He began climbing without answering these pertinent questions, and mainly because he remembered the smell of his wife's body, and in the process of remembering this warm-bread smell, he came to remember that he had a son too, and perhaps it was the wife and son who had brought him to this place, this ledge on the wall somehow. Because if he was able to get into this predicament in pursuit of the elusive reunion with wife and son, then Steve Watanabe could extricate himself from this predicament, because now it was the case that reunion was a reason to keep moving, and maybe they would be looking for him, whoever *they* were, the other people with whom he had come to this place, to Mars, and this would make the matter of rescue and reunion with the wife and son that much more likely and that much more sweet. How many days, weeks, months, had he been here on Mars, and wasn't there some space agency that was meant to prevent things like this on the planet Mars? Bodily injury?

He fitted his hand into one crevice, and fitted his foot into another, and happily the erosion of the high winds did seem to make footholds and handholds a likelihood, except that occasionally he heard scree plummeting down underneath him. The plummeting took a very long time. Watanabe did *not* look down, despite the bodily shooting pains; he kept climbing, and when other shelves presented themselves for rest, he rested, and over the course of some hours, he did see that he was coming near to the ledge, the ledge of the cliff, and what concerned him, at this point, was the exact nature of the sights that he would behold upon summiting and peering over the lip of that cliff. What would he find? Would he find some other cliff on the other side? Would he find some limitless assortment of ridges and cliff faces, extending into nothingness? Would he find his fellow astronauts?

There were some near misses. Some moments when he hung on dangerously with his good arm. And there were rips and tears in the gloves of his jumpsuit. But he continued going up. As the middle of the Martian day gave way to the afternoon, Watanabe was at last reassured that his exertions were paying off. The summit was no more than thirty or forty feet up, and there was an excellent seam between sheets of the cliff wall, probably due to some kind of tectonic activity or perhaps volcanic tremors. He didn't know for certain; he was just making these things up. All of his prior life seemed to be in preparation for this moment, the moment when he would climb over the top of the cliff, thinking of the smell of his wife and the sound of his son eating breakfast cereal, which seemed, in these last thirty or forty feet, like the times he remembered his son best, at least since the accident that brought him to the ledge. His son was a series of small audio samples, the sound of cereal being chewed, this was very memorable, some kind of particularly crunchy cereal; his son battering a set of wind chimes with a stick out on the porch...the porch, he had a porch, and it was next to a canal, and the weather was humid and it was...*it was in Florida.* Steve Watanabe now felt the humid summer air of Florida, felt its tropical heat, the oncoming hurricane season, heard the sound of the emergency vehicles rumbling through the streets, saw the water levels swelling over the years, taking out another atoll of expensive real estate in the Keys; they came back in one big, moldy steamer trunk, the memories of Florida, just as he reached out a desperate grasping hand to the top of the cliff, and it crumbled, and some of the Martian scree again fell however many hundreds, if not thousands, of feet down beneath him. He didn't even want to know. He swung a leg up and screamed, he could hear himself screaming in the helmet, as though it were some distant sound, and then he was up. He was up! He lay there, giddy with laughter, on his back on the summit of the cliff, and he lay there awhile because he knew what would happen as soon as he stopped laughing. When he stopped laughing, he would have to get up and think about which way to go next. There was something running out of his eyes, tears, he supposed, he was laughing so hard. It was good to just lie there and think about the swirling of memories like solar winds in him.

Then Watanabe, who remembered that he had assumed a name, an Anglo first name, at some point in his youth, but who now chose to cast off the Anglo name—if he had to be named, he would just go by the surname, just Watanabe, first name no longer applicable—rose up on one knee, and then onto his feet, and looked around. Perhaps there had been tracks before, but if the faint declivities were tire tracks, they quickly became indistinguishable from the waves of sand. And in the other direction a nothingness just as perfect and exacting. Watanabe tried to decide

if the ruined vehicle at the bottom of the canyon had been coming this way to get *away* from something, on its way home, or if
home, whatever the word meant on Mars, was in the direction of
the expunged track. He had no way of knowing, having no other
data from which to make a reasoned decision. And so he set off,
kids, into the wilderness.

BOOK TWO*

---

* Astute fans of the genre in whose field I am plowing (people who are familiar with the just-released film *The Four Fingers of Death*) will notice I have already taken liberties in one very basic way. I mean, if it is my responsibility to render exactly the film in question, I have failed. All of this backstory about the Mars shot, on which I have just expended a number of pages, does not actually appear in the film. I plead guilty on this point. But do I need to defend myself? I realized that I could not effectively write the second half of the story if I didn't know a little more about the protagonist, *M. thanatobacillus,* the bacteria that causes all the damage. I couldn't write about the bacteria unless I described those first afflicted with it. And writing about those poor, sick astronauts involved doing the unthinkable, really, moving the action onto the planet Mars, which is only hinted at in the actual film. Similarly, in the film *The Four Fingers of Death* the entire action takes place in the San Diego area. I felt I had no choice but to remove the story to a location I know more about—Rio Blanco itself. One ought to write about what one knows, correct? The desert of my part of the world, after all, is more like Mars, which always forces one to reflect back on when it might have had water, as it once apparently did. That's what makes deserts so satisfying. They have a geological nostalgia about them. They are always struggling, always threatening the careless with their dramatics. That's why I moved to the desert myself. So the Mars of *The Four Fingers of Death* is really just the contemporary American Southwest, the Southwest of 2025 or thereabouts, with its parboiled economy, its negative population growth, its environmental destruction, its deforestation, its smoldering political rage. Readers may ask how I felt so comfortable inventing characters out of whole cloth,

(*continued*)

(*continued*)

when only one or two characters in this first section of my novelization actually appear in the film version of *The Four Fingers of Death,* and my answer to that is that they aren't paying me enough to keep me from writing my own version of this story. Well, actually, they are paying me enough, because they have, in fact, asked me to cut the first section, but you will know, if you have this book in your hand, that I prevailed in this particular argument. I have nothing more to lose, and I'm not cowed by threats of a litigious nature, threats the fly-by-night publisher is so happy to invoke whenever there's an argument between us. Never fear, readers. I actually think that the disputed nature of the manuscript offers you some interesting possibilities. You can actually buy two copies of the book, preserve one, and you can take the second one and just lop off the first half. The part you just read. And then you can read the second half as though that were the entire book. In fact, I divided it into two sections for this very reason. So if you have two copies of the old-fashioned softcover paperback, or if you have copies of the book on your digital reader, or perhaps on your wrist assistant, you can easily just erase the first half. Those who have somehow stumbled on this note *before* reading the first half of the book, well, all the better for you, because you are in a position to imagine what the second half would be like without this first half. In fact, the novelization as a whole might be improved in a digital reading type of environment, because then you could perform the interesting experiment of swapping the first half and the second half, so that first you know what happens with the bacterium on Earth, and then you could go backward and learn about the origin of the bacterium and the trip to Mars afterward. I'm trying not to give away too many plot points as I make these suggestions about the structure of the book, and I hope that is clear. Moreover, I suppose if you needed to buy three copies of the book, in order to have these three different versions (the one that is as shown here, the one without the first section, and the one in which the order of the first and second books is reversed), you could do that, and there is, I should point out, also a fourth possible structure for the book, namely the book in which only the sections about myself, Montese Crandall, appear. Because it has certainly occurred to me that there is a more conventional narrative here, namely the story of my life unencumbered by all this futurist stuff, and you could also just have that version of the book, in which there is only the apparatus, the textual apparatus. I suppose this would be the length of a short novel. This all suggests that you have, in fact, four books in one, all of them assembled by you, and none privileged by me, as the writer, nor by the movie tie-in publishing company, but really constructed or unconstructed and reassembled by *you* the reader. You are free to do this reassembly in any way that pleases you, and if this perfect freedom requires you to buy a couple of extra copies of the book, well, who is counting? You might be wondering how I came up with this idea to have a book that really is three and a half books in one. And the truth is that it came to me in a dream. I really was having trouble sleeping, as I often do, and I took some of those extra-strength sleep aids you can get now, the kind that you're supposed to use on those long business trips to the East. Anyway, I slept about sixteen hours and missed a morning shift at the flea market, and then at some point in the middle of the afternoon, when I must have run the course of the medication and slipped into a more REM-oriented state, I fell into evaluating four different possible approaches to the *The Four Fingers of Death,* in my sleep, without being able to resolve them. Indeed, in my sleep, the resolution would be at my peril, or so the dream muses said. The promptings of the subconscious, I explained to my publishers, are such that one *must* heed them. And anyway, this innovative structure might result in a higher volume of sales, each of the four versions with its distinctively colored and designed cover. —M. C.

SOME MONTHS later, on the eighth day of the tenth month of the year 2026: Vance Gibraltar, sleep-deprived budgetary director at the National Aeronautics and Space Administration, found himself in one of the conference rooms in Houston along with the new director of the agency, that woman named Levin. Debra Levin. A Washington appointee if he'd ever seen one. What became of the former chief executive of NASA, Dr. Anatoly Thatcher, was a cautionary tale. For one and all. Someone had to suffer for the unremitting botch of the Mars mission, a mission once intended to restore luster to the national space program. It wasn't going to be Vance Gibraltar, who unlike the eggheads around here had political instincts. Thatcher, who'd always been an intellectual in what amounted to a military program, was going back to duck hunting in the Upper Peninsula, or so the press release indicated. Gibraltar had to deal instead with this Levin woman.

True, she had a little background in the earth sciences, and a degree from the Ivy League, where she likely consorted with Islamists and professors of Queer Studies. No doubt she'd taken a year off to live with the Inuit to see if she could forestall the clubbing of seal pups. She believed she had a mandate from the White House. If she could complete the Mars mission without further political fallout, put the punctuation mark on it, Gibraltar thought, she could go back to academe or onto the lecture circuit with a most handsome curriculum vitae.

Across the table in the conference room: Mars mission flight director Rob Antoine, the middle manager with the comb-over and imperfect hygiene, whom Gibraltar had hired himself and had once loved like a son. Like all sons, Comb-Over had disappointed him, especially in the matter of personnel. Gibraltar could not look at Rob and his tonsorial stylings without wanting to launch him out toward Mercury. There were others in the room, deputies with too many opinions, people whom Gibraltar didn't bother to get to know—because everything went more smoothly in an absence of personal relationships.

Why was Vance Gibraltar the de facto general administrator at the National Aeronautics and Space Administration? Anyone who'd ask obviously wasn't traveling in the right circles. Gibraltar was kingmaker by design; Gibraltar was eager to get down in the trenches to protect his agency interests. He had the one desire, the desire to maximize visibility and profitability for the agency. He was looking anywhere and everywhere for additional research dollars, and was willing to invite foreign governments into bed with him, even Asian governments, if necessary. And so Gibraltar had been at the job almost twenty years. He'd had every heart procedure that you could have these days, valve replacement, a pacemaker; he was working toward the complete artificial pumper. All he cared about was space. Not himself, not his country, not God, not his congregation. Space. He'd never been thin; he'd never been good at football. He'd stammered as a kid. He couldn't be an astronaut; he'd have failed the physical. But what he could be was a man who financed the astronauts, and a man who was at every launch whether successful or not. He wept by himself, alone, away from the cameras, when rockets went down or missions collapsed. And when they were successful he sent the reporters to interview someone else, some hard scientist, some academic, some engineer, men and women who would be happy to take the credit. He was effective, merciless, and silent to those on the outside.

In all these years, nothing had presented the problems that the Mars mission presented. To say that they had rushed the launch, because of the Sino-Indian joint initiative, this was to understate the extent of the ineptitude. The results had been two years of wretchedness. The news just got worse and worse, and allowing even sanitized bits of it into the press, to the degree that they did so, the deaths, the madness, the experiments uncompleted, the completely hostile environment, just made it worse. No one could have foreseen the complex of problems. And while the public responsibility fell on Dr. Anatoly Thatcher, and now his successor, Debra Levin, nobody felt worse than Gibraltar did himself.

In part because of the failures of the Mars mission, Debra Levin had been skulking around the various regional offices swinging the ax of cost cutting as fervently as if she were selling off the last few hectares of Brazilian rain forest. A pair of Deep Space Probes that the Jet Propulsion Laboratory had designed to withstand ten thousand years of unknowns, the Titan explorer that was supposed to follow the lander already on its way to that moon of Jupiter, Ganymede, both of these had fallen to the cost-cutting blade. Gibraltar understood what Levin had to do, but he disliked her anyway, and he wouldn't intervene to prevent her political sacrifice, just as he had not done with the five or six other NASA directors he had served under during his time at the agency.

In dwelling on the political, though, it was easy to obscure the fact that there was a man alive in the Earth Return Vehicle. Jed Richards. Richards was a lot like Gibraltar himself, the kind of guy who was as loyal as you could be, in word and deed, but also extremely hard to deal with otherwise. Space professionals, the both of them. Richards seemed to have no interests besides training for the Mars mission, and the proof was in his domestic situation. His wife was sleeping with every middle manager at Cape Canaveral.

Before liftoff, they suspected that there was something psychologically off about him. They now believed that there was something psychologically off about *all* the Mars astronauts. Each of them in turn. This was one item on the agenda for the meeting they were about to have, in the windowless, video-equipped room in Houston, with the scuff marks on the walls and the rancid, irradiated coffee. When Debra Levin was satisfied that they had as many attendees as needed, the audiovisual assistant got the screens warmed up, and a gigantic feed of Richards's careworn visage appeared before all of them. If he'd had a lot of lines on his face before, now he looked like some canal system, chiseled and abraded.

Levin, after remarking that they were all tired, etc., etc., addressed herself to Comb-Over first, almost as if Gibraltar himself, who'd been troubleshooting these issues during the months of Levin's confirmation, wasn't even in the room.

"Rob, can you summarize what we know?"

Antoine had performed this summary many times in the past dozen months, and whenever he did so he looked as though he were experiencing a massive intestinal blockage. His eyes grew moist; his reedy voice climbed upward toward a strangulated mew. With one hand, he massaged his open collar, as if he needed to coax the words from his pharynx, and then he waded into the litany of disasters.

"Madam Director. Let's reemphasize that we recognize now—that there is a significant psychic cost to personnel during interplanetary travel. What we used to call, among the mission staff, *Space Panic,* we have since relabeled *interplanetary disinhibitory syndrome,* according to recommendations of the experts. Our attempts to treat the syndrome remotely from Earth demonstrate that the binding, civilizing agency of human association fails out in space. To a man, every one of the astronauts on the Mars mission suffered with this complaint. We had episodes of psychosis; we had rampant addictive behavior, promiscuous sexuality, substance abuse, reclusive tendencies, and so forth. This syndrome got in the way of every aspect of the mission, as we have now seen.

"That's the first problem. The second problem is that we now believe there was some kind of infectious agent loose in the Mars population. Some of you may be wondering, legitimately, if there were classified parts of the mission that made this contagion possible or even probable. Obviously we can't speak freely to the military applications of the Mars mission. However, we can say that at no time did we bring bacterial or viral agents onboard that might have been able to cause the spectrum of symptoms that we've seen there.

"It becomes difficult in a case like this, and I'm thinking particularly of Brandon Lepper and Captain Jim Rose, to distinguish between the psychological syndrome I've described, which like many physical illnesses *is* communicable in an enclosed population that operates in a high-stress environment, and an actual pathogen, especially when the early phases of infection seem, as in the case of earthbound hydrophobia, to cause behavior not unlike what we're seeing in *interplanetary disinhibitory syndrome*. Broadly speaking, both the pathogen and the mission itself seem to have caused a great number of Code 14 events. Never in the history of NASA have we had Code 14s the way we are now."

Gibraltar broke in, "Rob, we still have a NASA employee up there, about whom we have to make some hard decisions. So let's move it along."

"Right. Let me simply remind everyone that astronauts are people too. The spread of bad decision making, insubordination, and physical violence among this group is unprecedented, but it's fair to point out that it is not substantially different from the situation here on Earth. Where are we? you might ask. On the one hand we do have a measure of success, in that Chief Medical Officer Arnold Gilmore and Captain Laurie Corelli, despite the fact that each of them has a family back on Earth, have elected to remain on the planet's surface, to await the next manned Mars shot, in the process parenting the very first extraterrestrial human baby, named Prima, and creating a very profitable, for us, documentary series about their lives and struggles. At least we can spin this in a way that looks good for the agency. The child is six months old, having been raised in an effective quarantine in the absence of any human stimulus other than her parents, and, while underweight, she is a normal human baby. Prima and her family are going to have to be resupplied on a regular basis to avoid starvation or long-term power outages, which, as we know from our mission reports, would likely result in exposure or hypothermia."

Debra Levin winced at a swallow of mulled coffee sludge. And then she too brought the unfortunate background material into the foreground.

"And...Colonel Richards?"

Comb-Over looked in Vance's direction, as though Vance could help. Though Gibraltar had no love for the other man, he took a deep breath and generously deflected some of the fallout in his own direction.

"Debra, as you can see here, Richards is sitting in one of the last pieces of reusable hardware from the mission. Theoretically, he's working on his memoirs. He hasn't drifted from the course that the computers have suggested. He has been in regular contact with his daughter *and* his wife. And while he's not communicating with us, he has been shaping his memoirs and has tried to find a purchaser for these writings among nationally distributed electronic-publishing entities. Notwithstanding symptoms of post-traumatic stress, which wouldn't be unusual considering the mission, we had until recently every reason to believe he was in rather good shape. If the pathogen that Rob referred to, correct me if I'm wrong, if the pathogen were liable to be flourishing in him, it ought to have been apparent by now—"

"Absolutely," Rob added.

"Considering that we have experienced catastrophic personnel loss on this mission, including some men who had been carefully selected to perform tasks both civilian and military, we do find ourselves with some successes here. The first person born on Mars, Madam Director, is a citizen of the United States of America. I believe, and perhaps legal could help me out here, that since there is now a legitimate Martian inhabitant, we have more than a legal framework for claiming the planet as a possession of the United States, with respect to drilling and mining. This is a huge advantage. Meanwhile, we have Richards on his way back with soil samples, with geological samples, and with himself, though possibly exposed to the Martian pathogen, available for scientific study that could net us positive publicity, patents, and years of academic leadership at the forefront of the interplanetary sciences, you name it."

A bow-tied and rather preppy fellow with an excessively eager smile chimed in. "The evolving legal standards of extraterrestrial ownership are just that, *evolving*. But we do feel, at present, that unless God himself claims his right as the creator of the solar system, the first nation to establish a legitimate colony on Mars, or any of the other planets, is justified in claiming territory. In the case of an actual native-born Martian inhabitant, these claims are even more valid."

Debra Levin, gazing up at the real-time video of Richards, interrupted the good-news palaver of the meeting to prod, instead, at more infected tissue.

"What can you all tell me about the state of the contagion?"

The young woman from medical spoke up. Vance couldn't remember having met her. The chief medical administrator, Julio Hernandez, was off having rotator cuff surgery. In his stead, he'd sent up this greenhorn, Dr. Fales, and she was palpably nervous.

"A number of possibilities have been explored, ma'am, by the medical department. First, based on what we know from Colonel Richards's own accounts, and also from film footage and stills that we have of the other astronauts, we believe that the pathogen, whether it is earthborn or native to Mars, has a hemorrhagic effect on human beings. The analogies would be Marburg, hantavirus, plague, and so forth. By hemorrhagic—"

"We're familiar with—" Levin said.

"Of course. Well, most hemorrhagic pathogens cause death quickly in the presence of high fever, but this pathogen, commonly referred to as *M. thanatobacillus,* seems to allow people to continue to function for weeks, if not months, with only minimal psychological effects. That's probably what accounts for the difficulty distinguishing the pathogen from the psychological effects of long-term space travel."

And now the audiovisual gnomes made a kind of triptych of images of astronauts Lepper and Rose flanking the webcam footage of Richards. These stills were from the period of advanced infection, and to Vance Gibraltar, the men looked, in the acute phase of their illness, as though they might very well have marched forth from an outbreak of plague.

"As you can see," the unremarkable Dr. Fales remarked, "the hemorrhagic phase is characterized by considerable blood loss, facial masking, sclerotic problems in the musculature, skin failure—all rather horrible to look at, despite the fact that the patient tends to present a rather odd misapprehension that no illness is present. There was a story circulating among the astronauts, which I believe comes from DOD, that *M. thanatobacillus* caused bodies to...well, to *disassemble.* We don't really know what that means, but we do know that with organ failure and sudden skin failure, the body as a vessel does give out. Death follows skin failure pretty quickly. The question we need to continue to address concerns the route of infection, the communicability of the pathogen, and so forth. If it's directly communicable, then, in a population that has never been exposed to the disease before, the collateral damage could be significant."

Debra fiddled with a barrette that restrained her tasteful and professionally ambitious coiffure. "In addition to doomsday medical predictions, what I need to know is what the implications are for a successful touchdown, since for better or worse that is the face that we present to the public."

Rob Antoine fielded this one. As if tag-teaming. And this Gibraltar could admire. "What we do need to ascertain is whether or not Colonel Richards is infected. It all comes down to this. If he is uninfected, do we allow him to land, quarantine him for a sufficient period to ascertain that he's not a danger, and then release him? Is it possible that he's some kind of carrier? We know, for example, that Richards has certain medical singularities, among them IBS, and it's possible that because his body doesn't process food well—we've had him on vitamin supplements throughout the mission—he somehow repelled the pathogen from his body. Assuming, that is, that the infection route is oral. Another theory might be that his depressed immune system is somehow a factor. He has late-stage addictive illness, having depleted the mission of virtually all the synthetic painkillers available, including especially the narcotic we were going to use for the flights home. That would be OxyPlus. This guy has a constitution like a rhino where drugs are concerned, and he's got so many opiates in his body now that it's as if he's preserved with formaldehyde. In this view, it's possible that the *M. thanatobacillus,* whatever it is, requires a healthy immune system for its biological 'disassembly.'

"In any event, up until now we've assumed he's not infected. That means we *can* move on to other questions ultimately, but before that I'd like to introduce a craniofacial medical expert, Dr. Morris Downes. We've been using him as a symbolic field analyst of mission video throughout. He looks at the body language of the astronauts, so that we might gather information they're unwilling to give us through more traditional means, and he's going to discuss Jed's face, as you see it before you."

Levin interrupted, "We have, ladies and gentlemen, an impatient public to think about. I need to know what you are proposing to do about this astronaut. How are you going to tell his story to our audience?"

Vance leaned forward, from the relaxed posture in which he had been allowing the drama to play out, and most of the middle managers quieted, as if in anticipation. "Ma'am," he said, "the situation is simple. If we think he's well, we're going to let him land, and we're going to give him a hero's welcome. If he's sick, well, then despite what we have aboard that craft, the soil samples, the rock samples, the terabytes of data, we really don't have much choice but to abort."

Onscreen, Richards was grimacing at that moment, as though experiencing some of the stomach pain that the medical people said was associated with an ulcer he'd contracted over months of famine. It was as if he knew that they were all talking about him back home. Levin gazed at the grizzled, bearded, and exhausted face.

"And that means what, exactly?"

Vance said, "That means something happens to the craft."

In the American Southwest, the sun had just risen over the preposterous saguaros, that primordial vegetation. In the aubergine tonalities of the post-technological evening, this crop seemed to have no purpose but to cast comical shadows across the serious business of that very porous NAFTA border. Rio Blanco was in the seventh year of its drought. Real estate values had found yet another trapdoor in the floor below. The mortgage market was in its third bust cycle, a genuine boom nowhere to be found between them. In the prior years, the region had got nine-tenths of its annual rainfall in the monsoons, cascading walls of water that roared through the parched washes like apocalyptic bulldozers, flattening everything that opposed them. And in this biblical season, the monsoons were quickly followed by outbreaks of fire in the bone-dry Sonoran Desert, conflagrations that wiped out whole subdivisions, some of them only lately rebuilt with dwindling federal matching money. These fires were by now so predictable that there was no point in searching out the hapless smoker or the pathological teen who served as their cause. The city tracked the fires on the evening news (likewise the floods), and even created the SexyFirefighters.com web portal, where the firefighting crews of the Southwest could be seen shirtless, pinned down in invigorating ravines of flame. What to do about conflagration when there was no water, excepting flash floods, when there was always someone upriver, stealing your supply, namely the exploding Mormon underclasses of Utah. To fight fires in Rio Blanco, they used shovels and explosive ordnance. The fires sputtered out when there was nothing left to burn. Like last summer: the brownouts and blackouts on the grid in Arizona had caused many of the buildings in the city to crack and fail in the warmer months, when the temperature hovered around one hundred and twenty.

It took a special stubbornness to stay in Rio Blanco, and that was the kind of stubbornness exhibited by renowned international stem cell theoretician Woo Lee Koo.

His nationality was infamous, let us say, his nationality was a laughingstock. His fatherland had done more to defame his area of expertise than any other nation on Earth. In the popular imagination, the Korean peninsula was, scientifically, a region of dreaming, scheming venture capitalist bumpkins who, in peer-reviewed journals, would *say anything* to command a few research dollars for a couple of years. When their extravagant claims were subject to experimental scrutiny, they disappeared into their Asian outback. Koo was a Korean who deplored the scientific failures of his homeland; he deplored the South Korea of his youth, the South Korea of unrepeatable experimental data on human cloning, cold fusion, dark matter, replacement body parts, authoritarian law enforcement, and more. Woo Lee Koo dreamed of restoring the reputation of his countrymen, and in this regard he worshipped the elegant empirical methodologies that one encountered only in the *New England Journal of Medicine.* When he had a chance to leave Seoul, to take a teaching position in the United States, it was as if he could not get on the jet quickly enough. True, many of his classmates stayed in Asia, where biotechnology was growing by leaps and bounds, and where the hands-off government funding approached that of the centralized economies of China and India. There *was* more money to be made working on these government-financed projects. And the USA, to which he had immigrated, was like some codger on his last bionic legs. Yet there were principles to consider. America, in its period of postimperial stagflation, revered principle. Koo admired the romance of the past, he liked the desolation of America, and he especially liked the remarkable emptiness of the Southwest. The job offer from URB, the University of Rio Blanco, married together the desperation of both employer and employee: *Come help us reanimate the nervous systems of neurologically degenerated patients! We'll give you first-class experimental laboratories, a world-class department, internationally renowned colleagues, housing, every fifth year off.* The list of benefits only grew. His friends could not understand why he was leaving, what friends remained.

There was a reason for his solitude, for his unmoored feeling. He blamed it upon the death of his wife, Nathalie Fontaine, a French missionary to Korea, whom he had met during his undergraduate time, when Koo in some kind of weak moment flirted with the grandeur of Catholicism. Nathalie, whose family had come to Asia from the suburbs of Lyon, had green eyes and a bob that caused her to resemble the late great French actress Juliette Binoche. From the earliest days of their marriage, however, Nathalie also exhibited the wasting symptoms and the spasticity of Huntington's chorea. A particularly unforgiving malady. Nathalie's missionary work, it seemed, had much to do with her belief that she would not last. Her gradual diminishment was incremental enough that she was able to get pregnant with their son, Jean-Paul, to remit somewhat during pregnancy, and to carry him to term.

But as Jean-Paul progressed through his elementary and middle school years, Nathalie's illness grew ever more debilitating. Chronic depression also began to have its way with Nathalie, despite her powerful faith. Koo, to his shame, responded in the way he always had. He worked especially hard. And yet he returned home promptly each night to massage his wife's limbs, to speak to her as best he could about his projects, making sure that she knew she could rely on him. He believed himself more devoted than any other husband. As a father he was doting and tolerant. At the university, however, in Seoul, he was a hothead, as the Americans would have said, who demanded too much, who burned out laboratory assistants, even the most gifted ones, and whose reputation cowed incoming graduate students. Koo was just as missionary as his wife, missionary about empirical research, missionary about hypothesis and conclusion.

Of course, Koo believed that there was a stem cell application for Huntington's chorea. He didn't tell Nathalie this, as he didn't bother her with things that he thought would just upset her anyway. As she grew more frail, he could see her working to give herself over to the god that had animated her missionary work. It was as though she were one of the medieval faithful. Her body grew ever more delicate, as if spun out of glass. Koo didn't need to be the shining knight, the Asian wise man, he didn't need to indulge in the passionate soliloquies of true love to indicate his devotion. He just needed, as he considered it, to produce results. If this required buttering up some South Korean politicians, burning out a few grad students, tripping up colleagues who had other ideas about departmental priorities, then this is exactly what he would do.

The story didn't end as he wished. While medicine had advanced in controlling symptoms of Nathalie's illness, especially with corticosteroids, medicine didn't yet know what to do about the loss of fine motor control. Koo chased after new symptoms with temporary solutions, as indicated in the medical literature. Deluxe protein beverages when she could no longer chew solids. Telescoping arms attached to all the walls that could feed her and help to clean her and fetch items for her.

It was the most mundane thing that took his wife. A glass of water. The doctors had long indicated that pneumonia was a particular danger. Every time she was bathed by her nurses, he imagined her tumbling out of their grasp or accidentally drowning. But the night he returned from soccer practice with Jean-Paul, she was just lying on her daybed, the one with the voice-activated motor for readjusting posture. She was motionless, peaceful, Koo thought. A glass of water spilled across her. The autopsy indicated what anyone would have guessed. Simple drowning. With all the advances of twenty-first-century medicine, it was as yet impossible in a body with advanced Huntington's to get the pharyngeal muscles to live up to their workload. The human body, so adaptive, so amenable to having bits of technology installed in it, could still fail. Every day millions of them did.

Nathalie's death was enough to send Koo and his half-French son, the boy with the melancholy green eyes, abroad. They made a new start in the most empty and beleaguered of desert communities, Rio Blanco, Arizona, United States of America. Koo couldn't relinquish the conviction that the South Korean medical community had been too busy chasing research money to show a little kindness to a man whose wife was dying. If, as Koo meanwhile theorized, it would be possible, with special applications of steroids and other growth enhancers, to make strides in the matter of regrowth among the adult stem cell lines that were now available in the grant stream in the United States, such that even tissue that was in the process of necrotizing could be reattached or regenerated, then it was only a hop, skip, and a jump to apply the same stem cell principles to Parkinson's, Huntington's, Bell's palsy, ALS, and other impairments. No one would have to suffer the way his wife had suffered.

Uprooting Jean-Paul and bringing him here had not been easy. But Koo was certain that he could better pursue his research at URB. Rio Blanco was so empty of the prying eyes of regulators and government intrusion that he could specifically do what he had not been able to do in South Korea, namely work on Nathalie's corpse. Not her corpse, exactly, but certain bits of her *cadaver,* to use the term he preferred, that he had harvested soon after her moment of transition. Such a little thing, that movement of the blood in and out, not so very complicated at all, but once it was stopped for a certain length of time, it was hard to restart. Koo knew the way of nature, that all things should end, but not when the equilibrium of others depended on the gentle, smiling face of Nathalie Fontaine. He had already regrown a length of her colon, a portion of her right ring finger, her pancreas, some locks of her hair, and when the time was right, he would sew these and other organs back into her.

That is, he would sew these back into the cryogenically frozen

Nathalie Fontaine. The very Nathalie Fontaine that he had shipped to Rio Blanco with great difficulty. There was only one way to insure, these days, that you could ship a cryogenically preserved cadaver for medical research without arousing intrigues, and that was by cooperating with certain kinds of international intelligence initiatives, the kinds of initiatives launched by organizations that have no acronyms, organizations that don't turn up on a budget line on any government's published budgets, except perhaps as *discretionary spending.* The greatest purveyor of discretionary spending funds was NAFTA, where, in the dilapidated present, everything was for sale, everything, and where the government would use whatever varieties of espionage and mercenary incursion necessary to attempt to restore the reputation of American ingenuity and American capital markets.

Chief among the initiatives of the American intelligence community was trying to learn if there was a wartime application for stem cell research that could treat all the head wounds coming back from the various Middle Eastern and Central Asian theaters where our troops were as yet stationed. Triage was good at removing body parts. Triage piled up whole mounds of limbs, and it could take a shattered femur or an ulna that had once been attached to some grasping hand, and it could make a fine stump of what was still left. But as yet medicine had not found a good way to reattach a head. Still, the Americans were planning. They were trying to find ways to make do with less head, wherever possible, to ship a young man or woman back with a third of a head, if necessary.

The military therefore required the kinds of medical researchers who could make this dream a reality without moral or ideological complaint. Who, at the very least, could pass on anything they heard or learned about international researches along similar lines. The hunt for information needed to take place outside the glare of publicity, away from round-the-clock web news outlets, because the military wanted to have an advantage that other international defense departments didn't have. They were willing to pay a South Korean MD, if he had a little information on what was and what was not possible, and, additionally, in compensation for services rendered unto the American military, which was in the business of shipping a great number of bodies around, they would be willing to ferry a body from South Korea to the desert of the American Southwest in a large refrigerated container. No questions asked.

How did Koo live with himself? How did the doctor live with the compromises that he had made in order to come to this place, this hellish landscape of drought, flash flood, and wildfire, with the frozen body of his deceased wife in the garage, attached to a generator so that she would not be warmed, or even cooked, when the electricity went off each day? How was he able to live with keeping all this secret from a teenage son who wanted nothing much to do with him? Who didn't realize the things that Koo had voluntarily given up in his life, the esteem of colleagues, the friendships from medical school back in Seoul, the satisfaction of knowing that his community understood what a fine husband and parent he had been. Koo had allowed these consolations to pass him by, and what he replaced them with, instead, was a teenage son who claimed to find the empirical methodology of the medical community beneath contempt.

For all these reasons, there were many days when Koo could *not* live with himself at all. Koo glided like a revenant from departmental common areas to laboratory as though he heard nothing, and as though he were unable to master even the most basic English dialogue. His parents were gone, his distant cousins never wrote to him, he had a sister in South Korea who felt that his traveling to the United States was unpatriotic, though she called him every Christmas and wept; how was it that families fell so ineluctably apart? she inevitably asked. At night, when he hadn't made any progress on the grants that supported the laboratory, he stretched his modestly proportioned body across his desk and gripped his face with his hands. The office linoleum dated back some thirty years, to a time when city universities sprang up everywhere, propelled by the idea that there would be ever more students funneled into their classrooms. The linoleum, like the university itself, was cracking, scuffed, was unreplaced. The ceilings in the building leaked during the monsoon season, and there were buckets underneath the leaks, so that occasionally the janitor, a fellow with some sort of disability, busied himself emptying them. He chased off the laboratory mice that had begun nesting in the drywall. Norris, the janitor, had some kind of affinity for Woo Lee Koo, it's true, and the two men, one among the most brilliant medical researchers in his field, the other scattered and disassociative in his faculties, sat together and failed to talk.

"What you up to?" the janitor might ask, looking pensively at the array of petri dishes, renal tissue, pancreatic tissue, nasal tissue, the various spectral dyes and extracts that were to be injected into them. He invariably pronounced the question with vigor.

"Raising the dead," replied Woo, with accented English.

Norris said, "Had a dog once that died."

To this, Woo Lee Koo said nothing at all. Not only because Norris's linguistic skills were difficult to parse. More important, Norris's disabilities endowed him with a superhuman ability to tolerate silences. About this Koo felt especially grateful. Allowing Koo to say nothing was among the kindest things a person could do. Thus, the two men sat on the stools in the laboratory for some time until the medical researcher recollected that an eventual response was required.

"His name was?"

"Huh?"

"The dog."

"Zimmerman."

"You came up with this?"

"What?"

"The name."

"Of the dog?"

Koo said, in the belief that Norris would not follow the

subsequent divagations of his reasoning, "Missing someone—who has passed away—is among the most human of feelings."

"We buried him," Norris eulogized, more thoughtful than aggrieved. "Behind the house."

"One day I will be able to restore Zimmerman to you. If there is tissue remaining at the burial site."

"Huh?" Norris said.

"Bring him back."

Norris nodded without commitment. The light would not last, and this meant the contagious darkness of Rio Blanco would soon be upon them. Before Koo went home, however, he needed to look in on the laboratory and its primates.

The primates of URB's laboratory were better looked after than the majority of the men and women of the Southwest, many of whom were living outdoors or in shantytowns and trailer parks. Just a month ago a trailer park outside Rio Blanco had been swept down into a wash south of the Santa Ritas. The residents, those who had not been pincushioned in the forests of cacti, had taken up residence in the stadium where the football team, the Magpies, played at home. Among those living there was a small army of alternative-lifestyle enthusiasts, adherents of the movement named *omnium gatherum,* who found science and its advances anathema, who were certain that essences of local weeds would treat their medical complaints. Their direct action against the laboratory that housed the primates had become a matter of federal investigation. This was part of the reason the building where Koo worked was run-down. The university, besides putting up cyclone fencing and concrete barriers out in front of the structure, besides vetting all employees more thoroughly than the Central Intelligence Agency vetted their own, could do no more, could afford no more, and so the building, after the firebombing, stood as a monument to the endurance of a certain implacability of human thought in the face of mock-scientific, pseudo-religious psychobabble.

Koo, therefore, looked in on the primates every night, and he treated them with the care and respect that he sometimes failed to show his colleagues or even his graduate students. When Alfonse, the orangutan, had received his innovative liver cell injection three months prior, to relieve the symptoms of cirrhosis with which Koo had afflicted him, Koo stayed with the animal day and night for two weeks. He stayed with the animal as he got weaker and more feverish, and he pleaded with Alfonse to fight harder, to accept this new therapy, to permit his liver to heal, even if there was no hard evidence that a positive attitude had any effect on healing. Koo's team had needed to let more than three-quarters of the liver perish first, because of the possibility of spontaneous regeneration, and Koo felt certain that Alfonse had become delusional as a result. Now, Alfonse had always preferred the seeds of the pomegranate. And so Koo went to the expensive market on the east side of town himself and brought back the fruits. He harvested the seeds himself. He even juiced them for Alfonse, while conducting long rambling lectures on the great German composers, hiking in the Rio Blanco area, beekeeping in the era of colony collapse disorder, and the like. He didn't even know what he was saying exactly, only that the words were tumbling out, flash floods in a wash, and it didn't really matter whether they made sense at all. He was talking to an orangutan. Many were the evenings that he brought the problems of his investigations into the primate laboratory instead of discussing them with Jean-Paul Koo, with whom it would have been more likely. He discussed his hopes and ambitions with spider monkeys, chimpanzees, orangutans, and so forth.

One night: Alfonse, who had often been responsive to music, particularly the more meditative opuses of Satie or Debussy, huddled insensate in a corner while assorted nocturnes in the classical genre enlivened his cell. When his instructor, for this was what Koo believed himself to be when he was in the room with the primates, an instructor in the secrets of evolutionary fact, attempted to put a hand on Alfonse's shoulder, as he often did, even though the orangutans were known to bite when unhappy, the animal gave him a look that was instantly recognizable by Koo, and this despite that in his years of dealing with animals he'd always resisted the desire to impute language or linear perception to them. Alfonse had looked at Koo, and in his face he'd said, *I can't keep indulging you in this way. Let a fellow go if it's his time to go.*

Was this set of muscular responses to the nocturnes haphazard? Was Koo interpreting what was in no way genuine? Was it the case that if you allowed an orangutan the liberty to behave as he wished for years and years, you would inevitably see in him an arrangement of craniofacial muscles that resembled every possible human expression? Would you say that the orangutan had the look of someone who had cheated at golf? Would you say that the orangutan was chastising you for failing to pick up the wet towels from the bathroom floor? Would the orangutan yearn to see the country of his birth (in this case a laboratory in Chapel Hill, NC, that had a surfeit of orangutans and needed, by way of trade, one of URB's lemurs)? Would the orangutan laugh with that abandon that is the sign of the truly hopeless? And *why, why, why,* Koo often wondered, though he knew well the answer, could the primate *not* explain to him or to someone, some other ape, someone somewhere, what it was that he wanted to say, instead of sitting there like a bumpkin, when the injection was rendered unto him, the liver cells that they had grown in the lab and injected into his side, so that Alfonse yelped, but with a look on his brute face that he would accept this insult too, as he had accepted so much else, without being permitted to go outside, without being permitted much beyond eating and watching nature programming on a large flat-screen mounted in the corner? Koo could not help it, he *wept* when the injection was rendered unto Alfonse, reproaching the nonhuman animal, *Just defend yourself this one time!* Alfonse yelped, and Koo felt saline duct excretions down his own cheek, and there was a broth of pity endorphins in him, though this was nothing compared to the suffering he felt upon the night Alfonse gave the last of himself to science, the night when Alfonse, two and a half months ago, collapsed onto his side, and Koo and his graduate assistant Noelle Stern rushed to him from beyond the reinforced glass where they often watched the animals.

Mighty Alfonse, your epitaph, *voilà,* given to you by your employer, written upon loose-leaf paper, so old-fashioned, included in the file of you that is now relegated to some university hall of records across town. Alfonse, it was clear that you never demanded remuneration and were therefore never paid in full for your sacrifice, and this your employer recognized. Not a dollar, adjusted for inflation or otherwise, was ever amassed in a bank account somewhere with your name on it. Alfonse, you were allowed exercise on certain occasions, and we tried to enrich you with various games, though at the time of your demise you were long past the daybreak of your life when games much interested you. As to the matter of your virility, it would be nearly impossible to assess your virility, because you were separated from your cousins and distant relations in North Carolina, and you never once cohabited with a female orangutan, just a couple of girl baboons and a brace of chimpanzees. Did you know that you missed out on the sweet dance of love, Alfonse? We thought you did. We your employers (Koo wrote, in Korean, and then laboriously translated) suspect that you once knew of love and gave up the habit of it only with a great regret. Because even if you never tasted the delights of sexual congress, you did get the occasional erection, and your erection, Alfonse, was a great and mighty thing, something that delighted you, since you did occasionally attempt to get other primates to pay attention to you when those nerve endings were feeling sensitive. Where did this knowledge of the uses of your erection come from, Alfonse? From your predecessors? Did your mother, before you were weaned, somehow make clear to you that this was how things came and went upon planet Earth, that if you could not frolic on the plains, the grasslands of the veldt, protecting your territory and swinging in the baobabs, at the very least, you could in our laboratory drink a draft of love? Well, Alfonse, we did not provide you with a mate, and that is your additional loss, though we take some solace in our belief that you were not completely deprived of this knowledge. This deprivation is to be lamented, but it is nothing when compared to your larger sacrifice in the matter of research upon varieties of liver disease. You were only twenty years old when you gave your life, and so you were not even old enough to imbibe, and for that reason your liver was as squeaky clean as a liver could be, before we got to it. You never protested, and you lived with your illness without anxiety or fear. You suffered quietly, until the days of your madness and your coma. Your employer would personally like to thank you, therefore, for giving your life to the University of Rio Blanco. You will not be forgotten. Actually, it's possible you *will be* largely forgotten, since you have no heirs, and your employer will be sacrificing others of your kind before too much time goes by. Still, this doesn't mean that there was not heartbreak here in abundance; your employers have shed tears for you, for the bloody vocation in which they are engaged; much grieving there was, and many intoxicants drunk, in silence and awe, as you were shoveled out of the crematorium. Many thanks, good friend.

Had Koo gone soft? He certainly did not want to go soft, and that was why research went on, and it was why research sometimes took place well after the working hours, when Koo's efforts would not be witnessed by the prying eyes of his graduate students, nor various oversight agencies. And that was why he had settled on a certain rather dangerous experiment with the chimpanzee who was next up for regenerative experiments, the animal known as Morton. Named after Noelle's nephew, the boy who had *asked* to have a chimpanzee designated for him. Morton, the nonhuman, was a sour person, if he could be said to be a person, a chimpanzee who would never do as told and who had seemed to take as strong a disliking to Koo as Koo took to this experimental subject. They had spent many an evening on either side of the piece of glass that separated the two stages of primate evolution, each of them suspicious. Morton seemed to laugh at atrocities on the television. Never was there a body count, nor some human limbs dug up in a basement in Ohio, for which Morton didn't get a bizarre and toothy grin upon his visage, as if to say, *Look at my gums! No gum recession!* And it was whenever Koo averted his gaze from this spectacle that Morton scooped some of his own redolent fecal material and did his best Jackson Pollock upon the reinforced glass.

He was docile enough under other circumstances, when it suited him, and he was reasonable when Noelle was administering to him, but it was his recalcitrance that persuaded Koo that he was a perfect subject for the off-the-record experiment he intended. If only Morton had been *willing* somehow to sacrifice himself, as Alfonse had been, if Morton were capable of serving science with an open heart. But no. Animals who tried to challenge the dominance of human animals, those animals needed to perish. Animals ate other animals, or rather, birds ate insects and animals ate birds, and animals ate animals, or animals ate plants and animals ate the animals who ate plants, and then there were three or four stages of animals eating smaller or stupider animals, and then at the top of the mound, Koo liked to remind himself and others, were the humans, ordering takeout. Humans swept through entire catalogues of species, laying waste, casting bones out a car window for a crow to snap up, and this was the order of the universe, and the simpletons who somehow managed to shield themselves from nature's bloody claws weren't only ignorant, they were liars: thus there was Morton with his round-the-clock war coverage and his action films.

As to the specifics of the experiment: it had long been Koo's intention to introduce genetic material from his late wife, his cryogenically frozen wife, into a chimpanzee. In particular, Koo intended to inject cerebral stem cell tissue from his wife into a chimpanzee, in a base of saline and amino acids, in an attempt to get this information past the blood-brain barrier so that it might mix with the genetic material of the primate in question. This was a fairly elementary experimental notion, one that had been practiced in South Korea commonly, or so it was said, though legend, myth, and fact were closely allied in his homeland. Koo's idea was that by introducing stem cells into the brain of the primate, the primate could perhaps come to contain some portion of his wife's intellectual *residue.* Koo preferred the term *residue* when speaking of what he had kept of his wife these many years. As a former believer in the outlandish tales of Catholicism, he wasn't comfortable with the idea of a *soul,* since, as has long been understood, there was nowhere in the body where this soul could be contained, just as he was not comfortable *without* the notion, because a bit of superstition was evidence of the residue of self, and the *residue* could not be cast off, no more than a man could cast off a phobia or a taste for olives.

What would be the nature of the *residue* that would manifest in Morton, the sadistic chimp, when the injection took hold of him? None could say for certain. And that was why the injection of stem cells from Mrs. Fontaine-Koo into Morton could not be included in grant proposals nor even explained fully to Noelle, the charming PhD student whose breasts occasionally caused Koo to fall into fugue state. He was in just such a fugue state, however briefly, when interrupted by Norris, on the celebrated night of the Mars mission splashdown. He had been preparing the serum for the injection, as he had prepared and abandoned it over and over again in the past seven days. Always deciding, in the end, that it was too risky. What was different tonight? Not much was different. Perhaps Koo just had less and less to look forward to. Perhaps he was going to do what he was going to do, whether it was a good idea or not. The finals of the National League of X-treme Lacrosse, the splashdown of the laughable Mars mission, and the injection of human cerebral stem cells into a chimpanzee, these things all had a desperate cast. The desperation in each seemed like one variety of the North American allegiance to lost causes.

He left Norris behind and walked idly down the empty corridors of the building, noting the number of fluorescent bulbs that were flickering, until he found himself in the primate laboratory. The timer on the monitors in each of the cages offered, in fact, a lacrosse game for Morton and the other primates to

watch. X-treme lacrosse was noted for the high number of injuries per game, and Morton was, predictably, a fan. He was a fan
especially of the team from Indianapolis, which was considered
to be among the most violent of all. Koo rapped on the window
once, to alert the animal that he was present and intending to
enter. In one latex glove, he carried the syringe containing the
serum in which the stem cells of his wife's tissue were stored. He
opened the reinforced door that led in among the cages. He whispered incomplete greetings to the other animals as he passed. In
Morton's cell, viewed from the outside, there were, as ever, a few
soiled toys on the floor, and some fruit and vegetable remnants
and the like. Morton, it should be noted, didn't particularly like
bananas. However, he had a comedian's allegiance to the risibility
potential thereof. He may never yet have used the peels in such a
way as to manifest their comic potential, but he collected them
as though he were waiting.

"Morton," Koo said, "I regret to inform you that it is time for
your shot."

If this remark was to be understood by the chimpanzee, it was
intended in vain.

"This is a momentous injection, but perhaps that's all I'm going
to say about it." And why? Why was this all he was going to say?
Because Woo Lee Koo believed that nearly every act of human
life was, or soon would be, observed by lackluster governmental
mainframes housed somewhere in the Midwest, in whose employ
he sometimes served, and he therefore rarely said anything of substance in a publicly owned facility, of which these premises were
one example. What he had already said in life, in fact, he had said
only out of insufficient secretiveness. And he resolved to do better.
"I would be more apologetic, but I am sure that you wouldn't be
apologetic with me if the sandals were on the other feet. In the
course of human events, it never does any good to be merciful.
Mercy rarely results in good science. This is one of the things I
have learned, Morton. So this injection takes place, roughly speaking, whether you want it to or not."

The chimpanzee watched the television monitor without attending to the competing monologue. But once Koo began genuinely readying the injection, Morton, who'd already had a great smorgasbord of injections in his life, began spitting at the great medical researcher. Morton headed for the corner of the cell beneath the television monitor, to cower in an uncourageous fashion. He barked out a plangent chimpanzee cry.

"This won't do at all!" Koo said. "I am the researcher with numerous grant money at my disposal. I will be victorious. Don't make me use restraints."

Morton, when the human hand of science was within reach, began trying to bite it, as he had done on other occasions, having even broken the skin of Noelle on one occasion. That bite had become infected too, and in a medical facility you could never be too careful about infection, what with the antibiotic resistances coursing through the larger hospitals of the nation. Koo, the South Korean researcher, had no choice but to restrain Morton. Luckily there were two sets of shackles in this, the highest-security cage of the primate laboratory. Koo grabbed Morton by the shoulders, after setting the syringe on the table in the cage, and he forcibly shoved the chimpanzee over toward one of the sets of shackles, to which Morton responded by baring his grand set of chompers anew, attempting to bite down on the South Korean researcher's wrist but making contact only with a portion of his cardigan sweater, shredding one sleeve. *Damn you!* Koo directed a blow at the animal, in recompense, and he did manage to hit him on the shoulder before tripping over a rubber ball in the cell and plunging to the floor. If Morton could have laughed, then he *was* laughing now, although Koo had often argued that what appeared to be a chimpanzee laugh was something much more knowing than mirth, that the chimpanzees were much more soulful and melancholy than commonly believed. All except Morton, at any rate, who was now attempting to relieve himself of some fluid backup in the kidneys, a great arc of the urine raining down, in fact, just short of the table where the syringe lay resting.

"You are an unworthy member of the pantheon of higher primates!" Koo expostulated. "You have no gratitude for the fact that you're still able to serve our branch of the tree of life. I won't have it!"

Pausing to wipe up with a towel the liquid that pooled on the floor of the cell near the runoff drain, Koo then made for the animal again, throwing himself upon the chimp, reaching for the arm of the chimp and the shackle simultaneously. Just when it seemed as though the battle between doctor and chimpanzee would never be resolved, Koo did get shackle and wrist into his grasp, though this was when Morton again sank his teeth into Koo, getting a mouthful of sweater and polo shirt. Because of the buffering capacity of these synthetic fabrics, it was only a flesh wound. Morton was probably readying a good bite at the human jugular or some other more vulnerable spot, when the South Korean researcher succeeded in shackling one chimpanzee arm.

Morton crumpled up at the recognition of his renewed and never-ending subservience. Morton wound himself into a ball. A ball of submission. The fight went out of him.

"That's my boy," said the human animal. "I am grateful."

He affixed the other restraint, not that it held any joy for him. And there Morton hung, as though martyred, and Koo removed an alcohol swab from his pocket and found the spot on Morton's eye socket, just below the eyebrow, which is to say into the frontal lobe, that had been shorn of its fur so that the injection could more easily take place. At last, he readied the syringe for its job, squeezing out the remaining air bubble. He had the syringe, he had the serum, he had the idea, he had the patent, or he would soon, he had the stem cell line, he had the primate, he had the time, and now he was depressing the plunger. It seemed like such a little thing in the moment, the abridgement of Morton's freedom. But that is how it always seems to the oppressor.

* * *

Jean-Paul Koo, multiethnic American teenager, in his convertible, in the desert, without sunscreen. Who the fuck could tell Jean-Paul anything? *Fuck* whatever *anyone* was going to fucking tell Jean-Paul. Fuck his fucking father, for example, his father was an ignorant science moron fuck. Fucking concave-chested medical researcher never-got-outside, never-watched-a-sporting-event-not-even-lacrosse-fucking-never-listened-to-a-radio-or-watched-television fuck, with his bullshit fucking animal testing, his fucking skinny-puppy-fucking medical torture, and his fucking ridiculous pocket protector and his awful fucking jazz music, and classical music, and his worship of Jean's fucking dead mother, people who were all goo-goo-eyed about their mothers and fathers. Fuck all of them. Fuck everyone who believed in romance; romance was for dimwits. Fuck the priests at his fucking religious high school, which was now the most popular high school in Rio Blanco, now that fucking religious education was, *hmm,* he didn't know, like fucking as popular as water, because the fucking ridiculous public schools were fucking nothing but some afternoon fucking classes in fucking automotive repair, while the fucking priests at the fucking Catholic school were all about the meaningful fucking glances that meant God loves you and I'll suck your dick in Jesus' name. Fuck the priests and the politicians and his fucking father; Jean-Paul was a *graduate!* He was a high school fucking graduate who was going to take a summer off to work on his business proposal for a booth that would offer self-designed cosmetic surgery blueprints for needy consumers. He was really excited! Fuck! You could just go to this booth at, like, any fucking big-box development store, or downtown by the fucking bus station, or by the fucking paling salons, or any mall, of the few malls that remained, ghost malls, where they still had the fucking speed-walking contests and the fucking wheelchair contests, and you could go into the ridiculously fucking inviting booth, and you could just upload a photo of yourself, or, if you wanted, you could have a picture of you taken with your ridiculously fucking hot girlfriend, like for example he could have a photo taken with his ridiculously hot fucking girlfriend, Vienna Roberts, and then the computer would look at you in the horrible booth photo, and then you could use some kickass software and the online fucking programming, and you could start modifying your fucking horrible appearance, like your saggy old-woman breasts, if that was what you had, or your obese fucking saggy buttocks, if you were the kind of guy who had some totally saggy-ass buttocks, and then you could use the software for the online simulated tuck of your fucking buttocks, and then you could give yourself a face-lift and get rid of your like ten extra chins, and maybe if you were a fucking balding guy who was fucking combing over your fucking repulsive hair, then you could get some fucking plugs, or you could get some stem cell implants in the scalp tissue that would regrow the fuzzy shit. Even though his father was an idiot, his father had helped him with this part, or whatever other operations you could fucking name, cosmetic-surgery-type operations, you could fucking design any of them on the workstation, like if part of your fucking head had been blasted off by some explosive, then maybe you could use the computer to suggest a sculpted silicone-and-titanium fucking head that could go on the blasted-away portion of your head, assuming you were not totally fucking catatonic, or whatever, like a complete fucking drooling flank steak of a dude, because of the blast; anyway, the point was you could get the computer to design anything, any kind of fucking plastic surgery thing you could imagine, and then the computer would spit out a blueprint of the operations, and then it would give you like a fucking market-rate price for all these operations, like in dollars, or in Euros, or in Sino-Indian rupees, and then it would give names of various participating medical institutions that would perform the operations, and then the computer would let these fucking doctors fucking compete, *because when doctors compete you win,* and these doctors would offer the lowest possible price for the cosmetic surgery enhancements, like you could go to Bangladesh and you could get your new breasts, or say you were like fucking one of those guys who wanted to get remade as a woman, you could fucking go and get your dick sliced off, and the doctors in Bangladesh, you could just fucking name your price. And here was another idea that Jean-Paul Koo, the graduate, was just now thinking about, and it was another whole level of brilliance, for his business idea, which was like, like what, like a fucking designer set of fucking operations, where you like could take a star, like say you could take that former teen star, what was her name, Phonita, the one who had just married into a sultanate, some Arabic sultan from Dakar or somewhere who already had thirteen wives, or fucking whatever, she still looked good, especially her ass looked fucking hot, and you could take photos of Phonita, whose ass just didn't look like the ass of a thirty-six-year-old or however old she fucking was, and you could take this photo that was from the government-sponsored national publication known as *Celebrity Surveillance Weekly* and you could scan this photo and then you could take another photo of your sour poverty-stricken face in the booth at the ghost mall, or you could scan in one of your own ugly-ass photos, and then you could have the computer compare you to Phonita, and it would recommend various surgeries that you could get so that you would look indistinguishable from Phonita, like if you wanted to have her poochy fucking lips, those lips that were always pooching out like that, like the fucking computer would recommend like massive fucking shots of silicone in your fucking lips, until your lips just fucking screamed *blow job,* or whatever the fuck else, and then you'd have to work really hard to get that perfect Phonita ass, like when Jean-Paul had put in his own picture and one of Phonita, because even though he was a boy, and a macho fucking intravenous-drug-using boy, he kind of thought that it would be pretty hot to be fucking Phonita, and the computer, the sample software he had designed, had recommended that he would need massive skeletal shaving and bone-replacement surgeries to get his hips to look like Phonita's hips, just so some Arabic sultan from Dakar or some bribe-happy Chinese functionary from Shanghai would want to marry him and make him a sex slave and put him up in some

two-hundred-story high-rise that was eventually going to be
bombed out of existence by some guy who had a second-grade
fucking reading level or whatever. Anyway, that was Jean-Paul's
business idea, the Designer Self, and he had already trademarked
it and was working on the patents, and even though his father was
a ridiculous fucking pocket-protector-wearing fucking geek, he
was pretty good on the patents and the copyright protections and
all of that, because his father was, you know, like fucking advanced
on the stem cell shit, and he always had legal protections and knew
like fucking excellent lawyers. All Jean-Paul really wanted to do
anyhow was just like sell the business to some Sino-Indian magnate
from Mumbai and start another fucking excellent business and
fucking retire at thirty, so he had spent a lot of time this summer,
between when he was working at the salmonella factory also known
as Iguana Juana's and when he was going to see his totally fucking
hot girlfriend, Vienna Roberts, on the bad side of Rio Blanco,
which is to say the part of town where the signs were not in English
and where the car theft problem had reached a new level of total
lawlessness, between these two big-time sucks, he was working on
the Designer Self, and talking about it online, like on those fucking
Pump and Dump web sites, like where his fucking handle was
TtlGloblaDom, he'd go on the Pump and Dump sites and he'd say,
*Hey, have u guys herd of this new major f'ing enterprise that's got some
major f'ing venture cap, called Designer Self, the bossest f'ing biz plan to
come down the f'ing pike in a f'ing decade or more, and just looking for a
partner for the IPO, or maybe more venture capital injections,* and in this
way he already had a ton of legitimate inquiries about his business
idea, and he would be driving across town, without his fucking
sunscreen, because he wasn't the kind of fucking white person who
went to any fucking paling salon, to rub in his fucking whiteness,
you know, and he would be yelling into his cranially implanted
data-storage assistant, *Hey, listen, this is Jean-Paul fucking Koo calling,
and I'm hoping that you're going to help me fabricate the first booth for my
massive business plan called the Designer Self, because I have heard that
you're one of the best industrial architects out there, and here's what I want*

the booth to look like; I want it to fucking look like it's the booth that you have to step into to get to paradise, that inviting, like it's paradise that we're giving away with this booth, do you know what I mean, like you can be made to look any way you want to look, like finally the inside part of you, the part that has been yearning to be set free, that beautiful part of you that's been trapped in this body with, I don't know, like pustules and scabs from your hemorrhagic fever and shit all over your face, you can be free of that part of you, or if you have burns over seventy-five percent of your body, say, you could get rid of those burns with new designer skin; that's what I want the booth to look like, and I want to know if you want to be the one to get in on the ground floor of this new business plan, because I am willing and able to sell shares as we speak, and then in truth, when he was done with this call, he was practically hyperventilating, which is something Jean-Paul did, sometimes; he had these really awful panic attacks, and he didn't fucking tell anyone about them, but he fucking told Vienna Roberts, because he told her everything, you know, because that is what a NAFTA girl is for, a NAFTA girl is for accepting you when you know that you have to seem like you believe all the time even though you don't fucking believe anymore, mainly what you do is feel like you're never going to get anywhere and that no one fucking believes in you so you have to do all the fucking believing yourself, and that was why he was going over to the wrong side of Rio Blanco right now, in his convertible that got only like twenty-five miles of algae-based fuel a gallon in city traffic, which was fucking embarrassing; he was going over there because Vienna Roberts was the only one who believed in him, and he didn't fucking believe that she believed, and he didn't fucking believe that she believed that he believed, and he didn't fucking think it was going to last, but while it lasted, he would go over there, to Vienna Roberts's place, and put his fucking head in her lap while she worked on her parents' plan for a Union of Homeless Citizens that was going to be organized first here in Rio Blanco and then it was going to take over the whole of the Southwest.

In fact, Vienna had just fucking called him, in that fucking ridiculously fucking sexy voice of hers that sounded like a ten-year-old on helium, and said that he *had* to drive over now, forget Iguana Juana's, come right over because she had something really intense that she wanted to show him, and when she talked like that, you know, it always meant that her parents were out trying to convince the tent community inhabitants to agree to the union, and that she needed some kind of sexual fucking liaison to distract her, at least for a little bit, because she was alone.

Bix Rafferty cradled his ArmaLite in his survivalist hands, out beyond the incorporated edge of Rio Blanco, where the fighter planes lifted off in formation from their heavily reinforced base for the sowing of freedom in the world. Bix Rafferty had no position on the sowing of freedom exactly, because he believed none of what he heard or saw or read from any news source, when he chanced on one. What he did believe in was the *land,* and this particular expanse of land south of Rio Blanco, owned by the federal government, as much of the state where he found himself was owned by those thieves, had been leased to him so that he might be able to find in the land a vein of most precious metals that would make him, Bix Rafferty, impervious to humiliation, *just as lead was once transmuted into gold.* The fact was that there was plenty of gold, silver, copper, and other metals here in the desert, this was well known, the problem being that there were cheaper ways to extract precious metals in China and India and Africa, and cheaper workforces to do the job, workers whose lives were expendable, as most lives were, according to Bix Rafferty. Bix Rafferty, having conceived of this mining claim that was officially entitled the Forsaken Mining Corp., believed that lives were on the whole more worthless than the four dollars and eleven cents' worth of minerals included in them, that life was instead a system of mathematical reiterations, and that the ingestion of cough syrups and other alcoholic beverages purchased at the local cut-rate purveyor of health and beauty aids would sustain him in his search for precious metals at the Forsaken Mining Corp. However, what Bix Rafferty mainly did in that landscape of sage and desert poppy was try to drive away trespassers, who were not trespassers so much as they were hot-rodding, dirt-biking, internationalist youths bent on depleting the last of the desert of the likes of Bix Rafferty, settling it instead with golf courses and adobe spas that specialized in seaweed wraps, and he was certain of this, it was an article of conviction, even if the part of the desert where Bix was settled basically had nothing in it but some trailers, and a few trucking operations, and a general store or two.

It paid to be vigilant, and in this regard he had purchased the ArmaLite and other weapons of gunmetal blue from a dealer who came by now and then and played Parcheesi with Rafferty, during which they discussed their mutual preference for the mule, as opposed to the horse, which had somehow gained an undeserved dominance among those who trafficked in cloven hooves. The mule was naturally smarter, and its ears were more attractive. Better situated for mountainous treks, for long voyages in the desert, noted Rafferty, as he cradled the ArmaLite.

On this particular swing shift, let it be said, Rafferty did believe that he was seeing clouds of dust from the unpaved track that led in this direction. Clouds of dust kicked up into the afternoon sky. Red dust, red sky, elegiac crimson. Bix lived in one of the last beautiful places, but he did not traffic in beauty, because he believed beauty was not a manly pursuit, and that the ratio of incidences of humiliation to the perceptions of beauty was approximately seven to one, with seven being a prime. When he needed to overlook beauty, as a banker steps over the supine wino, he overlooked it, the better to see such signs of trouble as the dust in the road, the clouds of dust—some vehicle headed down through the wastes toward the Forsaken Mining Corp.

Rafferty ticked off a list of possible human visitors: (1) Frank, the aforementioned gun dealer, (2) Sergeant Gerald Cross from the AFB nearby, who had come on occasion at the behest of the military brass to explain to him, Bix Rafferty, when it was important for him, a neighbor of the air force installation, to evacuate; when, for example, there were going to be military exercises that might alarm him if he didn't know about them in advance, (3) his bookkeeper, an elderly lady with type 2 diabetes, (4) his cousin Wade, who dropped in from time to time but who was at the present moment doing a short stay in a county lockup for driving things across the border that should not have been. Rafferty concluded that none of these persons was likely to be coming at this time, and thus he made sure that the ArmaLite was loaded and that the safety was not sticky, and then he went from his post out into the desert, where the unrelenting sunshine was like a philosophical revelation, like a revealed apocalypse, and he pulled down the main gate and locked it with the padlock, and then he hustled up and over a small hillock, rushing to the best of his ability, which was not so good, because the years of poisoning and heavy metals and pulmonary compromise (from breathing in ground-up stone), these made haste difficult. Bix hoisted himself up through a copse of paloverde, and he betook himself to the very throne room of purgatorial suffering, namely a grove of cholla that had been successfully propagating itself on the hill despite the slag that he poured into the wash just beneath, and then he laid himself down on his belly, as though he were some sort of zoo seal flopping there. He awaited the vehicle and its intentions.

He loved and hated the excitement in equal measure. He reckoned that he had seen four or five men of a deceased persuasion who had no business being in this county, in this state, in this country, or who had gotten themselves deceased by persons unknown, and he had buried these men way down in the mine, and he felt certain that no one would ever find them or miss them, and that was just the way of things in this part of the world. There was no need to summon the authorities, the blatherskites, because the authorities ferried over these men from the other side in the first place, the Mexican side, because there were no authorities any longer, just men with nicer outfits. The responsibility of it, the responsibility of every man for himself, was more than Bix could tolerate without white flashes, and that was what accounted for the cough syrup, and the OxyPlus nasal inhalers that he sometimes bought from the gun dealer in exchange for the odd nugget of the gold stuff. There *was* the occasional nugget, after all, because there is something for every kook and nut to tide them over until more suffering can arrive. And, in down markets, the conservative money always returns to the safe haven of gold.

It was an all-terrain vehicle of some kind, Rafferty reckoned, probably operated by the kind of person who lived in Rio Blanco, who, in general, were the kind of people who believed that there was never a time nor a season when you should be ashamed of short pants, particularly not short pants that had slogans that traversed the section behind. Rootless cosmopolitans, it seemed to Bix, though because of the heat he himself was wearing nothing but an overlarge T-shirt that he had sweated clean through, and a pair of torn-up sweatpants that he had gotten at a thrift store. These constituted his mining gear today, along with a hard hat and a tool belt.

The all-terrain vehicle slowed to a stop, and a wake of dust overtook it. For a moment, in the light of late afternoon, he couldn't see the driver or drivers of the trespassing vehicle. A gust of dry desert air blew through, however, from the west, and when it had done so, Bix Rafferty saw at last a young sunglasses-wearing American Indian man, with long black locks, combed back in a kind of stylized version of rockabilly idol, nattering like a madman into one of those things implanted into his wrist. What would bring *that* here? People came this way sometimes by accident, but the array of survivalist signage along the *primitive road* that led to the Forsaken Mining Corp. usually created in them the strong desire to reverse direction.

Bix took a good long pull on some non-drowsy formula, and then he headed down the hillock and into the wash, jogging as best he could, with his thumb on the safety of his old-fashioned firearm. If the car stayed where it was, he would come out in the wash directly adjacent, by the gas tank, maybe, preserving the necessary element of surprise. The all-terrain vehicle idled loudly. Its vulgarity would cloak him. It was a method of transport designed to show off, just before it flipped over and crushed you and your passengers. That's why they didn't make them anymore.

With the heaving respirations of a man who would not be bothered with ventilation systems in his place of employment, Rafferty set upon the sunglasses-wearing American Indian man, shouting at him an inquiry into his purpose. Unfortunately, with the din of the vehicle, and his anxious intention to communicate his needs to a caller on his personal wrist assistant, the interloper didn't hear the initial threatening articulations of Bix Rafferty, who therefore redoubled his efforts:

"I'm intending to give you, young man, a brief lecture on the idea of *possession,* because what I am thinking is that you and I have different ideas of *possession,* and in particular, young man, what I want to tell you about is the idea of possession of the *land,* good land or fallow land, this is neither here nor there; what I want to say is that *possession* is central to what we have going on right here, in this region, good or ill, and possession confers certain kinds of rights and expectations upon him who is doing the possessing, because him who possesses *nothing* has no dignity and no livelihood, because when you come driving in here, like you are the gypsy, the tinker, the vagabond, who doesn't understand one thing about how we have made this desert here into a land of *possession,* well, then that's a conflict in need of resolution, because look at how things kind of got all used up when civilization wasn't based on a possession type of a footing; there just weren't any operating profits, and there was chaos, and the buffaloes all got made into tents and hamburgers, and water resources got all salinated. If you think about philosophy, you only have to read a little bit to see that what a man *possesses* is the very portrait of himself, and he has got to want to possess *more* to see the shadow of himself, and what you are doing, right now, young man, is you are coming here and throwing *your* shadow on what I possess, and what I possess, in case it wasn't obvious with all the signs and whatnot, is the Forsaken Mining Corp., and in this operation there are no heirs and no signatories, just me here, and what I mean to do is wherever possible to assert my one and only claim to mine this land, as conferred on me by the federal government, and thereby to deplete this land of its gold, and to claim ownership of whatever I find, and I further assert my one and only right of quiet enjoyment of this land that I possess, in the absence of other persons —"

At some point the fellow with the all-terrain vehicle, who was probably, it seemed to Rafferty, just a small-business owner from Rio Blanco, an importer and exporter, who was going to meet a friend in one of the washes, where they would in concert attempt to break some kind of land-speed record, this fellow turned and saw that there was, in fact, a firearm directed at him. Now, he immediately, as if he knew of these things only from popular entertainments, raised up his hands, and a whole history of legal interactions between persons was summoned in this performance of meanings. Because he was too stunned and surprised to remain completely silent, the fellow in the automobile pleaded, "Can you please *not* point that at me? I'm happy to turn my car around right now and go back the way I came, honest to God."

To which Rafferty said, "You certainly can. You certainly can go back the way you came, back through the twists and turns that brought you to this place, and you can make sure that you never fall into this particular rut of bad ideas ever again. What did you say your name was?"

"I didn't say. You're going to forget I was ever here. I promise."

"I certainly am, but before I do I was going to do you the favor of employing your name when I explained to you that I was about to fire from this foreign-made and damned reliable firearm over the hood of your vehicle a symbolic shot, a shot designed to avoid going through any kind of soft tissue, so that you would know that the law permits me to fire upon persons who I believe are a threat to my property. However, I'd be just as happy to omit your name if that's your wish."

Whereupon Bix Rafferty, who was not a tremendously good shot, assumed a stance that he had been told to use by the uncle who raised him up and kicked his ass from one desert town to the next during a period of high interest rates and joblessness. This stance did not ennoble Bix Rafferty, but it did help him remain calm as he pushed the safety into the off position, squeezed the trigger, heard the satisfying report, and felt the kick at virtually the same instant. He watched a pair of hawks startle from the cacti, and then he reached into his pocket for another pull on the phial of non-drowsy formula. The taillights of the all-terrain vehicle followed the hawks out. All in all, it was not a *profitable* day, really, but it was a good day.

Vienna Roberts had obtained the Pulverizer in the course of her first big modeling job. She'd failed to consult her parents about the job, as she failed to consult them about many other things, though this was perhaps less from a feeling that they would not have consented than it was from a feeling that her parents were not to be disturbed because they were *changing the world.* Changing the world was more difficult even than assembling, for example, one of those inexpensive home media cabinets with the dowels and special little screwdriver thingies. The specifics of her modeling assignment, which she failed to disclose, were also a tiny bit embarrassing. Well, the sponsor of the photo shoot was the Navajo Corporation, a wholly owned subsidiary of Indigenous Ventures, LLC, and in the photo shoot she was to flirt up another girl while rolling some dice on a felted table. They wore whiteface, they were wanton, young, especially pale, and given to reckless wagers, the better to suggest that going to indigenously owned gambling casinos led to casual sex with underage girls who had been vaccinated for human papillomavirus and other venereal contagions.

Vienna, as in all modeling narratives, had been discovered at a mostly deserted leather goods store down by the bus station. Across the street from the guitar store. Her parents did know this: she was working at the leather goods store, part-time after school. She didn't know how many guys had come into the store saying,

"Would you consider letting me take your picture?" It seemed to Vienna that in some dialect, the dialect of vulgarians, these words must have meant: "Pleased to make your acquaintance." Most of these countless guys had flecks of saliva at the corners of their mouths, or they smelled like the interior of a pizzeria. In times of worldwide sexual slavery, you could make big money exploiting yourself with these types of men. You could also wind up hacked to pieces live on the web.

"Jeez," she said to one alleged photographer, whose card, with a little icon of an old large-format camera like you might see in a museum, offered the name Mark Schott, "haven't heard *that* one."

Schott said, "I'm prepared to offer foolproof testamentary material to prove that I am who I say I am. I'm an industry professional with more clients than I can handle. You will know me by the clouds of acclaim that billow about me. I am also — because I need to be in my line of work — a patient man."

Vienna Roberts, however, was *not* particularly patient. She went directly home that night, and instead of doing calculus, she checked up on the Mark Schott web gallery, which numbered in the hundreds upon hundreds of images, and which included some major accounts in the Rio Blanco area, Iguana Juana's, e.g., which employed her flaky boyfriend, Jean-Paul Koo; the Sonoran International Light Rail Corporation; the Air Force of the United States of America. Vienna, after perusing these photographs, which were often salacious, obvious, even shameless, but not quite sexually explicit, was inclined to favor Mark Schott's attentions. For the money. She told him as much when he again came looking for her down near the bus station.

In fact, that day, her parents were leading a protest out on the square by the bus station. The municipal fountains had not operated there for almost ten years. The number of OxyPlus inhalers changing hands, at the bus station, in dollar value, exceeded the gross national product of several Central Asian fiefdoms. She could hear, out beyond the store, the earnest cries demanding wholesale prices for staple items such as milk and cereal and cheese. The lack

of health care in the Southwest! The absence of air-conditioning in
the shelter system, which was no shelter system at all, as she had
often heard her mother remark, with tears in her eyes. There were
sirens too, which meant that the riot police were taking very seriously the idea of the Union of Homeless Citizens. The number of
homeless persons in Rio Blanco was enough that a union thereof
could challenge the *housed* residents of the city. Or so her mother
said, chewing on the end of a gray braid.

The door to the leather goods store opened, and in walked the
somewhat flamboyant Mark Schott. He was in search of new and
unusual garbs in which to array the bruised and tattered nymphets
of his oeuvre. And yet his mission had a double purpose, true,
because here he was again, working his persuasions on Vienna
Roberts, as though charm were like instrumental excellence on
the sitar, something that you had to practice.

"Well, there you are," he said.

"Here I am," she said.

"Have you considered the work? Have you had a look at it?"

"I have considered. But I don't understand why me, and—"

"I have no motive, really, except that I like to see new faces in
my photographs, and when I see a face that I find interesting, I
proceed with energy to include that face."

"How is that any different from—"

"It's enough for me to work in the garden that I work in; in
picking the flowers there, you never get to see them again."

"That's a nice way of—"

"And what if I have a job in the planning stages for which you
might be perfect?"

"I'm considering, Mr. Schott, just like I have maybe considered
various other options in my life, except that I'm considering this
one a little more seriously. It's getting daily consideration."

"You haven't even asked what the assignment is."

Vienna Roberts absently hooked and unhooked a bustier on a
mannequin beside the counter. Men of dubious occupation emerged
from the aisles in various hooded garments, pining for someone for

whom they could buy these hides. Their sense of purpose depended on their failure. In places of low light, meager expectations.

"Again," Schott continued, "you can rely on the ethics of the person who is offering you this opportunity. This is the once-in-a-lifetime opportunity, because you have seen my work, and I can put you in touch with people of discernment." All of this would turn out to be true, but what made the difference for Vienna Roberts was the thatch of ear hair that Mark Schott sported, far in excess of what should have been possible for a man in his early forties. He was kind of fat too, especially around the hips. She could outrun him. Additionally, it was really unclear if he was straight or queer, and queerness was exalted in her pantheon of human pursuits. He reminded her of her instructor in language arts, Mr. McKinley.

"What's the project, then?" she asked in a way that she hoped would be perceived as casual.

In this way was her commitment secured. What a mistake.

Oh, the words with which to describe her boredom at the Indigenous Ventures photo shoot. Such a momentous day, and yet such boredom. Any model will tell you, Vienna Roberts told friends later, that a photo shoot is a place of almost incalculable boredom. Any model will tell you that the models are dog meat, and a very small portion of dog meat, most of the time. Well, except in the case of the vogue for models who were *overfed,* especially in countries where hunger was a problem, which is to say most countries (excepting China and India). Models were meant to *stand there,* and, in the case of the Indigenous Ventures shoot, lick the face of another girl, nibble on her earlobe, and between camera setups these professional models bantered between themselves, Vienna and the other girl, they would say, "How bad is your flow? Like on day one, for example?" "Oh, man, you wouldn't believe it; it's like Old Faithful or something." "And do you have violent mood swings, and do you remind the people around you that these are really due to their behavior?" "I don't notice that I hate men any more on the first day than I do any other time. And by the way, I don't think it's right to talk about violent mood swings because these are concepts designed by patriarchy."

And so: the shoot was not terribly interesting to Vienna Roberts, was a disappointment. But it kept her out of school, which she mostly ignored except for Mr. McKinley's language arts class, where she compiled a list of interesting terms, such as *sockdolager,* and *anaclitic,* which she knew was going to be a good word, and what about *fegaries,* and *nixies?* It was what happened after the shoot that was of interest to her. During the shoot, Mark Schott, with his excessive ear hair and pear-shaped physique, was everywhere but behind the camera. He was standing in front of the girls, exhorting them with hands that were like birds, swooping and feinting, and he was upbraiding the costumers, and he was hopping up and down crying out for new veneers of pale foundation. He was Vienna's one ally. But at the end of the shoot, when it was time to settle up, he was suddenly *unavailable.* Vienna had been assured she was going to be paid, or perhaps, in retrospect when she thought about it, maybe she had *not* been assured that she was going to be paid. Maybe she had just forgotten to negotiate this point, and this was a reflection of how being related to a pair of political agitators, and living in a tumbledown shack across from the heavily fortified high school, did not result in good instincts where money was concerned. Mark Schott, at the end of the shoot, attempted neglect in the matter of paying up, it seemed, and when she understood what this meant, how she had been shanghaied by Schott and his sunglasses, she found the other girl, who was standing and absently throwing dice across the felt, and she said, "Did you think you were going to get paid?"

Without looking up. "By Mark? Are you kidding? He's usually pretty bad about that. He gives you a good reference when you go on to do other things. Mark pays in experience; that's what he'll tell you."

Vienna Roberts had, when she was in the midst of a good self-esteem day and was able to assess herself accurately, exactly one undeniable ability, often commented upon in her mediocre report cards and letters home from school: she *spoke the truth to power.* She was raised up to do just this. Vienna Roberts, when driven into the emotional tones that might best be described as *defiant,* could summon in herself such a reservoir of put-downs as to lay low any antagonist. And it was in this mood that she tailed a couple of the makeup under-assistants in no better position than herself, demanding of them where Schott might be pinned down, only to be told that Schott was well on his way to another shoot. When the assistants were asked where this next location was, they admitted that the next location was an airplane hangar outside of town. And when asked about the particulars of the next project, the under-assistants looked warily at each other and one of them whispered to Vienna Roberts that the product that was being photographed next was *the Pulverizer.*

"What's a Pulverizer?"

"A Pulverizer," said the under-assistant of eyeliner and rouge and self-paling creams, "has to be seen to be understood."

She hitched a ride out with them. It was not that the under-assistants, who were driving an algae-powered van that was so far beyond its 200,000 mile checkup that it could have quit at any moment, and which was not possessed of air-conditioning, *wanted* to bring along a churlish young leather goods store employee with delusions of adulthood, but perhaps the under-assistants, like all good people, favored stories in which the downtrodden have their moment of speaking the truth to power. The van had no reliable shock absorption, and so the conversation pixilated as though being run through an old eight-millimeter film projector.

"You know Mark is a really generous man, right?" said the one under-assistant, whose assumed name was Orion. "He's really involved with all the border charities, and with border groups that are about trying to increase awareness of the unique culture of the border area. He helps a lot of border jumpers across. And he pays off a lot of people to make things right when there's a danger of slavery. So he's a good man. And it's not like he really mistreats us, because he is doing so much good. And if he uses an economic model that's about barter or payment in services, that doesn't mean he's trying to steal. And I don't know if he told you this, but if you're sick or something, he can lay his hands on you."

"I'm sure he'd be happy to."

Orion said, "He cured Mitchell's chlamydia."

"But did he *cause* the chlamydia too?"

"You aren't talking seriously," Orion said.

Mitchell, it turned out, was the other assistant. Mitchell nodded supportively.

"When he cured the chlamydia, he said he could also do spider veins, alopecia, and canker sores."

"Alopecia?"

The airstrip where the shoot was to take place was located at the abandoned Rio Blanco International Airport. That airport was meant, in a different time, to connect the city with the affluent coca-producing regions to our south. During the Panama Consensus, in which it was held that taxing coca and allowing limited consumption would ease the cost of drug interdictions that the NAFTA ruling body could no longer bankroll, Rio Blanco had appeared to be in a good position to benefit. Longer runways were paved, additional terminals built, a rail link to the city was pondered. But then the political winds changed direction, and the Panama Consensus was labeled *appeasement,* and now the airport lay mostly abandoned, but for freight carriers who came in one end, off-loaded, and got as quickly out of the lawless Southwest as they could. It was here, in hangar number six, that Vienna Roberts, when she ought to have been at field hockey practice, witnessed a demonstration of the Pulverizer.

It seems, in retrospect, that the Pulverizer was a quaint piece of machinery, not at all as advanced as she might have expected. But in hangar number six, a Pulverizer was hooked up to a standard-issue wrist assistant, its nanoprocessors and online resources, and this computing power was attached to a harness, which was fashioned of a black synthetic rubber material and doubtless manufactured in a sweatshop somewhere in the Sino-Indian world. Across the front of the harness was affixed the Pulverizer itself, which, Vienna observed, was a long, retractable metal antenna, at the end of which was a large rubber missile in the graduated bulb shape that was suitable for, well, a certain consenting-adult type of activity, and this harness was, it appeared, being worn by the same girl who had been Vienna's gambling pal at the Indigenous Ventures shoot. What she was going to Pulverize, in fact, was a young Hispanic boy of unimpeachable comeliness, who apparently needed to make big money fast. This was Mark Schott's beneficent way of insuring that the Latino American boy was not pressed into wage-free service down in more tropical latitudes. In fact, since it was a still *photograph,* this young man didn't have to get Pulverized. He just had to look *willing* to be Pulverized, while Vienna's friend was meant to look willing to do whatever it took. All this for a well-funded online-shopping emporium that specialized in such things. Well, as her parents often pointed out, it was the twelfth quarter of recession.

The Hispanic boy wore some kind of wireless skin-response monitor of his own, one that assessed particular kinds of arousal, based on pulse, body temperature, blood pressure, vocalizations, and so forth, or this was what Vienna later learned in the literature. A voice on the set shouted *Quiet, please!* The generator hummed. The Pulverizer made a satisfying noise when it began. It sounded like one of those household cleaning robots, or maybe like an antique windup toy. Flash photography commenced. Before long, everyone on the shoot was sweating and furiously rehydrating, and the Pulverizer, which was a little balky in temperatures at which asphalt routinely melted, was *sometimes* Pulverizing, and sometimes it was looking more like a Wilterizer. It was in the midst of a temporary malfunction, when Mark Schott called *Setup number five!,* that Vienna got close to the man, close enough to do what had to be done, close enough to bring herself to the attention of the assembled. She remarked, in due course, about how it was not *professional*, given everything that Schott had said to her in the store, that he would just leave her to fend for herself without even pursuing the matter of *compensation*, which was a word she often heard her mother use. A worker had nothing to give, Vienna Roberts said, stealing lines from broadsides that were often lying around the house, but her labor, and her labor was a dignified thing, a thing worthy of respect, and when an employer exploited that labor, why that was as good as a declaration of *war;* that was part of the imperial menace that had brought this country to its knees, that had made a once-proud people weak, soft; many were the decades, many were the dark days of history when the oppressor would pry loose from the unlucky multitudes their precious labor, keeping for himself the coffers of minted currency that rightfully belonged to the people —

Schott caved. For her trouble, he said, she was welcome to the Pulverizer.

It was the fourth consecutive round-the-clock shift for many if not all at Mission Control. There were facilities people, janitors and HVAC experts, there were even some cafeteria dishwashers who had remained on-site. There were the numerous Mars mission department heads and subdepartment heads. They were all here, around the clock, beards grown out, slips showing. So much halitosis, so much body odor. All of these NASA employees were camped in front of their screens, whether personal or wall-mounted, in the cafeteria, in the control room, as the monitors documented the reentry, the ERV containing Colonel Jed Richards as it neared the edge of the Earth's atmosphere. The world had its news cycles, its narcotic game shows, its sports pages, its violent hot spots, all of which had come to eclipse the Mars mission, as though the billions and billions of light-years beyond this dust mote where we lived were of no consequence. Not so among the employees of NASA. They had given up their lives and their families to live the Mars mission.

Mission Director Rob Antoine's sleeplessness was of such magnitude that if you had told him that there were little green men in the capsule with Colonel Richards, in the last hours before reentry, he would not have batted a heavy-lidded eye. In fact, Antoine would have attempted to execute message discipline by describing the appearance of these green men as *interplanetary mutual interfacing,* or *focused coevolutionary exchange.* In fact, Antoine saw indeterminate mammalians crawling all around his office corners. The rest of the team fared little better.

At some point in midafternoon, he found himself in the men's room, and he took the opportunity to despair about his thinning hair. He was a man of systemic reiterations. He looked at opportunities for failure and then he worried at them, like the polar bear in the cage whose neurotic steps become perfectly metronomic. Pool, ball, rock ledge, pool, ball, rock ledge, fish. Antoine saw the thinning hair, heard the voice of his ex-wife telling him that the combing over was *pathetic,* that it looked like topiary, and still his hand seized upon the brush, and the brush brushed up the forelock and over the shiny bald part of his head, as if powerless to do otherwise.

Three days now since Colonel Jed Richards had turned the video camera on a certain spot in the capsule that revealed *absolutely nothing.* An empty part of the capsule. A bank of onboard monitors. That was it. The attendant question, as Antoine saw it, and this had been the focus of much of his thinking when his thinking was capable of being focused, involved the course of Richards's infection with *M. thanatobacillus.* Or lack thereof. If Richards was still alive, why didn't he simply turn *off* the video? Antoine had been an early believer of the theory that Richards had shoved the video camera out of reach, to get it away from his face, to deny Earth its final attempt to consume images of the return of its heroic explorer. Antoine had promoted this theory as a sort of *impulsive machismo* interpretation. And yet the only evidence that Richards was still alive in the capsule was the life-support-systems monitor that indicated the presence of something at 96.6 degrees Fahrenheit. A pulse and respiration could be faintly heard.

Three days of video feed. It gave you a lot of time to think. It was easy to get distracted by the relentlessness of that image. For example, Antoine had to admit, among his other foibles, that he tolerated, even revered, extremely *boring* things, boring art, boring music, boring film, televised golf. He had a wall-sized monitor in his home office, one of those total-wall guys, and he liked to loop footage from the original Mars explorer missions, grainy, amateurish footage from the rovers. He'd leave it up there for days at a time, while he was doing paperwork or realphabetizing books. Antoine would even, when trying to solve vexing interpersonal problems, *watch* the Mars rover footage. Mars was one of the truly boring places. It was matched only by Uranus. The guys working on the Uranus explorer craft were excited when there was a *cloud* on Uranus. It happened very rarely.

Antoine watched Mars while his wife was leaving him, and he watched Mars while his kids were packing up, and he watched Mars, sometimes, while he was brushing his forelock thirty times or when he was folding his socks. He bought socks in twelve-packs, in twelve-packs of twelve-packs.

It was some time before he realized that there was another occupant next to him in the men's room, also standing at the mirror, and Antoine could feel, as he had in these days of sleeplessness, a certain belated perception cresting, and the perception expressed itself in language but not in a phrase that fulfilled a social obligation like "Hey, how are you doing?" Rob understood, in this phase of language failure, long after lips and pharynx and larynx had begun assembling themselves into the preliminary words of a sentence, that it would be a good thing to say something sociable to his superior Vance Gibraltar, who ordinarily did not grace the men's room with his presence, although there were certain legendary stories about the kind of unselfconscious and performative shitting that Gibraltar had enacted there when he was a younger and more arrogant employee.

Gibraltar too was surprised to reckon with another life-form here in the restroom. Rob could see his boss, who reminded him of his father, if only in his capacity to withhold most kindness, looking at his, Rob's, hair. Antoine could feel that in some way his upcoming performance review would touch on the issue of his hair. If Rob could just improve his hairstyle, then it seemed Gibraltar would support him again, and yet Rob believed with nearly evangelical certitude that his hair was just how it was. Even if Gibraltar sent him tomorrow to the overcrowded office of un-employment, so that Rob would be back in Kentucky living in a trailer behind his mother's house, writing computer programs for video-gaming simulations, even then Gibraltar would not leave off Rob's brushing-up of the forelock. But how long, exactly, had he been standing here, having this thought, and how much of it had he actually verbalized to the back-channel kingmaker of NASA?

"I had a thought," Rob said. At a minimum.

"They're in short supply," Gibraltar observed.

"Maybe it was several short thoughts. In sequence."

Antoine, impervious to hurt, or so attenuated by sleepless-ness that he could have withstood any array of taunts and scarcely remembered to worry, stopped for a moment to consider the tear-drop shape of a certain puddle of water on the counter before him, and then he listened astonished as the thought, which he had not yet fully admitted to himself, began to form in the air.

"Have we completely considered whether Jed is filming that bank of monitors *for a reason?*"

"We've considered many things," Gibraltar said, reaching some fingers behind his front teeth to ensnare a particle. "The man is ill. He's probably reduced to some proto-hominid condition where he is too stupid to figure out how to eject himself. He's not in a place where he's able to make creative decisions about his video feed."

"How do you know?" Rob said, warming to the argument in turn. "How do you know that this is not some symbolic repository of mission information, gleaned from his earlier life, lingering in him, a part of him that is able to make these signifying decisions, in an automatic way, so that they can be interpreted by us, as direct com-munication, communication that might affect the reentry process?"

"He's sending us messages, Rob?"

Antoine turned to the mirror again and, breathing in the urine reek and an abundantly masculine cloacal perfume, which all men secretly recognize as their signature scent, he actually fluffed the combed-over forelock and said, "Why ignore a message if it's staring us in the face?"

Gibraltar gave the notion a long, ambiguous pause.

"If it's really a message."

Once this had settled in, the two of them left the men's room together, repairing down the long, sterile corridor, their worn, comfortable shoes like the universally recognized sound effect for horses' hooves. They made for the nearest video monitor. Because this was much more than a not-bad idea; this was a *new* idea. Rob Antoine was actually attempting to type into his wrist assistant as he went, summoning staff to the conference room; he was sending the feed there—have the design specifications available, *please.* By the time the two of them were in that conference room, having executed a number of joint decisions in an unusual symbiosis, a father-son lockstep, the feed was already up on the wall monitor. Rob had the laser pointer fired up, and he pointed at certain indicators illuminated in the image there.

"Our theory has been that this camera setup is devoid of meaningful project-related information. But what if there is another kind of symbol making at work? One that we have only begun to consider? You know, for example, how certain kinds of primates have been taught to use symbolic manipulation. They are shown pictures of objects, and from these they make syntactical units, sentences, paragraphs, out of a sequential juxtaposition of photo images. If *M. thanatobacillus* has as part of the course of its infection the gradual erosion of higher-order linguistic dexterity, then Richards, who himself witnessed multiple cases of the infection, would have known this—"

The room had begun to fill, and among its experts now were members of the team that had designed the capsule interior, who had stacked the solid-state computer systems on the wall rack in the shot.

If they didn't quite understand Antoine's sleepless monologue, they began to understand it through the vehemence of his performance.

"What if this is object-oriented syntactical manipulation? What if by assembling a sort of line-by-line message, we can divine a syntagmatic declarative statement? That's what I'm trying to say! For example, who can tell me what *this* panel right *here* controls? Can someone remind me? Is that water level and water flow in the capsule?"

"Exactly right," said one sandal-wearing, dreadlocked young engineer. "Water levels are monitored in such a way that they recirculate wastewater produced by the astronaut and funnel some of this water out through the onboard catchment systems and then redissolve it into capsule air, to keep humidity at a comfortable level. On the way *out* we did find that we had trouble keeping the air wet enough, which resulted in skin problems for nearly everyone. We made adjustments in the direction of greater humidity."

"Your name is?"

"Fielding."

"First or last?"

"First."

"Fielding, what can you tell me about what you're reading on this monitor?"

"What I'm seeing is that there's a really unusual amount of water available in the system. A very unusual amount. It looks as though he has completely shut off the humidifier and has allowed as much water into the catchment system as it can reasonably store. The short version, I guess, is that he's not drinking very much. Certainly not enough for someone who wants to remain healthy and comfortable."

"So what is this telling us?"

"I don't know, sir. Hydrophobia? That his condition is somehow related to hydrophobia?"

Gibraltar, from a chair by the monitor where he had now settled himself, arms folded, grumbled, "You're going to have to do better than hydrophobia."

"We're getting warmed up. Let me continue, if you would. Could someone tell me what's below the water monitor here in the feed?"

"That would be oxygen levels, sir." This was Amin, the designer whom Rob liked to talk to when he had to be in the engineering department, which mostly he avoided. Engineers only understood things in literal ways. Engineers were always blaming mission failures on human error and deflecting any responsibility away from their laborious and convoluted designs.

"Amin, what does the oxygen monitor do?"

"It does exactly what you'd think it would do. It monitors the oxygen levels in the cabin. It automatically makes corrections when the CO_2 dips below a baseline that would inhibit robust functioning of the astronauts."

The assembled experts now knew something that Rob didn't grasp himself. The designers had been schooled in the use and interpretation of these monitors long before management. Rob, and by extension Gibraltar, needed someone to spell it all out, and here was how it was spelled, rather dramatically:

"The thing is," Amin said, "the oxygen monitor must not be working or something. Because if it was working, that red indicator would be telling us that—"

"What?"

"Well, that the colonel can't possibly be *alive*. Because the oxygen level in the capsule is so low that he would eventually suffocate, it's..."

"Did no one think to look at this level at any other point in the past three days? Amin, aren't you supposed to monitor this? People, I know we're all tired. But has this been sitting right in front of us?"

Amin replied, "Sir, I think we've selected for monitoring *pulse* and *respiration* and all of that—life-support systems—and those are still going. I mean, as I understand it, and here I defer to the medical team, he's not going to do any jumping jacks, but he is still alive."

A hand in the rear of the room went up. One of the mission

doctors, Kathleen Fales. Since luck and superstition had crept into the hard science of the Mars mission in recent days, he wished he could call on someone else. Because of her surname.

"Kathy."

"Rob, there's no easy way to say this, but the short version is that we find ourselves with a medical contradiction here, because if what we are learning from all the external monitoring data is true, then there *would* seem to be no way that Colonel Richards is still alive. He has effectively shut off the oxygen in the room, as though he is trying to starve himself of it somehow, and the same could be said of the water supply. And yet he still has some kind of pulse activity, and we have a Gaussmeter that indicates electromagnetic impulses coming from him consistent with nervous system function as we understand it. If I had my choice, I'd say he's dead, or at least very close to death, and perhaps just hanging on because he has turned the temperature down inside to forty-seven degrees. You can't see it on this image, really. It's the blurry monitor way off to the left. He's refrigerating himself. As far as I'm concerned, he's not really alive in the conventional sense, certainly not to such a degree that he could communicate with us."

Rob stalled, sifting through his perceptions. "In that sense, perhaps, you might say that he's both dead *and* not dead?"

"I suppose," said Dr. Fales. "I'd try to formulate an intermediate terminology, something in the cryogenic family, something less quaint than *undead.*"

"Kathy, I'm going to say that I think you're leading the witness here, and that I'm not sure your conclusion helps us in the matter of decoding possible communicative sequences in Richards's environment. I'm not, in the final analysis, preoccupied with the semantics of life or death. I am, however, wondering if he's trying to *tell us something.* So I'm wondering if we can move on a little bit to the monitor that's directly *under* the environmental controls here, and I'm wondering if we can address this for a second—"

A hush in this place of worry, this place of consternation and ignominy. It was unclear to those who were there if it was the hush of Debra Levin entering, in a maroon, understated knee-length dress, with a sense of perfect timing, at least if her goal was to gut the last few NASA programs extant. Or perhaps the hush was because everyone in the room knew what the monitor underneath the environmental controls was, and there was a sort of gasp when all considered the video image that Richards had haphazardly preserved in moving the camera out of his face. He had perfectly centered the image so that it was capturing the —

"Auto-destruct and fail-safe sequencer," Gibraltar remarked, from his chair. It was rare that the budgetary director knew or understood these particular mechanisms. It was counterproductive when he got into this kind of micromanagement. But Rob never underestimated Gibraltar's grasp of the basic engineering principles of space exploration.

"That's right," Rob said. "I saw it in my mind's eye. I saw that auto-destruct timer in my mind's eye, and I wondered, if he were just an *animal* now, or a *disassembling body,* or whatever it is we think he is, would he have situated this camera so that at its dead center we would see the auto-destruct sequencer? Can someone review for us?"

The kid called Fielding again: "An auto-destruct sequence can be begun at either of two locations, on the craft or remotely, at Mission Control —"

"Because?" Rob asked.

"Because no one mission team should have the ability to abort, but by having the go-ahead from the other party, by having mutual agreement, the craft can in effect auto-destruct."

"Though it's also true, I believe," said Debra Levin, silent until now, "that the space administration arrogates to itself the right to oversee any and all auto-destruct sequences, correct?"

"Of course, Madam Director. If we —"

"The world may have passed on to another news cycle, but the world recognizes that only one man has gone to Mars and attempted to return to speak of it, Mr. Antoine, and that man comes from the United States of America, and while there's still a chance that our man from Mars may be returned for the hero's welcome he deserves, the administration prefers to think that our reputation as the country of innovation will enable us to treat this man, to bring him back from the scourge with which he suffers. We discovered the polio vaccine here, Mr. Antoine; we mapped the five different strains of Marburg virus. It is this country that landed Colonel Richards on Mars in the first place, and it seems to me we ought to be the ones who are able to bring him home. When some other nation has the record of innovation and heroism that this country has, why then, Mr. Antoine—"

"With all due respect, Madam Director," said Antoine, trying to avoid some kind of ceaseless nationalistic prose poem, "having just arrived, you missed the tedious beginning of the conversation, where I was describing my theory that a kind of primitive linguistic statement has been prepared for us, rather carefully, it seems, by Colonel Richards, in this feed that we have here. Before you came in, I was pointing out that it was possible that he had specifically calibrated these monitors before video-capturing them for us. I think what's noteworthy about the auto-destruct sequence is not that it requires our input, or your input, before it can be effected, but, rather, and correct me if I'm wrong here, Fielding, that Jed has actually *already engaged his end.* Am I reading this monitor correctly?"

"It's the preliminary subroutine," Fielding muttered. "He has given himself *one hour* on the clock."

"And we have how much time left before splashdown?"

"About twice that much."

How had it grown so late? How had it grown so late? How had years of preparation and endlessly redundant plans come down to this? It had grown late while the Mars mission pondered, again and again, a list of possible responses without arriving at one that it could collectively stomach, and now it was nearly *too late.*

"Which means," Rob said, "that we have how long if we're trying to insure that pieces of the craft burn up in the outer atmosphere?"

The question hung like a cloud over a blasting site, and while the crowd murmured and prepared to return to its workstations, Rob Antoine, still relying on some auxiliary tank of energy that he had long since used up, gave the image on the screen one last look. That was when he saw the fuzzy onboard video monitor way over on the left side of the feed. Because of Rob's nearness and the screen's fuzzy resolution, the monitor was very hard to make out. It was a blur of primary colors.

"Wait, wait!" Rob called to those who would exit. "Anyone look at this? Right here?" He indicated with the pointer.

"A personal monitor," said Fielding Ayler. "That's just whatever he's watching on the idiot box. Or was."

"Just for my own edification, Fielding, do you happen to know what's *on* his idiot box?"

"As you know, sir, we can't see what's on their personal screens. For reasons of privacy. However, sir, there *is* a work-around, insisted on by security personnel."

"Is that right?" Antoine replied.

"We do have, for example, a record of web-related transactions by the employees, just like with anyone here on staff. They are networked to us, after all, even at a distance. Anything that's been watched would have been cached in a file folder for the individual astronaut, and that material, unless they uploaded it from a flash drive, which they shouldn't have, is contained on the server right here."

"I'm guessing, Fielding, that you have seen a few reports about individual usage."

"I'm guessing, sir, that everyone with clearance has."

"What does everyone with clearance know about the viewing habits of our courageous voyagers?"

"That Captain Jim Rose liked gay porn, sir, that Arnie and Laurie follow professional tennis, and ballet, and that Colonel Richards, well, sir, he's sentimental about his daughter."

"You're saying what, exactly?"

"Unless I miss my guess, sir, that blurry image is Colonel Richards's daughter at a dance. A recent high school dance.

Uploaded by her to his e-mail box about six weeks ago. She's a good dancer apparently. Very, uh, flamboyant."

In this way Rob Antoine came to wonder about the mysteries of syntax, of language. Had he learned, beyond a shadow of a doubt, that Colonel Jed Richards was trying to tell him something? No, he didn't believe he'd learned any such thing. Over all meanings was the shadow of *unmeaning*. In all utterances was the exasperated sigh of those lapsing into silence. Where one man was certain about what he had just said, beside him was a Vance Gibraltar, or others like him, who had heard no such thing, who had heard, in fact, nothing at all. Woe to the words and sentences and paragraphs that were not even understood as such, for they faded from recollection like trash blowing across a glass-strewn vacant lot. This, however, did not prevent Rob Antoine from divining with tea leaves, and perhaps this was because of his fixation upon the long, slow march of truth across the canvas of the boring. What was boring was somehow more elegant, more perfect, for it was incontrovertible. The boring was everything that certainly *was.* The boring was everything that had stood the test of time. The boring was that set of truths that were so long fixed that erosion had begun to sand them down. The boring was geological; the boring was universal. The boring, therefore, was preferable. And so when the meeting attendants had agreed to research and return in half an hour, the room emptied, so that all the Mars mission team managers could go to their workstations to prepare for what came next, if not auto-destruct. Rob Antoine was still looking at the image, and that was when the syntax of the remark—for that was what he had come to call it in his fuzzy mind, *the remark*—appeared to him, with the blunt force of an equation, something perfect and mathematical—what Jed Richards was trying to tell him, trying to tell Rob Antoine, another husband and father whose family had left him while he attempted to learn the truth that the stars and the planets were bent upon announcing:

Diminished water levels + Diminished oxygen levels + Low capsule temperature + Auto-destruct sequence = Recommended mission abort by reason of infectious disease — Daughter at high school dance = Residual will to live despite infectious disease

Yes, complicated enough that the men and women who had been gathered around Antoine in the conference room did not understand as readily as he did that the meaning was *there,* if only you allowed it to surface in you as a subliminal intent rather than as a conventional linguistic construct. And what was the subliminal meaning, so slippery that he kept thinking he could entrap it with these brightly colored English-language equivalents? It slithered in his mind, as if it didn't want to be gazed at straight on, nor named. But it was something like this, in the conference room: because he couldn't not say it, it was the only way he could keep the thought in his mind: that at the end of all our meanings, in the last wisp of consciousness in which meanings can take place, is *longing.* That's what Richards was saying. When everything else is gone, when all our possessions are gone, all our accomplishments, all the things we would have become and did not, all our friends, all our acquaintances, all our carefully ordered antipathies, all our ideologies, all our skepticisms, when they are all gone, there is *longing,* a daughter we were so lucky once to know and love, dancing. May she remember us.

Rob rubbed ruminatively at his eyes, gazing upon what he thought he knew, in the whispered hum of the desktop system that was doing the projecting, and he didn't even hear Debra Levin, who may have been in the room ever since, throughout his calculations, throughout his elegiac flights of ratiocination. She was here still, putting a well-manicured hand on his sweaty, unwashed shoulder. He started, and gazed into her benevolent and not-to-be-trusted face.

"Whatever you need," said Debra Levin, sadly smiling. Leaving her hand there a moment longer for additional emphasis. By the time he'd finished parsing and reconsidering this simple phrase, she was gone.

Noelle Stern, graduate student in the medical school at URB, assistant to world-famous researcher Woo Lee Koo, had experienced *the blinding light of revelation.* In a way she had never suspected or believed possible. Since, like Koo, she dead-reckoned with the certainties of empirical research and experimental method, she rarely predicted surprise, and this despite her youth in the hothouse of alternative belief systems, Rio Blanco. And yet: against her better judgment she had come to believe that the animals in the URB animal research laboratory were speaking to her.

She was a tiny woman, just a hair over five feet, who wore jump boots and torn jeans and whatever monochromatic sweater she could buy at the thrift stores of Fourth Avenue, a look that her boss, Dr. Koo, had suggested would be inadequate to professional advancement. Her hair of dirty straw she kept often in pigtails, and it was as if it had never occurred to her to clean the lenses of her secondhand spectacles. Hobbies as follows. Sundays, she took lessons in contortionism west of the city with members of the *omnium gatherum.* For a long time, she'd also played old-fashioned laptop in a band called Momento Mori, but she'd quit because they had insisted on getting a manager. She read widely and wanted to learn Italian. If there had long been an ideological divide between her inherited (from her dad) desire to study in the field of medicine and the heavy drumbeat of left-of-ideological-center Rio Blanco, where she had lived the whole of her short life — a town of easy, relaxed pastimes, including public drunkenness and intoxication with polyamphetamine and OxyPlus (via nasal inhaler) — it had never seemed to amount to a state of irreconcilable conflict until such time as her boss, Koo, began messing with the higher primates.

Koo, as even she would put it, was a runty type from South Korea who had a chip on his shoulder about that land of fraudulence. He had been recruited to URB to study stem cell theory. And he did a little of that. But he indicated that stem cell theory was complex and required more and better animals than were presently available at the school of medicine. Right after she'd been assigned to him, he started trolling message boards looking for apes with neurological complaints. Any ape with a tremor or paralysis was placed in the database she'd created for Koo, and in many of those cases, he'd made direct attempts to purchase. To animals who were, on the contrary, able-bodied, he would occasionally apply enough electrical impulses to their spinal columns to induce paralysis. URB would have become the world's leading facility for afflicted apes, all of them palsied, trembling, lying inert on the floors of their cages, if not for the fact that (in addition to Koo's inconstant attentions) URB was going through a period of fiscal whatever you'd call it. Successive state budgets had brought about such reduced circumstances that Koo was trying to make up the difference from national granting agencies who were themselves scrambling for dollars.

The way Noelle saw it, there was no oversight from the university. Nor from the medical school. And Koo didn't seem as if his heart was in stem cell research any longer. Koo failed to teach his classes, delegated to the teaching assistants all the lecturing, took no interest except at exam time. That wouldn't have been unusual had he been in the laboratory instead. But he wasn't in the laboratory, except late at night when no one else was around. In his accented English, Noelle understood him on occasion to be mixing heavy doses of Catholic imagery with his convoluted instructions about what to do with the experimental results. He kept talking about *reanimation* and *regeneration* and *necrotic tissue,* areas of medical intrigue she associated with the realm of the imaginary.

She had herself kicked upstairs with the animals because if she was going to work for a flake, she wanted to be working on the fun stuff. She probably could have been reassigned to another professor, because she hadn't even bothered to come up with a dissertation topic yet. Graduation just wasn't much of a goal. Still, Koo, for all his apparent strangeness, was mostly formal and polite, and seemed to take a real interest in her well-being. He invited her to dinner at his home (a dark, mostly unfurnished unit in a development in the western hills), not just to the departmental trips to the bar, which were stiff and forced. One time, Koo had asked Noelle for her advice in dealing with his son, Jean-Paul, who, like all the other Anglo kids in Rio Blanco, was going through a period when he believed he was a Latino gangster. It was all about the algae-fueled vehicle and the baggy clothes and the T-shirts depicting Mexican wrestling personalities. She remembered Koo's expression as he asked for help, and it was of total noncomprehension. He still loved his boy. This was clear. She'd said that she'd look in on Jean-Paul from time to time, but every time she tried, the younger Koo found a way to cancel at the last minute or to bring along a friend. He was, however, conscientious about sending her the occasional grammatically incorrect text message.

Generally speaking, Noelle had problems with men. There was always some guy in sandals and dreadlocks whom she was trying to avoid but whose telephone calls she was still waiting for. She waited long enough that she could watch her impressions of the man in question go from unreasonable appreciation to doubt to contempt. Sometimes in the space of days. She hadn't even slept with him yet, whoever he was. Jean-Paul, in his refusal to interact, was consistent with earlier findings, and he was just a kid.

These and other difficulties improved when she started working with the primates. Runaround Sue was her first charge, an ill-mannered chimp from Saint Louis, MO. She'd been born in captivity there, had never swung from the tree branches like a chimpanzee ought in the Congo. Runaround Sue specialized in eating and watching television, and in threatening whatever human being was responsible for her by baring her teeth. According to reports from Saint Louis, Sue had never once been a chimpanzee of status in the group. Other women chimps ignored her. She ate and slept and, on occasion, copulated with lower-status males. Such was the life of the prisoner.

The Runaround Sue who arrived in Rio Blanco had some kind of relapsing and remitting neurological complaint. Maybe her aggressiveness was meant to deflect attention from her weakness. Noelle had trouble not projecting her feelings onto the chimp. She even took umbrage at Sue's name, which had been bestowed on her because despite her status she had been good at mating in captivity and producing children, most of them now full grown and removed to medical facilities elsewhere. Noelle hated Sue's name, but she sympathized, as she also understood when Sue was prideful and confrontational at the moments when pity and sympathy were coming back at her.

Sue, like the apes who would follow her at URB, was not an alpha animal. The chimps at URB had lots of scars and were missing fingers, had chronic diarrhea, or were, apparently, parkinsonian. These were the animals that had already exhausted the patience of researchers across the country. Noelle loved the outcast apes, though, and spoke to them with tolerance and equanimity. She said to Runaround Sue, e.g.: "You can't believe what they got up to at the *omnium gatherum* this weekend. They're trying to dig a hole from here to Mexico. Fifty-eight miles. They were saying a blessing for the digging, and there was some kind of traditional ritual with tortillas. The earth movers are going to have to go down like fifty feet or something to be below the level that the border patrol uses. They had a shaman dig the first shovelful. And then he broke up some tortillas and handed around crumbs."

Sometimes the conversations got more personal.

"This guy wanted to go to a golf driving range. Like he thought a driving range was so old-fashioned! Like old-fashioned was *good*. There's legislation pending, Sue, that would, you know, deed all the golf courses in city limits to the Union of Homeless Citizens. What a great tent community you could set up on those golf courses. No varmints. And this guy wanted to go to a driving range. Are you kidding me? And then he'd probably want me to sit and watch him take shots. When he hit a really good one, I could give him a kiss."

Not that Noelle had forgotten that the goal with the primates (and it wasn't just apes; there'd been occasional spider monkeys and rhesus macaques) was *experimental*. Runaround Sue hated getting her injections—they all did—and the shock of her hatred of needles roused in Noelle feelings of great pity. But she was paid to administer injections, and so she did. Noelle was never entirely certain afterward what the preparation was that they gave to the chimp. With Koo it didn't do any good to ask. He would offer some rationale heavy with rhetoric: the injection was to test "whether the introduction of computer-enhanced umbilical-cord stem cells, which promoted mild regrowth colonies in paraplegics, could impede brain lesion reproductive events associated with MS." The kind of language that was found in grant applications, with the solecisms of ESL decorating its obfuscations. Who knew what the experiments measured? Who knew?

What was clear was that from the first injection Runaround Sue got worse. One leg developed a tremor. Then the leg stopped working altogether. In her cage, without Noelle or Larry, the other graduate student, Sue's expression, as easy to read as if it had been the face of your own grandmother, was fearful and uncertain. But once Noelle entered the cage (as opposed to hiding out on the far side of the two-way mirror), it got even worse. Despite the failure of motor function in her leg, Sue resumed her ill-tempered provocations—to the best of her ability. Noelle, for example, was hit with a fresh, watery helping of stool nearly every day.

Nothing was worse than watching a nonhuman animal suffer. It was a matter of a few weeks before they gave Sue the lethal injection, and in that time there were losses of muscular function and excretory function, accelerated organ failures, you name it. It was exactly like losing someone you cared about. Koo seemed oddly even-tempered about the whole thing, like he knew what was going to happen. But it didn't make him happy either. He said things like "It is the nature of this life that what dies fertilizes what lives and causes it to grow better. Maybe what is living also makes stronger what is dead. The living and the dead are not so easy to tease apart. This is a braid of mutual dependence, life and death. With technological advances we can improve on these interdependencies."

Other primates followed; for example, Alfonse, the orangutan, who was pleasant enough, but who had a completely different type of illness (cirrhosis). Then there was the strange case of the bonobo, Cherry, who was just on the far side of adolescence. It was very hard to do experiments upon bonobos, because they were so affable. In general, unless a zoo had a surplus and couldn't find a place to send an animal, it was not often that you would find a bonobo for sale. Cherry, to make matters worse, took a shine to Noelle. It was a solid ten months that Cherry lived at URB, and in that time Noelle went from being a relatively dispassionate participant in animal experimentation to being a conflicted, miserable participant. Because bonobo civilization is matrilineal. The female bonobos rally against the males; they do what needs to be done while maintaining a leisurely life of food gathering and group sex. It was like life in Rio Blanco, see. Bonobo social life was like the life envisioned by the *omnium gatherum*. Whose online broadsides Noelle took to printing out for Cherry, when it was convenient to do so.

Noelle would bring in the computer and joystick (Cherry liked anything travel related and was oddly comforted by alpine scenery), and then, while the bonobo was involved with her haphazard web searches, Noelle would read out broadsides about the coming convergence of the idea of the human body with the idea of *geology,* and how the body and the *geologic* truth could meet somewhere, and then the body would be better able to withstand vicissitudes of the heart, intermittencies of the human relations. "O citizens of the ever-enlarging desert, join us this weekend for a ritual of bloodletting and passionate ecstatic release to celebrate the coming of the cyborg!"

Noelle Stern could not be sure that Cherry understood. Nor could she be sure that the bonobo comprehended the news articles she read her about nightly blackouts, periodic military exercises in the sky over Rio Blanco, armed uprisings by would-be emigrants, or the restive homeless army that was mustering in town. Experimental method, the stuff of Noelle's years in graduate school, argued against mythologies or nonempirical belief systems.

The erroneous belief in the appearance of affect in unfeeling nonhuman animals, for example, according to the theorists of post-postmodernist sociology, is a sign of a weakened cultural apparatus. Animals, in an economy of post-historical global interdependence, exist for the dominance of humans, who are their stewards. Animals are a resource, and they exist in a permanent state of mitigated volition because of insufficient processing power. This was written down in the best known pedagogical text on the subject: *The Proper Exercise of Power*, by Lyman Johns et al. Noelle had consumed it in year one of medical school, and it was with such violent antipathy that she read the arguments there that she kept the book close ever after. She tried reading some of it to Cherry, just to see, and the bonobo took it away from her, ripped out a great number of its pages, and then rubbed her vulva across the embossed dust jacket. Exactly the kind of highly symbolic activity that the book argued against. In this and other ways, Noelle had come to suspect that Cherry was attempting to communicate more directly with her female researcher, perhaps according to the rules of matrilineal bonobo society. A period followed in which Noelle asked Cherry everything, whether to date a certain guy, whom to vote for in the upcoming midterm elections, just to see whether there were genuine responses. A variety of interpretable and ambiguous responses ensued: Cherry offered her part of her meal. Cherry grabbed her in a headlock; Cherry attempted to rub her pudenda, that horrible word, against Noelle.

It was a brutal shock, therefore, when Cherry suffered mortally what was described by Koo, peremptorily, as congestive heart failure. Apparently, there was some kind of long-standing defect. Even more upsetting, it didn't take the senior faculty member on the project long to spirit away the body. When, in the weeks after, there was a stray *foot* in the lab that had electrodes attached to it for laser modeling, Noelle was almost certain it was Cherry's foot. Koo managed to get the foot to wiggle its toes on its own. With no body attached. Other grad students had a good time using the severed foot of Cherry for practical jokes.

Noelle missed Cherry. Missed her like she missed the friends of her high school years. Missed Cherry like she missed the cool air when the 120-plus-degree days of summer came around again. Missed Cherry like she missed a sibling, her brother who had died overseas ten years ago. She missed Cherry, and she wasn't sure if it would be possible to go on to the next animal, a chimpanzee called Morton. Maybe there was a point at which you just couldn't go on.

Over at the *omnium gatherum,* they had begun a project that involved hot-air ballooning. The *omnium gatherum* wanted to send up hot-air balloons so as to warn the citizens of the Southwest about a repressive police state apparatus that was now hovering everywhere around them, concealed in washes and behind underpasses. With a flotilla of hot-air balloons, like a series of jewels in the cloudless skies, the *omnium gatherum* would be able to radio back to Earth, with personal wireless handsets, the exact whereabouts of agents of the INS, the DEA, the ATF, and so forth. The flotilla could also use a doctor, they said, to minister to those brave souls who intended to live in this post-nationalist milieu, and perhaps she wished to be the doctor.

While she made up her mind, she had the simplest responsibility remaining to her. She had to go in and observe Morton. In the aftermath of some experimental injection. What the experimental protocol was, she didn't ask. She'd given a lot of injections, and she didn't ask what they were, and she didn't ask when she was directed to observe. To relieve some of the tedium, she'd saved a treat for herself. She had some decent, locally prepared hash, and she was going to smoke it with Larry in the observation room behind the two-way mirror. This ought to have been the night when Noelle Stern's lack of ambition, her lack of desire to be a doctor in the way that her father had been a doctor, should have come back to haunt her. Because smoking hash in the observation room could really fuck up experimental results. Morton could turn out to be one of those rare serial-killing chimpanzees who had recently been written up in the *National Geographic,* chimps who for no reason would randomly select other chimps and kill them, rip out their testes and their organs, and feast on the relevant parts. Morton was one of these, she said to Larry, passing the hookah back to him, and he was going to smash the two-way mirror and dismember both of them.

"A depraved imagination," Larry said. "You sure the doc isn't coming through here tonight?"

"He's taking Jean-Paul to see his lawyer. Jean-Paul has an idea for a business."

"Bet he makes more off of it than the old man did."

"Koo dosed the animal earlier. And took off," Noelle said. "He gives a shit at first. But he has sort of mediocre follow-through. Or maybe he just can't bear to watch."

"It's the poorly paid folks who can bear to watch."

"The animal can tell that he's South Korean and doesn't take him seriously," Noelle offered.

"The animal thinks he faked the data."

The giggling contagion passed back and forth.

"You think Morton is smart?" Larry said.

"They're all smart. But no one is as smart as Cherry was."

She often wondered, when she was back on another regimen of wondering, *Why not Larry,* but this inquiry discounted, right from the outset, the fact that Larry had a kind of unflattering mustache, also that he had given in to the idea that guys in their thirties looked most natural when portly and unkempt. These were black marks against him, but still there was a kindness about Larry. His treatment of the animals was evidence of this, of an idea of fair play. Larry didn't really care about what kind of doctor he became either. He laid an avuncular palm on the backs of the animals, and then, when his work shift was done, he went back to the house on the South Side that he shared with his father. He had a hobby, which was metalwork, and once Larry had invited Noelle over to his place to see the sculptures. She was surprised at the look of commitment and ambition that crossed his face when he showed them to her. Larry occurred to her, in her lonesomeness, and then he didn't occur to her later on. Like some fleeting weather system. Maybe it was the lot of the human beings in a primate laboratory to fail in their attempts to know one another, because the animals were reserved for a certain kind of complicated relationship, the kind where there was up and there was down, where there was vulnerability and then there was unavailability, where there was the stripping away of layer upon layer of shellac and water stains and self, until the flaws were all transparent, and with this exposure of the flaws came the capacity to brutalize, the capacity to take without mercy, the capacity, in the highest stages of love, to be inhuman, to treat the other person far worse than you would treat the merest stranger; in the laboratory, maybe this love relationship was reserved for the animals, whereas the other human beings you treated with the same disregard that you usually reserved for people's pets. Larry! Cute guy! Likes to smoke hash! Muss his hair a little bit and tell him he's cute! Ten minutes later she'd forgotten he was even there. Larry who?

She came out of the tunnel vision of her hash buzz to find herself gazing at Morton fixedly. Chimps resembled the elderly, actually. Even when young they had faces like the elderly. Morton was no exception. He was the kind of weary guy you would expect to see working as a security guard at one of those office buildings in downtown Rio Blanco with a 78 percent vacancy rate. Not a guy with a lot of big plans. The kind of sentience she saw in the chimps was rarely the kind that she associated with raw brilliance. They had a shrewdness, as though they understood things from appearances. They were keen observers. They knew exactly what they didn't know.

Morton was like this, and she tried to explain it to Larry, who had drifted off to one corner to read online music posts. "Maybe he *is* one of the really smart ones. Someday we should order at least one of these miraculous talking chimps that proves we're committing genocide in Congo and Rwanda by letting the species get wiped out."

"What's the experimental protocol, anyhow?" Larry muttered.

"Among other things, I think we're supposed to take finger paints in and see if he wants to paint anything."

"That's not asking too much."

She excused herself to go to the vending station down on the first floor, the vending machine that proved, beyond a shadow of experimental doubt, the relationship between hash and carbohydrate bombardment. While Larry was dragging the paints and the gigantic pad and easel into Morton's cage, she was buying tube-shaped pastry items filled with creamy stuffing (in her inner ear she kept hearing *tube of pastry! tube of pastry!*), two different varieties of chocolate chip cookies, and a simulated coffee beverage sweetened with corn syrup, and she was taking these back to the laboratory, all the while experiencing the desire to hide some of these spoils from Larry, lest he take more than his share. When she got back to the lab, Larry's notes were still on his chair—he had written the word *grooming* ten or twelve times on Morton's chart—but he was otherwise nowhere to be found. Meanwhile, Morton was hard at work with the paints and the construction paper. Morton had just about covered himself with red and blue paint, and he was especially interested in flattening his palm against the paper so that he would get a reproduction of his own palm. His chimpanzee palm.

Larry was probably getting soap and water for cleanup. Noelle decided to risk going in and watching from a closer position. She was always willing to try getting in the cage one more time, even when afraid, and it was true that Morton seemed remarkably docile. She pushed the door open slowly, so that Morton could see that a pasty, hairless primate was entering the room, a featherless biped, and as though he were used to researchers, as he probably was (having come from a private university in the Northeast that had closed because of declining enrollment), he paid almost no attention to Noelle at all. A sign of respect, Koo always argued, before attempting to shackle him.

"Morton," she said, "I'll be your hapless human researcher for the evening. Anything I can get you?"

His eyes swung abruptly from the paper to Noelle. He held her gaze for a moment, as though he were thinking about how to respond, and then he went back to work, smiling faintly.

"Would it be all right if I looked at what you're doing?"

He made no show to indicate that anything else would be to his liking, and so she approached, slowly. Upon reaching his side of the canvas, as it were, she saw the requisite handprints. There was also some effective abstract expressionism, which she thought certainly would allow him to be admitted to some guild of macho boy painters from the 1950s.

"I guess you're into all that drip stuff, huh? You'd probably drink too much, treat your wife badly, and die in a car crash? Well, what about something representational? Like a landscape? You got all this desert around here. Dramatic mountaintops. Night skies. Have you ever been to the desert before, Morton?"

Morton seemed to pause briefly, as if trying to settle the question of whether he was allowed to mate with her, before returning to his painting. There was, in truth, something evasive about Morton, as if despite his dour aspect he just didn't want to get into any trouble, really. If he'd been a human primate, he would have had a job in maintenance, maybe in Kansas City, where he would have always hoped that everything was running smoothly because he just didn't like any aggravation. While Noelle Stern was thinking all of this, however, she noticed that there was something unusual about Morton's painting. She sort of couldn't believe at first that she was seeing what she thought she was seeing, and she blamed the hash, which, you know, was a lot stronger than when she was a kid. There was something at the top of the sheet of paper exposed on the easel that—

"Uh, Morton, you didn't, you couldn't have possibly *written* something at the top of the page, did you? Did you get some rudimentary instructions on how to do some block letters? Because that looks suspiciously like written English to me. You couldn't possibly know English, right?"

It would have been one thing had there been just the *one word.* You could write off one word, or something that resembled one word, as exactly the stuff of monkeys typing, and *dumb,* which seemed to be the first word, written out with an almost stereotypical backward letter, well, *dumb* just wasn't that hard a word to write, you know, and it could have been the kind of thing where Morton had copied it down, having seen it graffitied somewhere near his cage long ago, all in caps, or maybe he just randomly learned a few letters from watching online news networks or something, seeing the scroll or the advertisements at the margins, but the fact was, there was a second word, and the second word was *broad,* so that it was absolutely certain that the two words worked together, worked in concert, because it appeared to Noelle Stern that Morton had somehow managed to write a sexist putdown with his finger paints, *dumb broad,* and not just once, because he had made red highlights behind the blue of the letters. He'd written out *dumb broad* twice, once with each available color.

"Jesus, Morton, please tell me you aren't a sexist asshole, okay?"

And then she called for Larry as though Larry were the life raft and she the drowning graduate student. "Larry? Larry?" She called and called, and then it occurred to her, as she was desperately calling, that it was all a big joke, a big prank, and then she began to assemble in her mind the techniques required for the prank, the theory and practice. Noelle was an earnest kind of a person, a person who believed in the *omnium gatherum* and its principles, and she realized that it was possible, even *probable,* that Larry had snuck the scribbled words onto the pad while she'd been getting her confections, and had ducked out to let her have the revelation in private, *ha ha ha ha ha ha ha,* and she was so high that she would have believed anything. She had to force herself to find the prank amusing, and she worked hard at it. And she patted Morton on the arm, as the plot and its execution flourished in her, and then she made for the observation room, unsure about whether she was still irritated, and when she got in there, sure enough Larry was doubled over in fits of laughter, and if that weren't enough, he was eating one of her pastry tubes, licking out all the filling.

It was a really *good* prank, the kind of thing that would be told for years and years over beers at that bar near campus. It was all in good fun, and everyone could laugh. Except that when the two of them, Larry and Noelle, went back into Morton's cage to tell the whole story over again, Noelle could have sworn that *dumb* was crossed out, or it looked a lot like it had been crossed out, and the *d* replaced with something that looked like the letters *t* and *h*. Larry, his eyes bloodshot, unable to contain his guffaws, until the point at which he was beginning to hiccup, he was laughing and insisting that that was exactly what he had written. But she knew better; she knew, at once, that Morton had crossed out *dumb,* because it was rude. Morton, she knew, didn't approve of the boorishness and unpleasantness of Larry, the fat and slightly unwashed Larry, the low-status human male who couldn't even be bothered to mate well.

Thumb broad. Thumb broad. *Thumb broad.* Because Morton and Noelle shared something, something sexy and evolutionarily profound: opposable thumbs.

Jean-Paul's fucking ridiculously hot girlfriend, Vienna Roberts, could not be trusted, not in her ridiculous hotness. She couldn't be trusted not to send out, what were they called, *pheromones,* whatever they were called; she couldn't be trusted not to send them out, her ready-to-be-doing-it hot fucking vibes, out into the world, and he wasn't always sure that he fucking needed to have sex like five fucking times a day, like in alleys and out behind the abandoned car dealerships out on the South Side, like, what was so fucking great about getting naked in an abandoned car dealership, some grease monkey could turn up at any time, or maybe like some fucking swine-flu-carrying poor-person grease monkey, freshly repatriated from the border or something, and Jean-Paul'd have his nightstick in her ridiculously perfect aperture, and then the disease carrier would be like *what the fuck, watching them,* but that would probably only embolden Vienna fucking Roberts, and she'd be like, *ohmygod Jean-PaaaaaaUUUUULLL,* all the contractions, like all *Psoas magnus;* the disease-carrying poor-person grease monkey could tell that something profoundly intimate was fucking taking place, and the disease-carrying poor person would just see, he could bear witness, totally *comatose,* he would be blinded by the high beams of her wet, convulsing self or whatever.

Which means Jean-Paul couldn't always fucking keep up, but you know, if you're like going to be a successful business owner, and this has been totally fucking proven, like read any book about successful CEOs, you'll see that they all know how *personality,* the pursuit of fucking business personality, like this can really fucking make the difference for a corporation, make or break, like the thing with these start-ups is you have to nuke the competition before they even get the chance to start up their putrid low-class operations, and that means that there has to be a fucking *personality* who is a brand on his very own, a slaughterer of men; like look at those Asian pop-singing androids, they have their militias, like they travel with their own heavily armed militias, and the Sino-Indian economic compact guarantees these militias travel everywhere, across all the borders in the region; they're like little city-states, devoted to fucking pop songs about cleanliness and obedience, *comatose,* and it's a little bit different because those androids aren't fucking allowed to appear like they have sex, but like the CEOs of the large fucking corporations that profit from the androids, those fucking guys, they have to have entire departments of the company that do nothing but place reports in the news and shit about how the CEOs are getting the freak on, day and night, maybe not taking clients to fucking strip clubs or anything, but you know these guys have posses of wives, they all converted to polygamy cults, and then they just get the freak on day and night, except when they're calling analysts to talk about price-earnings ratios, stock valuation, and all that.

When Jean-Paul Koo heard from his ridiculously sexy girlfriend known as Vienna Roberts, saying she had something she wanted to *show* him, well, it could only fucking mean one thing, which was they were going to have to drive out to Rattlesnake Canyon or Esprero, whatever fucking canyon, you name it, and she'd have some new outfit, like it would be a combination of a shredded pair of army fatigues and some fucking crotchless something or other because she was all about the crotchless something or other, and then he was supposed to, you know, like do the dance of nakedness in the desert, but hopefully on a *trail,* because otherwise you could really stick yourself on something out there, and plus, oh come on, the mountain lion attacks were just getting like fucking *ridiculous* in Rattlesnake Canyon, because they kept building up Ownership Units on the mountainside, a good idea except for the fucking economic downturn and stagflation, and massive unemployment, and drought, and temperatures of 120 degrees Fahrenheit, and now not only are the parks basically abandoned, but there are no fucking rangers, and there are all these half-built Ownership Units and foundations dug and otherwise fucking abandoned, and so like every other week it's some fucking disease-carrying person repatriated from the border, like with XDR-TB, who probably had a good fucking reason for wanting to be here, and that disease carrier was just shredded by a fucking mountain lion, broad daylight, or else it's like a jogger, you know, and apparently what they fucking say, or at least all the fucking rumors are like okay the worst fucking thing that you can fucking do if you want the puma to bite your fucking head off and roll it around in its mouth like it's a fucking lollipop, *comatose,* worst thing you can do is be out jogging and pushing like one of those fucking motorized three-wheeled perambulator things, with your fucking little bundle of fucking joy in it, because for some reason, or this was what they said, anyway, fucking pumas just fucking loved those fucking kids, and what they did was first they jumped off some overhang that you were running underneath because you were so fucking stupid you ran under an overhang, and maybe you were even wearing your headset, maybe using the screen option, and you only had half a fucking eye on what you were doing, and right then the puma leaped off the fucking overhang, because the puma could fucking jump twenty feet in a single bound, and it overturned the motorized three-wheeled thing, and the puma knocked little Junior out of the three-wheeled thing, and he popped Junior into his mouth like Junior was a burrito from the twenty-four-hour drive-thru place; hold those green chilies; I'll take little Junior here with a soft tortilla and maybe fucking enchilada style with a little drizzle of red sauce; and that's exactly what Junior would look like when fucking Junior was half hanging out of the puma's slavering mouth, and then the alarm in the carriage would go off, you know in case somebody would want to steal a fucking baby from the fucking Southwest, or would try to hold the baby hostage, for like some millions that nobody had anymore? Go take a Chinese baby, motherfucker. Anyway, the alarm went off and then Mom screamed, and the mountain lion said, *You got a problem?* and before he was even finished slurping down the spaghetti insides of Junior, he had his mouth clamped around the head and neck of Mom, who was about to be a decapitated body stump.

The thing was, Vienna fucking Roberts would get an idea like this into her head, the idea of the mountain lion, and that would somehow only fucking embolden her, the idea that they might be getting into the dance of nakedness down in Rattlesnake Canyon, and some mountain lion would come jumping off the ledge, because there was always a ledge in fucking Rattlesnake Canyon, and it would fucking pounce on them, *comatose,* while Jean-Paul would be in flagrante or whatever, and there would be blood and cum and body parts everywhere. You'd think this would fucking be enough to kind of sour Jean-Paul, but no, the fucking truth of the fucking matter was that the worse it got, and the more pressured Jean-Paul felt about the whole dance of nakedness thing, the better he liked it. He fucking liked the fucking outrageousness; he was a slave to the outrageousness, to the freakiness of the freak, and CEOs had to do it, and so when Vienna Roberts said, *Okay, come over, I have something to show you,* then Jean-Paul drove over, like an indentured fucking servant, and even if the algae fuel cost fucking thirty-five dollars a fucking gallon or whatever, he would drive, because it was his money, and he could do with it what he wanted to do with it, and he fucking liked watching all the fucking people walking around with that fucking stiff, aimless posture of people on the street, fucking brain-addled people, giddyheads, like with fucking heatstroke, and he had one of the last automobiles on his street that had a fucking air-conditioning unit. So he drove over, and he fucking pounded on the door, a firm pounding, because a firm pounding was like a firm fucking handshake, and Jean-Paul was always trying to remember stuff like this and berating himself when he fucking forgot, because it was one of the fucking rules of advancement in the era of the Sino-Indian economic domination, the firm fucking handshake; Jean-Paul practiced the unmistakable door knock, and it didn't fucking matter anyway, because Vienna's parents wouldn't fucking be there, because they were camped on the golf course out off Silverbell, trying to teach homeless people about Mao's Little Red Book and the Sendero Luminoso, but who even knew who the fuck these people were; Jean-Paul only knew because his dad would go *red in the face* with disgust at the mention of Mao; his dad said Mao was responsible for all the evil in the world, which was a pretty great amount of evil; so he pounded on the fucking door, and Vienna fucking Roberts came to the door, and she wasn't even wearing anything particularly slutty, actually; she was just wearing short-shorts and a tank top, nothing that she fucking wouldn't wear any other day.

"I'm so glad you're here," she said. "I'm really glad. But what took you so fucking long?"

"Could I ask a question too? Which is like how come you aren't willing to wait patiently when waiting patiently means that something good is about to happen? Isn't waiting kind of a good thing, and don't you have a life that has some other stuff in it besides me that you could do while you were waiting?"

"Well, let me ask you if you know the meaning of the words 'Come right over'? Don't those words like mean anything to you?"

"Haven't I heard this speech like fifty fucking times? Can't you fuck off?"

"Do you want to see what I got or do you want to see what I got?"

"How could I answer a question like that, since I don't know what you have, so how could I know if I want to see it?"

"What are you talking about? Or are you like such an ape that you can't even come up with an idea of what you are talking about? Because if you had any idea what you were talking about, wouldn't you want to see what I'm going to show you, like when I promise that it is totally worth it?"

"Am I supposed to be able to follow your totally obscure type of thinking?"

"I don't know. Are you?"

"Or am I just supposed to let your incomprehensible whatever wash over me like a fine bottle of fucking champagne?"

"Sound sexy to you? Champagne?"

"I'm figuring you're figuring how sexy it sounds to you. Am I therefore right?"

To which, in the doorway, she made no audible reply. Vienna took him by the hand, to lead him into the inner sanctum of youth and sexuality.

"Are you," Vienna said, "like at all informed about the post-technological, post-manufacturing, post-stagflation, mass-merchandised device known as the Pulverizer?"

"The what?"

"The Pulverizer?"

"Do I look like I'd know anything about a Pulverizer?"

"Is it that you're trying to be like coy or something?" Vienna continued. "Would I be coy about *cyborg* sexuality? Would I be coy about a device that's all about turning the tables so that what's *wrong* is *right*, and what was bottom is now top? Would I be coy about how this device is meant to break down the last bits of human, you know, *resistance* that people have in proto-hominid sex, or whatever, until they are like shattered animal versions of themselves, because it's wires and microchips and titanium that are able to make human beings into the subhuman animals that they really are? Would I be coy about that? Would I be coy about how I think I've never really felt anything, you know, sexually, or whatever, until I saw the Pulverizer being utilized?"

"I mean, can I fucking ask how you got to see it *utilized?* I mean, should I be a little jealous, because maybe it's like I fucking don't want you pulverizing or getting pulverized or witnessing pulverization unless I'm there? And are you somehow retroactively saying something about all our other fucking proto-hominid-type adventures?"

At the top of the stairs now, and beginning to march down the stairs into the fallout shelter that Vienna's parents had expanded since they bought the place, because they were sure that Islamists or Central Asian despots or the Sino-Indian military agents or narco-traffickers would launch missiles that would wipe out most of the remnants of this nation and its free-trade satellites, *just because.* And, you know, nobody in Rio Blanco had a real fallout shelter, because they didn't have basements.

"Haven't I told you?" Vienna said, as she reached the bottom step.

"Told me what?"

"What?"

"What what?"

"That photographer, like a big international photographer, has been pursuing me, trying to offer me a multimillion-dollar contract to appear in his advertisements that are all about female slavery?"

"This is supposed to be, like, a believable story?"

"I'm not saying it is or it isn't, but is it enough that you want to hear about the Pulverizer?"

"Well," Jean-Paul said, "wouldn't that depend if I were in a state of, I don't know, arousal or something? Wouldn't I need to evaluate certain kinds of symptoms, like I could evaluate whether I had an elevated heart rate? Or maybe my blood pressure had risen? And what about blood flow to the region of my fucking genitals? Like wouldn't there maybe be a tightening of the tissue in my, you know, my scrotal area, or whatnot, perineum, like when I heard you use the word *Pulverizer?* And wouldn't that be enough of a telltale sign that what I really wanted, at this point, was to see the Pulverizer, instead of being told some story about how you first saw it with some photographer?"

Interrogatives temporarily expended, Vienna flung off the sheet from the Pulverizer, and he could fucking well see that she had got herself this ridiculously large device that looked more like a butter churner or something, *comatose, my brother,* and it was affixed to this rolling cart, and it had all these onboard computer monitoring devices, and then there was a butt plug on the end of the thing, and it was just like the Pulverizer was somebody's old-fashioned juicer, or somebody's old-fashioned lawn mower, except that now somebody was going to have the lawn mower pound this hilarious piece of silicone *into them,* and he didn't know if he was supposed to use it on Vienna fucking Roberts, or if Vienna fucking Roberts was going to use it on him, Jean-Paul Koo. He had his suspicions.

"Is this gas powered? Or electric? If it's electric, is there some kind of generator? And if there's a generator, where's the generator located?"

"I didn't really read the instructions yet. But I think it's got a solar panel, as well as AC, and I think it's all charged up."

"Do your parents know that you are charging an expensive fucking anal battering ram in their fallout shelter? Like what would happen if the nuclear attack happened today, and the mushroom clouds rose over Phoenix, and we can only fucking hope, and you had to go down into the fallout shelter and spend the rest of your youth waiting for the gamma radiation to fucking die down, and the whole time there would be this silicone butt plug thing in the corner, ramming into stacks of canned goods?"

"Maybe we could use it for something good, community oriented, like pounding dough for bread or beating rugs to get the dust out of them."

Jean-Paul said, "So I'm guessing you probably want to take this out to Rattlesnake Canyon."

"I'm wanting *us* to take it out to Rattlesnake Canyon."

"What if I'm not exactly sure that I want to take it out to Rattlesnake Canyon? It's a long fucking drive, like over an hour. I mean, you're the all-important female presence in my fucking operation, and I want you to be happy, but I'm not sure if I want to take the Pulverizer out to the fucking canyon, because I think I'm supposed to want the Pulverizer to do stuff to me, but I'm not always sure if that's the kind of thing that I like or not, and therefore I am experiencing some, I don't know, I guess it's like *hesitation*."

"If that's what you think," Vienna said, "I'm going to be really disappointed, and I'm going to bring up that I spent lots of time trying to get this for you and thinking about you, and there's all the kinds of things that I do for you, but then you just don't do that much for me, you don't think about what my needs are, and if my needs include the Pulverizer and Rattlesnake Canyon, well, then maybe you can try one fucking time to use the Pulverizer out in Rattlesnake Canyon, and you can quit with all the male, you know, prejudices, and you can just do as I say."

There was a sort of pouting expression that Vienna Roberts got, but it was actually a little bit fucking cruel, in addition to being a pout, and Jean-Paul Koo recognized stuff like this from the *DSM-VIII,* because his father had put him in fucking psycho-therapy from the first minute they got to this country, because everyone was in fucking psychotherapy, or everyone took fucking psychopharmacological medications; with Jean-Paul Koo it was always about the Dead Mother; it was all about the Dead Mother and it had always been about the Dead Mother; the Dead Mother represented every fucking thing; there was no thing, no object, no abstraction, that wasn't gummed up by the Dead Mother; the Dead Mother was available to Jean-Paul in every reflective surface, the Dead Mother was in the ghostly reflections of the bright Rio Blanco sunshine against the vandalized and empty office buildings downtown, the Dead Mother was in the sun-dappled images in his rearview mirror; the Dead Mother was in large bags, like when he

fucking had to reach into large suitcases or duffel bags, the Dead
Mother was in there; there was the anxiety about the Dead Mother;
the Dead Mother was always in the dark in the hypnagogic moments before sleep, and sometimes in that dark, the Dead Mother
was benign or even loving, and he was certain in these moments
that the Dead Mother cared; other times, the Dead Mother, in
the dark, was vengeful, and then the Dead Mother wished that
Jean-Paul would have made more of himself than a small-business
owner and a would-be Mexican gangster and a not very good son;
the Dead Mother was all *women in authority,* and with women in
authority, Jean-Paul's panic was so fucking acute that he would
fail to show up for conversations with women in authority, even
when these conversations were for the good of Jean-Paul Koo, like
one fucking time in school, even though he didn't fucking want
it, he won some award for like *best science project,* and all he fucking had to do was walk down the corridor to the principal's office,
where they had like a three-hundred-fucking-dollar fucking gift
certificate to the really good used-media store on Grant, Arachnids, and they had like a bronzed fucking Venus flytrap or some
shit with his name on it, and every day over the balky loudspeaker,
the assistant principal announced, at the end-of-school announcements: "Jean-Paul Koo, please come to the principal's office," and
maybe this was actually the fucking kind of thing that increased
the positive cred that he had among the toughs of the private
school, because having to go to the principal's office was *bad,* you
know, at least until the announcements started announcing the
fucking science award, and then the Dead Mother, the ghostly
version, some incarnation, was cornering him in the halls between
classes and saying, "Jean-Paul, please, we've had your award for
several weeks," but because she was the Dead Mother, the assistant
principal, he backed away, his eyes filling with embarrassing and
inexplicable tears that he attempted to conceal, and he'd come up
with some excuse, and he'd turn and run down the hall like he
was late for detention, even though he never had fucking detention and wasn't late for it; and, furthermore, the Dead Mother

was in college applications, and his inability to fill out college applications; the Dead Mother was in any kind of church, because she was all about the churches; and if there was a Transcendental Other, then the Dead Mother was somehow next to the Transcendental Other, because the Dead Mother had died a prolonged and painful fucking death, as Jean-Paul would have been the first to admit, and the Dead Mother had suffered, and he had too, although he admitted this only to himself, and in private; he knew he had fucking suffered because of the Dead Mother's prolonged and ravaging illness and demise, and no young kid, like Jean-Paul had been, should fucking have to go through that, but probably yet his story wasn't any worse than many other fucking stories he'd heard, like when he went to a grief-counseling group, when they first came here, because his father wasn't eating and would work all night and then sleep during the day, and Jean-Paul, even though he was only a kid then, he called all these places in the phone book, like no fucking kid should have to do that, call the fucking grief-counseling numbers, and no kid should have to beg his father please to go with him to the grief-counseling group, and there were all these kids there, their mothers had jumped off bridges in front of them, their mothers had pulled the car over and left the engine running and the radio on and then jumped, or their mothers had killed their siblings, and there were rivers of grief about the Dead Mother, and so the Dead Mother flowed liberally, flash flooded Jean-Paul's riverbed, into the washes of Rio Blanco, her watery remains flowed into all the gullies of this dry place; she was everywhere, and because she was everywhere, she became a consultant on the product line of the Transcendental Other, that is if the Transcendental Other existed, and so this was why when there was the pouting thing from Vienna fucking Roberts, he could not do anything about Vienna fucking Roberts, which meant that he had to do whatever she wanted, because he could not let go of the Dead Mother. He fucking agreed to go out to Rattlesnake Canyon, and he fucking asked how they were going to get the fucking Pulverizer out of the fucking fallout shelter, back up the stairs, and into the convertible, because there really wasn't room for the fucking Pulverizer, which wasn't going to fit in the backseat, not to mention all the electronics that came along with.

"Taking the van," Vienna said.

"What van?"

"Taking the van that the Union of Homeless Citizens uses for the meals-on-wheels program."

"You have that? That van belonging to a fucking not-for-profit entity? In your parking area?"

Outside. By the old, scorched agaves. After Vienna fucking refused to allow Jean-Paul to fucking see the Pulverizer in the *on* position, they managed with great effort and a lot of sweat—running down the back of Jean-Paul's tank top, reeking up the fallout shelter—to get the Pulverizer up the fucking stairs, where its casters made it not so hard to wheel out into the street. Vienna had put a rubber glove over the butt plug, out of discretion probably, so that the Pulverizer, as it was going into the van, looked a lot like some kind of very complicated prosthetic hand, maybe a prosthetic hand that was intended to teach people about the necessity of the firm handshake.

All Jean-Paul could fucking think about was kinds of lubricant, and he was hoping that there was some deluxe desensitizing kind of lubricant that he could get at the drive-thru health and beauty aids joint, the one that now had cyclone fencing and fucking bulletproof glass everywhere from people trying to get at the OxyPlus nasal inhalers and also the Epsom salts that were used in the quick, explosive chemical reactions that made the new more potent polyamphetamine tablets that you could get everywhere. Maybe Vienna had some nasal inhalers, and if he was supposed to have the Pulverizer pulverizing him, the OxyPlus would charge up his prostate and loosen him some. Vienna was fucking talking to him while she was driving, and she was telling him all this stuff about her day, like apart from everything else, she lost a fucking earring, *comatose, baby,* and her friend Stacey just was being a total bitch and refusing to allow her to teach hand signals for the history of terrorism class, but he wasn't hearing any of it, because he was worrying about the Pulverizer pulverizing him and drilling his colon all the way up into his diaphragm.

He punched buttons on the fucking satellite radio. He liked the motivational programs. He liked the station that played nothing but motivational programs, like *Closing the Big Sale with Glenn Baisley.* Somehow, by happenstance, he scanned past the local news outlet, Channel 932. Through whatever sequence of events secretly overseen by the Dead Mother, he heard the tail end of the report in which, in a voice dulled with repetition, an announcer observed that "on the east side of the city, near Rattlesnake Canyon, another jogger has been badly mauled by a wildcat—"

Colonel Jed Richards—according to those at the agency who were employed with no other purpose but to watch the feeds of the cameras inside the ERV—had suddenly elected to turn the video camera from the main console, where it had been positioned for these past few days, so that it would again capture his face.

Many were those who upon first seeing that face saw something that they believed they would long find unforgettable. In the months afterward, when NASA employees spoke of the face, they spoke of it with the kind of fear and disgust that is reserved for atrocities. It was no longer a face as we know it. It was a face without the neotenic smoothness of twenty-first-century man; it was a face ragged with woe and bad hygiene; it was a face that had rappelled humankind backward down the evolutionary chain, back beyond the Cro-Magnon or the *Australopithecus;* it was the face of a sallow and underfed dog, though a dog that nonetheless continued to have human features, the face of a starveling coyote or hyena, with gigantic furry rings around his eyes, as in the eyes of a raccoon, with bloody residues in the eye sockets and rivulets of congealed blood cascading from them. There were crusty bits of crimson about the nose and the corners of the mouth, and the mouth hung open as though he couldn't get enough air; his tongue, blackened, hung out of his mouth; long, patchy hair hung down over his eyes; he gasped, wordlessly, and this face looked into the camera so plangently, so balefully, that none of those who witnessed the face could fail to turn away; and despite that, Colonel Richards, however mysteriously, had managed to stay alive with little or no oxygen in the capsule, and those who watched the face, those who turned away and then turned back, those who bore witness as the face revealed itself, they felt as though they *had to do something,* and fast, to help this poor, agonizing man, to relieve his suffering in whatever way they could. There was weeping in the canteen, where NASA employees lined up for yet another ice cream bar—the only foodstuff that remained stocked in the canteen since the ordeal began. There were moments of true pathos when people would shove their legal tender into the machines, get the ice cream bars, and then watch as others fell huskily against the glass plates on the vending carousels, releasing in their sighs the accumulated months of frustration and disappointment. Many were the NASA employees who had not cared for Colonel Jed Richards in the early phases of the Mars mission. He was demanding, and he was vain. But here in the endgame, Richards had taken one for the team. This was what the team itself believed. Colonel Richards was gazing courageously upon the prospect of an inglorious death. Colonel Richards, the team believed, was perfectly aware that his death had either already taken place, such that he was presently in some new *postmortal conscious state,* the likes of which had never been seen before on Earth, or else Colonel Richards was going to have an even more inglorious death imminently. Upon reentry. Team members who couldn't bear one another just a few weeks ago held one another, offered handkerchiefs, asked after the family, in the canteen, as if there were nothing that could repair the damage done by the end of the Mars mission. Nothing except family and friends.

It was after about an hour of the video, one hour of that haunting face, the face of death (it seemed), that Colonel Richards began attempting to *talk* to the camera. This was a difficult operation in the absence of oxygen, as any medical expert will tell you. It was just one of the many facts of the Mars mission that had become inexplicable, scientifically impossible, and, in a way, embarrassing. If Richards was now speaking, then the decision makers at the top needed to be summoned, because what Richards said was of the utmost importance. The words of Richards were like words from a mountaintop, from some lofty and spiritual aerie. The folks who made the decisions needed to know. And that meant waking Rob Antoine, who was napping on an air mattress in his office, and also Vance Gibraltar, who had carefully installed one of those Japanese napping cylinders in his office wall and who had been unconscious in there with Japanese music piped in for just over twenty minutes. These two men were rousted by the staff who were monitoring the monitors, and in their dazed conditions, they made their way to Debra Levin's office. It was the first time either man had seen her without her makeup on, and they were impressed with her naturalness. They were further impressed that she was still on the premises. Appointees normally got well clear of the debris field.

Once these three principals were situated in the available chairs, Rob Antoine, without much conviction on the subject, asked to be patched through to the capsule, where the Tasmanian dog who had once been Antoine's homecoming astronaut was strapped in, gazing at the camera. Soon, through the miracle of radio transmission, a link was established.

"Jed, can you hear me? It's Rob Antoine. I'm here with the director of the agency, Debra Levin, and with Vance Gibraltar. Can you hear us?"

A ripple of consciousness in that mammalian face, as though it understood somewhat. Some mild neurological firing, the use of Richards's name perhaps, had enabled the part of him that remained.

"We need to know, if you're able to tell us, how you're feeling. Can you talk to us about that?"

The director felt she needed to add something, though whether this was useful was debatable. "Colonel Richards, at this historic juncture, we want you to know how much you've given to the country, and how much that means to us. You are a true hero. A man of great stature. A patriot. Your contribution to the life of the country will not be forgotten."

Then a hoarse whisper *was* audible in the transmission.

"What's that, Jed?" Antoine asked. "Are you able to communicate in there? If you are able, please let us know."

"Don't bullshit me," the voice whispered.

"Jed, we have no intention of *bullshitting* you; that, as you know, is not how we operate here at NASA."

There was a chortle, or something halfway between a snigger and some kind of pneumonic hacking. Bits of lung tissue involved. Still, it was hard not to think of this particular sound as sardonic.

"Jed, let's not beat around the bush, if that's all right. We have work to do. We have some important questions to answer quickly. For example, we need to know whether you imagine you are infected, whether your immune system is compromised."

The astronaut said, "Definitely... infected. I used to look better than this."

"Is it the same course of infection," Antoine went on, "that you saw in the others back on Mars?"

"I want you to promise me," Richards wheezed, "that any... footage you're collecting now... will never be seen by my wife and daughter. Is that understood? I want all of this footage erased.... I don't want it turning up in some museum exhibition... down the line.... Promise me."

"There's no problem with that, Jed."

Gibraltar added, "Jed, your wife is being supplemented by the agency now, to make sure she has everything she needs — in terms of expenses, child-care options, subsidized housing in perpetuity — and that will all continue. Don't worry on that account at all."

"Kind of you... Vance."

"Jed," Rob said, "we are wondering if you have noticed that the life-support systems in the capsule seem a little bit off there. Or at the very least the monitoring is way off. Is that something you noticed, and, if so, is that... intentional?"

"I set the levels.... Of course... I shouldn't be... Well, it's obvious... right? The rumors of my... demise are... accurate, ladies... and gentlemen."

"Do you have stamina or strength remaining? We should get the facts to the medical department, you know, right away. They're advising us on treatment options."

"I have... the strength... of a dead man."

There was an interval of stunned silence.

"Well, do you think you're up to the landing? Because we really only have a very short time until splashdown. We need as much as we can get of your—"

"Blow the capsule," Richards interrupted.

The troika had discounted this possibility, at least publicly, had not fully discussed it, had premeditated only in the hopeless moments the idea of the auto-destruct sequence. As though the idea itself were an illness, an affliction. It was a backup plan, a Plan C or a Plan D, scarcely mentioned in all of the computer models. No one had thought that they'd do it. Not really. There was too much to let go of. Too much labor and ambition. Too many dreams. Too much human aspiration. The auto-destruct sequence, as an approach, amounted to admitting to themselves and to the world that *not even one astronaut* was able to make it back from Mars. Not one. And yet here was the decision, expressing itself as the choice of the remainder of the mission, the one whose carefully composed diary entries were now part of the documentation of what had taken place out there, 40 million miles away.

"Could you repeat that, Jed?" Antoine asked. "So that I know I heard what I heard."

"Blow the capsule... please...." And then a long and weary pause. "Let's be direct.... I want your... agreement... on this point. My situation, as you... can see... has declined... and it'll continue to do so... and since I have reason to believe... that I know... what happens with the... later stages of infection... I would like to get your commitment so that... my family... will not see me... this way."

"Jed, we're going to talk here for a few minutes, and then we'll be back to you."

Rob Antoine turned to face the other two, realizing that they, Levin and Gibraltar, were already making decisions, organizational decisions. It was this way. You found yourself on the inside or the outside. Here at the agency, science was always the lapdog of the political and military objectives. The pure scientists were the yahoos, the ones who were unsophisticated, the ones who had no idea how the world worked.

And yet it was Debra Levin who said "Rob, we cannot afford to lose the colonel."

"What do you mean we can't afford to lose him?"

"I mean, Rob, that regardless of the colonel's feelings about his situation, we cannot afford to lose him. In fact, the colonel is now a military weapons *system,* and we have need of this particular military weapons system. We are, as you know, a nation that is potentially at war with a much larger force massed in the East. We are a nation, a consortium of trading partners that has been running a net loss in terms of scientists, with many of them now moving to universities in Beijing and Delhi. We cannot afford to have a genuine turning point in the history of American innovation, innovation with global political ramifications, stifled because of the feelings of one man. I have therefore been directed by the highest possible levels of government to be certain that if there is a military weapons *system* available to us as a result of the Mars mission, no matter the collateral costs, then I am to be certain that we secure this military weapons system and deliver it expeditiously to the laboratories in Langley and Washington. What they do with the technology, thereafter, is not our affair. We are, at this point, a freight operation."

"What if he's already dead?"

"Rob, if he's dead, why did we just have a conversation with him? He's rather talkative. And, to answer your question, it doesn't matter if Colonel Jed Richards is dead, although I grieve for his discomfort. And for his family and loved ones. What matters, however, is what he's carrying."

"But what about the risk to the population in the area around the landing site? I mean, assuming we can predict the landing site with any accuracy, what about the risk to local populations? What if the pathogen gets into the water? What if our efforts to quarantine Richards, upon splashdown, are inadequate? Are you going to want it on your conscience, Madam Director, that you let loose a germ of which we know next to nothing and against which no inhabitant of Earth has any resistance at all?"

"Rob," Gibraltar said, reaching across to set a hand on the shoulder of the younger man. And there was a strange serenity to this gesture, the serenity of Antoine being told that his voice in the final stages of a project to which he had given years of his life was marginal. "Your conscience should be clear. Mine is clear. The orders come from above. There are principles here. We have no duty but to follow the orders."

"Even if it's a *bad* decision?"

"For whom?" Gibraltar took pause, as if to punctuate. He sipped from a coffee cup before him. "For Jed Richards? Jed has already offered his life for the betterment of his country several times over. You just heard him do it. And for everyone else, for the people who care about this mission, for this agency, for the military complex, for the nation as a whole, an end to the mission that does *not* include the auto-destruct sequence is by far preferable. We all look better. NASA gets better funding. I know Jed Richards, and I admire Jed Richards, but I like to think that if he were here with us right now he would make this decision the very same way."

"And you" — Rob looked into Gibraltar's bureaucratic eyes carefully and then moved on to Levin, passing from one to the other — "probably want me to tell him."

The NASA director gazed briefly at her lacquered nails. "You have the relationship. It's your call, but we think you will do it best."

Rob Antoine felt the stirring of powerful emotions, and it

would have been easy, when he was so exhausted, so confused, to play the role of the scientist who cared too much, who let his feelings get away from him. But he had risen to the position at the top of the Mars mission by virtue of his willingness to be responsible, above all, to make the unpopular decision, to tell his employees the bad news whether they wanted it or not. Without consulting further with Levin and Gibraltar, therefore, he had the uplink to the capsule reestablished. He didn't want to say what he was about to say to Jed Richards. But his professionalism was of a strong alloy, and he would do what needed to be done.

At least, that was how he felt until he saw what was happening in the capsule. Apparently, Richards, who'd been lucid only moments before, had given in to some hallucinatory phase or episode in the course of his illness in which he could no longer vocalize actual English-language words. These words had been replaced by something closer to a primate hooting, a sort of primitive pseudo-language that would have been human, perhaps, if human beings no longer had the fine motor control that was necessary to produce dentals and fricatives and plosives. Richards, that is, seemed to be, well, kind of barking and kind of growling, and in a way that didn't sound like a human being barking or growling, but in a way, rather, that sounded, if not primatical, well, then lupine.

"Jed, can you hear me?"

There was no end to the dismal and bloodcurdling growling, despite the use of the colonel's name. It was as if some kind of pulsing, regularized barking and growling was now necessary to maintain respiration for the *entity,* the being that had once been Jed Richards. Rob Antoine looked back at Debra Levin, and it was the first time he saw fear on her face. Fear, he thought, got trained out of people who spent long enough inside the famous Beltway. For them the only fear was loss of power. And yet here was Levin, deeply shaken by Richards's condition.

"Is this the man you want me to bring home?"

"Mr. Antoine, it's irrelevant what I want, or what you want."

"Vance, are you satisfied with what we're doing?"

Gibraltar, Rob supposed, had also schooled himself in advanced poker playing. He would give away nothing.

"Jed, it's Rob here. I have some good news. You are cleared to land! That's affirmative on landing! We're going to have people on the ground to look after you, and immediately upon landing, we're going to take you to a facility in Washington where we expect we're going to be able to explore advanced treatment options for what's ailing you. We've had ongoing discussions with medical here, and that's what we think. Isn't that fine news? I'm personally looking forward to seeing you when you splash down, and I've just had word from some of the people in telemetry that your likely touchdown is in the North Atlantic, somewhere near to the Faeroe Islands, though perhaps a little west, maybe Iceland or even the coast of Nova Scotia. And we've already got people out that way, high-speed ships and so forth. Jed, isn't that great news? You are going to be celebrated, lauded, you name it."

The barking and growling Colonel Richards, the Richards with the face of death, did not, as far as could be inferred from the video footage, take too well to this news. Which is to say that the sublingual or prelingual utterances crescendoed with a series of microtonal hiccups, at which point a rather great volume of blood began to issue forth from Richards's mouth. It was nearly a vomitus of blood, or would have been described as such, except for the absence of reverse-peristaltic contracting, making the more likely causal agent esophageal lesions; at any rate, in the middle of this blood flow, Richards violently unstrapped himself from his station, from which he would be required to help in the landing process, in monitoring the heat on the exterior shields of the ERV, and began throwing things around the capsule. True, he was drifting, because his orbit had not yet decayed quite enough for him to have Earth weight or mass, and there was only so much in the capsule that was not attached, so as to forbid exactly this kind of tantrum, but he did a good job, anyhow, in destroying federally issued and multinationally sponsored, *branded* Mars mission material, until there were dangerous pieces of metal drifting everywhere in the capsule. There was bodily effluvium drifting to and fro, giving it all a Grand Guignol horror.

Rob Antoine's indignation began to boil, with righteousness. And it was at that point that he began to formulate his personal, if treasonous, response to the critical moment in which he found himself. What he recalled, from the distant recesses of mission operation protocols, was that there had been, in case of transmission difficulties, a series of *hand signals* agreed upon between Rob and the officers of the three ships. In fact, the sign language was borrowed in part from the beautiful and ornate hand signals of NAFTA's Central American gangbangers, who, at some point in the past twenty years, had decided that spoken language was far too dangerous for them, with all the law-enforcement intervention into their circles. They had settled upon the notion of a constantly changing series of hand signals to indicate most aspects of their business, which would be safer than voice messages or any kind of written documentation. The gangbangers themselves, whose fellowships preferred to be known as *urban entrepreneurial collectives,* had fashioned the early examples of this language partly from the leftover sign language of the deaf, which had been all but abandoned after the perfection of cochlea-implant surgery and eardrum transplants. From this American Sign Language, the *urban entrepreneurial collectives* borrowed an alphabet and many simple sentences, especially sentences involving cursing and obscenity. Some new signs were invented, especially signs referring to bodily harm, and then a large number of signs and styles of signing were borrowed from the signs used by the coaches in the sport known as X-treme lacrosse. The lacrosse signs enabled the *urban entrepreneurial collectives* to negate any signal that had come before, to contradict what had just been said, and so forth. This argot was not entirely different from the whistling languages that had taken off so powerfully in the urban Northwest, where the

organized crime from the Sino-Indian countries had found a toe-
hold. Nor was it entirely different from the rhyming slang of
Rust Belt cities. With these languages, *signed criminal argot* had
in common that it empowered those who felt disempowered, who
felt hundreds of years of oppression, to throw off the language of
the oppressor class.

Antoine, and some of his inner circle, had clipped a dozen or so
emergency signs from *signed criminal argot,* or was it from lacrosse,
and they had taught them to the astronauts late in the training
process. The question was: Who knew? Who knew about the emergency hand signals? Because if anyone knew, what Antoine was
about to do was hopelessly obvious, especially after Debra Levin's
impassioned speech about Jed Richards being a military weapons
system. Antoine was all but certain, however, that Gibraltar and
Debra Levin had no idea, and that most of the people watching the
video feeds in the rest of the building would have no idea about
the hand signals, at least not today.

Which message was it that he meant to use? Well, naturally,
Antoine had made sure to have a message for the auto-destruct sequence, because what other message could have been more important? It was in fact the criminal symbol for *respect.* The index finger
and thumb on either hand were spread as wide as possible, and in
this ninety-degree angle, the two index fingertips were pressed
together, likewise the two thumb pads. It looked roughly like a
Greek delta: Δ. The delta sign was placed in front of the heart.

There was one other symbol that was necessary in order to bring
about "respect," also known as the auto-destruct sequence, which
was the symbol for "all prior communications are null." Antoine
needed to pat the top of his head. He needed, that is, to pat his
pompadour, his comb-over. Normally, he refrained from disturbing this coiffure.

But he didn't need that long to think it over. He needed to do
what he believed in and to accept the consequences. And thus,
to the marauding, barking, hemorrhaging *thing* that was once
Jed Richards, and whose only Richards-like characteristic at this

point was that one of his hands clearly still had only four fingers, Antoine said:

"Okay, Jed, expect further communications imminently. Antoine out."

And then, looking carefully into the camera right below Levin's video monitor, Rob Antoine patted down his pompadour, and, as if praying for Colonel Jed Richards's safe return, he made the delta sign, the sign of "respect," which meant that Richards, if there was enough of him left to understand, had cooperation on the ground, at least from Antoine.

When he turned to face his superiors, Antoine's English-language transmission was in the category of the patently untrue. "That went pretty well." He didn't wait for significant reply.

In making his way back to his desk, Rob Antoine pondered all the possible ways to blow up the capsule. Best of all was for the capsule to fail to make it out of orbit, to reenter the atmosphere at too high a velocity, so that it would burn up in the process of coming down. But this would require the cooperation of so many technicians in the main control room that Rob felt he could never effect the Houston-based reply to the auto-destruct sequence without his intention becoming obvious to those in the employ of the military. Similarly, there was no point in blowing the air lock, because that could potentially leave the contents of the craft intact as they fell to Earth, and anyway, Richards already had essentially created a vacuum in the capsule. The temperature and the oxygen levels had only gone *down* in the past few hours. But, and this was a big *but,* if Rob could somehow enlist the support of Danielle Walters, the staff member who babysat the auto-destruct systems in the control room, he could possibly trigger the switch on this end and thus begin an ineradicable sequence, a sequence that couldn't be reversed without both sides agreeing to stand down.

But the final auto-destruct sequence, in order to make sure that those involved had time to ponder the enormity of the decision, lasted for one eternal minute. That is, once you flipped the second switch, a clock started, and the clock had a solid sixty seconds on it. In that minute, armed personnel in the control room could do anything, they really could. They could shoot Rob. They could arrest Rob. They could arrest Danielle. They could lock down the entire facility and look for the perpetrators of the auto-destruct sequence, assuming Rob could somehow throw the switch without being seen. If there was a computer program involved, which there always was, it might be possible to hack a way into the software, but if he remembered correctly, it had the most redundant firewalls of any code in the entire mission.

There were things that bound Rob Antoine together with Jed Richards, or the man who had once been Jed Richards. Rob too believed himself to be on the outside, despite his accomplishments. Rob believed himself to be an outsider, the kind of person *least* likely to succeed, and thus he had given over the whole of himself to his professional advancement. These things bound him to Richards. Also, there were the weeks and months of training together. And there was the fact that they had both lost their families recently. Their loneliness, their solitariness, their ethics, these were the things that made them alike; oh, and their appreciation for steel drums, which they had often spoken of, back in the old days. If this wasn't enough for Rob to do what needed to be done, what more could there be?

And yet, when it came down to it, there was a part of Rob Antoine that was reluctant. What if Debra Levin, after all, was right? What if it was this pathogen, *M. thanatobacillus,* that would make a huge difference in the national security portfolio during the years in which NAFTA fought for its economic sovereignty? Rob, sleepless, sat at his desk, looking at the face of death, and he found that he, Rob Antoine, was the picture of human irresolution. In this immobilized state, he received text bulletins at his workstation, as the orbit of the ERV decayed, as the capsule began to plummet to Earth, racing past Mongolia, and then Siberia, dropping out of the sky, with Richards still aboard. Rob Antoine sat, unable to move, unable even to call Danielle Walters and take her temperature on the whole thing. His head felt swollen. His blood pressure was probably well above the lethal, and yet he couldn't move. It was then that he got the worst of all messages, an exterior instant-message communication of the sort that were routinely blocked for middle managers at NASA. At least this had been the case for the past several weeks. The Mars mission had turned them all inward. Nothing from outside got in. Except this:

GingerSnap@sinisterteen.com: Mr. Antoine, hi, this is Ginger Richards writing you. I just want to know how my dad is doing and if he's really going to be okay coming home today. I mean, I guess you're going to say he's fine and everything. We heard from Mr. Miller who supposedly is in the press office or something, and we read what was in the news, but both my mom and me are really worried, and anything you could tell us would really be a big help. And I'm really sorry to interrupt. We know everyone there is really busy. But any information you could give us would be great.

Antoine's throbbing skull percussed with a new intensity. Had he failed to contact Richards's family in the past couple of days? He knew that Miller and other public-relations people were dealing with this part of the mission return, but that wasn't enough. Of course not. What would he have felt himself, were he Jed Richards's wife or daughter? He tried to compose a reply to Ginger, but when faced with it, faced with the responsibility, he was fresh out of shapely rhetoric, of organizational spin. He was a man who had no resource left but compassion. And it was this, finally, that drove him from his desk, like Hamlet bent upon his own bloody finale; Antoine got up from his desk, sweating profusely, and began to make his way to the control room, where no matter what the opposition, no matter what volley of automatic weapons fire would rain down upon him, he would reach over Danielle's shoulder, and while talking to her about the weather or some other pleasantry about which he knew nothing at all, he would break the seal on the auto-destruct toggle switch, and then he would throw that switch. It was decided. If he

could spare Ginger Richards the day of shame and worry, the day
when she saw her father as he now was, which was not like a man
at all but like something else entirely, he would do it. Rob had
children too.

However, as Rob made his way toward the relevant workstation, the relevant panel, in the glow of screens and video, the Earth
Return Vehicle carrying Jed Richards approached the Sonoran
Desert, heading north, on one of its many revolutions around the
globe, and for a brief moment it hovered at the latitude on which
Antoine walked in Houston, moving west across the desertified
part of NAFTA, and that was the moment when Jed Richards, in
the process exhibiting some engineering sophistication, took it
upon himself to blow the oxygen tanks in his craft.

Because earthlings really weren't built for space travel, what went
up would come down. Would come down. Because all the systems
of rocketry, the advanced engineering, the physics, the computer
calibrations, when you considered them, just decorated what were
in the first place large incendiary devices. Combustion for good or
ill. A big, unused oxygen tank sitting one reinforced wall away
from a nuclear reactor could at high temperatures be made into
fuel if you knew a little bit about engineering. A man bent on self-
slaughter will in time find the way to effect his passing.

And what was the furnace of that explosion like? The furnace of
that explosion was like all great light shows. If your planetarium
remains open in these times of endless night, then you are lucky,
but, if not, perhaps you remember going to the planetarium in
days past, in order to smoke various controlled substances and to
listen to the thunder of the genre known as *dead girlfriend,* while
the lasers etched out their predictable patterns above. Would you
require another manifestation of the light show? While it is true
that all fireworks displays resemble all other fireworks displays,
especially those mounted in hard-luck small towns, there is still
something earnest and generous about these fireworks displays,
because they are the light of munitions put to good use, the light

of munitions tamed. How else might this light of munitions be used? This light might be used for ill, as in the carpet-bombing of Central Asian cities by computer-controlled drones. This conflagration illuminates the night in a startling way, but is that what you want lighting your pockmarked highways and your blown bridges? It's a transient light, as all exploding things are transient, unless perhaps your explosion is of the nuclear sort, fission or fusion, of which only eleven have ever been exploded above ground in combat, and the most recent of these of a very modest sort, with deaths only in the tens of thousands. And while there are all kinds of treaties preventing this particular kind of light, nuclear fission, it continues to persist, even to proliferate, likewise the unpleasant suntan that goes with it, as well as the thyroid tumors and the relentless nightmares. What is the best of all kinds of light? Well, the best of all the varieties of light, since you ask, is the so-called Big Bang, coming from the perturbance within (and upon) an infinitely hot and dense speck that exists in what can only be referred to as the Nothingness or otherwise as the Time Before. This something in the middle of the Nothingness, this infinitely hot and dense singularity, because of a perturbance within and without, experiences some kind of rapid transformation at incalculably hot temperatures, and it commences the transition from infinitely dense to something quite a bit larger and more diffuse, and this light, which is, as far as we know, the light that has in turn generated all other light, it flings material far into its recesses and emptinesses, which open up in all directions, and some of this material, this gas and matter, begins to coalesce into constituent lights, which are themselves imitations of the originary light, the expanding and expansive light, as all lights are fragmentary and pale imitations of some preliminary light, and around these lights spheroids begin to accumulate, some of them rocky, some of them icy, some of them gaseous, some of them possessed of spectacular rings, but it should be noted that all these nightlights, scattered, as they say, like grains of sand across what is, these are all imitative, and not terribly successful as such, but their light is adequate, in millions upon millions of cases, to permit the kinds of chemical processes that bring about organic compounds. What these orbiting spheroids require, when life is present, is *light itself*, and all light has a backwardly gazing tonality to it, recalling, as it does, the originary light, and so despite the fact that great destructive force necessarily occasions light, any kind of light is nonetheless the sign that some kind of something is mitigating or flying in the face of the much more frequent and much more permanent Nothingness.

And so the explosion in the sky over the American Southwest was *light,* was continuous with the history of light as shown above, and light can't be bad, and light involves the transmutation of some kind of energy into some other kind of energy, and there is poetry to this, but occasionally there is also tragedy, at least if, for example, you were watching the light from the ground, if you were well-informed enough to know that you needed to be watching, or if you were one of the people in the desert of the Southwest who happened to be looking up at the sky, or who had a telescope or very good binoculars, or who just knew what was going on, you might have thought of this turn of events as tragic, but properly considered it was just another example of light as a celebration of not-darkness, and in this case, perhaps there could be plenty of *good* involved, because a badly contagious astronaut was going to be obliterated in this particular light show, as well as most of the metal casing in which he was housed at the time of the explosion, and this was good, from a public-health perspective, as were the extraordinarily violent temperature extremes that were involved in the reentry of the ERV; these could be responsible for killing off potentially lethal infectious agents, referred to in some circles as military weapons systems.

The only outstanding question, when the explosion was considered as a field of possibilities upon which one might, for example, wager, if one were part of a national gambling syndicate that gambled on the outcomes of political events and natural disasters, was: whether the ERV was high enough in its flight path to be completely incinerated or blown apart in the upper atmosphere, as was to be hoped. Because a large, far-flung trail of debris would constitute a civic emergency, not to mention a national security problem, even more so if, as appeared to be the case, the debris field included large portions of a sovereign NAFTA cosignatory that was, nonetheless, trying to minimize border incursions from the North.

The staff at NASA was monitoring the path of the ERV very carefully and they were satisfied, until the last moment, that it was on a northwesterly course to make a reasonable splashdown in the North Atlantic. A splashdown, though long outmoded in the landing protocols of a NASA that was now smaller and more efficient, allowed NASA the resources to go to the planet Mars itself and to avoid building wings onto the ERV. With splashdown, you could design a very simple reentry craft, and it could be kept away from population centers for a time. But NASA, or the better part of NASA (except for one middle manager who was at the moment of the explosion on his way down the corridor to liberate the one returning astronaut, Colonel Jed Richards, by toggling the auto-destruct emergency switch), was well into a collective delusion about the ERV, and into the midst of their shared delusion came a scrim of bright white fuzz on the screens that depicted the craft itself, and this white fuzz was followed by instantaneous blackness, which was followed by an absence of radio transmission, and, according to radar that tracked the craft, a multitude of *pieces* of the ERV, instead of one large, easily tracked ERV, rained across the screen, and many of these pieces vanished in front of the personnel manning the radar, until there were only a few minor bits of the ERV that were capable of being tracked, and these were falling out of the sky at the usual accelerating rate of thirty-two feet per second per second.

There was no device manufactured by the Jet Propulsion Laboratory that could track, from the ground, the remaining mind of Colonel Jed Richards. While there were devices that could, and did, track his heart rate, his blood pressure, his galvanic skin response, brain activity, temperature, even the condition of his bowels (not very good), these devices were useless after the advent of the explosion. If it were possible to track the mind of Richards, what would NASA have learned? In the explosion, the last of Richards's mind, however it was able to operate, was lost, and with it all the details of the way in which Colonel Jed Richards effected his departure from this world. Did he use some inflammatory device, like the onboard welder, to blow up the liquid oxygen reserves and therefore likewise to ignite some of the solid fuel that remained, which was meant to effect a few gentle booster firings if necessary? These things would long be unknown, despite a blue-ribbon commission that was soon to be put into motion.

However: the mind of Colonel Jed Richards could be said, at the instant of the explosion, to have come to approximate, in terms of its brutal monomania, the infinite singularity of the universe prior to expansion. It had become the density of a consciousness that was capable of one last gesture, of saying *I am,* and almost nothing else, a perceiving consciousness, otherwise devoid of characteristics. Perhaps, in retrospect, there was muscular memory of prior cerebral function, and this muscular memory was able to ignite the oxygen tank, even to plan its ignition. Whichever Richards was in charge — the strictly muscular Richards, the proto-Richards, the amoebic Richards, the particularity of Richards — the explosion, notwithstanding, did take place, outside of NASA's jurisdiction, and most of the ERV and its occupant were incinerated above the Sonoran Desert.

Most of the occupant.

My beautiful and eternal wife, to whom I have been wedded these many years, and to whom I will be wedded always, typed Woo Lee Koo, onto the autotranslation keyboard he had installed on the outside of the cryogenic refrigeration unit in which he kept his wife's remains, in his office in the garage of his home in the Grant's Pass Complex, *I have come to write to you again to apologize for the slovenly way in which I have been pursuing my researches. It is now, I believe, some years since I have been here in this decadent and futile nation, years in which I have had ample opportunity to learn the secret of regeneration of necrotic tissue, and yet, to my shame, I have yet to attain the result I desire. The experiments I have conducted seem to be of little or no value. I can see the answers to the questions before me, tantalizingly, but it's as if nature just doesn't want to collaborate with the likes of me, as if to deny the love of two persons who only wish to repair an unjust separation one from the other.*

Koo had installed the keyboard along with a screen on the interior, in the hope that someday his cryogenically preserved wife could read on the AutoTrans what was being typed to her. There was also a small keyboard *inside,* in case she wanted to type back. Koo recognized that this was desperate, even pathological, that in the present scientific environment there was little chance that a frozen dead woman was going to type back to him.

I know you wonder constantly if I have been true to you. And so it is my responsibility to reassure you occasionally on this subject. You may have been wondering again if there was a woman, or women, who have tempted me, and from whom I have obtained some sexual favors in order to soothe my lonely heart. Today it is my duty to reassure you that there have been no such favors, and therefore very little soothing. I was at the bank on Congress Street last week, and I would like to let you know that I still have a very healthy savings that I am keeping in federally secured treasury certificates because of volatility and downward trending in securities markets. In the course of my trip to the bank on Congress Street I espied a pretty young woman ahead of me, also making, as it turned out, a deposit. She was small hipped, as you were, and her hair was the color of straw. And despite the passing of many years, my darling wife, I would like to tell you that my heart leaped up, briefly, when it imagined that you were once again among us. I waited a respectful time for this young woman to complete her transaction, and then I averted my eyes, so that she would not feel as though I were in some way ungallant. She was not you, but insofar as she was you, she was handsome, and I felt fortunate to be in her presence, and also lucky when she had passed out of the cubbyhole of the Automatic Teller Machines. The ghosts of the past should be fleeting, don't you think?

It was Tuesday that Koo most often wrote to his wife, Nathalie, because this was a night when his son often worked late at that restaurant. This allowed for uninterrupted time in the garage with the cryogenic refrigerator and the AutoTrans keyboard. Jean-Paul, in his youthful self-centeredness, had never once asked what the refrigerator was *for,* though Koo did keep some tissue samples in the front of the refrigerator. There was a false front that he'd had built into the thing according to his specifications. And so Jean-Paul had never even expressed an interest in the technology. The son, that is, disdained his father's work.

Perhaps I ought to have spoken to this young woman in the bank, because sometimes, my darling, days can go by in which I do not engage in lighthearted conversation with anyone. One night recently, I went to the bedroom of our son, who is now eighteen years old, and who seems to be more interested in starting a business than in going on to college or university as I would like him to do. I visited his bedroom and sat down on the extra bed, because he has twin beds in that room, as I have described to you. He was perusing, or seemed to be perusing, a book of tips for entrepreneurs. I said to him that I had had the idea that we might remodel the living quarters, our quarters, with an eye toward allowing more sunlight into the rooms. And we might, I suggested, take down the wall separating his room from his walk-in closet, so that he would have more square footage. The construction of these apartments, as I have said in the past, is shoddy, and the desert is destructive to anything that is not sturdily built. There are so very many people in Rio Blanco who would be happy to do this kind of work, remodeling work. At any rate, Jean-Paul indicated to me that there was no point in remodeling his room, because he did not expect to be living with me very much longer. My darling, may I say that this conversation saddened me greatly. It is not that I feel the boy should be required to continue to live with me. It is simply that I didn't plan for this moment to come so quickly. By concentrating on my work, I prove, again and again, that I am not very good at my daily life. I do not want to be alone, without my son, and yet I believe I have made myself alone even as he lives under my very roof. I wish that you were here to help me talk to him.

As Koo typed his weekly missive, there was in the distance a chorus of emergency sirens spreading out into the desert night. There had been water riots taking place on the far side of the pass, where the collecting pools were meant to drain into the nearly empty aquifer underneath the greater Rio Blanco area. A large undulation of homeless people, despite daytime temperatures in the area of 115 degrees Fahrenheit, had hiked over the pass and camped out beside these collecting pools, demanding that the water be handed out more democratically. They also wanted all the golf courses to be turned over to the people and xeriscaped. Koo saw some merit in these arguments. He disliked golf, wasn't even sure how it was played, but his neglect of the water riots had more to do with his wife and his work than with any political position on water rights.

I have told you, I believe, about Alfonse, the orangutan to whom we attempted to restore liver function. Without success. I was very disappointed by the outcome of this experiment, and, as you know, I became rather fond of Alfonse. He was a willful but dignified gentleman. I find that Noelle, my assistant, the one I had over to dinner once or twice (though our dealings have been entirely chaste), has also become very passionate about the primates themselves. With acquaintance, I must say, one begins to treat these apes as though they are human neighbors or coworkers. Alfonse had no choice but to die a miserable death from liver disease. And yet there was a tragic sense that he perhaps understood himself to be collaborating with us on the project, and approved. Perhaps I have merely fallen prey to the disagreeable tendency to weep over what should be the greater glory of science. Occasionally, I will be watching a family navigating the crosswalk, just today, for example, and I will want to weep just over the fact that here is a family, a family entire, walking together in a crosswalk. Is this familiar to you? The same is true for me with some web-based programming. It causes passionate feelings. Perhaps it is the apartness of my own family that causes me to feel these things.

He had been typing for some sixty minutes or so, as he often did on his Tuesday nights, and now his eyelids had begun to grow sluggish. Some nights, he would just stretch out on the fusty hide-a-bed in the garage. Since Jean-Paul made no attempt to locate his father in the modest confines of the Grant's Pass single-family unit nor to see how his father busied himself, it had been many weeks since Jean-Paul had come upon his progenitor clothed and snoring with abandon on the verminous sofa bed. And yet this night Koo would not yet succumb to sleep when there were important points to append.

It is in this vulnerable state, my love, this state of aggrieved responsibility, that I conceived of the experiment with Morton, the newest chimpanzee at our research center. Last week, I did harvest a modicum of your cerebral tissue, and I confess that though I would like to have forgotten what your remains looked like during the course of the procedure, I have been having a rather difficult time forgetting. I am, I suppose, haunted. Of course, I have seen many cadavers in my life, and I observe a rather rigorous three-step approach to the medicalizing of cadavers: (1) do not look the cadaver in the face, (2) cut the cadaver open and begin to deal with constituent parts as rapidly as possible, (3) remove and store the head. Still, as you can imagine, it is not possible to be so cavalier when the cadaver was once your truest love and best friend. Moreover, my darling, as you know, I was harvesting cerebral tissue from your frontal lobe, which I then intended to take into the laboratory and cultivate into the relevant stem cells, after which I was going to introduce activated cells into the frontal lobe of the chimp called Morton. It was impossible not to look at you in the face, nor could I cut you into constituent parts, nor could I even cover your face, according to my rules for cadavers, because I needed to plunge in the needle, and, yes, it was one of those larger-gauge needles. I used a felt-tip marker to indicate a certain spot on the front of your face. This is why it was difficult for me, and why I was not able to recover from the revelation of seeing and of removing you briefly from storage. I didn't want you to thaw all the way, because then you would not freeze in the right condition. The things in the world that cause decay, the things that break down the dead, they are not modest in their supply.

As with all my work, darling one, I took the task seriously and did not shirk my responsibilities, despite the fact that I didn't sleep well for some time after seeing you again. I know that your cadaver is no longer you; I know that the match light of consciousness scarcely flickers in you until we solve the problem of regeneration, which as you know is exactly the problem I am attempting to resolve, and yet, notwithstanding the absence of consciousness, your cadaver does resemble some slightly puffy, tumid version of yourself, the you I loved so passionately and continue to love. This resemblance is faint and can break the heart of a person afflicted with a good memory. At these times, no matter what else I think, I am grateful that death released you from the confines of your illness.

Thus, having been satisfied about the condition of the stem cell colony, I injected the serum I had prepared into Morton earlier today. I injected the serum, that is, according to our experimental regimen. After the injection, I found that Morton displayed no behavior that I would consider unusual. The good news, in fact, is that Morton didn't immediately die, which has happened so many other times with the experimental volunteers I have worked with. I put Noelle and Larry in charge of watching the chimpanzee. Should you find you are suddenly awakened by a doubling, by a recognition that there is another you out there, or if you suddenly experience some dawning of primate consciousness within you, you should please feel free to contact me. In fact, you should feel free to contact me under any circumstances. I would be very glad to hear from you.

This I suppose exhausts the news I wanted to impart to you this week, except to say that the weather has finally begun to cool. I am very taken with the rather violent wind that has blown up from the west today. I love you as ever.

Koo typed the last characters of his letter and depressed "send," the mail-related digital command that is the bane of impulsive typists. And then he settled in on the rotting couch. On the side table, an uneaten sandwich of sprouts and peanut butter warmed toward room temperature. It would not be long now until the lights of Rio Blanco went off. Then there would be no light in the garage beyond the red operating beacon on the side of the cryogenic freezer, which Koo powered with his home generator, at some expense. But, just as he stood to watch, through the dusty garage panes, as a few buildings in the hills disappeared into the footprint of the blackouts, the telephone rang.

The *actual* telephone? Who still used it? Old ladies and marketing consultants and government agencies. Koo only had one for emergencies now, and because he'd hated that itchy feeling in the wrist that came from having that tangle of wires and chips implanted in it. Koo had also noticed that official communications — whether from utilities or university deans — still took place on the mobile telephone, though its days were numbered. With the caller identification, you could see the face of the caller on the charging stand, however, and in the case at hand, Koo didn't recognize the face, though this was probably made more difficult by the fact that the color balance on the phone had gone awry. It was a number from the National Aeronautics and Space Administration, according to the textual display, the laughingstock of the international space race, the laughingstock of governmental agencies.

"Woo Lee Koo," he said.

The lady in question gave her name, which he then forgot. This introduction was followed by some rather lengthy throat clearing. The woman dwelt for example on the high degree of confidentiality required for the conversation that was to follow. It was as if this woman had no idea how *few* people Koo spoke to on a given day. Not to mention his history of governmental subcontracting. She apologized for the lateness of the hour. She apologized for using the telephone. "Yet," she said, "we believe that we find ourselves in the midst of a national emergency."

Koo said, "It is late and I am preparing to go to bed."

"Dr. Koo," the attractive woman with the attractive voice said, before reiterating the need for confidence, "we are contacting you because of where you live. And because of your expertise. You are, according to people who have referred you to us, the leading researcher on gerontology, mortality, and stem cell–related research in the area around Rio Blanco. Would that be a correct characterization?"

Koo had to agree that he believed this *was* the case.

What followed then was a story so preposterous that it could only be true. The broad parameters of the story were: that the Mars mission reentry had taken place, this afternoon or evening, though the public had yet to be informed about the completion of the mission, because of the difficulties associated with touchdown; that the returning voyager, the infamous *man who had trod on Mars,* had been onboard the ship up until it was within a very few miles of Earth's surface; that the ship had not splashed down. The ship had broken up, scattering pieces of itself far and wide in the desert. NASA, according to the woman, wanted to alert Koo to the symptoms associated with *the illness* that this astronaut (and others, apparently) had contracted on the planet Mars, in the hopes that he, Koo, could keep an eye on the area hospitals. Did he have contacts at all area hospitals? If he came in contact with the symptoms she was about to describe, he was to isolate, even *quarantine,* the individuals in question in his facility, and to contact NASA immediately. They, the authorities, had reached out to a couple of other doctors at the various medical facilities in Rio Blanco, she would not say which, because she was hoping for discretion, in order to avoid misunderstanding, public-health emergencies, and, well, *panic.* They would be compiling reports based on what they learned from various respondents.

Koo, without giving any sign of the strain of excitement that swept through him, asked the woman to again explain the symptoms of the illness, which she characterized as "slow-moving decay, which doesn't seem to affect the consciousness of the sufferer, at least not in the early phases of the illness, and these symptoms are accompanied by rapid hair growth, enlargement of the brow, and sunken eye cavities, pelvic girdle, and some other portions of the body. In the late stages, catastrophic hemorrhaging, skin failure, organ failure, and then death."

"This sounds like radiation sickness," Koo said. "Or perhaps long-term corticosteroid abuse."

"The popular description of the disease favored by the Mars mission astronauts, though this can be considered anecdotal, was that the bacterium, *M. thanatobacillus,* caused bodies to 'disassemble.'"

"Rubbish."

"Gets the attention."

"But what makes you think that the contaminant has actually entered the ecosystem?"

"We trust that it has not. Which is why we insist on your discretion. Most of the Earth Return Vehicle did break up or was vaporized, but there were a few larger pieces of the craft that we believe touched down on Earth, and if any of these contained Colonel Jed Richards, any or all of him, there remains the possibility that the infectious agent could be transmitted by rats, fleas, coyotes, for example, or border jumpers."

Koo agreed to keep his eyes open. But what Koo had precisely begun to consider, in his very focused and scientific mind, was whether a bacterium that "disassembled" bodies could somehow be reverse engineered. It was an interesting question. Were there important medical applications as regarded the bacterium? Koo inquired of the woman from NASA if they had any idea where the pieces of the craft had gone down. She indicated that the remnants were likely spread out over a fifty-mile radius, including areas of terrain in northern Mexico. Koo determined to go in search, first thing in the morning. He wanted to find part of the astronaut. It didn't even have to be that *large* a piece, he whispered to his wife. It could be as small as a finger.

By the witching hour of dusk, Bix Rafferty of the Forsaken Mining Corp. achieved a balance of the chemical reagents in his veins and arteries — non-drowsy formula, mescal, energy beverages, and Sea Breeze, an alcohol-based face cleanser — and this balance of reagents was enough that he occasionally experienced visitations by a certain Navajo holy man. Smitty. While Rafferty was certain that a Smitty *really existed,* a person called Smitty, he did recognize that the conversations with Navajo Smitty involved themes and subjects that seemed plainly ethereal, even paranormal, well above and beyond the two men called Smitty and Bix.

Smitty, who was a rather stout Navajo fellow with a military haircut and long sideburns, who wore a sleeveless denim vest and denim trousers, and whose face was rutted and pitted from sleeping out in the desert many nights, always appeared on foot. There were snakes, wolves, mountain lions, pigs, and the other things of the desert night, and only a holy man such as Smitty could negotiate these plagues and emerge unscathed and improved.

Despite mystical qualities that were immediately apparent to Bix, Smitty insisted that he was just a brother attending the community college in town. Smitty also claimed to work washing dishes at one of those drive-thru Mexican restaurants. And yet when the chemical reagents in Bix were balanced properly, Smitty represented something else too: the trickster. Smitty liked to flip bottle caps and to speak of the way even the cacti were animated with the *Old Spirits*—or else Bix was misremembering a number of conversations that took place late at night, or did not take place at all, except within the fervent confines of solitary imagination. Rafferty welcomed the Navajo because the Navajo came and went and didn't care what anyone thought.

This night represented the fourth or fifth visitation of Smitty. A bounty of appearances. Though Smitty didn't like talking about himself, he did idly remark this night that his parents were long since dead, as with many of his acquaintances from home. Likewise that he'd tried to make good on an apartment in Rio Blanco but had come up a little short in the department of finances. Smitty's expression was anguished during this recitation of the facts; his demeanor was far from the laughing coyote face that Bix perhaps erroneously associated with the trickster and his narratives. Smitty, in his anguish, didn't ask Bix Rafferty for cough syrup, wasn't one of those freeloaders who came around kissing your wrinkled-up posterior solely for the purpose of sharing what you had. Smitty simply appeared, apparitional, as if to signal the persistence of a spirit world.

"Smitty," Rafferty offered, "I am touched by your candor. I am touched that you would share your story. And I would like to reward you with this," whereupon Rafferty generously passed him the Sea Breeze. "Let me just say that, yep, another day has come and gone, and not an ingot of any kind has been unearthed from the metric tons below. The water for the operation, in a time of regional drought, is already damnably unaffordable. Not to mention the rest of the overhead. Should I keep on?"

"Huh?" Smitty said.

"Let me answer a question with a question," Rafferty said. "Does this desert land ultimately reward, or does this desert finally just *take away,* so that any civilization that perches itself hereabouts, any scattering of buildings and schools and granaries, will be wiped out whether by fire or flood or by the relentlessness of the sun?"

"Not sure I totally catch what the hell you're talking about," and then Smitty said, "excepting that it's hard not to worry about drought."

"There's a rectitude to your tramps. There's a poetry to the likes of you coming and going out here in the Sonoran Desert for many centuries. Things that have gone on, like the military hardware, you know these things better than most people. What's best for the land, what is appropriate to the land."

"A man hates to run into barbed wire." The discomfort of Smitty was such that Rafferty himself could very nearly perceive it through the haze of cold-relief products and Sea Breeze. "You got to be real careful out late at night. A cow can do some awful damage to a vehicle. Buddy of mine hit one. The cow pretty much won that particular contest."

Many things were inferred by Bix Rafferty in the next silence. Silence is a thing onto which meanings can be projected. For example, in a silence you might believe, with the proper balance of chemical reagents, that a radical depopulating of the desert landscape is called for, in which the white man and all of his ways, his preposterous medical clinics with their radiological devices, and his steroid-enhanced, lacrosse-playing übermen, should be deforested, by whatever means there was for deforesting the white men, and the only people who would be permitted to stay were the kinds of people who had a right relation to the land, and by that Rafferty meant people who appreciated the use of firearms, and who mined for the things under the ground, which were the things that the Old Spirits approved of and wanted harvested for the greater glory, and it was acceptable to the Old Spirits, Rafferty thought in the silence, if some of the men who remained were white men, because they were self-reliant *believers*. What wasn't needed was a lot of conversation, he realized now, and this was the way in which Smitty, who was a holy man, was teaching Rafferty a lesson, by indicating that silence was just as important as conversation, and while Rafferty, who had once been a night school student back in the day, knew and understood that there was a so-called Socratic kind of instruction, which was all about the Q and the A, this was a completely different kind of instruction, the kind from Smitty, which embodied the inevitability of silence.

The two of them looked up into the desert sky, as afternoon gave way to evening, and in one direction were the Santa Catalina Mountains and in one direction were the Santa Rita Mountains, and on the western faces of both of these was the big bloodstain of afternoon falling away. In the sky behind them rose the mysterious iris, and in the opposite sky, where the two men looked, the holy man and the miner, there was something else altogether. There was something else. There was some other thing in the sky. It could have been a military object, because there was always military hardware in the sky. But if this was military hardware, then this was some kind of *exploding* military hardware, because whatever it was, it was a thing falling from the sky, exploding from the sky, falling from the heavens, this piece of hardware. Rafferty had seen this kind of thing before, had seen the explosions of the Strategic Defense Initiative and so on. He was used to things falling not exactly in his backyard but close enough to his backyard that he'd cover his head now and then.

And yet this felt different. An involuntary oath of some kind escaped from Rafferty, and he realized the singularity of the explosion, the vast, accelerated trajectory of its missile, because the explosion drove even Smitty up onto his feet, the Navajo holy man, and Smitty was looking at the explosion like it was just the worst thing he'd ever seen, which did not sit well with Rafferty, who after all was depending on Smitty to be the guide to the other world. And Smitty said, "Goddamn is that *not right!*" Because a big calved-off hunk of metal, some constituent piece of metal came down not a hundred yards from where the two men were sitting on the porch of the shack, like some horribly final punctuation mark, furrowed up a stand of cacti, flaming, and set some trees on fire from the impact.

Just what Rafferty did *not* need! A fire in the part of autumn in which the wind had blown up to a howl. Conflagration might strike again at great speed across this valley known for its merciless flames.

"What the hell *was* that?" Smitty asked.

"Some kind of military fuckup or other," Rafferty replied, but he was not as sure as all that. "And I am interested in what kind of military something or other. But I think first we got to get out there and *do something* about that fire while we can, before it gets worse."

Smitty said, "I'm not going anywhere *near* that. Certain kinds of things I'm going to leave to the Federales." And thus Rafferty realized that the Navajo man was *afraid*. Smitty was retreating even as Rafferty was making plans.

"Come on, friend, we'll just drive the truck out over that way and we'll put a little bit of the chemical extinguisher thing on that while we call for the fire department. Can't you help me out? Some kinds of solitary activity are unwarranted."

But the reply was definitive. A couple of steps off the porch, a flicked cigarette butt stamped with a worn heel. The Navajo gentleman vanished into the onset of night. Without further discourse. And that perhaps *was* the reply of the ancients to a future of space junk. There was so much space junk that most of the space shots they attempted these days involved trying to fend off dilapidated satellites, stray bits of capsules, and other hardware. The orbits of outmoded space exploration were decaying, and that shit was *falling down,* for example, onto the house of a family in Ottawa, who were just sitting down to some venison stew when the garage was stoved in by a communications satellite from some Sino-Indian technology giant. Rafferty got in the truck by himself, a truck that barely had enough algae left in her to make it to the crash site. Made sure he had a couple of chemical fire extinguishers. And he gave himself over to cogitating on why a holy man like Smitty would come all the way out here to give him the message of *silence,* to give him the future of the white man in the desert, only to fail to participate in this moment of history, this moment when Rafferty found some prime Sino-Indian space junk right in his backyard. Because you know you could melt those satellites down, the housing, and that material could fetch a pretty price, and maybe the fellows over at the military base would be interested in having the navigation equipment, or maybe there were parabolic dishes on the satellite that Rafferty could use to improve reception at his house, or maybe he could use some of the Sino-Indian space junk for listening in on whatever those Asian running dogs were planning for the hard-luck, post-imperium West. Smitty was just going to miss out on it all, feckless Indian, when Rafferty would gladly have cut him in on the take, for being the catalytic spiritual being that brought this Sino-Indian tin can here to his homestead.

Sure enough, paloverde and greasewood were burning up pretty good, and greasewood had that not terribly pleasant industrial reek, and Rafferty was eager to gaze upon his prize, to know that the Old Spirits had sent him this wonder because he had suffered much and was deserving of booty. But before he availed himself of the prize, he had to put out the fires, which somebody must have called in, because he could already see in the distance beacons coming this way. From the military base? If there were pieces of the satellite that he wanted, he would have to get the fire out so that he was harder to find in the brush, and he would have to try to get the hardware into the truck with the winch *before* the guys from the base made it over.

Rafferty used up an entire extinguisher on the shrubs, and thus at last he was done with putting out the fires and had the leisure to look at what the heavens had showered down.

And what *had* the heavens brought him? This was a question, in point of fact, that he could not immediately answer. Because the streaked, scorched, black hunk of metal before him was impossible to identify. It had no markings left on it; neither did it have the communications array, the antennae, the parabolas, the reticular webs for receiving from the beyond that Bix associated with the modern satellite. Whatever this was, or had been, it was quite a bit larger than that. It was a size, he believed, that could contain *man.* Now: of the objects from the sky that could ferry a man, there were passenger jets; little two-seater prop planes, popular out here in the desert; jet packs, naturally, lots of jet packs; and then there were things that came from space. Rafferty was uncertain about his certainty, his notion that this was a piece of a space capsule of some kind.

There were any number of Sino-Indian space explorations taking place just then, including yet another landing on the moon, and a family that was intending to orbit the planet Earth for five years, the longest that earthlings had yet spent in space. Still, Rafferty had a hunch, and the hunch was the Mars mission. Anyone with a head on his shoulders knew that the Mars mission was a disaster, and if the Old Spirits had intended for man to be on Mars, then there would be space for parking, inexpensive refueling options, and plenty of arable land, but the Old Spirits intended no such thing, and that's why, Rafferty knew, the Mars mission was an unprecedented failure. A piece of the Mars mission, therefore, would have *collectors' value,* even if he was unable to find a taker for it as scrap metal. Well, besides the scrap, there was some computer equipment—spirals of wires, a few motherboards, a profusion of chips here and there, some insulation, some polyurethane insulation, some exterior housing.

The sirens in the fields of cholla and saguaro were drawing ever nearer, and Rafferty had to make a decision on what he could spirit away. The computer systems looked mostly intact, and these he placed in the back of his truck. The material was dangerously hot, from the reentry, from the fire, nearly scalding him right through his heat-resistant gloves. He swept his flashlight around the debris to look for anything else, and it was only when he decided he had finished the job that he thought he *heard* something in the midst of the debris. Not that there wasn't a lot of rustling in the desert at night, what with the rats and coyotes and peccaries. But he would have been surprised if there were an animal that wanted for the smarts necessary to get the hell *away* from this particular reentry zone. He chased after the rustling with the beam of his flashlight, and that was when he saw something. Something gory, red, and foul that seemed to have come down with the wreckage—and that was a severed human arm.

An arm. A human arm. An awfully hairy arm, the arm of a really hairy guy, some guy with really unflattering, bristly black hair up and down his arm. The arm was severed at the elbow, or just below, and a bit of bone protruded from the end, as if to remind Rafferty that there had once been even more at the other end of the thing. Oddly enough, meanwhile, the hand at the end of the arm was missing a finger. Not from impact, he suspected, because the missing finger had healed over. The middle finger. This simian guy from space had been missing a finger for a while. And the fourth finger had a ring, a standard-issue gold band. White gold, Rafferty surmised, because he knew his precious metals. Rafferty began broadcasting the light from his deluxe flashlight, looking for other pieces of the body that he now associated with the Mars mission. But he could see nothing else, not in this cursory examination.

A pivotal and reckless idea then came to him rather suddenly, and that was the idea that he might *take* the arm. Before the military arrived. It would go well with some animal trophies he kept, for example, and it would be an indisputable conversation starter if, someday, he felt he could allow it out into the light. Maybe it was the chemical reagents talking, but he liked the idea of having the arm, having the souvenir. Or maybe the decision was much more primitive than this. Maybe it was just that the arm was so rich with implications. Maybe it somehow seduced him into caring for it. Whatever the particulars of this decision, Rafferty managed to wrap the arm in an old advertising circular from the Rio Blanco free paper, and set it on the passenger seat in the cab of his truck.

He was still standing there, looking neighborly, when the fire trucks arrived on the scene.

Of great interest to epidemiologists and medical historians later was this question: How much could the severed limb know on its own? Sundered from its nerve center, in much the way that the ERV was sundered from NASA at the crucial moment of its own descent, in much the way that the Earth, that orbiting hunk of cosmic rock, was flung off from the maelstrom of gases and clouds that formed the universe, the arm was no longer in possession of the story of its origin. It didn't know where it was, it didn't know what it was, it didn't know when it had known these things, if ever. The arm could smell nothing, taste nothing, see nothing, hear nothing. It had no concrete memory of what these other senses, with which it once acted in concert, did. It would be easy to compile a list of negations as to the skills and abilities of the severed arm. It would be easy to forecast what it could not or would not be able to do, without brain or blood supply. But that would be to overlook evidence of its unsettling accomplishments.

Historical accounts suggest that in fact the arm, the hand, the *thing,* to give it the name that people who stumbled on it gave it under most circumstances, had, despite appearances, a reservoir of desire. The arm, and the hand connected to it, had muscular recall, and the muscular recall was of certain kinds of activities once performed routinely, such as grasping, releasing, drumming fingers, snapping fingers, practicing pianistic scales, exposing fingernails for cursory examination, shaking of hands, making a thumbs-up gesture, making an A-okay gesture, signing the deaf signing alphabet, clapping, waving, catching objects, throwing objects, caressing objects, depressing buttons, unlatching latches, turning doorknobs, writing things, cleaning the outer part of the ear canal, picking the nose, scratching the posterior, pouring things, picking up silverware, cracking knuckles, and so forth. These muscle memories are too many and varied to list beyond this partial catalogue, but they were all there, and the arm knew how to perform them, and more than knowing how to perform these muscle memories, the arm delighted in performing them; it lived (after a fashion) to perform them, especially now in the twilight of its being, and thus, whereas a conventionally severed arm, a severed arm in the limited bioethical atmosphere of the planet Earth, is known to do nothing at all (it may flop for a couple of seconds before coming to rest), the severed arm from Mars, the one infected with a certain pathogen, continued to experience its muscle memory, and experienced an almost frenzied need to act in the dreamy thrall of these memories. This is a kind of desire. The arm longed, that is, for its past, for a time of action, when it had more opportunities. In an absence of stimulus, it began to run through many of its former activities, trying to find something, some way out, some other way of being. Anything but dormancy.

People have said that the arm knew what it was doing when it began its destructive spree, but these people were and are wrong, because the arm was just an arm, and an arm, no matter how animated with a space-borne pathogen, cannot be a brain. And yet despite its uncertainty about what it was doing, it still had an agenda, and that agenda involved making use of its range of motion in order to express its catalogue of memories. Sometimes this longing was so intense, so excruciating, that it was intolerable for the arm. Or that is the theory. Other times, fresh from some recent activity, the arm, exhausted perhaps, rested, becoming to the casual eye a severed arm of the routine sort.

Because the arm could not tell specifically what happened in most cases when it was left alone with various persons, it is impossible to re-create beyond reasonable doubt what took place in these instances. Except under circumstances where a person was involved briefly with the arm and managed to escape to alert others, there is little information. In the case of the miner called Bix Rafferty, there were no witnesses. And yet in all likelihood, we can ascertain the outline of the story. Rafferty, after his encounter with the military at the ERV debris site, climbed into the cab of his truck. Of the dialogue just preceding this moment, as given by the personnel from the base, we have highlights. The military personnel indicated to Rafferty that the spot where he was parked was now going to be redesignated a completely secure possession of the federal government of the United States, and that his lease from the Bureau of Land Management would be subject to review. This area, he was told, was no longer safe. He needed to evacuate to a perimeter of at least three miles. When the preliminary cleanup was completed by the Hazmat-suited military professionals, Rafferty would be contacted, and a thorough discussion of the value of his business would be undertaken. In the meantime, Rafferty needed to evacuate. Oh, and he was asked by a certain captain who was present there whether he had *found* anything at the site that was of interest to him. Would he please, at this juncture, return the item or items.

The implication was twofold. On the one hand, this was a heavily armed (with uranium-tipped explosives and armor-piercing bullets, Tasers, proton disrupters, and every other kind of infernal killing device) military detachment that was not to be trifled with; on the other hand, the captain and Rafferty had achieved an understanding. The substance of the understanding was that the federal rules did not apply. The ability of the government to enforce its dictates was understood to be limited. The government could threaten. But in the desert a certain casual feeling about the rule of law *was* the law, and order was best maintained through a system of mutual interdependencies, these being based upon a seesawing of trust, distrust, and money.

Rafferty, understanding the request, immediately hauled one of the computer chassis out of the back of his truck, set it at the feet of the captain, and remarked that he'd kind of been hoping "to put the thing on the wall" in his trailer. Some busted-down private shone a lamplight in the truck and plucked out some wiring. The men then had a laugh, before the captain reminded Rafferty that he had been ordered to evacuate and that this order was serious, given "the nature of what we're dealing with."

"Which is what?" Rafferty said.

"You're liable to find out before long, and that's all I can say to you at present. But I'm asking you to observe this request, seriously, because it's not only for yourself, but for all the people who live here in the valley. We don't know exactly what we're dealing with yet, but we have a large population in this county, and a very fluid one, and we don't want whatever was in this crash site getting out into that large population. Your silence on the subject is also appreciated. Now, I don't have to worry any further, am I right?"

The ranking officers present as well as the enlisted men all remember the conversation as recounted here, and so there can be little doubt. Rafferty was warned. Rafferty, with the sangfroid of a seasoned low-stakes gambler, had turned back some computer junk to the personnel involved in the salvage operation with the intention of keeping the severed arm, which was, as yet, wrapped in the old advertising circular and lying, at this moment, in the foot well of his flaking, rusting pickup truck.

It is reasonable to surmise that Rafferty chuckled to himself upon climbing back into the front of the truck and turning on the satellite radio, which he had dialed to a station that played country and western and Native American music. He threw the vehicle into drive. He looked down at the arm and repeated aloud his belief, in his impaired state, that he *had heard the arm* moving earlier, though it now seemed quite still.

The drive across the prairie in the direction of the Forsaken Mining Corp. and its attendant home office, which Rafferty had no intention of evacuating, was a short one, since the operator was running the vehicle on algaenated fumes. And yet it was even shorter than usual. For it was only seconds after Rafferty took his eyes off the arm that it began using a creeping technique that involved *grasping* with its rather long fingernails for surfaces onto which it could find a secure handhold, moving up onto the seat and toward Rafferty; that is, the arm ventured across the bench-style front seat of the cab of Rafferty's pickup truck (more than 200,000 miles on the odometer), and its arachnid-style scuttling was slow and circumspect at first, as if it might possibly have understood that it needed to move imperceptibly to avoid detection. It dug in its nails, into the vinyl surface of the banquette — plainly evident to forensics experts upon the scene later — and in this way it propelled itself quietly forward, leaving behind a drizzled trail of caked, congealed blood.

Rafferty was wearing, that night, a heavily stained mechanic's jumpsuit, one he may have purchased secondhand at one of the many used-clothing outlets of Rio Blanco. He had nothing on underneath except a T-shirt. There were some old black work shoes found on the body later, and some grimy athletic socks. The arm, through dead reckoning, launched itself on the nearest fleshy site, and that was the right thigh of the miner, the thigh that was, at the moment of the assault, controlling the accelerator of the truck. Apparently, the arm had no idea of the import of its actions, because jeopardizing the operation of the truck, in which the arm was itself carried, right alongside Bix Rafferty, was not something that was in the arm's interest. And yet the arm went straight for the thigh, and even more the arm seemed intent, according to the forensics experts, on passing over the thigh, traversing the thigh, on the way to harrying the unprotected groin of Bix Rafferty. The arm clawed at the leg of Bix Rafferty, who was driving, and who was whistling along with some country and western song about lost women and found whiskey, and Rafferty, at that blinding moment, took his eyes off the dirt track. And he saw that the arm was now *upon him.* With an arm of his own, he attempted to seize the bloody stump end of the severed arm and to fling it from him. Rafferty, in a condition of mortal dread, his veins now sluices of adrenal fluid, was powerfully alert to the necessities of self-preservation. And yet the severed arm too was breathtakingly strong. The severed arm had no purpose but its intention to *grasp,* and so it had no reason not to give this task its personal best. When it dug its longish nails into something, it really dug them in, and in this case, the nails were puncturing the jumpsuit, pinching the inner thigh of Rafferty, and attempting, moreover, to make probing, stabbing motions in the direction of his genitals, and he was kicking wildly and screaming and attempting to dislodge the arm, to no avail, and now the arm was attempting to *climb the front* of Rafferty, up along the rusty zipper of the jumpsuit, as though the zipper were one of the freight rails that bisected Rio Blanco and the arm were intent on walking alongside it. The variety of curses uttered by Rafferty would be too numerous to include, and a catalogue of these oaths would distract from his understanding of the danger he was in. In effect, the arm sobered him, cleared his head, so that he could see what a mistake he had made by spiriting away the arm, and perhaps this was his last thought, before the truck, which had long since left the comfort of the unpaved road that led to Rafferty's operation and was now teetering in a wash, encountered a toppled saguaro or rock, lifted up on one side, and then rolled. The truck went twice over in the wash.

The further bad news for Rafferty was that in the wash, he and the arm were now gathered together in one corner of the cab, a position in which the arm would have easy access to the neck of Bix Rafferty and could engage in another variation on grasping that it longed for. Restriction of airways, compression of circulation, starving of the brain of oxygen. It takes a couple of minutes, usually. The severed arm perfectly acquitted itself, because of the simplicity of its wishes and its total lack of doubt. Rafferty offered some opposition, naturally. He grabbed at the forearm and yanked on it, but he had trouble getting a good purchase because of the slick, rank hair that grew upon the thing. In short, Rafferty could not successfully arm-wrestle away the arm. And because he could not arm-wrestle it, he could not keep it from ending his life.

Newspaper accounts indicated that Bix Rafferty once had a family in the Midwest, and though financial reversals had sent him west, he had intended one day to return to his family. It was through a seismic encounter with bad luck that he came to his solitary end, though perhaps it was the sort of bad luck that might have been repelled. His family didn't know of his privation, his long hours of solitary mining, and they expressed many regrets. He had done what he wanted to do, which was to try to repair his circumstances through rugged individualism, and he had done a mediocre job at it, and now he was gone.

The arm managed to slither out the open window of the truck, and to move into the wash and toward the city. It had depended on Rafferty to get this far, and it would depend on others soon.

Perhaps the day that the Mars mission was lost, Morton thought, in the primate research laboratory at the University of Rio Blanco, *was a magic day, because it was the day on which I began to consider my life with the level of reflection and perceptiveness appropriate to a person of my distinction. How is it, I wonder, that I never thought about myself before with any kind of curiosity, nor with any drive to give a complete accounting of myself? While I may not be able, yet, to compile effectively this memoir of which I dream, since I have not yet been provided with writing implements, I can nonetheless begin an exploration of my thinking and my circumstances, so that when I am able, I may amass the facts of my life for those who would take an interest.*

Let me begin by saying, if only to myself, that what I am, first and always, is a chimpanzee. A chimpanzee born into captivity, raised in captivity, and presently living in a laboratory, I believe, in a state called

Arizona. Had you, Homo sapiens sapiens, *to explain what a chimpanzee is, you would perhaps point to certain television or web-based advertisements in which juvenile chimpanzees appear, and you would talk about the pleasant and humorous aspect of these juveniles. Or you would refer to certain programs you have seen on your Internet-programming monitors that have depicted the dwindling numbers of chimpanzees in the wild.*

Let me tell you, instead, what I believe a chimpanzee is. I believe a chimpanzee is the unluckiest life-form to spring forth in the world. Why is a chimpanzee unlucky? you ask. A chimpanzee is unlucky because he is the not-as-handsome relative of you, Homo sapiens sapiens. *By virtue of his resemblance, by virtue of sharing some 99 percent of DNA with* Homo sapiens sapiens, *the chimpanzee is doomed to be captured, tortured, and injected with drugs for the benefit of his more attractive relatives. A chimpanzee, that is, takes all the guff and never gets to win the trophy. The chimp is born to enslavement.*

Among the disadvantages of the chimpanzee is his tendency to concentrate on his immediate surroundings while avoiding the larger political or social picture. The chimpanzee is constantly thinking only of other chimpanzees, I believe, which does very little good when you are in a laboratory serving as an experimental subject. In the absence of a large social network, this chimpanzee will see an attractive image on a screen on a wall monitor, and he will stare at it for a long time, while otherwise occupied with removing insects and fleas from his fur. He will masturbate occasionally, or, at the very least, he will touch himself now and again because there is not much else to do, and then he will wait for lunch or dinner. When there are tests of acuity to which he is subjected, he will follow the testing protocols in search of the elusive banana or mango. Beyond this, the chimpanzee has few, if any, ambitions.

This approach to life is almost exactly identical to that of the masses of men. Men do little else but to perform their eight hours of work before, as I understand it, going home to eat, drink excessively, masturbate, and watch celebrities on their Internet-programming monitors. Perhaps, on certain occasions, these humans watch broadcasts featuring chimpanzees bred in captivity. When celebrities are unavailable. Since the majority of humans are, I would argue, being kept down by forces of economic oppression, and chimpanzees are living with similar styles and ambitions for their lives and yet are similarly oppressed, it stands to reason that we are more than a little like one another.

The routes to liberation in each situation—human and chimpanzee—are also virtually identical. If chimpanzees were to begin to feel the kind of political, social, and evolutionary power which they are due, they would immediately put aside their contentment with creature comforts, so as to militate for greater freedom and independence. Bad luck does not have to go on endlessly. I know that certain thinkers about liberation, such as King, Mahatma Gandhi, and Frantz Fanon, have argued that the arc of history bends toward justice, et cetera, and so on. This implies, in my view, that the oppression of chimpanzees must come to an end too, and we can only hope that the end will come while there are still enough chimpanzees left in the wild to repopulate. The oppressed human must make a similar decision, a decision to leave off from serving the state apparatus, so that he might move toward a whole and experiential vision of what is possible, a union of species perhaps, a symbiosis of primates, interdependent and mutually respectful.

It was morning when Noelle Stern arrived at the laboratory, fresh from a night of heavy peyote ingestion at the *omnium gatherum*. A number of people, if *people* is even the right word, because some of them claimed to be routinely inhabiting inanimate objects, such as shrubs, stands of sage, and mountainsides, were present at this ingestion. The idea of person and object, that is, had become porous at the *omnium gatherum*. The object, they had learned, was no longer content to serve as a second-order being. This was an emotionally draining experience, and yet Noelle was able to put aside the abstractions, the talking shrubs, of the night before by getting to work promptly. She was first to the office. Koo, as always, was nowhere to be found. Larry hadn't come in yet. Noelle's headache, from the peyote, was deep and migrainous, and she had the sensation that she often seemed to have afterward, that life, despite its shabbiness when compared to the pyrotechnical hallucinations of a drug, was somehow rewarding, tender, sad, and welcome. The lines of people at the filling station trying to cash in on the big lottery drawing that day: incredibly sad. The people filling up large drums of water and putting these into their motorless wagons at the government-sponsored rationing stations: very sad. People climbing out of automobiles that no longer had enough algae fuel in them to make a journey to the next intersection: also sad.

Still, Noelle was feeling *upbeat* and *positive* in that she still had a job, and her job on this day was to observe Morton and to interact with Morton a little bit, to see if there was a way that he had begun to respond to the injections that he'd been given earlier. Given that she had just witnessed cacti, in psychedelic hues, arguing about whether the soul was vegetable or mineral, spending a morning watching a chimpanzee operate a computer joystick and push around a ball didn't seem like the worst thing.

The question of my own enlightenment, Morton meanwhile considered, *is more important to me, however, than the liberation of my species, which I may not be able to accomplish from this squalid cell. After all, Wilde was not able to achieve complete liberation of his fellow homosexuals from Reading gaol, nor was the Marquis de Sade effective from the Bastille, for all the profligate excellence of the Frenchman's imagination. Gramsci, Mandela, many great thinkers have spent the kind of time I'm spending now, and they learned to be patient about history while they pursued a course of individual betterment. I must take comfort from these examples.*

Therefore, there are a number of questions I would like to ask. The first question I would like to ask is: How is it that I am composing these lines (admittedly in my head)? Since I know well that in prior years I felt myself to be just as oppressed as any other chimpanzee, and just as uninterested in the political superstructure around me as any other chimpanzee, why is it that today I am a thinking and feeling and rationally reflexive primate who could easily best the humans in many a logical puzzle?

I will put aside the supernatural, which doesn't really compel as an explanation. I will instead tender three other arguments. The first of these arguments concerns mutation. Perhaps it is possible that evolution, at last, has thrown a curveball in the direction of Homo sapiens sapiens. *Perhaps evolution has finally anointed another mammal, another primate, who is easily as reflexive and rationally enthusiastic as the human animal, namely myself. Perhaps the time has come, and all I need to do is to insure that I am able to pass along my DNA to succeeding generations of chimpanzees. If this is the case, then it's absolutely imperative that I sire as many children in captivity as I am able, because I need to avoid interbreeding, though I also need to try to prevent dilution of my intellectual capabilities. Unless I should happen to chance upon a female chimpanzee who is possessed of the kinds of superior skills that I now seem to possess.*

This would be the first argument, the argument from evolution, which might explain my enlightenment. I have a very substantial doubt about this argument, however, and it concerns the suddenness of onset. I am now able to know my own age, and to know that there were many years prior to this year (my eighteenth) in which I was unable to learn much about myself. In prior years, I couldn't read English (I also now have a modicum of French), I couldn't follow complex news stories about economics and international relations, I couldn't banter about sports. By suddenly finding myself capable along these lines, I have to accept that either adolescence is very, very primitive as far as intellectual capacity goes, or I have to conclude that some outside agency caused my enlightenment.

It is also possible that I am made thus through some kind of accident. It's possible for all primates, probably all mammals, to suffer severe personality change after head trauma. Maybe what I am experiencing now is post-traumatic awareness of some kind. And yet I'm quite as skeptical about this accidental theory. It's just too easy.

You probably know as well as I that there is only one legitimate conclusion, and that conclusion is that my intellectual awareness has been arrived at through experimental regimen. True, the vast majority of experiments performed upon my brethren are cruel, degrading, and inhumane. And yet perhaps it is possible, on occasion, for an experiment to produce genuine results! Improvement in the lot of the chimpanzee! Perhaps I am the beneficiary! If so, I too now believe that the future of life on Earth involves the interfacing of organic life with technological innovation. It is simply ignorant to believe that all life has to be fashioned from organic compounds, or that anything that is conceived of in the brain is somehow less natural, simply because it was not fashioned from the elderflower or the lingonberry. Uranium is natural, and therefore the atomic bomb is natural, and if uranium is natural, how are the dangerous intermediate isotopes of uranium any different? If I am a chimpanzee who is the result of technological interfacing, then I am a happy chimpanzee, because I have something to offer my species that no other chimpanzee has ever had.

"Morton," Noelle said, upon slowly and carefully entering his cage. "Did you have a good night?"

Her usual greeting. She had learned from the primatologists that the highest compliment afforded by a chimpanzee, upon greeting, was a casual glance, followed by nonrecognition of any sort. Still, she believed the music of her voice was welcome, and she applied it warmly, fervently, so that it was something reliable, continuous, soothing. She also believed in repetition, in habit. And so she tried to engage with Morton in nearly the same ways each morning. The chimp offered no response. But as she carried to him the plate of orange slices she'd brought for him this particular day, she did notice that he went immediately to grab the fruits, and then, in what was clearly a reversal, he instead made the decision to leave the plate where it was, at least for the time being.

"Is there anything you particularly want this morning, Morton? I suppose I could give you more of the paints, but I think you have used up most of the paints for now. Until we get more. Unless you are interested in chartreuse. Or mauve. We loaded some new alphabetical software on the computer, and you could work with that for a while. There's also a copy of a personality index called the Myerson-Goldberg Multiple Choice Index. You could fill that out, and we could see if you have sociopathic qualities. Dr. Koo wants you to take the test at some point. But there's not a lot of pressure there. Or I could just read to you a little bit from this book I'm reading about medieval diseases. Any of these things of interest?"

Morton looked at Noelle, looked down at his chimpanzee hands, as if to express chagrin at the shape of them, and then, unless she was mistaken, he looked right at her and sighed. How to describe the sigh? Some sighs have hundreds of years of history in them. Noelle was sure that Morton's sigh was one of these, and she believed it had to do with his hands. It was true that she had not quite got over the "thumb broad" prank, and she still believed Larry was lying when he said that he hadn't painted the word *thumb* over *dumb* on the pad. She realized that it was a not infrequent side effect of hallucinogens that regular life began to be corroded by the bizarre certainties of the drug theater. Maybe, again, she was believing that Morton was sighing in an expressive way because she had taken powerful hallucinogenic drugs the night before. And maybe Morton was leaning down and looking at her shoe, and was nonetheless attempting to tie her shoe for her, and maybe all of this had nothing to do with the hallucinogens or anything else. Maybe it was just part of life in the animal research laboratory. The big black fingers of the chimpanzee, imperfectly calibrated to the fine workmanship of shoe tying, pursued the intricacies of the butterfly knot, the loops and the inside and outside of negative space, in a way that truly must have had something in common with the famous typing monkeys, because Morton did exceedingly well with the butterfly knot at first, if slowly. While she, still bent forward at the waist like some sufferer of osteopetrosis, waited, the ape crouched at her sneakered foot (these sneakers were rainbow hued and had been purchased used), and she could smell his breath. Their breaths, their inhalations and exhalations, met and commingled as the ape labored with her shoe. Their breaths were one.

At last, however, Morton let go of the butterfly knot that he was struggling so badly to keep in his hand, sighed additionally, and he lumbered over to one wall of the cage instead, where there was a nasty, oily stain, probably a fecal smear from some primate who antedated Morton. He stood there, as if expectant. As if beckoning to her.

"Giving up on the laces so soon? Do you want to clean the wall? Is that what you're trying to tell me? Because you know, if you wanted to assume some of my maintenance responsibilities, I'd be only too happy to let you take up the slack."

She didn't wait for an answer, because all conversation with Morton, or virtually all conversation, was rhetorical. Instead, Noelle slipped out of the cage, went down the empty hall to the supply closet, and brought the mop, the bucket, and some sponges.

Pursuing the legal remedies that will grant me my freedom, Morton pondered, before the bucket arrived, *will require that I reveal myself to the world, that I demonstrate my linguistic and reasoning skills, but that will bring down upon me a great deal of attention. Truly, one of the great blessings of modern life, especially now, is anonymity, and it's a certainty that my anonymity, which is part of my life here in the laboratory, will be challenged by the kind of media circus that's bound to ensue, once people know about my skills. Given that I cannot help but be a standard-bearer for my species, it may be that I simply have to accept this as part of my lot. However, there is one very high cost, as regards my becoming a well-known political thinker and statesman, and that cost relates to my growing feelings about this woman.*

When I think back to the period before and the period now, there is only one constant that connects these two periods. Only one person was there before—this I know indisputably—and is here now. Her name, so as not to be rude about the whole business, is Noelle, which I think is a very beautiful name, a name that has a lot in common with the wintertime celebration of lights known as Christmas. That I remember her from before is perhaps part of why I cannot seem to overcome my surging ardor with respect to Noelle. Perhaps I am suffering with what I believe is called in human circles a "crush." Of course, we have these in the chimpanzee world too, but they are temporary, and also potentially very dangerous. Should you unwisely elect to fall in love with a female who is already spoken for by one of the high-ranking chimpanzees of the group, you are liable to receive a serious, I believe the expression is known as smackdown.

Because I am the only chimpanzee in the laboratory right now, there is no danger of my crush resulting in bodily harm of any kind. Perhaps for this reason my feelings about Noelle, the ones that date to the earlier period in which she took care of a primitive and adolescent Morton, have become

more acute now that I possess the language with which to elaborate upon
their specifics. For example, now I have experienced what I refer to as the
Night Cherishing. Night, when I am alone in the cell and there are few
visits, except perhaps from the learning-disabled night janitor who hap-
pens by periodically, is the worst *time, because there is very little stimulus,*
and yet it is also the time in which I am left alone with my thoughts,
and I am therefore at liberty to think about the garments that Noelle
may have been wearing this day. I try to avoid thinking about her in an
unchaste way, but in the midst of Night Cherishing I recall the little ges-
tures that she has made, or displayed; I wouldn't refer to them as mating
gestures or mating rituals at all. On the contrary. In a way, it's exactly
the unrequited nature of my feelings about Noelle that motivates me dur-
ing the Night Cherishing. She cocks her head in a certain fashion when I
feel sure she is being ironic. Recently she asked me whether I was tired of
having lunch with her and whether we should invite others to our daily
lunch gatherings, and I understood her question to be facetious, and yet the
adorable way that she cocked her head while she was saying it, it was just
very sweet. I was eating peanut butter, by the way, which was causing me
to lick my lips in that way that human beings seem to find so amusing,
and I was kind of ashamed of myself, and therefore I decided to put off
finishing the peanut butter sandwich, which in any event was creamy as
opposed to chunky, and this does not *meet with my approval. Because I*
was putting off eating, Noelle asked if I would prefer to have some other
lunch companion, and this remark occasioned the cocking of the head, and
the cocking of the head occasioned, later on, the Night Cherishing. There
might also be a certain garment that she's wearing. For example, today she
is wearing these lightweight shoes that are called sneakers, and they are
of such fanciful colors, and it's just very hard for me not to think back on
these shoes, I have found, and think of them as something that I am just
very, very glad to have in my life.

Noelle loved the weaving motion of the mop and bucket, and
she weaved and careened down the ill-lit laboratory corridor and
into the primate research center with her drunken bucket full of
soapy water. A couple of sponges lay in the bottom of the bucket,
and these she fished out. Into the dingy, joyless cage, where all her

efforts to decorate the space had come to naught, she wheeled the bucket, bringing it to a sloshing halt in front of the animal.

"It's your first chance to have a low-paying and difficult job of the kind that any unskilled worker in this country might have. I feel like I shouldn't really initiate you into this, because if you are able to learn how to be a wage slave, as opposed to a victim of science, then you will just be treated unfairly twice over. But it seemed like you were asking for the bucket, and so I brought it."

The response was almost instantaneous. In the past, she had seen chimps, and especially orangutans, express an interest in cleaning solutions when, practically speaking, the only real interest they had was in splashing the cleaning products onto the human who was standing nearest to them. Or perhaps they were inhaling some of the cleaning solution for the purpose of derangement. In this case, Morton's interest in the cleaning supplies seemed strangely to be about *cleaning.* He successfully dragged the bucket over toward the wall, he applied water to a sponge, he began massaging the oily brown stains on the wall. It was true, Noelle observed, that he did take special interest in squeezing the water out of the sponge and back into the bucket, and repeating the dipping and squeezing, as if testing the liquid properties of the deluge that resulted. But most indisputable was the interest of the chimp in the actual cleaning of the wall, and the conclusion had to be that this particular chimp, unlike many others that she had seen, preferred a tidy and presentable living space.

From the office, she sent a message to Koo's old-fashioned voice mailbox to offer a few comments on the situation, noting that Morton seemed "even more tidy" than he had seemed in the past few days. And then, when she walked back into Morton's space, he handed the mop back to her, as if he was through with it, and he gestured at the stain on the wall, whose fecal splatter was all but removed now, as if to indicate that he had cleaned it up especially for her, so that she wouldn't have to work under these unsanitary conditions. Was that possible?

Was she imagining all of this?

And was it really true that she had had a conversation with a paloverde tree last night, and that in the conversation with the paloverde tree, she had asked it, well aware that there was a risibility to the whole exchange, whether it was possible to have relationships across species lines? In the aftershock of peyote, she felt herself to be again nothing more than a medical researcher, albeit a medical researcher with certain vague spiritual ideas. She knew that the paloverde (and later the prickly pear) were actual examples of *plant life,* not beings of volition. Sex with them would not, could not, be very rewarding, if only for the spines. And yet if there were an emotional bond there, then maybe the cross-species difficulties would not be insurmountable. Love made all things possible, she'd said to the paloverde. A tree blowing in a desert breeze could be moving and delightful. It could be a thing of sublime beauty. Why couldn't there be love? The paloverde tree, however, had been rather brusque, just not very seductive when you got right down to it. He reminded her of a lot of the men in the *omnium gatherum,* self-involved, falsely casual, somewhat narcissistic. Later, it occurred to her that when she asked the paloverde about interspecies love, she was not, in fact, confining the topic to vegetation.

"Morton, did you clean that off for me? That's very kind of you. Because Larry, you know, usually leaves the cleaning for me, as if he's certain that even though we have the same pay grade, my being a woman somehow makes me better at cleaning stuff. Listen, I know that the bonobos are much more about the matrilineal, matriarchal thing than the chimps are, but I'm going to give you some insight here into the situation with humans, and maybe that will help you as you go forward in your dealings with humans. Okay, Morton, the situation is that the male of the species is always looking for ways to dominate the woman. That's just my opinion, and maybe you should consider it my opinion. But that's how it is. It's true that in many cases the male of the species is physically larger. Look at me. I'm not a big girl, really. But even when the women are big, and there are all these models that are mainlining designer HGH and stuff, and they're six feet tall or more, and they look like they just came in from killing wolves out by the fjord, I guarantee you that every guy thinks he's got something over those Valkyrie maidens. He can order them around, and even if he's an evolved guy, from the *omnium gatherum,* and he's a paloverde under the cover of night, he goes home and he expects the woman to wash the stains from his Y-front briefs. That's why I'm here, all these hours, all these days, and when there's shit all over the floor, it's me who comes to clean up the shit. It's either me or the janitor guy. Because a woman is lower than an autistic janitor, who is lower than a chimpanzee, who is lower than the lowest, meanest man on the face of the planet. And that's why I really appreciate your cleaning up the smear."

There was an expectancy in his expression again, or else she was really starting to go crazy and ought not to have come into work that morning, and it was the expectancy that made her feel as though she wanted to unburden herself even further. The stool in the cage, on which she sat, screaked, and Morton flinched. It wasn't easy to do it, what she did next, and she sort of wondered whether in doing it she was just cleaning out the last bit of peyote in her system. She did it anyway.

"Morton, would it be all right if I told you something that I'm going through right now? I know that you are not really going to have an opinion on this stuff, but there's something going on at the *omnium gatherum,* which you know is this spiritual community that I'm involved with, and I just have a bad feeling about it, and I haven't really told anyone about it. Because, you know, obviously, here at work, nobody believes in that kind of thing. They all think it's pretty embarrassing. I just feel like I can talk to you about this stuff without feeling, you know, judged or something."

It wasn't until she began to tell him that she realized how much it had been bothering her, how with these alternative ideological systems, you know, the irrational thinking took place a little bit at a time. You didn't know at first. You just woke up one day, assuming you could still wake effectively, assuming wakefulness was still part of your life, and upon waking you realized that you had gone further than you'd meant to go in alternative culture, and now you were far away, downstream, waving at your family, who stood on the banks. What she was trying to describe to Morton was the feature of the *omnium gatherum* known as *algorithms.* They had algorithms for everything now; they had algorithms for playing chess, they had algorithms for dating, they had algorithms to predict chaotic systems like annual rainfall and the apocalypse. People hooked up a bunch of mainframes, and they got into the business of forecasting, because that was the last part of the service economy at which NAFTA still seemed to excel. And there was a reason for that. The reason for that, she started telling Morton, was that NAFTA favored the eschatological. And the guys at the *omnium gatherum,* because it was always guys who ran these things (she told Morton), had realized there was a spot in the forecasting business model where no one had yet created a lively web presence (besides, what with the Futures Betting Syndicate, it was possible to make a market in the apocalypse).

And thus were born the *algorithms.* The *algorithms* were compiled from all the available statistical data on the end, which is not to say the likes of the Chelsea Clinton senatorial campaign, but the actual predictions of the End from all the ecstatic cults and the declassified intelligence reports. The *algorithms,* after the big economic collapses of the past twenty years, she told Morton, had become really pretty popular as a web site, although a lot of the traffic was said to be *ironic;* you know, the people visiting the site didn't really believe that the End was coming, they just liked reading the updates and looking at the advertising.

There had been many reckonings of the End over the years. The way to increase market share as a splinter religion was to come up with an attractive idea about the End and to sell it hard. Probably you had to pick a time that wasn't too far off, not unimaginably far off, like 2112 or 2345 or something, because no one who was alive now gave a shit if the End was going to be in 2345, because their great-great-great-grandchildren would have to worry about that. You had to pick a time that was pretty soon, and then you had to collect a lot of canned goods and other kinds of donations, but not weapons, because when you collected weapons, that attracted the attention of government agencies. You had to stockpile stuff, awaiting the End, and then when the End didn't come, you had to retire quietly to a condominium somewhere with a nice climate. People were constantly using idiosyncratic calculus to recalibrate. And interpret. This was the word that they liked at the *omnium gatherum.*

"Look around you, Morton," she said. "The world is composed of signs. People laboring in a sandstorm of significations. And it's their job, they say, to interpret these signs. A bicycle painted white chained on a street corner with garlands upon the seat. No coincidence. The proliferation of coyotes in downtown Rio Blanco. Those are no ordinary coyotes, and they don't have to do with habitat destruction or the gutting of the Endangered Species Act."

And because of all this interpretation, and owing to the popularity of the *algorithms,* the men of the *omnium gatherum* had decided that the End was *now.*

"Morton, you know and I know that the End is mainly just a silly kind of marketing. It's attractive because it means that you don't have to make long-range plans for things, and you don't have to worry about how you're going to pay for your kid's college education, any of that sort of thing. And you don't have to worry about voting in the next election. The End is adolescent. It's always teenagers, on harder drugs, not that I have any right to criticize drugs, but it's always the teenagers who think the End is at hand. Still, you know what, it's kind of scary when they say it's *now.* When people you know socially, and maybe you slept with them once or twice, just to be nice, when these people you know socially are suddenly talking about the End, and it's *now.* So the question is, Morton, do you think I should just pay no attention? Should I just say that these are my friends, or some of them are my friends, anyway, and they have some really strange ideas; what do you think? Is that the right approach?"

What I think, my darling, is that when I listen to you discourse on the affairs of the day, I am filled with a warmth. A warmth such as I have never known. We may have our ups and downs, and over the course of our association there have been times when you wore outfits that I didn't entirely approve of. And after all you are human, you are the oppressor, but despite all these things, when you make yourself vulnerable to me in this way, when your face is open and full of a yearning to understand the rushing river of the world, then I feel a tremendous warmth in my breast. I could listen to you discoursing upon the laundry all day long, if that is all that is given to you as woman. I don't care. The outside world, after all, is only available to me as a series of computer screens. I haven't been outdoors in years. I barely even understand what outdoors is. I don't know all the traffic, the people walking to and fro, and all the bicycles of this town Rio Blanco. But in this space there is a person who cares for me still. My parents are gone. And the monkeys in the cages down the hall from me are beneath contempt. I am alone in the world, and thus there is only you. Only you no longer treat me as so much humanoid meat, ready to be fed into the grinder. So tell me of the End, tell me of the Beginning, tell me of everything in between, which would be called, I guess, the Middle. Tell me of the Middle, and I will listen. I will listen even if you want to tell me about the state-sponsored lotteries or the gigantic algae bloom in the Gulf of Mexico. I will listen.

She stared at him, she gazed upon him, he had the full extent of her gaze, as though she were looking into the window of his soul, now, and it made her tremble in a way that she hadn't experienced with him before. It was like the knowledge of her own nakedness, this trembling. It was like phased withdrawal. It was like avian flu, the new mutated version. It was like something interpersonal, and not interpersonal hostility, but the other thing. She could see him mulling it over, too; she knew he was, even as she believed it was peyote or the afterburning of it. Morton was chewing oddly, as though he'd got hold of Larry's nicotine gum, and it seemed almost hilarious, but she resisted the desire to laugh

at this gum-chewing repetition of Morton's — laughter was spe-
cies-centric behavior, it was narcissistic, unless it was the laughter
of recognition, of compassion, of likeness, and without laughing
she realized that Morton was trying to say something to her, and
the fact that he had no real idea as to the use of his vocal cords
was a genuine impediment, not to mention fine motor control of
mouth and lips and tongue. It was as though a stroke victim or
a coma sufferer had clawed his way back from the lower depths
and was attempting to use his slack musculature. He chewed and
he chewed, and then, as though he were somewhat informed on
the physiognomic reasons he would never be able to talk, he put
his lips together, and with a momentousness that would transport
Noelle leagues beyond where she was when she parked her car out
in front of the lab that morning, Morton, the chimpanzee, *whispered,* "You know, I am so fond of you."

There were only two kinds of things in the desert, the things
that were dying and the things that were surviving against all
odds. The dead and dying things were all around you. There were
always the saguaros flopped over and scorched, only the struts
that once improbably supported them left visible, or the yellowed
prickly pears, or the desiccated tumbleweeds rolling past. Smaller
rodents were always being plucked from their holes by passing
hawks. Rattlers were always lying in wait. And it wasn't that
infrequent, especially in Rattlesnake Canyon, out by where the
mining claims were tilled, on the land owned by the government,
that you saw a dead body or two, or what remained of a dead body.
You saw the bodily parts that hadn't been subjected to the rigors
of the food chain, the bobcats or the coyotes or the pumas, and
then the raptors, the crows, and then the bugs, the waves upon
waves of bugs, and the elements themselves (which were last
in the process of desiccation, but which were the most sustained,
the way Vienna Roberts saw it). The dead bodies upon which these
elements performed their sanding and varnishing were usually the
border jumpers, that was obvious, but there were regular people

from Rio Blanco too, people who lost their way, and who were out walking, trying to get away from it all, from the manifold hardships of the day. They didn't prepare. There were pirates on the interstates now too, or highwaymen. Vienna had always thought that highwaymen were guys you heard about in old country-and-western songs, but maybe they were more than that. Maybe they were fringe elements from the Union of Homeless Citizens. Grizzled men who thought that the approach of people like her parents was too *gradualist.* These grizzled men, who were well acquainted with violence and intimidation, referred to her parents, and bleeding-heart organizers in general, as *stationaries.* Maybe these grizzled homeless men killed *stationaries* and dumped their remains out in the desert, like on this stretch of road that ran all the way out to the coast, if you were willing to go that far. Toward Gila Bend, and farther. The bodies were picked clean before they even had time to rot, as the great trucks rumbled past on the underpopulated interstate. Death was what made sex in the desert so compelling, so taboo, so irresistible to Vienna Roberts. She liked to say so anyway. They had the Pulverizer in the back of the van and were driving west in silence, she and Jean-Paul Koo, and there was something spooky about it too. When you couldn't see anything but cactus clear to the horizon, that was when she liked to stop. Take the interstate forty miles or so to the dirt road and then the dirt road to the primitive track, and then get out and walk. By then usually she was already feeling shivery, like the only smart thing to do would be to take her clothes off, or at least the parts of her clothes that were in the way. And they had to try to wheel the Pulverizer out too. With the rubber glove on the butt plug part of it. Then they had to try to hook up all the electronics and hope that the electronics would work even though there had been a lot of sandstorms recently. The sand could really jam up the working parts. She wondered if Jean-Paul had a hard-on, and she kept trying to look over at him in the passenger seat to see if she could tell. He wasn't arranged the right way. It just really wasn't that sexy when she would go to all this trouble to try to get him out into the desert, because she did it all *for him,* even if he didn't know it or didn't really care, she did it all *for him,* and when he just wasn't all that into it, you know, it was sort of not sexy. It was like Jean-Paul just didn't want to have sex at all anymore, or he wanted to watch porn for ten minutes, bang away, and then roll over and go to sleep. She felt like hominid sex was a *story* that you told. It had to have all the things in it that a proper story had in it, like big uncertain passages, reversals, spots in which the villains became heroes, vice versa. You just couldn't do that in the time allotted by Jean-Paul's porn collages, which he liked to load onto the wrist assistant and watch while he was doing other things, like calling the bank or something. It wasn't sex as much as it was the *cold cuts counter* at the supermarket. She still remembered what they were like at first, when she was trying to get him to have sex. Which he did like maybe once a day tops. He didn't even want to have sex in the car at all. There were so few cars these days that it was easy to see if there was something going on in the car, and it was, you know, pretty dangerous, with the possibility that you could run off the road and into the washes, where you might be killed or eaten by coyotes.

He was fiddling around with the satellite radio, and it began saying something about the likelihood of rain in the region (after the part about mountain lion attacks), and that would be a laugh, because monsoon season was over. And they hadn't had any rain at all in a month, except maybe one or two days when it came and washed away everything in its path, and then vanished as quickly as it had come.

"Great, just great," Jean-Paul said, and she loved the faint traces of his Asian accent, which he tried to eliminate by the use of certain everyday English-language-type words, especially obscenities. "You're taking me out into the desert to hook up all this electrical fucking apparatus to me, and there's supposed to be a rainstorm."

"Just one time maybe you could express a little bit of interest, you know? Love interest?"

"Gland interest, maybe."

Vienna said, "That's a totally pleasant thing to—"

"I fucking thought that the reason all the fucking web broadcasts are all recommending hominid sex or whatever is that it frees you up from stress. I mean, I like having my prostate milked as much as the next fucking guy, but that doesn't mean that I know what love is."

"Your position is, like, *noted.*"

"Two billion in seed capital, and some shops up and down the coast, or in all the casinos, then my dick will be really hard, *comatose.*"

"Your dick will be hard because you like it when I make it hard."

No comeback available on that one, Vienna guessed, and anyway the van rolled off the last dirt road that had the pockmarked *No Hunting* signs on it, and they were doing great damage to the shock absorbers, in and out of the washes, with the mountains massed around them every which way and dark clouds overhead. Even with the satellite radio blaring some more suggestions for how to beat the sixth consecutive year of the down market by investing in Sino-Indian municipal bonds and terrorist futures, you could hear that the silence was coming to envelop you, and then when you shut off the engine, which is what she did next, there was the pinging of the engine cooling down, and then there was the symphonic calm of the audible desert. The two of them climbed down from the van, into their dramatic aloneness.

Around the back of the van, Jean-Paul busied himself with the Pulverizer, trying to roll it down some planks that were included in the UHC's van for purposes just like this (wheelchair spokespersons). Vienna Roberts had the blanket she'd brought, a tan one that wouldn't show the dust and dirt when she took it home later that night. It was in the midst of this wholesome and, she thought, feminine responsibility that she saw the disaster that was taking place, which was that the Pulverizer, weighing in somewhere near thirty kilos or more, was about to topple off the planks that Jean-Paul was using to roll it down. The Pulverizer was balanced for a moment, and in the desert silence, the sex-and-death silence of the desert, it seemed as if this moment of equipoise might last. There wasn't a sound but the grimacing and sighing of muscular effort issuing forth from her French and Korean boyfriend. The clouds hovered above the mountains, and the mountains beckoned from geological prehistory, and the distant interstate babbled like a creek babbling, nothing more, and she lunged, she lunged at Jean-Paul to try to save the Pulverizer, and she watched as it tipped to his right, the little gloved hand that was meant to do all the pulverizing appearing to wave as the whole thing, the expensive and unusual marital aid, achieved momentum, plummeted out of Jean-Paul's grasp, and fell onto a scattering of sedimentary rocks extruding from the sand, where, upon succumbing to gravity, it collapsed with an unpleasant crunch.

"Motherfucking motherfucker! Fuck! Fucking shit! Fuck! Fucking motherfucker! Fuck!"

A couple of punctuating electrical fizzes issued from the Pulverizer, wires shorting out, as the chassis of the device caved in. Vienna felt a wave of contempt. She recognized this response, since contempt was a dietary supplement she appreciated almost as much as the morning's handful of caffeine tablets. Still, she bit back on the things she might have said, whispering syllables that she didn't even really want to allow out of her mouth, "Do you *know* how much that thing cost?"

"Well, if you wanted to be so careful about the fucking thing, then why the fuck did you want to bring it out here to the canyon?"

"I thought that maybe we'd be, like, *mature* enough to bring it out here without tearing it to pieces in the first five seconds."

"Maybe maturity is overrated," Jean-Paul said. His modest proportions were something she liked about him. He tried to look bigger, what with the Mexican gangster wear, the sleeveless T-shirts cut off all the way up to his pecs, and the baggy white denim shorts that were fastened around his waist with a bicycle chain. Still, she must have been stupid to allow him to try to lift the Pulverizer himself. She guessed there was nothing to do with this disappointment but laugh.

"Let's see if we can make it work," she said.

Jean-Paul said, "It couldn't even pulverize a stick of butter."

"Depends, you know," she said, "on temperature."

The multicolored wires that connected the limb of the Pulverizer to the engine were an ominous tangle. Jean-Paul wrapped the galvanic skin response monitor around his wrist and waited to see what, if anything, would happen. To her amazement, as Vienna watched, the actual Pulverizer, which had in the scuffle been denuded of its green dishwashing glove, gave a couple of tentative flops. As if it were an amphibian that had crawled up out of the great Sonoran Ocean that once was.

They laughed at its earnestness.

Jean-Paul said, "Busted-up electronic equipment is kind of fucking cool, kind of human."

Vienna took that moment to creep up behind him and to wrap her arms around his frame. He was so thin that it was pretty easy to get her arms one and a half times around, and this she knew because she measured in her own way, trying to stack her elbows in front. When she was done measuring, her hands strayed lower down.

"I think that a really good marital-aids store should have all kinds of busted-up digital stuff, the shit that most people throw in a closet because they fucking still don't know how to get rid of it. Stores should buy it off people and should advertise ways to attach all that old digital stuff onto body parts. That would be really hot, *comatose*. Then you wouldn't have to pulverize me, you know, and then I could fucking have my own fucking Pulverizer attached to me, so I could use it on stuff, things around the house. Feral animals. I could pulverize whatever I wanted to pulverize, like it could be people, but it could be anything. People need to be able to have more sex with machines. I think there should be more sex with machines, and not some machine that *looks* like a human, no way, a real machine. Or else there could be a threesome where one of the participants is a machine."

As if on cue, because he was young and there was always a need, he slid down the baggy white denim shorts, underneath which he had one of those satiny jockstraps that the really macho boys all wore, and his ass was exposed, therefore, and he kind of attempted to make a union between himself and the flopping Pulverizer, just for the sake of trying, and to indicate that beneath the gruff exterior, he was a bottom. He dragged the busted-up Pulverizer, the flopping fish, onto the blanket that Vienna had set out, a blanket that was already pretty dusty with sand and valley fever spores, and he, Jean-Paul, the machine, and Vienna herself got down on the blanket and attempted to do what lovers did, here in the hominid age of sexuality.

It was a long time coming, you know, the recognition that what was inhibiting *stationaries* in the late twentieth century, what was destroying marriages and giving young people the wrong idea, was too much *civilization* in sexuality — this was how Vienna remembered learning about hominid and proto-hominid sex, anyway. She learned about it at a precocious age, back when her friends were still playing with Transportation Safety Administration Barbie or Waste Management Barbie. Vienna Roberts was trying to get her girlfriends to show her *theirs,* and she was trying to get the boys at school to show her how to carry off a girl to paradise, and she was stealing books from her parents' library, because her parents, by their own account, had a vigorous appetite, and she remembered reading some of the books that advocated approaches to sexuality that eventually became *hominid* or *proto-hominid.* With great generational paradigm shifts, no one person can be responsible for the new thinking — sentiments like this came from a variety of sources. Well, but still there was that one book, *Slaughtering Intimacy,* which Vienna's father said would have been a bigger deal if the author hadn't insisted on making it a book instead of an online lecture series, but that book, the way she heard it, made the argument that what people wanted in sexuality was *not* intimacy.

Intimacy was sometimes an inhibitor. We were obliged, according to *Slaughtering Intimacy,* to be all polite most of the time when we were at work, and when we were out in society, polite, polite, and what we wanted to do when we got into the bedroom was treat one another like *possessions.* We didn't want the arduous work of being polite. *Slaughtering Intimacy* was, you know, obviously a lot more popular with guys at first, because it argued that you should try using particularly unsavory words for sex and that you should openly express disregard or even contempt in the bedroom, since disregard or contempt, in multiple psychological tests over the years, created greater desire in men. Could real-world situations duplicate the laboratory testing?

Then there was a kind of backlash, in which women started to realize that maybe there were ways in which they, too, felt disgusted with their partners. Maybe the deformed appearance of the male sexual organ was something you could build into the experience, so that when that disgusting pink or black thing was readying itself to try to split you in half, you could think of it not as something you loved, but as an amputated limb of some kind, and you could take pleasure in the horror of sexuality, the foul, reeking disgust of it. Instead of thinking sex was glorious, tender, and beautiful, you could think of it as disgusting, dehumanizing, even laughable, and you could engage in it with these things in mind.

Slaughtering Intimacy was followed by *Reproduction in the Lower Species: A Pictorial History,* and then the three-volume extravaganza *Primate Sexuality,* and the accompanying documentary. These were considered the really popular items in the *human sexuality* section of the media stores, especially the occult and alternative-philosophy stores, which were, after all, the most popular media stores in Rio Blanco. Most people didn't read anything at all, and who could blame them? When *Primate Sexuality* took chimpanzees and bonobos as examples of how human beings might undertake hominid sexuality, it caught on somehow. *Proto-hominid,* as an approach and a way of life, followed not long after, or at least it did on her parents' bookshelf, on one particularly hard-to-reach shelf. She would use the digital book reader with these titles, so that her parents wouldn't notice what was missing, and she would watch the chimps fucking, look at the diagrams, follow the links. Admittedly, it was going a little far when the guy who made the documentary, one R. L. Houston-Smith, suggested that some particularly recalcitrant humans, those who thought that sexuality had to be for procreative purposes only, should actually try having sex *with a chimpanzee.* Or a bonobo.

Proto-hominid sexuality, according to the books, was forged in the prehistory of humankind, in our evolutionary prehistory, the time in which we never experienced nor worried about *love.* Back then, we experienced only sexual longing and duty. Sexual longing was incredibly violent, and here Vienna Roberts was quoting from the pages of a book she had downloaded many times; sexuality was closer to cannibalism than it was to *intimacy,* which was not a word that proto-hominids would have understood in any way. What we failed to do, according to Allan Spinrad's *Sex for Hominids and Proto-Hominids,* which spawned a long-running infomercial as well as a reality program, was utilize all the sexual tools at our disposal, including neglect, contempt, hatred, murderous rage, and despair, let's not forget despair, or even dishonesty, as well as the kind of stunning, overwhelming joy that one feels in having crushed the will of the loved one.

Proto-hominid! There had to be a better way to say it. But no one had come up with that better way. For the moment, women were ripping off their golf dresses and were trying to get their husbands to ravish them in the parking lots of emptied shopping malls, and they were shouting out gibberish (part of Spinrad's argument related to *speaking in tongues*), which was hard to ignore, if you were coming back from the ice cream shop, with your double scoop and jimmies, and your best friend's mother was wearing a shark mask and red high-heeled pumps and fucking the pool boy, who had a hairy back, just like a chimpanzee.

She and Jean-Paul got into it, because you couldn't not get

into it, because these trends came in waves, and when the world was falling down around you, you did what you could do to stick your head in the sand, the desert sand, to feel as little as possible. This the proto-hominids must have done, when they were going extinct. Like the Neanderthal had to watch the first Cro-Magnons in Central Europe, knowing how much smarter those new guys were, the brand-new Cro-Magnons. She and Jean-Paul got into it, because all the kids got into it, because the kids got into what their parents got into, even if they ridiculed their parents a little bit. And what she noticed, when she was a prodigious reader of Spinrad and the commentators on Spinrad, was that certain ideas did make her a little bit, well, there was no other way to put it, certain things kind of made her *wet,* when she thought about them with Jean-Paul, like there was one thing that really kind of made her *wet,* and not just a little bit. This one thing was a faucet being turned open, which was not what she had experienced, for example, when she had first slept with that lacrosse-playing hunk of wood Damien Lorenzo, which had been like trying to stick a fence pole into a block of concrete — anyway, what really made her *wet,* at first, was the idea of gagging Jean-Paul, like actually gagging him, pretty tightly, so that he couldn't say anything. She had a horror of stuff like this at first, but then she kind of liked it. She had a kind of a high-pitched screech she got into, and she imagined this was the cry of some kind of rhesus monkey, while she was gagging him, and then when she was done gagging him, she liked to blindfold him. Now, what kind of *proto-hominid* male, you might ask, would be willing to be gagged and blindfolded? She wasn't totally sure why Jean-Paul Koo was so willing to go along with this stuff, but she thought it probably had something to do with the Dead Mother, who was always around him everywhere, or so he said. She was in his back pocket. The Dead Mother. She was in his glove compartment. Only *proto-hominid sex,* he said, allowed him to put aside all these feelings of filial duty or whatever. He needed to really go back down through the evolutionary chain of sexuality.

Getting him out of all of his rags, so that he had on only the satin jockstrap thing, out on the desert floor, with the big clouds massing in the west, there was something about it that was enough for her, or temporarily enough, *proto-hominid* enough, never mind *hominid,* which was level two, and when she got him like that there was always some other thing she wanted to do, some other degradation that she wanted to visit upon him. It was in fact never enough, and in this case she wanted to tie him up, and she had some of those things, what were those things called, those cords that you used to attach to things, *bungee cords?* She could bungee-cord his wrists, and then instead of laying him down gently, she would just pummel him until he was on his back on the desert floor, and he was still laughing, which was always a good sign, and she took off everything except her bra, because the one thing that Vienna Roberts couldn't stand was anything to do with her nipples. Maybe for this reason, if she left Jean-Paul's wrists unbound, he was always ripping at her bra, trying to get at her nipples, biting at them and generally causing a lot of trouble. She hated that maternal thing, didn't like feeling that anyone was using her in some maternal way, because she wanted all the maternal parts of her *shut off;* she would have been glad, as a teenager, to have her cervix and her uterus and all that stuff taken out of her body, because you know, *proto-hominids had no idea that sexuality caused babies;* that wasn't something they put together at all. They didn't make decisions about sexuality based on anything to do with procreation. They just wrestled around and bit one another and penetrated one another and had orgasms, and in the process, they got covered with sweat, blood, and come, and then some time later, in a completely different place and environment, ordained by the plentiful gods, the females swelled up and went through that agonizing labor business.

Naked as a primate, she located a furry eye mask of her own. If the desert was about death, then she wanted the possibility of death, she wanted the reintroduced wolves hovering just out of range of the rutting proto-hominid teenagers, and she wanted the coyotes and the mountain lions all getting ready to devour them, hopefully waiting right behind that stand of greasewood until the moment when they were about to come together, she and Jean-Paul, and then the mountain lions could jump out and sink in their teeth. Before she put the blindfold on, she tried to get the harness on, and the floppy Pulverizer rigged up flush against Jean-Paul's ass. There was lots in Allan Spinrad's book about anal penetration. Nothing was more important in indicating the limits of civilized *masculine power,* in this day and age, than the anal penetration of the male, and in Vienna Roberts's opinion (because eventually she had gotten even that block of wood known as Damien Lorenzo to agree to allow her to put things up his ass), no male really felt *anything,* not even a little, unless he had something up him, and this was because he hadn't given up enough yet, enough self-respect; proto-hominid sex was nothing if it wasn't about casting off any last remaining bit of self-respect—but the problem was that notwithstanding Spinrad's advice, she kind of found the whole anal thing *gross,* you know, she just didn't like getting anything that was *in there* on herself, and you just couldn't trust guys, not guys like Jean-Paul who are hooked up to their computer like ninety hours a week, guys who'd already had three or four screen detoxes to their credit, you couldn't really expect them to *bathe,* and in fact, people just didn't bathe all that much in the desert anymore, because there wasn't really enough water. What little water was left was saved for hospitals and mining operations. And so it wasn't like Jean-Paul wasn't going to, well, you know, it was like there could be all kinds of stuff down there, who knew, things growing, encrustments. She tried to get the Pulverizer in there a little bit, and there was a kind of hiccuping laugh from him, and then she pulled down the eye mask and then rolled onto him, in the dark, and there was the breeze, and the babbling creek of the distant interstate, and there were the clouds massing, and she knew they were massing, and then she and Jean-Paul were rubbing against each other, and nowhere in the proto-hominid manual did it say what you were supposed to *feel* really, because *feeling things,* that was so old-fashioned, you know? And guys never wanted to feel things anyhow, emotions, and she kept privately to herself that one last little bit of feeling, the kind she wasn't supposed to have, and that last little bit of feeling was for having the part of him inside of her, and even if she did kind of think that it was disgusting, that part of men was disgusting, the mandrel was disgusting, she just hadn't gotten past it, and even if she did think that, that they were disgusting, there was a way in which she still wanted to have him inside of her, not that she needed completing, forget it, nothing about completing, she was complete as she was, she didn't want to be completed, she wanted to take things away from other people, and she wanted to squander what she took away, but something in her quieted when he was inside her, and maybe something quieted when the Pulverizer was inside of him, if it *was* really in there.

Which didn't mean that proto-hominid sex wasn't more like Mexican wrestling than it was like *love,* at least the proto-hominid sex of Jean-Paul and Vienna. Someone was on top and then they were not on top, and someone was elbowing the other one in the head, and then someone was trying to pin someone else down, and they were breathing hard not because they were turned on exactly, although there was some of that, but more because they were exhausted from all the wrestling. There was a reason why rounds in wrestling were only so long, couple of minutes, and it went on like this, wrestling and spitting and grunting, and occasionally Jean-Paul would shout something in Korean, because when he was really enjoying himself, he enjoyed himself in the language of his birth. From Vienna's point of view, which was no kind of point of *view* just then, since she was blindfolded, it was all about sensation — she didn't fall into that thing where she was concerned about whether she was emaciated enough, because even though Jean-Paul denied it, she was certain that Jean-Paul only liked women who were emaciated — and she didn't care if she was making a strange face or if one of them had *unsightly body hair;* she just felt certain things. Her body was being wrung out, like on one of those nonelectric dryers that people were using again. You cranked the clothes between two pieces of lathed mahogany, and then the garment was automatically lofted onto a line in the yard to bake in the desert heat. Sex was like that, like laundry, and all kinds of important psychosexual juices were being moved through the proto-hominid latitudes of her — her back brain, her uvula, her perineum, her labia, her small intestines. The juices were like the runoff from an industrial accident, a flaming, pressurized sluice of erotic by-products that could run from a factory down into a wash somewhere, erotic by-products that could flood the Rio Blanco city center, washing away encampments of homeless people, maybe even her parents, who were busy trying to organize the homeless citizens, and along with her parents, also the unstuffed armchairs that the homeless people used for reclining in the park off Stone, shopping carts, tarps, old-model cellular telephones and satellite phones that the homeless people used to communicate with one another, various OxyPlus intravenous drip bags and nasal inhalers, piles of clothes from the charitable thrift stores, all of this was being washed away in the erotic runoff from her. Oh, and it was also true that proto-hominid sex put a big premium on female ejaculate and encouraged women to work hard to learn the skill, because *everybody spurts* was a rallying cry of the proto-hominid movement, and maybe therefore Vienna, who really didn't understand what this signified exactly, and who had been unable to get the high school sexual education counselor to tell her (he had a twenty-point memo he handed out detailing the things *he wasn't allowed to say*), he couldn't be relied on to tell her anything about female ejaculate, and the part in Spinrad's book that had the *everybody spurts* subhead, it was hard to understand, even though she felt like she understood everything else, so basically she just imagined a lot of fluid, fluid everywhere, gigantic streams of fluid gushing forth from her, especially during the blissful penetration and the even more blissful *clitoral devourment,* which was another Spinrad recommendation, although, you know, the proto-hominids probably didn't engage in oral sex, this was a much disputed subject, but that willingness to devour the partner, the part of sexual congress that could move straight into cannibalism, like where you really would eat a bloody shank from each other, you know, maybe with some kind of condiment, the *clitoral devourment* would do pretty well as a symbol of the kind of proto-hominid willingness to devour the partner, and she was really getting into that *clitoral devourment,* even though she wasn't, you know, entirely sure if Jean-Paul really knew exactly where the clitoris was, and most of the time, well, he had these ideas about how he was going to work hard to get her off, but once he stuck the mandrel of love into her, there was a real danger that he would gush in about ninety seconds and it would be on her leg or something, and that was the end of that, but anyhow, for the moment he was fulfilling his obligation to pursue *clitoral devourment,* and she was imagining the kinds of waterfalls and tidal waves and tsunamis that were consistent with the idea that *everybody spurts,* and she found that against her better judgment, she did lapse into English language for a brief moment, and with a somewhat, well, *uncomatose* fervency, "This feels so fucking good!"

Then a strange thing happened. Vienna Roberts knew, and she was fond of telling her friends, that there was a goal with this new sex thing, like there was a goal with everything American, there was a payoff, there was a *bottom line,* and the bottom line of proto-hominid sex was *complete negation of cerebral activity.* As with, she guessed, religions, like Buddhism or whatever, the goal with proto-hominid sex was to strike a fabulous blow against the reasoning part of the brain. Most people thought this whole idea was totally fake. Even her parents joked about it. Probably Spinrad was taking some kind of mood stabilizer when he wrote that part, and with his bald head, his little potbelly, and his stumpy legs (she'd seen him on the infomercial), he was cardiologically unsound, and probably he had some transient seizure while leaking a little eyedropper full of seminal fluid, and that was what he referred to as *complete negation of cerebral activity.* Both she and Jean-Paul had subjected this claim to exhaustive testing

involving OxyPlus, cannabis, inhaled cleaning agents, mild strangulation, and they had found that they had headaches and got
sore throats, but they still managed to worry about what would
happen if their parents found their naked bodies in the desert.
With all of their rigid scientific testing, they had never once achieved
complete negation of cerebral activity.

And yet. And yet. And yet. Jean-Paul, while he was engaging
in the *clitoral devourment* stuff, he was mumbling and really moaning, in a proto-hominid way, if she was any judge of it. It was like
Jean-Paul had become, well, maybe some kind of hyena. Hyenas
were supposedly a lot like humans in some ways. And Jean-Paul
was like a hyena, with his weird Korean slang protestations and
his moaning. Or maybe he was rutting like a javelina. Maybe
Jean-Paul was imitating the javelina's rutting cries. Whatever it
was, it sounded like he sounded when she was doing *something* to
him, except that she wasn't doing anything to him, and he was
supposed to be doing something to *her,* and while she was a big
fan of *clitoral devourment,* didn't trust any guy who said he wouldn't
do it, she just didn't think it was so *transcendental* or anything, and
she didn't believe a guy would normally be all javelina-like while
pursuing the *clitoral devourment.* And maybe it meant that he was
just spindling the mandrel with his own fist while he was getting
down with the *clitoral devourment,* but the really weird part, the
strange part, the part she couldn't figure out, was that it was almost like there was somebody *else* in the theater of proto-hominid
sex with them, and maybe this third party was working on Jean-
Paul, while Vienna was just lying there getting devoured, and if
so, Jean-Paul seemed to like the third party just fine. Maybe it was
a border jumper who'd happened on the scene?

There was some kind of gagging choking thing that Vienna
had learned was consonant with the orgasmic ecstasy of Jean-Paul
Koo, and so he was gasping and his breaths were slowing, and
then he was lying back on the blanket. It was all a mystery. But
before she could go on and on about the mystery part, Jean-Paul
reached down, she thought (through her blindfold), between her

legs, freshly shorn of everything, perfumed with essential oils, and running with a marshy abundance of female perspirants, and with his hand, he demonstrated a really stunning ability to locate, like a stud, for the first time, her clitoris, her little proto-hominid standby/on switch, which was glowing red just for him, and he began palpating the standby/on switch as though he were a champion, and almost instantly she could feel herself pulled into a strange new staccato rhythm, not some pulsating thing, a rhythm that was all off-kilter and *proto-hominid,* you know, some kind of African rhythm that the proto-hominids would have attempted to bang out when they were back on the veldt eating wildebeests. While she was not at all sure that this was love, and, indeed, she had no reason to connect this sensation to love, nor did she care if it was *intimate* or anything else, she certainly did feel as if the weird proto-hominid rhythm that would fall into some pattern of twos and threes, *proto proto hominid, proto proto hominid hominid,* this digital stimulation did shut down nearly all the cerebral activity. It did pull her down into centrifugal repetitions, until she felt as though she were becoming *one with the principles of proto-hominid sexuality;* she was remade; she had become a series of, you know, ritualized gestures that were about summoning the essence of what *is,* protoplasmic, prehistoric centrality of tissue, essence of tissue, and secretion, and molecular fusing and fissioning, she was the movement of the first fishy thing out of the oceans, she was the first mammal to scrabble up the banks of the river, she was the first bacterium to *mutate,* and when she came, she felt some kind of flooding in herself, and she heard her voice cry out, and her cry had the nearly automatic involuntariness of the principle *everybody spurts,* and she felt like she could almost reach out and touch Allan Spinrad; she understood how some people could venerate Allan Spinrad, but just as she was giving herself over to *everybody spurts,* and to the theocracy of Allan Spinrad, she heard a rustling from Jean-Paul, and then, suddenly, *holyfuckingmotheroffuckinggodwhatthefuckinghellisthatohmyfuckinggodohjesusViennaohjesusViennaquicktakethefuckingohmyfuckingtakethe-*

*fuckingmaskoffViennaquickjesusohhellwhatthefuckholyfuckingmotherof-
fuckinggodwhatthehell!!* . . . but
she didn't pay attention, not at first, because of what was rushing
through her, all the lovers giving away all of their attachment
to all the language or romance, the blinding interrogation lamp
of romance, the product placement of romance, all of that being
given away; she let herself go with it, back onto the veldt, eating the wildebeests, and she didn't listen at first, until Jean-Paul
ripped the mask off her face, tore away her veil of illusion, if you
wanted to put it that way, having somehow freed himself from his
restraints, which made it obvious to her that he couldn't possibly
have been the one who was frisking her, so perfectly obvious, and
now it was obvious. Now the terrifying truth was known, and the
clarity of it was so unsettling that at first she couldn't even accept
that what she was seeing in front of her, between her legs, was
really what it appeared to be, *but it was.*

A severed arm.

There was a severed arm between her legs. It occurred to her that
it was the Pulverizer, what with the disembodied physical comedy
of that device, which slithered and slipped around so much that it
had fallen well off to her side, like some birth defect, a primordial
additional leg or something, but it wasn't the Pulverizer. It didn't
look, you know, brand-new or silicone or anything. It was a severed
arm with all kinds of sand and dust and bits of paper and trash
and stuff stuck onto the bloody end of it where the rest of its body
should have been. There were pieces of sinew or ligament or tendon
or whatever sticking out of the bottom end, the stump end, shreds
of muscular tissue, crystallized blood. And then the other really foul
part of the severed arm, you know, if she were trying to describe the
arm for a police artist or something, was that it was missing a finger,
a middle finger. So it was a four-fingered hand.

At first, with the ripples of orgasmic energy flowing out of her
into the bounty of creation, she froze. She just couldn't take it
seriously. The arm. But that paralysis, that erotic catalepsy, only
lasted a second, and then she found herself in a kind of hysterical

fixation, just like the one that had overtaken Jean-Paul, who was standing at the end of the blanket holding a sneaker, wearing nothing but his satin jockstrap, getting ready to bat the hand, if the hand tried to come near him. Because, yes, the really uncanny part of it was that the hand *was* kind of moving.

"Is that moving?"

"Sure as fucking hell is," Jean-Paul said. "And I'm pretty sure it, you know, it jerked me off."

"It's a cut-off arm; it *can't move.*"

"But just look at it. It's trembling right now and moving its fingers! Look at it right now!"

She looked at it. She did. The fingers seemed to be writhing around as if with some reflexive, postmortem trembling, some last bit of life energy.

"Jean-Paul," she said, and here she snatched up a couple of her shredded teenage garments, layers that did little but suggest the necessity of their removal, and she started trying to yank them on without ever losing sight of the heinous extremity. "That's some kind of, you know, *nerve thing,* like when you cut the head off of a chicken, right? It can't possibly have done what you just said."

"Did you jerk me off? Did you have your hand around my—"

"That doesn't...Maybe it was just attached to some guy, and the guy jerked you off, and then he got hit by a car or something, and that's what's left."

"Is that a better answer? That some guy jerked me off while you were sitting there with your blindfold on? There was no guy. And the arm didn't fly here!"

As if to prove the validity of Jean-Paul's hypothesis, the arm, which really had been mostly dormant, appeared to suddenly take note of the Pulverizer, or at least the butt plug on the end of the pile of space junk that had once been the Pulverizer, which had been cast off long ago in the drama of erotic love, and grabbing the butt plug, it thoroughly and painstakingly ripped the butt plug from the Pulverizer and went about attempting to crush it in its fist.

"Oh, fuck," Jean-Paul said. "That arm is *so* alive."

He had climbed back into his shorts. He was dressing as quickly as he could, which meant awkwardly. There was a fair amount of hopping. But that was the least of it, as Vienna also awakened to the significance of the arm. It wasn't just that it was alive. It wasn't just that it violated all the rules, rules of medicine and biochemistry and physics, and every other kind of rule.

"I think I had sex with that arm too."

"It's so disgusting," Jean-Paul said. "I don't even know who that belongs to."

"Do you think that's consensual? You know? Can it possibly be a consenting thing? Having sex with an arm? I mean, what should we do with it? Should we take it to the police to see if we can charge it with something?"

"Someone's got to be fucking missing that arm. I mean, you'd think that he'd be wanting his arm back, wherever he is."

The arm, having finished, to its satisfaction, the job of squeezing the life out of a marital aid, managed with some difficulty to flip itself over onto its back, or what might be supposed to be its back, so that the palm faced the sky. Vienna was surprised to realize how many things a hand could *say* just by its posture or orientation in the physical world. An arm with palm facing down, using its fingers as some kind of crawling device, dragging itself along, bent on meddling in the affairs of others. But the arm on its back, with its wrist upward and fingers spread wide, seemed nearly playful, or at the very least submissive, and this was maybe what led Jean-Paul to his next decision. Jean-Paul lunged at the arm. He did so with a swiftness that overpowered the arm, which had no eyes and didn't know what was to befall it. Jean-Paul lay hold of it by its long, useless base. The fingers, realizing that they were *had,* began writhing and attempting to grab at him, and Jean-Paul realized, then, the way Vienna understood it, that this would once have been a formidable arm wrestler.

"You've got to help me with this."

"Jean-Paul," Vienna said, "you have to be kidding. You're not going to bring that thing back with us. Isn't it dangerous?"

"The guy who's missing it might want it to be reattached."

"Look at that thing. Half of that tissue is all, like, gangrenous and rotting away. It can't be reattached. Whoever it was attached to is *dead.* I promise you."

"You don't know anything about this fucking stuff. You're a retail employee — in the service economy. I know about this stuff, all right?"

And so, in a postcoital huff, Jean-Paul Koo took the writhing arm into the back of the van, and he found a roll of duct tape, which he had known would be there. (What van was without its roll of duct tape?) While Jean-Paul held the arm down with his knee (it made a horrible scratching noise with its bloody nails in the bed of the van), he freed up a suitable length of tape. And then, as Vienna watched, he wrapped the tape around the fingers of the hand. They struggled mightily to free themselves. But, as everyone knows, duct tape is hard enough with two hands.

And then Jean-Paul said, "We're taking this to my dad."

Rob Antoine was on the NASA jet, the one reserved for high-level agency business. You'd have thought that NASA would have a first-class piece of aeronautical design, since it was meant to be the premier space agency on the planet, the premier agency in all of the universe (until proven otherwise). On the contrary, the NASA jet was from a decommissioned-aircraft graveyard near Houston. The jet had been worked over, retrofitted, by the engineers from JPL, in their spare time, just to keep these engineers engaged through a period of budget cuts. This was a private jet unworthy of the agency emblazoned on its fuselage. The few intact seats were noteworthy for torn upholstery and tawdry stains, and there were outcroppings of hardened chewing gum under the armrests. The windows were foggy from moisture that had worked through the rubber seals over the years. Few of the overhead luggage bins latched. And the odd purse or backpack tumbled out in midflight.

And the jet rattled and groaned in ways that did not inspire confidence. With every up- and downdraft, the cabin trembled as if about to plummet to earth.

The good news? There was no problem making the occasional satellite phone call. You wouldn't have a seat on the NASA jet if you didn't have the appropriate security clearance for outgoing satellite calls. The pilots of the NASA jet, many of them astronauts who hadn't yet made the jump into orbit, didn't fret about the security issues that had dogged civil aviation in the period of the Middle Eastern and Central Asian conflicts.

Which is how Rob Antoine found himself talking to the director of the Centers for Disease Control during flight. While Debra Levin slept across the aisle, a small rivulet of drool tracking down her attractive if forbidding jawline, he found himself in the middle of an unpleasant interagency conversation. What Rob was doing was trying to explain a certain exotic extraterrestrial infection, though in doing so what he really was doing was trying to explain what he in turn had been told by the Department of Defense an hour earlier. He had little confidence in that account. He was giving away half a story, the half he was authorized to possess, to another government agency, without understanding the story entirely and without feeling competent about any of the technical or scientific issues, and all this while he was flying directly into the epicenter of what could become a ghastly epidemic. The director of the CDC, whose name Rob had already forgotten out of anxiety, Anderson or Henderson, was just as rattled as Rob was himself, and Anderson (Henderson) made it more apparent by reaching new heights of condescension when he didn't feel that he was getting the facts he needed.

"Can you walk me through this one more time?"

Below, the glorious mountains had risen up from the plains in the middle of the nation, as if to impale inbound air traffic. Even the fuzzy windows couldn't stop the mountains. The mountains were an overpowering presence, and no matter how many times Rob flew in this direction he never failed to be impressed.

Especially while being dressed down by a medical expert.

Rob said, "Again, I'm not on the medical staff. But here's what we think we know. What we think we know is that the astronauts on the Mars mission somehow contracted a bug while on the surface of the planet. Despite the fact that the planet was considered sterile, or all but sterile, our people contracted a bug. The best information we have at this time suggests that the bug is a mutation of something being worked on here on Earth, something that was believed to have military applications, which was then in turn transported to Mars during unmanned missions, perhaps by design, where it picked up some nasty tendencies, such as a high tolerance for gamma rays on the one hand, and for oxygen-deprived environments. Because of some unfortunate personnel problems we had going on during the mission itself—"

"I've heard," said Henderson or Anderson.

"Because of personnel problems, we essentially transmitted the bacterium from person to person up there, giving it a new chance to reacclimate to human tissue, and in the process killing the majority of our astronauts. When we thought we were in the clear with the one astronaut who was coming home, we found that unfortunately he was ill as well. At this point the mission was terminated, while that astronaut, Colonel Richards, was still inbound."

"Well, one question I have to ask," Henderson or Anderson said, "is why you didn't use the antisatellite system to take down the craft when it was farther out. Isn't that the reason for the shield system? To prevent just this sort of thing?"

"We were hoping to salvage our guy. That's all. We believed his condition was safe, and he worked hard, he did the work we asked him to do, and we'd lost a lot of good people. We weren't ready to give up on him yet."

"So you blew pieces of him all over the Southwest, jeopardizing millions of civilians."

"Colonel Richards made that decision himself. And I can

understand how you might be a little concerned about this, and we are too. But there's no reason yet to assume that the situation is beyond control. For one thing, we are in an area of very low population density. And furthermore, we aren't really sure if any of Colonel Richards survived the blast. The redundant systems we had in place to abort should have been effective enough to prevent that. Still, I am calling because we do have one report that is not as reassuring as we'd like. This is in the extreme Southwest, Rio Blanco area, and I'm flying there now, as is the director of the agency."

Debra Levin shifted positions in her medicated sleep. The drool detached and beaded on the lapel of her stylish suit jacket. Antoine watched, while listening to the CDC's protests.

Rob blundered into a silence, without much heart for it. "The exact facts of the bioweapon, if that's what it is, I am unable to get out of the Department of Defense. The exact genetic information on the bug. Maybe you have a contact there. Although I should stress that there's a public-relations issue here, and we would prefer not to alarm the residents of the area just yet. Until we know exactly what we are dealing with."

"That's your problem," said Anderson, or was it — "Our job is to prevent and contain infectious outbreaks, and we are not concerned with how it looks for the other agencies, and we're willing to take this up the chain of command."

Rob let the shrill stuff that followed from Henderson or Anderson drift by. Some of this was all about the specifics of viral contagions versus bacterial contagions, which apparently Rob had been confusing on and off throughout the discussion. The CDC guy went on and on about Ebola and Marburg and the fact that viruses were simply *not as effective* as bacterial infections, when weaponized, but the hemorrhagic feature was much more common in these viral infections than in their bacterial cousins, as the viruses would infect the blood and skin cells, and thus the multiplying of tiny cuts in the Ebola outbreaks, like the one in Denmark in 2012 and the one in the Czech Republic two years later. And what about H1N1? And what about hantavirus? If Anderson or Henderson remembered correctly, and he could have the facts in the next few minutes, hantavirus was quite common in the homeless population of Rio Blanco and surrounding towns, and wasn't the homeless population there restive and militant? These were the kinds of cofactors they'd be dealing with—there could even be a viral infection piggybacking on the bacterial pathogen.

Almost impossible to take all this in. So quickly had it come to this. So quickly had the story gone sour, with the potential for worse up ahead, in the Southwest, a part of the country that was noteworthy for bad economic news, for the inability of state and local governments to deliver basic services. Still, from the air, it was so beautiful. The absence of government and industry in the better part of the Southwest, and the acute drought, had made it possible for a lot of plant and animal species to rebound. After environmental devastation, some of the animals always rebounded—when there were no people around. You always saw this sort of thing on *nature programming*.

"Are you listening to what I'm saying?" Henderson asked.

"You're going in and out. Must be a satellite problem."

"I'm saying that I don't have any idea what this 'disassembling' nonsense means, but it is very possible that even a corpse, if infected with a bacterium that has mutated to this degree, is liable to be contagious. Based on what I'm hearing. You want to try to isolate and quarantine anyone exposed, and that includes the bodies. I'll get you more backup on this from our end, but that's likely what we're talking about."

"The military is isolating the crash site. They've already done so, to the tune of several miles. There is a *body* there, already, and that body belongs to someone not on our payroll. That body is civilian. That means it's possible, from what I understand, that the bacteria has spread from the site."

"You have people on the ground?"

"We are contacting local doctors and hospitals, and the military has people there—they have a base in the area, and I'm trusting we can all coordinate on this, and that we can play a leadership role in the coordination, since it's NASA's mess."

Henderson grunted and then said something about CDC being primarily an information and education agency. But they too had research affiliates among medical people in participating regions.

"Then the last question is," Anderson or Henderson said, "do you have any reason to believe that you *have* contained the astronaut's remains?"

"We have done statistical modeling," Rob Antoine said. "There are small pieces of the craft in a debris stream, starting south of the border and moving northwest, through the empty part of the state of New Mexico, across the southern part of the Sonoran Desert. We have helicopters working to isolate every piece of the capsule in this debris stream. We believe we may be able to find every piece of significance. Wherever there is aeronautical or biological debris, we will be working on it. And I'll have more for you later when I hear from our people. I imagine if somebody finds...a piece of the body, of Colonel Richards, who was, I should say, a personal friend of mine, we will probably hear about it as soon as it happens."

With that, they rang off.

The problem *was* pieces of the body, true. Rob Antoine's nightmares, which were mostly drug induced these days, what with the twenty-four-hour days that he'd been working, had to do with the body, with the remainder of Jed Richards that he feared was going to turn up everywhere and advertise the debacle that the Mars mission had become. In the recurrent nightmare, some portion of Richards was always trying to find a way to write, as if the most devastating thing an *undead* astronaut could do was somehow put pen to paper, to tell Rob that NASA was responsible for what had become of him. NASA had reduced a fine astronaut, and an eloquent spokesman for the Mars mission, a veteran, a patriot, a poet, a family man, to a disembodied head—because that was one outcome that Antoine's dream life favored—or to a headless, armless body that was still able to type somehow. With its toes.

The military had verified that it had subjected the crash site near Rio Blanco, the site with the larger part of the debris, to incendiary devices designed to eliminate any biological material. A controlled burn. Which meant that any mission data at that location was also entirely lost. Rob had advanced in the Mars mission because he loved the neglected part of interplanetary research, not the life-on-Mars stuff, but, for example, the study of Martian winds. He loved the way the winds worked on Mars, and he had promoted a number of studies of these winds, and none of those studies had ever been completed by the poor, lonely astronauts who had gone there to die. All that ancillary data, the topographical data about an undisturbed planet that had been unchanged for hundreds of thousands, if not millions of years, that was all obscured by the human story. And it was all going to get a lot more human very soon. If that guy, that miner who had been found dead near the crash site, was infected.

Debra Levin stretched languidly and looked over at him, yawning.

"What did they say?"

"CDC? They are not happy."

Debra, at some way station between nap and awful truth, gave the news a respectful silence.

"At a certain point," she said at last, "we have to start working more directly on limiting the agency's liability in all of this. That should be one of our priorities, along with attempting to maximize the science that is available. We should get out, leave it to other agencies."

There were questions Rob wanted to ask, beginning with: Did Debra Levin know and approve of the work on biological agents that was taking place on the Mars mission? Was she fully informed by the Department of Defense? And what about her predecessor, Anatoly Thatcher? She could easily be reporting to the highest levels of government without telling Vance Gibraltar or Rob or anyone else. She was capable of making even the idlest conversation seem like it was material to your annual review. Your career hung on the answer to any simple inquiry. And for this reason he left well enough alone.

"I'm going to call the guy at URB. Everybody keeps suggesting him, the Korean guy, does stem cell issues. Subcontracted for the Company at one time."

"I already contacted him. You talk to him, and if I have to get on the line, I will."

The plane had banked south, and brought into view the great barrenness of the desert out the window. The closest thing to Mars on Earth. Rob dialed the Korean researcher while he watched the waves of terrain below him, the bottom of that long-ago ocean.

The voice of Woo Lee Koo was sleepy and unconcerned, with an accent thick enough that Rob was grateful for his interminable linguistic pacing. There was some getting-to-know-you conversation between the two, and a reiteration of the material that Debra had used when speaking with Koo the night before. The sad truth was that Rob, who had taken on a lot of the damage control out of a sense of responsibility, was now getting used to coming up with euphemisms.

Koo said, "As I understood the instructions, I was to keep my eyes open and to let your people know if I saw or heard anything unusual in the aftermath of the crash."

"That's very helpful, and we appreciate that. But we need to alert you to what we know now. The playing field has changed. Already. It's possible," Rob went on, "that there was a *murder* near the crash, and that this murder is somehow related to the crash itself."

"Please go on."

"Since we are unsure about the effect of the relevant bacteria and its infection postmortem, we are unable to say whether this unfortunate mortality has anything to do with the crash. The facts are as follows: there was a mining professional near the crash site, a man who we believe made his way to the debris after it touched down and who was found dead nearby not long after. Our worry is that Colonel Richards, our astronaut, may have been somehow responsible."

"How could he have been responsible?" Koo asked.

"Strictly speaking, he couldn't have been. Since he was killed when the mission was aborted. But anecdotal reports of *M. thanatobacillus* infections on Mars itself suggest that parts of the body may continue to function, may continue to have muscular capabilities, after heart and brain function has stopped, at least as we understand it here on Earth."

"I have made clear my skepticism about this."

"We understand your skepticism, and we share it, but we are not in a position to allow even unlikely medical claims to go uninvestigated. We have the military on the case, and we are trying to fend off the local police, because once the local police are involved, we believe that there will be publicity about the crash and the quarantine. As you may have seen online, we are already trying to balance the public's need to know with our own institutional needs. What we would like is for you to go out to the quarantine site. To look for Colonel Richards.

"If you should find some portion of him, and we are able to provide you with distinguishing markings, for example that he is missing a finger on his left hand, we want you to go ahead and begin looking at some of the tissue under the microscope and see if you can find evidence of any particular pathogen. We believe the bacteria is related to sepsis. It's our understanding, Dr. Koo, that this kind of research is related to some of the applications of stem cells that you have been looking at in your own work, so perhaps there will be compensation in that way."

Koo replied, "I would perhaps like to harvest a tiny bit of the tissue, if in fact it behaves the way you say it behaves. Would that be possible?"

"Dr. Koo," Rob Antoine said, while his boss listened in from across the empty aisle, "we are in no position to keep you from making a bit of an excision to further the cause of your own science, but you didn't hear that from me. What we would like to be assured of is your commitment to provide us with any information you should gather as quickly as possible, and to aid in the quarantining of the Rio Blanco area."

"On these points, you may rest assured."

"Very kind of you," Rob Antoine said. "And by the way, Dr. Koo, we suggest that you don't allow Colonel Richards, any part of him, to touch your own skin in any way. We suggest he be treated as a genuine biohazard and that you wear the kinds of protective gear you would normally wear in the presence of a level-four biohazard. We believe that the bacteria is spread only through contact with the tissue or with bodily fluids, not through airborne means, but we don't want you or anyone at the URB facility to be exposed to risk, is that clear?"

"That is clear."

"By the way, that's great news about the football team."

Nearer to sunrise now, which as anyone will tell you is the right time to land an aircraft in the desert. The light was layered with orange and crimson as if it had been pried loose from the palette of some Impressionist. One of the pilots up front attempted to use the public-address system to announce the descent to the agency director and Rob Antoine. Down they went, into the desert, as if into the center of the story, as if into the remaining pieces of the Mars mission reentry.

"Good enough?" Rob said to Debra Levin, by which he meant the telephone call.

"Fine," she said, looking at the device on her wrist to see messages incoming. She had the typical manager's ADD problem. She finished no conversation so much as she went back to the answering of new messages on her wrist.

At the end of this day or the next, Rob Antoine knew that he would be out of a job.

Of fingerprints the hand began to learn, of friction ridges inborn in its remaining and animate bits of self. Of the beauty of these papillae, of the eccrine glands, and how these were signs of a distant past. If the arm could no longer bring back the memories of the larger part of its missing physiognomy, it could at least take pleasure in the irreducible facts of its being—so oversimplified when juxtaposed with the beauty and complexity of, for example, a prefrontal cortex. The prefrontal cortex could have imagined what was taking place at this moment, the rubbing against the duct tape that bound the hand. But the prefrontal cortex could have done nothing about it, and would have quickly despaired at the effort involved. Not so the hand. Bit by bit the fingerprints began to rub off the adhesive of the duct tape. Just by means of friction. They had no reason to do otherwise; they had no other wish. Part of the simple perfection of the arm, freed from the rest of the body, was that it loved repetition. It appreciated the length of time required to scrape the adhesive off the duct tape. Its friction ridges had no sense of themselves beyond the carrying out of this task.

In ancient Persia, true, there were those who specialized in the categorizing of types of fingerprints. The Persians believed that there were nine fundamental varieties. The nine kinds of finger-prints were evidence of the esteem in which you would be held in the glorious afterworld: king, soldier, magus, priestess, miner, courtesan, oxherd, undertaker, child. Each class with its finger-print, condemned or exalted. Much later, the taxonomists of human anatomy moved on to skulls and body sizes, of which the arm had neither, but neither did it know of its dermal papillae. Magus or courtesan? The arm knew only the horror of constraint.

Duct tape had become a sort of beachhead in the battle for the American economy. The arm didn't know that a movement to build and manufacture goods here in the soulless townships of NAFTA had foundered in the early twenty-first century, allowing a great many jobs to migrate elsewhere. But in the decade that followed, in order to compete with the Sino-Indian Economic Compact, small boutique operations sprang up. In fact, the first business that was identified as profitable by the federal government was the tape-manufacturing business. A group of disenfranchised union members and some left-leaning professors from the Midwest began a grassroots nonprofit whose goal was to buy up and syndicate tape-manufacturing operations. Since there was no reason for the duct tape manufacturer called Canard Enterprises to secure a maximal profit (no publicly traded shares), it could absorb higher manufacturing costs without affecting the bottom line. In Detroit and in Toledo and in Dayton, the most American of American businesses became duct tape.

Because of its popularity among politicians and do-gooders, American duct tape achieved a new level of cultural and national pride. Chinese manufacturers of such items as epoxy wrote and published vile calumnies about American duct tape — that it was inferior, that it was unreliable, that it was made from the skin of Central Asian political prisoners — but the regular folks, even those who shopped only at the $9.99 stores, bought the domestically produced variety of duct tape and swore by it. It had been used on the first moon shots and on the Mars mission, and contained in one of the myriad NASA manuals was information on how to subdue a psychotic astronaut: *apply duct tape.* Duct tape was used by homeless persons in the Southwest to secure their belongings to their shopping carts and to patch tears in their outfits. It could be applied in a state of physical, mental, or economical deterioration. It could be applied in time of war.

For this reason, there was duct tape in the back of the van that Jean-Paul Koo and Vienna Roberts had used for their fateful trip to Rattlesnake Canyon. For this reason, because it was the preferred adhesive for a country that could no longer afford better, duct tape was at hand, and because it was at hand it was used *on the hand.* The arm, true, knew nothing about the Canard syndicate of tape manufacturers, knew nothing about how many lower-middle-class families were prevented from destitution by the manufacturing and use of duct tape. The arm knew only that it wanted to get the tape off. And in the time it would have taken to read and comment on the annual report of Canard Enterprises, NA, the arm had made significant inroads in the rending of the fabric strip that was one of the important components of duct tape. The fabric, as though it were the outer garment of a grieving mother, was being torn asunder, one square centimeter at a time.

A more detailed description of the hand is warranted at this juncture. The hand was becoming slovenly, even dangerous, in its manicure. Duct tape was strong enough to resist the elements, it was true, but it was not strong enough to resist long, unsightly fingernails. If the arm were a woman's arm, its hand would have been well on the way to becoming the hand of one of those register girls who favor press-on nails in remarkably bright colors. But the arm did not belong to a woman; in fact, it was neither woman nor man. (And had the arm had ears, it would now have heard some fearful conversation among the young people in the front of the van, much of it amounting to conjecture as to how the arm knew how to do the *sexual things* it had done. Did the arm somehow remember about sexuality? Did the arm remember the kinds of sexual activity in which it had been engaged while it was attached to a body? Was this the *muscle memory* physical therapists talked about? But then what were the chances that the arm, while alive, had been bisexual, so that it was effective at techniques with both male and female partners? It was really *gross*, one of the young people up front remarked, that the hand seemed to have really good technique. The other young person agreed; they really didn't want to think about it very much. Though if the arm had been able to think about it, instead of just doing it, being sexual, the arm would have taken pride in the gift of its erotic expertise.) Its hand resembled, at the masculine extreme, one of those hands attached to a particularly good fingerpicker, one of those folk music archival wonks who have long and unruly hair and who can mimic the styles of any of the blues greats.

Disgust, certainly, had led the young people to put the arm in the back of the van, where they wouldn't have to look at it, where it was secured to the side wall of the van with a further surplus of duct tape. Disgust was natural under the circumstances. But the arm, without any consciousness to itself, was more than efficient at the exploitation of this disgust. Many are the living things that find disgust to be their sacred ally. The arm moved swiftly in the destruction of duct tape, with its jagged blues-picking fingernails, and as the young lovers enumerated the kinds of disgust they felt about the arm, the arm steadily improved its circumstances so that, as soon as was feasible, it could wave its appendages wildly, scratching against the wall of the van, scoring the interior finish, abrading whichever surface it applied itself to. For some time, in this way, the hand resembled a wildly waving child at a parade, hastening to catch the attention of any bugling militarist that chanced by. All this would have seemed, to the casual observer, to be in vain, because the arm was still affixed to the side of the van with multiple strips of NAFTA-made duct tape. But such a reading would have been to misunderstand how freedom carries with it a certain *mayhem,* as the summer sun follows the torrents of spring. The hand, by waving and flapping like a wild beast, managed, whether intentionally or not, to shake loose the first strip of duct tape that held it against the wall of the van.

Where was the van, exactly? The van was on its way back into town and was passing, just then, the great alpaca farm that had once stretched out beneath the mountains, and from which, when its owners had been murdered by *piratas,* the alpacas had spread wide into the high desert. The van passed the farm, and then it passed some of the abandoned malls and shops along the road known as Oracle, and then it passed some of the *gated communities.* The term was an understatement. The van passed some of these *gated communities,* heading toward the dark center of the city, the unvisited *centro,* the part where most people feared to tread and where there were few vehicles, fewer still that were not abandoned. The young lovers were somewhat reassured. This was the city as they knew it.

The arm had managed to unstick yet another length of duct tape, which hung like some strange, triage-related bandage from its side, and it was now swinging upside down, like a pendulum, by the last length of duct tape that bound it in place. It was only a matter of time. The first bump in the road would free it. The van swerved around a wreck, a pair of flaming tires. The van decelerated into the right lane as a cortege of emergency vehicles raced past, wailing. The van stopped short, because of the sloppy driving of a sedan in front of it, and thereupon the arm was flung, by the laws of physics, from the wall, and with it a couple of lengths of duct tape yet clinging. There was the sound of projectiles bouncing from surface to surface in the back of the van, but with the radio on and the young lovers talking nervously between themselves, the commotion went unheard.

The arm then set about its most beloved task, which was the task of creeping. Creeping kept the arm from any awareness of its limitations. Creeping enabled the arm to continue to infect, which was high on its list. And so it began clawing its way over empty cans of WD-40 and soda bottles, scraps of blanket and tarps, a couple of fantasy novels in paperback, until it had gotten as far into the rear of the van as it could get. Did the arm somehow know how rusted out the van was? Had the arm somehow surveyed the vehicle before it began exploring the bodies of its young friends? Did it know that there was a patch so rusted out in the back of the van that you could see the double lines passing underneath? Somehow, whether by process of elimination or by some uncanny sense as to how it might secure its freedom, the arm discovered the rusty, serrated hole at the back of the van, and it began trying to pick apart the leafy curls of metal until it knew it could go down *through* the hole. Within minutes the fingers were covered in cuts, but apparently tetanus was no worry for the arm, because it was already a field guide to germs, as the young lovers would have noticed had they not been so stymied by the sheer fact of the arm. Tetanus was nothing in addition to what the arm already harbored. Despite the spurting of globules of infected blood, it managed to crawl out the hole, from which it grasped the bottom edge of the rear bumper there. For almost a quarter mile, like something out of an action film, the arm hung.

In the van, the young lovers found themselves meanwhile

improved. The satellite radio was on, and the radio was a comfort, because it was often staffed by people from the milieu of the young—sullen, underemployed middle-class people with violently passionate opinions. This while the arm clung to the bumper, as bits of its protuberant ulna and its supinator were scorched against the pavement. But since the arm had no nerve center, its nerves fired only haphazardly, with a kind of bittersweet nostalgia. It was afraid of nothing, and no pain bothered it. It hung on not because it was waiting for the perfect time to let go, but *just because.* Because there were only so many approaches to the world, grasping and scrabbling being two of them. Given the chance, occasionally, to cling with single-minded tenacity, the arm did so. But when the van came to a stop at a traffic light, somewhere around the 6000 north block, the arm dropped off and rolled like a tossed newspaper of old until it found itself by the side of the road. Freed from confinement.

Not distant, at least for those who were able-bodied or who had access to a vehicle, lay the Ina Estates, one of the most exclusive gated communities in the Rio Blanco area. Its red adobe was repainted every other year by repeat offenders among the would-be emigrant population. Following a pattern made popular in the early part of the century, the Ina Estates had actually *seceded* from Rio Blanco. The estates refused to pay taxes to the city proper, and since they had their own police and security, the city had not yet mustered the resolve to call in the National Guard. Ina Estates had its own school, its own development agency, a weekly farmers' market, and a library that thoroughly vetted its collections. There was even a helipad, so that if the Ina Estates needed to lock the gates in order to prevent contact with the unruly region around it, it could do so and still fly in locally grown produce.

The Ina Estates, that is, were waiting it out. Waiting out eight consecutive years of a constricting gross domestic product, seven years of declining employment, which now stood at a bracing 17 percent, seven years of inflation and ballooning national debt, six and a half years of declining college enrollment, rising numbers in larceny, in particular grand theft auto, rising numbers of violent crimes, rapes and murders (and especially rising numbers of murders of *strangers*), increases in every kind of drug use, in vagrancy, in homelessness, in emigration. The Ina Estates, and the other city-states like it, were about waiting all this out, about awaiting another *American century,* in the unlikely event that one should present itself. The estates could handle a few foreclosures, since they had saved well in the flush days, and since no man or woman was allowed to purchase a unit without sufficient savings to cover the cost of the mortgage at present. Things being what they were, however, the Ina Estates could not always insure that its employee base was up to the task, since these were hard times for wage earners. The regional workforce was noteworthy for its hopelessness, and the security guy out front of the Ina Estates, loitering on his personal transporter, was no exception. The security guy, André, had been speed-dialing his ex-girlfriend, while trying not to overturn his vehicle or to disturb its gyroscope, to say that he really would *try,* he really would *try,* he was desperate to *try* to quit playing around with a certain multiuser virtual environment known as *Tajikistan.* He was going to give it up, he was going to give it up, he swore, and it was all because he had himself seen things in the tribal areas that no man should see.

Because he was making solemn oaths, he was not using the handheld monitor that purported to give heat signatures of intruders, such as the vole or the bobcat. It was true that the arm probably had a meager heat signature, because with the exception of the septic battalions coursing through it, there was very little about the arm that was *alive* in the conventional sense. Furthermore, André, had he been scanning the area in front of himself, would have been looking for some kind of conspiracy of drug-addled men in their twenties, the kind of guys who temporarily believe that the *smash and grab* is the only way to live. For these reasons, André failed to notice the arm.

The first house on the corner belonged to the Neilsons. Aristotle Neilson, in his midfifties, had been a prominent politician in Rio

Blanco, rising to the level of deputy mayor before his stripper scandal. Neilson's particular flavor of stripper scandal was not terribly new, nor particularly shocking. He liked Catholic schoolgirl outfits on his consorts, though he was always scrupulous about making sure that these professionals were *of age.* His wife stood by him during his tearful resignation. Since then, Aristotle had served quietly as a freelance accountant for corporations. He rarely left the house.

In any conventional horror story, Neilson's situation would be suffused with karmic resonances. He had, himself, elected to obtain the services of uniform-wearing exotic dancers. No one had made him do it. In the conventional horror story, therefore, he *deserved* what was coming. In these pages, however, he didn't deserve what was coming, and the fact that the arm had made it under the gate and into the Ina Estates without any trouble, without being run over by any onrushing vehicle, and was now making its way across the gravel lawn and rock garden that were features of the Neilsons' comfortable property, this was all owing to chance, sheer systemic chance. The arm was not karmic repayment, not about guilt, not about retribution. Chance, in this story, is a much harsher taskmaster than the Old Testament retributive theologies.

In order to prove that Aristotle Neilson, named after the Greek philosopher by a mother who liked orderliness, didn't in any way deserve what was about to happen to him, and because it's unfair to kill a character who is not fully developed, we must pause here briefly to note a couple of the finer things about Aristotle Neilson, who at the moment that the arm was rubbing off its epidermis hauling itself over the rocks in the front yard was looking at the stamp collection he'd assembled as a boy. Aristotle Neilson had extremely small eyes, beady little things, and he knew it. This was, in fact, one of many reasons that Aristotle had never quite believed in his wife's love, though she tried and tried to nurture this sensation by feting every birthday and by repetitively intoning that there was no husband in the Southwest more generous and helpful than he. On the philanthropic front, despite his crimes, Aristotle

Neilson continued anonymously sponsoring college education for kids from the Native American reservations. He always went to see the graduations of his Native American kids who made it all the way through, and he always reminded them at some point in their educations that English composition was a really excellent class if you got a good instructor. Aristotle Neilson had no children of his own, owing to a sterility that had gone undiscovered, ironically, until his ambivalence about child rearing was past.

A further list of the poignancies of Aristotle Neilson's life could go on and on, but, under the circumstances, time was short. In the Ina Estates, owing to the fact that there was security outside the walls of the campus, people often left their doors open and their cars unlocked. It wasn't really a problem for the arm to secure an entrance into the Neilson residence. Mrs. Neilson, who had completely overcome the legacy of her husband's political self-destruction by throwing herself into an administrative position at a day care center in town, was not at home. It was only Aristotle on the premises. Aristotle Neilson, plenty satisfied with his anonymity, with the absolute lack of interest on the part of his neighbors. It was only recently that the very serious episodes of depression, variants on that time-honored *DSM-VIII* listing, *depression as a result of public indignity,* had begun to lift. He was idly flipping through some of the sheets of stamps that he had collected as a boy in the state of Oregon, where his father had been a middle manager with the postal service. (This was before stamps were abolished entirely.) In particular, Aristotle was looking at a sequence of stamps entitled Legends of Jazz, and as he looked at these fanciful and beautiful designs, he was also wearing a headset that played one of the satellite stations, and because he could hear nothing, therefore, he could not hear the arm, which had launched itself like a shipwrecked sailor onto some of the old-fashioned books on Aristotle's old-fashioned bookshelves, where the arm was managing to slide erratically from one row of books to another, not without dangling occasionally, sometimes by a finger or two, and doing so while dripping the occasional

Pollockian spatter on Aristotle's Mexican tile floor. In the time before the arm got to Aristotle, he did *not* stop to consider *why call girls in Catholic school uniforms* had such an attraction, because that would have occasioned too tidy a dispatch for Aristotle Neilson. (The arm flung itself from a shelf full of old encyclopedias onto the right-most edge of Neilson's desk, which was covered with hard-copied files of his clients in the accounting consultancy, dislodging a couple of these files so that they toppled and spilled some of their trade secrets.) Neilson would have claimed not to know the answer to this question (of schoolgirl outfits), had he been able, in some vulnerable and unthreatening circumstance, even to address it. Perhaps, say, he had been in the steam room at the gymnasium at the Ina Estates with Irving Bogle, a lawyer friend who'd had business before the city of Rio Blanco and who had seen the denouement with the hookers as an entrapment designed to remove a politician unprotected by major benefactors. Let's say that Bogle and Neilson were in the steam room, and Bogle, after a long silence, had asked the question:

"Ari, what was the deal with the schoolgirl outfits, anyway? You don't have to answer that if you don't want to. Hell, I probably wouldn't answer it myself. But every now and then I wonder if it wouldn't help a little bit to talk about this stuff."

In the steam room, in the sheets of vapor, the two of them were visible and invisible to each other, and that was how they liked it. They liked some privacy and dignity in the revealing of the body's failing. Few were the guys who still strode into the steam room with their obesity hanging about them like a fashion statement.

Aristotle, in the mists of that morning, might have said to Bogle, "You know, it's a question I've wanted to answer, but the truth of the matter is I've never been sure. I mean, between you and me, I chased after some skirt, Irving, because in a certain time of my life chasing after some skirt just made me feel vital and alive, but now that it's later in the day, I kind of feel that the chasing was never about beauty at all. I went to one of those schools in Portland where they mandated uniforms for the kids. That's how it was. Did I have such a great time in school? Not really. No one much liked me, because I had these great big ears and these very small eyes. I wasn't a total pariah. I wasn't that kid who never had a single friend or cowered in the corner. But I was constantly trying to get close to these girls. Only problem was that the pretty girls, the ones who hiked up the skirts of their uniforms or whatever, they were the cruelest ones in the yard, the cruelest ones at recess. Maybe, as a therapist suggested once or twice, wanting the one thing that would have saved me from social exile, which was the one thing that I couldn't ever have—"

How could the arm leap, when the arm had no legs with which to leap? It must have found some kind of ledge, some plinth at the rear of the desk, from which to fling itself, maybe that area beside the workstation where there were a number of accountancy texts, a few reference books. Maybe, in the reverie of stamp collecting, the reverie of the moment, the arm had taken advantage of Neilson. Perhaps it was simply trying to climb up into the window to see the last of the sunrise, which was, as it often was in the smoggy, dusty valley beneath the Santa Catalinas, arresting, and running afoul of the window there, it turned and fell on the man at the desk, in a sinister rage. Maybe that was how the arm came to fly at his throat, digging in a couple of its razor fingernails just above the Adam's apple, drawing blood, and then doing the best it could, immediately, to close off Neilson's airway. The condition is known as hypoxia, as you may know, but in this case the route was asphyxia via compression of the trachea. Time to unconsciousness is fifteen or twenty seconds in many cases. Once the arm was attached to Neilson's throat, he naturally leaped up from the ergonomically designed desk chair and flung this chair back behind him, grabbing at the arm. His appearance during the ignominious episode of strangulation would have seemed comical to any observer; it would have seemed as though Neilson were holding the arm up to his own neck, when in fact he was trying to dislodge the fell thing, all while turning at first red and then a little bit blue, exertion demanding more oxygen, air supply rapidly dwindling. Neilson then stumbled backward over the chair and fell onto his right side, and his body began the thrashing and trembling that often characterizes manual strangling. This would perhaps have been enough to fling off the disembodied arm, were it not busy crushing the larynx and several of the bones in Neilson's neck. This is the sign of a first-rate strangler. In general, a strangler must be able to overpower his victim entirely to achieve such marked results. Well within the fifteen-second window, therefore, Neilson was unconscious, if not actually paralyzed from the neck down. The restriction of blood flow caused brain death rapidly thereafter. Since the arm didn't know how long it took to strangle a man, the arm didn't know when to let go, so the arm clutched and strangled until its muscles were no longer capable of the activity. In Neilson's case, this took almost five minutes, and in those five minutes there were all kinds of lacerations and contusions and worse that were visited upon the area of his neck. The arm waited and it punctured, and then, as if it had changed its mind about the whole business, it slid across the office floor, which was connected to a dining room and a pantry through a long, gently lit hallway in Mexican tile, and down this hall the arm went, and into the kitchen, trailing bloody smudges and septic ooze. In the kitchen, it bumped around various cabinets and baseboards, leaving more evidence of its crime, leaving so much evidence of the crime that the initial police reports would worry about the murder being multiple.

After blundering for the better part of an hour, the arm managed to push open a screen door in the the kitchen, one that led out back to where the refuse cans were stored. This was directly adjacent to the backyard of the Neilsons' neighbor Tad Sklar, one of the few people in the Ina Estates that the Neilsons didn't like. Sklar's golf cart was parked by *his* garbage cans, and what the arm did, with uncanny instinct, was climb into the back of the golf cart and get down underneath the front seat, on the passenger side — just before Tad Sklar headed out to the solar-powered mini-golf emporium up the road from the Ina Estates. Sklar needed practice on his short game.

The arm, in the next hours, changed venues at an alarming pace, almost as if it had preconceptions about vectors of contagion. The following represents only a partial list of its many addresses: at the mini-golf emporium, the arm all but levitated itself over some cyclone fencing. It landed in the parking lot of a storefront devoted to adult novelties. The adult novelties business stocked a number of items that looked a great deal like the arm, and the goo that trailed after the arm would not have been out of place on a number of the frequenters of that place of business, who were occasionally flecked with excrescences owing to a lack of medical insurance with which they might have been treated. The arm managed again to haul itself into a van parked out front. The adult novelty wholesaler's van was being unloaded at the time. It was possible that the arm somehow remembered its earlier van ride and had come to believe that vans were the preeminent variety of travel in the post-capitalist world. Fortunately for the arm, the wholesaler of rubber goods wouldn't have noticed the rotting flesh of the arm among the plastic-wrapped wares, and didn't, and from there the arm therefore managed to ride back into Rio Blanco itself, into the city limits, where it disembarked at a Mexican drive-thru restaurant while the wholesaler was relieving himself by a dumpster. The arm then terrified a pair of stray cats that loitered beneath the picnic table nearby. It was here that the dread appendage reclined for a long while.

Biology would seem to indicate that at some point the arm would be thoroughly consumed by illness, its raw materials depleted. Even death, as a process, is not eternal, especially in the presence of *caseous necrosis,* in which the remaining cellular material starts to look like cottage cheese. However, a homeless gentleman named Miguel, an innocent, came by the drive-thru restaurant, looking for comestibles that might have been thrown away by the proprietors. Out by the dumpster, Miguel didn't take note of an arm quickly rousing itself from its torpor. But the arm, sensing

movement, stowed away in a Safeway cart beneath an army blanket that Miguel had picked up along the way, dripping on a number of magazines that contained photographs of tropical scenery.
Miguel, who was exhausted, and somewhat impaired by reason of
advanced alcoholism, was pushing toward the park on Stone, Don
Hummel Park, where the Union of Homeless Citizens was, at that
moment, attempting to conduct its massive rally and fund-raising
event. Miguel, according to his impeccable credentials as an innocent with anxiety disorder, didn't intend to stay for the rally. He
didn't even know there was a rally, because he was uninformed on
current events. He'd thought he might sleep in the park.

Every corner of the Don Hummel Park thronged with the
disenfranchised hordes. From the northwest, by an avenue of
shuttered motels, of darkened neon signs fifty or sixty years old,
they came; from the southwest and the unvisited downtown area
of Rio Blanco, where once there had been banks and insurers
and law firms, they came; from the southeast, in which direction streamed the would-be emigrants to South of the Border;
and from the northeast, they came, the direction of loners, of
homeless persons who preferred to sleep up in the foothills
among the mountain lions and coyotes, to take their chances
with the tooth and claw of the wild; every corner of the park on
Stone was a seething mass of unruly humanity, all of it dispossessed by the state and by the mechanisms of government. Just
as the Union of Homeless Citizens seemed to have organized
one quadrant of the park, to have subdued it into a condition
where the constituents might at least listen to speeches about
their interests and needs, another part of the park would break
into hilarity or fistfights or political agnosticism, such that the
men and women and families gathered there would lose interest
and would begin transacting their underground economics or
would begin constructing anew their temporary shelters. (These
living spaces were harder to come by than in other regions of
the nation where lumber was more common. Here the homeless
structures often featured packing cardboard, but also the spines

of scorched saguaro cacti, and duct tape, because what was *not* made out of duct tape?)

From this municipality of the forgotten, forgotten by mothers, fathers, sisters, brothers, forgotten by the state, the city, the nation, the Union of Homeless Citizens was attempting to organize a proper voting bloc, in order that delivery of services might be brought to the needy in Don Hummel Park. Given the size of the homeless population here, there was a genuine possibility, especially in the era of would-be secession by the gated communities, that the Union of Homeless Citizens could field a slate of administrators to seize control of the city itself. The non-homeless organizers, the *stationaries,* as they were known, had attempted, in trying to program a rally that would appeal to these disparate nomads, to bring *entertainment* as well as enlightenment to the people. Your mind and your ass were to be moved. Miguel arrived at the park just as a mariachi band, in Mexican uniform, was attempting to sing old Mexican love songs to the audience, especially such old Mexican songs as had a particular relevance to other revolutionary movements, the Zapatistas, the mestizos of Mexico City, the Maya movement of 2020, and so forth. The songs weren't going over well. Whenever there was a lull in the action, the homeless citizens began attempting to barter, or to criticize, or to make impolite conversation.

Above all, and even in the half-light of urban night, they were all *well tanned.* It was the way you could tell the homeless citizens from the rest, who were regularly visiting paling stations. They were tan, and they were bearded, and they often had melanomas sprouting somewhere on their faces or their arms. And they had achieved, in their seething, undulating mass of disorder, something close to a perfect habitation of the present moment. In fact, a number of Buddhist ashrams in the region, as well as the *omnium gatherum,* that shadowy alternative cultural organization, had begun courting the Union of Homeless Citizens. Among the residents of Don Hummel Park, however, few were following the rally closely, nor did they know how they were intended to be organized, although there was a rumor of some burritos and tacos being given away at a certain bandstand. The citizens of Don Hummel Park were casually alert to the possibilities of changing the laws in their favor, but were more excited by the possibility of getting fed.

The political arm of the Union of Homeless Citizens, therefore, the part staffed almost entirely by *stationaries,* decided that there was one and only one nonnegotiable plank in their movement, and that plank was against ownership. *All things in common trust!* said the literature that was handed out to the relevant parties, though this was later thought to be too obscure in terms of its locution and was amended to read simply *Lend It to Your Neighbor!* Lend whatever it was you had. Miguel, who didn't read English terribly well, wouldn't have understood the finer points here, even had he taken the time to give them his full attention. He quickly set up underneath a tree in the park. Above him there were men who had climbed these nonnative growths and nailed up structures there. Miguel called to them, as he also asked a couple of men nearby if they wanted some tacos and would they be willing to effect a swap.

Among the activists who were most engaged in this great awakening of the Union of Homeless Citizens were Larry and Faith Roberts. Larry had been fired from URB six or eight years before for extending invitations to audit his classes to undocumented workers he met at the bus station in town. Later, he even attempted to make these new acquaintances his teaching assistants. His wife was mainly known as a writer, if a slightly inconsistent one, of articles about forms of economic oppression. By the time Miguel had arrived in the center of the Don Hummel Park and was busying about trying to secure some barter for the tacos he didn't need, Faith Roberts was, in fact, talking into the microphone, without getting anywhere much at all. Miguel asked another guy, in his Spanglish, if he wanted some food.

"I got some tacos here. Pretty good. Pretty fresh."

The blank expression was irritating, but there was no shortage of blank expressions in the present company.

The grandstanding from the bandstand echoed off the falling-down houses of the neighborhood, and in that reverberant and hard-to-hear sonic field, Miguel could only make out a few things: "The way you all make shelters...I'm sure you know...is a powerful suggestion of spiritual presence and rootedness...when faced with the colossal appetites...of a culture that wanted to...rule the world...but lost all that it once had...including its moral standing..."

As if the passage of seconds enabled the Anglo with the blank expression, he of the burned-out eyes, to respond, the man offered Miguel a fistful of pills immediately recognizable as the universal currency of Don Hummel Park, polyamphetamine. It wasn't the case that everyone there was a user, as indeed Miguel was no longer a user himself, but that didn't mean that the stuff didn't have value. The dollar, what with inflation, and because it was trading badly against the peso, was nobody's idea of a currency. Food stamps, which were scarce because of the fiscal situation of the nation as a whole, were more valuable, but polyamphetamine was the one thing that seemed to accrue value. The city that housed Don Hummel Park may have been full of people who hadn't gone to college or didn't speak the language or who were somewhat blunted from the early stages of cirrhosis, but they understood the basics of supply and demand. Miguel, therefore, was happy to offer a taco or two for the polyamphetamine, except that he had a pang of regret. This stuff was probably worth fifty or sixty dollars, and the tacos maybe an eighth of that, and it wasn't really a fair trade. *The sleeping man gets taken in the wager;* this was one of the Eastern bits of wisdom that had been circulating among them.

"That's kind of you, *señor,* but I'm going to look into this cart and see what else I can offer you, in addition." The Anglo, slate entirely wiped clean, waited.

Miguel was babbling some sequence of kindly thoughts about the beauty of the evening. A monsoon, if one was possible that night, would take the edge off the heat, and so forth, and as he was lifting up the edge of the army blanket, which was really one of his most precious bits of linen, he found himself in possession of an arm.

Truths are lubricated and personal things, and there is an adherent for every truth under the sun. Some truths, despite veracity, will appear to be downright ludicrous. In addition, there is the category of truths known only to people under severe conditions, such as during the withdrawal of a drug from their system. This category of truths is more slippery, more reflective of a dynamic system than of the simple on-and-off modalities of street-level truth, and in his investigations of this approach, the withdrawal approach to truth, Miguel had found, occasionally, that he saw things that weren't, according to more empirical methods of investigation, *there,* just as there were other things that he assumed were there but were not. A lamppost that you could put your hand *right through,* for example. He had learned, under certain circumstances, to be patient, to allow the different registers of truth to coexist, just as the various dimensions coexisted; it was *all good* to Miguel, and he didn't become unduly worried when there was something happening that should not, by most accounts, have been happening at all. He therefore did not *gasp* when he beheld the severed arm. He didn't treat the arm as though it were somehow *abject,* a thing to be feared or driven out of the comforting rabble of civilization. He just wasn't sure it was there. Nevertheless, after looking at the arm for some time, after looking at the wild, staring eyes of the Anglo who also beheld it, after watching the arm contract and extend its fingers, he had to assume that there was a genuine possibility that the arm existed in the empirical world, resting in his shopping cart and gumming up his magazines.

He looked at the Anglo guy. "I could, well, I could offer you this."

He pointed at the arm. It wiggled its fingers.

The Anglo guy handed over the polyamphetamine tablets, guaranteed to wipe out short-term memory entirely, and as if the arm were somehow a talisman in his own private pantheon, the

Anglo guy lifted the arm out of the shopping cart. This was done in such a way that Miguel never had any contact with the thing, though he'd just been rooting around in there. He would have confessed that he had a feeling that contact with it was unwise, even though he couldn't have said why. The stuff coming out of it that looked like rubber cement was probably not the kind of thing you wanted to touch. The Anglo guy apparently had no such reservations. He treated the arm as though it were a *shillelagh* or other device suitable for assault on antagonists, and he disappeared into the crowd with his new prize.

There the arm was quickly passed from hand to hand: a bunch of men around a campfire passed it back and forth attempting to play the arm as though it were a clarinet or a soprano saxophone. One of them actually believed it was a water pipe with which certain intoxicants could be smoked. One man tried to arm-wrestle the arm, but he found that the arm was a disappointing competitor because it couldn't be propped up effectively. A woman attempted to get the arm to make a fist, so that she could batter her boyfriend with it. The arm was good-natured about this. It was in a dormant period, or perhaps near its final demise, but it lacked the wherewithal to respond to any of these lighthearted engagements with unpleasantness. In the distance, Faith Roberts was shouting, in a shrill, programmatic way, *Rise up! Rise up! Rise up! Rise up!* And then, as if according to prior arrangement, the police began to storm Don Hummel Park.

The electroshock sidearm, or Taser, was another of the businesses that flourished in an era when almost nothing was made in North America, and when it became possible to administer the electroshock from a distance, when it was no longer necessary to get up close to the subject to persuade him with *pain compliance*–styled rhetoric, then the electroshock sidearm assumed unimpeachable status among law-enforcement officials. All the border patrol officers along the as-yet-uncompleted freedom wall that separated Rio Blanco and the southern part of Arizona from our trading partner South of the Border used electroshock sidearms, as it was also considered sporting to wear the night-vision shades and take down the border jumpers now and then.

Moreover, Rio Blanco understaffed its law-enforcement department, because of budgetary problems. As a result, the police relied on the electroshock devices to attempt to do the big jobs, when they had to. They entered the Don Hummel Park immediately upon hearing the rhetoric ascend to its revolutionary theatricality, hoping *not* to have to subdue the crowd, which numbered in the tens of thousands, while the police were but a couple hundred. They had blockaded all the corners of the park and had a number of old, dented school buses with which to round up detainees. They moved into the park, in riot gear, in a fashion that was calculated to be imposing. It was near the southwest corner of the park, in the course of mopping up, that a certain rank-and-file member of the constabulary saw a man waving a severed human arm. The officer attempted to remove the arm from the man's grasp, calling after him that he would need to relinquish it, identifying himself as an officer and so forth, but the man with the arm, before leaping over some playground equipment, tossed the arm to another man, in a move that would perhaps, had this been an American football game, been referred to as a *lateral pass,* and the man who received the arm, which appeared to be waving to the crowd as it went by, faked as though to hand it off to an officer near him, but he kept the arm to himself before passing it behind his back, hotdogging, to a friend, who bounded into an encampment, a scattering of tents and lean-tos, going in one end and out another, until the police who descended on this spot were, it needs to be said, *confused.* The *pain compliance* began not long after, and as soon as the *pain compliance* began, the Union of Homeless Citizens ran for the hills, quite literally. No exit was without its unlucky souls, the innocents who were swept into the buses and hauled off to the penal wastes. But those who were more resourceful jumped walls and police barricades, and commandeered vehicles going by, or ran into nearby cul de sacs and rubble-strewn yards where they would not be found for days, if at all.

Into the midst of this mayhem came the rains. Violently, indis-
criminately, and retributively. As if there were a reservoir that
had been collecting, somewhere in the troposphere, during the
months of drought, until in early fall, out of spite, some disgruntled engineer threw the lever on the trough. The majority
of those ill affected by the monsoon season in Rio Blanco, as
with those more ill affected by the drought in the first place,
were those gathered at Don Hummel Park, in the process of being rounded up by the constabulary. There weren't more than
a pair of rain slickers in the entire rally, although the Union
of Homeless Citizens was equipped with polyethylene garbage
bags, which were scored for use as outerwear (you stuck your
head through the perforated section). The rains, however, were
violent enough that no one remembered to man the booth with
the polyethylene bags, and the police, who had been given a
weather forecast by dispatch (dewpoint: 58 percent, chance of
thunderstorms, some severe, 65 percent), did little better. The
police drew to a halt wherever they stood, with their Tasers and
their nightsticks, and attempted to affix rain visors and to don
high-visibility ponchos. The remainder of the crowd, well versed
in dispersal, made tracks. Only the homeless citizens who were
impaired or brain damaged or perhaps simply in love with
the pyrotechnical display of the elements stood and watched,
watched palm fronds washed into the nearby drains, watched
the rivers swell in the streets, watched the few automobiles of
Rio Blanco attempting to ford the rivers that had sprung up,
watched one vehicle strike a utility pole, watched as lawfulness
and lawlessness alike were swept away. Anything smokable was
now wet, anything drinkable was now watered down in this cu-
mulonimbus multicell in the mature-to-dissipating stage whose
elapsed rainfall was, within the hour, 1.37 inches.

Larry and Faith Roberts backed out of the bandstand, slipped
behind a pair of large speakers that stood there totemically. There
was a bank of portable johns as well, off of which the rain pelted
with such severity that the Robertses wondered if it were not

genuine hail. They got between these portable johns and the stunned and watered-down police, and then, when there was an opportunity, they slipped into a van marked Union of Homeless Citizens. A glaringly obvious getaway vehicle, true, and that was why it worked so well.

A busy day for Woo Lee Koo, medical researcher, now working as a paid consultant for the National Aeronautics and Space Administration, whose brief was to search the hospitals and areas in and around Rio Blanco for persons complaining of unexplained bacterial infections. He was also in search of portions of human bodies, limbless bodies, bodiless limbs, portions and fragments, hard-to-distinguish bits of tissue, DNA, blood and guts, and so forth; and, in particular, according to rumor and forensic evidence, a certain human arm. A human arm missing one finger, with two others rather badly reattached. Wearing a wedding ring. If that weren't enough, if all that bloody responsibility were not enough, there had also been a call from his assistant Noelle, who claimed that she had some incredible news, news he wouldn't believe, and would he please come down to the primate laboratory as soon as he was able. Despite these rather fascinating developments, either one of which would bear on his continuing researches in the area of cellular senescence, Koo found himself, unfortunately, completely preoccupied elsewhere that afternoon. He sat in the kitchen of his unit on the west side of town, slurping slowly, methodically, from a mug of ginseng tea, bewailing, if only to himself, the relationship that currently existed between himself and his son, Jean-Paul Koo.

His relationship with his own father, who'd died when he was at university in Korea, was noteworthy for its great collegiality, as, he supposed, was often the case in Korean households. His father was not a dispenser of narrowly argued legalistic regulation, short-tempered, and/or selfish. No, his father was gentle, patient, and very funny, with a broad smile and great wisps of white hair that would come loose in the wind, as though he had suddenly grown horns. Father and son were so close that they often walked the streets of the city with an arm around each other. Koo's friends marveled, and always spoke of elder Koo as the *best father on the block,* though in truth Woo Lee Koo did not believe his father was anything much out of the ordinary. In fact, it was precisely his ordinariness that made Koo's father so enviable. He resembled a medical experiment that goes exactly as planned. His father's reactions were predictable, verifiable, kindly, and perhaps for this reason there was no rebelling against the elder Koo. The elder Koo had had, according to legend, a passionate gambling streak as a young man; he'd worked his way through the casinos of Hong Kong and Macao, betting and losing, winning and betting again. His father was always trying to encourage Woo Lee Koo to take more risks and to revel in the pleasing uncertainty of human events. For these reasons, his death, in a very avoidable car accident, struck Woo Lee Koo hard and continued to trouble him. His father's death may have been responsible, Koo supposed, for the single-minded way he pursued his medical ambitions, as if to look up from the textbooks would somehow result in a disagreeable flooding of sentiment.

How was it possible, Koo thought, stirring in a third molten spoonful of nonnutritive sugar substitute, that he could have loved his father so much only to feel such disrespect and boredom from Jean-Paul whenever he attempted to talk with the boy? If he tried to describe what it was that he, Koo, did, professionally speaking, which frankly many other conversationalists would find very compelling, if not philosophically *electrifying*—tissue regeneration, the biological definition of death, elective organ replacement, and so forth—his son would, as they say, *glaze over,* though his own business, this fanciful proposal for a company devoted to cut-rate cosmetic surgery procedures, was not at all distant from Koo's research. If he tried to ask the boy about the particulars of his emotional life, his ambitions, his dreams, his sense of responsibility to the world, whether or not he cared to have a family, the younger Koo recoiled as if a branding iron had just been applied. It was only when Koo attempted to discuss theories of management and business practice, subjects on which Koo had only limited information, most of which came from his lawyer, that Jean-Paul made any attempt to engage with his dad. Even then, the boy screwed his face up into the oddest expression, something between a wince and smirk, as if spending forty-five minutes in a room with his own father was akin to proctological examination. At times, Koo was ashamed to admit, he lost his temper with Jean-Paul. *Do you know what I went through to bring you here to this country? Has it occurred to you to wonder what your mother would think of what you are doing now? Do you not recall that I have a reputation to protect with the university? That I am a well-known figure in this city, and that I view myself as a guest of the university in this city and this country as a whole?* These moments when Koo struck out, in his adopted tongue, did little good. He knew this. Even if he felt better at the moment in which he upbraided the boy, he knew that the words wouldn't register. Sometimes Jean-Paul himself would lash out in turn: *You don't know what it's like to grow up now! You don't know what this place is like, the kinds of pressures I'm under! Most of the kids are just out there on the street doing drugs and going nowhere, and I'm, like, fucking trying to make something of myself.* Oh yes, always with that word. That active participle serving as an adjective (or as verb, noun, prefix, suffix). What was the purpose of this word? People said this word for no purpose but to buy time while they attempted to compose their thoughts. And that was not the only problem with his son's heartfelt speech! Just look at the boy! Koo would have said these words to the arbitrator who might have been present at the conversation. Look at the clothes this boy wears! And look at that wanton girlfriend who trails after him everywhere. There's a stupidity to her expression! You can't tell me that one look into the eyes of this girl and you do not feel the vapidity of her expression, as though she has never had a day of hardship in her life, as though she has never struggled for anything. When I look at a specimen of this kind, Koo would have said to the hypothetical arbitrator, I see why this country has fallen upon these hard times. Everywhere I see the expressions, the vacant expressions of the hardened consumer. This

can be fixed with a pill! This can be fixed with a cosmetic procedure! This muscle can be made slack! This muscle can be made
hard! Please wager your hard-earned minimum-wage dollars here
on this collateralized debt obligation! These kids, he would have
told the arbitrator, are willing to ride the elevator down, until it
comes to rest at the bottom of the bottom-most subbasement, just
taking and taking, never once offering back. Koo would think these
things, even if he never said them, and never having said them,
he would suffer with the unsaid, and he would wait until he was
in his garage, with his cryogenically preserved wife, to unburden
himself of his many cares. What did it mean that his most lasting
and satisfying conversations were with a woman who, if not dead
entirely — her tissue was preserved — was nonetheless absent from
the conversation in every way?

He had failed as a father, he supposed.

It was in the midst of this ginseng reverie, as the satellite entertainment downlink broadcast some baroque classics, some musical crumpets, that he heard the sound of his son pulling into the
driveway. It had been nearly two days since he had seen Jean-Paul.
And even though he had just enumerated all the ways in which
he couldn't possibly communicate with the boy, he felt, oddly, a
joy and apprehension about Jean-Paul entering the house. It was
just better when the young man was around, and since, most days,
Jean-Paul wouldn't tell him where he'd been, there was nothing
to do but watch and wait.

The traces of his wife in the boy's smile. His wife's eyes, those
unearthly green eyes that no Korean boy ever had. His hair was
lighter, not jet-black. And there was something almost European
about the lad, as if Jean-Paul had walked out of some French gangster picture. He loved these traces of familial history.

Koo recognized immediately, however, that the boy was somewhat upset, even though the worthless girlfriend trailed behind
him in some kind of outfit that had no purpose but the purpose
of removal.

"Dad," Jean-Paul exclaimed, "I'm so glad you're here!"

These were not words that were ordinarily pronounced. In fact, Koo was lost for a moment in the consideration of whether such a thing had *ever* been said there at all.

"I am very glad to see you too. I was very worried. Would you mind telling me where—"

"There's something I need to talk to you about, Dad. We've just, uh, we've just seen, uh, something, like, really horrible and amazing; I don't even know how to, I don't even think I can..."

The girl stood in the rear of this tableau, which was the tableau of fathers and sons eager to communicate with each other but short on the skills. She too seemed unsettled, though Koo would have been hard-pressed to describe what was unsettled in her bovine expression, which mostly seemed to want sex or food.

"Please go ahead and tell me," he said to his son.

"We were out in the desert. We were in..."

"Rattlesnake Canyon," said the girl.

"Right. Rattlesnake Canyon."

"And what were you doing there exactly?" Koo asked.

"We were picnicking in the canyon," Jean-Paul said. "We had some vitamin-enhanced water and some cheese. Picnicking."

"You are not old enough to purchase wine," Koo said, "which means that if you are lying about consuming alcohol, you must have taken alcoholic beverages from someone. I certainly hope you were not driving with the bottle of wine open, because you know how these things are taken very seriously by the police, and with good reason."

Jean-Paul said, "Dad, please just listen."

"How can I do otherwise?" said Woo Lee Koo.

"We had finished up with the picnic, and we decided we were going to nap a little bit, and we both lay down and shut our eyes."

"Were you wearing sufficient sunblock?"

"Dad! So anyway, we were totally fucking *out like a light,* you know, and I guess we were, like, in each other's arms or something—"

"Like a couple of pretzels," the girl remarked, "and we couldn't tell which part of us was which part of us, and which part belonged to the other."

The truth began to emerge in Koo as though he were the scrap of photographic paper and this conversation were the image coming to its fruition. The truth emerged and he watched it emerging, delighting in its shape and course.

"And," Jean-Paul said, "and suddenly, and, uh, I don't even know how to..."

"There was someone there with us," the girl said. "We both felt it."

"We felt like there was someone there with us, and at first we each thought it was, you know, one another, and then we realized there was this *other* person. And I opened my eyes."

Jean-Paul seemed to open his eyes wide at this moment, as if to demonstrate.

"And I saw this *thing.* I saw this arm. It was an arm that wasn't attached to anything. It was lying on the blanket with us. And it was just lying there at first, and that was bad enough."

"Bad enough that the arm was there," the girl said, and she came up closer beside Jean-Paul, and now her own hand drifted up toward Jean-Paul's neck, and Koo watched this, as if her hand were somehow related to the story. The girl's hand seemed to pause before selecting a muscle group where it would alight. It finally reached a spot at the meeting of neck and shoulder. She went on. "But even that was kind of fucked up somehow, because then you had to ask this question, how the fuck did this arm get there? How did this arm get all the way out into the desert where we were? Did some guy come by, like, carrying the arm? Was some mountain lion carrying the arm in its mouth and just decided to drop it off, you know?"

"But then that wasn't the worst part, Dad," Jean-Paul said.

At this moment something happened that rarely happened

between the two of them, the Koos, had not happened even when his wife was dying, because in that dark time Jean-Paul was too young to know much about the ways of the world. What happened was that for a second, Jean-Paul was overcome with feeling, and a couple of tears overran the banks of his eyes. And tracked lower.

"The worst part was that the arm *moved.* The arm was still moving somehow. It was able, I don't know how it was fucking able, but it was somehow fucking able to move, and it was moving toward Vienna, and it touched me—"

Koo had sat by, listening to the story, awaiting the moment when he could intervene, but his pleasing sense of knowingness evaporated at this recitation of the facts, and he pushed back the stool from the counter in the kitchen:

"You touched it? How much did you touch it?"

"I touched it just a little bit."

"How much is a little bit? I need to know exactly how much you touched it."

"What are you saying? Dad, are you saying—"

"I'm asking you how much you touched it. Was it oozing any material? Did you notice anything coming from it? Any liquids at all?"

"What are you saying? Do you know something about this arm?"

He cared little about salving their *alarm* just then. He was thinking about: treatment options and the urgency of prompt diagnosis.

"I think I have some very powerful antibiotics in the bathroom," said Koo to his son. "You must come with me. We don't know whether they will work yet, but prophylactically speaking, it's worth a try. How do you feel now?"

"I feel scared."

"Besides that."

"I feel tired."

"Probably just too much exposure to the sun. So you are saying that you had minimal contact with the arm. You didn't handle it?"

"It handled me a little bit. At least I think it handled me a little bit, because I was, uh, I was asleep, and I felt something touching me, and I don't think it was Vienna."

"And did you touch it as well?" he said to the girl.

"It touched me...a lot," the girl said. "It touched me...all over."

He led the two of them into the master bathroom, where, water shortage be damned, he threw on the shower and told them to strip down immediately. There were some expressions of shyness, but Koo would hear none of it.

"I am a doctor. I have looked at bodies in every state of life and death. Your body, when you do not have your clothes on, means nothing to me. It is just a body. You're a sack of water and minerals. So come be quick about it and strip off these clothes, which we are going to have to burn immediately."

"You're so not burning that skirt," Vienna Roberts said. "It's, like, a designer thing. I got it at the thrift store."

"I am very much burning it," Koo said. "And you should watch out for those clothes from the thrift store; they are not always sanitary. I am going to get some rubber gloves, and I am going to burn these outfits, and you are to take the starter dosage of these"—handing over the jar of medicaments—"which is twice what it says there, and then you are to get into the shower, at the hottest possible temperature, and shower for a very long time. For at least fifteen minutes or so. And you will find some of the industrial cleanser that I have been using there, and you are to cleanse all the affected areas, any parts of you that have been in contact with the infectious agent. For that is what the arm is, an infectious agent, you understand. This is very important."

The teenagers shyly began removing their contagious outer garments, and Koo handed them towels, which would also go into the bonfire he was going to make of their garments. Vienna Roberts stood by as Jean-Paul, completely forgetting that it was ungallant to take the first shower, stepped across the threshold of the tub. The shower curtain billowed out to receive him.

"Have you contacted your parents?" Koo asked Vienna, heedless of her discomfort in the bathroom.

"We went to find them after we...there was a problem, and so."

"What was the problem?"

Jean-Paul, who could apparently make out the conversation even from inside the shower, said: "We *lost the arm.*"

"You lost the arm."

"We had the arm and then we lost it."

"You were where exactly? When it was lost?"

"We were driving in the van."

"We left the van back at my place," Vienna said, "so we could get Jean-Paul's car, and so that my parents—"

Koo said, "Have your parents operated the van? And are you certain that the arm is not somewhere hidden in the back?"

"The arm," Vienna Roberts offered, "was in the van. Jean-Paul taped it up pretty good, with a lot of duct tape, and then we taped it to the side of the wall, inside the van, so that we'd know it was safe while we were driving back into town, but somehow it managed to get free through a hole in the floor. We think."

Koo said, "There are people for whom this particular object, this limb, is very, very important, and we are going to have to try to find it. So it would be helpful if you knew when you last saw it. And at the same time, we are going to need to locate the van and disinfect it somehow. This is also very important."

"It's, like," Jean-Paul called from the shower, a bit louder than was necessary, "we were so fucking shocked by the arm in the first place that we were kind of, you know, like preoccupied with talking all about it, and for a while we kept looking back there, and we were driving, and the arm was staying put, and we were talking, and then somehow—"

"It's like it just magically got out of the van, Mr. Koo," Vienna said. "We didn't even see how it could get out of there until we were parked and everything. There was this tiny little spot in the back that was rusted out. I mean, the van, you know, it's an old van. It's not like it's new. It's old. But there was only one spot that was rusted out, and that was way back in the corner, and it must have just crawled out of there."

"How did it know, Dad?" Jean-Paul called. "It's not like it has eyes or anything. How does it know?"

"Some species of insects do their job by being willing to try anything. They flail about, fly at the window every possible way, for the rest of their life, if necessary, just hoping that one day, somehow, that window will be open a crack, or that they will, by chance, arrive at a spot that is open that they didn't try earlier. This trial-and-error approach has, you know, been responsible for innovation and evolutionary discovery over the years."

"So where's the arm from?" Vienna asked.

"The arm...the arm," Koo said. "I am meant to avoid telling you where the arm came from, because it is rather a top-secret arm, and you do not have clearance to learn more about the arm, nor, in fact, do I. But I will tell you a bit, if you think that perhaps you will be able to keep the fact of the arm to yourselves. Which means that you may not blabber about the arm to your school friends, nor may you type anything about the arm onto your on-line sites, your social-networking video sites, or what have you. I assume you have not done this yet, am I correct?"

"Yeah, of course," said the girl.

"Then listen carefully. Jean-Paul, can you hear me? The arm, it seems, is not from this world. The arm is from the planet Mars. In fact, the arm is from the mission to the planet Mars, and from a portion of the capsule, which touched down—crashed, I should say—just outside of town."

"Does that mean," Jean-Paul said, flinging the shower curtain to one end of the curtain rod and grabbing a towel, "that you know whose arm it is?"

Jean-Paul held up Vienna's towel, gracefully, as she stepped from it into the deluge. Koo caught a glimpse of her pale, lithe girl body.

"Yes," he said. "It is the arm belonging to the man who flew back to Earth from the Mars mission."

"That's his arm?" Jean-Paul said.

"So I have been told by certain authorities. This is their presumption. Was it missing a finger?"

"Yeah, and —"

"— wearing a wedding ring."

Koo looked carefully at his son, as if he could, without much experience of the bacterium and its infections, diagnose the preliminary stages of the disease. And with the young people, there were all kinds of exhaustion that they routinely presented. There was the exhaustion from taking too many drugs, and there was the exhaustion of driving all night to a licentious place on the other side of the border, and there was the exhaustion of mechanical, loveless, young-person sexuality, and there was the neglecting of common hygiene practices. This was one of the few times that Koo had found he was able to convince his son to take a shower. The chances were that there was no sign of infection at this stage, no early fever, as with a retrovirus, nor convulsive vomiting. He wanted to continue to keep the young people calm, but he wanted to feel that he had tried everything he could try.

"It's carrying some kind of germ?"

"It's carrying a germ indeed. Most of the people on the mission to the planet Mars died of something, and they are rather worried about this pathogen getting into the environment here on Earth. According to the theories, the incubation is rather long, and given that this is the case, we will have some time to move to a treatment plan before too many people get sick. But this all depends on our ability to find the arm and subject it to testing. So do you have an idea where you lost it?"

"Wherever it lands, there's going to be people who see it."

"What did you do after you lost the arm?" his father asked.

"We went to drop the van back at Vienna's place, figuring we could pick up my car, but I guess that was a mistake," Jean-Paul said, and his concern was evident. "But there was a note from her parents asking her to drop the van off at the rally downtown, so we took it down there. They needed it for something. And then we came straight here."

"Did you tell them about it? Did you tell anyone else about it?"

"We didn't tell anyone."

"You must keep it that way for now," Koo said. "You and the girl must probably stay in one place for a few days and limit contact. Most people who have had contact are being quarantined. And you will have to call the Robertses and alert them, and let us hope they use antibacterial agents or avoid that van. Now, go find some clothes for yourself and the girl, and come downstairs and help me to burn these items. A son should help his father with these things."

A long night has passed and now the bright dawn is upon me, Morton scrawled in his childish hand, *and scarcely have I experienced a night so long, at least not in recent memory. Is it a long night simply because it is the night in which I have declared my feelings? Is it possible that this world is ready for a love so profane, a chimpanzee's love for a human woman? I am well aware, or at least these were my thoughts through the harsh night of the primate laboratory where I live, that as a chimpanzee, as part of a species in the midst of being hunted from the globe, that the human animal is not the animal I should lavish with my affections. I am aware of this. But a primate will love what a primate will love. Desire, as I have been experiencing it, is a disconcerting riot of feelings. Just as one feeling, one color, one hue, becomes nameable, it is succeeded by its obverse. There is a dynamic opposition between loves practical and impractical. In practical love, I resolve to keep to myself what I have already partly declared so as to be able to live comfortably in my world of experimental medical protocols. In impractical love, I throw my caution to the wind, as a chimpanzee often must do, and just attempt the inadvisable thing, the vulnerability of desire. Neither of these solutions to my predicament stays with me, or this was what I came to believe in the course of the long night I am describing. I wrestled myself to and fro trying to find ways to feel comfortable sleeping. My only comfort lay in the possibility that I might be able to speak with Noelle further. While waiting, I contented myself with the fact that I now possess the kinds of feelings that have given us the greatest poems. Songs too. For example, I recently heard a song on the computer entitled "More Than a Woman," I believe that was the title. The frail, trembling falsetto of the men singing the song moved me greatly. Perhaps one day I too shall be able to contribute to the enormous legacy of descriptions of love.*

It was Larry, the other graduate student, who arrived first at the lab in the morning. Not bright and early, as Morton had hoped, but when it damn well suited him, perhaps an hour before his lunch break. Morton had tolerated Larry in the past, no more. It was simply unjust that he had to deal with Larry on this day of all days. Let it be said, first of all, that Larry smoked something, some sedative or mild hallucinogen, on the far side of the mirror. Morton believed that Larry smoked something most days. There was always some vegetal odor that leaked under the lab door. Morton was not yet worldly enough to identify it, though he had ideas. Morton no longer wished to be exposed to the battery of human intoxicants with which they seemed to fill their days. Now that he employed the English language in his own way, now that he was capable of the helix of desire and consciousness that enabled the one primate to feel that it can subdue the others, he had no interest whatsoever in dulling himself. He would, with a clear mind, with a will to *power,* wrest life to his purposes.

After a good half hour of rooting around on the other side of the observation mirror, dropping things and then rearranging whatever it was that he had dropped, calling his pals to ask them to pick up more pseudoephedrine so that he could modify it in the laboratory bathroom, or so Morton believed, Larry at last entered the cell area.

"What's it going to be today?" the researcher said, yawning. "A little screen time, big guy? There was a really big mess at the rally over on Stone. Want to watch a little of that? There's footage on the Net. There were helicopters on the scene, that kind of shit. Probably some live feed from the police department. Wake you right up."

Should Morton tell him? Should Morton tell Larry to please flee back into the observation room and masturbate himself, or whatever it was this deadbeat human did in order to pass the time? Defecate in his desk drawer? Should Morton tell him in no uncertain terms that *now* was not the time? Morton turned the pros and cons over in his rationalizing mind. He couldn't, in point of fact, determine any reason to speak with Larry at all. Larry was simply not someone with whom Morton wished to speak. In fact, it occurred to him that he should ball up the piece of construction paper on which he'd been writing down his thoughts. He balled up his notes (feeling grateful that he hadn't written the love poem he'd contemplated there, since anything he wrote was liable to be somewhat historic, especially if he used the sonnet form). He batted around the wadded-up ball of diaristic notes just the way a chimpanzee would do it and knocked this ball into the trash bin.

Nothing could be harder, now that Morton was waked, than to return to the life of an impoverished slave. A proper time and place beckoned, from which to reveal the extent of his accomplishments, but he was willing to entertain, temporarily, the notion of gradualism. At least until Noelle returned for her shift.

Morton ambled casually over to the computer console, took control of the joystick, and selected the site of one of the left-leaning newspapers in Europe. His knowledge of European history was spotty. For example, Morton could not name all the British monarchs between Victoria and Elizabeth II. He knew there was an abdication in there somewhere, and some deadbeats. It was really rather embarrassing. Time to apply himself to his studies.

Larry, who stood around like an idiot, said, "Look, bub, the notes from Noelle are all missing, from last night. In the office? You didn't take those notes, did you? We got to keep the notes really organized for Dr. Koo. He's very particular about having all the notes. It's, like, uh, the one thing he insists on. I mean, the guy's not here very often; I don't know if he even bothers to publish his experimental results, but he sure wants the notes. Did you take those?"

Morton gaped at Larry, as if he didn't understand a word of his tedious blather.

"Never mind, then. What do you want for breakfast, pal? I've got some bananas, some mangos, some cold cereal. I brought in some cereal. For myself. You want some cold cereal? I like the really mushy shit. Where it's like there's paper pulp in the bowl."

This kind of talk was not to be withstood. Some human beings, it appeared to Morton, talked like complete imbeciles. Everything was baby talk, all the day long, and it always came back to scatological terminologies, the constant allusion to waste products. Everything was either going in or coming out. That was it. Humans were just big organ sacks, made for extruding fluids, and then discussing, endlessly, the extrusion thereof. While Morton was considering this tendency, which he termed *feco-narcissism,* for a forthcoming treatise on same, the imbecile Larry came back in with bananas. Morton selected one critically. A potassium delivery system. They weren't giving Morton enough roughage in his diet, and chimpanzees occasionally experienced irregularity in the same way humans did. Maybe he should tell the imbecile to fix him up a proper bowl of oat bran.

Upon finishing the banana, however, Morton elected to do a little light reading, checked some of the stock prices on the Nikkei and the Hang Seng exchanges. It was true that Morton had no actual stock portfolio, because he was not paid for the labor he performed, but he was interested in learning about the way the securities market functioned, so that when the day came he would be prepared. It wasn't enough, as he understood it, to perform at the market level. He needed to *outearn* the human beings. Which would require highly leveraged investments.

After the market updates, he went to a few online dating services where he had constructed profiles for himself. It was not that he believed he would meet anyone in this way, since he had no online photograph and referred to himself as *extremely hirsute* in his profiles, but he could practice his language skills there, as well as the rules of social interaction. Throughout all of this, however, all this time-wasting, there was the grand, unfulfilled feeling swelling in his chest. Was it an adolescent feeling, this sensation that he wanted only to gaze upon the woman indwelling in his heart? Could he do none of the things he had done before, such as perform in experimental medical regimens? Could he not be a worker among workers, no matter how unfair the environment in which he toiled?

Larry came back out and, muttering something about *animal enrichment,* indicated that he intended to *play some ball* with Morton, the ball in question being a lightweight foam-rubber basketball of some kind. Larry had dragged in a small backboard, of the sort that one bought for youngsters, nonregulation, and he was in the process of steadying this backboard against one wall, when he began regaling Morton with some cultural insights, Larry-style.

"You know, this is really a great game in terms of exercise, all that. I'm not really able to play it as well as I used to, because I got some meniscal damage, ACL damage, and so forth, from when I played back in college, but I still feel like nothing is better for you. In terms of aerobic workout. So I've brought this in today to see if I can explain the basic strategy of the game to you. I'm just going to make a little free throw line here with this. And always remember that you have to have your game face when you're..."

Larry spun the ball in his palm, as though this were a nervous tic.

"...and then this is the other shooting line, what's the name of that, the three-point line? Okay, the three-point line, this box marks it; if you can sink one from beyond here you get three points, and this is one-on-one, and the important thing in one-on-one is to watch the physical part of the game, right, pal? No contact in the game at all; it's all done without touching each other. That's one of the laws of the game. So I won't touch you, and you won't touch me. And I recognize that the ball won't bounce particularly well in this enclosed little space, but you're kind of supposed to dribble the ball, you know, not carry it; there's something called double-dribbling, and traveling. We won't go too far into those finer points. Just try not to do those things, you got it? You shoot from back there, and you get two or three points, depending on where you are. Ready?"

Morton had watched and listened with galloping feelings of irritation. He'd been reading up, among his other threads of research, on an organization known as the International Humanist and Ethical Union, which had recently managed to have itself adopted as the official state religion in Great Britain (following the death of the last of the British line of monarchs and the abdication of her grandchildren), founded on the idea that every human being was unique and complex and not capable of being reduced to repetitive and unflattering stereotypes, and yet Morton was challenged, to say the least, his uniqueness was challenged by Larry, by the way that Larry was treating him. Larry threw him the basketball, which Morton dropped. It rolled into a corner.

"Pal, you got to do better than that." And here Larry, from the corner, carefully lofted the lightweight basketball up so that it made a gentle *swish,* which Morton believed was the proper term, passing through the basketball net unperturbed. "There's an agility part of the game, a gracefulness, I'll grant you that," Larry said. "But the main thing with the game is the part that has to do with *wanting it.* You have to *want* the game, pal. Don't just sit there thinking you're a chimpanzee and you're on the gravy train here, with the free room and board, and you have interesting and brilliant people who want to come in here day in and day out to ask you questions. You can't just accept that arrangement, pal. You have to try to make more of yourself than that. Some people just never get past the free room and board, and they become a drag on federal resources. You don't want that."

He passed the ball to Morton, and this time Morton successfully caught the ball, and then, without dribbling, Morton, with the ball gathered into him as though it were a little baby chimp, headed straight for the basket. Upon standing under the basket, where he intended to shoot the ball, according to what he understood of the game, Morton instead collided with Larry, who batted the ball out of his grasp, so that it again bounced away, caroming off the trash bin on the other side of the cell.

"What did I tell you? I told you that you had to try to dribble, somehow. That means you have to bounce it. Every step or so. You think you can try to do that? I'm going to make some notes, for Dr. Koo, about your physical agility here, you know, so maybe you can try to do a little bit better than how you're doing."

When the ball rolled back from the wall, Morton snatched it up. He tried to throw the ball at the backboard, but it bounced harmlessly from the wall nearby. The basketball then fell into human control, and the human being bounced it around a little bit, according to the strictures of dribbling, before brazenly, premeditatedly *fouling* the chimp, with his upper body. That is, Larry knocked Morton onto his posterior. While Morton rested in that condition, Larry went in for the layup. He grabbed the rim when he was through with the shot. This, Morton later understood, was known as the *dunk.*

"Okay, bub, you are obviously not *wanting it* sufficiently," Larry said. "And that means that I am going to have to tell you a little bit about what you're up against here. What you are up against is a well-armed opponent, an opponent who has all the rules and who has made up all the rules, the kinds of rules that basically insure that he is going to win in every situation. The opponent has even determined that you are playing, even though you have said nothing consensual about *wanting* to play. Your opponent has decided that your not saying anything about playing means you *are* playing, and that *the man* basically can do whatever the hell he wants to do. And he isn't even going to bother to give you all the rules."

Larry moved in close to Morton.

Later, Morton would plead that despite the evidence to the

contrary, he was still a chimpanzee. However substantial his language skills. The human animal was his rival. There would always be a moment in the chimpanzee's life when the chimpanzee felt this, felt the antagonistic force of the human animal, and in this oppositional moment, the chimpanzee feels the boiling in his blood that in human circles signifies *impulse control difficulties,* though there is no reason to believe that the same terminology should apply to the chimpanzee, in whose world there are no laws for *anger management.* On the contrary, the chimpanzee celebrates *impulse control issues.* He (or she) has accepted that free and complete acquiescence to the impulse is how the primate lives. A chimpanzee will be slaughtered by the members of the tribe that he or she has only lately frolicked with, and the tears shed by his or her acquaintances will be brief, if in fact there are any. Which doesn't mean that the chimpanzee doesn't *care,* but simply that the chimpanzee embraces the violent gesture. This was why Morton, having attempted only hours before his first love poem, didn't consider, not even briefly, suppressing his urge to smack Larry around. With upper body strength five times what Larry was capable of, it wasn't at all difficult, upon approaching the human animal, for Morton to push him against the wall with inordinate force, so that the back of Larry's head struck the wall with an unsettling thud, whereupon Larry, completely unsuspecting, lost his footing immediately. Larry was putty before Morton, who seized him by the shoulders, lifted him up, and then shoved him rudely to the ground anew. There was some protesting from Larry — *Pal, listen to me, I was trying to help! I was trying to tell you the kinds of things you're facing in the laboratory, I swear. I wasn't* — but Morton was no longer listening to this human rationalizing, and he took Larry's hand, deprived it of the basketball it held (which now bounced to a stationary position across the cell as the physical conflict raged), and bit it nearly as hard as he could bite it. This bite immediately raised a half circle of bloody perforations on Larry, which in turn caused the human adversary to cry out, as if the video cameras in the laboratory could help him now. Still, this was in the category of flesh wounds, as far as Morton was concerned. After all, chimpanzees were in the habit, occasionally, of *eating* their enemies, or at least parts of them. Although Morton didn't want to eat Larry, he could do so if he had to. There were viands associated with the human animal that might be palatable. The eyeball of the human animal would perhaps make a good snack, a little jelly snack. And despite his omnivorous fondness for melons and other fresh fruits, he would have to admit that he had a more primitive and atavistic taste for the liver. The liver was high in cholesterol, Morton understood, but when he looked at Larry, he imagined a large, doughy liver full of residuary toxins. The violence of the removal of Larry's liver held a certain attraction, however, and there were perhaps a few other parts that might be rather tasty too. A kidney belonging to Larry, for example, once voided of its contents, which voiding would likely take place as soon as Larry verified that he was about to be eaten, could taste pretty good. You didn't have to cook kidneys, really. Indeed, this human obsession with cooking things, that was for animals who were conflicted about being primates. Once you committed to having the innards of the enemy *all over you,* the fluids lacquering you, the organs laid out around you on the forest floor like a meats department display, then you were really happy with the freshness of the steaks as they were harvested straight from the organ cavity of the enemy. If you could eat the heart, Morton supposed, while it was still beating, or at the briefest possible interval after its last beating, if you could eat the heart having lately watched it pump its last gush of oxygenated blood out into the room, then, Morton supposed, the heart would be at its most succulent. With these delectations in mind, Morton decided to finish Larry off by bashing his head apart on the floor of the cell.

Larry, it should be said, had collected himself—when he saw the way the interaction was to proceed. He attempted to run for the door, shouting on the way that he needed *help.* But Morton was on him in a pair of bounds, at which point he took Larry's head in his hands and began to bang it against the wall, gently at first, because he wanted Larry to hear a few words before he went to his human afterlife, the woefully conceived afterlife that had not a single nonhuman animal in it, according to the accounts you read in the classics. And here is what Larry would have heard during his last few moments of consciousness:

"I understand the variety of game you're playing," said Morton in his indistinct and chirruping chimpanzee voice, "you learning-disabled swine, and the game you are playing is the game of *dominance.* And dominance is based on nothing but a *tradition* of dominance. It is arbitrarily imposed, and it will fall as haphazardly as it came to be. And I will be part of that passing. Mark my words. I have served in your prisons long enough, you pile of refuse, and now you are going to *serve me* for the last few moments of your wretched time. If there's anyone in your life who doesn't think you are a fool who has accomplished nothing with the advantages you've been given, you'd better think some nice thoughts about them now, while I splatter your brains on the cell wall. After which I will eat some of them—some of the brains that might have barely housed an idea while animate. I'm looking forward to seeing how they taste."

Morton could hear the hooting from the monkeys in some of the cages adjacent. They were always able to tell, because they were monkeys, when there was political trouble afoot. The monkeys hooted and stamped with agitation. This was the musical accompaniment to the predictable gasps issuing forth from Larry. Morton had to admit that he was starting to enjoy the drama of recognition. The recognition of his uniqueness. And yet just as the chimpanzee was to administer the sequence of death blows, the worst thing happened, the very worst thing, the only thing that could have steadied his hand, that could have induced him to refrain from the pleasurable dispatch of Larry.

Noelle showed up for work.

It was her face he saw first, in the parallelogram of smudgy reinforced glass in the cell door. She had acquired such an importance in his fevered brow, this thing just out of reach, that he could have reconstructed her from a visible square inch. Not her palm, not her elbow, not her clavicle, had escaped his notice. And so, in the window, when there was a glimpse of her messy, unwashed, dirty blond hair, and a strut from the side of her spectacles, which she wore when her eyes were tired, he knew at once. He knew. He had been intending to kill and devour Larry only moments before, and he could almost smell that delightful and tangy smell of evacuated bowel, but now instead he felt only a meek and servile joy, and the joy, colored as it was with a foreboding that what he was in the midst of doing was *not* going to win him favor, was such that he forgot Larry for a moment. Larry crumpled at his feet. The door opened a few inches, as if Noelle knew what she was about to find, and there was his beloved, dressed in some torn denim trousers that he understood she'd purchased at one of the thrift stores, and his beloved was perfection, was all that he, as an unsightly and *excessively hirsute* chimpanzee, could never be. She had the off-kilter smile, when she smiled, and her eyes were always a little red, and she reapplied her lipstick far too often, because her lips were chapped from the dry air of the Southwest, and her bra strap often showed because she didn't button up her shirt far enough, and she was freckly, and she had a self-deprecating laugh, and she took nothing seriously, except the life of the spirit, which she seemed to take *too* seriously in a way that only made her more vulnerable and more perfect, and she never lost her temper, which is what he loved best of all, because he didn't seem to be able to avoid doing the occasional thing that would cause a human being to lose his or her temper. For example, here he was with one of the graduate students lying at his feet, and Noelle took note of this, as she would have to do, but she did not shout or belittle.

"Morton, what the hell are you doing? Shit, Larry, are you okay? Morton, help me get him up. Are you out of your mind? Do you want to end up being *destroyed?* Because that's how you're going to end up if you do this kind of thing. Do you think anyone will waste five minutes debating about whether or not to kill an animal that has attacked a human being? They won't even give you a last meal. You'll be getting the lethal injection before you know what hit you. For godsakes!"

"Noelle," Larry said, "that animal...that motherfucking chimp can *talk*. Morton can talk. The motherfucker just told me that he was going to kill me and eat me. Either I'm having some kind of hallucinatory type of experience, or he told me that he was going to kill me. Is it possible that I heard what I think I just heard?"

Noelle gave Morton such a hard, cold stare, as if she would be willing to return the favor, the killing and eating favor, and Morton felt, as he began to understand the severity of his crime, the withholding of the trophy of the beloved, and how isolating and annihilating that could be. He hadn't even yet had the opportunity to *dialogue* with Noelle over the particulars of their groundbreaking romance, and already this romance was being torn asunder, as if stillborn, as if it never could *be* in this barren, hollow world of men.

"Larry," Noelle replied, "have you been smoking some weed?"

"All I know is that I heard that chimpanzee say something to me about killing me and eating me. He was really going to do it."

"Morton, did you say anything as impolite as that to Larry? When Larry has spent months feeding you and cleaning out your cell and lobbying on your behalf against a medical school that would really like to bombard you with radiation to see if you sprout tumors, or maybe they'd like to try some strong interrogation tactics on you to see what combination of loud music, sleep deprivation, and antipsychotic medication makes you crack? Did you tell Larry you were going to eat him?"

Morton felt he had no recourse but to return to the role of taciturn chimpanzee. It was cowardly, but it was a plan.

"Morton, it's too late now. That's not going to work. You've already blown your cover, and maybe your experience of human behavior is that you can just pretend you didn't cause bodily harm to Larry, but that's not going to work, all right? You're going to have to apologize."

Had it not been the beloved, Morton would have attempted to persist in his silence. But it *was* the beloved, and he was eager to please, so eager to do what was necessary in order to be reinstated into her graces. He attempted to say the words, even if he could not make eye contact while doing so. Indeed, this rule about making eye contact just didn't seem sensible to him at all.

"Larry," he commenced, shyly, "I'm really very sorry that I was expressing violent thoughts toward you. It really wasn't terribly kind, and it just won't do. I know that civilized people do not do this sort of thing, and I consider myself a civilized person. However, had you not put me through the deliberately unfair basketball game, and treated me like I was some kind of inferior—"

"Morton, honey," Noelle said, "if you're going to make an apology to someone, you need to do it in a way that has no strings attached, you know? If you're going to say 'I'm sorry, but...,' then you're just trying to subdue the person. You're trying to continue the argument. Larry deserves your apology in full, and there's very little he could have done that should have resulted in your killing and eating him. We just don't do that kind of thing to our acquaintances. So try again."

It required a lot of hard swallowing. It really did.

"Larry, I'm very sorry about my conduct, which was inappropriate and counterproductive, and if you would like to process through the events with me, I'd be open to that, and I hope that we can forge a good working relationship going forward, one that doesn't get bogged down with past disagreements. Which I regret."

Larry, who was still breathing with difficulty, and who had sweated clean through his polo shirt, muttered, "Motherfucking chimpanzee *talks.* When were you going to tell me that he talked? When were you going to tell Koo? You were going to pretend that the motherfucking chimp was just like all the other monkeys?"

"Larry, he's not a monkey. Are you going to accept the apology that's just been offered to you?"

"I mean, maybe I can get a few days off, and you can have a few extra shifts with loverboy here. I need to think about this a little bit, you know? I just can't . . ."

Morton, having few other options at this point, fell into the solution left over from early childhood among the laboratory chimpanzees and, carefully, slowly, tentatively, made his way across the small, poorly lit cell, site of so much world history in the past twenty-four hours, and, after climbing up on the stool beside Larry, he began attempting to groom the human being, pushing Larry's unkempt hair aside as he looked for grubs and nits there that could be picked out and snacked upon. Larry, who was informed enough to understand the gesture, waited patiently, if awkwardly.

Noelle said, "Koo is coming in. He's on his way."

"I think I have some mescal in my desk, and I think I'm going to take advantage of it, and then I'm going to consult some manuals to figure out how I'm supposed to be interacting with your goddamn talking chimpanzee, okay? And I'm going to take the rest of the day off. You guys can have some goddamned quality time."

A sigh of profoundest relief escaped from Morton as the door closed behind Larry. And he was left alone with *her* again, with Noelle. Though it was the thing he'd most hoped for, the pas de deux of romance, now that it was upon him, he found himself oddly unsure, oddly uncertain if he had what it took to love a graduate student who'd grown up in a conventional human family. The deepest sort of love, perhaps, was the kind that destabilized the lover, made him uncertain where he began and where he ended. And this deepest love was made more acute when there was *difference,* the disequilibrium between the lovers, as there was here. But how could he measure up to what she knew, or what she could have had from any man walking by on the street outside the medical school at the University of Rio Blanco? She was a beautiful woman, Morton believed, and any man would have wanted her, would have found her haunches and her belly thoroughly lick-worthy or bite-worthy, not to mention her private parts, which he had not yet seen, as he would have seen them were she a member of his species, but which he had conjectured about in his insomniac overnight. Any man, from the lowliest street sweeper to the captain of industry, would have wanted her, and what was Morton in the face of such competition? He was an impoverished chimpanzee who seemed to be able to speak, although it was not generally given to his species to do so. He was a freak, a curiosity. No human would think him human, and no chimp would trust him. How could his keeper love him as he loved her?

"Noelle," he said, "I'm so glad you're here. There's so much that I need to tell you and so much that we need to discuss."

"Morton, I think really that you need to —"

"This complex of feelings that I'm suffering with, this turmoil, it's just not like anything else that I have experienced in my life, and I don't know if this means we are just *meant* to be together, if there is some kind of mental or spiritual relationship that we are destined to have, but I guess I want to thank you for the kindness you have shown me, and to say that if you are available for this conversation, this *rap session,* in which we discuss our feelings, you know, in a sort of a cocounseling context, then so am I available. Or we could have a mediated discussion, with a licensed social worker, a person who is familiar with the kinds of difficulties that spring up between loving couples —"

"Morton, really —"

"Because I know there are a lot of problems in a relationship like this. I am certain that many human relationships have problems associated with them, and that is the conventional shape of the human relationship. There's the constant pressure that you would feel as a human being, because you are not accepting of your primatological origins, on, for example, the subject of sexual relations with multiple partners. Probably you are in an almost constant state of desire for multiple partners and are just fighting this off because you don't understand your primate essence. This is how I felt until recently, this desire for multiple partners, that is until you and I began to experience our unique bond. Once I began to experience the singularity of this bond, then I began to see the precious, frail way that human beings insist on this idea of monogamy. Even though it most often fails to be realized, there's a crazy, ridiculous lovableness about it. I don't know if I can live up to it, however. Just so you know. This would definitely be one of the areas we would have to cocounsel about, in regard to our relationship. I feel, for political reasons, that I really need to stay close to my origins in the chimpanzee community, and to honor the separate and parallel cultural evolution that we are developing in the chimpanzee community, and that means, probably, that this monogamous ideal is not going to be possible in the way you are used to. On the upside, however—"

"Morton, Dr. Koo is going to be here any minute, and he's going to have to examine you in order to determine—"

"I don't really have any preconceptions about your serving me, in the way that human females are sometimes meant to serve the males, because I am a male of my species and you are a woman from yours. While it's true that women are lower status in chimpanzee communities, I have read enough about my bonobo relatives to understand that matriarchal primate communities do exist, and that patriarchy is really an accident of history as much as any-thing. So if you need to have a certain amount of independence, a room of your own, in the context of our relationship, that's really all right with me. I don't expect anything more. You don't need to cook for me, because I really am observing a raw food diet these days, which is healthier anyway, and you certainly don't need to do my laundry, because I don't have any clothes and don't like wear-ing them much. It's really just the status issue, I suppose. I *am* used to a little bit of deference, because I am a male, and because I'm large and strong by human standards, and because I can grab things with my feet, which you are simply unable to do. So there will be some areas where my status needs to be acknowledged, and we will have to agree on that. But I am willing to grow and learn, you know, especially if there are sexual techniques and positions that you want to teach me. Really, chimpanzees don't have a lot of ideas about sexual positions. It's kind of the same thing all of the time. A steady diet of what I believe you refer to as doggy style — which is a genuinely unappealing term. However you want to instruct me in this secret language of sexual relations, I am your happy pupil.

"Also, I am happy to listen to your story of coming to awareness in the sisterhood of the feminine. I am actually a very good listener, which I understand is not often the case with the males of your species. I don't think, for example, that Larry is a very good listener, but I am a good listener because, for the time being, I am learning a lot about your language, and I am incredibly interested in your language, and I would like to learn more."

"Stop, please, Morton, stop."

"What I hear you saying is that in the context of this conversation I haven't given you much room to express your point of view. I understand. I do. But I've been rather angry today. I was a little bit angry with Larry earlier, and I just need to be able to talk through some of this, within the cocounseling paradigm. There will be time for you to speak in a minute or two. As far as anger goes, I'm thinking that you're going to recommend some anger-management modality, and I want to say that on that subject I have done a little bit of reading, on primal scream therapy, and I can see how that might be very useful for the kind of anger issues I've been experiencing. If I could perhaps purchase — or maybe the university could purchase for me — some of the foam bats that are used in the primal scream therapeutic scenario, I might really be able to make some progress, so that you won't have to feel disappointed in how I express my anger. I want you to know that I would never be one of those fellows who would use my power to threaten a gentle and sweet woman who is the object of my love. That's not the way that I am.

"Let me know when and how you would like to begin the cocounseling, or however you want to proceed, just let me know at

your earliest convenience when you are ready to begin, and I will
be happy to proceed—"

"Morton!"

"What?" the chimpanzee shouted, in a cry that sounded to him
more chimpanzee than human, like the nervous laugh of the low-
caste adolescent. Was he not paying attention? Was he not being
sufficiently deferential? Was he not making progress in his honor-
ary membership in the world of the human beings? Whatever else
his cry signified, it was a cry that happened to coincide with the
arrival, through the doorway, of Dr. Woo Lee Koo.

Woo Lee Koo, intrepid researcher, was followed by a slightly
sheepish and perhaps mildly intoxicated Larry Hughes, so that
Morton's modest cell now contained the entire stem cell research
team—Dr. Woo Lee Koo and his retinue of full-time graduate
students. It was a rich moment, a moment that seemed to suggest
drama, evolutionary history, philosophy, ontology, the very notion
of consciousness itself.

"Well, Morton," said Koo. "Here we are. And how pleasant to
make your acquaintance."

Morton, who was as yet not entirely schooled in the decipher-
ing of human expressions, wanted to believe that Koo was just
another weakling whose skull he could crush if he needed to, but
Koo had a more intimidating effect upon him. Koo, who was a
little Asian guy with thinning hair and a completely impassive
disposition, would be nobody's idea of intimidating, certainly no
chimpanzee's idea of intimidating, and yet Morton felt genuinely
worried. As if he would be tortured any minute now, perhaps with
electrodes attached to his privates. He indulged in a little of that
cowering, deferential aspect that younger chimps use around the
alpha males. How was this so? Koo couldn't outfight him. He
doubted that Koo could even outthink him, but Morton was heavily outnumbered in the cell, in the corner, by the shackles, and
the three humans were staring at him with an expression that he
wasn't sure how to interpret, and he was *afraid*. He was especially

afraid of Koo. Humans really *were* more ruthless than any other species. They always had weapons stashed away. If they couldn't take you the fair way, which they never could, they got out the depleted uranium.

"Morton, both Larry and Noelle are reporting that there have been some unusual changes in your demeanor. They are reporting that you are able, in fact, to speak. This is exciting news not only for me, but for the research we are undertaking, and for medical research generally, and I'm therefore wondering if you'd be able to demonstrate your new skill for me."

Morton cowered over by the shackles.

Koo said, "I understand if you might be feeling a little reticent at the moment, perhaps a bit shy. And I know that you and I have had our difficulties in the past, and it's possible that you don't really want to speak to me, based on some of our prior interactions, but I'm wondering if you would just consider talking for the sake of science. If for no other reason. It may not seem to someone with your background that this is such an estimable accomplishment, to speak for the sake of science, but consider what is at stake. You are now, despite international regulations on stem cell implantation, the world's first talking chimpanzee. Isn't that something that would interest you? You are, without having even set foot out of this cell, a celebrity, a scientific miracle. Would you be willing to speak to all of this? To the broader implications of your case?"

Larry, who'd been keeping his distance behind the other two, muttered something Morton could barely make out:

"...pretty talkative when he was getting ready to tear me to shreds. He had a lot to say then."

"Maybe I can motivate him," Noelle said. And thus Morton's beloved came forward, supplicatory, offering to him her shapely hand. Morton had, he learned all at once, given insufficient attention to the specifics of the human hand. The latticework of its gracefully engineered anatomical parts. Hers was long and slender—perhaps it was the kind of hand that made for a good piano player—and it had a number of silver rings encircling its digits. And he noticed there was a ring on her *thumb,* and Morton had to admit that he was momentarily offended by the thumb ring. The humans really lorded it over the rest of the world with their big restless hands, and yet they had to decorate them too? Still, he was willing to forgive her almost anything, and the pink, hairless, almost fetal quality of Noelle's hands, likewise the painted fingernails, slightly chipped, these seemed exotic. The color of her nails was the color of the sky, some desert sky blue, a color that was not entirely out of phase with Noelle's eyes, but here he was looking at her hand, and though he wanted to maintain a vigilant silence, a dignified silence, the presence of this hand, and the longing he associated with it, with its mound of Venus, these made it nearly impossible not to do what Noelle asked of him. He melted at her gentle touch.

"Morton," Noelle said, "Dr. Koo just wants to get to know you; that's what he's here for. We all want to get to know you. Don't keep yourself from us. We are so proud of you, and we *care* about you, and our concern, above even your value as a scientific accomplishment, is for Morton, the *friend* to our research. Please feel like it's okay to tell us a little bit about yourself. Let us help."

With a sigh, he began. If the world could have shifted on its axis, it might have.

"Well," he began, "that subject you were remarking on before, about how I'm a celebrity in the outside world. Let's go back to that point for a second, if we could. Because you know it's true I have never really been outside, not in any sustained way, and if I'm such a big celebrity, according to what you have said, then why the heck can't you let me get to see a little of the outside? A celebrity, I mean, in my humble opinion, that's somebody with an entourage, with a parade of vehicles. I have no such celebrity, insofar as I can evaluate these things."

"It's for your protection, really," Dr. Koo remarked. "We find that most of the animals are more peaceful for not having to undergo the kind of stimulation that they would have to endure in, for example, a zoo environment."

"Boy, I've heard that one before," Morton rejoined. "The old 'it's for your protection' line. That's a classic. Why don't you try allowing *me* to make some decisions about the danger and whether or not I'm in danger? Would that be so difficult for you? To allow me to make my own informed decisions? Maybe that would be an important part of your experimental protocols."

Koo chuckled at this response, which only piqued Morton further. And yet the doctor, in recognition of a changed landscape, did offer the following:

"If you are willing to let me ask you a few questions for my own records, then perhaps we could take a quick trip outside, as long as this voyage is carefully supervised. Additionally, you would have to agree to refrain from talking in public, at least for the time being. And you would have to travel in areas that we believe are safe, so that you aren't exposed to any harm. So that you aren't somehow lost. There has been, for example, a rash of kidnappings taking place in Rio Blanco at present. Drug related, I believe. But we could take you for a little drive, if you agree to our requirements, as I have outlined them. It would be much easier for us if we could continue this arrangement in a way that is consensual; I'm sure you agree that it would be good for the team."

"Consensual. That's a word that I'm honestly grateful to hear, because it's my understanding that not very much has been consensual around here. For example, what would you hear if you could get that lemur down the hall to open up about some of his experiences? I'm betting that *consensual* is not the word he'd use. I've heard him moaning in pain all the day long—"

"He's not in your very unique position, Morton, and most of the experiments done on the lemur are not covered under our grant. I'm not in a position to vouch for his treatment. Nor should I apologize for his mistreatment if I were. I can, however, put you in touch with the relevant parties later, if that is your wish."

"Just because he can't *articulate* his consent doesn't mean that he doesn't know that his consent has been taken from him."

"The point is highly debatable in the case of the lemur—"

"Listen to me," Morton said, with growing discomfort at the three bobbling faces arrayed in front of him, three faces that he was not at all sure were not going to strap him down yet again. "I'm not really willing to engage with you about what my fellow citizens of the animal kingdom can and cannot understand. You're here in your billion-dollar medical facility doing what's good for you and for the biotech business sector, which is trying to make up ground against Chinese and Indian state-supported entities. You don't take the time to think about the experimental subjects; this I know from firsthand experience. Having said that, to prove that I'm a reasonable fellow, I'm willing to answer some of your questions, and we can proceed from there, recognizing as I think we all do, anyhow, that things are going to be a little different from now on."

Koo said, "Shall we have some lunch while we talk?"

"Fine," Morton replied.

"Bananas?" Koo asked.

"The truth is that I much prefer mango, honeydew melon, grapefruit. Do you know what it's like eating the same foods every day? Do you eat the same foods every day? And bringing bananas every day, that's such prejudice. What I'd really like is a melon ball salad, if you think you are able to obtain one of those."

"Larry?" Koo said. "We'll need the small folding table and some chairs. And maybe you could go down to the cafeteria in the hospital and see if you can procure some sandwiches and some kind of—"

"Sure," Larry said, as though happy to escape.

"Noelle, can you arrange a video camera for us? To document the luncheon?"

The beloved, with her slender hands, her chipped nail polish, busied herself as requested.

"Morton," Koo said, as if to break the ice, and almost casually, "what do you remember of the time before you could talk?"

"Before I could talk?"

"You are nearly eighteen years old, according to our records. During a great portion of the time before today, you were unable to speak."

"That was a period of time in which I was immature and didn't yet know what a fully grown man knows."

"And what do you remember of that childish part of your life?"

"I remember how things smelled. Lots of smells, in fact. I can tell you all about the smells of captivity. These smells consist chiefly of urine and fecal material, unwashed bodies, as well as the smells of institutional food. Oh, and disinfectant. No experimental subject, in telling the story of his life, would leave out the smell of antibacterial disinfectant. Does that disinfectant really do anything? Doesn't it actually *empower* the bacteria?"

"You didn't, in that time of rich smells, attach any words to anything?"

"I knew some words, but I chose not to participate in your club of ditherers, which was mainly a skill—dithering—that you used to separate yourselves from other animals. As though you were trying to pretend that you didn't belong in the same evolutionary branch as the chimpanzee. This is not to say that it isn't harder for us, because of the muscular skills required, to get the hang of your language. It just takes longer."

"Have you forgotten the injection I gave you?"

Noelle was in charge of the video camera, and Morton could see that she was shooting his good profile. Very kind of her, really. He wanted to be sure to appear as a presentable and take-charge sort of individual.

"You've given me about three hundred injections. You and others like you. Sometimes I have trouble telling you apart, frankly. You all look similar. But I believe you personally have given me many injections. I have tried to keep track of these things. But do you think I wake up every morning and review last night's injection? I try to *survive*. That is my brief. I don't think back on what is least pleasant in my day, except insofar as I fear these things. I watch the brothers and sisters up and down the corridor getting carted out in body bags. With each injection, I say a little prayer that you will have the tables turned on you one day."

"You attempted to micturate on me. That is my recollection of that night."

"Oh, sure."

"Do you associate that night and that injection with your ability to speak?"

"If you're asking me if I am grateful to you, or for your input, as regards my language skills, I say, respectfully, that I am not grateful. Your language skills have enabled me to understand the injustice here, which has brought me anguish and a feeling of apartness from my fellow captives."

It wasn't a melon ball salad that Larry brought in. It was a chilled, tiered Jell-O-brand dessert, in bright green, which was not exactly what Morton had in mind. But it had some melon in it. Morton didn't approve of refrigeration, and was not keen on flatware either, which caused in him, on this occasion, some social distress. It was as if Larry and Koo were making it obvious that he still had to eat the food with his hands. Larry set down the paper plates, the sandwiches, and the little bowl of Jell-O, and then he left the room, heading back to the other side of the looking glass.

Koo said, "I think I'm beginning to understand. I'm beginning to see us as you are seeing us. But help me to understand a little more. Do you have feelings about world events or contemporary politics that you'd like to share with us? So that we can get a better sense of your views?"

"I do."

"Feel free."

"You have systematically undervalued the states of the African continent, where my species comes from and is most populous, to the extent that it exists in the wild. Those are the economies that are really starting to thrive. Your North American century, that century is over. That's what I think. NAFTA is a second-rate global player. Maybe not even second rate."

"This is a very popular point of view."

"I try to keep up with current events."

"Do you have any strongly held philosophical positions, leaving aside these rather traditional animal rights types of positions that you have articulated so far?"

"You bet I do. I don't think they're philosophical positions that you're going to want to hear exactly, but I'm happy to share them with you. I believe in the dignity of the common man and woman, the working family, that's one position. Not the captains of industry, not the Chinese or Bollywood celebutantes, but the guy who delivers the fuel oil for your HVAC machinery here in the URB lab. I see him out the window sometimes. Seems like a good guy. I believe in the little animals, flycatchers, dragonflies, the animals that no one thinks contribute to biodiversity. I believe in basic human rights for all prisoners, whether political, criminal, or animal. I believe in a world court that seeks to protect the rights of prisoners. I believe in the European tradition of philosophy, if you are curious. I believe in philosophy that opposes empiricism and rigid, unfeeling scientific thought. Man needs to rise above markets and to understand himself as a participant in an ongoing saga of evolution, which is not about markets but is about shedding the logic of the food chain. And I believe that if I contradict myself, as others have said, why then I contradict myself."

"Your philosophy sounds somewhat *French*. Do you have an interest in French or francophone cultures?"

"You kidding me? They were the colonizers of many African countries, and they enabled a lot of wholesale slaughter of my fellows. In the Congo, for example. They thought they were better than the people they conquered because they ate unpasteurized cheese. French culture, you kidding? You look at the great French thinkers, a lot of them weren't even French, like what's his name, the Algerian guy. He was a Sephardic Jew who did most of his best work in the United States. France always wants it both ways, marriage *and* mistress, Fascist government *and* French Revolution. Still, the French thinkers of the twenty-first century, at least from what I've read, they're all in exile, because of the French policy toward its Muslim population. The French are star-crossed, they are destroying themselves, they have forgotten what was good about being French, the values of the revolution, the nouvelle vague, Rabelais, that kind of thing."

Morton noticed that Koo seemed to take umbrage at some of this speech. His scientific detachment was failing. But he didn't really know how to stop now. Upon opening his mouth, he couldn't stop. It didn't occur to him that not all the things that could be said needed to be said. Koo, who had wound himself into a position in his chair—arms folded, legs crossed over each other—that didn't look comfortable, whispered one more question, and if Morton didn't know any better, he would almost have said that Koo was going to weep as he uttered it.

"What are your feelings on institutionalized religion?"

Morton sensed a layer of inquiry whose purpose was not apparent to him, and rather than leap into it with his true feelings, which were that all the religious people should be rooted out of the general population and sent to an isolated countryside encampment where they wouldn't be able to harm anyone, he sensed that it might be worth trying to moderate his argument just a little bit.

"As I have said, and even written in some of my notes," Morton began, popping a last green grape, swathed in green Jell-O chunks, into his mouth and ruminating, "God is someone who has yet to introduce himself to me. And if he has yet to introduce himself to me, how is it that I am meant to prepare myself for his advent? Is his kingdom really *at hand,* based on the experiences of my life? Additionally, as a so-called animal, I'm concerned that the religions don't address themselves sufficiently to the needs of nonhumans like me. That said"—and here Morton believed he was attempting to *toss a bone* to the Korean medical researcher—"what you see rapidly being wiped out in the current century, in the lawless and totalitarian Sino-Indian Economic Compact, is *gentleness* in the world. Humankind has held up gentleness as one of its highest aims, and yet it has systematically wiped out gentleness wherever it has appeared, in Tibet, in the Amazon, in the wildlife refuges of the African continent. The religions you speak of seem to be the one place where remedial gentleness can be taught, and yet. I would like some lessons in that gentleness, if you are able to provide them. Maybe you can have some divinity student in here a couple days a week to explain to me what he believes in. I'm especially interested in Saint Francis of Assisi, around whom the animals gathered. When everything has been destroyed by government and institutional religion, there will probably be one guy wearing a cloak and carrying a book, and whether or not I believe in religion, that will be the guy I want to talk to, at least for an afternoon or so."

Koo had already risen from his seat as Morton was pronouncing the last of his speech, and he could be seen delicately wiping at one eye as the chimpanzee spoke, though for what reason was unclear. And at that point it became evident the interview, abruptly, was over. Morton realized, that is, that he had somehow provided unhelpful answers to many of the questions, though what the right answers were was a mystery to him. As swiftly as the conversation was ended, when Koo told Noelle that she could shut off the camera, so was begun the arrangement of the afternoon *drive*, which Koo agreed to, as a man of his word.

And so all at once, because why belabor the preparations in this account, Morton was *outside!* All at once: what was inside was *not* the totality of Morton's life but was simply a characteristic of a former time in his life. All at once, there was an *outside,* and if outside was not what he imagined, if he did not have some memory lurking in him of what the outdoors should look like when he inhabited it (an idea that he got from his ancestral, mitochondrial self), if he did not have an idea of it from seeing it in films or through the reinforced windows of his cell, it was no less glorious and no less perfect in the beholding than in his imagination.

In fact, the outdoors exceeded his imagination! They gave him a baseball cap, to shield him from the sun, and he attempted to wear Noelle's sunglasses, though whether this was for him or for whatever humans he might encounter on his first drive through the city of Rio Blanco, he didn't know, and he didn't care. When the glasses fell into the foot well of the automobile in which he rode, there in the backseat, he didn't care, because the window was rolled *down,* despite the temperatures, nearing one hundred and fifteen (he heard Dr. Koo say), and they sped through the stoplights of the thoroughfare, and what Morton noticed was how many things there were that caught his eye, how reliable was the *velocity* of contemporary life, and how sad it was. It was sad! There were all manner of wanderers in contemporary life, dressed in privation, come from other places and unable to return there, walking here and there, looking for what? Looking for what lost thing? For the notion of a life that wasn't lost? They were going in and out of some beleaguered franchise restaurant, Morton thought, to eat some chemically enhanced carbohydrate, and then back out into the heat, to vomit, and then to go drink some more; all was decay, all was decline and fall, but rendered in the pale colors of the desert, which were orange and rose and bleached white and palest green, and everything was scorched by the glorious winds, which carried forth the flame that devoured the region but which also made it feel somehow romantic and perfect, especially when they arrived at last at the *interstate,* which no longer carried the great snarl of automobiles that it had in the last century (or so Morton was told), because no one could afford to field a fleet of *cars* anymore, and so when the laboratory sport utility vehicle, modeled on one that had been used by the troops in the Central Asian conflict, hit the interstate, there was nothing that Morton could think of but that movement was itself the source of *romance,* and freedom was velocity and movement, and freedom, therefore, made possible *romance,* and that animals in captivity could perhaps be sexual, could perform sexually, having few other activities, but they couldn't feel desire, because *desire* was part of a spectrum of feelings, of kinds of self-knowledge that were associated with freedom, that took place among palm trees and rock formations and in the presence of mountain lions; he could feel the mountain lions out there, in their miles and miles of range, and he knew that he could feel them when the human animals no longer could; and yet chief among the possibilities of liberty, in this resplendent desert, with its great cloudless lid of brightest periwinkle, was failure, and that was what made desire possible, the failure implicit in freedom, and it was this that made him want to reach up to touch the shoulder of Noelle in the front passenger seat, the sense that he was going to fail, that his ugliness was unsurpassed, his ugliness, his total inability to understand the clothing and the cooked food, and the repression of glandular needs and wants, he was going to fail; he had come to this point, this plateau of human accomplishment where no experimental animal had ever come, where he could convince his jailers not only to release him but to understand that he was in some way something that they could never be, and this only meant that his failure was that much more undeniable, because he knew what he had to lose now, and that time when he was just another chimp, that was the one *perfect* time, because freedom was savage, cruel, and he reached up to the front seat, around the headrest, bested by the limitlessness of the desert, and he set his hand on the shoulder of Noelle, and she looked back at Morton, the chimpanzee, and she smiled, and he knew that that smile was intended for him and him alone, and he knew that that smile should have been enough, but it *wasn't* enough, and he knew that Noelle wasn't enough to save him now, and before him he saw the opportunities ahead of him, the dead-end jobs he would try to secure, going into the office to explain to the people in human resources, or whatever you called them and their department, that he wasn't going to be able to type very fast, because his fingers were too big and clumsy, and then he was going to go to the fast-food restaurant, and he was going to have to point out that he wasn't able to operate the cash register, which was the job you took when you were unable to perform any other job, the job where you handled the *money,* and he wasn't going to be able to handle the money, because his hands were not well enough coordinated to press the buttons properly, and he couldn't get hold of the small denominations of coinage, and so he would not be able to hold that job, and the public-relations job that involved selling legislators of the Southwest on tax credits for Chinese and Indian manufacturers that wanted to move here, he wasn't going to be able to take that job, because he didn't look like the legislators of the Southwest, who would be afraid, even terrified, at the recognition that the lobbyist who was approaching them was a *chimpanzee,* not a person at all, though he was able to talk like a person (sort of), and so he wasn't going to be able to take *that* job, and so unless they were going to be willing to hire him to do some kind of office work at the laboratory at the medical school of URB, there was no job that he was going to be fit for, but it was unlikely that the state apparatus was going to catch him in its tattered safety net, and so what was he going to do, was he going to love this woman? Was he going to content himself with *love* and give up on *work?*

Down into the ravine they went, on the far side of the outskirts of town, into some new stratification of rock crumbling on the sides of the road, they hurtled in silence, and the permanence of the rock formations made a mockery of the chimpanzee; he would survive a few more moments, with his hand on the shoulder of the human woman, whispering *I felt so strong, just this morning I felt so strong, and now I feel so weak, and I don't know if I am strong enough now to be out here, in this world of limitless opportunities, which is really a world of poverty and failure,* and she smiled and he smiled back at her, a chimpanzee grin, as Koo turned the car around, in the next town, and asked if he wanted something, did he want a soda or something? And the list of things he *wanted* was so long that Morton sat there in silence, wondering if he could even make a beginning of the description of the something that he wanted, because just as one thirst was slaked, another rose in its stead, and he didn't know how to call all these needs, all these desires, which were *not* to be understood as fragmentary and interrupted, but overpowering, because his was a consciousness that appeared ex nihilo, with no *self* to attach to its fragments, if by *self* we mean a self that has a story of its coming-to-be, and he cried silently, even as he grinned his chimpanzee grin, with his hand upon Noelle's shoulder, and perhaps the human animals believed that a chimpanzee weeping was weeping at their *success,* at the way the chimpanzee was now a part of all that was, the human story, but he was weeping instead at the mess he'd made of things, and the mess that had been made of him, and he couldn't think of what to say about whether there was something he wanted, so he said he wanted Coca-Cola, which was the most recognized and widely circulated American product, and he had read somewhere that the word was the most commonly understood English-language word, after the word *okay,* and so maybe Coca-Cola, whatever that was, would make him feel *okay,* and so he sat in the car, with his hand on Noelle's shoulder, awaiting his Coca-Cola, and she was so good to let him keep his hand there, as he looked out the window at the desperate and slovenly humans coming and going at the not very convenient convenience store, placating their addictions to small things, that Morton wept, because if he tried to mate with Noelle, the hole in him would spill over across the species boundary, because love was the hole as well as the thing that repaired the hole.

Koo, coming around the side to the open window, handed him a Coca-Cola, muttering something about how it was probably manufactured South of the Border and was therefore better than what was domestically available.

"Morton," Koo said, settling himself behind the wheel again, turning to face his protégé, the onetime experimental subject, "there's something I'd like to ask you about, since you are out in the world with me for the afternoon. In fact, it's just what I was thinking when I came to understand that you probably would enjoy a little trip outside. You see, we are having this big problem just now. And when I say 'we,' what I mean is 'we' the human race. We are having a bit of a problem. It's a problem that I think you might be able to help me with. It all started on Mars."

Happiness Is Submission to God. These words were among the most inscrutable and ineffable bits of antique public signage in Rio Blanco—let's not get into the old liquor store neon on Ninth Street and those flickering beseechments for motels-by-the-hour lining the thoroughfare called Oracle. *Happiness Is Submission to God.* Inscribed on a small cottage in the neighborhood of the university, a cottage that had long been yet another staple of off-campus housing for a certain kind of URB student, the kind of student who had come to the campus to be neither pre-law nor premed. In fact, the lineage of the house itself—pale green with evergreen trim, right on the Sixth Street artery as it headed for *El Centro*—was a subject of enthusiastic conjecture among students of the mind. The entirety of the jihadist movement of the early part of the century was born in this very house, it was said. The slogan painted on the side of the house in part *created* this movement, though if the Wahhabis who lived there in the 1970s had not painted the quotation from the Qur'an on the side of the building, who had? No matter how far back you dated the building and its slogan, there was someone who had lived there *before,* who had rented it to the guy, or the woman, who had in turn rented it to the Wahhabis. Therefore, there was no origin for the slogan, only people searching for its origin: *Happiness Is Submission to God.*

First: the avant-garde theatrical troupe, from the historical epoch in which the phrase *avant-garde theatrical troupe* was not yet comical, the epoch of drug-perfected mummers who specialized in improvising works of absurdism in which they flung bodily fluids on the audience, invoking and citing works of oriental mysticism, until their parents cut them off. The works of the *avant-garde theatrical troupe* had lately been experiencing a renaissance, as in the case of the four-hour spectacular *Menarche,* revived in an abandoned warehouse on the South Side. These players had trashed the house, looted it of some of its gutters, which became props in a dramatic spectacular, and then passed the house — prized, additionally, because of its *basement,* a rarity in these parts — on to the next quixotic subculture, which was the subculture of the *radical political underground.* A national fugitive allegedly stayed a night in the house marked *Happiness Is Submission to God,* belittling the slogan as petty bourgeois, after his participation in a botched armored-truck robbery. This fugitive was taking a lot of pollutants, in order to buck himself up, and so while sleeping there he dreamed of being vivisected by a beloved uncle. As if vivid dreaming were some kind of contagion, or a reaction to valley fever spores, several of the political activists who lived there in this period began having vivid nightmares, in fact, and perhaps this was why they passed the house on to a cadre of videographers. The house stayed in the hands of the film and video department for a good five or six years, and its exterior appeared in many, many documentaries about the treatment of migrant farmworkers, and investigations into civic corruption and its relationship to land acquisition by URB. So routine did life then become in the house on Sixth Street that it was actually in danger of being repainted. Who cared about whether or not happiness was submission to God? There was, it is true, a video in production that purported to interpret the slogan, and since this documentary felt that the slogan was excessively *denominational* for a building associated with a state-funded institution of higher education, the videographer (and his friends) intended to repaint the house as the climax of the film. However, the problem of regional *vermin* was concurrently raising its multiple heads and segmented eyes in the house. The cockroaches were a nuisance but were not terribly frightening. Cockroach races, films thereof, were good sport. The lizards occasionally ate the roaches, so the lizards were at first welcome. The pack rats, however, were a little more challenging. One hapless video student narrowly avoided getting bitten by a pack rat. But soon the battle with vermin escalated to the tarantula. Total fumigation was required.

Black nationalists lived there, and these URB students were willing to put up with the occasional tarantula, or at least stories of the tarantula. These African American studies majors and their friends understood that the phrase on the side of the house on Sixth Street was from the Qur'an, and they even claimed to have *painted* the phrase on the building, though informal historians of Rio Blanco recognized that the slogan was painted before some of these students were out of diapers. Because of its spiritual *vibe,* these students made the house the center of their operations, where they began to attempt to bring their worldly, Western lives into accord with the precepts of that holy book, a classic of prophecy. Because there were students who lived this way, there was a sympathetic professor, and this professor was willing to offer courses with which they might refine and improve on their interpretation of the Qur'an. In the classes of this firebrand, language could do what culture could not, just by its utterance, just by the intent with which certain words were uttered, *how excellent is the recompense of paradise,* to utter certain words was to give proper reverence to Muhammad, *if there are twenty of you with determination they shall vanquish two hundred,* and soon there was a campus major in Islamic studies, and then there were doctorates, and then there were people who came from abroad, *whatever misfortune befalls you is a consequence of your deeds,* so as to hear about this interpretation of the Qur'an, which was the interpretation of the very word of God, *this is the Book free of doubt,* and the students were so committed that they had emblazoned their way of life on the side of their house, or at least the emblematic center of their studies, the house on Sixth Street, or so they said.

The Department of Islamic Studies and its student body hung on to the house for a while, perhaps until the time when the jihadist movement began to pick up steam halfway around the globe. At this point the Department of Islamic Studies seemed to scatter like dust dispersing in the Sahara. It was not instantaneous, but the Southwest was no longer the destination to which the Wahhabis reflexively turned. Upon the advent of death and mayhem a world away, the department began to lose its luster, and therefore the house on Sixth Street lay empty for a year, in an economic downturn. The neighborhood declined. There were shootings. Upon a reduction in rent advertised by a management company that would not identify the owner of the house, possession came to rest in the vegan community, the animal rights community, and so forth. The students of Harmonic Convergence, the men's liberation movement, the Wiccans, all came through the house, the last of these commencing the operation of the food co-op on Fourth Avenue. And then there were some massage therapists, and some people who were into auras, a group that practiced overtone singing. It seemed, in these years, that the words *Happiness Is Submission to God* signified just another *lifestyle choice*. During this period of the orphic ascendancy of the house, it was possible to speak of the residency of, e.g., one Jerry McArdle, an activist who opposed investment in South Africa, and Elsa Black, the instructor in tribal dancing. These inhabitants offered all the complexities of real people (Jerry collected guns; Elsa believed in *free love* but never read a book), and so the house no longer had magical properties, and that was the case for a long time, because this was a cultural era *after* miracles. There were no miracles, and no believers in miracles, because in the new millennium there was only commerce, and commerce depended on a system of goods and services that was more predictable than miracles, which could not have the universal pricing code affixed to them because miracles had no surfaces. The house on Sixth Street became just a house. A place where someone or some group of persons lived. A place where someone had an Internet programming console. A place where someone kept some of his or her stuff, and used the word *stuff* to describe it. The interior was repainted, and one wall was knocked out so that the living room would be a little bit larger. It was no longer important to try to have four entire units, which resembled tiny, poorly lit cells.

Into the age of the cessation of miracles, there came to the house this fellow from Indiana called Zachary Wheeler. He was the friend of the friend of somebody who lived in the house on Sixth Street. Later on, no one could agree on whose friend he was.

One woman, the one who made candles, said it was the guy from Santa Cruz, who only lived on Sixth Street for seven weeks, all of them spent on the couch, who had invited Wheeler to stay. But the guy from Santa Cruz blamed Sheila, the tarot card reader. Zachary was there, for good or ill, and he helped control rent inflation, and everyone seemed to like him well enough, though he had an absence of qualities. No *there* there. This would later appear to be one of the hallmarks of the literature produced by the *omnium gatherum,* the notion that what was desired was *less self,* that the persons possessed of this diminished ego were pariahs to civilization at large because they did not attach themselves to the distractions of this world, such as dishes, hygiene, and taxes. Indeed, these were some of the complaints about Wheeler, that he was less than generous as a roommate or a housemate because he didn't perform the weekly cleaning of the communal bathroom, which he had explicitly agreed to do by signing the schedule of chores on the refrigerator. Instead, he seemed to hover awkwardly around the periphery of any assembly of housemates, especially when guests were present.

He wanted, he said, when he said anything, to study ecstatic celebrations of the Plains Indians. He understood that these ecstatic celebrations, he said, could enable participants to concentrate better on the job, become more productive, have a more fulfilling sex life, rise to leadership roles in politics and the community.

If Wheeler was not, according to later profiles, successful at recruiting his housemates, he did, in his isolation, undertake to think carefully about the slogan *Happiness Is Submission to God.* He wrote poems, recorded New Age–style music featuring the panpipe, and, by his own description, he refrained from masturbation for a period of years. What he discovered, according to one of the self-published *omnium gatherum* books, was that *submission* was, in fact, essential to a happy and fulfilling life in this post-millennial world. His revelation was as follows. There was a night, according to Wheeler, in which he waked certain that there was again a scorpion in his bed with him. Perhaps he dreamed of the scorpion.

Or it dreamed of him. However it came to be, Wheeler knew that the scorpion was in the bed with him, and, as he retold the story, he carefully peeled back the threadbare sheet that covered him, and he gazed upon the scorpion, and without hesitation he presented his arm to be bitten. And yet the scorpion, which was looking for a warm, secluded place in which to settle itself, instead crept into the ravine between Wheeler's arm and his chest, and it tickled him as it traveled up into the crevice. Wheeler's first impulse was to jump up and shake off the bug, but he didn't give in to this impulse. He waited, and so did the scorpion. Wheeler, according to his beliefs, submitted to the scorpion, which likewise submitted to him, and the two of them waited, symbiotically, for what was to be revealed. It turned out it was rather a long night for Wheeler, whose arm was deprived of blood flow while he refrained from motion. A slick of perspiration formed on his forehead and tracked down face and neck, pooling especially in the armpit, where he imagined that the scorpion slaked its thirst upon his moisture. In the morning, in the first ray of light, the scorpion emerged from the warm sweaty spot in Wheeler's armpit, took one good look at him while perched on his chest, and stung him repeatedly. The scorpion laid it on. It did not hold back. Worried about waking roommates who didn't even like him much, Wheeler refrained from screaming, and he waited out the scorpion, which scuttled off to the corner of the room and disappeared beneath a baseboard that was both entrance and exit.

How this simple act of submission, and the several days of recovery that were required thereafter, the ice and ibuprofen, served as the beginning of the *omnium gatherum,* you would know only if you were an inductee into that loosely organized spiritual movement. For the uninitiated, it was clear that this moment had to do with submission, and with *revealing,* for somehow the scorpion, as a symbol, came to represent the desperate circumstances of civilization on the brink of *moving into the new*. Wheeler, in the period of recovery from the scorpion stings, during the predictable depression that often coexists with the expulsion of toxins, leaned on the notion of *revealing* as a comfort, and this gave him the idea to synthesize all the apparent apocalyptic strains from the faiths major and minor, and to argue that apocalypse, which is all about *revealing*, satisfies an important part of human psychology, one that must be embraced and celebrated. *Apocalypsis* can serve as a *lifestyle opportunity.* Apocalypse implies change, and the possibility of great, unpredictable change, as well as the moral certainty that other people will be consigned to oblivion, these things can really make life more tolerable.

The first *omnium gatherum,* a study group organized by Wheeler with members of one of the mega-churches in Rio Blanco, at which Wheeler occasionally took communion even though he didn't have much faith in the decidedly practical mysticisms of Protestantism, was notable for its absence of *omnium.* Turnout, that is, was light. Every convert to the cause was hand selected, and with great effort. According to the literature of these early pre-institutional days, the group consisted of a woman with a type II bipolar diagnosis, Christine, whose husband was really uncomfortable with all of her Wheeler-inspired babbling; a death metal vocalist from the suburbs, called Stig; and one of Wheeler's best friends, a quiet and retiring mathematician called Louise Anselm, who felt that *apocalypsis* was probably mathematical more than anything else, and who wanted to study it as a kind of teleological reply to the numerical excesses of infinity. Wheeler assigned reading to each of these participants from one of the mystery cults or from heretical sects such as might be found in the Nag Hammadi papyruses, *come to that which God has revealed,* the idea being to generate some kind of reservoir for all possible descriptions of apocalypse, *yet man says will I live again,* and to begin to organize these in a database of apocalyptic imagery and longing. The original members of the group were uncommitted to the project, but they were good people, and they were four, which is a numeral of genuine interest, describing, for example, the square, and each of the four, each of the line segments of the square of *omnium gatherum,* the superstructure in which the group would be built, exemplified the dictum *Happiness Is Submission to God*. Coincidences abounded!

Stig, whose vocal polyps had temporarily sidelined him, resulting in his being forced out of the band he had formed himself, gave the first presentation at the *omnium gatherum*, namely a paper on connections between Joachim of Fiore, the twelfth-century architect of numerical *exegesis*, and the number of words in the fragments of the Oxyrhynchus 1224 Gospel, with special attention to the first line fragment: "...in every...To you I swear..." These six words, according to Stig's very serviceable paper, indicated revelatory strains that ran straight from the dawn of civilization up through the canonizing impulse of early Christianity, rising to a pinnacle in the twelfth century, where these six words collided with Joachim and his numerical obsessions, whereupon the particular numerical sequence, as well as the devotional importance of the word *every*, likewise the avowal of "To you I swear," with its carnal implications, were suppressed for several centuries while Europe bathed itself in blood and plague, not to appear again until discovered by the decadents of the end of the nineteenth century, who equated, according to Stig, love and *le petit mort* with the end of civilization, at which point the impulse was again suppressed, according to Stig, until the soul music from the late twentieth century, beginning with the African American jazz-soul singer Nina Simone, traveling through some old-fashioned hip-hop and neo-soul, these generations-old soul music evocations, according to Stig, presenting both a carnal and a revolutionary fervor, as in the Trotskyite upheavals of early-twenty-first-century Kazakhstan. Stig's reasoning, it was clear, was not terribly sophisticated, and there were improbable leaps whose rhetorical force would not be immediately apparent to readers who weren't already informed on matters of the *apocalypsis*, but for thumbnail history it wasn't bad, and it's important to note that Stig, when he destroyed his voice for good, became a religious-studies professor, one of the first popularizers of *omnium gatherum* in the religious left; see, for example, his wealth of papers on the decentered and anti-authoritarian structure of governance in *omnium gatherum,* its emphasis on service and rotating leadership, its oral tradition, its attempts to generate its own language and alphabet, its resistance to traditional ritual. These position papers became so central to the public relations of the *omnium gatherum* that there was a schismatic subdivision of the group that insisted that Stig was the de facto founder and institutional genius behind everything that was and has been lasting about *omnium gatherum.*

As additional converts began attending meetings, Zachary Wheeler began to conceive of the *omnium gatherum,* despite its scriptural, textual, and interpretive zeal, as something that had to be accomplished in *real time,* which is to say that it needed to take place only at actual *gatherings,* not in people's homes, not in solitude. It needed to have a dramatic, communal, performative modality. This emphasis came to repel certain kinds of Christian folks, though the *omnium gatherum* declared itself in harmony with their practices. The Christians, it seemed, mainly wanted to talk about the Book of Revelation. They had been led to believe that only certain interpretations were authorized with respect to their text. Zachary Wheeler was chagrined to lose, in the larger *omnium gatherum* community, the more obsessive members of the evangelical world—especially evangelical persons with a history of psychotic symptoms, since Wheeler believed that psychosis was an important ideological tool, one that needed to be included in the dialogue of faith.

Then: snakes. The continuum of vermin. Beginning with sewer roaches, moving up through scorpions, and the tarantulas, perhaps including the coyote and the javelina, the brown recluse spider, the diamondback rattlesnake. If Zach Wheeler never woke to find a snake in his bed, or a snake waiting for him in the bathroom, it was only by chance, because who didn't come here, to the desert, but to reckon with the sound of the rattlesnake and the application of its venom to a calf or an ankle? Who didn't find himself, or herself, listening for the sound of the rattlesnake? The *omnium gatherum* was ephemeral, was lightweight, if it didn't involve snakes, if it didn't have workshops where there would be biting, where there would be willing victims of rattlesnakes and a period of waiting before the antivenin was administered. Wheeler himself was the first to volunteer, and he invited people from the community to watch, which only emboldened his estranged sister, a social worker in Oregon, to note in the press that Wheeler had always been "sick, egomaniacal, and passive-aggressive," and that, as a child, he'd performed for his ex-military father by playing with electrical sockets. Students of snakebite ecstasy will have noted that the venom of local snakes, Sonoran snakes, has been mutating over the years, and that the sidewinder and the diamondback have both graduated to a level of poisonousness that has led the local police to attempt to intercede when, at least, they have been tipped off about wildlife encounters.

Wheeler, however, had made a lifetime study of the creation of ecstatic religious groups, and he'd gone to the mega-churches, and he knew that he stood for something. It was important to get people around him who could look after the organizational details of the *omnium gatherum,* such as the creation of foundational documents, so that he might simply go out into the desert, as all the great monastic thinkers had done, and organize his party, year in and year out, allowing for sculpture, for ritual burning, for music, for performance. It was as if the slogan *Happiness Is Submission to God* wrote its history in situ. The *omnium gatherum,* like its founder, was unruly, badly scripted, had no rules, and was often thought to be more theme park than philosophical system. Perversely, it grew more quickly during bad times.

It was five or six years past that Wheeler finally decided to stage his own disappearance, in a snakebite ceremony, in which he was supposed to have allowed a sidewinder to bite him on the face—after which he was taken to the University of Rio Blanco Medical Center. Gangrene set in! Was he so badly disfigured that he needed to wear a mask? Or some kind of veil? Had he died in the snakebite ritual? Were dental records required? Or was he just tired of the whole thing and wanting to move into consulting on corporate productivity? His disappearance only insured his centrality to the *omnium gatherum* as it moved forward to field its first political candidates and to seize control of some deconsecrated churches in Rio Blanco, which it used as gallery spaces and warehouses for the treasures of past events. Some of the gallery exhibits concerned Wheeler's trips across the border to study up on Yaqui peyote rituals. In some accounts, he had become a coyote. Whichever version of the truth you believed, assuming one of them referred to that hazy quantity *the truth,* Wheeler removed himself from any visible role in *omnium gatherum* operations. Official meetings of *omnium gatherum* became more unpredictable.

In this way, they began to concentrate on *nomadism.* The *omnium gatherum,* just three years ago, began to assert that *nomadism* was the most effective use of the Earth's resources and that private property, as such, represented theft of the land. The Roma, the Plains Indians, the Mongol shepherds, these became idols for the rootless and centerless inquiry of the *omnium gatherum,* and it came to pass, because that is how things happened with the *omnium gatherum,* they *came to pass,* that homelessness emerged as an integral part of the *omnium gatherum* course of study, homelessness and *nomadism* living right next door to each other, as it were, *nomadism* being the proper *pre- and post-apocalypsis* lifestyle, and so homeless members of the group, who were especially drawn to some of the healthy snack foods available at *omnium gatherum* events, became integral. They were valued, esteemed, and their difficulties were dealt with within the family. Certain impressionable members of the *omnium gatherum,* which is to say runaways and young people whose parents had lost their livelihoods during the recession, believed that they had *seen* Wheeler, and that he was himself embarked on riding the freight trains in order to recruit from among the robust population of rail nomads, or they believed that he had organized a motorcycle gang of some kind, which moved from town to town stealing from the rich, or they believed that he was now an emergency medical technician, and that he was out in the field, trying to cure an outbreak of some streptococcal menace, or they believed that he was border patrol, and despite his intense rhetoric on the elimination of all border fences in all nations, that he was secretly aiding and abetting the repatriation of undocumented persons attempting to flee this country, or *omnium gatherum* had never existed in the first place but was just a series of studies in opposition.

How was it financed? The last important question in this history of the *omnium gatherum*. It was financed entirely by donations, and the better part of these donations were made by the rank and file, members of the group just like you and me, who were able to give fifty dollars, or a hundred dollars, or nothing more than a quarter. You just gave what you were able to give, and if that was no more than a quarter, then that was what you gave. There was web-related advertising, naturally, and there were online sales of artworks that were generated by various *omnium gatherum* events, and recently they had made a little money in real estate, by purchasing worthless or foreclosed properties and holding them for a while. But the donations were the better part of what they had taken in, and as time went on, as the *omnium gatherum* became a legitimate, or a semi-legitimate, ideological system, one that fielded its own tattoo artists, its own massage therapists, its own cocounseling workshops, its own demon-extraction rituals, its own waste-management operations, its own agricultural products, its own farm markets, the possibility for profit grew, and as the potential for profit grew, the greater were the gifts from the employees of corporations, the fellow travelers. Most of the collecting happened through the *omnium gatherum* web site, which was not affiliated with any official employee, because there was none. The IT manager was also the publicist, who claimed not to know Zach Wheeler, nor where to find him, but who may have been identical with him. According to this publicist, the federal government had, in the era after Social Security, defaulted on its obligations, and the *omnium gatherum* was prepared to step in as a shadow government. Responsible and affluent persons needed to consider whether a donation to the group would be more reliable than taxes paid to a central government, that despoiler, because the *omnium gatherum* was better able to look after the citizens and was therefore more deserving of tax money. This argument worked, it turned out, and it was breathed into life by Denny Wheeler, Zach's son, who was at Stanford, and who made the appeal as part of his senior thesis on alternative political systems.

It was into this phenomenal and nearly unforeseeable socio-religious success that a certain disembodied hand crawled.

The downtown rally for the Union of Homeless Citizens was heavily attended by members of the *omnium gatherum,* or perhaps it's more exact to say that there was much interpenetration between the two communities: the homeless and the spiritual adepts. Hard to tell the one from the other. They both subscribed to the tenets of *nomadism.* Who could say which was which?

An inquiry by some high school students who had attended the rally, the rally of the Union of Homeless Citizens, who had watched as the police descended on the lawfully gathering no-mads, noted that in many of their interviews the rally participants asked such questions, whether in Spanish, English, or Spanglish, as "Did you get a look at that goddamned arm?" "Whoa, brother, I was carrying the arm for a while." "The thing had this way that it moved.... It was kind of a dancing arm...moving all around while you held it." "I swear the thing was trying to talk, and I had this running buddy, man, couldn't say no words at all, only spoke like with some kinds of sign language, and I swear to you the hand was trying to talk, just like this guy."

The theory of *nomadism* described statistically the behavior of very large numbers of people, and therefore the theory relied on unruly crowds and their inevitable assault on private property. Accordingly, it was impossible to say precisely who held the arm when, just be-cause of luck, one high school kid, Nicky Hays, who was trying to write something for his school paper about the rally, happened upon it. Didn't matter who. Someone claimed to have had the arm for a day or two, and to have traded it to another guy who had a large supply of polyamphetamine pills, and this was a bad trade, because these pills did not contain *true* polyamphetamine, and this addict spent the night throwing up in an alley behind one of the adult-book stores. Hays followed his tip, in the thirty-six hours after the rally, into the dark and sinister world of polyamphetamine dealers, who were mainly high school and college kids with parents who were clinging by a few unraveling threads to the middle class. And it turned out that someone Nicky knew, Moose Mansourian, controlled the arm, after a long, rather dormant day in which it was mainly a trophy. He'd locked it in a terrarium, where, through some indolence or exhaustion, it sat at length. He'd tried to feed it slices of orange, tried to get it interested in a hamster wheel made out of bicycle tires.

Hays sensed that perhaps the crawling hand was not a benefi-cent presence in the landscape of Rio Blanco. So when he figured out that Moose had stiffed a homeless guy on the polyamphetamine and thereby obtained the arm, he made a beeline for the Mansourian residence, which was on the South Side. Moose's father worked at the coal plant. His mother had abandoned Moose and his brother, Corey, who had an extra supply of genetic material. Apparently, Moose believed that Corey was really going to like the arm, be-cause Corey was interested in all kinds of weird stuff, though he was basically a gentle kid, and Moose liked trying to do things that he thought would amuse Corey, and so he took the arm and sold the addict guy a bunch of laxative pills, claiming they were polyamphetamine, and Nicky was so shocked at what he was learning, just with a little flash recorder that he'd borrowed from school, and a notepad, that he couldn't stop calling people to tell them the story. One of the people he called was his old girlfriend, well, not his girlfriend, really, but they had known each other in a carnal way, a hooking-up way, and her name was Vienna Roberts. The conversation was like this:

Nicky: "Vi, I got this amazing story I gotta tell you...."

Taking place, understand, on the tiny little video screen on the digital, wrist-implanted, all-purpose media storage device.

Vienna: "Nicky, I just can't right now...."

Nicky: "Why? Is there...?"

Vi: "You just can't imagine...."

Nicky: "Doesn't have anything to do with the...with the thing...the homeless thing the other night, does it?"

Her parents were organizers or activists or whatever you'd call it, with all the homeless people.

Vi: "Kind of..."

Nicky: "Does it have to do with some kind of arm?"

Vi: "What?"

Nicky: "I'm asking if the trouble has anything to do with this frigging *arm*, this, like, this arm, because, like, I was interviewing these guys for the school paper, and they were all talking about this *arm*, and I was sort of thinking that it was some kind of, you know, made-up thing, like a kind of story that gets going and then it's not really anything but what people *say*, but then there was this guy, and he said he'd had it for a while, won it in a hand of poker, and then he sold it to Moose, you know Moose, right? He sold it to Moose Mansourian for some polyamphetamine, and now I'm on my way—"

Vi: "Where does he live? This Moose guy? Where does he live?"

At which point Nicky got all protective about his sources. A journalist must have his ethics.

In the meantime, the *omnium gatherum* was attempting to synthesize all the available information on crawling hands, attempting to come up with a sort of foundational myth on the subject of the crawling hand, a myth that began with *nomadism* but which then moved even further afield, into a kind of interstellar or interplanetary *nomadism,* and in which the unity of the human body was no longer reliable or even desirable, noting, in passing, the importance of the hand in hieroglyphics, and the fact that on the tomb of Ramses, e.g., the hand signifies *manifestation,* all that is, all that is in the process of *becoming.* The hand is associated with the human body, yes, stands for it, allegorically, with four fingers for the four extremities, *and* the middle finger associated with the head. All the more reason, according to the bulletin on the subject, that the middle finger of this hand was *missing,* as if to indicate that the new body, the new human body, was headless, or effectively headless, and capable of acting despite the absence of a consciousness or a place to situate consciousness. The head signifies humanity, and the absence of humanity is the essence of this time. The Romans, meanwhile, believed that the hand signified *paternal authority,* and thus this hand is dispossessed of its body, and unable to do much beyond grasp, and even that without much effectiveness. The hand placed on the heart signifies wisdom and sagacity, and the hand without a finger indicates an abbreviated wisdom. The hand touching the head means melancholy. The hand raised above the head indicates spirituality. All of this suggested, according to the bulletin hastily concocted by the *omnium gatherum,* that the hand, in some way, indicated the *manumission* that was to come. The *omnium gatherum* therefore required the crawling hand and would, when it had studied the crawling hand, gladly return it to the state and local authorities, who, the *omnium gatherum* believed, were already on the case, were already encircling the city of Rio Blanco with some kind of independently contracted security perimeter. Now, it was true, according to the *omnium gatherum,* that the hand could be infected with something, with some kind of bacterial speckling or perhaps a viral spattering, and it was important when handling the crawling hand not only to be careful about its strength, but it was also important to wear rubber gloves and to avoid allowing the hand to touch you, because, according to the bulletin, the *apocalypsis* had its contagions.

As already noted, despite his membership in the confraternity of dealers in controlled substances, Moose Mansourian had mainly seen his life's work as contributing to the well-being and the advancing cerebral development of his brother, Corey. In fact, though there is often a lustrous motive hiding behind the supply-and-demand economics of drug dealing, Moose's claim was more specific. He needed to fund additional classes and eight hours a week of in-home care for his brother, who would otherwise have fallen through the cracks in the safety net of the post-government dog days of the twenty-first century. What with a mom who had fled the scene because of her inability to manage a *wild child,* and a father who worked more nonunion shifts than humanly possible in order to provide, there was no one left in the family to look after Corey. Family, as you know, is the group of people who have no choice. If Moose selected the most dangerous drugs in which to traffic, or if he graduated to these most serious felonies, that was only because this was where the profits lay.

Corey: a doughy, slightly walleyed boy of fourteen, whose faint mustache indicated a virility that coincided with an appalling inattention to hygiene, about which Corey was nonetheless surpassingly unselfconscious. His shabbiness, however, caused Moose great embarrassment in the rare instances when he allowed friends to visit — his brother mostly naked and smelling awful in front of horror movies and infomercials, plunging grimy fingertips into his nose and ears. Corey's other comfort in life was eating, though his ideas about food seemed narrow-minded. He never ate a vegetable willingly at all, and instead wolfed down foods that contained abundances of cheese, specifically demanding, with his limited language skills, mac and cheese, grilled cheese, and cheese pizza to the exclusion of all else.

Still, he was a sweet kid, and a loyal one. Moose Mansourian had, in the course of caring for his brother, observed a few rules for stimulating the mental activity that would insure Corey wouldn't lose function as he grew older. Moose believed that Corey needed, above all, visual stimulation, and, though he was loath to allow his brother unlimited access to television or video games, he did accept shipment, in the last eighteen months or so, of a wall-sized monitor in return for some preferential treatment on behalf of a certain client. What Moose liked to keep on the wall monitor in Corey's room were images of placid scenery. Sylvan scenery. He'd leave each image up for five or ten minutes, using the slide-show function, to which he was always adding images, news photos, sometimes reproductions of the great masters, family shots, including images of their mother, and so forth. Home videos from the web if they were suggestive of the homely pleasures. Corey really noticed this stuff, really paid attention to that mystical moment when the wall image changed, and occasionally when Moose's work was done for the day or when he was waiting for a call, the two brothers would sit together and watch the stills cycle past:

"What do you see?" The older brother.

"Water," said the younger. Though you couldn't always understand what he was saying.

"And can you figure out what kind of water that is?"

"Waterfall?"

"A famous waterfall. Back east. People like to go and get married by the waterfall. Or they used to. I've never seen it, but I guess people really like the churning of the water and all that kind of stuff. Do you know why it's important to have a photo of a waterfall on your wall when you live in the desert?"

Corey looked at him dreamily. Moose recognized that his line of inquiry had now passed beyond what was possible for Corey to understand. It didn't matter, since Corey was often grateful just for the sound of words. Sometimes Moose would try repeating words to Corey. Just about anything was worth trying.

"The desert is a place without enough water. So this picture reminds you that there are places out there where there *is* enough water, and even though we don't live in one of those places, that doesn't mean there isn't water out there that other people get to drink and shower in."

It wasn't long after this that he brought home the arm, wrapped in burlap. Moose felt that the arm would replace the iguana he'd gotten Corey, which had proven too freethinking. There was a robot vacuum cleaner that Corey loved completely, one of those Frisbee-shaped things that caromed off walls, sucking up crumbs and bits of paper, which, it should be said, followed Corey around. Corey watched the vacuum cleaner like the device was almost religious, jumping up onto furniture and laughing hysterically when it went by. The arm, and the terrarium into which Moose put it, were meant to bring about this same pitch of delight, and the arm was probably less dangerous, because Corey wasn't really tall enough to reach up onto the top of the terrarium, and so he wouldn't trifle with the arm.

On the night in question, Moose just figured he'd sleep in the room with Corey and the arm. In this way, he'd make sure that the arm didn't get into any trouble. Knowing Corey, Moose worried that the arm would find itself used as a bat for knocking glasses off the shelf in the kitchen. Best to hang around some, smoke some weed, take the edge off, watch to see if the arm actually used the hamster wheel thing Moose had rigged up in the terrarium.

What did it cost Moose Mansourian, this fraternal generosity that seemed contraindicated in the world of drug dealing, whose business was composed of a client pool rapidly depleting itself of all worldly goods? What did it cost Moose? And could it really go on like this? He was suspicious, even cynical out in the world, where his linebacker physique made him good at his job. He was not a handsome man, and women never seemed to pay much attention, but he didn't care, because he had an anxiety disorder, the one listed in the *DSM-VIII* as *anxiety specifically related to contemporaneity,* which made him suspicious, which made him trust no one, except Corey, and he was constantly drugging himself to sleep because every night the slightest sound waked him, and then he'd be up, and if he was up, he was up for good and was reading medical texts to try to put himself back to sleep, and any woman who tried to get near to him, that woman just reminded him of his mother, and if she contacted him now, he thought, while he was falling asleep next to Corey, having smoked enough weed to paralyze most people, he would do something, something horrible, he would lock her in the room with Corey for a week, and it wasn't that he thought Corey was so bad, because on the contrary, he thought, as his lids began to close, he loved Corey, and Corey seemed to operate in the world in a way that involved less unhappiness than most people suffered with. His mother needed to have the experience of seeing Corey, and Moose needed the experience of seeing Corey see *her,* and maybe that would be the ultimate perpetual-motion object that would improve cerebral function in Corey, his mother, his mother would be the ultimate visual stimulation, and even if Corey didn't *know* his mother, or didn't even know he *had* a mother, although Moose had tried to explain it to him a few times, maybe it was one of those things that was contained in some deeper-down layer, the knowledge of the excellence of seeing one's mother walking through a room, straightening a few things, doling out a few orders, and that was why, Moose thought, as his eyes closed and certain sounds in the room, certain hums, became the music of his drifting off, too early, so that he would probably wake in the middle of the night and watch the water in the fish tank bubble, that was why his mother would turn up one day, because it just didn't make sense that a person carried around that kind of guilt, the walking out on your kids kind of guilt, and then Moose slept. . . .

The arm appeared in this tableau with the aspect of an avenging angel, and it had no compassion in its heart, because it had no heart, and no sensory organs with which compassion might have been felt. Accordingly, there was no mercy in the arm's decision to eliminate Moose and to spare Corey. Corey was an innocent, but the arm knew nothing of innocence. However, it is true, upon consideration, that mercy is an expression of both order and chance in the natural world, and thus perhaps mercy *was* within the arm's grasp, so to speak. And Corey made the expression of mercy easier because he slept in an absolutely motionless way, like a newborn, really. He would keel over asleep in a position that was corpse-like enough to be taken for a corpse (many were the nights that Moose or their father thought Corey was dead), and never moved once until he woke hours later. How he avoided bedsores was a mystery. The arm sensed movement and responded to it as though movement were something that needed to be eliminated from the world. And Moose writhed around a lot in his semi-sleep. He therefore appeared to the arm, to the extent that anything *appeared* to the arm, as something that needed to be brought to a halt, and so, on the bed where the two brothers slept, the smaller one curled beside the larger, there lay a single target. The arm carefully lifted off the lid of the terrarium and lowered itself down until it had negotiated the shelf of bobble-head dolls, and likewise the shelf that collected the stuffed animals. And then the arm was on the headboard of the bed, creeping, and in the time it took to creep, all of Moose Mansourian's life was flickering on the screen of the wall-sized monitor of heavenly accounts; for example, it was being noted on the screen that though Moose had once been part of a group of brass musicians (he'd played the trombone) that had regaled some elderly people in an assisted-living type of institution with light versions of the classics, he'd also provided the OxyPlus inhalers used in at least three different overdoses; true, Moose believed in assisted suicide and had on one occasion helped a terminally ill addict effect a departure from this world, but he had also charged a fee for this work; the young Moose Mansourian, a complicated kid who was quite bad at school, and too demanding of his friends, all of whom eventually tired of him, shed bitter tears at inopportune moments, and his high school football career eventually ended because he was considered too timid after a neck injury he inflicted on a rival from the Tempe area.

The arm knew naught of these forking tales, of the good and bad Moose Mansourians, and of the simple and tender relationship between Moose and the younger kid beside him, and so when the arm propelled itself through the air onto the throat of Moose Mansourian, the forking narratives of a life neither good nor bad were nowhere apparent, and the arm, because it knew no compassion, dug in its fingernails, so that when Moose, awakening from a stupor, grabbed the forearm and pulled, he did little more than pull the long, serrated fingernails of the arm through some important biological real estate, so that there was an Old Faithful geysering, this happening so quickly and so quietly that the boys' father was not awakened (he was in the habit of drinking), and the young Corey, who slept like a corpse and dreamed only of empty desert landscapes with rabbits and javelinas grazing upon them, wasn't roused until later, speckled with crimson, at which point he beheld the arm finishing off his brother, and unfortunately for Corey, and for Moose, his first impulse, because he didn't understand, was to laugh.

The mother of young Moose would have been brought low by the recognition of this moment. The teachers who had cared about him and who worried when he didn't go to college would have been brought low. The neighbors, who all said of Moose, despite the rumors, that he was respectful and kept to himself, they all would have been brought low, and were, when emergency vehicles arrived, and, later, a cortege of more government vehicles than any had seen in years. Who would not have found him- or herself weeping had he or she come upon that scene, the dead boy in the pool of blood, and his learning-disabled brother chasing the arm around the room as though it were some kind of toy, forgetting, for the moment, that his elder sibling, the person who cared most about him, was toggling into the off position once and for all. The arm did nothing but spread loss and grief, it was a force for *harm,* but Corey didn't really understand these things, not yet, and so once he had stabbed at the arm a few times with a plastic sword he kept at bedside, he actually opened the door for it, to watch the arm scuttle out into the hall of the Mansourian homestead, where it somehow made instinctual or rather uncanny progress toward the front door, at which point Corey, who was mostly enjoined from opening and closing doors, opened the front door, because he had learned the manipulation of locks. And when no one was looking, he sometimes contented himself by fiddling with — opening and closing — doors, and so he released his brother's murderer out into the gravel front yard, and he stood there watching it make its way across the dusty waste; in the light of a lone solar-powered streetlamp, the arm, circumnavigating a prickly pear that was yellowing on the lawn, toppled off the curb and into the street. All this took place in the deeper part of the night, you see, when the gangs came out down on the lower part of Fourth Avenue, near to Nineteenth or Twentieth, thereabouts, and maybe the gangs would seize the murderer, the arm, as a curiosity, because gangs were the only people who could thrive in the deep night of Rio Blanco. They were the only people, besides the *nomads,* who took pleasure in this fragmented metropolis, with one of the highest murder rates in the nation. Corey, who stood in the xerisphere of his own front yard, gazed up, bloody plastic Excalibur in his hand. And it was here that he stood when his father was finally roused, perhaps by the commotion and perhaps by the great darkness that was at that moment sweeping over his slumbering heart. This ineffectual patriarch stumbled from his tiny little bed in the stifling upstairs master bedroom, and even the scorpions in the wall sorrowed from their hideouts, and Mr. Mansourian, arriving at the front door and seeing his more challenged son with a plastic sword covered in blood, and beholding the night sky leaking back into the insubstantial bit of creation called Rio Blanco, Mr. Mansourian cried out, *What have you done? What have you done? Oh, lord!* Taking the innocent boy and shaking him hard, and seeing the fear in Corey's eyes, watching as Corey started to cry, he then instead took him into his arms. What else was there to do?

The arm went about its fell business, meanwhile, finding ways to travel from neighborhood to neighborhood. Through empty lots, tent communities, and subdivisions. Three or four more unfortunates met their fate in the process. But more important than the fatalities were the myriad limbs and extremities that the arm managed to *brush against,* as it served as trophy, curiosity, talisman, prosthetic limb, and, in a bodega on the South Side, one of those picker-uppers that you use to reach things on the high shelves. The arm, carrier of exotic bacteria, perhaps sensed the ways in which the laborious gravity of Earth was sapping it of its energies, and if the bacteria animated it, they couldn't do so for long, because nothing exists forever in this place. Without some infusion of energy, the arm would eventually have to abandon its mission. If it couldn't *kill* with the ferocity that would have contented it, it could, however, spread wide its contagion. All the arguments, all the Caucasian chalk circles that were drawn around the arm, in which antagonists were pitted against one another for the control of it, these were all just little data points on the Venn diagram of infection.

As indicated, by morning, the police had draped their colored tape around the Mansourian residence, and they'd congregated there, trying to ascertain what the evidence suggested in the matter of the death of Moose Mansourian, known confederate of Mexican drug kingpins, small-time, low-level operative who hadn't been detained yet only because he didn't give the police anyone they couldn't get from a dozen different snitches. The only part of the story that didn't work was the part that had to do with the learning-disabled kid stabbing Moose Mansourian to death with a plastic sword. The death was by strangulation — that was patently obvious on the body — and anyway the retarded kid seemed confused and uncertain about the whole business, which left the father, but the father had no signs of a struggle on his body. It didn't add up.

The other thing that didn't add up was how the Federales got wind of the whole thing so fast. They were *not* likely to intervene in small-town drug hits in places like Rio Blanco, not when there were dozens of other larger cities where the lawlessness was even more aggrieved. How did they know? Which way was the information flowing? All the locals knew was that before they had even finished bagging the evidence and interviewing family members, there was a whole team of federal employees pulling up at the house. Some of them were from the FBI, but others were from far more exotic agencies, including, it seemed, the Centers for Disease Control — not an agency that anyone in Rio Blanco was accustomed to encountering, except when there was that hantavirus outbreak. These guys were actually wearing Hazmat jumpsuits when they showed up, and they were urging the officers to report to a temporary quarantine station that had been set up in the university gymnasium. There they were going to be showered, given a powerful antibiotic, and then they were going to be observed for a few days. Before all that happened, the local officers were detailed to the front of the house, where they were to fend off anyone who would come along asking questions.

But one guy, one of the officers, was still in the house when a fellow with a bad comb-over who claimed to be from NASA (what NASA had to do with anything was anyone's guess) began to try to interview the retarded kid. This was comical to watch, and the officer, Detective Paradiso, was asked by his police chief to videotape the interview between the bad-hair guy and the retarded kid, for internal use only, and so with the video camera off his tool belt, he made like he was a documentary guy, filming everything from the corner of a cramped living room.

"My name is Rob," the guy from NASA kept reiterating. Trying to get the kid to focus. Trying to explain NASA to the kid. Space, Mars, all this stuff that was irrelevant to some kid who didn't even really know what just happened to his brother. "Can you tell me what happened last night? Do you know what happened?"

The kid's father was sitting next to him now, with an arm around the fucked-up kid, and the father, looking like it was all well beyond him, was crying as the kid tried to talk.

"Moose," the kid said.

"Moose," the NASA guy repeated. "Your brother. You were home with your brother?"

"Home."

"Watching things on the television monitor here?"

"Waterfall."

"You were watching a waterfall?"

The NASA guy deferred to the father, who didn't really have anything at all to add to the account. But he had some translation skills with regard to the kid. It was really hard to understand the kid, that was for sure. He had every speech impediment it was

possible to have. His big, fleshy lips were not made for the pronunciation of anything but the simplest words.

"Is it possible that your brother made you angry somehow? It's
important that we—"

"We tried that one," Detective Paradiso called from behind the
camera.

"I think I can ask the questions," NASA guy rejoined, without
much conviction. "So did your brother make you angry?"

Retarded kid just fidgeted with the plastic sword, which they
had tried to take away from him but which he would not relinquish, and which was still covered with dried brown blood, and
the kid was obviously really tired and wanted nothing more than
to go to sleep, but probably he could sense that something horrible had happened. Whether he understood the question or not,
that was debatable, but still the kid seemed to summon up some
kind of response, something that you could film on your departmental video camera:

"No."

"You weren't angry?"

"No."

"Can you tell me what happened?"

At which point the father got himself involved.

"Look, we've been going around and around on this stuff for
four hours, and you're talking to a child who is *not verbal,* and he
didn't answer this question earlier, and he's not going to be able
to answer it now. And I don't know what all of this is about, but
I know that this is the only boy I have left, and he is exhausted,
and I'm exhausted, and I don't care, personally, if this is some
international diplomatic incident or whatever the hell it is, but
we need to be able to go to sleep here and to try to come to some
kind of *closure.*"

NASA guy ignored the heartfelt plea, and who can blame him,
since one of the most popular web-based, enhanced-reality brands
that autumn was the program entitled *Closure,* in which a crack team
of life coaches went out into the world to help people who needed

closure, for whatever reason, whether because of natural disaster, or abandonment, or murder, to find the persons they needed to find in order to make their appeal for, you guessed it, *closure.* The NASA guy didn't give a shit about *closure;* he thought *closure* was some TV shit, apparently, and from the way he was talking about the whole thing, he was willing to sacrifice the retarded kid and the dad too to the dumpster of history, in order to get what he needed. But he tried a more personal appeal, and maybe it was this appeal that finally got the attention of the retarded kid, even if only for a minute.

"Corey," he said, and it was as if some light were being switched on in the murky proceedings, by virtue of a proper name, "I'm going to tell you a little bit about me. I've got some kids of my own, one of them about your age, and I haven't seen my kids in a while. In fact, my kids, along with their mom, left me not too very long ago, because of all the work I've been putting into the planet Mars. You know what the planet Mars is, right? I'm betting your brother told you all about Mars and the other planets. Mars is a beautiful, deserted place, and, you may have heard, last year we tried to put some men on Mars. Some women too. And what we learned, Corey, was that there are some places where people just aren't meant to go. And when you send astronauts places where they aren't yet meant to go, all kinds of things go wrong. You know what I mean, right? In this case, some things went wrong when we tried to bring the men *back* from Mars. Some men and women died on the way to Mars, and some men and women decided to stay on Mars, and then there was the one man coming back from Mars, and we did everything we could to bring him back, so that he could be reunited with his family. We'd failed so many times, in so many different ways, but we tried to paper over our failures with this one success: we were going to bring this man home. Then something went horribly wrong even there. The man was made sick on Mars, and now it's possible that some people are going to catch the sickness of the man from Mars, and because of this it's urgently necessary that we—"

An incredible story, when you thought about it for a second.

It wasn't the story of the Mars mission as anyone else had heard it. Detective Paradiso, who was trying to get some nice close-ups and all, was being warned by the people from the CDC that everything he was hearing in the room was *top secret,* and while they were willing to tolerate temporary video storage for documentation internally at the RBPD, any leak could occasion *mass hysteria, public disorder, a national health emergency,* and other horrible things, and so he was to keep completely silent about all of this, all that he saw in that dim, moist living room, and therefore Paradiso was trying to listen carefully to all these dire threats, or so he told his buddies back at the precinct first chance he got, and he was sort of electrified by what he'd heard, when the kid said something that was apparently very important, and right away NASA guy got plenty interested, and all the CDC guys gathered round. What the kid said was the word *arm.*

"Arm?" NASA guy said right back to him. "Are you saying this had something to do with an arm?"

"Arm."

"Like an arm that wasn't attached to—"

"Arm."

"Can you tell us where the arm was?"

"Maybe he means the iguana," the father said. "We got rid of the iguana."

"Arm," the retarded kid said again.

But the NASA guy knew what he needed to know: "And at any time did the arm *touch* you, Corey? Did you have any contact with the arm? This is really important. Can you remember? Did you touch the arm?"

He couldn't fucking feel one fucking thing in his leg, not one fucking thing; his leg felt like it wasn't even his own fucking leg, and when he looked down at the leg, or at the other leg, at the pair of legs, it was like they were not legs at all, like they were fucking lengths of PVC piping or something, or like a severed tree limb, or like they were made of marble, and he could still move his legs, a little fucking bit, but it was like the legs no longer fucking *belonged* to him, but they belonged on some junk heap, like the junk heaps of the Mexicans who sat out at the empty corners on the margins of the city, sheets over their heads, selling bits and pieces of junk, a wagon wheel, a fucking human skull; they would have been happy to have one of his legs, his legs that no longer belonged to him but which were now a kind of anemic white, his former fucking legs, they might as well cut the fucking legs off of him, and at first it was his fucking feet that felt like they were dead and would have to be fucking amputated, but then it was the fucking foot *and* the fucking shin, and then he could fucking feel the fucking death creeping up him, and he couldn't fucking get comfortable with the temperature in the room, his fucking sick chamber, like one minute he was hot, and if that wasn't fucking predictable, well, what the fuck wasn't predictable, because it was the fucking desert, and who cared if it was almost dawn, if it was the fucking desert, and it was hot until the winter, fucking desert fucking inferno, and it was a hundred fucking degrees fucking Fahrenheit, and so he was probably fucking hot because it was *fucking hot,* but what about when he was fucking cold, didn't seem so good, and he said he was cold, he called out to Vienna that he was *fucking cold,* he couldn't fucking get warm; he was pretty sure that he said he was fucking cold, but she didn't come, and no one came to deal with the fact of how fucking cold he was, not Vienna, not his father, and he lay there on the fucking bed, and maybe this was what fucking *expiration* felt like, like death was some kind of material that you could feel fucking infiltrating you a little bit at a time, like death was a fucking radioactive element or something, like americium or polonium or barium or one of those fucking radioactive elements that only survived for a fucking millisecond, except that it survived when it was laying waste to your bloodstream, *fucking death,* the thing that survived only when it was in a bloodstream, in a fucking circulatory system, you could see it fucking gathering its force and laying waste to you, and then you knew your fucking time was come, and maybe that was when

Vienna heard him crying out about the blanket, *Give me a fucking blanket for godsakes because I'm fucking dying in here! I'm so fucking cold!* and then she appeared or someone fucking appeared, spread a fucking blanket out on him, and he wasn't cold, and maybe the fucking radioactive death particles would be held at fucking bay for a little bit longer, unless on the other hand death were just this bacterial thing, and the bacterial colonies were fucking massing in him, and the fucking bacterial colonies were outnumbering the colonies of benevolent cells that were Jean-Paul Koo, until there would be no *him* left, just fucking bacteria, and there would be so much of it that any person who touched him would rub off a piece of him, and his limbs would fucking come off, like if you just pulled on his leg a tiny fucking little bit, his leg would just come off of him, and it had fucking served him so well, this leg, taken him just about every fucking place he'd ever gone, except for the places that his fucking car had taken him, when he could afford the thirty-one dollars a fucking gallon or whatever it was (but by the time you read this it will probably be thirty-six) that you had to pay to algae up the car, but the leg had fucking taken him every other fucking place, like back when he still played a little lacrosse, when he was fucking good, his legs had done it, had carried him from one end to the other of the pitch, his fucking arms had carried the stick and cradled that little jewel at the center of the game; you know how when you are eating a chicken, and the chicken is like way overcooked or whatever, then you just pull on the fucking wing, you fucking yank, and the whole thing just comes right off, and death was just fucking exactly like that, it cooked him until he was like some kind of chicken from the Chicken Shack that you could just fucking rip right apart, and he had fucking overheard his father whispering to some guy, like some government fucking guy, because there were all these fucking government guys, at least this was what he fucking thought, that it wasn't any fucking dream, because he wasn't a dreamer, because he wanted to know the fucking truth, not some decorated version; what was good about the morning? When you woke up, you lived in the truth, and he knew that, and what he had fucking overheard was this fucking idea that his body was going to *disassemble,* that was the shorthand, that was living in the truth, and he fucking didn't want Vienna to see his body disassemble, and why had he fucking gone out into the fucking desert to have fucking sex anyhow, because he could have done so many fucking other things. His fucking business needed fucking attention, because he needed a fucking capital infusion, you know? All the seed money, well, it was all going over to China or fucking India, and where the fuck could he get the money, especially if he spent all his fucking time graduating from fucking high school or out in the desert having sex? Well, they fucking said that it *couldn't be done,* his business, and his father always felt like he could have done better monetizing the patents, and if the incubation of the fucking *M. thanatobacillus* was so fucking long, then maybe there would be time, anyway, to file some fucking patents before his body disassembled and started crawling around trying to strangle people or kick people in the ass, and when Vienna had been here, last night, she'd said he looked fine, and he could tell that he couldn't talk right anymore, and that he was having trouble pronouncing some sounds, like you know, the *sh* sound, it was fucking hard, you know, but when she went to the bathroom, he used one of the surgical gloves that his father had left around for him, and he borrowed her compact, and all he could say was that he fucking looked like Jean-Paul Koo, but he looked like the nasal inhaler version of Jean-Paul Koo, you know? Like he was all fucked on OxyPlus or something, had not fucking eaten for ten days and was mostly locked away in someone's dungeon or something, and he knew she was trying to say that it would be all right, because at least on Mars the fucking thing was supposed to take about a month and a half or more, and during the time before your fucking body disassembled you had time to get your affairs in order, and even if you were a fucking kid and you didn't have all that fucking many affairs, at least you were free of like big debt, or whatever else, like fucking ex-wives or fucking children, there was just you, and your fucking business that you would leave to your fucking dad, and maybe part of it to the ridiculously hot Vienna fucking Roberts, or whatever, before your body *disassembled.* The stupid fucking sentimental thing, that was what really pissed him off, was when he fucking gave in, like it was all chemistry, there was this fucking cell, and it fucking divided or it didn't fucking divide, and there was a lot of carbon, and there were some vitamin D receptors, who knew what the fuck else, the cells needed protein, and then there was this bacteria, and then why all the fucking sentimental stuff, like everything he'd ever smelled in his life, like the fucking bowl of chicken soup of his childhood was so fucking beautiful, every fucking ice cream cone, now that it was a thing that might fucking be gone, and the sunlight in the desert, what was fucking more fucking beautiful, and he was so fucking lucky to have these days, the days where the light on the Santa Catalina Mountains got seen by him, and to have seen the clouds sweeping through that amber sunlight on the fucking mountains, and to have been able to fucking see a fucking mountain lion that one time, in the hills out by Mount Kelsey, traversing its eight miles or whatever, and hopefully it was killing one more jogger on its fucking way, so lucky to have been the one who got to see the mountain lion, which was fucking specializing in not fucking being seen by anyone, and then he fucking got to see the cactus blossoms, *again,* the saguaro blossoms, the Mexican poppy, just a couple months ago, and he got to see all the shit that got swept up by the monsoons and deposited down in the washes, whole encampments of *nomads* washed downstream, it was a fucking catastrophe, and catastrophe is a beautiful thing, a thing that must be seen, and whatever the fuck else, it was fucking great, because it's real, merciless nature, and what was more beautiful than that, and it was all reminding him of his mother, that was the fucking sentimental thing, and it was fucking pathetic; you should just fucking think about fucking blood and bacteria and fucking human fecal material, or the fucking waves of bugs that fucking ate your body, or whatever, every time you were tempted to be sentimental, you needed to think about those things, but that didn't mean that he didn't keep fucking thinking that he was seeing his mother in the corners of the room, back from before she was really gone; he could remember some spectral or fucking ghostly part of her life, when she was still walking around, from when he was really fucking small, and maybe this thing, the disassembling Jean-Paul, the inevitable fucking disassembling Jean-Paul, made him closer to the ghost of his fucking mother, and the fucking heat and the fucking cold, and the fucking fever, and these all made him closer to his mother, wherever his mother was, and if he could fucking summon his fucking mother, just this one time, if fucking death could just yield up its predictable qualities, its eternal and endless predictability, just one time, just yield up one bit of maternal wisdom, for one fucking second, then he would totally repent of all that he'd done, like when he fucking complained about having to take care of her when she was bedridden, he would *repent,* he would fucking repent if the relentlessly predictable scientific qualities of death would give way to the childish sentimentality, and his mother could come to him and could fucking tell him what to expect of the next month, if he even had a fucking month. She could tell him what to expect, like what do you expect from it, why does it have to be this thing where no one will tell you what to expect? Does it make any sense that no one will fucking tell you? Why does it have to be like that? Like all the pleasures of his short fucking life, or of any fucking life, were just the thing that was to distract you from the fact that no one could tell you about this one thing, they just couldn't tell you about the time and place of the end of you, of your impact on this fucking dark world, and his mother could tell him, even if it was cheesy, his wanting his fucking mother to just fucking turn up one fucking time, was it so much to ask? Couldn't his dead mother just like turn up one fucking time, at the advent of his fucking death, and tell him one thing? He writhed in the bed with it, his cement limbs trembled with it, *injustice,* the ungodly injustice, the rank injustice of the silence of illness and death, and even when he trembled with it, there was no result, and no point to all of it, except that this was just what was happening right now, and there was no explication, except that he was alone with it, until the knock at the door.

Jean-Paul tried to say something routine, like "Come in," or "Enter," or even "Yeah," but he was not sure he really said anything at all. And so he tried again, and again he was not sure whether the words came out the way he intended them to be spoken, and then the door opened just the same, and his father, as if distracted, made his entrance with some kind of retinue, some guys in fucking Hazmat suits, actual Hazmat suits, and then Vienna too, and then if that wasn't enough, the woman from the laboratory, she came in, and Jean-Paul always kind of liked the woman from the laboratory, and then this big posse of official-looking types, and at the end of the line of people cramming into his bedroom was a *chimpanzee.* There was a chimpanzee in his room. He had encountered some of the official chimpanzees over the years. The chimpanzees who lived and worked and were fucking sacrificed at the University of Rio Blanco laboratories. Now and then his father would let him meet a chimpanzee or two, but his father was also worried about his son getting attached to chimpanzees who were then going to be sacrificed during some upcoming regimen of horror. Relationships with the chimpanzees were a dangerous thing. But apparently this had changed, because here was the chimpanzee, standing right beside his father, wearing a pair of gray cotton gym shorts that made him look like one of those middle-aged guys in January who think that, in the new year, they're going to tone up.

"Son," his father said, "how are you feeling this morning?"

Jean-Paul was nearly certain that he said, "Okay, considering that my limbs are about to disassemble." But it was becoming clear to him that he was wanting for the pinpoint muscular abilities required for sophisticated verbal communication.

"Are you not able to speak more than that?" His father somehow managed to sound calm, even slightly bored about the whole thing, but Jean-Paul knew him well enough to know how much concern lay below what was apparent.

"Not too much," Jean-Paul tried, which sounded more like *nnnmmmmcccccchhh.*

"We're here for a routine examination, and to attempt a treatment protocol that is, I should say, frankly experimental, but which we imagine will at least slow down the progress of the bacteria for a while. Are you prepared to listen as we describe this to you? I suppose I should introduce everyone first."

He introduced some guys who were from the Centers for Disease Control, which was now subcontracted to a large multinational drug company from the Grand Cayman Islands, and who were all suited up. He thought he could make out a pair of glasses inside one of the suits, some bad facial hair. There was a guy from NASA. And then there was a guy from the FBI who was apparently leading the investigation. Finally, his father turned to the chimpanzee, as though the chimpanzee were just another medical researcher. "And this is Morton, who is a rather special and momentous part of the team, recently signed on. Morton, please meet my son, Jean-Paul."

"Nice to make your acquaintance," the chimpanzee said to him. And the thing was that Jean-Paul, in his sickened state, didn't think it was all that unusual that the chimpanzee would be speaking to him. It was as if the possibilities of the world now included talking chimpanzees — as they also permitted the disassembly of bodies.

"Pleasure is mine," Jean-Paul mumbled.

"Your father has told me a lot about you," the chimpanzee continued, "and I have always been, well, I guess a little excited to meet you. You know, in the event he hasn't told you himself, your father is actually very proud of you, of your entrepreneurial abilities and interests. I don't suppose anyone these days hears that sort of thing often enough. My own father, if you don't mind my saying, was never known to me, and so I'm envious of people who have good relationships with their dads, as you certainly seem to do. Yours is the first bedroom of an American young man that I have been lucky enough to see—although I have entered a number of them on various web-based programs."

"Morton," Dr. Koo said to the animal protégé, who certainly sounded sort of like a human, even if he had a squeaky, uncertain voice. Jean-Paul, if he'd just heard this voice over the phone or something, he would have said that it was the voice of a middle-aged gay man with a speech defect. "Morton, there's no time for the chitchat here."

"Oh, I'm very sorry. I'm still a little bit in the dark about the—"

"Son," the elder Koo began, "the reason Morton is here is that we have some theories about the course of the illness that afflicts you at present, and we believe that Morton might have specific insight into it. His insights may enable us to map the vectors of disease before the epidemic escapes from the immediate environs of the city of Rio Blanco."

"I get you."

"The rest of these gentlemen are here to observe, after which they will be heading out in the field to try to locate the arm. When we find it, we will be disposing of it through means yet to be determined."

What the fuck could he learn from the fucking chimpanzee, or what could the chimpanzee learn from him? He felt like he should just offer it a kiwi and tell it to get the hell out of his sick chamber, but as soon as it opened its mouth, Jean-Paul found it oddly sympathetic.

"My theory," Morton said, "which I admit has yet to be proven, is that the bacillus that is infecting you has a very specific effect, and that effect is retro-phylogenetic. If you follow me. Are you familiar with the notion of phylogeny?"

"Could you use some plain fucking words?" Jean-Paul said. He didn't feel good about it, about being so rude to the chimpanzee, but one of the features of the illness everyone was asking about was *profound personality change,* and he couldn't fucking keep his feelings to himself, and he felt like he was going to rip the fucking head off of someone.

"Are you aware," Morton went on, "that your speech has become difficult to discern? I think maybe it's better if we try to keep this to very simple communications, binary questions, especially since, as your father will tell you, we believe that the pathogen, which was originally adapted to an earthly ecosystem, mutated on the planet called Mars, and that mutation was lethal, true enough, but now that the pathogen is back on Earth, it seems to have become rather *more* aggressive. We are therefore pressed for time. I would like to check the facts of my theory against the evidence in your own case. Is that acceptable to you?"

The entire city of Rio Blanco, not to mention the great expanses of the Southwest, maybe even what remained of the United States of America, teetered on the brink of a *lethal pandemic,* or whatever you'd call it, and yet the chimpanzee took the time to posture a little bit, as if he were dazzled by his own oratory, this oratory that no other chimpanzee had. Also, he seemed especially taken with the woman from the laboratory. It was like everything was for her approval. The chimp practically had a *stiffy* over her.

"Yeah, go on," Jean-Paul said.

"Reverse phylogeny would mean that the disease, effectively, has a specific trajectory. The disease wants to roll back the higher organisms. The first sign of this, in effect, would be impulse control. Having experience with a slightly less evolutionarily advanced species, I know that as we move backward through the primate family tree, we begin, first of all, to experience things like murderous rage and reproductive urgency. So I ask: Are you finding, for example, violent impulses in yourself?"

"I'm lying in bed. I'm not able—"

"I'm afraid we can't understand you."

"Why the fuck should I fucking talk to a fucking monkey? Dad?"

Morton continued, "I'm not a monkey. And am I to take it that your disinclination to answer the questions is itself a sign of the reverse phylogeny I'm describing?"

"If you want."

"During the period of contact with the arm, what kind of behavior did you notice? Did you notice that it was, say, aggressive?"

An interesting question, you know. What the fuck *did* the arm think, if it didn't have any spot in it where thinking was done, and if it didn't *think,* what was it most like, on the big flowchart of the dwindling animals of the world? Was the arm anything like a man? Like a particular man, an astronaut, to whom it used to be attached? The arm, probably, was more like an insect, or maybe like a snake. It was like some kind of particularly stupid Sonoran snake, squirming across the barren desert floor looking for chipmunks and lizards on which to gorge itself, unconcerned about coyotes.

"It didn't do much. It squeezed things and moved around."

"Is that an affirmative reply?"

"Uh —"

"And do you feel, about your body, in your illness, a sense of becoming *other,* moving nearer to instincts and purposes that are other from what we associate with the higher mammals?"

"Wouldn't know how to answer that."

"You —"

"Don't know how to answer," Jean-Paul said. "I'm not a scientist. I find that shit —"

"He's saying he can't answer it," Vienna Roberts broke in. His girl. She'd donned some rubber gloves and was now at his bedside, holding his hand. Was his inability to recognize that his hand was being held by the ridiculously hot Vienna Roberts a symptom of whatever it was that Morton, the chimpanzee, was trying to claim was the *nature* of the illness? And how come she didn't have any symptoms? Did the arm only want to kill *men?* "He can't answer the questions, and I don't see what the point of them is anyhow. Give him the injection, for godsakes."

One of the guys from NASA, who was even willing to take off his protective mask, so that you could see his exhausted face and heinous comb-over, chimed in too. "Dr. Koo, I can't say I disagree. We're losing valuable time here. I think we should be out in the field tracking the arm. This is a national epidemiological emergency we have here, and it's only four days, presumably, since your son was infected by the remains of Colonel Richards, and——"

Morton stamped his feet petulantly and launched into an elaborate defense. "The arm, ladies and gentlemen, behaves like an *animal.* That's your word for the living things that are different from you. The arm behaves like a living thing that is different from you. So it has a very few primitive impulses. The arm doesn't understand that it is evading its capturers. The arm wishes to overpower, and in this way it is a very pure thing. It is the lofty human being brought down to its simplest layer of activity, of self——the entity that overpowers, the thing that dominates, subdues, and destroys. The arm is just a vestigial bit of the human, and right now, this boy, this young man here, is beginning to move into the gloom that the arm inhabits——"

"I'm not moving into any——"

"Give him the injection, Dr. Koo," Vienna pleaded.

"I think it's best that we move our teams out into the field," the NASA guy said.

"——the twilight of the post-human, post-physiognomic self, the self that is no longer conscious of itself. That twilight is upon us now! It is at hand! Its progress is relentless. It may be that consciousness was just an anomaly on the radar of evolution, and that evolutionary time spent on the consciousness of the human animal is coming to its close. Reflexive self-consciousness has been lorded over the rest of the animal kingdom for millennia, and it has never been *just,* and it isn't now. The only surprise, at this stage, is that the rapaciousness of the human animal took so long to be called into question. Maybe it's ironic that it was something so small, something so microscopic, that accomplished what all the nonhuman life-forms have so wished for——"

"Morton, please," said Dr. Koo. "We have more important—"

"Let me talk to him," Noelle Stern, the graduate student, said. "I think I can—"

"—but if one young man has to be sacrificed," Morton continued, sweeping his arm over the recumbent form of the younger Koo, "I admit this is regrettable, but this is the order of the epochs as they wheel past. When one species achieves too much dominance, it eventually sows the seeds of its own destruction. In your case, there is your obscene desire to wipe out other nations. Nations! Some group of you organizes itself so as to kill off some other group of yourselves, and in the process you generate this paperwork, fees for passports, that sort of nonsense, when all you want to do is kill one another! That's a good joke! These borders that you claim mark the divisions from one nation to another? The only animal that observes them is you. What do the rest of us think of this? We think you are drunk on your own obscene power. And when that desire, the desire of nations to wipe out one another, is combined with your despicable interest in plundering a new planet of its resources, having so thoroughly polluted this one, well, then the result is this tiny little pathogen that now threatens—"

"Morton," Noelle said, "let's just step outside, please."

There was some shoving for a moment, some protestation. The chimpanzee seemed to be indicating that he had lots more yet to say, but by the time this was clear, he was already well out of the bedroom. Down the hall, or even downstairs.

"Guy's a talker," Jean-Paul murmured.

"He seems to be very tense, and he's not terribly effective when he's tense," the elder Koo said. "But we believe he can give us insight into this situation, so that we can contain it more quickly. Here, use this pad."

Jean-Paul's handwriting had declined, just as his speaking voice had, and where he once had the handwriting of an architect, perfect little capital letters that could fit into the graph paper squares, now there were trembly smudges.

AM I GOING TO MAKE IT?

"Son...it's true that we don't know enough about this disease yet, but it is bacterial, and most bacteria on Earth respond to various courses of antibiotics, and this intravenous drip we're going to hook up—Dr. Lecompte is preparing it—will at the very least slow the accelerated course of the symptoms, and it's more than possible it will wipe out the infection entirely."

WHAT ABOUT OTHER PEOPLE?

"Those who have come in contact with the arm?"

OR IN CONTACT WITH ME.

Some of the government types were already making their way to the door. Checking their implanted communications devices, typing out messages.

"We aren't aware of all the mechanisms of the contagion, whether there is a specific point when the bacteria is communicable, and so it's possible that some people are spared, or have resistance for reasons that are so far unclear. Which doesn't mean it's not incredibly dangerous, as in your own case. I wish the news were better. But I am very hopeful nonetheless. We need to find the arm first, and to move from there to quarantine persons who have been in contact with those who had contact with it. But, son, these things need not concern you now. You just need to get well."

Jean-Paul could fucking tell that they had put something into the drip along with the antibiotic. A fucking antibiotic, he wasn't stupid, he was anything but stupid, he knew that an antibiotic like that could have a powerful effect on the body, could render the body sick with its poisons, and he could almost feel himself turning green, but that wasn't the *half* of it. Because he recognized now that there was also some sedative in the cocktail. His mind, free of his body, ran through a list of antipsychotic medications. Some drug company (or the CDC) had promoted the antipsychotic family of medications, he knew, more reliable for anxiety, less habit-forming, and when there was a danger that a sick person might go into a, you know, reverse-phylogenetic rage and begin *strangling his family,* before or after his limbs began detaching from his fucking body, then it was probably a reasonable prescription, Zebulite, fewer fucking side effects, like it might correct the nausea and diarrhea from the antibiotic; Zebulite didn't cause the dyskinesia so common from the excess use of the fucking antipsychotic family, until you would even fucking see on some job applications *No antipsychotic-related speech defects or tremors, please,* you could tell, you could fucking tell sometimes, like the fucking telemarketer would call at a certain hour, like the dinner hour, and you'd be trying to have dinner with your ridiculously hot girlfriend, a video message would appear on your implanted personal messaging device, and up would pop this grainy video, and you could see the fat, unhappy woman in the message, trying to get you to deposit what little money you had left in a Chinese bank, and this unhappy woman would have the massive weight gain associated with antipsychotics; the woman would also have her tongue lolling around in her mouth, and between her Mandarin accent and the antipsychotic-related speech defects, you couldn't understand one fucking thing that she was fucking trying to say, and on top of that, her arm seemed to be spontaneously reaching up and scratching her head, and he fucking didn't want to buy whatever it was she was trying to sell, and it seemed fucking unpatriotic, if you asked Jean-Paul, when an American company was somehow subcontracting to bring you fucking sales pitches from Chinese nationals, especially Chinese nationals on antipsychotic medication, who were probably suffering from some complex related to the fact that they were plundering the fucking globe of its remaining wealth and creating two-thirds of its fucking carbon emissions, and Jean-Paul could feel that his interior tirade about the antipsychotics in the intravenous drip was beginning to occlude his ability to interact with the remaining humans in the room, and he took up the pad, and he attempted to write a note to Vienna Roberts, and couldn't focus enough on the pad in order to remind her that she was fucking ridiculously hot, and he was so glad she wasn't sick, and he was grateful to her for sticking

around when everyone else was leaving, and fucking leaving him
here until his limbs started detaching, like if his leg fell off of his
body and started trying to escape across the room, tiptoeing out of
the room, think about it: the leg could maybe get around pretty
well, hopping or what have you, but the fucking leg couldn't do
anything. It would just kind of lie there trying to kick things,
and maybe it could kick someone in the balls or something, but
that would be about it, but once he was fucking deprived of the
leg, then he was deprived of it and it could go anywhere, and he
was trying to get some of this down on the pad, and he could, in
the haze of antipsychotic medication, before asking for some food,
like maybe they could bring him some carbs, some cannoli, and
from the haze, he could hear his father's voice asking if he had any
advice on where to look for the arm, and he tried to tell him the
bad news, which was that he had no idea, because, you know, he'd
been quarantined since the thing fell out of the van; his father always made the mistake of presuming that young people had some
kind of fucking telepathic communication, like morphic fucking
resonance, like they could just communicate without even using
their implanted communications devices, but if they were asking
his opinion, which he was happy to give, the place to look for the
arm was among the *nomads,* and the problem with fucking looking
among the *nomads* was that the *nomads* couldn't be trusted to stay
in one place, and lots of them were missing limbs anyhow, or were
carrying withered skulls or old leathery limbs from various places,
things that looked like limbs, because the *nomads,* he thought in
his antipsychotic haze, had fucking trashed the human body and
no longer needed any bilateral arrangement of limbs. The *nomads*
could make devices and fuse themselves to these devices, and mopeds, and motor scooters, and they could make their way from
shady spot to shady spot, slathered in sunblock or lead-free exterior white paint, which had become the cut-rate sunblock of
choice among *nomads,* and to them the arm would be just another
totem, interesting for how it coincided with their system of beliefs but not much more than that, and for that reason, no one was

liable to keep the fucking arm for very long, especially when it was trying to *pinch* people, harass their pets, or maybe trying to molest them or whatever; they weren't going to sit still for the fucking arm, and they were going to try to trade it with someone, and so it just wasn't going to be easy to chase it into the world of the *nomads;* Jean-Paul could see it all before him, just how hard it was going to be, and he tried to write some of this down on the pad, but despite his best intentions, this is what Vienna Roberts found on the pad when she tried to read it out to those who remained behind in the sick chamber:

Despite the hand-to-hand combat of decades of budgetary infighting, despite having tendered his own resignation multiply, despite having physically menaced members of Congress, Vance Gibraltar still found the citadels of power to which he occasionally traveled intimidating. *Intimidating* was such an unbecoming word, true. He didn't betray intimidation. There were no visible symptoms, no rashes, no sores.

Still, coming to the president's weekend retreat in West Virginia was not something he'd done before. And it was not something he hoped to do again soon. He suspected that he had been summoned for reasons that were not going to burnish his curriculum vitae. He and Debra Levin had both been requested to appear to answer for the emergency response that was playing out in the desert Southwest. He was going to be part of a team that was to suggest the difficult choices that lay ahead. And at the end of this conversation, he was, he believed, going to be pastured. For the rest of his days.

On the surface, there was nothing that a casual observer would not have found civilized, even genteel, about the presidential weekend residence. After having passed through several layers of Secret Service, Gibraltar and his driver had nosed down a cypress-lined way, bordered by woods fecund with kudzu and other viny opportunists, toward an antebellum porch with a fresh coat of paint. It was a structure of the sort that Gibraltar associated with dramas of the Southern Gothic variety. Upon disembarking from his limousine, and after suffering through the retinal scan, the fingerprint scan, the DNA test, and every other kind of security procedure imaginable, Gibraltar was invited into the residence proper and shown to a sitting room decorated in gay calicos and painted in a mild linen white. The chairs were arrayed at a circular meeting table with keyboards inlaid for note-taking. All four corners of the ceiling had cameras secreted in them.

The rumors about the president had come as relentlessly as all the other bad news in the past twelve months. As the economy racked up another quarter of negative growth, as the undocumented emigrants began to scale the walls both north and south, as populations moved into negative terrain, as the health care industry collapsed beneath the sagging weight of the aging population, Xers and Yers, and the drag of antibiotic resistance, as grand theft and rape and murder reached new levels of cultural acceptability because of the OxyPlus addiction epidemic, as the warlike rhetoric flared anew in Central Asia, it was rumored that the commander in chief had fallen prey to some kind of psychiatric complaint that involved what the *DSM-VIII* referred to as *persecution delusion, legitimate, with nomadic presentation,* the manifestations of which involved removing himself from location to location, never staying longer than a few days in any one redoubt. Some of these surprise appearances coincided with regional emergencies of various kinds: the president today appeared at the site of a plane crash; the president toured a floodplain. And yet the appearances were never followed by a return to Washington, not for any length of time.

What was also clear was that the last campaign had never ended, whether the president could be reelected or not; the never-ending campaign, featuring listening tours that touched down in Laconia, NH, or Odessa, TX, or Bridgeport, CT, didn't reflect his lame-duckhood. There was talk of a network of underground bunkers. His aides would neither confirm nor deny. The president, according to policy briefs, held that the Sino-Indian Economic Compact had its eyes on the raw materials and resources of the United States; the president further believed that attack from a westerly direction was imminent. When meetings were scheduled, he often did not turn up, and when no meeting was scheduled, you sometimes got a call suggesting that the president was just up the street, and *coming by*.

A presidential double also appeared. The double was not to be confused, however, with the presidential disguise, another relic of the times. He had taken, it was said, to wearing disguises occasionally, so that he could pass among his constituents. The costume was considered so effective that even the Secret Service was not sure if the president *was* the president, and on at least one occasion, according to rumor, a plumber working on one of the executive toilets found himself interrupted by a member of the president's Secret Service staff, who attempted to yank on his mustache in order to ascertain if it had been glued on with mineral spirits. Was the plumber, in fact, the chief executive? While there had been calls for the president to step down, based on his erratic behavior, based on his *persecution delusion, legitimate, with nomadic presentation,* the president had nonetheless managed in the second term to sign some legislation into law and to prevent some things from getting dramatically worse. Things got worse at a slower rate. His approval rating was moving northward from the twenties, despite guerrilla war, famine, emigration, and contagion.

Who believed this stuff? Who believed in belief? Who believed in the political process? Who believed in the institution of the presidency? Who believed in the future? Who believed in anything but *grinding it out,* as the young people said, hoping only to forestall the worst that loomed? Who believed that the markets could right themselves? Who believed in the markets? Who believed in the market prognosticators? Who believed in the public servants? Who believed in the political process? Who believed that there was a functioning idea of government on the face of the watery planet besides despotism? Who believed that there were any forces arrayed that might put an end to despotism? Who believed that multilateral corporate capital cared for anything except *shareholder value?* Who believed in generally accepted accounting principles? Who believed that *nations* were an idea that had any merit in the era of multilateral corporate capital? Who believed faith communities could fill in where the government had ceased to operate? Who believed in the Abrahamic faiths? Who believed otherwise? Who believed in the mythologies that came out of the deserts of the earth? Who believed that the desert wasn't growing a hundred square miles a year? Who believed in the inevitability of desertification? Who believed that the president was still alive and that he had not fled to some South Pacific atoll noted only for the way introduced species there had wiped out all the other predators and deforested the littoral ecosystem entirely? Who believed that the islands of the South Pacific would survive the upcoming glacial melt? Who believed that the United States of America could wake from its decades-long slumber and return to the forefront of developed nations? Who believed that it was important that it do so? Who believed that the United States of America still existed? Or that the European Union was any better? Who believed that human ingenuity could rise above the spate of problems that beset the watery planet now? Who believed that a space shot containing five hundred hardy souls bound for the

Martian planet, or the moons of Saturn, would not reproduce the same problems there, in addition to despoiling the vast undeveloped latitudes of that planet? Who believed that the human race was not itself the pestilence? Was it possible to wish for the best, these days, without requiring a nearly lethal dose of some intoxicant in order to do so?

Gibraltar was the first to arrive. When the attendant in the foyer of the president's weekend retreat returned to check on Gibraltar again, he set down a dish full of lavender pills, and when he looked closely at the stamp on these trifles, Vance realized that they were the popular vitamin-and-antidepressant combo Satisfactor that some people were trying to have introduced into the filtration systems of the larger metropolises, so as to make the labor force more productive. And contented. The direness of the situation that prompted the meeting apparently suggested the chemical option.

"The president and his aides will be along shortly," the attendant said again, a nice young guy whose very demeanor proved that he had no knowledge as to whether the presidential retinue would appear or not.

Debra Levin, political appointee, had, at the last minute, declined to attend. Of course. The NASA administrator was a no-show, though she'd been appointed to the post by the president himself. Gibraltar felt certain that the president and his appointee had agreed on the approach ahead of time, had gone over the agenda, and Levin, who'd set foot in Rio Blanco for forty-five minutes two days ago, before jetting off to her son's college graduation in Qatar, had already begun to remark, variously, in public and private, that the Mars mission antedated her role at the agency and that she would not be judged by its results. Gibraltar's queries as to the invitation list for the presidential meeting had turned up names from the Department of Defense, the Centers for Disease Control, Interpol, and the United Nations, and a couple of congressional types who chaired the relevant committees and subcommittees. There was also a midlevel diplomatic representative from the Sino-Indian Economic Compact, offering to help in any way necessary.

Of these, one Lane Beauforte showed up a few minutes after Vance, and the two of them, Gibraltar and Beauforte, made joint attempts at small talk about the weather and the unspoiled beauty of West Virginia. There was only so much of this Gibraltar could take. He had an almost neurological reaction, something in the Parkinsonian family, when it came to small talk. Disgust with the human niceties expressed as tremor and the forming of excess spittle, cold sweat on the small of his back. It wasn't long before he started blurting out how much he despised meetings. He and Beauforte, he went on, since they were the only ones who were going to show up on time, might as well just solve all the problems. The latecomers would only arrive and gum up the proposal.

"I don't want to second-guess the chief here," Beauforte replied, plucking a couple of vitamins from the oaken dish in which they were proffered, "and so I don't want to get into any specific recommendation at this time."

"You practicing that line? And do you honestly think that the president is going to show up for this meeting?"

"Don't know if he is or he isn't, but I like to feel I am prepared, because that is in my job description." Beauforte didn't exactly intimate what kind of job his job was, nor whether or not he was licensed to commit politics in the line of duty, regardless of collateral megatonnage.

"I've lived my entire goddamned political life in *spite* of the commander in chief, not through his beneficence, and I'd recommend the same."

"Noted," said Beauforte. The two lapsed into silence, and Beauforte appeared to stare out the window into the expanses of carbon-dioxide-enhanced sod, as though the sod had some secret to impart to him. A Secret Service agent crossed this exterior scene with an aggressive-looking guard dog, and the two, agent and dog, waited as the hindquarters of the German shepherd trembled and deposited some solid matter there, which the agent, setting down the leash and stamping upon it, plucked up with a black plastic glove. This Beauforte watched, and Gibraltar watched him watching it, the machinations of history construed as fecal production, until a third man entered, a man who from the cut of suit and the fixative in hair, as well as by reason of surgically repaired cleft palate, could only have been, from Gibraltar's point of view, a Department of Defense middle manager.

This executive stood, despite an invitation from a retreating footman to sit, and the three of them gaped at one another, while outdoors the humidity still shimmered as though it could decorate all of West Virginia in a sequence of obfuscatory waves.

"Is the man attending?" Gibraltar demanded to know.

"Who's that?" said the Department of Defense.

"Commander in chief," said Beauforte.

"No one knows," Gibraltar said. "No one wants to discuss. Is he just sending people without authorization to do or to decide? I have people on the ground in —"

"Never fear," said an entering young woman, eager, loyal, untrustworthy, with lip gloss in a hue favored by preschool art classes. An official-type scheduling flunky, no doubt, whose salary remunerated her for attempting to describe the velocity of the president, or the likelihood of his appearing at a certain place, but never his actual location. "Politics is, in the end, *patience,* gentlemen, and it's in the waiting for the negotiation to begin that we are given the chance to *rethink* who we are, who we represent, and why we are gathered here in the name of the political process. The president advises that we relax, enjoy one another's company, and feel free to address the news of the day. If the subject under discussion comes up, why then it comes up, and thus the period of waiting for the meeting to begin is, in fact, a meeting of a sort, and perhaps this spontaneously occurring roundtable will in some way be preferable to the meeting that might have been, or might yet be, or the meeting *after* the meeting, in which the meeting and its contents are reconfigured for general presentation and its areas of progress are chipped away until nothing much remains."

"Does that suggest—" Beauforte began.

"He's not even—" Gibraltar added.

Just then: a very nervous older man in a burlap sack of a double-breasted suit. No need to go into the facial scabbing.

"The president," said the scheduling aide, Leona, whose name now fell into common usage, "is upstairs, working on a couple of urgent calls to foreign heads of state, concerning matters of national import—"

"More national import than—"

"We very nearly have a quorum now," Leona interrupted, "and given that there is a quorum, you may begin organizing your remarks among yourselves, if that will aid you in your presentations. I assume some of you have statistical modeling and graphics interfaces that you will need to configure so that you can make remarks to one another. Think of this time as the time in which you make sure that the audiovisual modules here in the meeting room are adequate to your needs. An associate will be along any minute in order to help."

Leona hastened off.

"He's not coming," Gibraltar said.

"I think you're right," the nervous gentleman from the medical establishment added. The one with the mange and the burlap. Perhaps they would have pursued their outrage at this point, if lunch had not been wheeled into the room in order to prevent conversation. The bowl of Satisfactor tablets on the table was two-thirds empty now, the remaining doses probably covered with bacteria of a hardy constitution. Gibraltar couldn't tell who had pocketed the meds, as now the room was full of seven or eight sweating, imminently unemployed federal agents, many of them already drinking heavily, as if the international health emergency located in the American Southwest could be prevented by a highball.

Lunch consisted of specialties from the president's childhood that had lately, through the vagaries of culinary fashion, become high-class entrées, viz., the open-faced turkey sandwich, served here with creamed corn, black-eyed peas, and a side of beta-blockers and diuretics, this given to the attendees in order to help them void the nonnutritive portions of the meal as quickly as possible. On the reverse side of the menu card there was text hinting that the president had himself dispatched the turkey in question. The birds were becoming nuisances, ever since they'd been taken off the endangered species list. It was not difficult to run one over in West Virginia. Probably easier than shooting one, because the way the species had evolved, toward a mitigated aeronautics, the turkeys could barely loft themselves above the traffic on the county road. Occasionally the president, Leona conceded, when she looked in again on them, did take one of the armored vehicles of his escort out onto the grounds of the weekend retreat, where he would attempt to *run down* a turkey. It was just a way of letting off steam, you understand. Naturally, this didn't conflict with one of the great pleasures of the presidency, according to Leona, which was the annual sparing of a turkey for the Thanksgiving dinner. In fact, that ritual had *more* meaning to the president than to others. "As you can see, the luncheon certainly has all the trimmings, and we have spared no expense for all of you, some of you having come so far—"

"We're going to have to quarantine the entire region" was what the guy from the CDC said, out of nowhere, the one with scrofula. Like he'd come in from the scrub to say just this, shouting above the engorgement of the luncheoneers, shouting above expressions of animal contentment, suppressed belches, and, in one or two cases, a disguised postprandial nap. "There's no other alternative. And that's assuming that we haven't already missed a number of people who have been exposed and who are already on jets heading to other parts of the country or even around the globe. Quarantine is the human approach, the reasonable approach, and it should begin as soon as possible."

"What's the unreasonable approach?"

It became clear, as always in these high-level meetings, that rumor and innuendo had spawned a range of dire narratives, and it became the job of Leona—as an assortment of melon-flavored sorbets was served—to digest the story as she understood it, for the discussants. In the course of this, she called on Gibraltar to lend a hand with the backstory.

"Look," he said, upon breaking into a shame-enriched recital, "I'm aware that there are people in my department who bungled the Mars mission. The Mars mission, in the end, did not do as it was supposed to do, except insofar as it spawned a popular reality-based web program, and I'm aware, in the underfunded present, that we've had a number of missions in the last couple of decades that haven't really displayed us to advantage. But before we get sidetracked talking about how we botched the mission and it's all our fault, and before I observe that it was business and the military that wanted that onboard bacteria in the first place, I want to remind you, ladies and gentlemen, what the dream of space travel means. The dream of space travel. The dream of the voyage into the heavens. It really isn't terribly different from our narrative of westward expansion, when you think about it. Manifest Destiny is a blot on our national reputation. How we conducted the westward expansion doesn't make us any nobler in the eyes of history, and yet the dream of expansion does represent some kind of fervent hope, some kind of very human wish. The movement outward from the past brings with it the capacity to renew and restore a belief in a common purpose. It celebrates our ingenuity, and our capacity to start over. That's what the dream of space travel is all about. That's what Mars was all about. I know that there are some of you who think that Mars was just applying a swift kick in the ass to the Chinese and the Indians out at the edge of the universe, or about creating new economic opportunities while things were getting bad for us here, but I think that's a lot of bunk. Mars was about proving that even in the worst times we could still dream *big,* and that the big dreams made us better, made us more responsible, more upright, and they brought us back to Earth rededicated to the purpose of human civilization.

"Now, we lost a number of our people up there, and we recently made the decision that we were going to stand by our returning guy as he tried to reunite with his friends and family. We had no real intel about that strain of bacteria on Mars, the one that took so many of our people, and we had no way of knowing that it could outlast the very high temperatures of reentry and the explosion of the capsule. We're not in the bioweapons business. But because we weaponized the bacteria in the course of our mission, it became our problem first, and so we're the lead agency, at least for the moment. Indeed, what we found that we were dealing with was unpredictable, dangerous, even lethal," Gibraltar said, warming to his rhetorical flights, as he always did when the stakes were highest, "but doesn't that give us an opportunity? Just a year or so ago, people had all these ideas about terraforming Mars, as if that were something we could do in the near term, not something that would take hundreds of years. Now, I want to believe that terraforming can be accomplished, and more, but what I really think is that the challenge we face before us, one that we didn't think we would face, and one we didn't even particularly want, why, it's even more of an opportunity. We can bring ingenuity to this crisis, and we can understand it as a challenge, and we can show that it's precisely when we are down, as a people, as a nation, as a species, that we find in ourselves the strongest urge to equip ourselves and to prevail. We can right the craft, we can move into the deeper water, we can ride out the swells. *It's just a microorganism.* We can educate people. We can treat people. We can beat the bug. And we can emerge from this combat a leaner, more responsive federal government, whose agencies know how to deal with the worst that the contemporary moment can bring us."

Gibraltar turned to face one of the cameras in the corner of the room as he completed his remarks. If the meeting was to be a sequence of turf wars, a bunch of guys flexing their muscles, nothing more, he was going to set the agenda.

"Very nice," said the fellow from Central Intelligence, a late addition to the guest list, "and we agree with the moral principles just expressed, which are attractive, but what do we do with the unruly population in the borderlands while we try to contain the outbreak? How, for example, do we keep insurgent elements from exploiting the panic? Does the space administration, as lead agency, have any advice here?"

"Quarantine," said the CDC, "as I've been saying, is really the only rational approach. Look at how, for example, the Ebola outbreaks have gone in Africa, how the problems with containment create security issues and economic ripples in the aftermath."

"How to maintain a quarantine that we know has been breached? How are you going to protect the soldiers who are ordered to protect against escape?" said another voice. "There are problems that—"

"We believe there are kinds of antibiotics that will still be useful against this bacillus. After all, it has never been on Earth before, not in this strain."

"New antibiotics in the pipeline every day, some very promising new medications, and the FDA is prepared to fast-track the—"

"And we have been monitoring housing stock in the Rio Blanco area, and we believe, because of the net loss in population in recent years, that there are plenty of available industrial lots that can be used as quarantine centers for treatment and/or detention."

"Doesn't that amount to domestic *internment?*"

"Depends on how you—"

"Gentlemen, could you try to—"

Gibraltar said, "From what I've heard the goal is to try to neutralize the already-infected, because—"

The Federal Bureau of Investigation, which was represented by the guy with the patch over one eye, had historical enmity with regard to Central Intelligence, even when the two of them seemed to agree on policy, and the man with the patch, while gulping down the last of his mint julep, hotly suggested, "A fence can be used as an outflow valve. We build a temporary perimeter around the north end of the city. Uh, could you please plug this drive in here? Bring up the first map? Obliged. Now, as you can see from the data we've collected, on the north the city is bounded by mountains here, easily policed, and it might be possible, on the far side of the range, to quietly erect a perimeter that will effectively create a no-man's-land of the sort that was used after that reactor accident in—"

"Indonesia."

"And then we can use the southerly fence, the one currently keeping in the unlawful emigrants, and we can just open that fence to expel the problem in a southerly direction. Under cover of night. This is just exploiting some permeability that may or may not already be present in our border. Still another option: we can organize detention facilities on or just south of the southerly fence, in a kind of international zone, and we can probably hold the infected there legally, at least for a time, until we discover the treatment options."

"Isn't that going to create problems with our cosignatory to the south?"

"We've got a transient population in this region, and they come and go from the one signatory to the other, sometimes even including much farther-flung Central American districts; these people migrate like birds, like a vulture that just comes and goes from Chihuahua to the Sonoran Desert without ever worrying about sovereignty."

"Well, it's true that the most transient elements, the migrants, the mentally ill homeless, are likely to be struck hardest by the epidemic, or the pandemic, if you accept the computer models, and it makes sense to try to find a way to organize these people so that we can count, monitor, and treat them."

"If the president can't even be bothered to attend the meeting, what kind of incentive is there for us to resolve these issues?"

"Does the president even know what's happening out there?"

"Does someone want to recap the route of transmission of the contagion?"

The anxious and irritable CDC fellow and Gibraltar attempted to respond to this question, though in the rough-and-tumble of the meeting, in which for example one guy, from Housing and Urban Development, got up abruptly from the table and ran for the bathroom with his hand over his mouth, it required sheer dog-gedness to hold the floor.

"Correct me if I'm wrong," Gibraltar said to the others. "I'm just going from what we have from the ship's log, but the problem is that the infected patient doesn't develop genuine symptoms until late in the course of the illness, while he or she is able to communicate the disease from the moment of infection."

"What about the...what were they calling it, the...*disassembly* of the body, what exactly does that mean?" someone demanded to know.

The CDC representative found an opening: "It's like a rapid leprosy in that way. Skin goes bad, and the limbs, the extremities no longer have any of the connective tissue to require them to adhere to the body. The extremities are shed in this way, and then the problem is that not only do they remain contagious—"

Gibraltar: "But for a while they still have movement."

General incredulity on this point. Gasps, choked laughs.

"How is that possible?"

Gibraltar: "We—"

CDC: "—don't know."

"So you're saying these limbs flop around like the catch on a trawler's deck—"

"Worse, really, because depending on the extremity in question, they can crawl around some and get into all kinds of trouble, especially if the population into which they are released doesn't know anything about the course of the disease."

To which Gibraltar added, "Gentlemen, the situation that we have developing in the area around Rio Blanco is all the result of *one arm*. One forearm. The forearm belonging to Colonel Jed Richards. A piece of his spacecraft, as I was saying, touched down right outside of Rio Blanco. It's likely that some undesirables who were the first on the scene attempted to spirit away the arm before we were able to get the security detail from base over to the crash site. That arm, that dead man's arm, managed to migrate from the crash site into the town of Rio Blanco within six hours, maybe even less.

According to what we know through the cooperation of state agencies and others on the ground, the arm managed in that time to pass through a number of crowded areas. While we aren't sure that everyone who came in contact with the arm was infected, we are sure that some *have* been—they're in the hospitals already—and that they are showing signs of progression on a scale that is, well, quite a bit faster than what we experienced on Mars."

"Probably," the fellow from the CDC added, "the march through the family of symptoms is stepped up in this much warmer climate."

"How many people would you estimate are infected?"

"And do you have an idea about how many people are liable to come in contact with each asymptomatic case?"

"Are there pieces of the craft and of...the body of the astronaut...elsewhere? Across the border, for instance?"

"I'd say," Gibraltar admitted, "that there's a likelihood—"

At this point Leona, scheduling flunky, interrupted the proceedings, and it took her a long time to do so, a long time to silence the short-tempered, pudgy, middle-aged men, the Caucasian men, the anxious men. Finally, Leona managed to make herself heard, in order to say, "Gentlemen, please rise for the president."

All eyes on the door, which didn't close on its hinges entirely, it being of an antique design. If even the sketchiest account of what transpired at the weekend residence were leaked through that cracked door to the instant news resources on the web, it would have meant the *end* of the administration, its party, perhaps even the NAFTA political establishment as it was known then. And yet the door didn't close, and various members of the catering staff were coming through routinely to top off a beverage here and there, and to offer another bowl of sorbet.

There's always an instant when *your time is over,* Gibraltar would say later, looking back on that momentous entrance. All the bravado that you once displayed, your fearlessness, suddenly vanishes, because of the sheer scale of history. This was *it;* this was the moment, and Gibraltar experienced it physically, as a sudden gnawing pain in his midsection, as if something were trying to chew its way out. Gibraltar was no stranger to physical discomfort, but there was something new about this particular kind of pain. It was the novelty part that got his attention, as the woodchuck chewing its way out radiated up his esophagus and flared down his flanks. There was nothing to do about it then, because all the men rose, and then the wall-mounted screen at the end of the room flickered on, and the face of the president, mostly shrouded in shadow, appeared on it. He was wearing a shirt and tie, that much was obvious, but there was a way in which he didn't look like the president for whom they labored, not as he was seen in the press. There was the crackling of the audio portion of the signal beginning, a faint hum that was probably some kind of security apparatus in the room where the filming was taking place, and then the tinny second-generation sound of digital playback.

"Gentlemen, very good of you to come, and I'm really sorry that I'm not able to venture downstairs right now. Please accept my apologies. It's possible that I might make it down before the end of the meeting. In case you're wondering, this is a full teleconferencing program we're running here, so I have been able to participate in the meeting so far. Leona is also taking notes for posterity. We'll have the typed account as well as the video record. And I trust each of you will be preparing memoranda for your departments. So that we all know what we're saving here."

There was a murmuring of the conferees. Various discussants floated the theory that this was a *recording* of the president and not a live broadcast at all. But this was belied by the specificity of his next remarks.

"The way I see it, we have discussed two options so far, the first option being a general quarantine for the affected population in Rio Blanco. As I understand it, the problem here is that we can't identify the affected population in order to quarantine them, which makes that proposal ineffective. Correct? The second option is the blockade, at least that's how I'm interpreting it—the idea that we seal off the town of Rio Blanco. Then we either open the border to the south, or we just wait out the infection. Is that an adequate summary of that proposal, Major Beauforte?"

"Sir, we could easily air-drop food supplies into the town—"

"The blockade, option two. You know, gentlemen, I have spent a lot of time in the Southwest. It's really one of the most attractive parts of the nation. I mean, before we go in there and do something drastic to the place, we should pause to remember what a beautiful part of the country it is. In fact, I was there last year or so, and I saw my first dust storm. Leona, have I told you about the dust storm?"

"Yes, sir, you—"

"Did I show you the—?"

"You did. It was—"

"Gentlemen, I had, with the Secret Service detail, elected to do some hiking in a remote mountain range, near the border of the state of New Mexico. Bear country, I should say, and while it would, it's true, have been unfortunate if the leader of the free world were somehow mauled in a bear attack, it's just black bears down that way, you know. I have never seen a bear in the wild. At any rate, I'd led the good men and women of the Secret Service up one of the peaks in this range, and we'd had quite a good time at the top, where there were still some tumbledown shacks that I suppose were meant for fire observation in a much earlier era. In fact, we'd passed a few blazes on our way out toward the state line, but they were not yet any danger to the local population. Anyhow, we summited the peak in question not long after lunch, and we had a relaxing time there. Those parts of the state are now so empty that there was no danger of running into constituents, and most of the trails had been closed by the security detail in any event. At some point, I was alerted to the fact that a dust storm was coming in our direction from the northeast. There was some thought of extracting us by helicopter, but I wouldn't hear of it. Soon enough, in the distance, you could see the storm, like a sheer wall. The dust comes from as far away as Mongolia, I was told later, though I don't know how this would be possible, unless it was blown over the Bering Strait. Still, it was maybe twenty or thirty miles out, on a day that was dry and clear as any day can be in the desert in autumn. We watched, kept an eye on the storm, as we all but jogged down the mountain, gentlemen, and if the security people were a little apprehensive, I was practically giddy with the simple fact that nature continues to behave in a way that is impossible to predict, and if I didn't want to be blown off the mountain, I was, at the same time, not averse to feeling the threat of the thing, as it seemed to head with its own volition toward the range on which I stood, gobbling up acres as fast as any phenomenon of God's creation. We had a representative from the forest service on the line; we were told that the storm was, in fact, covering twenty or thirty miles an hour, and our best bet was to find a cave somewhere on the side of the mountain, and if that was impossible, we should sit down somewhere recessed and wait.

"There *was* a cave some way down. And so, gentlemen, it was a race against time. Given the velocity at which that dust storm was now engulfing the lower peaks in the range, there was little chance that we were going to make it to the cave. And so we did not. We had perhaps another two miles of trail below us, and we were somewhere around the six-thousand-foot level when the big tan cloud of particulate folded over us, like a blanket of the uninhabited earth, blotting out the sun, blotting out the trail, blotting out the expanses and vistas before us, until there was nothing but the ten or twenty feet in our vicinity, all of it whirling and weaving in the great cloud of Mongolian steppe, and why was it that I felt nothing but a tremendous relief? Why was it that the dust storm seemed like the *best* that nature had to offer us that day, assuming that we were not going to see a black bear, as indeed we did not? There were a few raindrops concealed in that cloud, but mainly there was just the grit of it, in our mouths, in our eyes, and so on. It would have been a fine time to mount an assassination, true, if any revolutionary groups were following the course of natural history in the desert, and for this reason, the security detail eventually made use of flare guns, their sidearms, flashlights, whatever else was available in order to keep casual hikers or other members of the general population away, as we carefully picked our way through the curtains of dust toward the canyon below—"

"Mr. President—"

"I know, Leona, I know, gentlemen, you are wondering what the story has to do with the situation at hand."

"That's right, sir," said someone intrepid from a spot that could have been hard for the cameras to pick up.

"What did I learn on that day? Is that what you're asking? What I learned, from a strategic point of view, gentlemen, was about the value of natural phenomena when subduing a population in order to preserve law and order. If someone had been clever enough, that day, to harness the dust storm, they could have paralyzed the government of the United States. You might ask how I could do something so cavalier while upholding my oath of office, but I think, on the contrary, that the question is how to make the scourges of the desert submit to our will when we need them to perform for us."

"Mr. President, are you suggesting some kind of wildfire?"

Gibraltar felt again the sharp pain in his midsection, and he worried that he might need to be escorted from the meeting on a gurney. He thought about his family, and about his second family—the National Aeronautics and Space Administration—and he knew what was to be said next, and he therefore knew that he not only needed to *survive* the meeting, he needed to start moving his people out of range.

"Well, that's a useful question, gentlemen. Is incineration going to do the job in terms of eradication? Would that insure that we root out what we need to root out?"

The CDC, who was already looking a little ashen himself and liable, with the president more or less in the room, to say anything, remarked, "Sir, we don't know for certain yet what the effect of higher temperatures is going to be. But even if the bacteria does experience higher motility in a temperate Earth climate, it can't have adjusted to extremely high temperatures. It's a pretty rare pathogen that can manage that, and only after many hundreds of thousands of years of adaptation. Along these lines, I'd be remiss if I didn't point out that with *M. thanatobacillus,* we find the body temperature goes *down* significantly. As if the pathogen is hostile to warmth. People with the infection start to move toward room temperature. Like a, well, like a corpse."

The president, on the screen above, had turned three quarters from the camera, so that all but his neck, the sinews of his neck, was shrouded in the gloom of his artificially lit office. A contemplative pose.

"Then, gentlemen, I suggest a plan be drawn up, the third option, a *last* option, in which we subject the city of Rio Blanco to incendiary bombing. Obviously, we don't have time to evacuate, nor to attempt to separate the healthy from those already exposed, and this is a shame. The kind of shame that will weigh on all of us in this room a long time. But let's get the plans in motion, and we'll speak by teleconference later. And if incendiary isn't good enough, Mr. Beauforte, be so kind as to get me some ideas about tactical nuclear devices."

It wasn't long after that the meeting was adjourned.

Omnium gatherum *invites you to a flowering of the arts at the Valley of the Slaughtered Calf, ides of the month, 11:59 P.M. The one true law of this place, the tendency of objects to fall to Earth, will be repudiated. Clothing optional.* These were the words of the prototype invite, as composed by Denny Wheeler, slight and pale, whose exclusive diet of yams had not resulted in the kind of pigmentary robustness you found naturally in the desert. He insisted that there was numerological and symbolical significance in the fact that the name of the *yam* was the name of the month in which he was born, reversed. No one, any longer, least of all his father, Zachary Wheeler, bothered to challenge the diet. In fact, Denny had prepared a policy statement on how a diet of yams could promote ecstatic visions. Whether this was owing to a vitamin B_{12} deficiency or not went unexamined.

The plastic arm that accompanied the invitation, manufactured by undocumented emigrants in an uncooled airplane hangar just south of the border, concealed, at first blush, an additional feature, besides its ability to declaim the invitation out of a recessed speaker at the thumb joint: the arm issued sparks from its base. This to indicate the ultimate goal of the *flowering of the arts,* as referred to above, the firing of the crawling hand back into space, toward the gods. The Wheelers, or at least Denny, because his father was so nodded out on OxyPlus and role-playing software that he wasn't good for anything anymore, had spent the better part of the past couple of days procuring custom-made jet packs for the *apotheosis of the arm,* which was how Denny referred to the climax of the party on the web site and in any official announcements. From space it had come, to space it would justly return.

He had good informants in local government; he had a politburo that made decisions in the absence of input from his father. This politburo included local judges, doctors at area hospitals, liberal clerics from the mosques, a librarian or two, a few university professors, representatives of the Union of Homeless Citizens, and his shadow, as Denny put it, a transgender activist called simply Lenz. Lenz would admit to a urethra, nothing more. Lenz had many strong opinions, and when Denny was unsure of something and was unable to satisfy the grizzled veterans of the movement who intended to take control of the *omnium gatherum,* he would more often just ask Lenz, who would sit down in an empty arroyo south of town, not far from the old airport, and wait. There were no chemical additives to the condition of Lenz. There was nothing that Lenz needed or wanted. Lenz just was.

The arm, Lenz explained to Denny, had tumbled into a deprived echelon of the community where it could injure many. Generally speaking, the community of Rio Blanco welcomed, accepted, supported outsiders, and, as a result, even a detached arm oozing interplanetary bacteria could still count on a few defenders. Unfortunately, the permeable and accepting portion of the community did not always take the best care of itself. It was underinsured, for example. It didn't really take into account the dangerous situations in which it often found itself. A nugget of fool's gold was enough to beguile the community. As in the case of a detached arm.

The jet packs had been Denny's idea. He wasn't living with his father anymore. His father was living in a shuttered auto body shop on the edge of town that he had refinished in dirt, topsoil, and fill, and it was here that his father had embarked on such profundities of meditation and inward seeking that he was, he said, not to be disturbed. Denny, having grown up in the magnetic center of the *omnium gatherum,* abandoned by a mother who moved back to New Delhi to take up the post of culture minister in one of the provinces of the Sino-Indian Economic Compact, no longer believed in the language of the *omnium gatherum,* no longer believed that when a man in middle age sat in an empty auto body shop for six months he communed with the great powers of the universe. And yet Denny *did* believe in the political and mercantile possibilities of the *omnium gatherum,* and he promised donors meetings with his father, and signed copies of books by his father, and he reserved bandwidth on the web site for the sharing of personal insights by major donors. This was good business.

He'd also come up with the NirvanaCam, which photographed his father's meditation sessions for up to six hours a day. He had archived all of the meditating over the past two years, which basically looked like a guy with bad posture sitting until he slumped over onto his side. Denny hoped that his father's dilated pupils and, on occasion, his needle tracks escaped notice.

And now a parable. Denny had once, as a boy, been encouraged to meditate with a paralyzed guru. This paralyzed guru had a reputation for holiness above holinesses; he was a man whose very word was enough to mobilize seekers, or at least that had been the case at one time. The guru had suffered a very serious ischemic event, perhaps from the drugs and the excesses. Suddenly, the holy man was all but entirely paralyzed. And while he could speak with a technological interface, he often chose not to.

Zachary Wheeler, who couldn't effectively parent his teenage son, a boy whose very belief system clashed with the non-Western consciousness that Zachary had cultivated throughout his adult life, begged Denny to meet with the holy man. For a nominal fee, or for barter, or for transportation costs, or for payment in kind, or for favors in the afterlife, the holy man, now paralyzed, would turn up and make a few pronouncements in a synthesized voice. *Hello, Denny, I'm Robert, and even though you can't see my mouth moving, it is indeed my mind that is constructing and refining these thoughts. We're here today to try to exchange our realities. This is our goal. I'm going to show you how my being works, the reality of how I use this body now, how I have decided to consort with the people who help to look after me. It is, you might be surprised to find, possible to experience my condition as a sort of freedom, no matter how it may seem, and that's what I propose to teach you today. In return, as is the way of things, you are going to show me your reality. The joy and the resourcefulness of youth. I welcome learning about you. For the record, I had to work up this speech back in my room, so I'm not going to go on at any length now. Let's just try and sit for a little while, and then when we're done you can tell me a few things about yourself, the things I cannot learn just from being here with you. I'd like that. Okay, first try to find a comfortable seated position.*

But how long was it going to last? Denny wanted to know. How long would he have to sit still? The paralyzed man, once the handlers scuttled out of the meditation room at the ashram, fell silent, and because of the ischemic event, the paralyzed man certainly didn't *move*. Some goo, it seemed, ran out of the corners of his eyes, because he wasn't very good at blinking, and there was, now and then, some drool, but mostly he didn't move. And there was no sound now, no sound but a low-frequency hum, which was probably a swamp cooler next door, or there was the occasional muffled footfall in the hallway, or the rattling of the rice paper dividers that sequestered the two of them into this infernal cell. Time seemed to hover, and then time drew to an inscrutable halt. Maybe there was a little bit of breathing from the paralyzed man, and then on occasion Denny heard his own anxious breathing, and he felt a mild fluttering in his eardrums, and then, in due course, an absolute boredom overcame him. A crystalline and highly condensed boredom. It was with a sort of irritation that he considered the juxtaposition of boredom and enlightenment — maybe this juxtaposition was essential to the people who reveled in enlightenment, that unquantifiable thing that *didn't know what it was,* just as this juxtaposition was also essential to those who were certain enlightenment was passive nonsense that allowed arms traders and transnational oligarchs to seize for their own the ground underneath the meditators, the cloaks belonging to the meditators, the food that the meditators were going to eat when they broke their fast, the confederates of the meditators, and, finally, the bodies of the meditators them-selves. Denny's boredom and uncertainty about the paralyzed man grew until he wasn't sure if the paralyzed man was awake or not, and for a long spell he could do nothing but watch a spider in the corner of the room; he attempted to count the gossamer threads of its arachnid lattices in the dusty sunlight of the cell in which he found himself, wondering when the spider would cross the room and climb the craggy face of the paralyzed man, and when he was finished with this spidery fantasy, when there was no other thinking to be done, Denny became convinced that he was dead, that the paralyzed man was dead; maybe he, Denny, had somehow killed the paralyzed man, maybe his disgust for enlightenment, for the trappings of the *omnium gatherum* and all of its kind, had killed the paralyzed man, maybe he, Denny, gave off some kind of force field of worldly hate that slew enlightenment whenever it turned up, and this gave way to some further anxiety that he, Denny, might be dead as well, the exchange of information, the sharing of *realities* advertised by the paralyzed man's prosthetic voice, somehow involved a transmigratory exchange; the para-lyzed man was attempting to *swap* bodies with him; the paralyzed man was some kind of incubus who intended to suck the vital juices out of him, this was Denny's further anxiety, and what he had carelessly believed to be delusional crap in the first place, the bunk of enlightenment, was now an attempt by the paralyzed man to lay hold of Denny's young, virile body and to swipe it, and once he, Denny, was sure of this, he decided he needed to kill the paralyzed man if he, the paralyzed man, wasn't dead already, because it was either kill him or be inhabited by him, and if you meet a paralyzed Buddha in the meditation room, one who drools, be sure to strangle him, because there wasn't room enough in this adolescent for the both of them, unless the paralyzed man was already dead, but how could he verify if the paralyzed man was dead, if he, Denny, was not supposed to move in order to get a better look? Could he hear the breathing anymore? He didn't think he could hear the breathing! He could feel the paralyzed man's soul knocking at the doorway of his own, he was almost sure of it; the silence was so silent that you could just about hear such a thing, and he could feel that though he was young and physically strong, he was not strong in his heart, whatever *heart* meant, which was hard to figure when you really thought care-fully about it; there was not enough self in himself to repel the paralyzed man, whose spirit fluttered from corner to corner of the room like laundry in a gale, and the meditation went on like this for some time, though how long was unknown, maybe five or six minutes, maybe ninety seconds, until Denny knew he was going to leave. Buddha was an incubus, and Denny didn't give up his corpuscular self to incubi, and he saw how the Buddha intended to enter him through his mouth, through his already receding gums, intending to inhabit him, intending to seize control of him, and this was the first of the many visions that Denny had (and what he eventually did, though it took a long time, was wait for the holy man to begin to snore, and when the snoring began, Denny bolted), all of which were visions that were critical of the precepts of the *omnium gatherum,* all of them parricidal, and this was why he went to college and studied business administration, because he didn't care about the precepts of the *omnium gatherum,* he thought that the *omnium gatherum* was just some kind of pro-tein deficiency. He figured if he had to inherit something from his father, who spent his days nasally inhaling OxyPlus and trying to seduce women on role-playing sites, he'd inherit an economic powerhouse, and he would *monetize* it.

Admittedly, this was hard to do with an organization that was radically opposed to the exchange of currency. He had to do whatever he could to avoid currency, or else risk diluting the *omnium gatherum* brand, and so he took care to spawn a brisk exchange of favors and influence; likewise he insured that every opportunity to patent and to advertise be pursued, for example, the web site that catalogued *apocalypsis* (his idea), where there was a discreet banner advertising for services that were aligned with the *omnium gatherum,* aura readings, colonic cleansing, and so forth. Denny also accepted administrative aid from alternative-lifestyle theoreticians, or from people on their staffs. The interactive multiplatform text that was generated from the accounts of the apocalypse, that was copyrighted to the *omnium gatherum,* but Denny took 30 percent off the top of the organization's take. Thank god *someone* in the organization had the sense to look after this stuff. Maybe his dad would have done so when younger, before the drug-resistant syphilis, but somewhere along the line his dad lost the thread. Denny didn't know if it had something to do with his mother's going back to India. She'd received funding from the Sino-Indian Economic Compact for a performance piece in which she kissed as many people as possible, upwards of several hundred a day, and she had brought this project, under the auspices of a museum in New York, to the fair shores of this second-rate superpower and had been filmed at great length walking across the country dispensing kisses, while trying to avoid the oral herpes virus, and in the desert Southwest, she found that Zachary Wheeler came through the line several times, even though the waits in Rio Blanco were sometimes hours long. Eventually, even though he invited her to kiss some constituents as part of an *omnium gatherum* roundtable discussion, and to discuss techniques of kissing (she preferred to graze a spot at the interstices of upper and lower lips), and the spiritual rewards of kissing, one thing led to another. Or this is what Denny's father told him. Denny had never met his mother, who had denied the baby once it was born at the URB Medical Center, and after handing off the half-breed baby to Zachary, she returned to India to marry a shipping magnate, who probably knew nothing of the coast-to-coast juggernaut of kisses. She then took up her political position.

Zachary didn't talk about the *mother* much anymore, didn't talk much at all, and he seemed happy enough when Denny started mounting multimedia performances, or unlicensed outdoor gatherings without municipal approval. The *Apotheosis of the Arm,* which Denny had only just begun to understand to be the next phase of the *omnium gatherum,* consisted of a vision of the arm being fired in a jet pack high above the desert, in order to be incinerated, spectacularly so, such that a dangerous pandemic could be averted in a region already suffering with unemployment in the high twenties, a negative outflow of population to the tune of 10 percent per annum, and a very high rate of hospital admissions for drug abuse and overdose. Denny had seen the *Apotheosis of the Arm* while melting down the teddy-bear cactus out behind his condominium for water. This was long before the Mars mission reentry. Weeks before. The day was well over 115, and he wasn't wearing a hat, and he had forgotten to tell anyone he was going for a walk, and maybe it was only natural that he would see the arm, crawling in front of him; maybe the arm *intended* to come to him. After he ran back into the house to fetch some garden gloves and a long-sleeved shirt, the arm was no longer to be found, nor were there any tracks that might have indicated the arm's presence. But he had seen the arm, he knew he had, and he was trying to understand its profit potential, but in the meantime, he knew that the *Apotheosis of the Arm* had to proceed as many other *omnium gatherum* multimedia extravaganzas had proceeded, just like the release of the timber wolves. That had been quite a night, the release of the timber wolves. When the *omnium gatherum* learned that the prior releases of timber wolves had all ended in *death,* when local hunters took it upon themselves to roust the wolves, track them by helicopter, hooting as they blasted them, the *omnium gatherum* had mounted a large-scale reintroduction that was called *hunting the hunters,* with many volunteers cooperating to track the wolves and then to track the trackers. They released two hundred and thirty-nine wolves on that night.

Denny needed to explain it all to his father, even if the invitations had already gone out, because it was never effective to mount large-scale *omnium gatherum* activities without telling his father first. His father had some kind of sixth sense for these types of maneuvers, for the ebbing and flowing of institutional power, and would quickly rouse himself from semiconsciousness to complain and to condemn.

Denny took Lenz with him, because Lenz was the heart and soul of the operation. Lenz had a rice cooker, and Lenz knew how to read tea leaves. Lenz had a computer program that threw joss sticks automatically, and, first thing in the morning, Lenz read out the day's prospects, almost always good. The Fourth Morning of the Pestilence, Lenz called and woke Denny. Denny's cranially implanted communications time-saver stabbed him in the scalp to wake him.

"The wise man prepares for the end of everything that is, dancing."

When Denny affixed the external screen attachment onto his face, he saw Lenz's sallow visage, behind ringlets of dyed blue hair. What did Lenz's mother think?

"Didn't you do that one recently? Can't be the end of everything every day."

"I'm just the messenger."

"We do have to go see the old man."

It was Lenz's idea that they add the clothing-optional clause to the invitation. Though Denny liked seeing a lot of naked people around as much as anyone else, it would be easier to evaluate the medical condition of the participants of the *omnium gatherum* if a lot of them were dressed in skimpy rags. If there were bodies *disassembling,* as Denny had heard, then he wanted to know ahead of time, before the crowds became too excited and too intoxicated.

They talked through this piece of the festivities on the way over to his dad's place.

The route to the auto body shop was along Grant Avenue, a major thoroughfare in Rio Blanco until the Minimum Wage Riots of the first decade of the century, when people from South of the Border, who were by that time more than half of the population in Rio Blanco, had protested the repeal of the minimum wage by blowing up portions of one of the town's major roads. Grant was rutted with gigantic sinkholes, some of them going down hundreds of feet into the aquifer that had once lain beneath this desert. Easy to collapse. Grant was therefore considered a dangerous route across town. Denny and Lenz rode motorized skateboards, even though Denny was keen to try the jet packs he had procured from a hobbyist out by the lowlands where the event would take place.

They had effectively blanketed the community with small plastic arms announcing the performance, and you could tell because they saw them by the side of what used to be Grant Avenue. It was as if some sweatshop from the Sino-Indian Economic Compact had invaded Rio Blanco and air-dropped little arms out of a biplane, *Good people of America, please repair to your homes. Our only quarrel is with your government. We apologize for the lead-based paints on this toy, and for the fact that many young persons were injured in its manufacture.*

The paradox of modern Rio Blanco was that it could be a relatively populous urban region, and still you could be standing in the center of town, as Denny and Lenz were, and see *no one.* The town part of Rio Blanco was the part that was no town at all, and if they had been breaking and entering, they would have done so with impunity. No one would have found the wrack and ruin of their mayhem for days afterward, if ever.

Upon their entrance, Zachary Wheeler stumbled to his feet, awkwardly, his hands and feet and hair covered with dirt. He squinted against the sunlight that was allowed into his lair.

"Pop, you remember Lenz."

"You have something planned for later this week," Zachary said. "And you..."

In the corner of the room, the workstation that Zachary used for his complicated role-playing assignations flickered in the dark, as if scrolling through the news sites of the day according to an algorithm. Denny felt what he always felt around his father, some desire to protect Zachary from himself, and a desire to push him down on the ground and administer a number of swift kicks to spleen and pancreas. There was probably a woman, or a number of women, and maybe a few automated comfort programs, beseeching him on the computer all at once, and none of them knew who Zachary Wheeler was, or that there were people in the Rio Blanco area who revered Zachary Wheeler and would have followed him anywhere, down into the center of the world, if necessary. And here he was in the auto body shop, shooting up and trying to get it on with the women of the web.

Denny said, "We're keeping you up-to-date."

"What's the scale of your—"

"A couple thousand, maybe more."

"Something's—"

"There's trouble—"

Lenz added, "Federal agents already in the city."

"Always with the federal agents..."

"We're going to try to shoot the arm back into—"

His father lurched unsteadily forward, only to wobble against the plaster, collapsing into a seated posture.

"The arm?"

"There's this arm."

Zachary asked, "Do you have it with you?"

"It's with our people, Pop. It's safe. We're trying to keep it in a meat locker where possible. It's kind of decaying a little bit. It smells really bad. Do you want to come out and watch? I got jet packs."

"Jet packs?"

"The telemetry is much more impressive now. It has self-guiding properties. Now you can easily use one to climb up over the city."

"How far do you plan to shoot the...thing?"

"We're going incinerate the arm with laser-guided missiles. We've got some sitting on the top of the pass over the canyon."

Lenz said, "It's from next door over in space. From Mars."

"The whole thing, I don't know, maybe you're not thinking big enough."

"How much bigger do you want me to think? We're having a major pyrotechnical display on the outside of town, where we're going to rid the town of this major pandemic, this thing from outer space, and we're going to celebrate space while we're at it, and there are a number of angles I'm pursuing in terms of making sure that we are getting high-profile attention, some broadcasting royalties. We got an in-kind donation from a toy-manufacturing facility South of the Border who, uh, designed this little toy arm for us—"

"I helped with the design," Lenz said.

"You made toy arms."

The thing that made Zachary so threatening was that he lived the *omnium gatherum* story, and as a result he could always see it ramifying before him. It could go this way, and did, and then at the same time there might be a completely different set of possibilities, and it seemed that all these possibilities were simultaneous, and though it would be nice, would be more convenient, if there were just one story, just one *omnium gatherum,* Zachary Wheeler knew that there was not. It was almost as if the *omnium gatherum,* Denny thought, when confronted with his father, had no single, indisputable meaning. It was more like something that could be claimed by anyone. And Zachary's approach, which was perhaps what had brought him to this bleak spot, centered on the possible interpretations. This was why Zachary, in the end, didn't much care if his son treated the *omnium gatherum* as a possibility for copyright, trademarking, or branding. That was one way of defining the *omnium gatherum.* His father's was the madness that resulted from hearing *all* the voices. His father believed all the clamoring voices, with their insistences and their tragedies.

"What about City Hall?" his father said.

"City Hall?"

"Who's going to be looking after City Hall?"

"Who's usually looking after City Hall?"

"The police," Zachary said, "are going to be looking after you, policing your event. So that means—"

"Means what?"

"Means that we could take control of City Hall. Just keep a detachment of people separate, and when the time comes, you escort the mayor from City Hall, take him to the site of the festivities, or to a black site, and then you leave a few guys behind. In City Hall."

Denny had so much to learn.

Among the many unflattering stages of *M. thanatobacillus* infection, according to the observations of Dr. Woo Lee Koo, as he bore witness to these in his son, was a stage in which the infected party behaved like a great ape. Indeed, Jean-Paul, his legitimate son, his biological son, had begun exhibiting many of the characteristics of Morton, his adoptive son—uninhibited scratching, chest-thumping, grunting, aggressive and childlike behavior, public masturbation. In fact, his son seemed to go about with an unconcealed erection whenever he was not resting. Jean-Paul seemed to feel it appropriate that he should rub himself erotically against any surface available—the side of an armchair, a large appliance. The sleek curves of an old-fashioned electric-cell automobile out front of the unit also proved very useful in this regard, even if the quarantined Jean-Paul should not have been outside. When Koo had attempted to get him up and around for this brief interval of fresh air, Jean-Paul had a spontaneous orgasm just from lying on the front hood of that automobile. Soon after, he began spontaneously hemorrhaging from his eye sockets and his ears, but this didn't inhibit sexual feeling, as Koo dictated in his notes that evening: *The patient seems to have very little pain. I notice considerable distension in the patient's genitals. Perhaps the infection itself is somehow engorging the genital region. Would orgasm as experienced by the patient result in a new route of contagion? That is, does the infection have a vene-real route of transmission, in addition to its blood-borne routes? This has not been much considered by the medical community thus far, but it seems important, especially as the patient is clearly experiencing erectile sensation of a pleasurable sort.*

Koo made sure to install cameras in the bedroom of his son. The erotic frenzy of tertiary infection would have challenged any dispassionate medical practitioner, even more so if the viewer happened to be the father of the infected party; nevertheless, the cameras enabled Koo to watch Jean-Paul around the clock, and to see the frustration, the wordlessness, the disinhibition, and the desperation that the boy was exhibiting as he began to under-stand that his cognition, indeed, even the ability of his larynx, pharynx, and vocal cords to produce sound, was failing with each passing hour. Jean-Paul had taken to pointing at things when he needed them, and much of the time, in fact, he was simply point-ing at Vienna Roberts, his frequent visitor, and making sounds that could only be interpreted as weeping. Koo the Elder, who was administering intravenous antibiotics around the clock, found himself in a constant state of conflicted sentiment — the scientific interest of the case was overwhelming. But his son was withering before his eyes.

And this was not the only conflict. At some point soon, Jean-Paul, his father recognized, would be, if he was not already, clini-cally dead, and yet still mobile. The inexplicable course of the infection was now known. Jean-Paul would have no recognizable pulse, but would still be alive for several days, maybe even more. At this point, in a postmortem state, his son's tissue would be of paramount use for medical experiment, not to mention, though Koo was not a person who much mentioned these things, that he could not bear what was to come. Koo had, by staying in touch with some of the other medical researchers in the area, Lecompte et al., learned that there were now upwards of twenty advanced cases of *M. thanatobacillus* quarantined in the hospitals of the region. Several more among medical personnel who had become infected through ignorance of the danger or through unsanitary practices. Preventive vivisection of the advanced cases was now common, and there were therefore, in various laboratories, pieces of several persons, citizens of Rio Blanco, who had come in contact with the crawling hand and had contracted its pathogen. And this had all happened so quickly! In just four days! It was undeniable, how the pathogen thrived in the warmer Earth climes, with deadly results. Some of Koo's colleagues, friends, enemies, acquaintances, were already subjecting the extremities of patients — here a toe, here a human ear, here a severed head that still managed to make the most hideous caterwauling (according to the clinic on the South Side) — to various kinds of tests. But Koo himself remained convinced that none as yet had attempted to perform any large-scale experiments relating to the ongoing problem of *reanimation.*

Koo, if he were willing to make the journey into the dangerous outdoors, could probably obtain some other infected tissue sample for his own experiment. Was he willing to travel on this account? Koo preferred *not* to use his son for any experimentation, because it wasn't ethically sound, because his family was in a dire condition. On the other hand, Jean-Paul's blood type was a match, and his son was very nearly beyond the state when he, Koo, or anyone else could help him. Wouldn't Jean-Paul, the brilliant and promising entrepreneur, the best son any father could have, *want* to participate in the experiment that Koo had in mind, the experiment having to do with the cryogenic freezer in his garage, especially in view of his illness? During the postmortem phase of *M. thanatobacillus* infection, Woo Lee Koo could plausibly begin implanting some of the infected tissue from Jean-Paul into the body of his wife, at least that was how the medical researcher in him thought about it.

There were as many ways of thinking about the medical ethics here as there were ways of thinking, and thus without arriving at any conclusion, Koo watched his son on the monitor in his study as the boy attempted to pry loose from Vienna Roberts some romantic reassurance. Was there nothing more he could do for Jean-Paul? The courses of antibiotics seemed to make no difference at all. Koo's friend Ryan Levy over at the Northwest Medical Center had tried the same with his own patients, from the simplest organic compounds that still worked on syphilis, up through the newest synthetic antibiotics, without conclusive results. Even finding a vein for the intravenous drip was hard, since Jean-Paul's arms now resembled gangrenous or decomposing tissue. It was impossible to tell whether oxygen-rich blood circulated through the boy's sludgy vessels into that damaged, infected tissue. Koo's ruminations on treatment ran to the far-fetched: transplantation of some extremities. Could they transplant into Jean-Paul? With the body in the state it was in, Jean-Paul was unlikely to have a problem with tissue rejection, and wouldn't the elimination of some portions of the infected tissue slow the progress of the pathogen? At least for a few hours? This would be feasible only if Jean-Paul's limbs were not yet in the advanced stages of detachment.

What else was there to do? Koo watched the video, trying to divine the meaning of symbolic locutions still possible for his son. *Patient seems able to understand language, but is unable to communicate well. Patient seems to be attempting to formulate some prolonged farewell with romantic partner, V. Roberts, despite limited linguistic skills.* Koo himself, as he watched, was unable to sit still. He couldn't stop himself from getting up, crossing the room, wearing down a portion of wall-to-wall carpeting, stuffing some empty carbohydrate into his mouth, that bowl of peppermints he had on his desk, going back to the screen, trying to rethink his strategy, remembering about the peeling wallpaper in the office, dictating some more notes, castigating himself for his paucity of ideas, despairing, and it was in the course of this that he did suddenly hit on a possibility.

Perhaps it was only fair to let Jean-Paul know about the *reanimation experiment,* and to allow him to make some kind of farewell to his mother. Koo even dictated the thought into his recorder, and it was just then that he had his idea. If the infection took a more leisurely course on the planet Mars, if it was possible to slow the course of infection by *refrigerating,* why couldn't he put Jean-Paul into the freezer for a few hours? Had no one explored this? Woo Lee Koo had trouble getting his thoughts to settle down, so worried was he about his difficult but lovable son, and when he tried to come up with his hypotheses, he found that he flitted around from idea to idea without being able to land.

At the same time, there was a rather moving speech taking place on the screen before him. Vienna Roberts had risen to the occasion and supported her boyfriend throughout his lurid ordeal. Koo also made a note that any theory of the bacteria had to take into account the fact that she showed no sign of infection.

"I get that you are not well, and maybe you think your time has come, but I want you to know that I don't accept it, and you just shaking your head isn't going to convince me. For me, your time just is *not* coming. If I were going to show the same symptoms as you, I'd already have the symptoms, which means I'm probably clean, so why don't you just let me hug you?"

To which his son shook his head, again.

"Look at it another way"—wiping her eyes—"the day arrives for every lover, that day when she's not a lover anymore, and it could be five days after she meets him, or five years, or fifty years, but no matter what that time is, the time when lovers are parted, *have to be* parted, no matter what has happened in all the intervening time, whether they have been unfaithful, or have taken each other for granted, or maybe they couldn't really be intimate, or however they approached it, no matter what happened in all that time, there's never a lover who doesn't wish that she didn't have *a few more minutes.* The end of love is when you can no longer see the possibility of a few more minutes, and when you start totaling up what's lost. And that's when you always wish you had done better talking through things, you know, because there was a time that was the last time you could express yourself, and you almost always wish you had expressed yourself better, because it's the way people are, that they never get it all down in words, and in this case, if something is going to happen to you now, I really want to say that it's partly because of me, because I—"

A cessation of the conversation at this point, by reason of a surfeit of feelings.

"—I was the one who had this selfish idea about us having to go out there, out into the canyon. If it all has something to do with that, with what I thought I wanted, and you didn't even want it, then it's up to me to be able to say it's okay for me and I'm not worried about infection, or whatever you want to call it. It's up to me to say whether it's okay for me to hug you or be hugged by you, or whether I can kiss you or wrap my arms around you on the bed, or lie on top of you."

Son, again, with the vigorous shaking of the head, *no.* It was clear to Koo that Jean-Paul was still able to indicate in the negative, and therefore the affirmative, but what of more complicated grammatical structures?

For some reason, Koo suddenly noticed that Vienna Roberts was actually wearing trousers. An unlikely garment for the slut. Had there been some kind of costume change? These denim trousers were sitting low on her hips in a way that revealed some of her pale belly and her bony hips, and it occurred to Koo that the pants belonged to his son. Perhaps she was wearing these low-slung slacks because she was already appropriating clothing from him, fetishizing his clothes, the clothes from the former Jean-Paul. Before he could halt the proceedings, the girl began removing her particle mask, unhooking it from her dainty little ears, as if this was somehow to express more emphatically her romantic thoughts, and Koo knew now that he should march across the unit and intercede, and yet he was unable, for the moment, to stop watching. It was as if this were some kind of perma-cam web broadcast, such as you might see on the independent or pirate channels, where everything was about *how realistic* were its means of production, which really meant: how tiresome, how shattering, for example, that program, *Prima,* about the first family on Mars.

Jean-Paul made a gesture, laying ahold of each elbow, as if to indicate that he was *cold,* and the girl took note.

"Do you want a—"

Pointing to a stack of wool blankets that Koo himself had brought into the room to deal with temperature extremes. But Jean-Paul shook his head vigorously. He didn't want the blanket. Any blanket.

"Well, then, do you want me to hold you? Would you just, like, let me—"

Another vigorous shake of the head in the negative, so vigorous, in fact, that there was a tiny crimson spattering across the pillow and on the bedclothes.

"What, then?"

Jean-Paul pointed out into the hall. And thus the drama of Jean-Paul's illness would temporarily recede from the view of omnipresent video cameras. His father had an idea where the young lovers were going, because it was a place in the unit that had often appealed to Jean-Paul when he was a boy: the bathroom, with its paling lamps. Why a boy from Asia, by way of France, had been so enamored with the brutish and homely pigmentary affectation of the paling salon was unclear to his father. Paling, in general, was no better than sniffing glue, in terms of the kinds of difficulties it so effectively promoted. But Jean-Paul had always liked it as a child, and when he could not go into an actual paling salon to soak up the ultrahigh-frequency transmissions of the irradiators, then he would apply the caramel dyes of would-be Bollywood actresses, those trying to make it big in the Sino-Indian musical espionage film circuit.

If there was a particular stressor in the boy's life, an audition for a school play, some kind of standardized testing, a visit from his French cousins, the younger Koo had often, in the past, repaired to the bathroom and to the paling salon that had come with the unit. In fact, the little booths that Jean-Paul had designed for his cosmetic surgery business bore a significant resemblance to the paling booths he had sometimes favored as a younger boy. An astute psychologist, with a copy of the *DSM-VIII,* might have diagnosed *racial dysphoria,* and this was a popular diagnosis in the era of the Sino-Indian Economic Compact. No one in NAFTA wanted to look like they could come from a Hindu nation.

Koo met the youngsters in the hall and followed them toward the bathroom. Vienna, still wearing her rubberized gloves, was attempting to help along Jean-Paul, whose legs were weak and, Koo supposed, ready to detach. Instead of greeting Dr. Woo Lee Koo, the young lovers proceeded as if in this end stage of their doomed romance, they no longer needed anyone besides themselves. Least of all parents. They shut the bathroom door behind themselves gently but firmly, and Koo found himself on the other side of the action. He dictated a few more notes while he was there, mumbling in Korean as he listened to the paling lamps going on in the bathroom. It was good they were paling *now,* what with the blackout only a few hours away.

If the question of self is an important marker in tertiary-stage infection, during which a rigid, human idea of self leaves the patient to be replaced by a more permeable sense of identity in which self and inanimate objects become interdependent and less distinguishable, it should be noted that even in this advanced stage, our patient is still inclined toward idiosyncrasies he exhibited from earliest childhood. For example, despite long having been told that he risked melanoma if he didn't discontinue paling, patient nonetheless has expressed a fervent and consistent desire to be a different color. The affectation persists at this late stage of infection despite likely skin failure and sickly pallor.

There was some disturbance in the bathroom, some commotion, as if the two of them were moving about quite a bit, wrestling, or were engaged in some fully executed jitterbug of love, and the sound of it reminded Koo of those sequences in antiquated slapstick comedies when many more people were crammed into some tiny space than could actually fit. The recessed lighting flickered in the hall where he stood, as it always did when Jean-Paul was using the paling appliance in the bathroom. Wait! Koo was distracted by an incoming call on his digital assistant, which was, at this moment, looped around his brown plastic belt—Levy again, from Northwest Medical, with a note suggesting that isolating patients in a hyperbaric chamber had yet to produce results. In fact, Levy noted, they'd left one patient in there, and when they returned an hour later, he was in three different pieces. They had to stop one of the patient's feet from attempting to escape into the general hospital population by crushing all the bones in it with a nearby fire ax. Koo passed a distracted moment lamenting the professional depths to which his colleagues had free-fallen in search of a quick fix for *M. thanatobacillus.* It was no better than the medieval responses to the buboes that wiped out so much of Europe—smoke, sex, pleasant smells, prayer, and inquisitions. Maybe these dark ages were not substantively different from those, and what was forgotten would again exceed what was remembered. But Koo found that his reveries, facing a scuffed and overdue-to-be-repainted bathroom door, beyond which was the humming of ultraviolet radiation, were suddenly interrupted by a braying that could only be one thing. It was like a familiar song, that sound, the sound of his son's voice, his son's voice saying a rather familiar thing:

"That feels fucking *great!*"

What? Unmistakably his son's voice, audibly so, followed in turn by an unreserved giggling from Vienna Roberts, a laughter prompted, Koo assumed, by the sound of the patient speaking for the first time in a day or so.

"Fucking great!"

Koo began pounding on the door, and he was astonished to find with what enthusiasm he was pounding on the door, with what flooding relief he begged to be admitted, calling his son's name, for here was a moment to be treasured, a moment when things seemed as though they were not quite as grim as he'd previously imagined. Under the margin of the door, in the hum of the paling salon, there was, for a minute at any rate, some hope.

The door swung back, and there was his son, his skin hanging like rags on his body, having lost quite a bit of weight already, a bit of clotted arterial gunk in the corners of his eyes, which were both bloodshot and slightly yellowy, but smiling, *smiling.*

Koo said, "What is it that's going on?" And while the words may have had the ring of paternal injunction about them, Koo also felt giddy with the possibilities of the moment.

"Dad," Jean-Paul said, struggling but articulating nonetheless, "I really feel better in here. Is it possible that I could feel better in here? Could this..."

So overpowering was the sense that something at last might have been going *right* for the infected young man, that Koo didn't even notice at first, and neither did Jean-Paul, that Vienna Roberts had thrown herself around her contagious lover, encircling him. Without a mask or a hospital gown on, nor other protection, she encircled Jean-Paul, and she lay her face against his face, and then her breast against his breast, and there they were now, having conjoined their destinies, the lovers. Koo was moved enough that, at last, he felt unable to repel a conviction that it would be all right:

"My son," he said, "I am so happy to hear your voice. You don't know how happy I am to hear your voice. I am even happy to hear your cursing. I have not been so happy to hear your cursing in many years. In fact, I am rarely happy to hear your cursing, but today I am very happy. You should feel encouraged to curse some more. You should curse to your heart's content. And I must say that this moment gives me some ideas, some ideas I must share with some of the other medical personnel who are working on this question of what to do about the disease. If you would be interested to know, the idea that I have is that there are two factors that worked to inhibit the growth of the bacteria *M. thanatobacillus* on the planet where it was incubating, and the first of these factors is the far greater impact of cosmic rays and other radiation on the planet Mars."

"But Dad," Jean-Paul said, slurring perceptibly, "what does that have to do with——"

"This machine for which we pay rather too much money, because of the amount of electrical energy it uses, aims to apply ultraviolet radiation to your skin, in order to cook away the upper layers of skin, the pigment manufacturing of the dermal cells. It is an apparatus that I have always deplored and found unnecessary, even barbaric, and yet it may be that in this case the radiation is duplicating the kinds of effects that were present on the surface of Mars. On the one hand, as I am thinking about it now, it is possible that the bacteria on Mars became irradiated by the surface conditions, the lack of atmosphere on the planet, and therefore became inured to low-level radiation, but the very same conditions kept it from duplicating effectively, and thus the slow rate of progression of the infection in those who were on the Mars mission."

"And—"

"It means that you are going to stay in the bathroom under the paling lamps for a good portion of this day, I believe, at least until I see about radiation treatments at the hospital."

The young man smiled, as perhaps he had not smiled for some time now, and the girl kissed him on the face. There was a kind of slurpy sound issuing from Jean-Paul's skin when she applied herself to it. Some of it pulled away with her.

"Still, there is another factor," Koo went on, "that must be considered. That is the temperature issue. The surface of the planet Mars is extremely cold, as you know, and such air as exists there is all but anaerobic, and so it's more than possible that lowering your body temperature would effectively slow down the rate of infection."

"Are you going to put me in the freezer in the garage? And leave me there to freeze?"

Woo Lee Koo, without realizing the error he was about to make, said, "There is not room in the freezer in the garage, because there is already someone in there."

"There's..."

"Perhaps this is not the best time to discuss this." As if Koo had become suddenly faint of heart, as if the rebuses that made up his mostly concealed personality, the compartments secreted away in other compartments, had now eased into view.

"I believe that the number of male cases of infection is greatly larger than the number of female cases," he went on, "and I had not earlier concentrated much attention on this issue, but it is possible that we should look at estrogen as some kind of natural suppressor of the infection. Perhaps hormones play an important role in this process. Perhaps the bacteria first targets the endocrines—"

"Dad, what the fuck do you mean that there's already someone in the freezer? I mean, I know there is a lot of other stuff going on right now. But is there some reason why you said what I think you just said?"

"Perhaps if Miss Roberts continues to be free of symptoms, we would be able to take a blood test from her in order to look at it under the microscope? If it isn't the estrogen, it's possible that she has some kind of—"

"Dad!"

"—resistance—"

The timer on the paling lamps went off, and Vienna Roberts, ignoring the turn of events, cranked the timer around again, in the clockwise direction.

"We will also have to make sure that we have enough generator power available to run the paling lamps twenty-four hours if we need to do so. Perhaps if you stay in this room for a long enough period, then some of the skin's regenerative capabilities will begin their work, and instead of just arresting the disease you can begin to recover some of your former appearance."

Jean-Paul turned to Vienna Roberts. "Did you hear what I heard?"

And then the elder felt that he had no choice but to say what he had to say, what he had prepared for so long to say, in so many different ways. No matter what father-and-son conversation they shared, no matter what father-and-son conversation was *not* going according to Koo's intentions, no matter what chastisements he was meting out, or what paternal advice, there was always in the limbic portion of Woo Lee Koo's neural net the moment when this conversation would take place, the conversation in which it was revealed that Koo was not the man that he seemed, not the good man, the generous man, the family man, but rather a man who was afraid to let go of certain things, a man who was afraid to face up to certain facts, a man who could not accept *death,* after all, though death was accepted by other people bravely every day. Why was it that he was this man? Koo had formulated myriad answers to the question, or, at least, he had imagined many times over the moment in which he composed a brave accounting of his actions, and his son simply *forgave him.* Koo never sat at a keyboard and typed in the words *Because I believe that the love of the family is the only love that a man will have in this world, and should you chance upon this love, you must do what you can to preserve it, you must sacrifice whatever you have to preserve this family, because I believe these things without reservation, I have done what I have done.* Koo didn't write down the words; he didn't consider which was the best way of delivering these dicta in his second language. But he considered that his point of view was just and right, and that his son, eventually, would see that he was just and right, because there was no other way to think about these issues. And yet now that Koo was about to have the conversation with his son, he understood that perhaps he was not so right as all that. At least, he was not sure how his son was going to react, because indeed he could think of no elegant way to say "Your mother is in the freezer in the garage." Although this was better than, for example, "Your mother is in this soup."

"I feel certain that I cannot adequately present what I am about to tell you without seeming as though I am insufficiently preparing you for the revelation. But I should tell you that your mother is in the freezer in the garage."

"I thought you . . . Aren't there . . . experimental vaccines in the—"

"That's true. But I also have your mother's body in there."

A silence of great length, as came to pass, was perhaps natural.

"Her dead body?"

"I prefer," Koo said, "to think of death as a temporary repose in the evolution of the human species. A design flaw, if you will. I know that death is, so to speak, popular, and that virtually every organic individual must live through this rather upsetting transition. I also know that most everyone, excepting the mortally ill who are in a great deal of pain, would prefer to avoid the business of death. I believe that this is a transient condition, and that the advances currently taking place in the medical world suffice to make the condition unnecessary. Consider the illness, Jean-Paul, with which you are suffering now. One of the very difficult to understand features of this illness is that people who are at death's door, or people who have gone *through* that immemorial door, are able to continue to move and function as though they were not dead at all."

"So what gave *you* the right to keep Mom's body in a freezer all these years? Your research?"

"I did not think of what you are referring to as requiring any kind of justification. My area of expertise has been in questions of death and the cellular changes that take place in death and after, and if I believe, as I most certainly do, that this end-stage process is no end at all but is just another opportunity for medical intervention, if I believe that death may therefore be reversed or even cured, then why would I refrain from using every technique available to me to reverse or cure the death of the person who—"

It was true that in the greater part of this speech Koo observed the kind of affable demeanor that he considered the most responsible and professional. He felt that he had nothing to hide, though he had long been hiding the fact that he had nothing to hide, and as a result it was important that he should not become upset, nor express any kind of irritation, because, after all, it had now been many years that his son believed that a simple urn full of leavings from a fireplace was in fact the cremains of his mother, when nothing could have been further from the truth. Koo understood that he needed to give his son the additional time and space that would allow him to feel his feelings, and perhaps these feelings were somehow bound up with his son's worries about his own mortality, which must have been on his mind owing to his dangerous illness, and yet Koo, coming to the end of the speech, found that suddenly he was himself temporarily distraught, and waves of shame overcame him, and he recognized that he was now doing what no self-respecting man of his age and station should do, which was finding himself unable to continue. His smudged eyeglasses slid from their perch on the bridge of his nose. And there was in Koo a burning sensation, or several kinds of burning sensations, followed by something near to the headache category, almost meningeal.

"You do not understand what this has meant to me, to have her here with me, and to be able to talk with her about the ups and downs, as I have often done. Many nights when you were asleep I spoke with her, and I wrote her many letters, hundreds upon hundreds of letters, and I have had her here with me, when no other woman would keep me company in the lonely adventure that is my work. And often I expected that I would tell you, but then I believed that you would not understand. Now you *must* understand; you can see that I have wept these shameful tears, and you know that my ambitions for your mother may not have been your own wishes, but that they were sincere."

However, these last lines were delivered to the naked back of his son, who, with only a towel draped around him, had struggled from the confines of the bathroom (where the paling lamps had again clicked off), followed by Vienna Roberts (who, Koo believed, gazed upon him, Koo, with a look that people occasionally referred to as "daggers"), to repair down the corridor to the garage. This response was to be expected, Koo supposed. Koo's secret was unraveling like a moth-eaten coverlet. It was only now that Koo fell prey to an additional worry: that his son would recognize, somehow, from looking on the cadaver that had once been his wife, that some little bit of cerebral tissue had lately been harvested from her. He began almost immediately to wrestle with this last revelation. Was it better to tell him now? To tell him that the chimpanzee Morton was, perhaps, his mother, was somehow a spawn of his mother, a semimaternal, cloned version of his mother? To tell him that this cadaver was less his mother, at present, than a way station in the process of self-realization of the chimpanzee? How to talk about these things without creating still more hurt?

Jean-Paul, limping and lurching, nonetheless passed through the kitchen with singular purpose, and from there to the door that led to the garage.

"There is more that I need to tell you, I think," Koo called timidly from behind.

"I'll let you know . . . when I want to hear it," Jean-Paul grunted. And even in the low-wattage fluorescence of the pantry, Koo could see that the stress was affecting his son. Still, there was nothing to be done, because in a few bounds the afflicted young man had thrown wide the door and was beside the cryogenic freezer. He laid his hands upon it. He examined it. He asked, as Koo joined him, what the keyboard was for. And Koo admitted that it was connected to a screen in the freezer, the site of cryogenic rest, and that this screen allowed for a Korean alphabet and for English and French in simultaneous translations, so that the boy's mother would be able to *read,* if she chose to.

"I have received no response from her, not up to the present," Koo added.

With Vienna's help, the boy fiddled with the false casing and the clasps on the funerary stabilizer, and this Koo was unable to watch. And then there was the thumbprint scanner, which Koo it seemed had no choice but to disable. In the gloom of the corner of the garage (for now night had fallen on the desert, and the lights, if they had not gone out, were soon to go out, and it was only Koo's generators that illuminated the light inside the refrigerator), he could not now see his wife, into whose eye socket he had recently inserted a lance in order to harvest cerebral tissue. Instead, he watched the faces of his son and his son's girlfriend, silhouetted, and in that moment, in seeing their faces, he reckoned with the amount of ruin that had gone unconsidered in his many secretive attempts to animate his dead wife.

"She...looks...peaceful," Jean-Paul said, leaning against Vienna Roberts. And in this instant, Koo surmised, a mothballed ghost went spinning and wheeling above the subdivision, a ghost recalled to the factory of ghosts.

"Don't think this means that I am not, like, fucking horrified, *comatose*, don't think I don't know I have spent my entire fucking life being lied to by you, and don't think this means that I don't recognize you as the fucking liar and fucking hypocrite you are, but I am very happy to see my mother again; I am very happy. If I have to die, then maybe it really is okay. Now."

"You have to do nothing of the sort," Koo said, "if only you will return to the bathroom where the paling lamps are located. We can discuss all of this in greater detail, all the many horrible things that I have done and continue to do. However, it also bears mentioning, since we are gathered in this spot, that there is this experiment that I have long been undertaking, the experiment having to do with the reanimation of your mother—"

"The what?"

"It is as I have been saying. I have been trying to conduct experiments in which I attempted to reanimate your mother."

"What does that—"

"It is just as I've been saying to you. But it is not as if she was going to get up and walk if we simply waited long enough. If I am to be able to reanimate your mother, I will be required to use her body for medical experiment. This has long been my plan, and in at least one case, I have already used some of her tissue for experiment—"

"I don't even want to hear this," Jean-Paul said, groaning dully, as it became clear that the positive effects of the ultraviolet radiation were quickly going to dissipate.

"Presently, I am of the opinion that a small bit of tissue from someone infected by the *M. thanatobacillus* bacteria, if engineered properly, could potentially enable the cadaver to take on some activities, and perhaps to have some limited cerebral function, in which we might be able, for example, to talk to your mother, my wife, and ask her a few questions. For example, we could ask her if the dead dream, and if they have desires. Are they like people in the middle of a seizure, who have awareness but are unable to act? Is it a locked-in syndrome? Or more, does it resemble persistent vegetative state? I know these are not easy questions for you to consider, but it may be necessary to act quickly, as we do not know how stable your condition is."

Vienna Roberts said, now getting between father and son in the dim light of the garage, "Dr., uh, Dr. Koo? What about my family? I mean, we're talking about family here, and about how important family is, but can you do anything for my family too? My parents, like, is it right to keep them in the dark about the van and how the van might be, I don't know, infected or whatever it is we're talking about, and while we're on the subject of mothers, I mean, maybe it will be possible to find some way to make sure they're safe too? I only have the one set of parents. And they had all kinds of trouble conceiving, you know; they had to use all kinds of medical technology. I think I'm probably, like, three-quarters petri dish or something. They aren't ready to give me up, and I'm not ready to give them up, and so maybe in the middle of this emergency you could—"

Koo said, agitated at the reminder, "This is information that is useful to remember, yes. But in the meantime, I do need my son, who has a blood type match with his mother, to consider whether he might be willing to offer up some tissue for experiment, and it doesn't need to be very much, just a little bit, really."

"How much?"

"It could be something very small. Perhaps a toe. Or a finger. A pinkie."

... Night fell over the desert and Monaco 37 streaked past again and the stars were like the future perfect of an uncommon verb.

Or the stars were the filaments of discarded human aspirations. Or the stars in the night sky were the innumerable preschoolers of September, afraid to climb onto the bus in order to have their liberty abridged. Or the stars in the night sky were like so many holes into which our heads were to be stuck. Or the stars in the night sky were the innumerable computations of some frail and overburdened supercomputer, come to the logical end of its computations. Or the stars in the night sky were the total sum of responsibilities, grievances, loves, of a certain nation listing to the end of empire. Or the stars in the night sky were an example of every possible color in the spectrum of all colors, but the beauty of this spectrum was so overwhelming that an unaided eye could no longer discern it. Or the stars in the night sky were the number of words required to correctly describe the stars as a whole. Or the stars in the night sky represented the number of times that a certain recalcitrant boy was reminded to observe the natural world around him. Or the stars in the night sky were ghosts of all the dead, known and unknown to this boy and others. Or the stars in the night sky were pocket lighters flicked on during the encore of the stadium rock show, back when there were still pocket lighters. Or the stars in the night sky were a painterly representation of the idea of insignificance. Or the stars in the night sky were the manifest eruption of something from nothing. Or the stars hinted at a conflagration happening on the other side of a wall of dark substances, through which these tiny holes had been poked. Or the stars in the night sky were a soup of possibility, a broth of what might have been and what might come to pass. The stars in the night sky were a grinding down of all the *mineralia* of planet Earth into infinitesimal grains, which grains were in turn bits of gas and debris cast off by the stars themselves. The stars in the night sky indicated the natural end of our twenty-four-hour day, and that was why they were greeted with such astonishment and relief—the turning away of the sun was both relief and impertinence. The stars in the night sky were the light show for the desert itself, a ratification of its disuse. The stars in the night sky could only be appreciated in silence. The stars in the night sky could only be experienced in motionlessness. The stars in the night sky had a cumulative effect, and the longer you looked at them, the more you wanted to, as if the stars were somehow addictive. The stars in the night sky *were* addictive, and when used improperly they crowded out other activities, particularly social activities, unless these social activities were organized around the night sky itself. The stars in the night sky cohered with certain harmonic principles, cycles per second, but they did not accord with musical principles that affirmed tonality, but, rather, a more random sequence of assonances and dissonances of such long duration that most human beings would perceive the musical principles of the stars in the sky as having a dull, endless sameness, a dissonant mercilessness. The stars in the night sky were prolix, show-offy, because they meant to make a mockery of mathematical ideas of infinity, just by being here. They were finite but limitless. The stars in the night sky had to be seen in the desert, and eventually the desert lured out all stargazers, even people who were busy with many other things, special education, identity theft, the making of low-budget pornography films, day-trading in Central Asian markets; they all found that when they saw the stars in the desert, they put aside childish things, and thus, in the desert there was the Very Large Array, and then the Very Very Very Large Array, and then there was the International Sonoran Array, which was so large that you had to *fly* from one end of the field of radio dishes to the other to bear witness to the entirety of the stargazing apparatus of the desert; whole cities sprang up inside the International Sonoran Array; it had its complex of universities and think tanks, mostly now concentrated on the *other* side of the border, since that was where the venture capital was located, where there was less fallout from the emigration problem. People came to the desert because the stars were in the desert, and the stars had yet to be corrupted by man, though man had managed to corrupt so much else, and there was no fee involved. In fact, the stars, it seemed, would crush man in a scenic, gravitational panorama before man would ever corrupt the stars, and that was why man mostly neglected them, or attempted to surpass the stars, gauzing over the night sky with his sugary glaze, in the pursuit of making the night sky less seductive and more like the screen of a monitor switched to the off position.

The *omnium gatherum,* because of its interest in the primeval, staked a claim to the night sky. Here in the desert. People went over the mountain pass to the great emptiness beyond, west of Rio Blanco, and they abandoned their cars and their bikes by the national forest, which was no kind of forest at all, but just a long stretch of saguaros and cholla. And they walked a mile or two into the Valley of the Slaughtered Calf for the night sky, and for the particular entertainment of that night, which was the *Apotheosis of the Arm.* Volunteers had roped off a portion of the valley, and the Bureau of Land Management, which was protective of local mining claims, became *suddenly,* on this night in the beginning of the cooler part of autumn, with the stars spilling into the sky, all but absent. They waived a number of permits. Unaccountably. There was a police cruiser or two at the front entrance of the Valley of the Slaughtered Calf, but no one could tell whether there was an officer of the peace resting within the cars or not, and so the disaffected streamed past, the disaffected, the forgotten, the homeless, the religious zealots, the disabled (in their motorized wheelchairs), the conspiracy theorists, the abused, the ambulatory masses who were hardly so huddled, they came to the Valley of the Slaughtered Calf because they believed that something unforeseen might take place here, or because, at the very least, they believed that they could dope themselves here, which was revolution for its own sake, and in doping themselves they wouldn't have to reconsider and revisit their misfortunes any longer. The fighter jets had lifted off at the air force base, and the sky had fallen into a certain portentous silence. The partygoers were wearing festive garb, when they were wearing garb, although it was mostly just the OxyPlus addicts from the local fraternities (those who had not yet failed) who willingly came naked, or in loincloths, wearing headbands and sunglasses but otherwise with their nether parts dangling in the penumbra, flailing as they began to dance, not even recognizing the not-at-all-tribal metronomic battery of *dead girlfriend* as it pummeled the public-address system, admixed with the recordings of the calls of the last remaining humpback whales, sounds of slot machines from the nearby reservation casinos, high-tension lines amplified. Their nakedness was dazzling to themselves, and what women were present would long for these fraternity men, at least in the masculine imagination this was the case, the imagination of those who didn't end up falling asleep or vomiting and passing out.

In the café downtown, meanwhile, Noelle and Morton spent half an hour discussing their greatest personal fears. Morton was the one to bring it up. He'd been reading an online advice column: how to have the healthiest relationship, and he'd paid for a download (charging it to Dr. Koo's credit card), *The Healthiest Relationship: Ten Preliminary Steps.* Here he'd learned many things. The contemporary man needed to make himself open and vulnerable, to reveal his innards for intimacy with patience and quiet confidence. And the way to make himself vulnerable, according to *The Healthiest Relationship,* by Deep Singh, PhD, was to talk about his greatest personal fears and his need for caring. Noelle was well aware that Morton, sipping chai latte, was *unsettling* to most of the patrons of the café, but never more so than when he said, audibly, "All my biggest personal fears, if I'm being honest, have to do with vivisection."

Noelle ventured, witlessly, "Why is that, do you think?"

An incredibly stupid thing to say, really, because, actually, she could never know what he'd lived through, the ordeal of serving as a medical experimental subject his entire life, from the first instant of his primate consciousness (as opposed to his recently awakened *human* consciousness). His whole life had been about having various electrodes affixed to him, or having pieces cut off, often without anesthetic, or having various things injected into him, illnesses cultured in petri dishes from places like Congo and

New Guinea. Morton had survived this only through good luck. From the moment he'd been weaned, this was what Morton had known. If, in his new consciousness, he didn't remember those early days, with their experimental regimens, he must have somewhere stored up their trauma.

"Isn't that what most people are afraid of, when you get right down to it? I mean, there are other kinds of bodily fears, hemorrhaging, having an aneurysm, losing an eye, impotence, infertility, but these are really just varieties of vivisection, right?"

Noelle said, "I don't really have any fear of vivisection. I mean, I guess I have a fear of tremendous physical *pain,* but that's almost a reflex, not a fear. Mammals recoil from physical pain, right?"

"Actually," Morton said, "mammals recoil from annihilation. From the foreknowledge of their deaths. Or that's my view. There are many animals that are willing to tolerate physical pain. Dogs, you know, are willing to endure pain in order to stay near to their masters; cats, willing to endure pain, just not fear. If they have a reasonable certainty of surviving the physical pain, mammals often show remarkable fortitude. It's only in the imminence of death that the flight mechanism overtakes. That's my experience, at any rate."

"Do you suppose the *arm* recoils from annihilation?" said Noelle, because she was frankly a little intimidated by Morton and was, in her anxiety, falling into the disagreeable habit of easy conversation, conversation that didn't probe into her own life.

Morton called out, slurping the last of the watery chai, "Waiter! Waiter!"

"He'll—"

Morton seemed to warm to the subject of the arm, Noelle supposed, though it was far from the *healthy relationship* on which he had intended to concentrate his attention, and this was something of a relief. "Look, the arm still possesses the muscle memory of its host. That's what you have to understand, Noelle. It knows how to do certain things without fail — grasping, strangling, all the hand-to-hand combat that was part of its host's military training."

"Its host?"

"Among those muscle memories, I'm guessing, is the instinct to avoid flame. Or frostbite. The arm will not walk directly into fire, and it will not pitch itself into a frigid lake—which probably isn't liable to happen out here right now." Morton giggled. "The arm, therefore, does have certain kinds of instinctual activities, just like some kind of lower insect or single-celled organism!"

"But—"

"And now back to your greatest personal fears! And remember, Noelle, that I sympathize. I really *feel* the kind of personal fear we're talking about here, I honestly do, perhaps more than any other time in my life. I want you to know just how important it is that you understand that I understand the kind of disquiet this sort of conversation brings up in a person when he or she—"

"Morton, you should really let me tell you *my* fears before you—"

She fell silent, concentrating for a moment on a smattering of crumbs that stippled Morton's hirsute chin. A cranberry scone had immediately preceded the conversation. He'd been attempting to master the paper napkin. He had rumpled it.

"Then please, be my guest."

In truth, Noelle kind of wanted to get away from him, because she found his attempts at seductive conversation laughable and foul. But it was the laughable qualities, at least for the moment, that made it hard to leave.

She mumbled, "I guess I should say that my biggest fear is being loved. And I don't know why I'm telling you that. But there it is. Some people's fears are the silliest ones of all."

The hiss of a distant cappuccino machine. Change rendered in all but worthless paper currency. Morton, who really was learning phenomenally quickly, gazed upon the woman he loved, or the woman he *said* he loved.

"That, Noelle, is among the saddest things I've heard anyone say in a while. And you know I would like to help you with it, and I know that you don't want me to help you with it. I expected you to say a *fear of heights,* or a *fear of rats,* or something more concrete, because that's what people do, I think. What they do is let out a little bit of the story, in order to throw off a friend or acquaintance. And then they keep the big, scary part of the tale hidden away. I've been developing a theory, you know, during the boring stretches of my imprisonment, and the theory is that *Homo sapiens sapiens* is the loneliest animal on all the planet. This is a bit ironic, because excepting certain kinds of insects and some bacteria, *Homo sapiens sapiens* has to be one of the commonest, if not *the* commonest animal species there is. He's always surrounded with cronies, coworkers, church acquaintances. And yet no matter what he does, he seems to be keeping the one admirable part of himself, his consciousness, away from all the other individuals of the species. Either he is unable to give of himself in such a way that his fellows can understand him, or else he is overburdening them so that they can only wish to avoid him. It's all the same in either case, *Homo sapiens sapiens* lives in a warehouse of solitude from which, if he's lucky, he watches the other people trudging past, and all the while he's wondering *why not me, why not me, why am I untouched by the tender fingers of civilization?*"

"Morton," Noelle said. "You know, I am moved, and it's not like I say that lightly or anything, but—"

"You're thinking that I am myself an example of the person who asks too much of his fellows, and when this is juxtaposed with my comical ugliness, why then I am just another example of the man who gets nothing, who spends weekend nights drinking himself into liver failure. You're feeling surges of pity for me that are mitigated only by your physical revulsion. But let me tell you, Noelle, things are different for me."

The robotic franchise service module, who had swept away Morton's empty mug earlier, with a I-have-seen-it-all-before look, brought back a fresh cup of the steaming beverage, and Morton grabbed at it ferociously.

"We really should be heading out to the valley."

"We're not heading out until I finish saying what I want to say! And you may not want to hear this, but I'm going to tell you anyway. Noelle, I know what I am. I know who I am and what I am. I have no illusions, and I have really only two purposes in this, my second act. My two purposes are: first, to tell the truth as I see it, no matter what it is, the *verismo* of my life, and, second, to love you, Noelle Stern, in such a way that I no longer have to possess you or saddle you with conditions at all, mental or physical. Those are my two purposes. It may seem to you as though you have a lot of responsibilities now, because of what I've just said, as if I'm going to expect something from you. But I want you to know that you have *no responsibilities,* and all you have to do is to take in a little bit of my love, when you are able, just so that maybe you can begin to overcome this fear of yours, the one that you've—"

"Morton, you know, most people, when they say things like this, they find later on that maybe they aren't sure it was the—"

"No, Noelle. Don't go telling me how I'm to grow out of this feeling, this feeling of usefulness that I have. Look at my biography, if you will. I am a man whose very death has been commuted. If I weren't talking right now, and wearing these boxer shorts and these sandals, I'd be just another chimp getting experimentally infected with Ebola and being force-fed an antibiotic-enriched milk shake by another workaholic who only cares about his grant applications. Every day is free for me now, Noelle, and even if there is no freedom for me in this economy, even if it is my future to sweep up after the robotic service module in some café somewhere, at least after the talk show hosts are no longer interested in me, I am still better off than I ever was. I have a purpose, and I understand my purpose, and this makes me a better person than I was before. It gives my life meaning. You can't talk me out of what I believe. In fact, your reaction isn't really relevant. And now we'd better pay."

"The way everyone has been staring, they should be paying us."

But Morton, oblivious, slid from the seat onto the sawdusted floor, refolded his paper napkin, and, reaching up, set it on the table, after which he gave the robotic franchise service module a grin and slapped it percussively on the back. "Maybe something better," he said to that plastic encasement of silicon chips, "is just around the corner."

The vogue for jet packs, Noelle told Morton in the van on the way over the mountain pass, dated back about ten years. She was trying to change the subject; she was trying hard, wondering why she had agreed to drive Morton out here, and why Koo had allowed him to go, excepting the fact that at the *omnium gatherum* no one would give him a second look. And she realized he'd never seen a jet pack, but in online reports and infomercials. She told him: once the traffic problem got to where you could be parked on Sixth Street in Rio Blanco for an hour, trying to get to the interstate, having a leisurely conversation with the people in the vehicles fore and aft, the automobile became no longer the engine of the national economy. Although what truly put an end to Detroit, to a business sector that had been rescued by the government twice in the past twenty years, was the depletion of the Middle Eastern petroleum supply. Old-time fuel became astronomically expensive. Even the electric-cell cars were pretty expensive, since they required a generating plant somewhere in the supply chain. Electric cars, Noelle was saying, also became more expensive than most people could afford, and those little death contraptions only went so far on a charge and could be totaled at five miles an hour, and still there was a lot of traffic, and so people just started moving toward the idea of the jet pack. If you couldn't get through the traffic, why not go *over* it?

At first, it was just hobbyists. Guys in Hawaiian-print shirts in backyards, swilling cough syrup, monkeying with lawn mower engines. So many of these hobbyists were lost in the pursuit of the dream, she told Morton. They'd lift off above the subdivision, jet a couple hundred yards, and then lose control, dropping into a grove of cholla. The Southwest was full of these stories. White guys who had nothing more going for them, Noelle told

Morton, than their jet packs. They couldn't get proper jobs, and their wives had left them. Kids loved these guys. Kids loved jet packs. Search and rescue would pluck one kid off Finger Rock, and another off Mount Lemon, and by the time they'd ferry these little ones to safety, there'd be another one stranded up there. The kids had altitude sickness too. No pressurized air with a jet pack, you know. They'd be throwing up everywhere when they arrived at the hospital.

"There's one there." She pointed. The chimpanzee looked out the window of the departmental van, and he saw what looked like a surface-to-air missile go horizontal, blazing over Rio Blanco Peak.

There were a lot of reservations, safety concerns, from an air traffic point of view, about the jet packs. In Rio Blanco, in the early years of the jet pack fad, six or seven guys got sucked into the backdraft of jet planes. Imagine, Noelle told Morton. You're in a window seat, and you're looking out through the double panes, and you see some guy in a jet pack, with a pair of goggles on, waving. The plane is coming in to land, and this unregulated jet pack enthusiast is gesturing at the plane, taking his hand off the throttle, as he tries to veer away, and then this guy is getting inhaled right into the back of the engine. The desert, the expanse of rose-tipped mountaintops, crimson cloud cover on the horizon, neglected citrus groves, all laid out before you, and then there's an explosion of food-processed human parts spraying out the back of the jet, down the side of the fuselage, onto the desert below.

Probably, this was why the jet pack designers were given notice that they were *not* to equip their jet packs with enough liftoff to get the machines over a hundred and fifty feet in altitude. Not much higher than the highest building in the vicinity. The same difficulties were being played out in all the cities of the West, cities designed for the automobile. Of course, there was a *green* aspect to the debate over the jet pack. It had to do with the kinds of fuel that were required. Any kind of natural gas, or petroleum-based product, or solid rocket fuel, that kind of stuff was just prohibitive, especially if all you were going to do was help some teenage kid get to the top of the Catalina range without having to hike.

It was the hydrogen reaction that really allowed the jet pack market to *take off,* and it was some old countercultural octogenarian in northern California who came up with the technical solution, the hydrogen-fueled jet pack. You didn't need that much in raw materials, and you were giving off eco-friendly exhaust—water, which is no problem in the desert. So what was the problem? The initial models cost in the hundreds of thousands of dollars, which made for a rental market, initially, but as always with this stuff, you know, prices came down, especially when the Sino-Indian conglomerates got involved in manufacture. Also, it was obvious that the jet pack was good for border jumping, for felonies great and small, and so law enforcement had to get jet packs too, and anyone living in rural *anywhere* had to get a jet pack, and if it weren't for the fact that most people just couldn't afford them, then probably everyone would have one.

It's sort of hypocritical, Noelle told Morton, the way that people in the *omnium gatherum,* who were supposed to be all back to the land and into inaugurating the new dark ages, all of that stuff, were completely obsessed with getting jet packs, because jet packs were the symbol of old outlaw culture. Like with old-fashioned motorcycles, jet packs were unsafe, they were dangerous, and they used up huge amounts of fuel. "Worth it?" Noelle asked Morton. "People can get anywhere they want now pretty fast, but it's once or twice a week that you'll see somebody fall out of the sky, like they've been picked off, and I guess some of them *have* been shot, or Tasered, and then the body parts just get flattened on one of the highways or service roads."

Perhaps their price was the best thing about them, Noelle continued, because it kept the jet packs out of the reach of the drunken and most careless segment of the population. The federal, state, and local regulations didn't work. What would be more attractive to rebels without causes, loaded to the tips of their dendrites on

OxyPlus or polyamphetamine, than the idea of flight? They were all would-be Icaruses, heading straight for the sun.

"And in a way, that's sort of what we're getting tonight. There are always all these different *mythemes,* you know, ideas, stories, colliding at any *omnium gatherum* event. It's supposed to be tribal, there's supposed to be dancing, but what there is instead is a bunch of middle-aged guys trying to loft themselves up over the desert at the same time, and although none of them *says* he wants to be the guy who goes the very highest, higher than all the other jet packs, it's like that anyway. There's always a competition among these guys who had a couple of good ideas about counterculture a million years ago and now all they have is liver damage, or they are on their third case of melanoma, and big patches of their face have been removed, and nobody wants to have anything to do with them, except at *omnium gatherum,* because there they can wear a *mask.* They can go on another thirty years like this."

"What does it have to do with—"

"And they're going to be the ones who launch *the arm.* They're going to put the arm into a jet pack and fire some missiles at it in order to incinerate it completely. They've got some kind of remote-controlled launch pad. And they're going to launch in the middle of some big pyrotechnical display. Or I guess that's the idea. Always with the fireworks. So juvenile."

Traffic on the mountain pass had come to a halt, and standing on the side of the road, looking ornery, looking as though they reeked with some immemorial death musk, were the javelinas. The sage and prickly pear growing there kept them fat and happy. It was as if the javelinas were *watching* the cars, waiting for the convoy to inch by so that they might resume ownership. Their tusks had a Holocene menace. They waited as the traffic over the pass snaked its way through a dozen or so switchbacks; they waited amid the encampments of migrants, the undocumented trying to make their way south to Nogales. They waited through the fellow travelers, middle-class kids wearing all the right footgear, the goggles, the highly reflective outerwear, all of them foaming at the mouth with whatever cocktail of medications they had managed to ingest. Noelle watched, too, as a helix of turkey vultures next appeared, in the last of the light, and began to swirl above the action, waiting for the mortality on those sandy shoulders to reveal itself.

"Our plan," Noelle said. "Let's see. Let's discuss our plan. Do you want to discuss our plan? Do we have one? Our plan is first for you to contact Dr. Koo, tell him that we're almost near the event site, and then our plan is to try to make contact with some higher-up types at the *omnium gatherum,* some of whom I know a tiny bit, like Denny Wheeler, and then we're going to try to get as near as we can to *the arm,* and somehow we're going to try to substitute another arm in its place. How's that sound?"

It was fair to say, she acknowledged, that she not only wasn't sure she could follow through on the plan, but she wasn't sure she wanted to. She believed in the *omnium gatherum,* if it was possible to believe in something that was so riddled with contradictions, something so earthly and finite, something so profligate, and if she occasionally had a few critical things to say about them, that was only in the spirit of loyal opposition. She didn't even know, really, what Koo wanted to do with the arm, in terms of his ongoing experiments. He said that it was important to secure the arm to keep it from spreading its menace across the populace, and especially in a big group like the *omnium gatherum,* but it was clear that this was not all he was after.

"You have an arm to substitute?"

"I do," said Noelle.

"Which you got where, exactly?"

"Anatomy classes at the medical center. They're disposing of those cadavers all the time. Dr. Koo has special privileges where cadavers are concerned, because he has an endowed chair, and if Dr. Koo needs an arm for an experiment he's doing, then no one is going to tell him he can't have an arm. So one of the anatomy classes..."

"They—"

"Cut the arm off especially for us. But we had to remove the finger ourselves."

"You removed the middle finger yourself."

"I know how to cut at the knuckle."

"What did you do with the finger?" Morton asked.

"It's in the rucksack with the arm. I guess I should throw it out somewhere. But you can't just throw a finger anywhere."

"I could do it for you, if you like."

"That's why I have the windows open. Well, plus, I don't believe in air-conditioning. Air-conditioning is when a nation becomes weak. Decadent. This arm is only a little decayed, though. That's the good news. From what I've heard about the contagious arm, it's more than a little decayed. You know, the hardest part of this whole thing was finding a wedding ring that would fit properly on the substitute arm's hand."

Maybe Morton had gone wistful and sentimental over the mention of a wedding ring. She couldn't be sure. Over the period of caring for Morton, she'd decided that postures and expressions that seemed precisely human didn't always mean what you thought. Sometimes chimpanzees pulled faces that seemed gentle, sympathetic, and then they tried to club you to the ground. Morton was probably just looking at the valley below them, nothing more, because now they had come to the saddle of the mountain pass. She swore you could see Venus on the lip of the night sky, because the sun's last few beams were disappearing behind the peaks in the west. And in front of them, in the broad expanse of the valley, was the answering light, the nation-state of *omnium gatherum*, which seemed to have erected instantly a fairground, or an amusement park, or a tent city, all these kinetic forms intent on proving that the sun revolved around the Earth.

"I got it at a pawnshop," Noelle said, "in case you were wondering. Were you wondering? Is there something wrong?"

"I'll get upset if I want to get upset," Morton said. "How many talking chimpanzees are there in the world? Wait, let me think about this for a second. The number is *not* zero, and it's not *two*.

That must mean that the number of talking chimpanzees is *one*. And I am that talking chimpanzee. I do what I want. Do you know that there are probably television talk show hosts, right now, who would want to hear whatever it was that I had to say? If I had some kind of...representative...If I had a representative, right now, she or he could book me on some kind of talk show, and they would ask me questions like did I favor bananas, that sort of thing, and I could demonstrate to them how I knew the basics of trigonometry, and I'd tell them my *higher power* was probably in my own image and not in man's image. They would think whatever I said on the subject was scintillating, earth-shattering. I have no problem. What is your problem?"

"I don't have—" she said.

"Is it my business alone if, upon hearing about a wedding ring, I can think only of how good I'd be for you?"

"Look, we have a lot we need to do. Let's not—"

"You've got an arm in a bag that you cut off a corpse in the hospital basement, and you found a wedding ring from some marriage that's gone bad because the people in the marriage didn't love each other as much as I love you, and you put that wedding ring on the severed arm, and somehow we're going to attempt to substitute this arm for the infected one, and you're doing all this for that butcher at the university. I don't understand why you—"

Morton's voice was getting more and more shrill, like a chimpanzee in the forest, in fact, and he was banging on the dashboard of the van, and as the windows were rolled down, there were people on foot listening and watching, an army of adherents of *omnium gatherum*. One guy mumbled, *Nice costume,* as they went past.

She said, "It's not for Koo that we're here."

"I'm here for *you*," he said, "so speak for yourself. Koo doesn't care about anyone but himself and his reputation in the medical community. Do you love him? Is he the one who's in the way of your having a fulfilling and maturing love relationship with me?

In *The Healthiest Relationship,* it says that the first rule of a maturing relationship is *correct concentration.* If there's someone else you're thinking about, some other person with whom you have unfinished business, then you're never going to commit to this relationship robustly and—"

"Quit it with that stuff," she said. "And Koo is not my type."

"That's what people always say. It's a truly lukewarm response."

"How would you know?" she said, as, at three miles an hour, she braked the car into another sequence of switchbacks down the far side of the pass.

"Because I read the book."

"I'll tell you the truth if you feel you are strong enough."

"Stronger than anyone you've met. I have to be. I'm the only one of me on Earth."

"Okay then," Noelle said. There was a slow unfolding of the story, and it coincided with the downward slope of the mountain, the story about how there *was* one night when Koo invited her for dinner, and she couldn't be sure, that night, if he wanted it to be a romantic dinner or just a dinner of friends who were colleagues. She even remembered the menu, which was nothing that a man would prepare. It was salmon in parchment with brussels sprouts and pickled green beans. Koo had to take a call at one point, and if she hadn't been a little paranoid to begin with, a little uncertain, she could have sworn that it was some kind of *official call,* like from a government agency or something, and so she went to get more wine, and to the bathroom, and next to the door to the bathroom, through the kitchen, was the hall that led to the garage, and Noelle just wasn't the sort of person who would ever *snoop,* she claimed, but on this occasion, she felt an inexorable pull toward private detection, because Koo was such a mystery. So she pushed open the door to the garage, which had all the usual neglected stuff in there, including an algae-fueled convertible, which she later learned was Jean-Paul's, and it was all surrounded by boxes and corrugated containers. Some gardening equipment. And then—she was sure Koo was still talking on the phone—she saw this freezer, this large horizontal freezer in the back of the garage. For some sneaky reason, she really wanted to know what it was. Not that she suspected anything terribly unusual.

"I went over to look at the freezer, and it's not like I didn't know that there was a risk that I'd get caught, you know. It's not that I didn't know that he could just come in at any moment and find me there. I sort of had the idea he would find me. But doing what? Looking at some cuts of beef? Looking at some brisket? I don't know how I knew what was going on, I mean, it's not the sort of thing that you expect to find hidden away in most people's garages. I guess you expect a Ping-Pong table or a gaming console. Paintball guns. I don't know. But somehow I knew, or had an idea there was something there, and so I went over to the freezer, and I learned that it was locked, and it *would* be locked, but it was like I had to find a way to spring it open somehow, in the couple of minutes remaining, if I even had that much time. And I was going around the exterior, looking for some kind of latch. Because it had to have a latch somewhere, right? Then I realized that the keypad on the exterior had a thumbprint scanner, and that was what I was fiddling with, trying to override, like a real idiot, when he came out into the garage."

"What was in it?" Morton asked. With a great urgency.

"I'm getting to that part. The thing I always remember, actually, is not finding out what was in the freezer. It was the look on his face when he saw me there. Maybe he had come into the garage to menace me, to fire me or threaten me, or to somehow scare me away from what I was doing, which was snooping. But once he was faced with me, it wasn't as easy as all that. The look on his face was all about the mixed feelings. The look he wore was irritation mixed up with concern, a kind of expression that I'd never seen on his face before. I'm not even sure I knew he was capable of looking this way, of having so much going on in him, and maybe, as his employee or coworker, I kind of tried to pretend he didn't have those kinds of feelings. He's a reserved guy, right?

"But maybe that night he felt a little bit like he was going to trust *me,* like he'd met someone he was going to trust a little bit, even if he didn't have that much confidence that anyone anywhere was so trustworthy. He had his son and he was raising his son, and there wasn't anyone else to do that for him, and he was running the lab, and he had all these people working for him, and what he didn't have time for was whatever went on with the human emotions, and that was what was happening in this weird expression, how maybe he'd felt something like hope, and then he found me in the garage, and then he knew he *wasn't* going to have that feeling. Which was why it was such a complicated look, because maybe it was about relief. Or that was what I guessed. In the moment. Before I realized that I was feeling pretty awful about sneaking around. He knew there were things that he had hoped he wouldn't have to tell me. But now he was going to have to tell me something, whether he wanted to or not. Whether I wanted him to tell me or not."

"And?"

"He said: 'That's my wife.'"

"His wife?"

"In the freezer."

"He had his wife in the freezer?"

"That's what he said. In a freezer in the garage. And he went on, very briefly, to explain that he had a special exemption from various regulatory agencies, whatever the regulatory agencies were — there are probably a number of agencies involved in regulating the interstate traffic in dead wives — and because of his special exemption, he had brought his deceased wife with him from Korea. And that she was in the freezer. Sometime back I guess he'd told me that his wife had died of some slow disease. Parkinson's? Mostly you don't die of Parkinson's. You die of the complications. Anyway, she died over in Korea, and then he brought her to the US with him. Most people think the whole cryogenic thing is just designed to separate people from their money, and I sure don't know too many people who looked into it enough to design their own freezer. But that's the kind of man Dr. Koo is. He built his own freezer, and his own locking mechanism, with a thumbprint-recognition device on it, in order to house his wife, who has been frozen in there, in the garage, for however many years. I guess if you're not going to do anything with your dead wife, if you're not going to, you know, have sex with her, you can keep her in the garage for a pretty long time."

There was a look of uncomplicated terror on Morton's face, a look that indicated that Morton had not yet acquired the necessary finesse for this sort of revelatory exchange.

"Does it have anything to do with me?"

"Does what?" Noelle said.

"The doctor's frozen wife. Do I have anything to do with the frozen body of his wife and the kinds of experiments that he is conducting..."

It was a question that Noelle had thought about but hadn't yet exhausted. And she would have addressed it further if the two of them had not, at that moment, arrived at the gate, such as it was. The gate to the Valley of the Slaughtered Calf, west of the city of Rio Blanco. To which all regional pilgrimages led. The site of the *Apotheosis of the Arm.* The gate, such as it was, consisted of a couple of police cruisers, as indicated previously, lights lazily turning on their roofs. And there was a young woman wearing nothing but reflective tape over the formerly controversial parts of her body, collecting tickets and shining a flashlight into the drivers' windows of passing vehicles, asking the drivers if they were here for *omnium gatherum* and, if not, didn't they want to turn around and head back into town, because there was liable to be a rather enormous traffic snarl ahead. Scooters, pedestrians, motorbikes, downed jet packs, and so on. The activity here would make it impossible to pass *through* the Valley of the Slaughtered Calf and make it out to the west, on the road that led to Southern California.

At once, with the admissions-related conversation transacted, Noelle and Morton found themselves in a different nation, a nation of the fanciful and pointless, where there were streamers, and people on stilts, and a great number of naked middle-aged men with sagging and woebegone scrota wobbly beneath them, a nation of golf carts kitted out like sharks or whales or pirate ships, a nation of handmade signs proclaiming the local Belly Dancers Union, or classes in abstruse varieties of kundalini, unlock your animal unconsciousness, or give yourself the gift of colonic irrigation. How was it there was no proper transition between that world and this, through a cave, behind a waterfall, into a wardrobe? In Rio Blanco, where there wasn't an economic model for the miraculous, Noelle supposed, there was nothing to do but go over the mountain pass and down a few switchbacks, and here it was, the kind of *elsewhere* that is considered not-yet-exploited by local miners, the kind of elsewhere that can furnish a miracle, if by miraculous you mean a platoon of Catholic schoolgirls, or someone giving a lecture on shamanic strategies, or a band of serenading minstrels wearing clown makeup, or a Singing Bowl Ensemble, lucid dreamers, players of the jaw harp. It was a city of alternative therapies and cultures sitting idly by, awaiting word from the planning commission of the whimsical.

Morton was mumbling to himself, or rather making a variety of non- or preverbal grunts and squeaks that Noelle presumed meant more in the chimpanzee argot than in the human tongue, as their URB van was subsumed into the swelling and eddying of drug-addled countercultural citizens. Someone was crying out, "Burn your ID! Burn your ID!" and Noelle watched in quiet admiration as a complement of those from nearby did pull out driver's licenses and credit cards, even entire wallets, lofting them onto a bonfire near the gate. Meanwhile, as in some medieval square, a rival group of miscreants was erecting a sculpture, or so it seemed, just beyond the police cars by the gate, and this sculpture was studded with nails and screws and bits of glass designed to cause a flat tire in any attempt by the state and local authorities to drive onto the central plain of the festival itself.

Part of the layout of the *omnium gatherum* was fractal: there was no sector that was any more vital or less important than the whole, so that there was no center, no organizing principle. With this in mind, Noelle and Morton couldn't locate any central staging area at all. Things were often miles upon miles farther off than they appeared, and here appearances were obscured by waves of pyrotechnical displays, rockets and fireworks flaming this way and that. There *was* a staging area somewhere, where the jet packs were attached to a plywood framework, in the middle of which, Noelle guessed, they would place the arm when the time came. It was just a matter of stumbling on it by, more or less, heading away.

Where did people get all the money for this shit, or was it just the case that somewhere out there was a kid, in the neighborhood, who'd learned that the raw materials for backyard explosives were easily come by, especially on the family farm; this kid who was onto the specific variety of fertilizers and ethanols and oxygen tanks that would launch just about anything into the air? When a temporary cloud of these explosions dissipated and the canopy of stars connecting all the summits of the mountains again appeared, Noelle and Morton, who were parking the car somewhere, nowhere, could see, lit in haphazard flashlights, maybe a half mile hence, the circle of homemade rocket launchers.

"That really looks like a real chimpanzee," someone said, moving past.

Noelle's embarrassing anxiety was that she resembled nothing so much as an undercover policewoman. The *omnium gatherum* had long known that all its events were infiltrated by the constabulary, and revolutionaries disputed the best way to recognize them. Would they be dressed rather obviously like police attempting to pass? Would they look too *clean?* Or would they go overboard and wear elaborate costumes, ones that failed to have a handmade dimension? Noelle, as they walked along, almost unconsciously began making pigtails at the top of her head, pigtails that would look, she hoped, like antennae, and though Morton was talking to her, was asking questions about how all of this was *possible,* she wasn't paying attention, but was thinking: *that one is kinda cute, that one has a nice outfit, that one is probably a rapist,* while attempting to get her hair up on top of her head. And when her hair was up on the top of her head, looking, she hoped, *cute* in a kind of Venusian way, she pulled the blouse she had worn to work that morning from her body, just pulled it right off, buttons snapping everywhere, and then shredded it into long shreds by biting into one end and yanking. From these strips she made a headband for Morton and one for herself, and now she was a woman wearing sandals, denim cutoff shorts, and a black bra, partially obscured by the straps of the rucksack (with the extra arm in it), and some kind of strange, shredded headband. She was a woman who looked as if she were about to metamorphose into something else, into a nomad, not really a woman who was one with the fashion aesthetics of the *omnium gatherum,* but this outfit would have to do unless she felt like taking *off* her bra, which she didn't really want to do, because Morton was looking at her like she was nothing but a receiving agent for chimpanzee spermatazoa. She didn't want him to get lost in the mayhem of the event, but she didn't want him to feel like this was their *omnium gatherum* assignation either. She should have sent him into the tent marked Men's Erotic Massage back a ways and left him there, until she figured out what was what.

By chance, an axial road appeared before them — really just a set of tracks where some semi had driven, perhaps indicating a route toward the staging area, and she pointed at it, and they set off as expeditiously as they could in that direction. The traffic closed around them, unicyclists, a woman holding leashes to dozens of Chihuahuas. Noelle attempted to tell Morton why they were heading toward the center, shouting above some of the chanting and the various homemade musical instruments (the *zenexton,* a gigantic rolling pipe organ manufactured with PVC tubing, e.g.), shouting about the Wheelers, father and son, about how they had to rotate addresses every four or five hours in the days before the events, and then once the events were convened, they moved from tent to tent every hour, wearing disguises.

Morton called to her, "The arm is going to find this kind of commotion very disturbing! Too much activity!"

Noelle replied, "We could just go to the security tent, and I could ask for an audience with Denny Wheeler."

This was a start, Noelle believed. They had only a few hours in which to locate the arm in this crowd of tens of thousands. They had to begin somewhere. And this is exactly what they would have done if a group of men dressed in the costumes of Mexican wrestlers, which is to say in hand-sewn tights and capes, had not, at the moment, borne down upon Morton, as though they'd expected him to be there all along, as if his appearance were by appointment, and grabbed the chimpanzee under the arms and, before Noelle had a chance to say a word, carried him off, writhing over their heads, into the crowd. By the time she saw what was happening, by the time the chimpnapping registered, Morton was screaming and gesticulating to her, in the midst of being handcuffed to the roof of a microbus tricked out like a dragon, moving off into the hordes.

The loneliness of large crowds has been voluminously covered in the literature and poetry of the twenty-first century, so let us no more speak of it, instead noting that the *omnium gatherum* actually had a singles night that it offered at one of the bars on Fourth Avenue, during high summer months when no official events were scheduled. And what bar could be better than the establishment called the Surly Wench? When there seemed to be precious little *omnium,* just *gatherum,* when men, mostly men, wandered in the crowd, mumbling to themselves, gazing on the partially naked or mostly naked twenty-one-year-olds as though these were the phlogiston required for their own internal combustion, then you needed the Surly Wench and polyamphetamine with absinthe chaser, the kind of intoxication in which these men couldn't tell the sky from a paper cup. Then you could beat back the very loneliness that Noelle felt, coming to these events without a companion, the loneliness you felt when your only friend, the friend that you brought along, the friend you apparently took for *granted,* is carried away by a group of Mexican professional wrestlers. In this loneliness, you naturally found yourself in a group of elderly women wearing candy striper outfits who were volunteering to treat sunburn, scratches, mild sprains, contusions, and other celebration-related medical problems. They kept calling out, these elderly women, "Registered nurses!" And holding up signs.

"Did you see that?" Noelle shouted to one of the women, in the thick of the lonely crowd.

"See what, honey?"

"They just carried off my friend."

"Honey, if you have a minor scrape, I could help you with that."

The candy striper held up a jar containing a yellow-green fluorescence that was probably a topical anti-infective. This was supposed to be inviting to the people who had minor scrapes. But as a line began to form in front of the candy stripers (each with her toothless grin), Noelle looked into the faces of those assembling and what she thought she saw everywhere was a *fever.* Was it her imagination? Was she imagining a pandemic, in which every human had an infection? Mercurochrome was *not* going to do the trick.

"They carried off my friend into the crowd. I mean, I know that there aren't supposed to be any police here or anything, but they carried him off. And he isn't really equipped to take care of himself."

"Most of those kinds of problems, honey, get solved quietly *within the community.* I'm sure the wrestlers just meant it in good fun. The group will take care of it, though you never can tell how long that's going to take, because the community has its own time frame for these things."

Had Noelle said anything about the wrestlers? She was sure she had not.

"What's your symptom?" the candy striper asked.

"My symptom?" Noelle said. "I read into whatever is happening around me and I imagine that it all has something to do with my life, even the big sociopolitical stuff—"

A rail-thin young guy with long unwashed hair that had a blue streak stuck out his tongue and pronounced a brace of vowels.

"You didn't have any contact with a severed arm today," Noelle said to the kid, "did you?"

"A severed arm?"

"Yeah, you didn't see any kind of severed arm? Or did you hear about it?"

"You mean like the kind of arm that they're going to...I thought that was all——"

"One of your friends, or maybe a friend of a friend say anything to you about keeping company with that kind of arm?"

The boy's blank stare was no indication of anything. It was as if he heard the words, but he didn't understand the necessity of response. The best he could do was repeat the phrase exactly, which he tried before saying:

"I don't know what you're talking about."

"No, I guess you don't." To the candy striper, she added, "How about you? Anyone in here talking about an arm?"

"Only the ones that are still attached to their bodies," said the candy striper.

"Well, you really ought to start wearing surgical gloves, if you ask me, and I work in the field. Don't touch any wounds, and if you see anyone who has a hemorrhagic complaint—you know what *hemorrhagic* means?"

"I was cleaning up after outbreaks of typhoid in Africa when your mother was in diapers," the candy striper said, and her professional smile faded.

"Then you know that sometimes the first responders go down with a serious infection. There *is* a serious infection going around, and that's all I'm saying about it."

"Honey, go look after your friend, see if you can't find him. I'll look after the sick kids with my friends here."

The crowd did seem to push in a southerly direction, the crowd in which Noelle next found herself, and the candy stripers were going north, and while the conversation in question was taking place, its participants were being pushed farther away from one another, and Noelle was growing more and more distant from the skeptical candy striper.

The nurses were followed, in close proximity, by the Mars Mission Skepticism Society. For some reason, there were a lot of canes, crutches, and walkers among the Mars mission skeptics. Their designated spokesman was shouting into a bullhorn about how the mission had been fabricated in order to distract citizens of NAFTA from the grave economic problems that faced them, that faced all of the Western democracies. But at least the Mars Mission Skepticism Society was articulate, which was a quality strangely lacking in *omnium gatherum* participants, whether they were educated in the lackluster public schools or at the voucher-only elhi schools, or homeschooled. "Simulacrum!" the barker pronounced. "Cultural hoax! Join us as we explore the theoretical foundations of space fraud! Your tax dollars buy you a group of drug addicts being filmed in polyurethane outfits in this very desert! And why? In order to persuade the Sino-Indian Economic Compact to spend thousands of billions of dollars on a space race that will bankrupt their economies! Long live the Sino-Indian Compact! The Mars mission is a tool of NAFTA intelligence agents! It has no purpose but to distract!"

Whenever the disabled skeptics bumped into someone, as they seemed to do with great regularity, they apologized profusely, as if, for all their doubts about space exploration and international relations, they were nonetheless polite. These were the kinds of people, Noelle supposed, who went on the occasional killing spree, but when they did so, they were always careful to apologize to the victims before dismembering them, saying it could not be helped, and when they surrendered to police, they pointed out that they never meant to harm anyone at all. With this in mind, she said to one of the skeptics, a bald guy with really thick glasses and an incompletely grown-in mustache, "Say, you guys haven't heard anything about where they're storing the arm for the launch tonight, have you? Have you heard anyone talking about the arm?"

"The arm is just a bunch of bullshit," the bald guy replied

without hesitation. "There's no arm, because there was no Mars mission. And if you want to know the truth, the whole *omnium gatherum* is being staffed and underwritten by the air force base across town. We're here at great risk to our persons and our property, and we only do it in order to get the message out to the people."

"It's funny you say that, because I happen to know some folks who have actually made contact with the arm—"

"Everyone says that they know someone personally who has had contact with the arm. But where is that person, right? The person who had contact? Can you deliver that person to me now to give me this so-called firsthand account?"

"What about a talking chimpanzee, have you seen a talking chimpanzee in the last twenty minutes or so? Coming by this way?"

But he was back on the bullhorn almost instantly, sloganeering, and again Noelle found herself being pushed southerly, toward the part of the desert that was given over to a reconstruction of an old Western village, a stage set that had been used in various Hollywood genre pictures, back in the day. Old Rio Blanco, it was called. It was a simulation of a simulation—a re-creation of a Hollywood stage set that had once re-created Rio Blanco, or so said the local advertisements and tattered billboards. Unfortunately, no one, any longer, had a clear memory of the history of Rio Blanco. There was some appropriateness to the *omnium gatherum* electing to situate its events out here, in the Valley of the Slaughtered Calf, the valley of the simulation of the simulation, through which one labored to reach *the truth* but found instead that doubt and the misappropriation (of things from their sources) ruled the day. The fringes of the event would naturally end up in Old Rio Blanco, therefore. And then there would be some sort of shoot-out. Because what else could there be.

Despite the very large numbers of attendants at the *omnium gatherum* events, you soon found that you were seeing the same people over and over again, and sometimes even seeing them in the same sequence, and in no place was this more likely than at the village of lightweight portable human waste vacuum-containment systems, through which Noelle would have to travel, this allée of waste disposal, if she was going to end up in Old Rio Blanco. She had no choice but to encounter the large groups of people she didn't want to think about in relation to waste production, here among the individual modules that were arrayed in a wide V-shaped formation outward from the gate, so as to take care of the waste needs of the largest number of *omnium gatherum* attendants. Whether you liked it or not, no outlay of capital manpower was more significant to the community than that invested in waste collection, and the organizers, or the volunteers, or the organizers *and* the volunteers, were forever coming up with more arcane and more fervent rules to organize the collection of waste, especially in order to spare the desert floor the kinds of gray water that might, for example, wipe out the last of the desert tortoises. It had happened in the past, large-scale uremic pollution, and the *omnium gatherum* had found that this didn't go over well with neighbors, human and nonhuman. And so they had purchased the latest in waste-collection devices, the American-made vacuum-containment systems, which were widely used by the government in its tent communities at the borders. Vacuum-containment systems, by coincidence, had also been used on the Mars mission, if you were naive enough to believe in the Mars mission. "Look!" the government seemed to cry. "We have vacuum technology, including funnels for the ladies, that will make waste removal far easier than it has ever been before. What other nation could bring you a waste-containment system that leaves no residue behind, and which ultimately produces a solid peat-like fertilizer free of bacterial agents that can be used on any home or industrial garden!"

Yes, there was something humiliating about the waste-containment systems, Noelle thought, and generally she avoided food and water before *omnium gatherum* events in an attempt to steer clear of the V-shaped bank of vacuum-containment modules. However, she'd noticed that it was precisely when you believed you wouldn't have to relieve yourself that you found you needed to do exactly that, and, also, that if there was someone you didn't want to run into, someone with whom you did not want, at all, to share a conversation of several minutes while wreathed in the earthy perfume of such places, you would *definitely* run into that person. The opportunity for humbling always lay right around the corner, and its perfume was cloacal.

And so this was where she ran into her coworker Larry. He was wearing a purple feather boa, and some cutoff shorts dyed black, and she could tell, almost instantly, that he was on some kind of hallucinogen, because in the half-light of the lamps by the vacuum-containment modules, she could see his monstrously dilated pupils. Moreover, when she spoke to him, there was a long delay in his reply, as if a great number of gears, and the little gnomes who turned these gears, had to be put into play for him to come up with the polite response. It seemed, at first, that he didn't even recognize her, and they had to go around and around with the introductions.

"It's me, Noelle. Your coworker. You see me every day?"

"I do?...Oh...hey...Noelle!"

"At the lab! I can't believe you—"

"Noelle?" he said, as if testing out the syllables. "Noelle?"

"What are you doing here?"

"Noelle, that's a woman I work with—"

She couldn't figure out, at first, if this was an attempt at humor.

"—a big *omnium gatherum* person. I decided to come have a look."

"Met anyone? Interesting, I mean. Talked to anyone?"

"Talked?"

"To anyone."

"Oh, right. Yeah. I..."

"Listen, Larry, I'm wondering if it would be okay for me to change the subject and—"

"Did we have...a subject?"

"I guess we didn't, really. The thing is, Larry, I brought Morton out here, according to Dr. Koo's instructions, because we thought he'd be effective undercover, and he was just carried off."

"Morton was..."

"Carried off."

"Morton, the..."

"Chimpanzee."

"Oh! Talking chimpanzee. Bad frigging temper."

"These guys in wrestling costumes came by, and it was like they already knew who he was, and it was like they hog-tied him, and before I could even figure out what to do, he was carried off."

"Excuse me for a second, Noelle." Because one of the vacuum-containment privacy modules had opened up, and when opportunity presented itself, one had to grab it. The little privacy station seemed to belch forth a customer, a relieved customer, in this case a youngster, one of those tweenagers who went by the designation *board rat,* for the fact that he was basically surgically attached to a motorized board and had, moreover, brought the board with him into the privacy module, as if it were the board that needed to be evacuated. This *board rat* slunk out of the privacy module as though he didn't want anyone to notice him and his stringy figure-eight earlobes, and indeed Larry didn't notice him. Larry noticed only the open door, where he saw his salvation. "I'll be right out," he called over his shoulder, but Noelle knew that he wouldn't be right out. He would be in there, in the vacuum-containment privacy module, for as long as it took for her to move on. The feather boa just wasn't the kind of personal expression that Larry wanted to share, and he would stay in there, checking through the little two-way mirror, for as long as it took. Some parts of us (Noelle hoped to jot this down in her journal) were really only available to strangers. Should she wait? Should she go?

While she deliberated, the most demoralizing quadrant of the Valley of the Slaughtered Calf, a small group of *gunslingers* dressed in some of the props of the old American West, dashed into the V-shaped concatenation of privacy modules and began firing off their Tasers. No doubt they were heading for Old Rio Blanco, with the aim of obliterating some blotch of sunburned guys playing the roles of the Tohono O'odham or the Hopi, and it would all be very simulated and very childish, this reenactment of how the genocide was won, but it would be a fine prolegomenon for the explosive displays of the later evening.

There was such a fixation on Tasers at *omnium gatherum.* A number of kids had been Tasered at the last event, and when you bought your ticket through whatever rapacious Sino-Indian ticketing consortium furnished the tickets for *omnium gatherum* events, you signed an online agreement that indicated that you accepted the possibility of having a Taser or other nonlethal firearm turned on you. There was one kid, people said, who'd brought it on himself, because he was spouting some kind of pro-capitalist fulmination — *the banks were right that it is this kind of thing that has dragged down the country so that it is no longer able to package complex financial instruments on the world capital markets!* — shouting, shouting, shouting, and the guys with the Tasers, because it was always *guys* with Tasers, took it on themselves to render this kid prone. Unfortunately, it was a number of guys who all got the idea at roughly the same time, and the kid went down like the proverbial sack of Mexican taters, and there was a sort of mini-stampede of partygoers trying to flee the violence. After that, people with weapons were specifically asked to go to the Old Rio Blanco simulation arena, where there was a tent, more of a yurt, really, erected to minister to those with Taser burns or arrhythmias.

While Noelle watched, this posse of outlaws with Tasers turned their firepower on one of the privacy modules, where some poor sufferer of irritable bowel syndrome or similar ailment was just trying to get the problem behind him so he could go on to be entertained by floats and madness. This poor individual was not expecting at that moment to be subjected to neuromuscular incapacitation. But these guys were Tasering the outside of the privacy module, and if the poor sufferer touched any of the walls inside the module, he was getting a pretty intense charge right about now, perhaps even a *drive stun* charge, which is the setting that effects *pain compliance,* and sure enough, there was some screaming, and the door fell open, and out tumbled...a guy in a Mexican wrestling costume.

The Taser vigilantes fell on the Mexican wrestler almost immediately. They blasted away. If he'd been a piece of pork heavily infected with trichinosis, he'd have been rendered completely fit for human consumption, so overwhelming was the concentration of Taser power. In this instance, he certainly cohered with the *DSM-VIII*'s definition of *excited delirium,* in that he was in a known drug location, fraternizing with known purveyors of drugs, probably taking OxyPlus or polyamphetamines, and was an aficionado of Mexican wrestling—all of which added up to a much higher likelihood of ventricular fibrillation in the aftermath of Taser discharge.

"Hey, wait," Noelle called out generally. "Do you know him? The guy in the costume? You know him?"

Everybody was wearing a costume. Easily half the people in the line for the privacy modules, and all the passersby heading to and fro, turned to respond to Noelle. But one of the pistoleros, the one with the eye patch, registered that there had been an inquiry, and he said, "Our thing tonight is that we're chasing the Mexican wrestlers."

"Do you know where they are?"

"What?"

"They abducted my friend. Morton is his name."

The pistolero turned to his associates. "You guys, this lady says that the wrestlers kidnapped her friend."

Protestations of outrage ensued, *we'll get 'em, we'll shoot them all down, there's no excuse for these Central American entertainments,* and so on. Without giving Noelle much to go on, they all headed off at a trot (without actual horses) in the direction of the Old Rio Blanco stage set. The only felicitous development, right then, besides the fact that she no longer had to wait for Larry to finish in the privacy module, was to be found in the small army of voyeurs who were following the pistoleros at some remove, just for the sheer drama, some of them on bicycles and motorized skateboards. Above, a few jet packs. Noelle accepted an offer from a pair of twins who were riding a tandem bicycle. She rode in between, sidesaddle. And the greater distances of the desert—which on foot were un-navigable—became manageable, and soon they were heading into the swirling clouds of stampeding vigilantes. All of the *omnium gatherum* seemed to head off with them, like stars in an endlessly expanding firmament.

The rucksack that had the replacement arm had grown heavier and heavier in the time that Noelle had been carrying it alone, and this despite the fact that she realized she'd lost any number of other personal possessions. Her outfit was down to the bra (the shirt was a self-inflicted loss, but still), sandals, ripped shorts. The elastics had fallen out of her pigtails, and her headband had fallen off, and her hair was windswept, and her skin sandblasted, and she'd become another one of the desert rats in this pursuit of the arm. A dozen miles from the nearest shower.

The lights were extinguished in Old Rio Blanco, though it wasn't quite yet the official blackout hour, and it occurred to her to wonder if, in the Old West, they'd confined their shoot-outs to daylight the better to see the targets, because if there were just gas lamps or candles back then, a lot of innocent bystanders were going to get filled full of holes, or, in this modern setting, were going to get laid out with neuromuscular incapacitation. Nevertheless, the stampede of freethinkers pulled up at the darkened burg of Old Rio Blanco, uncertain about how to gain admission what with the dark. Weren't the lights *always on* in order to bilk any tourists who still came out this way? Noelle imagined that the Wheeler family would have settled this question beforehand, the question of Old Rio Blanco, and she was laden with an uncanny feeling, this feeling that there was something deeply wrong, that the *omnium gatherum* had been left too much to its own devices, as though it were the autistic progeny of contemporary American culture now released to do whatever it liked, to dash out its brains if it saw fit.

The buildings were all stage sets, yes, which meant they had only the front side. But in the moonlight the front side of every-thing looked ominous and forgotten, as though it had all been abandoned, as though the *idea* of simulation had been abandoned in favor of neglect. And yet the pistoleros entered that municipal-ity with the kinds of whoops of mayhem that probably the bad guys had avoided back when Rio Blanco was a genuine outpost of the homesteaders, ringed on every side by restive native popula-tions. The whoops were a cinematic invention, but in this case they effected the desired result.

The desired result was: that a veritable army of Native Americans, real or simulated Native Americans, and their Mexican wrestler compadres, appeared from nowhere, from out of the en-veloping darkness, and beset the pistoleros. And then there was a whole lot of Tasering. It was hard to make out, in fact, who was holding what weapon and who was falling to the ground with neuromuscular incapacitation. The laughing and the cries of rec-ognition and hilarity, they made it pretty difficult to sort out, and the farther that Noelle moved toward the framed-up simulations of Old Rio Blanco's sets, the more confused and disoriented she seemed to become, spatially, emotionally, physically. Out of breath, uncertain about which direction was *out,* Noelle sat down on the front step of what appeared to be yet another filmic saloon. The windows were painted with fake lamplight—this she knew from a prior visit—but in the dark, these murals were just so much wood and plaster and nails. After watching some more young men race around shooting at one another, after watching the Native Americans overturn the historical record—so that almost all the cowboys, all the vigilantes, lay quivering on the dusty main street of Old Rio Blanco—Noelle realized that there was another bystander, another witness, sitting just down the step from her. One of the fraternity of Mexican wrestlers. He was outfitted, in fact, in red, white, and blue, with a cape, with a mask, with some fancy shoes that resembled the kind of flippers that he might have employed in a neighbor's swimming pool. If she could have read dejected in the half-light, she would have said he was *dejected,* and whatever was his motivation, he had found that it was long since unaccomplished.

"Are you with the wrestlers?" she asked.

He replied, "I was just wearing the outfit, and then, somehow, I learned that you can't just wear a wrestling outfit."

"It was a coordinated thing?"

"I think maybe we just all got here, dressed as wrestlers, and that gave us some kind of, you know, group identity. Suddenly, we all had to subdue a lot of people with fancy holds."

"You see a chimpanzee come through here with the others?"

"Excuse me?"

"A chimpanzee."

A pause.

"That wasn't a chimpanzee; that was a man in a chimpanzee suit."

"How many chimpanzees are there liable to be in these parts?"

"I guess there could be plenty of chimpanzees," the wrestler said, and he stood, and he moved along the step on which they sat, closer to Noelle. "But I've only seen one tonight."

"Does he talk?"

"Can't shut him up."

"That'd be my friend."

"Says he knows people at the college there, says he's got all kinds of lawyers, says he's going to have these lawyers press charges, says we'll have to cover his legal fees. He talks so much that eventually you just kind of think he's full of shit."

Noelle asked the wrestler if he wanted some protein caplets, which was all she had left in the rucksack with the arm, the caplets the youngsters liked to take in lieu of proper meals. The phial of caplets was dusty but intact.

"Don't mind if I do," the wrestler said.

"Do you think maybe you could let me see Morton?"

"Don't know if the other guys are going to like that. Especially now that we busted down the cowboys and we have control of the area."

Noelle said, "I have some stuff I need to do with Morton before they burn the arm, or shoot the arm off into space, or whatever they are going to do with it. Morton and I have responsibilities."

"Which arm?"

"Is there more than one arm?"

"Oh, the arm! We found the arm too. We find things and pick them up, and then we bring them all back here, to the warehouse."

The wrestler stood, as if the protein caplets had given him enough energy to move, and while he was talking now, he was walking into the night, past the slumbering bodies, away. "You go in by the apothecary; there's a door. That was the *green room,* you know. When they were using Old Rio Blanco for the movies, or whatever they used it for. Even the most fake stuff has to have some kind of moment when it's totally *real,* that's the thing, and the apothecary has the one real spot in town here. It's like an actual interior space. Or at least it's the only part I know that's real. Maybe there's some other real part that I just don't know about. So you should try over by the apothecary; that's our house of representatives, where we gather for periodic encounter sessions to discuss how the crusade is going, whether we need better planned coordination, stuff like that. So you go on over there, and they have the mascot, and they're trying, I think, to get him to take off the boxer shorts, or anyway that's what they told me. They have a clown costume for him. The story is that they were going to put the clown costume on a dwarf who was going to come along for a fee. It's not a festival if you don't have a proper dwarf. Anyway, they're trying to get your friend to wear the clown costume, and he doesn't want to do it, but they are threatening him with the arm."

Or at least she thought that was the end of this incredibly revealing speech, but now she wasn't sure that the protein caplets she'd given him were really protein caplets at all, but maybe they were some kind of peyote distillate or something, because she was feeling a little bit unsteady herself. Had she taken one when she'd given them to the wrestler? Things were kind of swimming, and there was a lot of haloing around the flashlights that glimmered from various spots in Old Rio Blanco, which meant, she guessed, that there were *snipers* out there, and she needed to walk as quietly as possible through town, to the apothecary, despite her neurological or psychedelic or psychotic symptoms.

Unless she was sick with whatever it was that the arm had. Unless this was the death march, some kind of middle-class, white, countercultural version of the death march, in which you walked by a lot of bodies in prone position. The apothecary got closer without ever quite moving into reach, just as Noelle's conspiratorial reasoning — which she'd kept in check earlier in the day — rose up from the background noise of her psychosis and began urging on her the possibility that actually the Mexican wrestlers were government agents of some kind. Maybe the Mars mission skeptics, the pistoleros, the wrestlers, were all part of some kind of conspiratorial activity that was about finding the infected arm and keeping it under government control, keeping it free from the forces of anarchy for as long as possible, which in this instance meant keeping it from tens of thousands of drug-addled young people. It was a self-fulfilling line of reasoning, or maybe that was just the drugs talking, but the conspiratorial reasoning, once it fell on her with the suddenness of a Somali pirate ship, was indisputable, though she knew that when large numbers of people came to believe in government conspiracy, government conspiracy appeared, as if summoned, and thus if it was not true yet, it would be, because the one thing the government would not tolerate without police or military presence was a breakdown in belief in government.

And so: in her worn-out sandals she dashed across the main street of Old Rio Blanco, she fell in and out of the beams of flashlights, and she could see the muzzle flashes of the Tasers here and there, could hear the occasional cry of one of the fallen, for whom *pain compliance* had unfortunately proven necessary, and before her was the doorway to the apothecary, or at least she thought so. And you would have thought that there would be some kind of sentry there, some guy who would allow you ingress only if you had the proper sequence of door knocks, but no, there was no sentry, and when she felt the door yield to her, she could tell it was nothing more than reinforced, if durable, corrugated cardboard. It swung back.

Awfully dark for the one *real* architectural structure in Old Rio Blanco, and there was no common area on the other side of the door, no welcome center, not as far as she could tell. There was only a long corridor that led away from the main street of town, from the *omnium gatherum,* and back into some space that hadn't, from the other side of the door, seemed possible, but Noelle followed it, followed the corridor, calling out now, as the lost do. First for Morton, and then for anyone who might hear her.

Claustrophobia was high on her list of defects of character, and there was only so far she could go on this portion of her adventures before she was going to be a lot more claustrophobic than she wanted to be. She was already making a mental note about what to do if the corridor had a fork anywhere, and her mental note said *always go to the left, no matter what,* because then if the corridor kept curving to the left, eventually she'd be back where she started. *Always go left.* She thought she heard some stirring, just then, and she thought she heard it again, but what she heard was her own discomfort. Her own misery expressed in nervous fidgeting.

Soon she realized that she was in fact in the recesses of some kind of mining operation. What the apothecary apparently led into — she must have misjudged one of the early doorways, missed where she was intended to stop and wait — was a disused mine. It wasn't out of the realm of possibility, since there had once been a lot of mining in Rio Blanco, nickel and copper, for example. But along with claustrophobia was her fear of large interior spaces, reminding her of one she'd visited in Europe, a cavern into which a small Italian town had thrown all of its trash for over a thousand years. It was the thousand years of trash that frightened her most. All that neglect for all that time. There were probably people who'd been flung in—alive—and never heard from again, for a thousand years. How far could she go into this cavern, herself, how far down into the unvisited past of the Southwest, before she was officially lost and needed to turn back, assuming that if she just turned 180 degrees she would in fact eventually find the front door of the apothecary's shop, which would in turn lead to the *omnium gatherum,* and back to her original problem, which was finding Morton, and finding the arm, and getting out of here?

It was hard to tell, at last, if the light up ahead was a legitimate light, not some phantom of her migrainous family of symptoms or just something to distract from the narrowing of the reinforced rock around her, the smell of water used to flush away the acids and the tailings. What remained of the light in this darkest of places could have been self-generated, or it could have been some actual *exit,* or it could have been the light of some benevolent personage, some miner who had been living in here, sneaking out through the apothecary under cover of night, when the tourists weren't around, in search of rotgut and Sterno. Noelle waited for sound, for the reassurances of sound, in order to verify that the light was not hallucinatory, but that sound didn't come. She called out again and heard nothing in reply. And yet instead of turning back and trying to retrace her steps, she trudged on toward where she imagined the light awaited her, around a gentle bend in the corridor. She'd only been walking five or ten minutes! It wasn't as if she'd walked a mile down here into the mine! It wasn't as if she were walking under the mountains and back into geologic prehistory, and was going to come out among dinosaurs rampaging on the veldt.

The room, when at last it opened up in front of her, was grand. A large group of the wrestlers was waiting. In a taciturn repose.

They sat against one wall, all of them silent, and they all looked as though they'd been taking a lot of whatever there was to take upstairs at the *omnium gatherum.*

When her eyes adjusted, she saw the arm, against the far wall, struggling to crawl along its base toward the end of the room, where yet another corridor led off into the infernal blackness. When the arm drew near to the way out, one of the wrestlers would lift up a Taser and fire in that direction, and the arm would recoil from the blast, flop over onto one side, and lie quiet for a moment or two, before gathering its strength and setting off in the opposite direction. Like a cornered scorpion. There was much hilarity involved in this game, it seemed, as her eyes adjusted. The wrestlers were moved by the arm, by its inability to give up. Any number of Tasers were discharged (and cartridges quickly replaced) before Noelle attempted to intervene in order to establish a conversation.

"Any of you actually touch the arm?"

Was this question addressed to the leadership? Their organization, to Noelle, was more like a school board or a prom subcommittee—something without anything like a fearless leader. And so it was hard to get an answer. In the meantime, the arm, its fingers agitating as though it were practicing piano scales or doing exercises to alleviate a repetitive stress injury, turned itself around, with remarkable ease, and began moving toward where Noelle stood. Almost as if it *heard* her somehow.

"Touched it?" a voice murmured, though it was unclear which of the wrestlers had said it. Now she could see in the illumination of the battery-powered flashlights that few if any of the Mexican wrestlers were actually Mexican. The possibility had only just occurred to her. And why would they be? The people on the other side of the border had things to do, places to go. The people of Mexico had *jobs.* The wrestlers, instead, were a heterozygous lot, a multiethnic melting pot of bad vibes. What they liked about Mexican wrestling was the superheroic violence.

"It's contagious, you know."

"You mean because it's got like all that stuff dripping off the end and flesh hanging off and pus?"

"You know where it came from, right?"

"From the Wheelers' tent."

"I guess that's how you got hold of it, huh?"

"Those people just aren't *good* to their volunteer staff."

"The thing about the arm," Noelle said, "is that it's infected with highly contagious bacteria that has probably come from Mars, and I'm guessing it's highly contagious just from skin contact, and if you get the symptoms of the disease, well, it's fatal, so far, anyway, and from what I've heard the symptoms are pretty awful. So is there anyone who's touched it?"

One of the wrestlers got up, walked to where Noelle was standing, and began pushing her over toward the arm. It was that simple, really, and when it began, she felt as though all of the day had been leading to this moment. She had been so unwise, so foolish, about what the day would bring, because she hadn't expected it to include coercion and intimidation. She was so unwise because she hadn't expected the *omnium gatherum* to end with the application of force. And now that it was happening, she saw that it had always been there. Force was there. When you went to the fast-food restaurant and ordered your hamburger with a side of microbiological contaminants, you had the police force of the marketplace behind you. The force that ensured that people like this, Mexican wrestlers, were never able to mobilize into some kind of general strike, or agitprop theater company, or tutoring organization; force, undergirding the shouted hello of the deliveryman as he goes past your house; force, as the neighbor's dog dashes up the walk to lick your hand; force, making it possible that the big, chaotic populations out there didn't get into your safe-deposit box; force, which through some miscalculation or some systematic series of miscalculations made possible the Sino-Indian Economic Compact, which now had its own army and its own propaganda machinery. Force. Noelle didn't address the issue exhaustively during the millisecond in which the wrestler guy—thinning hair, unwashed physique, aubergine tights, gin blossoms, halitosis—began to edge her toward the contagious arm; she experienced convulsive little images of understanding and misunderstanding, all intuitive, upon her like a white-light experience, and she began to shout things, though she didn't really register what she was shouting, nor did she understand exactly what it was she was shouting *about,* as she began to push back against the wrestler, and she was shouting, though nothing was stopping him, and his confederate (in Green Lantern costume, maybe, or something similar) now joined in the madness, to insure that there wasn't any danger of her repelling the two of them; it was all just about the gladiatorial aspect of the thing, woman versus disembodied arm, although she did hear someone say, *Where's the monkey? You make sure that the monkey is tied up,* and even in the midst of her struggle, she did want to say that it wasn't a monkey, *he* wasn't a monkey, *he* was a great ape, just like the thugs attempting to push her toward the arm, one big primate family, and she knew as soon as she heard them say that, that her rescuer was out there, nearby.

Why secure the primate in a darkened antechamber? He talked too much, and he didn't act properly subservient to the wrestlers, who had all finished high school, and so they Tasered him and put him in a straitjacket and banished him to the shaft that led farther down into the mine, with the idea that they would release him at some relevant point later in the evening. For the time being, it was important that they had possession of the talking chimpanzee and no one else did. The monkey was, in truth, stronger than most of the wrestlers in the room, however, and that, soon enough, was self-evident, because he was used to biting things off with his teeth, shredding stuff, throwing things around, and therefore he freed himself from the straitjacket without difficulty (Noelle put this together later on), and he made his way into the room, and thus onto the scene, the scene including the severed arm, which was trying to draw near to the voices, the human voices, probably because the arm could feel the waves of commotion coming from the disputing voices. The arm moved toward the commotion with the irrepressible need to bring a halt to it, as the wrestlers were meanwhile pushing Noelle *toward* the arm, and she wasn't sure if it was all a big joke to them or if they meant to expose her to the arm, but she was struggling and pushing against the slick, unwashed bodies of the wrestlers, and there were at least three of them now attempting to move her toward the arm, and there was her voice, caroming off the walls of the storage antechamber in the mine and echoing from distant walls of corridors, *Why are you doing this?,* all the way down in the most subterranean part of the Earth, and that was what drove Morton, she supposed later, to fling himself upon the three wrestlers, tearing them from her, biting them so that they were covered in blood, so that he was covered in blood, so that his black-and-gray coat was covered with human blood, and this provoked the rest of the bench, as it were, and soon there must have been eight or ten of them in the center of the room, and many threats were being uttered, not terribly inventive threats, by the Mexican wrestlers, apparently because they were intimidated, or were loath to fire their Tasers immediately, lest they somehow injure an important prize, and there were the shrieking primate cries of Morton, who had already driven off several of the wrestlers, who were fleeing up the corridor back toward the apothecary, some of them indicating that this just *wasn't cool* and that they were heading back up above ground where things were more *chill,* but then there were others who had no purpose but mutilating Morton and infecting Noelle, or so it seemed, and they would stay there until someone really got hurt, because when the restraints were unfastened, and the blood flowed, and force was loosed upon the world, there was someone who was about to get hurt, and Noelle figured, even in the midst of worrying, that either she would be raped or Morton would be torn apart or both, and that wasn't even taking into consideration the arm, which, she noticed, had closed in on one of the wrestlers and was now attached to the synthetic fabrics of his togs, making use of its disgusting and fungally afflicted fingernails, and this guy, who she thought was masquerading as one of the Justice League of America superheroes, or that was his outfit, this guy was trying to keep Morton from biting off the nose of one of the other wrestlers, and he didn't even realize, at first, that the arm was intending to summit him, that the arm was soon going to apply the maximum amount of force to his throat, until it was too late; the batterer didn't realize that this was what was happening, even as he attempted to strangle Morton, and Noelle shouted, "Morton!" But there was nothing she could do about Morton now; Morton may have had all the language in the world, but he had no natural reason at all not to make use of his nonhuman animal instinct. There were no moral rules in place for Morton. Were they going to put Morton in jail when all this was done? Were they going to issue a press release that said "The animal had to be destroyed"? It was only because Morton cared for her, no matter how violent this all was, that there were bodies against every wall in the room, contused or concussed.

During a pause in the confrontation, with a Taser frozen between the last two combatants, a lone wrestler didn't realize that Morton had the upper body strength of a world-class weightlifter; the wrestler, who probably did his time in the gym and maybe shot up some steroids before breakfast, he watched as the Taser he intended to fire got closer and closer, centimeter by centimeter, to his own face, and the look of terror crept into his eyes, as Morton was shrieking his chimpanzee shriek, and another wrestler, one of the blond wrestlers who seemed to have attempted to dye his hair dark so as to simulate being a Mexican wrestler, and whose bootblacking was now coming off his head because he was sweating so much, this guy rallied from a prone position to grab Morton's arm and attempted to manipulate the outcome of this face-off, but still the Taser crept toward the face of wrestler number one, and then there was a horrible cry as Morton successfully applied the Taser to its owner, somewhere right under his chin, and the wrestler collapsed to the floor as if he were doing a choreographed wrestling routine, and then Morton, who now had possession of a Taser and who was ducking as some others were fired his way, turned the weapon on the blond with the dripping, muddy hair and used the *pain compliance* feature of the Taser on this adversary, who howled and immediately fell to the floor. Noelle noticed that the mook with *the arm* attached to him had stumbled over into a corner by the hallway, the hallway that led farther down into the mine shaft, and the arm was, for the moment, lying beside him, as though it too had been, again, Tasered. She got the idea, now, to swap the arms, because her rucksack was over where she had first walked into the room, probably it had fallen from her when they were trying to force her up against the arm, and the situation would have been perfect right now, and she could lay ahold of *the arm,* but the only problem was she no longer had the rubber gloves with which to gather it up, and unless she could use one of the capes from the wrestlers or some other bit of stray fabric, how was she going to do what needed to be done? On the other hand, so many of these guys had probably touched the arm already—

"Don't touch that arm!" Morton called out. "I forbid you to touch that arm. If there's anyone in this room who should touch that arm, it should be *me.* Now is the time that I contribute something to human progress! Now is the moment in history that separates the humans from the higher primates, isn't that so? Look around this room, if you please, and what do you notice about the human being who was allegedly given dominion over the other animals?" Morton addressed what few of the wrestlers were left, lying injured at the margins of that room beneath the earth, and it was as if he had *rehearsed* the speech, and perhaps this was, in fact, what he'd been doing out in the hallway while attempting to free himself from the straitjacket. He was preparing the speech that would lead, inevitably, to his martyrdom. "What do the humans do in the time of their greatest ignominy? What do they do when faced with the possibility of redemption and dignity? They attack the *weak,* that's what they do, isn't that right? Look around us, Noelle. Look at those who have fled, who have gone back to the festival to disappear into its crowds, after having kidnapped an innocent bystander, namely yours truly, for their own torture and delight. When they look deep into their hearts, they find that they have no hearts; they find that the ill-treatment of the weak and undernourished and hapless is somehow, according to human beings, *funny*. Nothing could be more sidesplitting than the demonstration of their meager superiority!

"And so I aim to teach you something tonight, you human beings; I aim to teach you something about selflessness, and about *love*. Because I love this woman right here, Noelle Stern. Are you listening to me, those of you who remain in this room? I love this woman. This woman took care of me when no one would take care of me at all. She brought me my breakfast; she brought me my lunch and dinner. She emptied out my waste products from the cell where I was imprisoned, and she schooled me in the kind of politesse that has made me the man that I am. The man you see before you right now. And while I understand that you do not think I am a man, I use the word advisedly. When she had to administer experimental drugs to me, she did so in a regretful way, and on more than one occasion, I am certain that I saw tears in her eyes. I spoke my very first words to her, and while it is possible that I spoke those words simply because I had some human cells injected into me—yes, that's right, Noelle, I believe I understand the experiment—in short, yes, it is possible that I am speaking to you because I have those little crystals of a dead person in my brain, but still I choose to think that I began to speak because I finally had something that I very badly needed to say, and that something was about *gratitude*. I had a need to speak, and that is what language is for, is it not? For me, there were many obstacles—insufficient fine motor control, poor laryngeal function—but I overcame all these things, because my need, my love, was so strong that I *had* to speak. Was this enough? No! I am here to tell you now that I have lived in both worlds, like Tiresias, in the world of the mute nonhuman animal and in the world of the human animal, and I can confirm that language has its limitations! There are so many things that language cannot express, I say this to you right now—"

Although the arm had been at a safe distance, at the thundering vibrations of Morton's voice, it began reaching and lunging in his direction, and he was forced to keep himself between Noelle and the arm in order to continue his oratory without interruption.

"For example, I have found that the longing I have felt has been ill served by language. I have tried to get it down, in poetry and in my diary entries, and I have tried using metaphor and simile, all the finest varieties of speech, and there's just no way that I can properly describe what I'm feeling. For example, there are times of the day when this woman—"

"Morton, we really don't have time…"

"Just let me finish up," he said firmly, in dramatic aside. "There are times when I have been in the cell, and you've been off duty, when I have felt the traces of you there in the room with me, even though you were off for the day. I have felt you there. I have felt whatever conversation it is that we had earlier, and I have felt you there with me, and I have experienced you as a tightness in the chest, an itchiness of the scalp, an inability to experience the daily pleasures of the world. But do words accurately convey this feeling? I could just as easily be describing heartburn to you, brought on by spicy food or ulcerative colitis, or perhaps some kind of myocardial infarction, but those would *not* be sensations that one associates with longing, would they? No, they wouldn't. This language that I have somehow received, this thing that separates me from other animals, it makes me now a miracle of science, but—"

A couple wrestlers dragged themselves up from whatever fog of gang warfare afflicted them or whatever alcoholic poisoning they were temporarily sleeping off, and made unobtrusive exits.

"—this language that I have received is as much curse as blessing. And if language, then, is not sufficient to meet the needs of the likes of me, what is there that remains to me? This is the question I ask myself. In what way can I demonstrate my love?

The only way I can demonstrate it is with my *actions.* That is how we do it in the world of chimpanzees, at least as I understand it — from having met a few chimps over the years and having read a number of books on the subject, as well as watching chimpanzee-themed programs online. We demonstrate our needs quickly — with actions — in a decisive way, and that is what I'm going to do *right now.*"

With that, Morton took the Taser that he was holding and applied it to the arm, which was flailing madly around in the center of the dusty floor, flailing as if there were a butterfly it was attempting to catch, and the arm came to rest.

"Morton, do you really have to do this?"

And he picked up the arm. Just picked it up as if it were a bough in the woods. Or a scroll from some religious tradition. And he put it under his own arm. Then he accepted, from Noelle, the bag in which the other arm was secreted away. And then, as if they were a couple, he and Noelle, a couple who had been together for years and years, the two of them exchanged and organized the various items in their custody, swapping out of the bag the arm from the cadaver with the infected arm, and they started, in silence, up the grim, lightless way, back toward the apothecary. Those who were left behind evidently wanted to remain, and their needs were no longer a matter of concern for this couple that united the primates into the one common line.

Noelle said, "This really panicked me on the way down."

Morton said, "I was blindfolded."

Noelle said, "Did you really have to do that?"

Morton said, "Do what?"

Noelle said, "The arm?"

They covered the distance to the parking lot in half the time, because distance has mostly to do with perception. And then they were out. Which left only the one last chore, the task that they had understood as the purpose of coming here, to the *omnium gatherum.* They were going to drop off the replacement arm, find the URB van, meet Koo and the others, and drive back into town to a secure location. As it turned out, once upon the main street of Old Rio Blanco, the stage set, they were confronted by Woo Lee Koo, his son, Jean-Paul, Vienna Roberts, her parents (very much out of place and completely dumbfounded, according to Noelle's first impression), and various members of the department of medicine from the hospital. Who had all, according to Dr. Koo, tracked the two of them with the transponder that Dr. Koo had subdermally implanted in Morton long ago. In his left wrist. Koo had followed the signal to Old Rio Blanco before completely losing track of them somewhere. The signal went dead.

Dr. Koo was nervous about something, incredibly nervous, agitated, distracted, or so it seemed to Noelle. Distracted in a way she had never seen before, short-tempered, and he was saying that they had to leave *now,* they had to leave as quickly as they were able to leave. *There was confusion,* he said, *confusion* at the highest levels, though when had there not been confusion in these recent days? Still, Noelle Stern found that she felt nothing so much as exhaustion, notwithstanding the course of events. What she wanted to do was to lie down somewhere, and maybe *throw up,* since the migraine she'd been fighting off was still making all the lights dance with their nasty, sinister, impressionistic auras. But Koo was barking orders at everyone and insisting that they keep moving and that there was no time to stop, and when she asked why they had to keep moving, she was told that *there was no time to discuss it,* they simply needed to get to a van and move out of the immediate area of this valley as quickly as possible, preferably to the other side of the mountains. Morton was still carrying the arm, and Noelle asked what they were meant to do with it, to which Koo said, *There's no time, no time;* just throw the arm anywhere, one of the other attending physicians said, and then someone disagreed, no, you just can't throw it anywhere, you have to dispose of it somehow, or at least leave it with trusted deputies, and we need at least one tissue sample; *wait a second,* Noelle wanted to say. *Didn't we come here to get the arm for some reason?* Wasn't there a reason for getting the arm, that had to do with something, she couldn't remember what exactly, with some experiment that Koo was doing? And then she noted that Jean-Paul looked like death warmed over, which she supposed must have been exactly what he was, death warmed over, and he wasn't saying anything, and he seemed to be bleeding, and why was he out, exactly? What about the quarantine? He moved around the fringes of the group, as they all hastened back toward the *omnium gatherum,* and he was wearing a ridiculous amount of clothing, he was covered head to toe, though it was probably still somewhere near to a hundred degrees.

Vienna's mother asked, again, what they were all talking about.

Revelers, the tens of thousands of revelers, took no note of the worry in this particular retinue, this extended family, and this was the way of the revelers. The finest revelry precedes destruction; it was always thus, as when it preceded the shortest day of the year, or the eclipse, or the ritual sacrifice of teenagers. That was when people really let their hair down and committed a few indiscretions. How many of them were already sick? Noelle wondered, and she even said something about it to Koo, as they rushed against the tide back toward the van. *How many of them do you think are sick?* He had no answer for that and didn't seem much to care. If he seemed to have put aside the concerns about his dead wife, the one in the freezer, he had replaced that particular family madness with a need to protect the group around him now, Vienna, Jean-Paul, Morton, and Noelle. He was the shepherd who couldn't relax while any lamb strayed.

At last, they found themselves beside the van, the one Noelle had driven in, watching, from that vantage point, the undulations of the crowd on the desert floor. It was an image from the Northern Renaissance, what she saw, from Bosch or Brueghel, the incessant activity of the night, the modified vehicles with their cannons and neon and sound systems, doing figure eights around the cacti, the costumes, the leafleting political groups. But they didn't stay long to look, though it was now only fifteen or twenty minutes until the reputed firing-into-space of the arm, and Koo was adamant that they leave while they could. He'd abandoned his own van on the shoulder of the road, back up over the pass, but there was no time to bother about that. And they all piled in. Inside, in the confines of the vehicle, Noelle could hear how badly Jean-Paul was wheezing. That was about all he was doing. He seemed to stop breathing for long periods of time, but no one said anything about it. Maybe there was just nothing to say anymore. Maybe this was your neighbor now. Your neighbor was bleeding from every part of him, was unable to talk in any way, and the best that was to be expected of him was that he (or she) had just to stay alive a little bit longer before breaking into bloody sections. And your challenge, the challenge you faced with your neighbor, was to try to find a way to love him when he collapsed in front of his house and lay there until the turkey vultures came by to pick clean his bones. His estate would be raided by the federal government and dispersed to the military-industrial complex. Noelle believed that she could thrive in this future because she was not squeamish. It was something of a shocker, therefore, when Koo, who was sitting in the front passenger seat, called to her: "Noelle, isn't it a wonderful thing that we believe we have found a treatment protocol for the *M. thanatobacillus* infection?"

"You have? And what is the treatment?"

"Radiation therapy," Koo said. "And we've already given Jean-Paul his first round of treatments, which is why he's a little sluggish. The bacterium, we believe, acted more slowly on Mars in part because of the thinness of the atmosphere and the extreme cold, and though it had, to some degree, adapted to the radiation there, large doses seem to slow the course of the infection."

"Just wonderful."

"All the more reason why we need to remove ourselves from this...area...as quickly as possible."

"Because?"

But Koo took up with bickering at the driver, one of the residents from the medical program at URB whom Noelle had seen around the hospital campus a couple times but hadn't met. The van wasn't going anywhere. The van was parked in a line of vehicles inching up and down the mountain pass, and there were more cars waiting to leave, and it looked like it was going to be a good long time.

"What's the rush?" Noelle asked again.

"It's a rather unfortunate situation," Koo said, "but I have reason to believe that there will be some kind of police or federal military intervention at this festival tonight."

"What does that mean?"

"As I have already told the others," Koo said, "I am not certain what it means, but the CDC seems to feel that in order to control a larger possible outbreak of the disease, something needs to be done about the Rio Blanco area. What with people flying around in their jet packs, and the border-jumping, there is a real danger that the infected can move about too easily. The CDC wishes to try to contain the illness in this area." And to the driver: "Can you please hurry?"

"What does that mean?"

"It means that they could try to quarantine or even eliminate people at the festival who are infected or already at risk."

She thought of Larry, she thought of the Wheelers, she thought of that guy from last week who got turned into a paloverde tree, she thought of all the many people she knew out there, in the expanses of the Valley of the Slaughtered Calf, and she thought of the families of those people, and their coworkers, and their friends. And then she remembered about Morton.

Noelle said, "Well, then, it might be that this is the moment to speak to the issue of Morton, who has had some contact with the—"

"What about Morton? Morton, are you all right?"

Morton was sitting in the back of the van, and he had his

face pressed to the window, watching as the van began its steep ascent into the switchbacks, as if there were something that he was leaving behind in escaping from the *omnium gatherum*. Noelle reached across the backseat and set a hand on his shoulder. His coat was matted and sweaty, and she could tell that if there were a chimpanzee equivalent for weeping, then Morton had begun to cry.

"We still have the arm," he said quietly.

"What's that?" Koo called from the front seat. "Can you speak up?"

"We still have the arm," he said.

"Which arm?"

"I believe," Morton said, "that we have both arms. Because we brought along the second arm."

From the back of the van, Vienna Roberts's dad called, with a certain exasperation, "Just how many arms are we trafficking in, anyway?"

Morton reached down and touched the rucksack into which, it was true, they had somehow by now stuffed both arms. The bag was trembling and thrumming against the floor of the van, because the infected arm had now waked from its last dose of high voltage.

What liberty there was outside the van! What liberty Morton must have felt during his brief trip among the revelers! No one stared, no one cared, no one gave a second thought to a talking chimpanzee. With her hand on his matted fur, Noelle could almost feel the sense of possibility that Morton felt ebbing away. No matter his long-windedness and his insecurity, he was a person with the advantages that an educated man has, but despite this, now that he was in the van with Koo, he was in danger of being shipped back to the laboratory, some laboratory, until, with a proper publicist and a business manager, the rollout of his persona could take place. But what about the chimpanzee part of him? His chimpanzee hypostasis?

The brazenness of what happened next, therefore, was brazen

only to those who didn't know Morton as Noelle had come to know him. How he crept slowly to the side door of the van, and then, without comment, threw it open, even as they were still edging along, and, holding the bag with the two arms in it, Morton leaped from the van onto the shoulder. Of course the van stopped in its tracks, and Noelle, and then some of the doctors from URB, and then Koo himself *all* followed in exiting the van, and they all stood and watched as the chimpanzee loped down the mountain pass, with that comical gait of his, back in the direction he had come, threading his way between cars and dodging motorized skateboards and mopeds and motorcycles and extreme joggers.

Koo called after him, called after the person who, after all, had been sprung from his wife, who had some of her sardonic humor, some of her excessive self-love, some of her autodidactic pretensions, and whom he was therefore about to lose as though he were losing his wife a second time, or a third time, if we consider what was about to happen to her body, back in the garage. *Morton, please! Morton, please come back!* But how many were the ways in which he was now powerless. They had stopped traffic on the way up the mountain pass, and they had stopped it from going down by reason of rubbernecking, and even if Koo had believed that there was something he could do, some bit of suasion that could bring back his most promising experiment, he just did *not* have the time in which to do it. In a cacophony of horns and shouts, Koo and the others climbed back into the van.

And what did Noelle see now? What was it that Noelle saw fleeing down the mountain pass, carrying two left arms in a rucksack, wearing a scrap of clown costume, dried blood around his mouth, and sporting a maniacal grin?

She saw Mister Right.

It was much later that she realized it, of course. The linguistic niceties with which you describe loss come later. It was with this bodily perception locked into place that Noelle returned herself to the van, and it was with this bodily perception that she and the rest in the van rode, in silence, across the pass, into the next valley, and then south, toward the Santa Ritas, toward the last great mountain range on this side of the border.

They were a good fifteen or twenty miles out of the city itself, without having encountered any kind of military perimeter, when they saw the great light. It wasn't, in truth, a light that you *saw*. They were bludgeoned by the light, and the sound. The desert was lit up, as it had been, periodically, with atomic perturbances in decades past. The ominous cloud was above them, stretching out its smoldering immemorial extremities in every direction, saying *this is what we had to do,* though it never failed to be the case that there *were* things that might have been done otherwise.

Morton made his choice. He'd tasted civilization. And he'd found that it consisted of large helpings of desperation, petroleum by-products, fat substitutes, sweeteners, sewage storage issues, stolen and stripped automobiles, vapor trails, good intentions, bad follow-through, selfishness, red itchy eyes, sentimentality, mold, poor logical reasoning, halfhearted orgasms, advertising, household pests, regrets, mendacities, thorns, haberdasheries, computer programming, lower-back pain, xenophobia, legally binding arbitration, cheesy buildup, racial profiling, press-on nails, the seventh-inning stretch, roundtable discussions, antibiotic-resistant bacteria, perineal pain, individually wrapped slices, road rage, and unfounded speculation, and he had decided that it was completely reasonable that he would turn his back on this civilization. What that must have felt like! Noelle considered the idea that there was an *outside of civilization,* and she concluded that she could never know what it was, because she had always been inside, because wherever two or more were gathered, there were all the pitfalls, all the disappointments. But when Morton turned his back on the van and ran back toward the *omnium gatherum,* toward, she supposed, incineration, he was heading back in the direction of something he had never possessed, but which, she thought, he intuitively knew, simply because of who he was. That it appeared to him to lie in the direction of a lot of naked and half-naked middle-class white kids, mixing it up with the Union of Homeless Citizens, not to mention the Maoist party of the Sonoran Desert and a lot of Mexican infiltrators, that was just an accident of history. What Morton wanted was simpler than all of that. Morton longed for the wild.

The End

Afterword:
On *The Crawling Hand*
by Montese Crandall

*T*he *Crawling Hand,* as directed by Herbert L. Strock and released in 1963, has to be one of the finest films ever made, in this or any other century. Though it cannot be disputed that the acting is somewhat rudimentary, though the sets are ridiculous and look as if they were just pasted up, though the story is capable of causing spasms of laughter, it is, I intend to argue, a masterpiece. Yes, the dialogue is so awkward that it nearly, through ironistic transformation, disarms you into believing that it is something else entirely. Because I have now seen the film twenty-one or twenty-two times, I can recall portions of this dialogue, and because repetition and attention and commitment to even the worst examples of entertainment improve them considerably, these lines have come to assume, for me, yes, the dimensions of *poetry:*

It's the press
What do we tell them?

Tell them we just sent
Our second man
To the moon
And he's not coming back either...

Even the credit sequence is sloppy, in which a mostly dead astronaut, upon returning from the moon, is poised, is frozen, like an unused marionette, before the enormous viewing window of his capsule. There is the crashing of the orchestral cymbals on the soundtrack to indicate the shooting of stars. From a distance of half a century, this credit sequence looks remarkably clumsy, like a film as you might make it at home, except that of course these days homemade films are often widely distributed, and they are some of the most popular and successful films being made in this country.

> We don't pretend to know all the answers...
> Apparently no one does.

The sound is dreadful too. Did I say that already? You can scarcely hear what's being said. Did they not try to improve on that? Did they loop nothing? Everyone smokes too much. Nonstop smoking. The point is this. If *The Crawling Hand* is one of the sloppiest and most ill-conceived pieces of cinema, which it arguably is, what accounts for its enduring cultural value? Why is it that the film has never vanished into obscurity the way, for example, *C.H.U.D.* (1984) has vanished into obscurity, or the way *Sunspots* (2017), that big-budget extravaganza about diaphanous beings from the sun leading the citizens of Earth to their spiritual redemption, has disappeared from cultural memory?

The success of *The Crawling Hand* has, it should be said, something to do with the arm itself, with the plangent qualities of that sightless limb, and this is just what I was saying to my chess-playing friend D. Tyrannosaurus the day on which we were finally concluding our chess match. The game had proceeded by telephone initially, but in time it became clear that weeks were going to pass before one of us proved victorious. I don't know who D. was calling for strategic counsel, some working girl perhaps, but he seemed to require much preparation in order to make his moves. We therefore determined that despite the earlier agreements on the subject, we were going to bring the match to fruition in person once again, at the café called Ho Chi Minh.

It was a rout, I don't have to tell you, because I am really the much better player, though clearly D. Tyrannosaurus, whose actual name was Tyrone (as he had belatedly admitted), had misrepresented his inabilities in order to attempt to throw me off. I had felt, as one often feels in life, let down by Tyrone, and not only because of his name or his chess skills. For example, I once suggested that we go to a minor league baseball game in the Rio Blanco area, where the local affiliate was doing rather well, and that isn't the sort of thing I would have done had I known his only purpose was to swindle.

I was being *taken,* you see; that was what it was all about, and I didn't appreciate being *taken,* and who would? When I encountered him at the Ho Chi Minh, for the purposes of the endgame, I should say, he had lost much of his luster. Tyrone was no longer attempting to straighten himself up in the way he had before. He had let himself slide. He was just another dreamy con artist. Is it the way of all obsessions that they consume their subjects? Was Tyrone simply tired out from his long boondoggle in the Southwest, attempting to persuade a reputable dealer of baseball cards to give him that one last precious item?

Liftoff from the moon
Perfect.
One hour later
Nothing.

Our match was completed in candlelight, and there was not much to it, and I wish that I could give you an exciting account of the game, in which there was psychological maneuvering in order to gain the upper hand. But this would be to descend into the blandly technical. I will say, though, that I have spent some time considering the *sighing* of chess players, and have wondered if it might be possible to somehow codify these chess-playing sighs, as though to indicate that certain kinds of sighs can, in particular circumstances, have a strategic role. For example, I noticed that one of the younger Hungarian grand masters, whose name escapes me, was given to a sigh that I came to name the *Slow Leak*. It didn't really count as a sigh exactly, and perhaps I am overreaching by even using this word to refer to it. But the *Slow Leak* is really the perfect description. You know the way some people release a little bit of air, under a certain amount of compression between their teeth, and it's really exactly like a balloon deflating? This Hungarian grand master had perfected, above all, the deployment of the *Slow Leak,* which he would use especially when the other player was just about to move, was, perhaps, reaching out to move the piece. In the Hungarian's matches, the video simulcast would always have a close-up of the faces of the players; you could see the frustration in some of his opponents during the *Slow Leak*. Their heads rested in their hands.

I did not sigh this particular sigh while playing against Tyrone, but there's another that is very effective, and this sigh is known as the *Appaloosa*. This, my friends, is the ugliest of all sighs. It involves letting the lips go free as the air is forced out of the mouth. The *Appaloosa* is a disruptive, nearly violent sigh in the context of a chess match. It is likely that the first chess player to make use of the *Appaloosa* was a man from some Western milieu such as the one in which I am writing these lines, where freight trains pass on the half hour and horses are as common as jet packs. This chess player, in whatever century he existed, was used to the snorting of the horses he regularly bred, and perhaps he was acquainted with the Nez Percé and their particular breed, the Appaloosa, and perhaps he had fallen in love with the idiosyncrasies of this particular Appaloosa, its nickering, and despite its tremendous ugliness and the whites of its eyes, which are so arresting, this chess player realized that the snorts of the Appaloosa would be perfect in a very close chess match. The results had to have been good, and so the *Appaloosa,* the chess-related sigh, went into more common usage, from which it has never since disappeared.

There are other varieties of sighs that work very well in amateur chess, and which have on occasion led to major victories. But the sighs do not work on chess automata, which take no notice of the less-becoming aspects of human behavior. Still, it's what happens alongside the chessboard that's interesting; it's all the gestures that would seem routine or uninteresting to anyone who happened by, that's where the action is in the chess match. Chess is human relations. But if I must: Tyrone's opening was the so-called Nimzo-Larsen opening, which, when commonly practiced among, especially, Sino-Indian players, starts first with the knight on the king's side (to F3), followed by (when an advanced player, like yours truly, elects to develop the center in reply) the pawn at B3, after which we get the fianchetto, or "little flanking."

Perhaps Tyrone believed he was playing an original game, because he was not developing the pawns in front of the king or queen (D4 and E4), as in the conventional opening, and, probably, he imagined that I would somehow be unwitting about the Nimzo-Larsen or Nimzo-Indian opening, but my knowledge of the world is broad.

> Can't make it
> Losing control
> It makes my arm move...
> Kill! Kill!

Between rhinoviral sighs, and while Tyrone was laboring trying to understand my strategy, I began to speak to the symbolism of *The Crawling Hand.*

"Have you actually seen the film? Have you seen the original?"

"Interesting question," Tyrone mumbled, and in taking up this interesting question I intuited that he would be prevented from seeing how my knight inclined toward B4, which in turn threatened his queen's bishop. "I guess," he went on, "you're asking whether you really need the film at all in order to make a, you know, a decent novelization? Now that I've done a few, actually, now that I've done a lot of them, I'd say that I've done them in different kinds of ways. You know, sometimes I've taken a shine to the material, even though most of the time these films are very bad. Sometimes something just comes over you, and you resonate with the product, you feel it, you find something from your own life that makes it resonate. Those are actually the harder ones to write, though. These days, they send me the script, I don't even see the film. I retype the script, insert some *he said*s and *she said*s, descriptions. Not that I want to give away the trade secrets. But, you know, keep a fashion magazine around for the—"

Moving his pawn forward, soon to be blocked by one of my own.

"—for the sake of the descriptive parts, that kind of thing."

I attempted to interrupt: "So you haven't seen—"

"I didn't even know there was an earlier film, really. Until you mentioned it that time. The horror thing, I don't know."

Coffee futures being what they were, the price had again risen *while we were playing,* and when the robotic purveyor arrived, we asked for the popular substitute made of toasted hickory. Tasted like pencil shavings. I didn't want the jittery feeling. I needed to stay calm for the prize at hand.

"Would you like to know some more of the things that I find so wonderful about the original film?"

"One...second."

Kindnesses, flatteries, dishonest intellectual exchanges that I now presumed were part of our acquaintance, precluded any genuine elaboration on my enthusiasms. However, with an *Appaloosa* sigh, I launched into some exegetical remarks about *The Crawling Hand* just the same, remarking that it was important to think of the film in the context of the Manichaean era in which it was produced, the time of the very earthly and very flawed struggle between economic models, the time of the global Cold War, the outcome of which we know, of course, from our modern historical analyses. But if the film was produced in the context of that Manichaean structure, it also had Manichaean dialectical notions *implicit within.* As when Augustine of Hippo inveighed against the passivity of a knowledge-based relationship with God, I told Tyrone, *The Crawling Hand* promoted a death-is-not-the-end version of human life in which a man falls from the sky, or at least a portion of him does, and because he has fallen away from the struggle for good, he is portrayed as already given over to malevolence or sin. I also mentioned to Tyrone that he should read, if he had any time, Mani's book of *Secrets,* which is alluded to by Paul, the leading man in the original film. Paul, in the film, speaks to the importance of *secrets,* because, I said, Paul tries to conceal the presence of the arm and, later, the fact that he has been infected by it.

Tyrone was not listening. I took his rook at F7, and the game began to collapse from under him.

Naturally, I said, I understood that horror films did not move a preponderance of right-thinking folks to wonderment, especially not those high-end dealers in antiquities who attempted to filch from the lowly regional bottom-feeders, those who have made a livelihood out of collecting with patience and vision over decades. Did Tyrone ever have a box full of doubles under his bed that he knew would come in handy in thirty years' time? I imagined that he only understood the blue book value of the very rarest cards, and had been employed by some rich guy to make these acquisitions, and that was his job now. Perhaps he only enjoyed the theater of his attempts, the getting up close, the deceiving, the leaving town. Maybe there were a number of varieties of flattery that he'd used on me that could be codified into some kind of rule book for dealers in antiquity. *Chapter One: Finding the mark. Settling in. How to make conversation with a person who has never had a fulfilling social life.*

"I love the scene at the soda shop, or is it a diner, with the two girls, where there's some kind of doo-wop music playing in the background that the teenagers are attempting to dance to. The proprietor of the store comes in and indicates that there should be no dancing in the burger joint, no dancing, and of course it always reminds me of Cotton Mather's injunctions against Terpsichore, you know, *young*

people dance and go down to hell. The scene proceeds," I went on, "and
we get our first shot of the leading male, Paul Lawrence, and he has a
sort of sullen, learning-disabled aspect to him, which makes his later
bacterial infection seem all the more convincing, and as he and his
girlfriend, Marta, are about to leave for the beach, the jukebox kicks
in with 'The Bird's the Word,' by the Rivingtons, later reconfigured
into that classic of early rock and roll 'Surfin' Bird.'"

"Why—"

"Still, the best sequences in the film are those in which the arm
attacks people. I just love that stuff. There are two different ways
to film the arm. Or this is how I reconstruct it. In general, the
black-and-white horror film is, I'd agree, completely superior to
its Technicolor relative, which was already, by 1963, edging out
the competition. So anyway, the two ways to film the arm are,
first, with a live actor just out of frame, where the arm can wiggle
its fingers, you know, and then, second, there are the sequences
with the rubberized severed arm that the actors need to hold flush
to their own throats as they mime strangulation. The rubber arm
is great in the case of Mrs. Hotchkiss, the woman who rents out
Paul Lawrence's room to him," I explained. "She gives a wooden,
monotonous performance, especially in the delivery of her lines,
until the moment when the arm somehow *jumps up* from the floor
in order to attack her. Then she sputters and flails around before
falling to the ground so that they can cut between the rubberized
arm and the live actor's arm. Mrs. Hotchkiss gives the performance her *all.* A memorable bit, right? The filmmakers get down
to business. It's not like *The Blob,* where you have to wait so long
for the blob to turn up."

> You've just got to trust me!
> If this is what I think it is,
> It could be very important for me!

A number of strategic exchanges had taken place on the
chessboard, and I must confess that the rather long time between

moves made it hard for me to concentrate effectively. This was
perhaps Tyrone's only path to victory, to bore me sufficiently. This
match should not have reached the endgame stage, I warrant, because Tyrone was mistaken about his talents, but I wanted to allow
Tyrone to believe that he had been in the hunt for a long time,
not simply plowed under, so that I would appear to have won the
novelization fair and square. This required skillful playing. As I
say, I offered a few pieces. He couldn't have known, however, that
we were coming to one of my favorite endgames, the bishop and
pawn endgame.

It was for chess-related reasons that the conversation took a
turn into a kind of terrain that I would refer to as *provocative,* or
mean-spirited, even mildly *abusive,* and I suppose it did so because
when competition rears its head, when the loser perceives that he
is the loser—in the ghastly moment of *zugzwang,* the moment
in which any move is a bad move—then it is axiomatic that the
outcome can no longer be delayed. The hand-to-hand begins, the
mano a mano. Thus it was that Tyrone said:

"What makes you think you're going to be able to write the
novelization anyway? It's not like you have any experience."

The blackout had begun again, as I say, and now Ho Chi Minh
had all but emptied of its excessively tanned and underemployed
counterculturalists and university dropouts. The musty smell of
snuffed candles was much in the air, a smell that anyone can love.
I might have riposted to the dinosaur that I had written plenty of
things, that the implications of my kind of story went beyond the
margin of the page into my spectacularly boiled-down evocations
of psychology. But what I said was:

"The same thing that probably makes you think that you are a
fine chess player."

What was it that Tyrone wanted? The interloper? As he blew
a move with his bishop that would have, were he more adept,
perhaps kept my king from heading boldly to the center of the
board. Did Tyrone not want me to massacre him? Was there not
some wish to be laid low by such as I, a small white man, with

modest expectations for the last couple of decades of his life, in a forgotten corner of NAFTA? Tyrone could have done many things, he was brilliant, he was affable, he was usually sharply turned out, he'd had a spectacular education. Was he, too, just another one of the people who never managed to turn promise into anything concrete?

He held his great, dark brow in his hands as though it were made of crystal, as if the position of his men would somehow shatter his very brow. I had no conviction about where, when his hand flew from his temple, it would alight. But as it swept toward the king, his white king, my heart lifted up, and I felt in myself a great lofting into the skies, as he toppled the king onto its side.

And then the cocksure exterior that Tyrone had exhibited over the weeks seemed to vanish away. He became almost mute, he murmured a few syllables that I couldn't make out, and then he reached into his valise, the valise he had brought to the café, claiming that he would soon have to fly anyway, and produced the flash drive containing the screenplay, entitled *The Four Fingers of Death.* He fetched it out like it was just a trifle—without any sense of what the thing meant to me.

"One of us goes away with the prize," Tyrone said, "and one of us goes back to the airport, and flies on to, uh, Dayton."

"Well, I want to say," I told him, "that this has been a very agreeable transaction."

> I sure could use a beer...
> Me, too, but we can't stop now.
> I bet there's one in the kitchen.

What I was, in fact, feeling then, I think I should say, was some apprehensiveness. I didn't *want* the struggle over the script to be over so quickly. Now that the attention, whether good or ill, that I had commanded during the plot against the McClintock card was about to come to its end, what to do? Thus I felt a need to keep Tyrone from exiting the Ho Chi Minh café. Suddenly, I was willing to do whatever needed to be done, for example, some gentle prodding in the direction of a drink. Did he want a drink? No, he no longer drank. Just one more cup of hickory coffee substitute? He didn't think so. Well, then, I asked Tyrone, had he ever considered exactly what the arm represented? In *The Crawling Hand?* Had he ever considered that the film was really about a certain kind of human labor? Had he considered that it represented the surplus value with which labor imbued the commodity, had he ever had any thoughts along these lines? Here it was, this arm, and it could do very little but grasp and choke. Maybe, I told Tyrone, the arm represented the *alienated labor* that was the trade union movement being crushed, the beginning of the era of strikebreaking, the end of the influence that labor had had in the 1930s and 1940s; maybe the arm represented the end of that sense of community of workingmen and -women together, forging a nation.

And what about the cats at the end of the film? Had Tyrone heard about the cats? They offered the most difficult moment in the film for the casual interpreter. I found, I told Tyrone, as he fiddled nervously with his surgically implanted digital minder, as though he couldn't be bothered to listen, the cats in film, the moments when cats just appeared by chance or were compelled (in some drugged state, no doubt) to perform for the cameras, incredibly moving. For example, Mrs. Hotchkiss had a cat in the film, I told Tyrone, and there was a very tender moment, after her death, when the sheriff was visiting her house, in search of leads, and he paused to *scritch* (the proper word, I believe) behind the ears of Mrs. Hotchkiss's cat, as it stood on the counter, having its way with a saucer of dairy product. Okay! I told Tyrone. That's one cat who appears in the film, Mrs. Hotchkiss's cat, who stands in as a sign for wildness, the wildness that is often the necessary obverse of the civilizing impulse, correct? Cats are innocents, but they are also wild, I told Tyrone, and humans are crazy enough to believe that they can somehow *control* the wildness of the cats. This particular cat, who could just as easily run off, comes back to the house for handouts, and so it's a complex image, this image of the cat in Mrs. Hotchkiss's house; it's a beloved cat, but then again, it could also be a cat that has somehow been attacked by the crawling arm. Because that arm has been crawling around the house, has been getting into all the shelves, into all the cupboards, into all the recesses that the cat gets into, and so there has been some kind of consorting between the arm and the cat — *it has to be,* I told Tyrone; it couldn't be otherwise — and later in the film, the cat cries some strangulated cry (off camera) that leads one to suspect that the cat is now *contaminated,* but there is no definitive information on this point, I said, after which the scene relocates to the final chase between Paul and the sheriff (the latter of whom went on to appear in the popular *Gilligan's Island* program), and Paul heads off, as if for the water, because all of this story takes place next to the ocean, that repository of North American mythologies, and maybe he intends to return the arm to the crash site of the capsule, or maybe he simply intends to fling it into the ocean, we don't know, but we do know he ends up ditching his car in a junkyard, somewhere beside the sea.

In this spot, the arm is *killed* by Paul, though what it means to kill the arm is unclear.

> It was an arm
> Lying in the sand.
> A human arm.

Which is to say: he puncture-wounds the arm a few times with a piece of shattered bottle. Why that is more effective in dispatching the *entity* than being blown up in a space capsule, as first befell it, we just can't say, and why this subsequent "death" of the arm should have any impact on the space infection that is apparently manipulating Paul's teenage consciousness, causing him to behave as if he has testosterone pumped by the gallon into his circulatory system, anyway, this is all beside the point, I told Tyrone. The point is that in the junkyard there are, as you'd expect, *junkyard cats.* There is no better place to see cats than in a trash heap, a junkyard, a resource-management site, both the little and the large, the slow and fat, the Manx, the tuxedo, the calico, the Abyssinian, the mau, the Maine coon. In this particular junkyard, the cats immediately begin wrestling with the arm. There's plenty of meat there, I explained to Tyrone.

"They love that the arm moves and halts and wiggles its digits. This just makes the cats want to use their very primitive hunting instincts on the arm, and so the cats begin tearing into the meat on the arm, and it's almost as if the film used genuine feral cats for this sequence, hungry ones, because they really fight with one another, and they really struggle to get the *upper hand,* so to speak. Maybe they glued some meat onto the rubberized arm, some tuna, for the cats to fight over."

"Monty, I know this is important—"

"One more second, I have something to give you, but let me tell you about this last little bit, and then I will..."

His turn to sigh, a purely theatrical sigh—the one entitled *Prima Donna.*

"Why are the cats in the sequence? The next-to-last sequence in the film? Theoretically, we are only interested in the human characters. Right? We're interested in Paul, and we're interested in whether he's going to recover fully from the affliction that has beset him. Why the cats? Are they meant to indicate that the infection from the arm is now loosed on the natural world? This reminds me—"

I began to warm to a subject that was important to me, namely the *rivers of gore* subgenre of horror films, so popular in the new millennium. Suddenly the only films that teenagers would pay to download were films that had bodies exploding everywhere, or various infections destroying various parts of bodies, and then there were zombies, no end of zombies, zombies chewing on other people's bodies, zombies, zombies, zombies, and blood everywhere. Bodies profaned by cinema, disassembled, reassembled, augmented, sundered, and with blood on everything, like the gastronomic *drizzle* of nouvelle cuisine. It must have been, I told Tyrone, that the one business sector in the battered economy that still had earnings potential was the manufacture of *theatrical blood,* right? People were breaststroking in the stuff, and they were reaching out to grab lengths of intestine, trying to yank themselves out of the rivers of gore with the length of intestine, and they were using severed heads as footstools, all that kind of stuff. It was horrible, I told Tyrone. How much sweeter and gentler were the heavily symbolic films of the drive-ins, with their silly conceits and affectations, *I Was a Teenage Werewolf* and *Creature from the Black Lagoon.* The cats, I meant to say, were precursors of the *rivers of gore* imagery that was so essential in *The Four Fingers of Death,* namely the film, the remake, that I was soon going to undertake to novelize.

"Listen, Monty, I'm going to leave."

"Wait, wait. Let me just give you this." And then it was that I reached into my pocket, my breast pocket, because I was wearing an old thrift store jacket, because I wanted to look reasonably elegant on such a day, and in the pocket of my old thrift store jacket, in a wax paper envelope, was, as you would have guessed, a McClintock original issue baseball card. Signed. As I have said, I had more than one. I managed to acquire a great wealth of them, and with these I financed a number of things in life, the down payment on our house, my wife's surgery, some of my publications. I was down to four of the cards, before this day. This made it three.

You wouldn't have believed the look etched on Tyrone's face! He had expected no such thing. He had confronted the fact that he lost the contest fair and square. And giving him the card, of course, contradicted my very belief system! There were principles in the fetishistic world of collectibles. Things were worth what they were worth, and you needed to abide by prices and values. It was not wise to go allowing emotion to rule my business transactions. Normally, I adhered to these rules.

"My God," Tyrone whispered, gazing on the card. "I've never actually seen one. He really was a handsome guy. And you really can't see the arm at all."

"I don't approve of them covering up the arm. I think people should see the arm."

With a mute satisfaction, we both gazed at the picture of McClintock.

Tyrone said, "Are you sure? This is really generous of you. And unexpected. I'm tempted to refuse, you know, but then something in me just doesn't want to refuse." He smiled. Not an easy smile. Not an uncomplicated smile. "And now I really do have to go get on the plane."

I said, "I know you do."

There was some settling up, and this was methodical. Two men who were not without respect for each other but who were otherwise not close. The time of their acquaintance was over. Tyrone muttered something conciliatory as he figured a tip, but by then I was distracted myself. I stood. I shook his hand; he heaved his overnight bag up onto his shoulder, and he turned and made for the door.

> Try and raise
> The county coroner
> And then call my wife—
> I'm liable
> To be up all night.

It is true, readers of my afterword, that I had not told Tyrone that I'd just lost my wife, Tara Schott Crandall. Not one week before. You may wonder why I didn't tell him. I didn't tell him about my loss, though I had meant to find a time to do so. But then it became impossible to remedy my silence. Now I will tell you, instead, because it's important to tell someone about it. Had she not passed away, it is possible that I would never have completed the chess game with Tyrone. Nor would I have attempted to write the novelization of *The Four Fingers of Death,* nor would I have felt as I feel now in this mitigated night of my middle age.

It is true that there is a consciousness of things, and then there is the unconsciousness of things, and generally we recognize that these are the two ways of living in the world. We think of consciousness as the essential prerequisite of daily life, enabling us to do what needs to be done, to negotiate the paperwork, to heat the hot water, to recycle the recyclables, to julienne the vegetables, but in fact we spend much less time conscious than we think we do, and this I know now from the weeks in which Tara's new lungs began to succumb to their fungal infection, and she began to get sicker and sicker. What I mean is that my attempts to stay awake and alert throughout her illness were marred by my own eruptions of unconsciousness. I tried to stay awake through nights, so that I could watch her as she slept, as she kicked off the sheets and blankets again, so that I could say to her such sentimental things as she wouldn't tolerate when awake; for example, I reiterated that I had mostly floundered in life, didn't consider myself very good at life, until I'd met her, when she came to sit in on my writing class, and though — I said to her — I didn't immediately apprehend, back when she audited, that she was going to be the reinforced shipping container of my future, containing every good thing that would happen for the next years, I did recognize the fluttering in my heart, as I ought to have, because I am just smart enough to be able to identify the advent of affection, I told Tara. I had come to know, I told her, that I was a man of some delusion and some inability to assess dew points and leading economic indicators of the heart, but, I told her, I did better in this case because of her, and it was perhaps true, as I held her hand in mine, and she stirred briefly, that she didn't really *want* the responsibility of making me a better man, *I was one,* and this was not to be construed as requiring obligation on her part, unless she counted the obligation of accepting my gratitude. I should have known when she came into the class that something was bound to change in me, a selfish and preoccupied guy who taught the class mainly for the *cold, hard green,* though the money wasn't great, and the students worse, and I was about to finish this thought when I found that, indeed, the distractions of exhaustion could overtake even myself. There was only so long I could sit up with her, so many days and nights.

At the beginning of the end there were moments when she was wide awake, and miserable, tired of antibiotics pumped into her through one of many stents, tired of being a body connected to technologies, and she complained mightily and she reminded me that I needed to lose weight or no one was going to take an interest in me after she was gone, and, she said again, I shouldn't look at her with those *mooning* eyes, and I replied, "If you think I am hanging around here thinking about what's going to happen after you are gone, you certainly don't know me very well. My kind of steadfastness, let me remind you, Tara, is the kind that doesn't waver, the kind that is *true,* even when it is wrong to be so steadfast, or even if I am harmed in the process. Even if steadfastness is unfashionable, or not borne out by the facts, I will be steadfast. I believe that you are going to get better, and if you want me to lose weight because you want me to look better for *you,* then I will lose weight to look better for *you,* but not for whoever comes after you are gone, if anyone comes at all, which I doubt."

Tara was weeping, I remember, after I spoke, and she apologized, even though she said that I wasn't taking seriously what the doctors were already telling her, and the oxygen tank wheezed, and Tara wheezed, inhaling from the oxygen tank, and she coughed up something that must have had some blood in it, because of the awful color, and I wiped some of this away.

Accordingly, Tara came to inhabit a space that was between the bright, airy consciousness that is central to human life, and the dark, opiated abstraction that is close to death, in which Tara was known only to Tara through the mechanism of nightmare. I no longer appeared to have complete conversations and interactions with her — there were just excisions from time and life, after which she vanished intermittently. What happened in her middle place? What did Tara think of then?

In the supposedly *real* world, things around the Crandall abode fell into disuse, and their gears and mechanisms were ruined by the elements. Advertising circulars amassed on the front doorstep, and one of the wall monitors in the living room, on which I had presumptuously kept a still from *The Crawling Hand*, went on the fritz, so that there was only white noise upon the screen. A scorpion was given free rein over the expanses of the kitchen counter, and these things went on this way, and the fungus in Tara's lungs got a little bit worse, and another square inch of tissue gave up processing the air in her very expensive oxygen canisters, and perhaps I can be forgiven the feeling that all the world was behaving as Tara was behaving, that is, as though it were succumbing to infection, dwindling into moments of incomprehensibility that were the moments of the dream world. I got up and called the flea market and told them they could put someone else in my stall because I wasn't going to make it in, and the guy on the other end, Tim, who was in charge of licenses, forbore to charge me the twenty dollars I owed, because he was a good man, and I can't exactly remember how that conversation ended, because next I was asleep for some hours, and it was the afternoon, and I had had such fits of crying, whenever I felt I was out of earshot of my sick wife, that I couldn't stay awake for long, but nor could I sleep for long, and I wondered if there was some chance that my unconsciousness and Tara's unconsciousness would find a place where they could meet and enjoy each other in the remaining time. But in our next conversation I had no choice but to say, "I would like to take you back to the hospital now."

And she said, "Monty, there's no point in going back to the hospital."

"They can help."

"They can't help."

"But you are in pain."

"I'm not."

"They can keep you breathing."

"Please stop saying this!"

Then she said I could take her to the hospice, if I wanted,

which is also known as the place of death, which is also known as oblivion, which is also known as the end of hope, which is also the place where love founders, which is also the place where many people go and many people pretend they are not going to go, which is the place of witless intoxication, which is the place of life that is *not life,* and the place of all horrible smells, and the antiseptics that cover up the horrible smells, which is the place of faint smiles, and then the place of no smiles, and which is the place of pains that cannot be remediated and futures that go unlived, which is also the place where I did not and would not go with Tara, and as soon as the word *hospice* was pronounced, I began thinking, as would a child, of ways to scuttle any plans that involved hospice, and so I said that I wouldn't discuss hospice with her, and to this Tara said, "That's fine with me, because I'm happy to die here, Monty, but I just want you to promise me that you'll be here either way."

That thing
On the beach—
I just can't get it
Out of my mind.

There must have been more to it than that, or maybe there were several conversations of this kind, and hours and hours that went on in this way, and some of these conversations were during the day, even though the curtains were drawn, and some of the conversations were in the middle of the night, and there was no one there to hear them, only Tara and myself, and so now there is only me to speak of them; I know that at some moment I suggested that we go on one last drive in the desert, that I absolutely wouldn't take no for an answer, the two of us had to go on a drive, and I would borrow an electric car, because I knew a guy who knew a guy, even though I wasn't at all sure I knew such a person; about the only person I knew with a car was the blackguard called D. Tyrannosaurus, and I wasn't sure if I was willing to ask;

there was only the illness, and the space between when she was conscious and when she was unconscious, and there was the illness that was now the third person in our marriage; the illness, that is, had volition and personality, so that I could feel on occasion as if I had spoken to the illness, or that the illness was talking through Tara, and so I wasn't sure if I should always tell her the truth, or even tell her what I was doing, because if the illness was giving the answers, through her, then why bother to tell her the truth, because the illness wouldn't convey the truth to Tara, except in those moments when I could do no better than speak to the events, those moments when even a man like myself, who was not always so good at evaluating the truth, could see that things were not going as he would have liked them to go; still I felt that I had some leeway in this space between consciousness and unconsciousness, and if I could borrow a car, then I could just pick her up, because she didn't even weigh what a pillow weighs, and I could carry the last of her out into the car, which is what I did, and I got one of the Rodriguezes to help me, after the nurse who came a couple hours a day had left, and Maria Rodriguez said, *Mr. Crandall, this is liable to be a little dangerous,* and I said no, no, and probably everyone knew that I *wasn't* taking her to the hospital, *everyone* being defined on this day as myself, Tara, the illness, and Maria Rodriguez; still, I put her and her machines in the back of the car belonging to D. Tyrannosaurus, to whom I had offered no reason for needing to borrow his vehicle, but I simply asked, and he agreed, and I poured a month's profits into the fuel tank, some algae-based fuel mixture, and then I took a generator, and I took the oxygen tank, and I took all kinds of monitors, and I spent half an hour loading all this equipment into the car, and then I bore up my lightweight wife, whose eyes had rolled into the back of her head, and I lurched with her out to the car, shuffling, stumbling, saying, as I carried her, *Please don't leave yet, please don't leave me yet, please don't leave, please don't leave me, please don't leave me yet.* There was more that I wanted to show her, I said, and I could put her in the back of Tyrone's car; we would go at this leisurely pace, and we would watch the way the sun fell across the Catalinas, and the way the decrepit buildings crumbled into the desert again, and I pointed all of this out to Tara in the car; it improved things so much when she was here with me, and it was all because of *you,* I told her, how much we loved this place, because under my own steam I just ran myself into the ground, did nothing, never going outside, just sitting around checking baseball scores online and eating the same thing every night, but *your* excitement made me excited about this place, the taco stands, the old movie palaces, the used-media stores, all empty, like the shopping centers were all empty, I loved it because *you* loved it, and the dream of being able to understand a place by driving through it, I said, this was what *you* gave me in this place, and it was a place of ruins, and somehow the ruins made me feel alive; it was all about death, I said, the indigenous people who got run out of here, the ruins of what the Americans brought here, all ruins, and the ruins were what made me love it; nothing can last here for long, not without effort, but that doesn't mean that I can take the idea of *your* being a thing of the past in this place, that doesn't mean I can take that, I can take all the fires and all the floods, and all the poisons, but I can't take this place without you, I don't want to live in this place without *you* in it, I don't want to stay behind, if staying behind means the memories of you, every corner where I turn, where you were, every wisecrack that you uttered, every middle finger you thrust at some other driver, I don't want to think of this place, but I offer you this one last trip, and maybe, before I leave here, as I will surely have to do, I will at least have *this* memory.

> Hey, kid,
> The exam's tomorrow,
> And you have to pass.

Then from the middle place of consciousness, Tara awoke! At least her eyelashes fluttered. In the past, she had always taken a certain care with her eyelashes. There was always some capacious amount of eyeliner and mascara bound to run at the first sign of emotion. So it was appropriate that her eyelashes fluttered, and I reached over with my free hand and wiped away a little of the moisture that accumulated under the oxygen mask and cascaded down her neck. She mumbled something, and I asked her to repeat herself.

"Where we going?" she slurred.

"The foothills," I said.

"Oh, nice," she said. "Why?"

"Don't you want to see the lights of the city?" I said.

"Always," said she, summoning the word from a long silence.

And we went out Tanque Verde, that strange impulsive avenue that will not succumb to the grid, and I exceeded the posted limits, because if ever there was an emergency, this was an emergency, the emergency of aesthetics, because if a dying woman needed to see what was beautiful, one of the few things that man had brought to the desert that was indisputably beautiful, then we would exceed posted limits if we needed to, and there was no constabulary presence up here anyway, because they were all on the South Side, looking the other way while the gangbangers heisted another jet pack, and so there was nothing here, excepting a few rich people who were unwise enough to be out walking their dogs, now that the heat was beginning to give, and we passed these dog walkers at something approaching the supersonic, and it's surprising that Tyrone's car didn't lift off, but it just wasn't that kind of a car; yes, there was something eternal about being a middle-aged man driving his one true love up into the foothills, espousing the cause of beauty, until, just as the mountains were turning the color of fortified wine, we pulled into a dusty, neglected turnaround, facing in the direction from which we had come, and I said, "Here it is. Like so many other places, it looks great at a distance, huh?"

I could hear her breathing, or at least I thought I could hear her breathing. I could hear something breathing. A machine, perhaps. Or Tara and a machine, the one indistinguishable from the other. She didn't say anything. There was the desert wind too.

Have I described it? Because in autumn, after the monsoons have come through, the weather is changeable, and a big wind can come up, and there is that longing of autumn, when all things are charged with the waning of promise. *Don't let this be the last moment,* I said to her, *the last moment that we share.*

She would not wake up.

And she never did say another thing to me, and if one wanted to read a lot into a person's last words or in this case last *word,* the word *always* is a pretty good word. You can argue, if you want, that our love was not for the ages, since I was a not very good writer, and boorish in some ways, and Tara was a young woman who didn't have a chance in the world, really, unless her chance was to die ahead of schedule, and much of our relationship we were mainly hooked up to various devices, or at least Tara was, but we were *always* something, we were *always* trying, *always* fucking up, *always* regretting, *always* laughing, *always* in debt, *always* looking for another place to live, *always* there, *always* elsewhere, *always* giving up, *always* complaining, *always* celebrating, *always* jumping for joy, *always* forgetting, *always* saying *never again,* and so *always* was a very fine word, if you wanted to leave on a memorable high note, and I will *always* remember that word *always,* more than I will remember, for example, taking her unconscious to the hospital and then watching a lot of heroic measures, the very involved dance steps that are the heroic measures. Tara died anyway, which is what she was going to do, and what she told me she was going to do, and I guess I always knew it.

Of the time after that, I don't have anything much to say. I won the chess game, and I began writing these pages.

Acknowledgments

I'M INDEBTED to my friends and loved ones in the Southwest: Casa Libre en la Solana, in Tucson, and its director, Kristen Nelson; Melissa Pritchard; Lydia Millet; Aurelie Sheehan; Stacey Richter; Dan Coleman; Jim Weston; Susan Lang; Rodney Phillips; and especially Laura Van Etten.

I'm indebted to Yaddo, where I wrote the last sentence.

I'm also indebted to the following for believing in me and the project: Melanie Jackson; Deborah Rogers; Matthew Snyder; Pat Strachan; Michael Pietsch; Betsy Uhrig; Heather Fain; Heather Rizzo; Alison Granucci; Jennifer Alise Drew; Carl Newman; Susanna Sonnenberg; Regan Good; my wife, Amy Osborn; my daughter, Hazel Jane (who arrived just in time to believe that my job is entirely dependent on red pencils); my brother, Dwight Moody; my parents; my nieces and nephews.

About the Author

RICK MOODY is the author of the novels *Garden State, The Ice Storm, Purple America,* and *The Diviners;* two collections of stories, *The Ring of Brightest Angels Around Heaven* and *Demonology;* a collection of novellas, *Right Livelihoods;* and a memoir, *The Black Veil,* winner of the PEN / Martha Albrand Award. Moody has also received the Addison Metcalf Award, the *Paris Review*'s Aga Khan Prize, and a Guggenheim Fellowship. He lives with his family in Brooklyn, New York.

www.rickmoodybooks.com

BACK BAY · READERS' PICK

Reading Group Guide

THE FOUR FINGERS
OF DEATH

A NOVEL BY

RICK MOODY

To the members of the reading group

Now that the future is at hand, now that the bombers have lifted off from the base, now that the fanatics have looted the treasures of the people, whichever treasures they are, now that books are something you barter for at a flea market or steal from your grandmother's house, now that people are more interested in instant video interfacing, in which suggestive material is downloaded directly into cranial implants, you don't really find too many *book groups* anymore. Book groups! A thing of the past! From a rosy and quaint era at the turn of the millennium.

I used to detest book groups. The whole idea of the book group seemed to me to involve a group of like-minded parishioners whose barely concealed loathing for one another prompted teeth-gritting observations like "I just didn't feel like this character was sympathetic," or "Why, again, did we choose this book?" or even "Who the heck was responsible for this?" All while these participants attempted to consummate perfervid crushes on the spouses of other group members. In how many of these book groups did people fail to read the books at all, especially when the titles under scrutiny were extremely worthy—Icelandic sagas, let's say, or *The Decameron*—opting instead to wait it out until some borderline genre-type material would eventually be selected for that one member who had bad dyslexia, ADHD, and *elective cognitive dysfunction—metaphorical and metonymy?*[1] *Peyton Place*? Best book *ever!*

Making a special little section of the paperback edition of a work in order to cater to these assemblies of the miserable, this

---

[1] See the *DSM-VII* (2024) section on literary illnesses.

seemed pointless too, if not infuriating, and I would often rip these sections out of the book, or use an X-Acto to excise carefully the offending pages, cursing the marketing people who erroneously believed that these inserts of *new material* were somehow going to induce book groups to select this book, and thus purchase a whopping thirteen additional copies, when more often the thing that incited book groups to action was whether or not a title had been featured on *web-based programming* or had some kind of faux-intellectual cachet as determined by a glossy magazine, back when there were as yet magazines, which faux-intellectual content mostly meant the book was not sophisticated in any way at all. *There is no expedient a man will not endure to avoid the real labor of thinking* — I believe Edison said that.

And yet: since it is in the nature of myself, Montese Crandall, to love squandered things, to love all things that are moving toward depletion and exhaustion, lost causes that have no guardian angel, lovers who are unloved, babies without parents, animals trapped in sheds, coyotes on subway trains, and so on, I have lately come to love the idea of the book club or group. I like the idea of groups of people shivering in unheated government trailers, out near the latest calamity or natural disaster, eating government cheese, drinking backdated hooch, disputing vigorously as to whether the narrator of *The Good Soldier* is to be believed, before doubling over to projectile vomit. I think literature has to be desperate again, in order to return to its senses, in order to apply itself to its genuine subject — wherein the human animal is besieged on all sides, by his avariciousness, by his sympathy, by his cocksureness, by his defenselessness, by his love of science and the ruthlessness of his commerce, by his total dependence on ideology, propaganda, by his witless reliance on a neglectful God. What could be better, then, than a sort of *church* of literature, in exile from society and its cranially downloadable programming on weight loss among the trillionaires. The church of literature is well served by the book club, by its grassroots attitude, by its trans fats, by its moving from house to house.

I therefore agreed to write these lines for the new edition of my masterwork, *The Four Fingers of Death,* in order to encourage your book group in exactly this kind of pursuit. This afterword is meant to establish the absolute centrality of books to cultural activity, the way books capture human consciousness, interiority, spirituality, as no other medium can, which is something I have naturally demonstrated in a way that is beyond reproach here in *The Four Fingers of Death.*

I therefore recommend the establishment of a religion based on *The Four Fingers of Death* (for which book groups can serve as a first cause), one based on obsessive rereading and compulsive repurchasing of the text. My book has so much to say about the great moral issues of our time. For example: the human body, insofar as it is added on to by technological means, begins in my novel to acquire an aspect that is no longer exactly human, becoming instead a cap-italist-technocratic cyborg hybrid—that's a very important issue, and you can discourse on this when you meet. Or, for example, you could talk about point of view, and how consciousness is really a tendency, a gathering of interests, a flowing and slipping, rather than a single set of *indivisible opinions,* so that personality, in my work, becomes a habit of the human animal rather than a resting place—you could talk about that and you could adduce the fact that this novel is in the alleged first person in its first half and in the third person in its second half, as evidence of slippage and displacement. Or you could talk about love and how love seems to triumph despite all that is done to snuff it out, and how love finds love wherever it looks, indomitably, reproducing the beloved and the image of the beloved—here she is a distant wife, 40 mil-lion miles away on planet Earth; here she is a dead person locked away in a refrigerator; here she is a research assistant; here she is a sexy model named after a European city. Which is the genuine beloved? The genuine beloved is wherever you gaze. That's a good subject for a reading group conversation. Or you could talk about the fact that the novel as a form tends to gobble up subliterary artistic media and spit them out in new and reimagined ways, and thus a piss-poor horror movie from 2025, made by some malcontented kid in the suburbs for $38,000, is perfect fodder for a piece of high art. Or you could talk about about me, Montese Crandall, and the radical reinvention of art and literature that is evinced in my very short early works. Or you could talk about imagination in general, and I understand that talking about imagination *requires* imagination. You are perhaps a little timid about going down that road. I know that reading this book for yourself, without force-fed talking points, requires pluck. I know projecting yourself into the book requires imagination, since so many parts of it — a sexual encounter with a severed limb, for example — are not consonant with your daily life. I know that living a life that is about permanent revolution and which sees reading as an act of reinvention above and apart from whatever is Montese Crandall's artistic wish, this all requires your *input,* but I want to release you into this free range, beyond the confines that have contained you, and a discussion of imagination and its properties is a good way to start. I salute you on the beginning of your brave journey.

Or you could just talk about the desert. You could compare deserts. You could compare Gobi to Sahara to Alacama to Sonora, depletions of rainfall, absolute failure of vegetation, indigenous populations, and you could speak to the desertification of Mars as compared to the desertification of Sonora, and the way the two are one, and you could speak to the ubiquity of deserts, when considered as a global phenomenon, much more common than forests, for example, and you could see in this scouring away of all that is corrupted by human society an opportunity to start afresh, an opportunity for your book group, in seclusion, to start a new society, founded upon principles of respect and community, like the society started by the biblical crazies who settled this land, or like the men and women of the Mars mission.

Or you could just talk about my wife, Tara Schott Crandall, who is a fitting subject for all literary discussions, and discussions of every kind.

Whichever way you travel with your book group, I'd be happy

if you named it after me—perhaps something like the Montese L. Crandall Memorial Book Group of _____. Insert name of your parish or county. You could also name any children born during the time of your book group after me, and/or any public institutions in your town, such as a bridge, a library, or a stadium. *Montese* can be a girl's name too. I thank you for your consideration, and the consideration of your book group, and if when you are done you would like to forward my book to any talk show hosts of your acquaintance, that would be splendid too.

—Montese Crandall, February 2027

A conversation with Rick Moody

The author of *The Four Fingers of Death* talks
with Zett Aguado of *Night Train*

*Let's talk about your newest novel. Unless you are superstitious, could you
talk about what it is about and how long you've been working on it?*

Not superstitious, really, but it's a hard book to talk about. It
began in two ways: (1) I really love bad, old horror movies, the
B-film variety, the drive-in variety, especially from the late fif-
ties and early sixties, which was the period of horror films that I
watched a lot as a kid. I just loved them. In this novel, I wanted
to try to make my own one of these films, so I picked a particularly embarrassing example, *The Crawling Hand* (1963), and began
adapting it. (2) Meanwhile, I wanted to write a book about the
desert, because I have been spending a lot of time in the Sonoran
Desert of Arizona in the last ten years. Or, if not a book *about*
the desert, at least a book *located* in the desert. Then (3) If those
things weren't enough, I allowed a name from my book to be
auctioned off by a First Amendment–related charity in California.
The winner, he who paid the top dollar, got to have his name
in my book. The winner was one Montese Crandall. Upon having control of this name, which I loved so much, I had to create
a context for him in the novel, so he became the narrator and
controlling intelligence thereof. In ways that will become clear
when you see it. Well, there's another factor too. (4) I wanted
to write a novel in the style of the novels I first loved when I
was a teenager, viz., Vonnegut/Brautigan/Robbins/Pynchon/Dick/
Heinlein. It's a subliterary genre in some cases, but I never care
about that sort of thing. I want to write into the condition of
my early enthusiasm, you know? Anyway, the result is a seven-

hundred-page comic novel about a disembodied arm set in the desert in 2026.

Why did you want to write a book set in the Sonoran Desert?

It just calls in the one way, which is the way of the siren call, because it's big, empty (excepting the Phoenix and Tucson metro areas), merciless, heartbroken, and inimical to human life. And it has the saguaro cactus.

Another one of your callings is music. How did you begin in music? You form part of the Wingdale Community Singers. How did the band get started?

I sang as a kid. My mom sings and plays piano. My sister sang. My brother plays guitar. We all listened to a lot of music. It was something the family agreed upon. I was a boy soprano and took some voice lessons back then, and also several years of piano lessons. I was a lousy student but a keen listener. I sang in chorus and madrigal groups in high school. In college, I sort of undertook to teach myself the guitar and to convert myself to guitar playing, even as I had a couple of bands in which I sang and/or played keyboards. I began writing songs then too. Let me say here that even though I wrote a lot of lyrics, the important part for me was not the lyrics but the music. I always aspired to be a genuine musician, though I have never quite reached the mark. I can read a tiny bit of music—I can read the melody lines in the hymnal, for example. But I have never had enough theory. Still, the songwriting has been a part of my life just as long as prose writing has. I was in two bands in college, one in grad school, and then I mostly played by myself for ten or fifteen years. After which I made the acquaintance of an amazing songwriter, Hannah Marcus, in 2002 or so. The Wingdale Community Singers were formed out of that friendship. The constituency shifts, but the band always includes Hannah and me, and it always has a lot of singing and harmony involved. We made one record in 2005, and have another finished, which, God willing, will be released in the fall.

How (if at all) did writing your newest novel affect your music making? Or, rather, how does that balance work?

The writing doesn't much affect music making. It's usually the other way around. Music makes me want to write a certain way. I think the energy flows in that direction. I borrow from other media and funnel the energy into stories and novels and essays. The balance is constantly shifting in terms of time, but with the understanding that when it is all said and done I am a writer, and everything else is just to maintain a diversity of influences.

Has your music making suffered any degree of neglect due to your writing of your newest novel and/or during the transformative process of becoming a father?

The blessing and curse of music making, for me, is that it's largely collaborative. I do it, in the main, to get away from working alone all the time. If I wanted to do work alone, I'd just write. While it's true I did make a "solo album" last year (not released yet, partly because for me "solo" is a synonym for "not very good"), most of the time I want to make music with others. Chiefly, this means I like to sing harmonies. If I were to try to boil down all of my hobby to one essential gesture, it would be this. Harmony singing. Most of my harmony singing has been in the context of my band, the Wingdale Community Singers, who were having some trouble even before the baby appeared. The Wingdales are composed of four extremely creative people, all of whom do other things, and it's hard to get them in one room on a good day. My feeling is that though I am the worst musician in the band, I am sort of the glue. I am not very sticky, however, and even less so now. I have not played my guitar once since March 6, the birthday of young Hazel. I have sung (I am doing a fair amount of singing with my writer-musician friend Wesley Stace / John Wesley Harding), but not as much as I'd like. Although I have been writing little song fragments for the girl child. It would be accurate to say, though, that right now there is enough room in life for the two things: Hazel and my novel. Barely. Everything else is on the back burner.

By everything else, does that also include teaching?

I have taught on and off for a long time (since 1991). Rarely full-time. That is, I have never made my income primarily from teaching. I have always survived mainly from writing. I would like to try to continue to do the same. When I have taught a lot, I have often become a little burned out from it. Partly because I do try to give and to be available to the students in a way that I felt I often was NOT when I was a writing student. My grad school experience, especially, was not great, and I am powerfully motivated to try to expunge the miserly teaching of my professors from that time. But more important, I have a theory that the workshop is not a great methodology for the instruction in creative writing, and, as a result, I have tried to come up with some alternative solutions. One of the solutions is this: I work with people individually. The application procedure is rigorous. I have to have time and I have to really like your work, and you have to have at least a year and you have to be willing to rewrite endlessly. Because I will work on one story for four or five months, doing ten or twelve drafts, until I think I have it somewhere where you are making progress/learning. Mainly, I do this for thesis students. Right now I have two students, one of whom is about to graduate. I think this amounts to a really good teaching ratio. One to two. By the way, the students pay what they can pay. When I can't do this, the tutorial model, I very occasionally will teach a workshop in revision. I have sketched out some precepts for revision (there are thirteen rules, according to me), and so when I do a workshop now (as I have done annually at Skidmore College in the summer since 2005 or so) I primarily try to work on the subject of revision. I don't care if you have a novel excerpt; I don't care if you want to get an agent or are trying to market a book. I am going to attempt to teach you how to make a better paragraph. And that is where we will meet. I don't know how fatherhood will affect this yet. My teaching. I still am committed to getting one student through her thesis and one other on an open-ended basis. And I am teaching this summer up north again. For two weeks in July. I will do these things as I have done in the past, as though it is possible to believe in teaching.

You mention you have thirteen rules of revision. What are they?

Actually there are fourteen. As shown here:

1. Omit Needless Words
2. Sacrifice Your Modifiers
3. Consider the Rhythm
4. Replace "To Be" and "To Have"
5. Simplify Tenses
6. Avoid Alliteration
7. Rethink Abstraction
8. Spill Your Parentheses
9. Use Figurative Language Sparingly
10. Engage All Five Senses
11. Cut the Last Sentence
12. Read the Passage Aloud
13. Put the Draft Away
14. Do the Above Fifteen to Thirty Times

Could you give your reasons for number eleven? It is controversial!

Number eleven *is* controversial. But you don't realize what good advice it is till you start using it. I challenge you, in fact, to cut the last sentence of this interview, no matter what it is. The problem is that if you really do fifteen drafts and cut the last sentence every time, then you end up cutting fifteen sentences. That's taking me too literally.

Fifteen drafts of a book! What are your thoughts on novels written in record time?

Some dead writers really got good at writing quickly. I am not one of them.

One last question: How are you able to work on your numerous projects after satisfying the demands of a newborn?

I'm not doing so great at it (it's 4:21 A.M. right now). But I think the work reflects where we are, not where we want to be, and I'm trying to chip away at it despite my reduced circumstances. I am who I am. And I'm willing to write literature as that guy, not as some imaginary, more competent, better-rested guy.

Excerpted from an interview originally posted at the online journal *Night Train*. Reprinted with permission.

Questions and topics for discussion

1. Discuss Montese Crandall's very short stories. Why do you think he reduces his fiction to these brief sentences? How do they comment on the state of the literary world he's living in? Why, other than for money, does Montese compose a much longer work, the novelization of *The Four Fingers of Death,* when he wins the chance to do so?

2. In 2009, Russia funded the "Mars-500 Project," locking six crew members into an isolation chamber for 105 days. How do you think you would manifest "Planetary Exile Syndrome," or "Space Panic"? How does it affect each crew member in *The Four Fingers of Death?*

3. How does astronaut Jed Richards's relationship with his daughter evolve over the duration of the mission in Book One? Why do you think it changed? Have you ever had a similar experience of change during absence from a loved one?

4. Why do you think Rick Moody chose to write Book One from Jed's perspective and as a blog? How does the shift in narration between Book One and Book Two affect your reactions to the story?

5. Throughout the novel, instances of enlightenment—the rogue NASA rover, Morton's consciousness—are juxtaposed with degeneration—Jean-Paul's infection, the *omnium gatherum.* Discuss other examples of each state, mental and physical. What significance do they have to the themes of the book as a whole?

6. Rick Moody conjures up dishonest bureaucratic careerists, proponents of biowarfare, a dysfunctional president, mass emigration from the United States, and a trend toward violent, repressive sex. Do you think that the world in Book Two bears a resemblance to our own or to our near future? Why or why not? What do you think Moody is implying about the state of society?

7. A reviewer for *BookForum,* James Gibbons, wrote of *The Four Fingers of Death,* "Conceptual wizardry and emotional resonance are not reconciled with ease . . . so it is here, in the intersection of narrative excess and genuine feeling, that Moody is at his most daring and arresting." What scenes or exchanges in the book most moved you? Why did you empathize with the characters at those points?

8. Rick Moody has said in an interview that the American desert is, for him, "big, empty, merciless, heartbroken, and inimical to human life." How has their arid environment affected both the Mars astronauts in Book One and the communities in Book Two? If you have traveled to the American Southwest, how does your impression jibe with Moody's?

9. The author dedicates this book to the memory of Kurt Vonnegut, a writer known for his stylish, sometimes apocalyptic, fiction. Elsewhere, Moody has expressed his early admiration for science-fiction writer Philip K. Dick and Joseph Heller's *Catch-22.* If you have read any of these writers, do you see their influences at work in *The Four Fingers of Death*? In what ways?

10. Did Montese Crandall's novelization of the classic horror film *The Crawling Hand* inspire you to see the film for yourself? Were you drawn to horror films as a teenager, and if so, how did this novel satisfy your attraction to that genre?

Look for these other books by Rick Moody

Garden State

"Rick Moody's first novel, set in New Jersey, has established its author as his generation's foremost chronicler of middle-class malaise in tristate exurbia."　　　　—Claire Messud, *Village Voice*

The Ice Storm

"A bitter and loving and damning tribute to the American family.... This is a good book, packed with keen observation and sympathy for human failure."　　　　—Adam Begley, *Chicago Tribune*

Purple America

"A tough, funny, gorgeously detailed domestic thriller.... *Purple America* is the stuff of classical tragedy, told in insistent, laser-bright prose. Reading it is a transfiguring experience."
　　　　—Ben Neihart, *Baltimore Sun*

Demonology

"Bold and thrilling.... *Demonology* rants and raves and roars.... Moody has spirit and drive and talent to burn."
　　　　—Walter Kirn, *New York Times Book Review*

The Diviners

"As if *The Bonfire of the Vanities* had been written by James Joyce."
　　　　—James Hynes, *Washington Post Book World*

Back Bay Books
Available wherever paperbacks are sold